2-13-10

ODD NUMBERS

Maria & Robin...
To a dear couple that
I truly love. Blessings
in Christ.
M.J.

ODD NUMBERS

By

M. Grace Bernardin

iUniverse, Inc.
New York   Bloomington

Odd Numbers

Copyright © 2009 by M. Grace Bernardin

All rights reserved. No part of this book may be used or reproduced by any means, graphic, electronic, or mechanical, including photocopying, recording, taping or by any information storage retrieval system without the written permission of the publisher except in the case of brief quotations embodied in critical articles and reviews.

This is a work of fiction. All of the characters, names, incidents, organizations, and dialogue in this novel are either the products of the author's imagination or are used fictitiously.

iUniverse books may be ordered through booksellers or by contacting:

iUniverse
1663 Liberty Drive
Bloomington, IN 47403
www.iuniverse.com
1-800-Authors (1-800-288-4677)

Because of the dynamic nature of the Internet, any Web addresses or links contained in this book may have changed since publication and may no longer be valid. The views expressed in this work are solely those of the author and do not necessarily reflect the views of the publisher, and the publisher hereby disclaims any responsibility for them.

ISBN: 978-1-4401-6256-5 (pbk)
ISBN: 978-1-4401-6258-9 (hc)
ISBN: 978-1-4401-6257-2 (ebk)

Printed in the United States of America

iUniverse rev. date: 11/03/2009

To John

Chapter 1
January 2006
Allison

Allison held the lipstick tube at arm's length and squinted. Moonlight and Roses, or at least that's what she thought it said. She moved the tube closer to her face, but it was no good. Just a blur. Her mother was about her age when she first got bifocals. Another concession to middle age. But then, as always, she tried to look on the positive side. *Let's see, the upside of bifocals. They might add a touch of class, make me look like an intellectual, or one of those gracefully aging ladies from old money.*

She moved in closer to the mirror then backed away again. She had a general idea where her mouth was. She began applying the balm to her upper lip. She thought of a crazy old lady she once knew who never got her lipstick on right. It was always smeared above and below her mouth. *She must've been too proud to wear bifocals*, Allison surmised. She could still see color at least, and one thing was for sure, the shade of her lipstick was all wrong. It didn't go with her black dress. It wasn't the Moonlight and Roses it was the Red Wine and Twilight she meant to grab before she left the house. It was too bright – bright red. Suddenly she was the crazy old lady with the smeared lipstick, only paler.

My God, I'm going blind. Blind and pale. I look like Elvira the Vampire Woman from Friday Night Fright Show: pale skin, black dress, and God-awful red lips–everything but the cleavage and black hair. Allison scrutinized the dark hair which peaked out of her scalp, afraid that the black roots made her shoulder-length dyed blond hair look a bit dirty. She imagined Elvira the Vampire Woman with bifocals as she dropped the lipstick into her black evening bag. The positive side of bifocals, along with everything else evaporated from her mind.

Allison hurried out the ladies room of the Lamasco Theater. She always hurried when in emotional pain. She schmoozed her way down the corridor to the lobby. Fortunately, she didn't have to walk too far without running into someone she knew. Allison Hamilton's smile flashed, her enthusiasm oozed, and her charm splattered out on everyone she met. "Wonderful concert!" "So good to see you again!" "You look great!" The social arena was her joy; looking in a mirror her agony.

As she approached the main foyer, the exiting crowd forced her to slow down. She thought of her three children and felt an ache of regret for the meager scraps of time which was all she seemed able to give them. She thought of Frank and every emotion known to womankind swirled through her chest–resentment, love, longing, disappointment, despair, and regret.

Ahead of her in the crowd was Tim Shultz, their dashing lawyer friend from the old days. Relieved to see someone she knew, Allison raised her hand, calling out, "Tim, darling!" She wormed her way to him and gave him a flirtatious little nudge until he turned around.

"Allison Hamilton! I swear you get more beautiful all the time." Tim gushed.

Allison threw her arms around him, giving him the customary rich lady hug: a light back patting, plenty of cheek pressing, and a smoochy noise, but no actual kiss.

"Frank is one lucky bastard."

"Flattery will get you everywhere."

"Never worked for me before."

"Oh, please, Tim. Stop. So what are you doing here anyway? I didn't think you went in for cultural events."

"I don't. I'm still the uncultured slob from the old days. My wife joined the Junior League and all her friends have season tickets, so here I am."

"I see," Allison smiled.

"Hey, I just talked to Frank out in the lobby. Still making him wait, huh?" Tim laughed boisterously.

"No, just keeping him on his toes, Tim. Mustn't let him get complacent you know."

"Hey, I was thinking about trying to get some of the old gang together; you know kind of a Camelot reunion. You ever think about the old Camelot days?"

"No," Allison abruptly replied.

"Why not?" Tim asked.

"Because it's in the past," she said smiling away the pain.

"I think about those days all the time. So you and Frank have been married how long now?"

"We just celebrated our twentieth anniversary last month." Allison caught the irony of the word "celebrate" as it slipped out, thinking how unlike a celebration it actually was. She felt her social veneer droop just a little.

"Twenty years. Well, I'll be damned. You're still as gorgeous as you were on your wedding day. Remember that day? That was one hell of a brew-ha-ha." Tim laughed again. Allison giggled behind her black evening bag, lifting it in front of her face, like a shy school girl laughing at a naughty joke.

If she really thought about her wedding day it would make her cry, not laugh. But instead she remembered only Tim's drunken proclamations of love toward her when he toasted her at the wedding reception. "I'm the best man, so I don't know why Allison picked Frank instead of me," he said with a slur, his champagne glass raised and his ascot tie sloppily pulled to the side.

Allison looked out from behind her black evening bag at Tim. She took in the image of his balding head and protruding stomach. He was definitely not the good-looking playboy she remembered from the old days, but then nothing was the same as she remembered.

"So how is..." Allison searched her mind for the name of Tim's newest wife. A skinny young blond thing he snatched from a college sorority. Or was it high school? Tim's wives kept getting younger and younger.

"Tiffany," he paused. "She's doing great. She's around here somewhere."

"Well, it was good seeing you, Tim, but I've got to go. I've kept Frank waiting long enough."

"See you later, sweetheart. Tell the kids hi for me."

"Will do. Bye. Let's get together soon." Allison squeezed his hand, furrowed her brow, and spoke the words as if she really meant them. She gave him one final smoochy air-kiss which landed inches from his right ear lobe. She left him smiling. She left all the men smiling. Except Frank.

Allison searched for Frank. She remembered the anticipation and excitement with which she used to search for Frank in a crowd and then she'd spot him and her heart would pound and her mouth would get dry. How different her search for him now. She was tired and wanted to go home. Her cheeks ached from all the phony smiling and she longed to be around someone with whom she didn't have to smile. That would be Frank.

Allison spotted Frank leaning against the large plate glass window by the lobby door. Frank leaned a lot these days. If he couldn't sit, he leaned. He complained that his back and legs ached if he stood for too long. Frank always complained, but he never used to lean. He'd even taken to slouching lately. Allison resented him for all the slouching and leaning, but especially for that pitiful far-away look on his face.

He looks like a basset hound, a starving basset hound that's just been kicked. He could at least force a smile when he's in public, but, no, then the world would never realize what a long-suffering martyr he is. Mister Melodrama, that's what he is. Allison muttered her contempt through smiling clenched teeth.

She was all set to despise Frank when, suddenly, the image of him standing there triggered a memory so vivid she found herself reliving it in that very instant. The unexpectedness of this deja vu caused her to stop in her tracks as if she'd run up against an invisible wall. Or maybe she only snagged the toe of her black poi de soi pumps on the carpeting beneath her feet. Allison looked down at her shoes, then up again, hoping the phantom before her would disappear. But there it was again, and the memory lingered for a few moments longer; Frank standing there, cradling her full-length mink coat in his arms like a sleeping child.

It was in La Guardia airport some thirteen, fourteen years earlier when she last saw him looking like that. They were returning from his father's home out east where they'd spent their Christmas vacation. It was late and he was tired. Their oldest son, Matthew, was about three or four years old at the time and was sound asleep in his arms. He looked utterly exhausted and the coat looked heavy in his arms, just like Matthew looked that night years ago, but no matter, he would stand there and hold that sleeping boy all night despite his aching back.

Allison broke her gaze away from Frank's dark sapphire eyes. It was always Frank's eyes that made her love him again. There was a depth to his eyes, like great pools which one couldn't resist diving into. In the past Allison found herself drowning inside those deep, mystical, endless pools of blue.

Basset Hound eyes, Allison told herself as the brief spell of love and longing vanished with the memory. Frank, himself, aided Allison in her efforts to stave off any more tender feelings with a long loud yawn which he made no attempt to cover. The yawn was so indiscreet that she thought she caught a glimpse of his bottom molar fillings. A few people standing near him yawned in sympathy. And then he spotted her and his sad tired look quickly changed to one of irritation as he heaved a loud sigh. Along with all the slouching and leaning came plenty of yawning and sighing. It's what Frank did best these days. In return Allison gave him a closed mouth smile. Frank called it her "polite but pissed" smile, and it was reserved for him alone.

Allison knew that Frank would quiz her about the second half of the concert which was Tchaikovsky's Sixth Symphony, the Pathétique. *Pathetic is right,* Allison thought. At least she would remember the name. It described Frank, and her marriage, and her life. *He really should have been a college professor,* Allison thought, for Frank was never more in his element than when he had some underling in his tutelage. Too often that had been her. He wasn't home much that week but when he was he followed her around the house giving her little scraps of information about the symphony and Tchaikovsky himself.

"You know it was totally radical. Nothing like it had ever been done before," he'd say as his image would suddenly appear in the mirror behind her left shoulder as she brushed her teeth.

"What are you talking about?" she'd say with toothpaste muffling her words and dripping out of her mouth.

"Tchaikovsky's sixth."

"Oh," she'd say spitting into the sink.

"His final movement was an Adagio, not an Allegro. That was totally new. I mean to end a symphony on a tragic rather than triumphant note," he'd say as she gargled and spit into the sink.

"Uh-huh," Allison would say as she pinned her hair back and daubed some white cream on her face, careful to make outward circular motions so as not to promote premature wrinkling.

"My back's killing me," he'd say, closing the lid to the toilet and plopping down on it.

"So what else is new?"

"Tchaikovsky suffered from melancholia, you know. But he wasn't melancholy when he wrote his sixth symphony. No, he was actually content, content and confident that he was composing something really worthwhile. He conducted the first performance himself in St. Petersburg in 1893, I believe. It was not well received."

"So I bet he was melancholy then, huh? All that hard work and nobody appreciated it."

"Genius is seldom appreciated," he'd say rising from the toilet, the sad Basset Hound look returning to his eyes. Then with one sweeping and dramatic gesture he'd exit the bathroom.

All week long Allison heard about that final movement and how tragic and beautiful it was. She fell asleep during it. She tried to stay awake. She rested her head on Frank's shoulder to avoid the embarrassment of it dropping and jerking. Tonight, however she was startled awake by a hard nudge delivered to her rib cage. She opened her eyes and he gave her a stern look like a professor reprimanding the naughty student. To Allison's horror she realized she had drooled on his camel's hair coat and discreetly wiped the corner of her mouth. She spent the remainder of the concert thinking about what she could eat when she got home: something with salt or chocolate?

"What in hell took you so long?" said Frank startling her back into reality.

She was relieved that he wasn't quizzing her about Tchaikovsky and the final movement of his sixth symphony, which she didn't hear. "What took me so long? I'll tell you what took me so long. The fact that men design women's restrooms and they never put in enough stalls. Until more women become architects or men become more in tune with women's needs, which I don't see happening anytime soon, I'll be destined to wait in line to go the john and you'll be destined to wait for me. So don't blame me for having to wait. Blame your own kind."

"At least you have stalls. You don't have some guy next to you urinating on your shoe."

"I can't help it if your species is uncivilized."

"If we're such uncivilized brutes then why do we stand around half the evening holding your coats? Yet we do it, even those of us with back trouble," Frank mumbled, helping her get the coat on. "It weighs a ton."

Allison's straight cut hair caught under the collar of her coat. Frank's cold fingers touched the back of her neck as he lifted the hair out, letting it fall in a symmetrical cascade upon her shoulders. In the old days this gesture was sexy.

"Your fingers are cold. Why are you so cold? You didn't even take your overcoat off during the concert."

"Maybe I didn't want to stand around holding two coats," Frank said putting on his leather gloves. "Let's get out of here." He held the heavy glass door open for Allison as she walked through. They stepped outside into the cold night air which stung Allison's face like a hard slap. It had stopped snowing, but the sky still looked like snow.

"No, I'm serious," Allison said, catching her breath. "I wonder if you have a thyroid condition. You have all the symptoms. I read about it recently."

"In one of your women's magazines, right? Al, those idiotic things are written on a fifth grade level."

"You're so damn superior. There're some very informative articles in some of those magazines."

"Yeah, right, like, 'How to Drive Him Crazy in Bed'. I can see you've gleaned a world of knowledge from those articles."

"Shut up! All I'm saying is you need a good check up. You have all the classic symptoms of hypothyroidism. You're cold all the time. You're tired, weak, forgetful. Of course you haven't gained weight, but then you are a man. Maybe it's different for men. Hey, why the hell are you moving so fast? Would you slow down," Allison called out to Frank who was several paces ahead of her.

"First you tell me I'm tired and weak. Then you tell me I'm moving too fast. Why don't you make up your mind?" he called back to her.

She quickened her pace to catch up with him, until at last they were walking side by side. "Passive aggressive bastard," she muttered.

"No, I just don't happen to think it's the kind of evening for a leisurely stroll."

"Would you please slow down before I fall and break my ass? There're slippery spots all over the place, and I don't exactly have on the best shoes."

"So don't wear such impractical shoes next time."

"What am I supposed to wear to such an event? Galoshes?" Allison looked down at her shoes. "Oh, no! Salt! My shoes are completely ruined!"

"So which would you rather have? A broken ass or ruined shoes?"

"Neither."

"Next time wear galoshes and don't complain."

"Next time park closer to the door."

"Next time don't take so damned long getting ready. Then maybe we won't be late and there might actually *be* a place to park closer to the door."

"I don't care if there ever is a next time."

"Well, at least we agree on something."

So ended Allison and Frank's longest and most intimate conversation of the day. They walked along in silence, the cold air making Allison's eyes water as she exhaled puffs of breath into the bitter night. They passed the Lutheran church where they were married. The full moon peeked out from behind the clouds and shone on the old Gothic style stone structure, with its arched doorway and windows and its tall narrow steeple. They passed by the church without saying a word. Allison deliberately looked down, focusing on her footsteps in the newly fallen layer of snow. Her only thoughts were on the car, the warmth of the heater, and getting there as quickly as possible. One more block to go, she thought keeping her eyes focused forward as they crossed the street. They stepped up on the curb, their car now in sight, parked at the end of the block. On this block were two buildings, a pawn shop and an old store which used to house a very posh women's clothing shop but now stood deserted, waiting for the wrecking ball to come along and turn it into rubble. A narrow alley divided the two structures built together so long ago.

Frank and Allison walked more quickly down this block, partly because of the cold and partly because this was a dangerous part of town. As they approached the alley between the two buildings, Allison felt a chill, a chill not caused by the cold night air but from something in her spirit. She felt dread and foreboding, like a large hand gripping her intestines. She wondered if Frank felt it too. She'd heard that people who'd seen ghosts often experienced a strange coldness. She dismissed the thought, wondering why she even had it.

She wondered what Frank was thinking. She never knew anymore. His arms were tight at his side, his hands in his coat pockets. Allison stuck her arm in his. She felt him jump at the same time she did when the sound of something crashed to the ground in the alley. Something or someone was in that alley. *Maybe it's just a stray cat*, Allison told herself as Frank quickly pulled her away from the building around to the street side.

"Just keep walking, Al. Keep walking," Frank said in a whisper as he firmly took hold of Allison's arm. Allison might have been touched by Frank's chivalry if she hadn't been so scared. She wanted to tell him she was scared, but she didn't. She just kept walking, her thoughts and her eyes focused ahead on the car. They were almost at the alley. *Just keep looking straight ahead*, Allison told herself. Out of her peripheral vision she saw a grey figure emerge from the alley. It startled her more than the noise, causing her to gasp out loud. Frank didn't jump this time though she felt his body tense up. "Keep moving, Al. Just keep moving," he said, not whispering this time.

The streetlight shone on the face of a woman. It was a worn face, accentuated by the disheveled and colorless hair which hung in matted rattails. She wore a coat which was ripped under the arm and looked like it was about two sizes too small. The wind blew the wrap open, revealing no lining in the coat, and only a tee shirt and an old pair of jeans worn much too thin to keep anyone warm on such a night. Allison recognized the woman's brown lace-up shoes as a style from her own high school years. One of them was completely worn through, revealing a socked toe hanging out. *At least she has socks on*, Allison thought, looking down at her own shoes.

The same wind that blew the woman's coat open blew the odor of alcohol mixed with dirty clothes her direction. The cold didn't seem to phase the woman, however, as she staggered toward them babbling incoherently. "You got any money. Gimme some money, man. Just a dollar. That's all. A dollar for a cup of hot coffee." Frank looked straight ahead, his hand gripping Allison's arm tightly, as he pulled her along. Allison shook her head and smiled nervously at the woman as they quickly passed her. She was still behind them, following them, her plea for money becoming more persistent and belligerent. "A dollar for a cup of coffee. That's all, man. Just a fuckin' dollar or two. C'mon, c'mon. I'm freezin' my ass off out here."

Something compelled Allison to turn around and look at the woman's face again. It was just a glance, just a moment, and she really didn't get a good look at her; but she thought she saw a scar on her cheek. There was something familiar around the eyes which stared back at Allison blankly. The light from the street lamp grew dimmer with each step away from it, and soon the woman's face was lost to the shadows of the night, as was her voice, which called out to them one last time in a gravelly and angry tone. "Bitch!"

The woman ceased following them. Allison turned back one last time to see the shadowy figure standing alone. "Don't look back, Al," Frank said to her.

They made it to the car without further incident. After Frank let Allison in, he quickly made it around to the driver's side, slipped into the seat of their new Lexus and flipped the automatic locks. The click of the locks, the sound of finality, Allison thought; she and Frank sealing themselves off from the dangers of the outside world. They were indeed safe now. The engine started and the car slowly inched away from the curb, the tires making a crackling noise over the ice and snow. But safe from what, Allison wondered. Even if the woman was dangerous, she was too drunk to do them any harm. Allison wasn't afraid anymore. The sight of the woman had removed her fear and replaced it with pity and revulsion. But there was something else gnawing at her. She reached in her black evening bag until her hand rested on the smooth surface of her cell phone.

"We should call the police, don't you think?" Allison turned and looked at Frank as she asked the question. He was staring straight ahead. His sad puppy dog look was long gone. He now had the intense look of the vigilante, the strong protector and provider. The primitive man standing in his fur loin cloth outside his cave with club tightly gripped in hand.

"Yeah. Probably so. She's most likely harmless, but you never know. Better give me the phone," said Frank, holding his gloved hand out to receive it.

"That's not the point, Frank."

"What's not the point?"

"Whether or not she's harmless. The point is she's out there alone in the freezing cold. Poor thing! She's undoubtedly in some kind of trouble."

"Poor thing? If that was a man back there you wouldn't be saying poor thing. You'd be all too willing to believe the worst about him. In your mind he wouldn't just be some harmless drunk. He'd be a thief, a rapist, a serial killer. But because it's a woman you automatically leap to the conclusion that she's in some kind of trouble."

"That's because your gender is more prone to violence," Allison said, wondering why everything between them got twisted into a battle of wits. Their bantering used to be fun, but somewhere along the line it had gotten ugly and tiresome. How funny that it was their mutual fear which connected them just moments before when they passed that alleyway, but now that the incident was over, they returned to their usual status of hostile adversaries.

"I'm calling the police." Allison pulled the cell phone out of her black evening bag.

"Give me the phone. With your sense of direction you'll send them to the other side of town."

"You want the phone? Here!" Allison threw the phone at Frank. He held his arm up in an attempt to block the flying object. It bounced off his arm and landed on the seat beside him.

"Damn! That could've hit me in the head and caused me to have an accident."

After a few moments of hostile silence, Allison saw the shadow of shock and rage leave Frank's face as he fought to regain his composure. "I thought your gender wasn't prone to violence." He smirked triumphantly and picked up the phone.

"Bastard!" Allison's pride hurt because she knew Frank was victorious. Whoever lost control, lost the battle. That was the unspoken rule they both played by. She blinked back the burning pool of tears which she longed to release in torrents down her cheeks. She was not about to let Frank see her cry.

Frank spoke officially into the phone. "Off of Fifth Street. Between Locust and Sycamore. Yes, that's correct. In the alley behind that old pawn shop. I'm sure it's nothing, you know, but maybe she's in some kind of trouble."

Allison closed her eyes and laid her head against the window as Frank talked with the dispatcher. In her mind she was back home in the warmth of her kitchen, sitting at the kitchen table all alone with a steaming cup of hot chocolate and a bag of chips before her. She could almost taste it as she imagined herself dipping a large perfectly formed potato chip into the cup of hot chocolate. A smile formed on her lips. Her fantasy was interrupted by Frank's voice.

"Police are on their way," Frank announced, his no-nonsense tone of voice reminding her of Joe Friday from Dragnet.

Allison let go a contemptuous little chuckle.

"What's so funny?"

"Nothing you'd understand." Allison pressed her cheek against the cold window as they drove on in silence through the dirty grey slush which a short while before had been clean, white, and glistening. Nothing stays pure and untainted. She thought of the woman. She remembered her face, the eyes, and the scar on the cheek. Realization struck her at that precise moment. It couldn't be. It couldn't possibly be. Could it?

"Frank, did you..." She stopped herself. She was about to ask him if he recognized the woman. Could it possibly be Vicky? She looked at him. He seemed totally unscathed, completely unruffled. If he did recognize her, he certainly wasn't letting on. No, he couldn't have recognized her. He wouldn't be acting so normal. Did he not get a good enough look at her face or had he blocked it out after all these years? Of course he didn't recognize her. Allison was surprised she did. It was the sick, bloated face of a drunk, not at all the face she remembered from twenty years ago.

Al, old dear, you're tired. It's late. You're jumping to conclusions. That was not Vicky. That's why Frank didn't recognize her. Because it wasn't her. Just some unfortunate drunk who looked a little like her. Allison's sensible voice reassured her.

"Did I what?"

"Huh?"

"You were about to ask me a question."

"Oh, nothing. Never mind."

"You seem upset."

"Uh, I, uh, think I forgot to turn the oven off before we left. I had a frozen pizza in there for the kids," she lied, remembering distinctly switching the dial to "off" and obsessively checking it several times before they left. "I hope Matthew caught it."

"Great. Now you got me worried." Frank stepped on the accelerator, the vigilante look returning to his eyes. "Damnit Al, you've got to quit this crap. I get tired of rushing home from places only to find out you turned everything off. One of these days you really will leave something on and we'll find our house up in smoke."

Allison was only half-listening. She was thinking about Vicky. The woman's face kept coming to her again and again. By the time they pulled into their driveway, she was convinced. It was Vicky standing out there in the cold cursing them. The ghost who so frequently haunted their marriage had returned.

Chapter 2
January 2006
Vicky

Vicky was lucky tonight. She found an old scrap of carpeting in the alley dumpster behind the pawn shop. It was large enough to wrap around her shoulders—an incredible find in such bitter cold weather. "Eureka" she shouted out loud when she found it. "I got me some insulation." With carpet remnant in hand, she tried to hoist a leg over the side of the dumpster and propel herself out. Holding on to the piece of carpet made her efforts more difficult, but she refused to let go of the prize possession. She tried again, but fell hopelessly back into the pile of garbage. She lay there and looked up at the night sky. "Oh, fuck it, I'll just sleep here. Warmer in here anyway." Vicky had the habit of talking to herself, and it had gotten worse. She didn't care if anyone heard her.

"I got my blankie," Vicky wrapped the piece of carpet around her shoulders. "I got a blankie and four walls." Vicky turned her head to look at the inside of the dumpster which was mostly rusted out. "Needs a paint job. I don't got a roof over my head. I got nothin' over my head but clouds. Wish I could see the stars."

The full moon appeared from behind some clouds. "Got no stars but I got a night light." The light dimmed as the moon disappeared again behind the heavy veil of white clouds. "Need to get some new light bulbs," Vicky said staring up at the vast ceiling which was now spinning out of control. "Ah shit!" Vicky rolled over onto her side in an attempt to make the spinning stop. She curled up in the fetal position and stuck her feet and legs under the garbage. The smell reminded her of her high school locker–gym shoes mixed with a brown paper sack lunch, consisting of a bologna sandwich and a banana. Not bad. Maybe it was the cold that kept the smell tolerable or maybe she just couldn't smell anymore. She wondered whether all of her senses were slowly fading away.

"I like bananas. Haven't had one in a while," she said to some strange object she couldn't make out in the dark, but which she adopted as a surrogate teddy bear. She held the thing close to her until it poked her in the cheek. "What the...?" She examined the object as closely as her dim eyes and the lack of light would allow her. She managed from sense of touch to determine that the thing was a broken umbrella. "*You* must go," she said as she hurled it out of the dumpster. "Fuck you!" she hollered at the umbrella and the world as the object hit the ground with a thud. She drew her knees to her chest, curling up again in an even tighter ball. She shivered from the cold, or was it her sickness? She didn't know which was worse... the pain in her throat and her stomach or the endless chill. Worst of all were her raw nerves: dread, panic, pain, and nightmares. A black shadow of a figure appeared before her each time the sickness got bad. She feared its return and had to think of some way to get more booze soon or she was in big trouble. Tonight she had to rest. She had no choice. She couldn't go anywhere.

Vicky's nerves weren't too bad now, in fact a strange feeling of relaxation and sleepiness came over her as She lay in the pile of garbage, staring at the rusted out wall of the dumpster. She didn't feel nearly as cold anymore. Not that she was warmer, simply number. She heard that this was how people froze to death. First there was the numbness, then the sleepiness, then slumber from which one would never awaken. "Good. Maybe I'll freeze to death tonight. Then I won't have to worry about how the hell to get more booze tomorrow." She wondered if she was really ready to die. "Shit, I ain't ready to burn in hell. Too busy raisin' hell here." Vicky laughed. "I ain't ready to die. Don't let me die. Please." She didn't laugh this time. "Who the hell am I talkin' to? Oh, yeah. Myself."

Vicky was on the precipice of sleep. Memories flashed before her eyes. None of them painful, mostly just dull. It was like being at a family get-together, being forced to sit through a slide show of some tedious family holiday. "So this is what it's like to have your life flash before your eyes. Geez, get to the good part."

She saw herself as a kid again running barefoot through the backyards of her childhood neighborhood in western Kentucky. It was a late afternoon in early summer. Bobby, her cousin and best friend, was breathlessly trying to keep up with her but couldn't. Nobody, not even the fastest boys, could run as fast as Vicky, even barefoot she'd beat them. The bottoms of her feet were permanently black. "Put some shoes on, girl," her Mama would call to her as she ran out the back door. "I'm gonna scour them filthy feet with the hottest water and the toughest scrub brush I can find."

"Won't bother me none, Mama" It was true that the bottom of her feet were so calloused she could run over broken glass and not feel a thing, or at least that's what she boasted of.

"Vicky Lee, stop!" Bobby called out to her. She looked back and he was on the ground. "I stepped on a dern acorn, or somethin' like that." Vicky ran back to her cousin.

"C'mon Bobby, don't be such a dang sissy," she said to the dark haired boy as he nursed his sore foot – rubbing it, blowing on it, and rocking back and forth. "You're always remindin' me we're over half Indian on the Miner side. So the way I figure it, you oughta be able to run barefoot too,"

"Hey," Bobby said quickly jumping to his feet, "You may be able to run faster than me in your bare feet, but I'm a faster swimmer and a better fisherman 'n you'll ever be."

"I know, I know. And you got the smarts. You're Tom Sawyer and I'm Huck Finn."

"And don't you forget it!"

"C'mon, Chief Tenderfoot, race ya to that tree. Bet I can climb to the top before you can."

So together they raced each other to the top of a tree amidst giggles and shrill cries of delight.

"I won. I won," Vicky said weakly from within the dumpster. A weakness and exhaustion overtook her and she felt as if something heavy were sitting on top of her. Even so, the memory lingered in her mind.

She was at the top of the twisted old tree, had scaled to the top like a monkey in her bare feet. Bobby sat on the branch below. There they were, two gangly kids, swinging their legs, laughing, bragging, and alive for the moment–and that moment only–until it was time to come down.

It had happened to Vicky one time before. She tried to get down, but couldn't. The last time she thought it was only a fluke, but here she was again, paralyzed with fear, even worse than the last time. She tried to look down but couldn't. The dizziness caused her to grab hold of the tree trunk and close her eyes tight. What was it that caused her to change so much in just one year, she wondered? She climbed up and down trees all the previous summer without giving it a second thought. It must've been the winter that did it; the long hard winter, being cooped up inside with her Daddy who was out of work and drank more and more, and had since become mean when he drank.

Bobby, who was halfway down the tree called up to her. "C'mon Vicky Lee! C'mon down or we'll both be late for supper."

"I caint, Bobby. I caint."

She was crying and shaking and holding on to the tree trunk as tight as she could. "This happened to me one other time," she called down to Bobby. "I don't know why. I'm just plumb crazy all of a sudden. I'm scared. Scared I'll fall."

"Hold on. I'm comin' back up there to git ya."

Bobby stood on the branch below her. "Here, grab hold of my hand."

"I caint."

"Yes, you can. I ain't gonna letcha fall. Now grab hold."

It took a good half hour of coaxing, encouraging, holding onto Bobby with one arm and the tree trunk with the other before Vicky was finally able to place her feet on solid ground.

"Promise you ain't gonna tell anyone about this." Vicky said to Bobby after a humbling thank you.

"I promise. It's just I don't git it. This ain't like you."

"I don't know. Maybe I just wanna stay in that ol' tree. I don't wanna go home. Maybe I oughta just build me a tree house and move up there–stay there forever."

Bobby placed a reassuring arm around Vicky, and spoke more quietly and seriously to her this time. "Remember, I told ya what to do if your Daddy whups ya agin?"

Vicky nodded her head and heaved a sniffling sob.

"Don't let him see ya cry. Bite on somethin' hard if ya have to. Remember, you got Shawnee blood. Be brave. Bobby reached in his pocket and pulled out a pocket knife. "I got an idea." He lifted his shirt, revealing his skinny frame, belly button, the waistband of his white underwear and the leather belt which he always wore in order to keep his britches up. He took the pocket knife and began sawing away at his leather belt until he was finally able to pull off a piece of it.

"Here." He handed her about two inches in length off the tip of the belt. "You bite on this. It ain't as hard a rock or nothin' so it won't hurt your teeth none. Just make sure you don't choke on it. Just close your eyes, bite on this, and imagine me all grown up comin' back to whup your Daddy's ass."

Vicky stuck the piece of leather in her pocket and smiled at Bobby."

"So how'd ya get down the last time this happened?" Bobby asked.

"I jumped."

"You dang fool. You say you're scared of fallin' and then you go jump?"

"I figured it was the only way down."

"And ya didn't hurt yourself none?"

"Not a scratch."

"Shoot, you was just plain lucky."

"Well, it wasn't as tall a tree as this one here, and besides, I landed on my feet. You know they're tougher n' hide."

"Now I know you're fibbin'."

"Yeah, the truth is I landed on my butt. It was black and blue and purple fer weeks. Worse than any whuppin' I ever got." They both laughed and Vicky forgot her fears, at least for the time being.

"Ah Bobby, whatever happened to you?" Vicky said inside the dumpster. "You still remember me? Wonder if you're even still alive. I never climbed another tree after that. But how come I could get up that tree but couldn't get back down again. Just like now. I can get in the dumpster but I can't get out. Story of my fuckin' life. I get into messes but can't get back out." She laughed feebly.

"Said the *F* word again. Owe ya a quarter. How many does that make today?" Vicky deliriously rambled on and on, an endless stream of unedited thoughts, not asleep but not conscious either. She was vaguely aware that it was snowing again. Little snowflakes landed on her cheeks and eyelids. "Ah, no, I gotta piss." A warm stream of urine rolled down her legs. She began to cry. The crying jags always came toward the end of a drunk. She sobbed and sobbed thinking how she would be found dead the next morning covered in garbage, snow, and urine.

The familiar squawk and intermittent static of a police radio filled Vicky's ears and became louder and louder until she realized it was coming from the alley. Headlight beams suddenly flooded their lights in her direction. The squad car was in the alley. Vicky heard two car doors slam. She decided then and there that spending the night in jail was preferable to spending it in a dumpster buried beneath a half foot of snow. She didn't care if it was the meanest cop on the beat, she had to find some way to get their attention. She banged on the side of the dumpster and hollered as loud as she could. "Hey pigs! I'm in here. Somebody get me out."

They shined their flashlights down on her.

Vicky looked up and saw the figure of two cops standing over her. "Is that you, Fat Ass?" Vicky hollered up, squinting into the glaring lights.

The two men laughed. "If you're referring to Officer Jones, he works days now," replied one of the cops.

"Thank God. I've had enough of his shit."

"Is that you Vicky?" The other cop inquired.

"Who the hell did you think it was? Oscar the Fuckin' Grouch?"

"Okay, Vicky, let's get you out of there. Can you stand up?" said the first cop.

"No. Hey you wanna kill that light, Officer Friendly!"

"You better watch that smart mouth of yours," said the second cop.

"Or what? You'll charge me with Public Intoxication again?"

"No, Vicky, we're way beyond that," said the first cop, reaching an arm down into the dumpster and pulling her up. "Just be a good girl and come along quietly. Don't make any trouble for us and we won't make any trouble for you." The second cop grabbed her other arm and together they helped her out of the dumpster. Cop number one ran quickly to the squad car where he fetched something out of the trunk. It was a blanket. He returned and placed it over her shoulders. "Here you go, Vick."

"Thanks Bobby," Vicky said as she planted a kiss on his cheek.

"Bobby! Who the hell's Bobby? I'm your old buddy Officer Graves. Remember me?"

"You don't have to shout. I'm just drunk. I ain't deaf." She thought he was repulsed by her kiss. She could tell by the look on his face as he wiped it off his cheek. "I had you worried. You thought I was gonna rape ya, didn't ya. So now you gonna charge me with sexual assault?"

"Just get in the car, Vicky. It's nice and warm in there." The first cop said holding a hand over the top of Vicky's head to shield it from bumping as she scooted into the back of the squad car.

"Sexually assaulting a police officer? That's a good one, Vicky," said the second cop laughing.

"I wouldn't wanna sexually assault your ugly ass."

"Thank God for small favors."

"Now c'mon, Vicky honey, don't go gettin' snippy or we'll have to cuff you. We haven't had to cuff you in a while," said cop number one, sticking his head in the door.

"I ain't your honey."

"Lucky for both of us," said cop number one as he leaned further in and strapped her in her seat.

The officers got in the squad car. A thick sheet of plexiglass separated them from the back seat.

"So tell me, Vick. You got a home these days?"

"What's that?"

"A home. As in place of residence. Abode. Domicile. You got some place to live?"

Vicky shook her head. "You just made me leave my newest domicile."

"Sorry Vicky, but it didn't look to me as if the heat was workin'." Cop number one radioed the police station and told them to prepare a cell.

"By the way Vick, yer damned lucky, " cop number two said as they backed out of the alley way into the streets of downtown Lamasco.

"How's that?"

"We just passed a garbage truck at the Chinese restaurant down the street. His next stop's the alley where you was sleepin'. Hell, had we not retrieved you from that dumpster, you'd been squished in the recycle bin."

"I bet if ol' Fat Ass was working he would've let 'em. He'd a had 'em haul my sorry ass off to the dump."

"You're more than likely right," said cop number one. They all laughed.

Vicky was beginning to fall over to one side. The shoulder strap of the seat belt chaffed against her neck, but she didn't care. She couldn't sit up straight if she tried.

"You all right back there, Vick?" said cop number one eyeing her in the rear view mirror. "You need to yark?"

"No, I'm fine."

"You sure? Cause we'll pull over if you need to yark."

"I don't need to yark," Vicky said more insistently.

"Just don't yark in the car again. Okay? Last time you yarked in one of our squad cars it took months to get the odor out."

"Still ain't out a hundred percent," cop number two added.

"You keep aggravatin' me, I'll stick my finger down my throat and make myself puke." By now Vicky was as horizontal as one can get while strapped into a seat belt. "You guys ain't gonna stick me in the drunk tank again tonight, are you? That place is disgusting. Just take me straight to my cell. Will ya do that for me?" She called out her request through a thick tongue and a throat that felt and sounded as if she'd swallowed sand.

"If you promise not to yark all over it."

"Look, I promise not to puke. What do you want me to do, take a dang oath? I, Vicky Lee Dooley, do hereby solemnly swear not to yark tonight, anywhere on or near the property or premises of the Lamasco Police Department. So help me, God." She let her raised hand drop with a thud onto the seat.

"Now if I'm a good girl and I don't back talk and I don't puke, will you grant me one more request?"

"What's that?"

"Could you bum me a cigarette?"

"You make good on that promise and I'll be more than happy to bum you a cigarette. Not until we get back to the station, you understand. And you gotta sit upright to smoke it."

Vicky smiled all the way into an unconscious state.

You couldn't really call it sleep, this fitful state of unconsciousness that overtook Vicky when the booze finally ran its course. It was a state somewhere between wakefulness and sleep. What real people would call a lousy night sleep, Vicky often thought. Her semi-consciousness was much more real and alive than her wakeful states, and without a doubt more frightening. She could achieve numb while awake, but never in this in-between state where memories and regrets and reality closed in on her. It was in such a state that she flopped restlessly from side to side and mumbled aloud to no one but herself in the small cell of the Lamasco jail.

The image of two people, a man and a woman, appeared before Vicky each time she closed her eyes. The woman was an attractive blond in a full-length fur coat; the man was tall, distinguished, and dark haired. The woman walked fast up and down the halls of the jail, her blond shoulder length hair bouncing right in time with each stride, and her little black purse which hung from a gold chain perched upon her shoulder danced about her hip as she moved quickly. She seemed to be running from something. The man moved much slower than the woman and lagged sorely behind her as the two paraded back and forth in front of the bars of her cell. He had the air of wealth, class, and aristocracy about him, but his shoulders were not held erect with pride as one might expect from such a man, but rather, were weighted down with something.

She recognized their movements first, then their faces. "Why, of course, if it isn't Mr. And Mrs. Frank Hamilton. Remember me, your ol' buddy Vicky? Remember me, Frank? Except you were never Frank to me. You were Francis. That's what your I-talian mama named you. If it was good enough for her, it was good enough for me. You were Francis to me. My Francis. What the hell kind of a name is Frank for a guy like you? Probably suits ya now. You done grown into it. Fuckwad Frank. Mr. and Mrs. Fuckwad Frank." Her laughter turned into a hacking cough which she couldn't control. The cough along with the pained laughter came from deep within her gut, it was so hard it made the veins in her neck and temples feel as if they would burst.

"Haven't changed a bit, Allison," the words squeaked out of her throat in one great wheeze. "Still running. And Francis still draggin' ass behind her. Haven't changed a bit. I wasn't good enough for either one of ya, was I? I was never good enough. Wasn't good enough to be your friend, Allison, and I sure as hell wasn't good enough to be... yours, Francis."

Vicky felt another crying jag come on, but she wouldn't let this one take over. "I'll be damned if I shed any more tears for you, Francis," she called out, mustering all the fight she had within her. "Frank the fuckwad," she cried out triumphantly. Anger had won out over self-pity this time, and it felt good. "Mr. and Mrs. Frank the fuckwad Hamilton. Mr. Frank fuckwad and his lovely bride of fucking Frankenstein. So, how many quarters do I owe ya now, Francis? Is that why you couldn't loan me a buck or two for a cheap ass bottle of booze? Figure I owe it to ya in quarters after all these years of sayin' the *F* word? Ain't none of us got nothin' to be proud of. You're yuppie scum and I'm a fuckin' drunk. We ain't got nothin' to be proud of." The anger spent itself, and exhausted, Vicky fell back on her cot.

"Ah shit, not again," she said, raising a shaking hand in front of her face. "Hold still," she said slapping one shaky hand with another shaky hand in a vain attempt to hold her hands still. "Here he comes again." There in the darkness outside her cell the dark phantom appeared. It wasn't the usual faceless hooded phantom like the Grim Reaper. It if was, then she would have a right to be scared, but it was a shapeless overgrown blob. Sometimes it would shrink very small then suddenly grow large again. It had a comic face like a cartoon character; a face which laughed at her and mocked her. It only laughed, it never spoke, and its laughter would fluctuate from very high and squeaky when small, to low and deep when large.

"Stop it. Stop it. Stop laughing at me. I've swept bigger dust bunnies than you out from under my bed. Now go away," she said closing her eyes and placing her shaking hands over her ears to stop the sound of the laughter. Booze was the only thing that would make it go away and she didn't have any booze. Maybe if she screamed one of the matrons would come in and take pity on her and get her something to drink. Most likely not. She was stuck with the stupid phantom unless she became unconscious. Maybe she could bang her head against the wall to induce a state of unconsciousness. Maybe not such a good idea. "Knowin' my luck I'd bang my head too hard and wind up a damn vegetable." She closed her eyes and tried to will it away. "I could always cast it out in the name of Jesus. Right Grandma?" She squeezed her eyes tight and willed herself to remember the face of her grandmother. She could no longer see the phantom though she could still hear it laughing at her. "If I see a friendly face then I can't see its face. Right?" She said trembling, afraid to open her eyes. She touched the small key which hung on a chain around her neck. It was the key to her grandma's hope chest–all she had left in the world.

She squeezed her eyes tight, rubbed the key, and tried to call to mind the little country church that she so often visited with her Pentecostal grandmother. The memory became more vivid as the laughter outside her cell door continued. "I ain't here. I'm far far away. Back at church with Grandma. You can't reach me here."

She remembered the uncomfortable wooden pews that caused her back and bottom to ache. Mostly she remembered the hardwood floor which invariably bade her to lie upon it when she'd finally had her fill of sitting up straight during the long services. She'd unabashedly hop off the pew and lay on that floor staring up at the ceiling of the church, with its wooden planks smartly painted white, arching up and up and up to the sky. The sound of the piano rang in her ear along with the voice of her grandmother, half whispering, half not. "Vicky Lee, get off that floor right now. You git right back up on this here pew. Now c'mon be a good girl. I don't wanna have to take a switch to yer hide." So Vicky would obey. She always obeyed her grandmother, unlike her mamma and daddy. Her grandmother would then place a large flabby arm around Vicky's shoulder, it was better than a cushion, and Vicky would snuggle against her sagging breasts which hung over the belt of her Sunday dress. Her grandmother smelled like Ivory soap and the fresh air of line dried clothes. All the while the voice of her grandmother and the rest of the congregation would swirl about in her head.

What a friend we have in Jesus
All our sins and griefs to bear!
What a privilege to carry
Everything to God in prayer!
O what peace we often forfeit
O what needless pain we bear
All because we do not carry
Everything to God in prayer!

Vicky opened her eyes. Her head was clear and the phantom was gone.

"Oh, so now you're gonna be my friend, after all the shit I've put up with. Don't you think it's a little late? Leave me alone. I don't believe in you. Who the hell am I talkin' to? Myself, myself, always my damned self."

The anxiety returned. Of course it did. Vicky knew it would. And with it came the apparitions of Francis and Allison, pacing back and forth in the hall outside her cell, completely oblivious to her imprisonment. "Oh, shit! Not you assholes again. Go away and leave me alone. I'm expecting another visitor. Maybe you've seen him. He's a twelve foot tall dust bunny and he eats drunks for supper." Vicky shuddered at the idea of the dark phantom returning. Then she got an idea which made her laugh, cough, and hack all at the same time. If the phantom returned, she'd simply command him to eat Allison and Francis. "Sic 'em! Go on and sic 'em," she laughed uncontrollably, not noticing the figure of the female guard standing over her.

"Vicky, are you all right?" She heard the voice say, sounding as if it was coming from inside a tunnel. "You've been making quite a ruckus."

"Grandma, is that you? I'm sick, grandma. I don't feel so good."

"Oh, my gosh! Shirley, get in here quick," Vicky heard the voice holler out to someone. There was commotion inside the cell, footsteps moving fast, two figures now standing over her, their voices hushed yet filled with concern. She only caught a word or phrases here and there. "Covered in sweat... A seizure?... No, not a seizure... Tremors... Hospital... Need to call an ambulance..."

"Don't make me go to the hospital, grandma. I ain't that sick. Just let me stay home from school. I don't need no doctor."

"Vicky, honey, do you know where you are?"

"Ain't sure. Make it go away. Just make it go away."

"We're trying, honey. We're gonna get someone to help you."

She was aware of someone touching her, stroking her forehead. She thought it seemed a concerned touch, but she wasn't sure. She wasn't sure of anything anymore. Was it her grandmother? Who was the other person with her? Was this a trick? Who were these two faces that hovered over her? Were they in cahoots with the phantom? Were they only pretending to be nice? What if they started to pull her hair out by the roots or dig their fingernails into her temple until she spurted blood?

The last thing Vicky remembered was the muffled sound of her own scream.

Allison

Chapter 3
Late January 2006

The lights and colors were unbearably bright while a cacophonic noise of buzzers, beeps, bells, and bubble gum pop music competed for the attention of the children, who ran wildly and aimlessly through the place. In the dining area flashing images of music videos played on three large screens, interrupted only by larger than life-size mechanically operated cartoon-like creatures, which appeared behind the curtain of a shrine-like stage every half hour to perform a second rate Vegas act.

Allison drummed her fingers on the table while Frank slouched in his chair and sighed helplessly. He wore his sad expression this evening, only more disoriented and agitated than usual. *Like an old basset hound that has to be put to sleep.* Allison thought of Frank, as she watched a ten-foot tall rodent sing and dance from the enshrined stage.

"I can't believe you brought me here," Frank said.

"Smile. It's your daughter's birthday. You're supposed to be enjoying yourself."

"I can't believe she wanted to come here. Why would she want to come here?"

"Because she's a kid, Frank. A kid. Not a midget."

"What's that supposed to mean?"

"It means you treat her like a small adult, not a child. You're the same way with Mattie and Alex. Always have been."

"She's eight years old, for crying out loud! How old does a kid have to be before they outgrow a place like this?"

"She's a kid! Where else would she want to go for her birthday? The Pump Room? But because she'd rather eat pizza than escargot on her eighth birthday, you automatically conclude there's something wrong with her."

"The only thing wrong with her is that you baby her. She could be exceptional if you wouldn't hold her back so much and just let her settle for mediocrity."

"Another dig at me! Let it go, Frank? She wasn't ready for that gifted program you tried to push her into. You're just angry because I stood my ground. I'm not going to allow that kind of pressure to be put on our child."

"She taught herself to read when she was three. You don't give your kids enough credit," Frank said with his all-knowing look.

"*Our* kids, Frank! They're our kids. Remember."

"It's difficult to remember they're my kids too with the way you smother them."

"Smother them!? I parent them, which is something you know nothing about. If I am guilty of smothering them then maybe it's overcompensation for your complete and total absence as a father." Even as the words were out of her mouth, Allison knew it was wrong to say, but she wanted to wound him in retaliation. It never worked. Frank's face reddened with anger and she knew she had pushed him too far; too far for a public place at any rate.

"Okay, let's just not go there. Could you go get us some beer," Allison said, desperate for a quick diversion, so as to spend Frank's angry energy and make him feel useful.

"They serve beer here?" Frank's face brightened.

Allison nodded.

"Why didn't you say so? I may actually make it through this whole ordeal."

So might I, Allison thought. *So might I.*

"I'll be back," said Frank, rising from his seat with a heave of great effort. Allison watched the slumped-shouldered husband turned stranger amble towards the front counter while avoiding wildly running children.

She wondered how exactly she would phrase it. She hadn't rehearsed anything, which was unusual for her. Organization and preparation were her strong points. Certainly Frank would agree. *A real go-getter*, Allison exhaled a little chortle filled with years of disappointment and cynicism as a Chipmunks rendition of *Stayin' Alive* blasted over the speakers.

Was it Vicky who finally pushed her into making this decision? It was the push she needed. *Funny*, she thought. She was sure it was Vicky that night, but as the days passed she grew less certain. A week had passed since then and she'd since convinced herself that maybe it wasn't Vicky after all. *Of course not. It couldn't be.* If it was then she would have to do something, even though she wasn't sure what. Nonetheless, the whole incident reminded her of Vicky and made her think about the past and how she and Frank married on the rebound. Mulling over these things, she glanced over at the next table where a little boy sat. The bottoms of his white socks were filthy black. She reached in her bag for anti-bacterial hand spray.

He wasn't over Vicky when we got married. Allison felt the relief of the waterless soap evaporate from her hands. *He said he was, but he wasn't. She's the one he left behind. Of course Mister Melodrama gets to pine away for his lost love while I sort his socks, press his shirts, and put the toilet lid down after him.*

Allison curiously studied a creature on stage–a web-footed winged cheerleader creature shaking a tambourine. *What the hell is that thing?* The *gorilla's groupie? They just let her play with the band every now and then to appease her.*

I guess this is a hell of a time to tell him he's got to move out. It's Kristy's birthday. But when else do I get a chance to talk to him. He works seventy hours a week, comes home, listens to his classical music, sighs and moans half the evening then falls into bed. She figured if she waited until the perfect moment when she had him alone it would be too late. She'd always been an action-oriented person. No time like the present.

The Vicky look-alike last week in the snow reopened an old festering wound and it was time to perform a debridement before it got any worse. This was the perfect setting. The kids were occupied–Kristy playing in the plastic tunnels and Matthew and Alex playing video games. Frank couldn't go anywhere; he'd have to listen. And a public place with children present, so they couldn't fight. Neutral territory, Allison thought, watching the long billed blond with the tambourine, wearing tennis shoes which Allison noted were especially designed for her webbed feet.

"Hi Mommy," Kristy said, as she hugged her mother's neck and awkwardly pulled her head down to her level.

"Don't yank, honey. Here, wash your hands." She held out the antibacterial hand spray. "You've been playing in those filthy tunnels" Allison sprayed the bottle into Kristen's palms. Kristen then hopped up on her mother's lap, once again throwing her arm around her neck. Allison was irritated at all the clinging. Allison had to admit that what Frank had said was true: she had indulged this one in particular and the immaturity drove her nuts.

"Mommy, I'm hungry. Where's Freddie Fieldmouse? When's he going to sing Happy Birthday to me?"

"Our pizza's coming. Freddie will be out as soon as we finish our pizza."

"But Mommy, I'm hungry."

"Don't whine, Kristen. I hate that. And for Pete's sake, stop tugging on me. I can't breathe." Allison felt the irritation growing within her as she pried the child's arms off from around her neck and scooted her off her lap. Kristen hung her head for a few painful seconds.

"Why are you so grouchy all the time?" she finally said looking up. "Are you and Daddy fighting again?"

Irritation turned to guilt as she saw the tears in the little girl's eyes, ready to fall with only a single blink. Kristen had Frank's blue eyes and the same thick dark hair, which was pulled back in a pink plastic clip today.

Kristen was what would have been known in Allison's day as a *crybaby*. Today she was called *a sensitive child*. Whatever you call it, she hadn't yet learned the coping mechanisms her brothers had. She was the only one of the children still young and unsophisticated enough to be honest about the family situation. She was a constant reminder to Frank and Allison that their kids knew what was going on. Kristen was the voice and conscience of the family. This broke Allison's heart. This was too big of a burden for a child so young to bear. The two oldest boys had their burdens too.

Their oldest son, Matthew, was a seventeen year old high school senior and recent recipient of a prestigious college scholarship. He was bound for Notre Dame in the fall. Of course he chose Notre Dame. It's where Frank wanted to go had his own father not insisted he go to the family alma mater, University of Pennsylvania. Sometimes when she looked at Matt she couldn't believe this seemingly perfect boy was her son. His blond hair, blue eyes, and rugged good looks bore a strong resemblance to her side of the family, but he had a quiet dignity and savoir-faire that her country bumpkin Brinkmeyer male relatives never had.

Matt was smart, mature, responsible, and confident. At least it looked that way. He had learned how to put his best foot forward. Allison had always been closest to Matt. He was a wonderful companion and great conversationalist, even as a small child, but now he was distant and secretive. She missed the days when he confided in her, when he was shy and awkward. They had a bond then but it had slipped away. He was like a shiny gold trophy she was happy to show off to others, but the thing itself was cold and lifeless and the best she could do was to stick it on a mantle and keep it dusted.

Then there was Alex, their middle child–fourteen years old and a disaster waiting to happen. He was an angry child and his anger leaked out all over the place. His anger was costing them money. He'd kicked his bedroom door so hard he'd left a hole behind. He'd thrown a lamp across the room. Then the countless trips to the emergency room, the stitches in his lip from the fight he got into at school, the broken arm from falling off his bike. "All boy," Frank would say. "Accident prone," Allison would say, but the child psychologist labeled it "aggressive" and "self-destructive". An Oppositional Disorder. ADHD. They had thrown away a wad of money on this child. Nothing any professional had done had helped. What would they be forking money out for next? Legal fees, fines, bail, drug rehab? Allison shuddered at the thought.

Then there was the rivalry between Alex and Matthew. Alex was perpetually flunking while Matthew was an "A" student who'd already tested out of several colleges classes. It seemed the more Matthew tried to be good, the more Alex tried to be bad. Allison knew there was no one to blame for this mess but herself and Frank And here it was–all this pain and heartbreak reflected on the face of her youngest child. *She's too young to have a face like that. Kritsy was supposed to be our redemption, our last chance, mid-life baby who would make us realize all the good we take for granted. She was supposed to revitalize our marriage. A hell of an expectation to put on a child.*

"Honey, please don't cry." Kristen's lower lip quivered and she swallowed hard, her blue sad puppy dog eyes staring up at her, completely guileless, making Allison want to cry instead.

"It's your birthday, honey. Please, don't cry. You look so pretty. Come here." The child stepped into her mother's arms. Allison couldn't put enough comfort into the hug.

What are we doing to these kids? She closed her eyes and squeezed tighter. *They won't have to see us fight after this. I just don't want them to see another fight.* She felt an ache in her chest as she thought of how the fights had increasingly turned uglier in recent years. How long before the verbal abuse would escalate into physical abuse? How often Matthew, who'd increasingly taken on the role of parent, ended up between her and Frank during a fight, pleading with them to stop? *He must know how close we are to taking swings at one another.* She remembered one night wanting to kick Frank so badly it took every ounce of energy to restrain herself. *This isn't like me. I hate what I've become. I want to put all this anger behind me. There's no other way to do it. Surely it will be better for the kids this way.*

"Everything's okay, Kristy. We're not fighting," Allison said, trying to get comfort from the lingering hug.

"Where's Daddy? He didn't leave, did he?"

"No, sweetie, he went to get some drinks. He'll be right back. You're hungry, aren't you? You're just like your mother. You get cranky when you're hungry."

Frank approached the table, moving slower than usual, a plastic cup filled with beer in each hand.

"Daddy!" Kristen, impulsive as always, ran up to Frank and threw her arms around his waist. The foam from the beer sloshed precariously from side to side, threatening to spill all over.

"Whoa! Watch it there birthday girl."

"You didn't leave," she said not wanting to release her father from her grip.

"Leave? Why would I leave?"

"Because you and Mom are fighting again."

Frank looked at Allison. She shrugged her shoulders.

"Nobody's fighting. Hey, let me put these drinks down before I spill them all over you."

"What took so long?" asked Allison taking a swig of beer.

"I had to wait for them to get their liquor license. I think they got some of the gorilla's relatives working the counter."

"I hear you. The pizza's not here yet either."

"Some service."

"Honey, go find your brothers and tell them to come to the table," said Allison. "We don't want to have to hunt them down when the pizza gets here."

Kristen ran off happy.

Should she tell him now? The impulse struck Allison, but only for a moment or two. They were both operating on an empty stomach, and besides there wasn't enough time. The kids were on their way to the table and the pizza would be here soon. No, she would proceed with her original plan and tell him after the pizza, and the birthday cake, and the visit from Freddie Fieldmouse. She would send the boys back to their games and Kristen back to the tunnels, and then she would tell him.

Allison focused her attention on the large TV screen. A music video with kids dressed in early sixties garb dancing to "It's My Party". "And I'll cry if I want to," Allison found herself singing along.

Frank looked at her.

"So what do you want?" she asked him.

"I want the giant animals to come out here and do their act again. I think I like them better than the music videos."

Allison laughed in spite of herself. Why ruin the last pleasant moment they would ever have together? They were becoming so rare. "Nothing like beer on an empty stomach to change your outlook on life."

"Cheers." Allison tapped her plastic cup against Frank's. She didn't notice her emotions until a small tear worked its way out of the corner of her eye. She wiped it away with a discreet rub of her index finger.

"Are you okay?" she was surprised to hear him inquire.

"Fine." He put his hand on her back. *Oh, great! Now he's going to be nice to me for the first time in about a year. His annual nice moment. Why did he pick now?* She looked at him. He looked happy. *It's just the beer. I haven't loved him in years. Tonight's the start of a new life. I will not back down.*

Luckily, the spell was broken by Kristen who came running up to the table with her big brother, Matthew, who was trailing behind with his cell phone in hand, rapidly texting a friend.

"Where's Alex.?"

"He's playing Alien Wars," Matthew said. "He said to go ahead and eat without him."

"Great, that's just what he needs. More mindlessly violent shooting games," Allison said in disgust.

That's all it took to set Frank off. The mad basset hound was back. Frank sprang from his chair so quickly he almost knocked it over. "I've had it with that kid! I don't care if I have to drag him to the table by his ears, he's going to eat with the rest of the family or he's not going to eat. Period!"

"I'll get him, Dad," Matt said.

"Daddy, don't!" Kristen's lower lip was quivering again.

"Sit down, Dad. Everything's cool. I'll go get him." Matt rose.

"Yeah, Dad, sit down and calm down. That vein in your temple is beginning to bulge," Allison added.

Frank acquiesced, plopping in his chair with a loud sigh of exasperation. "All right, go get him. But if the two of you aren't back here in two minutes, I'll, I'll..."

"Drag him to the table by the ears," Allison said. "We all heard you the first time, dear. Now calm down before you have a stroke."

The pizza arrived at the table as soon as Matthew left to get Alex.

"Two large pizzas," came the dull and depressed voice of a teenage girl with dyed black hair, matching black fingernails, pierced eyebrow, pierced nose, and ears pierced up to the cartilage.

"Is that a question or a statement?" Frank asked the waitress as she reached across Allison to set the pizzas down, nearly dropping one on her lap in the whole awkward process.

"Huh?"

"Were you announcing that these are in fact our pizzas or were you asking us? I couldn't tell." The waitress stared at him blankly unaware of what he even meant.

"Never mind him," Allison said to the waitress. "Frank, don't be such a smart aleck."

"Will there be anything else?" the waitress responded with all the zest of a poorly programmed robot.

"Yes, as a matter of fact there is. When does Freddie Freeloader..."

"That's Freddie Fieldmouse, Frank." Allison corrected.

"Whatever. When does he come out to sing Happy Birthday to our daughter?"

"We've been here close to an hour," Allison remarked, "and I haven't seen him out here once. Doesn't he generally come out every so often, walk around, and say hi to the kids?"

A suspicious looking smile formed on the girl's pursed purple lipps.

"Well, like, not all the time."

"What's that supposed to mean? We have a birthday girl who's counting on Freddie," said Frank touching the top of Kristen's head.

"Usually he comes out to sing 'Happy Birthday' after you're finished eating."

"*Usually?* What do you mean 'usually'?" Allison felt her face flush with the heat of irritation.

"Well, like, he's had a few problems tonight with his costume and all so it may take a little longer than usual." The suspicious looking smile was beginning to break into a grin, and something like a snorting sound emitted from the waitress' pierced nose, a stifled giggle, Allison guessed. "He could probably be out in, like, a half hour if that's okay," she said quickly regaining her zombie-like composure.

"A half hour? Why so long?"

"It's, like, a really long story." She made another snorting noise and stifled her laughter until she could control it no longer. She let out a loud blast like the blare of a trumpet, turned and quickly bolted from the table, her shoulders heaving with laughter as she sprinted back to the kitchen. Frank, Allison, and Kristen all stared at one another in baffled silence.

"Well, whatever it is it must be pretty funny if it made the Stepford waitress laugh," Frank said. "I like this place. I really like this place, Al."

"Here wash your hands before you eat," Allison said, handing Kristen the anti-bacterial spray.

"But Mom, I didn't go back in the tunnels."

"It doesn't matter. Those game machines are filthy too, sweetie."

"What do you expect from a place whose mascot is a rodent?" Frank said.

Kristen used the spray then handed it back to her mother.

"Here," Allison said handing the anti-bacterial spray to Frank. "Wash your hands. You don't need to get sick again. You're no good to me when you're sick."

"My, my, aren't we the paragon of compassion?" Frank said, spraying his hands.

"Is Freddie coming to sing 'Happy Birthday' to me?" Kristen's little face looked worried.

"Yes, sweetie, he's coming if I have to drag him to the table by his mouse ears. Now how about some pizza? I'm starved." Frank distributed the paper plates and cut the pizza slices free with a plastic knife.

Matthew came back to the table with Alex dragging defiantly behind, right along with the frayed hems of his bell bottom blue jeans, earplugs in place, blocking out the rest of the world. Alex looked up at Allison, his face sullen and sad, mostly hidden behind his dark bangs. He hid his painful adolescent self-consciousness behind those bangs and an air of bravado. His prominent nose seemed to have grown faster than the rest of his features, and to make matters worse, his skin had recently erupted with the first signs of puberty. The other day she passed by him as he leaned over his bathroom sink, eyes affixed to the mirror, compulsively picking at his acne. She admonished him to just leave his face alone and that the picking would just make it worse. He told her to get off his ass and that this was his way of dealing with the acne. He said she ought to be lucky he didn't take a blow torch to his face. She offered to take him to a dermatologist but he said what was the f-ing point? She ignored the cussing and tried to console him by telling him she was sure he would outgrow it like she did and end up a very handsome man.

"You know, in France they call acne *fleur de jeunesse*. It means 'flowers of youth'."

"Well, in the U.S. they'll always be known as zits," he hollered, right before kicking the bathroom door shut in her face and slamming her out of his life once again.

Matthew looked like her. Kristen looked like Frank. Alex was a strange combination of the two. On more than one occasion Alex had asked if he was adopted. When did this loneliness set in, Allison wondered? He was the happiest baby of the three. The heartiest and most robust. He used to laugh in his sleep. Where did that smile and little boy laughter go that he would now question his parentage and think himself an orphan? *I've killed his spirit.*

Allison noticed everyone at the table seemed completely absorbed in the pizza. Matthew studied his slice carefully from every angle after each huge bite. Alex gulped and inhaled with a vehemence. Allison was uncertain if it was hunger, anger, or simply a desire to get away from the table as soon as possible. Kristen bit and chewed happily and steadily, shifting around in her chair, swinging her legs, and humming along with the music. Frank cut his pizza up with a plastic fork and knife and ate it European style. Only the sound of chewing and swallowing could be heard as the curtain once again opened on the singing animals. Allison pulled an overcooked mushroom off her slice and tested the elasticity of the mozzarella cheese beneath.

"What's wrong, Mommy?" Kristen asked. Her finger always seemed to be on the emotional pulse of the family.

"Nothing. I just think your brother could slow down a little on his pizza. And maybe acknowledge some of his family members. You haven't said one word to any of us all evening, Alex."

"I got nothin' to say," he said with a mouth full of food.

"Then sit up straight and chew with your mouth closed. You keep eating like that and we'll have to perform the Heimlich maneuver on you," Frank said.

"Don't do me any favors. If I start to choke just let me die," came the sad response from the young Alex.

"Could I have that in writing?" Frank replied.

"Frank, don't talk like that. Don't even joke like that. It's not funny."

"I'm done. I'm gonna go play some more games." Alex carelessly wiped his hands on a paper napkin which he threw on the table as he stood up. "Hey, all you said was I had to come to the table and eat. I did that. Now I'm leavin'."

"Fine! Go! Just remember, you use up all your allowance on those idiotic games and you're not getting another red cent from me. And Matthew, I don't want you giving him any of your money. Do you understand?"

"I won't, Dad," Matthew said as his parents watched Alex walk away from the table in long deliberate strides.

"Go keep an eye on him, will you?" Frank commanded more than asked.

"Let him finish eating first," Allison said, feeling the unfairness of making poor Mattie the watchdog.

"No, it's okay. I'm finished," Matthew said. Allison thought he was as anxious to get away from the table as Alex was. "May I please be excused?"

"You're excused," said Frank, blowing out a long and heavy sigh.

"Don't worry, Kristen. I'll come back to the table to sing 'Happy Birthday'. I'll keep an eye out for Freddie Fieldmouse for you," Matthew reassured his little sister with a pat on the shoulder.

"I wish you wouldn't make him spy on Alex. It's just going to cause resentment between them," Allison said as Matthew walked away.

"So? They already resent each other."

"Yeah, and you've contributed to that."

"Please don't fight," Kristen whined.

"We're not fighting. Just discussing, sweetie," Allison tried to reassure her.

"Then don't discuss. Not on my birthday. Don't discuss anymore," Allison marveled at the speed with which this child could produce tears–real tears–expelled with such force from somewhere deep within her being, staining her cheeks and eyelashes as they made their way down her face.

"Honey don't."

Frank and Allison suddenly encircled the child, laying hands on her, first one clutching her then the other. Frank took his monogrammed handkerchief from his hip pocket and wiped the child's tears.

"Here, blow," he said placing the handkerchief over her nose.

Allison pushed his hand away and shoved a wad of Kleenex in front of her face. "No, here! That has your germs on it."

"I haven't used it all day."

"You'll stick it back in your pocket and forget about it, then pull it out tonight and use it. That's how germs get passed around. That's how an entire household gets sick."

"Stop!" Kristen wailed in one great sob, so loud that it made the kid with the filthy socks and his mother turn to look at them.

"Sweetie please. We're not angry. We're having a great time. We're here at Freddie Fieldmouse. You've been looking forward to this all week."

"By the way, where is that damned mouse?" Frank said looking around. "Would you like Freddie to come out now? Would that make everything all better?" Kristen nodded. "Fantastic! We'll get him out here then," Frank said, then turned his attention to Allison. "I think I see our waitress. I'm going to have a little chat with her."

Allison watched him move purposefully across the large room. She could tell he was mad because that was the only time he moved fast anymore. He descended upon the poor waitress, nearly startling her out of her wits. She watched the exchange between them. The angrier Frank became, the more amused the waitress seemed to become. Had she not been female, he would have punched her. Whenever he got really mad, Frank's Italian blood would bubble to the surface, drowning out any trace of his cool rational half-WASP heritage. He had reached that point, Allison thought, as she watched him throwing his arms around in large dramatic gestures. The waitress regained her zombie-like composure and headed back to the kitchen.

Frank returned to the table, his fists and teeth clenched in unison.

"Well, what's the story?" Allison asked.

He gave her a look then turned his attention to Kristen.

"Honey, you go play for a little bit. Here are some tokens." He picked up a plastic cup and rattled the metal coins inside, offering it to her.

"Is Freddie coming out?"

"Yes, honey, but it'll be a few minutes. We'll come get you when he comes."

"Promise?"

"Promise," they said together as the child scooted off her chair.

"All right so what's the status on the mouse?" Allison asked.

"According to Miss Congeniality he can't make an appearance until his costume dries out."

"What!?"

"Apparently he had a mishap. All she could tell me was that it involved a trash can and a water hose."

"What?! So what did you say?"

"I told her I don't care if he drips all over us, I expect him to get his rat's ass out here in ten minutes to sing Happy Birthday to my kid."

"Great. Now it'll be another half hour. We need to talk to the manager about this."

"I'll do more than talk to the manager. I'll go back in that kitchen and make an ugly scene."

"Calm down, Frank."

"First you imply I'm not being assertive enough then you tell me to calm down. Which is it?"

"Look, I don't want to fight about this."

"Neither do I. It's ridiculous."

This is it, Allison thought. *The way this evening's been going this will be my only opportunity.*

"Frank," Allison cleared her throat. "There's something I need to talk to you about." She sized him up quickly to see if there was any trace of anger left. He was scowling but seemed to be breathing regularly. *Dive right in, girl. It's the only way.*

"So talk."

"It's just not working, Frank. We've tried everything and we need to do something different this time." Allison avoided his eyes and looked instead at the paper napkin she'd been folding repeatedly until now it was a small thick wad.

"What's not working? What are you talking about?"

"Us. Our marriage."

"What are you saying?"

"I'm not sure. I just think we need some space from each other, some time to figure things out."

"Do you want a divorce?"

"I didn't say that. Do you?"

"No!"

"I don't know what I want. I just know I can't figure it out until I get some distance from you. We need to separate."

"Separate!"

"Maybe only for a time. You know, like a trial separation. Everything we've tried hasn't worked. We've been to three marriage counselors in the past five year, but it just keeps getting worse and worse. I can't take the fighting anymore, Frank. I just can't take it!"

"Yeah, but separate," he said, seeming suddenly pale.

"Why are you so shocked? Look at you! You're obviously not happy. Give me one good reason why we should stay together.

"The kids."

"The kids. That's a very good reason why we should separate right now. Look at what our fighting is doing to them. Matthew's skipped childhood.

He's more parent to us than we are to him. Alex is like a time bomb. We both know he's headed for big trouble if something doesn't change. And Kristen. She's so insecure and overly sensitive. And I know she's immature, and I know that's partly my fault, but I guess I've just spoiled her because I feel so bad that she's had to endure all this. If we stay together it'll only make everything worse for the kids. Don't you see?!"

"It sure sounds like you're asking for a divorce."

"You're the one who keeps saying that. I've never once mentioned the "D" word. Look, Frank, I'm so confused I don't know what I'm asking for—just more time."

"Why the hell did you pick now to spring this on me?"

"This is the only chance we've had to talk all week."

"It's Kristen's birthday!"

"We're not going to tell her tonight. In fact I think we should wait a few days before we talk to the kids about this. You know, give us some time to prepare. In the meantime you need to start looking for a place to live."

"A place to live? You're kicking me out of my home?"

"Look, the kids need to stay in their home while all this is going on and they need to be with me. I'm the one that knows what they need, what their schedules are, when they need to be here and there and at what time. You're gone so much of the time anyway. It only makes sense that you be the one to move out. For now."

Frank slammed his fist on the table.

"Why are you fighting this?" Allison said. "If it's the money you're worried about…"

"It's not the money."

"I'm going back to work. I've already got a new resume made up and I've actually got a few leads. So you don't need to worry about what it'll cost to run two households. You know me, I'll find something soon. And if I don't find anything right away, I've got the money that my grandmother left me. You know I re-invested it and it's done pretty well over the last year. I won't ask you for anything more than what's fair and reasonable to support our children."

"I see you've thought all this out. So how long have you been thinking about it, huh Al?"

"A long time."

"And just what made you decide for sure?"

"Oh, something happened that triggered old memories, made me think about our courtship and wedding. We were both on the rebound when we got married, you know."

"I know," Frank said, his eyes downcast, his voice full of pain.

"Look, I don't want this to get ugly. I know you don't either." Frank said nothing. He just continued looking down. "So, are we agreed?"

He nodded in resignation. "I'll call Tim Shultz first thing Monday morning. Maybe he can, you know, help draw up a legal agreement."

"Now it sounds like *you're* talking divorce."

"No, but a legal separation maybe; you know, so we can get all the visitation stuff worked out. Besides, Tim has that guest house on his property. Maybe he'll let me stay there until I get my feet on the ground. That is if you don't mind me saying something to Tim."

"Why should I mind? He's an old friend," Allison said remembering how they'd just seen Tim a week ago after the concert and how they stood there reminiscing about her and Frank's wedding day.

"Good. I'll call him tomorrow."

"You don't have to be out that soon."

"I'll be out tomorrow. One way or another." His words were emphatic as they sounded forth from his clenched jaw.

"Okay! Okay! I just don't want to fight. There's been enough fighting."

Frank withdrew with a sigh. He was deep in his cave where Allison was never invited and dare never venture. The moments of silence passed between them as Allison tried to think of something constructive to say.

I want it to work, Frank. She wanted to say it but didn't dare. She needed to know if *he* wanted it to work. Really work. Not just stay together, status quo, in a dying marriage for the sake of the kids or the favorable image it presented to the public, or whatever other reason. *Do you really want it to work, Frank, because you love me and you don't want to lose me. Please Frank please*, Allison pleaded inside her head. *Do something... anything to prove you still love me. Fight for me, damnit! Fight for me, not against me.*

Frank startled himself out of his solitary world of pain with a quick jerk of his shoulders and a hurried glance at his watch. "Okay, so it's been every bit of ten minutes. Where is that damned mouse?" Allison's eyes burned and felt heavy with the weight of restrained tears. She pushed them all back down with one great swallow.

Frank flagged down the waitress with a frantic wave of both arms. She strolled over as if she had all the time in the world and nothing better to do.

"Can I help you?" The waitress nonchalantly replied.

"Hell yes, you can help me. I want to speak to your manager. And you better not tell me he's drying his clothes out too. Now will you go get him or shall I?" Frank's voice was controlled but his face was nearly purple with rage.

The girls eyes widened in shock. "I'll get him, sir. Right away."

"Geez! Is that what it takes to finally get a reaction out of you people? Let me give you a little tip on how to be a better waitress. **Smoke dope on your own time!**" Frank yelled out to the startled waitress as she ran back to the kitchen. Everyone in the restaurant turned to look at them. Allison covered her face.

"I think it's time to go get Kristen," Allison jumped up from the table and headed back toward the play area. She stopped hard as she bumped into a child, practically falling over the little person. "Excuse me," she said looking down on the child, surprised to see the little face of Kristen looking back up at her.

"Kristen!"

"Mommy, I was just coming back to the table to see if Freddie's here yet."

"He'll be here any second. C'mon, let's go."

Allison saw a man leaning over a chair at their table, his arms straight like poles gripping either edge of the chair. Allison guessed he was in his mid to late twenties, but he had the aura of a much older man. He appeared beige from the tip of his dishwater brown hair to the hem of his khaki pants and plain brown street shoes. He would've blended in perfectly to the natural environment had he been in the desert, but here at Freddie Fieldmouse he peculiarly stuck out as the one neutral shade in the midst of bright primary colors. He looked very serious and intently at Frank. *At long last the manager of this wonderful establishment,* Allison thought, wondering if she should run back and hide in the tunnels with Kristen.

They heard Frank's raised voice as they approached the table. "I run a business myself. I believe in hiring the disabled, but geez, must they all be mentally deficient? Everyone I've talked to around here acts like they've had a frontal lobotomy."

"We're very sorry, sir. We can arrange for you to get a free large pizza the next time you come in."

"Next time? What about now? I think I should get a free large pizza now."

"We can't do that, sir."

"Why the hell not?"

"Because you already paid at the counter when you ordered the pizzas."

"So give me my money back. Or is that too complicated for the incompetents up front?"

"Frank," Allison said leaning down and breathing the words into his ear. "You're upsetting Kristen."

"I'm very, very sorry, sir."

"Oh, *two* 'verys'. Never mind, then. I take it all back."

"Cut the sarcasm, Frank."

"Freddie Fieldmouse will be out directly, sir. I apologize to your family for this terrible inconvenience," the beige manager said with new resolve as he straightened his shoulders for probably the first time in years.

"Don't lecture me now, Al," Frank said as the manger made a fast trek back to the kitchen. "I've had it! I've absolutely had it!"

"Daddy," Kristen sobbed, the tears that brimmed in large pools now rolling at great speeds down her cheeks.

"Oh, geez!"

"Calm down, Frank You're making a huge scene. Everybody's watching."

"Is that all you care about, Al? What other people think? God forbid I should make a poor impression on the patrons of Freddie Fieldmouse.

"Soooo," Frank said to Kristen with a phoney smile, changing moods with a sudden strained effort at cheerfulness. "Looks like Freddie's going to be out any minute to pay a visit on our birthday girl."

"Oh, Daddy!"

"Why are you crying? What's wrong, honey? No tears on your birthday."

"I will think positive thoughts. I will think positive thoughts," Allison mumbled over and over again until it became a mantra.

"You son-of-a....!" the terse words of an angry male voice coming from the kitchen suddenly startled everyone as they drowned out the volume of the singing animals on stage and interrupted Allison's efforts at self-meditation. Everyone in the restaurant quieted down and strained to listen. A terrible din amidst raised male voices shouting angry words could be heard from the kitchen. Every adult in the place had a look of alarm, as their children vied for their attention asking : "What's wrong Mommy?" "What's wrong Daddy? "What's going on?" Meanwhile Kristen sobbed into her Mother's chest.

The crescendo of the kitchen conflict finally came with a frenzied rustling noise, a loud banging like someone falling hard against the wall, and a woman screaming. A deathly silence followed as the animals continued to sing up on stage. Moments later Freddie emerged from the kitchen.

Oh, my, he looks more depressed than Frank, Allison thought as she watched Freddie's large mouse feet shuffle slowly across the floor. A waitress walked beside him, seemingly leading him in the direction of their table. His large brown mouse head with the permanently fixed grin, revealing two prominent front mouth teeth stared back at them surrealistically.

"Kristy honey, Freddie's here! Look!" Allison shook Kristen who was now heaving great aftermaths of sobs into her chest.

The child looked at Freddie, looked down, and said, "Who cares!"

Oh, great, Allison thought. *She picks now to lose her innocence; her faith in Santa Claus, the tooth fairy, and walking stuffed animals.*

"Where's Mattie? He said he would come back to sing Happy Birthday to me," Kristen said with a fretful look on her face.

"I guess he's still up front playing games with Alex. It's too late to go look for them. We'll just have to sing Happy Birthday without him this time." Kristen's lower lip quivered again, threatening to bring forth yet another round of sobbing.

"Oh, please, Kristen, do not cry again. I beseech you," Frank said. Kristen sucked in rapid little breaths of air in an effort to ward off the impending tears.

"Careful honey, you'll hyperventilate. Calm down. Take a deep breath," Allison said, coaching the child.

"Yeah, we finally got the damn mouse here. We don't need you to faint on us," Frank added.

Meanwhile several children ran up to the slump shouldered Freddie, who held up his large mouse paw-hands in front of his chest, as if shielding himself from a mauling. He seemed to take special care not to stumble over any of the children as they gleefully danced about him.

He arrived at the table and promptly patted Frank on the head with his large mouse paw-hand and began tying a balloon to the back of his chair.

"Hey, it's not my birthday. It's the kid's."

Freddie slowly and painfully made his way over to Kristen and patted the tearful child on the head then proceeded to tie the balloon around her chair.

"Hey, let's get a picture of you with Freddie, sweetie," Allison said reaching for her camera. "C'mon, honey, dry your tears," Allison said, handing Kristen a wad of fresh tissues. "Smile and say 'birthday'," Allison said holding the camera up.

Kristen, realizing some of the staff had gathered around the table to sing Happy Birthday and that all eyes were on her, wiped her face and managed to pull herself together. She stood up next to Freddie who put his furry arm around the child's shoulder to pose for the picture. Kristen forced the smile at first but after a few moments it became more natural.

"That's my birthday girl! Smile and say cheese," Click. Flash. A successful picture of Kristen on her eighth birthday. Just then, Matthew ran up with Alex dragging sadly behind.

"I hope I'm not too late to sing Happy Birthday," Matt said.

At the sight of her brothers, the past few minutes were forgotten and Kristen broke into a smile.

"Yeah!!! You're here," Kristy said and in her usual impulsive manner she jumped up, clapped her hands and grabbed Freddie Fieldmouse around the waist in a too-tight hug.

"Oooh Freddie, you're wet!" The astounded child remarked shaking out her arms as if to quickly air-dry out the dampness of Freddie's matted fur. The large mouse simply shrugged his shoulders in response. A dirge-like chorus of Happy Birthday soon followed. Freddie Fieldmouse patted Kristen on the head one final time then shuffled slowly back to the kitchen, warding off the enthusiastic entourage of children that crowded all around him.

Later that night Allison lay on her bed ruminating. Would it ever be *their* bed again, she wondered. Frank lay curled up in a small corner at the opposite end. An invisible line ran down the middle of the bed, and Frank, even in his sleep, seemed determined not to cross that line. He offered to sleep on the couch, but Allison told him that wasn't necessary. It would only raise questions in the children's minds. Their conversation over the sleeping arrangements were the only words exchanged since the drowned rat fiasco at Freddie Fieldmouse.

Frank went right off to bed and fell asleep instantly. Allison watched him sleep. He barely moved, tucked away in his little corner. She lay on her back staring up at the ceiling, her fingers nervously tapping together. The hall light flooded through their bedroom door, casting shadows on the wall. Kristen always insisted on going to bed with the hall light on and her bedroom door wide open. They usually turned the hall light off after she'd fallen asleep. Allison couldn't sleep unless it was completely dark, but tonight she couldn't bring herself to turn that hall light off. She didn't know why. Perhaps she felt compelled to keep vigil on their last night together in the same bed.

Her mind raced and her body felt as if it had to follow. She wondered if this could be Restless Leg Syndrome. She'd read an article about it in one of her women's magazines. It described exactly what she felt at this moment, like she had to move or she'd go crazy. She needed to get up and do something– house work maybe. But then her busy presence in the house might awaken her family, like a haunted spirit, what with all that restless energy passing by their doors and leaking in like radiation. No, what she needed was to move outside in the open air. She wanted to get up, put her running shoes on, and go for a jog, but of course she couldn't do that. She might get hit by a car in the dark. She might twist her ankle and, unable to move; lie outside in the cold all night only to die of exposure in the first early rays of sunrise. What a cruel farce that would be. Allison decided against a midnight jog.

She would have to turn that hall light off if she wanted to get any sleep. Why was she so reluctant to do that? What ghosts might appear in the void of complete darkness? If only she could turn her mind off with the flip of a switch.

She got up and flipped the hall light off, her long quick strides returning her back to bed in an instant. She felt the comfort of the sheets beneath her, still warm from where she laid just moments before. She closed her eyes. Something bade her go back to where it all began. She didn't want to go back. It wasn't Allison's way. The past was the past and she couldn't change it. Why look back? She breathed in deeply. She smelled Polo. No wonder her mind kept slipping back to the eighties. It was the cologne that Frank wore when they first met. She carefully leaned over the invisible line down the middle of the bed, and sniffed Frank. As far as she could tell it wasn't coming from him. She didn't think so anyway. He hadn't worn Polo in years. It was too passe. Too eighties.

Great ! Now I'm having olfactory hallucinations. She sniffed Frank again. Now she thought maybe she did smell it. *Stupid allergies! That's what comes from living in the Ohio River Valley too long. Everyone in this town has a screwed up sense of smell. But why would Frank put a cologne on he hasn't worn in years right before he went to bed? Or did he? I don't know.*

Allison collapsed back onto her pillow and closed her eyes. She stopped fighting it. She went back.

Chapter 4
June 1983

There was hardly a hint of blue on that early summer day in 1983. All along the horizon was a murky grey, contrasting with the dark green of the trees that flew past Allison's window. A cornfield blurred out of her peripheral vision as she rolled up the window of her red Trans Am and turned the AC up two notches.

My sinuses are bothering me already. She could always tell when she was getting close to Lamasco because of her inability to breathe, an invisible hand holding a warm, damp rag over her face. *The three H's. Hot, hazy, and humid.*

She had to remind herself why exactly a successful, upwardly mobile, young professional such as herself would choose to move back to her boring little hometown nestled on the Ohio River valley. Lamasco had a population of one hundred and fifty thousand, but it was small-minded. This was 1983. The Reagan era of the yuppie. Why would anyone who'd experienced life outside southern Indiana ever return? And why was she returning? *Because I love Kent,* she told herself, *and because Lamasco is a great place to raise a family.* Or so her fiancé Kent always said.

For those seeking stability and security Lamasco was a great town. That was the up side. But the down side was the conservatism and lack of adventure that had permeated the town. That's why her fiancé Kent had never left Lamasco. The fearful could never quite break free and neither could the dutiful. Many returned after attending college elsewhere due to family ties, often to a family business. And then there were those, like herself, who returned because of romantic ties. She was tied to Kent, and he was tied to Lamasco, and that's why she was coming back. She had of course argued that if he really loved her and really wanted to marry her, then he should make the move to Chicago. That's when she realized that his fear ran far deeper than his love, and she wasn't sure she felt the same about him since.

Allison looked in her rear view mirror at her father's pick up truck, which held half of her belongings. Behind him was Kent in his pick up with the other half. The rest of her things were crammed in the back seat of her Trans Am. She tried to get a look at her father's face so as to gauge his present mood, but he was too far back. She knew he was probably still mad at her. He wanted to lead the convoy back from Chicago to Lamasco. Allison shook her head as she remembered their discussion about it before they left.

"Let me lead, Dad. I'll get us out of Chicago without getting lost."

"Lost? What makes you think I'll get lost? You got no confidence in me."

"You're the one who has no confidence in me. I'm not a helpless little girl anymore, Dad. May I remind you that I've spent five years away from home; four years at college, one of those years in France as an exchange student, and one year after college living and working completely on my own in Chicago. I thought you raised me to be independent."

"I raised you to take care of yourself, not to be no women's libber."

"Not to be *a* women's libber. Not to be *no* women's libber is a double negative, and what the hell are you talking about anyway?"

"And I didn't raise you to be too big for your britches either. I know why you want to lead. I know. I know," he said, his voice and his words trailing off. Her dad had a habit of mumbling to himself.

"Maybe I could lead," Kent politely interjected. Up until now he had been standing, watching the interchange between Allison and her father like a spectator at a tennis match.

"I know why you wanna lead," her father mumbled again to the ground, ignoring Kent's suggestion.

Allison clenched her fists and rolled her eyes with one great growl of frustration, "You drive me crazy!"

"You wanna leave us behind in a cloud of smoke. Mario Andretti couldn't keep up with you."

"Did anyone ever tell you, Dad, that it's just as dangerous to drive too slow as it is to drive too fast?"

"Oh, and drivin' twenty miles over the speed limit ain't gonna cause no accident?"

Kent tried to speak, but was only able to squeak out a single syllable before being cut off by Allison.

"Would you please stop with the double negatives? And I do not drive twenty miles over the speed limit. I drive sixty-five. Which is what the speed limit should be. Fifty-five miles per hour is a complete joke."

"You drive seventy-five. And if they up'd the speed limit to sixty-five then you'd drive eighty-five."

"Oh, please!"

"I didn't raise you to be no speed demon with a lead foot. Know what I think?" he said mumbling again.

"Enlighten me, please."

"I think if you're so dag-nabbed independent then you can pay your own speeding tickets from now on."

"All right. All right. I'll drive the stupid speed limit. Just let me lead."

"You can lead if you promise to keep to that speed limit." Allison's father made the statement like a bold command from the king to his half-witted servant, not an act of surrender. "Deal?"

"Deal. *Mon cher papa*," she said, feigning a smile as she got into her car leaving Chicago and her other life behind.

"And don't be speakin' no French to me neither."

"How's this for a deal, Dad? I won't speak to you in French if you promise to speak to me in correct English," she said hanging out the car window.

"You're too dang big for your britches, little miss."

"And please don't speak to me like John Wayne either," she said rolling up the window.

Her father was still angry with her and hardly spoke to her at their various stops for gas and lunch. Kent tried to make polite conversation so as to ease the tension between the two. Allison found this mildly annoying and she sensed her dad did too. Couldn't Kent see they didn't want to make small talk? They wanted to sulk. And they wanted to see who would cave in first. It was the stubborn Brinkmeyer way. Kent's small talk simply interfered.

Allison tried to talk herself out of this growing irritation she felt for Kent when a green light suddenly turned yellow, snapping her out of her highway hypnosis. She braked just in time as the light turned red.

"Truck stops and stop lights," Allison said to herself. "Welcome to Lamasco! The only town in the civilized world that still has stoplights in the middle of a four lane highway."

The light turned green and Allison, solely for her father's benefit, deliberately floored the accelerator for a few gleeful seconds, squealing her tires through the intersection,. *I hope he gets a shot of exhaust through his AC vents. Except that Dad never turns the AC on,* she remembered.

She tried to tune in to a radio station. Her restlessness wouldn't allow her to stay on any particular station for very long. She then reached for the glove compartment where she fished out a cassette tape of Kool & the Gang and stuck it in the tape player. The music made her smile. It was upbeat. She didn't like anything too sad; sad movies, sad music. She couldn't sit still with sadness for very long. When she felt sad she went for a jog or worked out to one of her aerobic tapes. "Celebrate good times. Come on!" The music made her smile. It reminded her of Bloomington, nothing more than farmland and limestone quarries if it weren't for the campus of Indiana University. Indeed a whole other world to Allison. Here she met people from all over the world. The music reminded her of parties at her sorority house: being young and free and away from Lamasco. Kent had really never forgiven her, not so much for leaving Lamasco as for enjoying Bloomington and Chicago so much.

Do I really still love him? The gnawing question surfaced again. *Of course*

I do. I'm moving back to Lamasco for him. She glanced down at the diamond ring on her left ring finger. They were engaged yet the whole thing happened without Allison taking much note of it. She put in another tape, turned up the music and pressed the accelerator, drowning her doubts, fleeing from her second thoughts.

After a time she noticed an anxious feeling which had moved in gradually like an unwelcome houseguest. It was a feeling of doom, of dread, like someone or something closing in on her. She looked in the rear view mirror and immediately identified the source of this uneasiness. It was a man in a white Ford following close behind her, too close. *I wish this joker would get off my tail. Why doesn't he just pass me?* She looked as far back as she could, but saw no sign of her father or Kent. *When did I lose them?* She looked again. The realization hit her like an unexpected slap in the face. The siren sounded and the blue lights flashed.

"Shit!" Allison said aloud banging her hand on the steering wheel as she pulled over to the shoulder. *Don't panic, Al. Just smile at the nice policeman. Maybe he'll go easy on you.* She quickly switched off Michael Jackson along with the engine and rolled down the windows. Just in front of her was a large road sign: Welcome to Lamasco–A Great Place to Raise a Family.

The police officer was a large man. He swaggered over to the car, adjusting his pants which rode low on his hips. His large protruding beer gut would not allow him to pull his trousers up any further, still he continued to tug, more out of nervous habit than actual necessity, Allison guessed. He approached the car, and to Allison's alarm, leaned his gigantic upper torso through the car window. She feared for a moment he may get stuck. *Oh, no, here it is! The Intimidating In Your Face Lean.* She'd been pulled over enough to know that the roughest cops always leaned in the window rather than stood back at a safe distance.

"Good afternoon, ma'am."

"Good afternoon, officer," Allison said looking at the distorted reflection of her smiling face in his mirrored sunglasses.

"You got any idea how fast you were goin' there?"

"Seventy maybe?"

"Try seventy-eight."

"Seventy-eight? You're kidding! Not that I doubt your word, officer." She'd tried the 'perhaps your radar's not working correctly' argument before, but it had not been well received, particularly with the type of cop that does the intimidating lean.

"License and registration please."

Allison took her wallet out of her purse and handed the officer her license with a calm and finesse that surprised even her. She even pulled the registration out of the glove compartment without disrupting the stacks of cassette tapes which lay on top. This was getting to be such a routine, her hands didn't even shake.

"Be back in a moment, Miss." She knew he was the type to call her "Miss". It seemed all Lamasco men over forty either talked like John Wayne or mumbled their words like her dad.

Now came the time of terrible waiting. She felt like she was back in school again as she remembered all the admonitions from teachers about misbehavior going on a permanent record. What did her permanent record look like? She imagined an off-white, yellowish card like the report cards from grade school . Hers' would be all marked up with the dreaded red ink. Of course, the large police officer had access to her permanent record through some mysterious source. He was looking it over right now in his white LTD. She imagined him, red pen in hand, mirthfully scribbling away on her card as he laughed an evil villainous laugh.

Her reverie was interrupted by the sound of a horn honking. She looked up just in time to see her father drive by. He slowed down and waved, a smug, satisfied smile on his face. Following close behind was Kent, who only gave her a quick baffled glance and shrug of his shoulders. "Shit. Shit. Shit," said Allison banging her head on the steering wheel.

"Careful. You do that too hard and you may knock some sense into that head of yours," came the voice of the big cop ready to lean into her face again as soon as she moved out of his way.

"Oh... Sorry Officer," spoke two grimacing caricatures of Allison who mocked her from his mirrored sunglasses.

He leaned his large body as far into the car as it could possibly go and let go a sadistic little chuckle. He had the same gloating smile on his face that she imagined her father might have had when he passed her. "Well, well, well. I see this isn't your first time to be pulled over. With this red car I figured as much. Three previous tickets and the Lord knows how many warnings along the way." He was enjoying this far too much. Allison thought he must've been the type of kid that enjoyed pulling the legs, one by one, off spiders. "But ya know what I'm gonna do? I'm gonna go easy on ya," he continued.

Allison's hope returned. Was it actually possible that he would let her off with just a warning? *Keep smiling, Al. Smile and grovel. Apologize all over yourself.*

"Thank you officer. I know I don't deserve it. I'm so sorry. This won't happen again."

"Hold it there now, little lady. I ain't finished yet. Like I was sayin', I oughta charge you with reckless driving, seein' as how you was goin' nearly twenty-five miles over the speed limit and couldn't decide which lane to stay

Odd Numbers

in. But I'm gonna let you off easy and charge you with speeding. I'll say here you was only goin' seventy," he said as he wrote the ticket. "You're a lucky lady. You just get to go back to school. Defensive Driving School, that is."

"Thank you officer," Allison said with a frozen smile on her face. He handed her the ticket, and at that moment she wished that she was the kind of woman who could produce tears at will. If she thought dramatics would do her any good, she would have given it a try, but she knew it wouldn't work with Officer Big Boy.

The huge man leaned his face into her car one last time. "You need to slow down, Miss. Stop and smell the roses. Young gal like you's gonna miss too much of life racin' around like you do. Aright then," he said finally lifting his enormous self out of her window. "You have a nice day and welcome to Lamasco."

"Yes, Officer." Allison sat in her car and watched the cop pull away. Her hands were shaking now. *Shit! Defensive Driving School. So what? It's only a few weeks out of my life. It's my own life. My own ticket. I'll pay my own damned fine.* She turned the engine back on. The sound of Vincent Price's crazy laugh at the close of the Thriller track blared in her ear. She quickly popped the tape out and on came the radio.

"Our love's in jeopardy... baby." *Ech! I hate that song.* She turned the radio off, then the engine. She leaned over and rolled down the passenger window, then just sat listening to the intermittent hum of passing vehicles, leaving in its space the sounds of nature, insects buzzing, birds chirping, and a warm breeze rustling through a nearby cornfield. After a while she started the car again and pulled slowly away from the curb, listening to the sound of the pavement beneath her wheels. *Maybe I'll adapt to life in Lamasco again. Maybe I can learn to go at a slower pace. I can do slow. Slow's not so bad,* Allison thought as she stayed in the right lane and watched car after car whiz past her. She thought how ridiculous it was that she should be the one slowing up traffic.

The after effects of the speeding ticket along with Allison's new found resolve to go more slowly and thoughtfully had worn off by the fifth consecutive red light. There was a stoplight on every corner in Lamasco and they were all timed so no one could hit two green lights in a row. It was an engineering feat that never ceased to both amaze and annoy Allison. By the time she neared her new home, she was in such a state of agitation she yelled, "I hate this town." *Cool it, Al. Get a grip on yourself. I will think positive thoughts. I will think positive thoughts. I am calm. I am in control. I'm starting a new life. Kent and I can finally be together. No more long distance relationship.* Allison took a deep breath as she drove into the apartment complex which would be her new home.

"Camelot Apartments—Welcome ye home!" the sign read in Old English lettering. "One and two bedroom luxury units available," another sign read as she passed the stone and brick manager's office. A few small trees had been newly planted in the grassy median that lined the drive. Each apartment building looked the same with its reddish-brown brick foundation; its white stucco with brown wood timber cross beams, criss-crossing in the English Tudor style around the window and door frames; and finally the trademark brick turrets built onto the side of each building, standing like sentries, tall and unmovable. Atop each turret waved a triangular white flag which bore the image of some mythological coat-of-arms type creature—part dog, part lion, part dragon breathing out tufts of flame and standing on its hind paws. She had seen real castles in Europe and this was about as close as she could get to one in Lamasco. As she fixed her gaze on one of the turrets far off in the distance and squinted, she imagined standing on the ancient ruins of a long lost world, like she had when she lived in Europe.

Allison opened her eyes wide. She was back in Lamasco at the brand new Camelot apartment complex on the far end of town amidst the suburban sprawl of commercial real estate; with its piles of brown dirt, workmen, bulldozers, and the all-around sights and sounds of new buildings going up. This was her little slice of romance and chivalry right here in the Midwest, situated between a cornfield and a strip mall.

Positive thoughts. Positive thoughts. Allison smiled until she saw her father and Kent parked in front of her new home; building 3300 Lancelot Lane, Camelot Apartments, Lamasco, Indiana. There they were, each of them respectively, leaning against their pick up trucks. *Damn! Of course they got here before me. Positive thoughts. Positive thoughts. Oh, to hell with it. My apologies to Zig Ziglar and Dennis Waitley, but my Dad is standing over there with a shit eating grin on his face. This is no time to smile.* Her father's sour mood was no match for her own, and just like the beginning of their journey, the end of their journey found Kent, once again, standing in the middle like a spectator at the ping pong championship.

Later that night when she and Kent were alone unpacking boxes in the new apartment, Allison confronted him on his reluctance to defend her. "Why don't you ever take my side when we're with my Dad?"

"As if you need anyone to take your side. You don't need my help. You do just fine on your own."

"What ever happened to chivalry?"

"You want chivalry? I thought you were a feminist."

"I am. I'm just get tired of fighting all my battles alone."

"He's your Dad, Al. Besides, most of the time he's right."

"All right now we're getting to the real reason. You're afraid to stand up to him."

"I'm not afraid of him. I just respect him. He's my future father-in-law."

"What really gets me is that you didn't even stop when you saw I got pulled over."

"Why should I? What good could it have possibly done?"

"You would've been there when I needed you. You could've offered moral support."

"Oh, yeah? You know who that cop was?"

"No."

"Ol' Fat Ass. "

"Who?"

"The cop that pulled you over. I got a good look at him. It was Ol' Fat Ass all right. The meanest cop in Lamasco. You remember him. He's the one who busted me and the guys back in high school. Caught us with a case of beer down by the river."

"So?"

"Moral support ain't gonna do you any good with Ol' Fat Ass."

* * * * * * *

It was Sunday morning, Allison's first morning as a resident of Camelot Apartments. She sat at the kitchen table of her new home indulging in her usual Sunday morning habit… reading the Sunday paper, eating donuts, and drinking coffee. She hadn't had a chance to get to the grocery store yet, so she picked up her breakfast at the nearest Donut Bank, a string of locally owned and operated donut shops run by an old Lamasco family. *This is the best thing about Lamasco,* Allison thought biting into the chocolate long john allowing the flavor to transport her into a place of near ecstasy. She swished down the bite with a big gulp of coffee. It tasted so wonderful it made her eyes water. She was hard pressed to think of any baked goods anywhere in all her travels that could even come close to matching the Donut Bank's. She figured it was how Ol' Fat Ass got in the shape he did. She thought of Defensive Driving School and stuffed the rest of the chocolate long john in her mouth.

Allison opened the box of the dozen assorted donuts and counted them. There were now nine left. She reached for another but stopped herself. She knew if she had another donut she'd have to starve herself the rest of the day. As it was she'd have to go for an extra long jog. *An extra long jog to work off the extra long john.* She spread the newspaper over the box of donuts so she wouldn't have to look at it anymore. Already the effects of the chocolate were wearing off and the guilt was setting in. *Get up, Al, and do something constructive,* she told herself looking around at all the boxes that needed to be unpacked. Suddenly she felt very sad. So sad to think this was her hometown but she no longer knew anybody here except Kent, his family, and her parents. She wished she could see Kent, but she knew she wouldn't today. He'd be tied up on the family farm for the rest of the day.

Kent loved that farm. He still lived there. He was trying to save up enough money for a down payment on a house, one that they could move into when they got married. Allison knew that Kent couldn't tear himself away from the family farm. She knew their first house would be somewhere on the rural outskirts of Lamasco, somewhere near that farm, which is why she chose to live on the opposite end of town. At least for now. At least during this short period of time when she was still her own person. If she had to live in Lamasco then she would get as far away as she could from her own farming and blue collar roots. During this brief period in her life that she could still call her own she would live on the other side of Lamasco, the newer and developing side where the newcomers and transients lived, the well educated and those not so deeply rooted in this town.

Kent asked why she had to live all the way on the other side of town where the rent was higher. "Why can't you get a place a little closer to me?" he asked. Because, she told him, she wanted something newer. She had had it with renting older places, with old appliances, and poor insulation, and constant repairs needed. It was a lame excuse for someone supposedly in love. Kent's face dropped when she told him where she planned to live until they could buy their first house. She was seeing that disappointed look more and more.

She and Kent were high school sweethearts. They'd been together since sophomore year. He was her first. Her only. They were crazy about each other and seemed like-minded on everything, until senior year. This is when they began to disagree. She wanted to leave Lamasco and he didn't. He got a basketball scholarship to Lamasco University. He had every reason to stay and she had no excuse to leave, other than a claustrophobia that made her feel like she would suffocate if she didn't. They had the conversation so many times. Lamasco U. was a great school. She could learn just as much there as she could at IU. He didn't understand what she meant by "broadening your horizons". So she left and he stayed. They were mature about the whole thing. They gave each other permission to date around, believing that if it was really meant to be, their love would survive four years. They broke up once during their second year, but only for a few miserable weeks. After that, they stepped up their weekend visits and ran up their long distance phone bills.

So their love had survived, not just four years but five. The fifth year was the hardest. After college graduation Allison landed a job with one of the most prestigious marketing firms in Chicago. Kent argued that she didn't love him enough to move back home and settle down. After all, hadn't she gotten all her wanderlust out of her? She argued that he had to love her enough to give her this freedom, this independence, this chance to live and work in a big city. The compromise was he'd give her one year then if she wasn't willing to move back, they were through.

Kent was an old habit that Allison just couldn't give up no matter how much she wanted to. For all of her so-called independence she was dreadfully afraid of not having someone to call her own. She was estranged from her own family. Kent was all the family she had anymore. If she gave him up then who would she have? And so she felt forever torn. The fifth year came and went and here she was. She gave up the promising career in Chicago to work for a small advertising agency here in Podunk, USA that dealt mostly in billboards and signs.

Allison thought of her new job which she would start the very next day. She knew the old boys' network was thick here in Lamasco. She feared they would call her "little Miss" and treat her as secretary rather than a consultant. And since the cost of living was lower here than in Chicago, she was taking a significant cut in pay. She guessed it was just one of the little sacrifices one had to make. But for what, she wondered.

Meanwhile Kent was working in the trust department of First Lamasco Bank and things looked promising for him. His boss had his eye on him. Plenty of opportunity for advancement, but still he didn't seem happy.

She opened a cardboard box marked "miscellaneous". She unwrapped some old newspaper from an unknown round object and pulled out a cheap ashtray with a picture of a Hawaiian hula dancer on it. It said "Greetings from Honolulu". She wondered where the hell she got it. It looked like many a cigarette had been put out on the hula dancer's face. She wrapped it back up again and tossed it on the couch with some of the junk she hadn't caught while she was packing. Her mom could sell it at one of her garage sales. Allison smiled. It probably belonged to her mom anyway. She unwrapped the next object. It was an old family photo taken when she was about twelve. It was the one reminder of her family of origin. She looked at it every day in her apartment in Chicago, but she never really saw it in the same way she saw it now. Maybe it was because she was back in Lamasco. The picture triggered a memory.

She was seven years old and had snuck out of bed one night. She crept downstairs and overheard her parents talking in the living room. They were talking about "divorce"… again. She was used to hearing the word. She'd heard it thrown around enough, but usually when they were hollering at one another. Tonight was different. They weren't fighting. They were actually polite; not like friends though, more polite like strangers. They said they couldn't get the "divorce" until Allie, their youngest, was all grown up and out of school. In the meantime they had to be "civilized", whatever that meant. They had to stay together "for the kids' sake". The next day her dad moved out of the master bedroom and onto the couch. He claimed it was because of his back problems and the couch was more comfortable, but little Allie knew the real reason. She knew she'd better hurry and grow up so they could get their divorce and finally be happy. She was the last ball and chain they had to unshackle themselves from before they could finally start to live. They filed for divorce shortly after her high school graduation.

When she looked at the picture the truth stared back at her with all its ugly harsh realities: her missed childhood, her parents' loveless marriage, just how far she and Kent had drifted, and the sad fact that Kent was merely playing the part of the upwardly mobile banker to please her when all he really wanted was to be a farmer. She turned the picture upside down and put it back in the box. *I need to go for a run right now.* Allison abruptly stood up. The donuts felt heavy in her gut. *I will not eat anymore fats or carbohydrates today. I'm healthy. I'm in control. I will go for a run.*

She found the box marked "shoes", grabbed her kitchen knife, and cut the thick cellophane tape which held the flaps of the box closed. She pulled her running shoes out and put them on her bare feet without socks. She wasn't sure where her socks were and she didn't want to take the time to look. Happily she'd already found her walkman and had been listening to it all morning since it was her only source of music until she set up her stereo. *Got my shoes. Got my walkman. We're ready to roll.* Allison clipped the walkman to her shorts, took one last look at the boxes piled on top of each other, heaved a sigh, and closed the door behind her.

Finding an interesting, scenic, and safe jogging route anywhere within the vicinity of Camelot apartments was a challenge. Allison got bored running around the apartment complex so she ventured out into the street. She had to be extra careful because there were no sidewalks, and even though it was Sunday, the traffic was heavy with people headed to Lamasco's newest chain restaurants (all of which were on this side of town) for Sunday brunch.

Jaunting along, she heard church bells ring. They came from the Catholic Church across the street and down a little ways from Camelot, in the opposite direction from which she was running. The church used to be the only thing out here save cornfields and a few scattered farm houses. The bells pealed ten o'clock. She remembered it was Sunday. She tried to remember how long it had been since she'd been to church. Just then the gust from an approaching car nearly knocked her off her feet. The car came close enough to clip her. She turned around and headed back to the apartments, deciding it was safer to do laps around the apartment complex than get killed her first day back in Lamasco.

As she bounced along, her breathing keeping pace with the pounding of her feet, her mind unwillingly returned again and again to the horrible thought of getting hit by a car, the impact, the crushing sensation, the helplessness of being flung into the air or worse yet, dragged. How horrible to be the driver, Allison thought, as she imagined pushing down with all her might on the brakes in some futile attempt to stop another human being from rolling up onto her hood and smashing into her windshield.

Death. Such a final word. This is where I'll die. Here in Lamasco. I wonder if I'll be buried next to Kent. Of course I'll be buried next to Kent. What am I thinking? Why am I thinking these morbid thoughts? She didn't have an answer. She was unaccustomed to thinking about death, at least not for very long. She turned up her walkman and let David Bowie seductively croon all her horrible thoughts away. *Let's dance. Put on your red shoes and dance the blues. Let's sway. Under the moonlight. The serious moonlight.*

A thrill of anticipated romance shot through her and made her shiver. Definitely a preferable emotion to the previous one. She was approaching her building when she saw him. It was not the first time she saw him. She met him last night as she was moving in. He was one of two young men who appeared quite suddenly on the scene and offered to help carry boxes and furniture. Now here he was again washing his car. His car stereo blared and the sound of his music clashed with hers. It sounded like opera. With animated gestures he sang along.

Now what was his name? She'd learned in her Dale Carnegie class to remember people's names and use them often. She tried to remember when the two young men introduced themselves. *Just what exactly did this one say his name was?* All she remembered was that Kent looked worried when they mentioned they lived in her building. She told him he had nothing to worry about. They seemed like a couple of hon-yock school boys trying to impress her, only she wasn't impressed. If they were that hard up that they had to wait around for a new girl to move in, like vultures circling around dying prey, then they must not be all that great.

Name. Name. I've got to remember his name. She used word association to help her. The other guy was easy. His name was Tim. She came up with the acronym Totally Impossible Man because he seemed like a jerk. She had a hard time finding something that stood out about this guy. And then she remembered his eyes. She noticed they were blue. *Blue eyes. Ol' Blue eyes. Frank Sinatra. That's it! Frank.*

He noticed her and looked suddenly embarrassed that she caught him singing along with his music. He smiled sheepishly then quickly turned his music down. Allison planned on waving and jogging right past her new neighbor, but she was suddenly and strangely endeared to him by his smile and this brief glimpse into his foolish and vulnerable side. She couldn't help but laugh.

Allison seldom stopped until she was entirely finished with a jog, but he seemed to want her to stop and talk, so she took her walkman headset off her ears, jogged over to him and continued running in place. "Hello Frank. Beautiful day, isn't it?" She panted, her feet pounding the pavement in place.

"Don't you ever slow down?" He laughed.

"I beg your pardon?"

"Yesterday when you moved in you were flying around between the parking lot and your apartment like an angry hornet, carrying boxes up and down those stairs. The way you worked, I would've thought you'd sleep 'til noon. But here you are, up and running."

"An angry hornet?"

"You don't like that one, huh? Okay, how about white tornado?"

"Do I get a third choice?"

"Well, maybe, if I saw you standing still for a change. So far all I've seen is a blur going by... am I holding you up?"

Now it was her turn to be embarrassed as she realized she was still running in place. "I'm sorry. I don't want to lose the aerobic effect," Allison explained. She took her pulse with one hand and looked at her watch with the other. She stopped. "I guess my heart rate's been accelerated for at least twenty minutes. I can take a rest."

"A sunrise."

"What?"

"You wanted a third choice. Now that I've seen you standing still I'm comparing you to a sunrise."

It was a schmaltzy thing to say but all the same it made Allison blush.

"Well, I do feel rather like a large planet today."

"The sun's not a large planet. It's a bright star."

"Sorry, I was never much for astronomy."

Suddenly he dropped to one knee and extended his hand toward her. "'What light through yonder window breaks? It is the East, and Juliet is the sun. Arise fair sun and kill the envious moon.'"

Either he's a hopeless romantic or he's just plain psychotic, she thought searching his eyes for a glimpse of sane reason. His pupils appeared equal and responsive to light. *My God, he has sexy eyes!*

Nervous and embarrassed, Allison laughed and blushed all at the same time. "So you sing opera and quote Shakespeare? Tell me I'm not in Lamasco.

Right? I went to sleep in Lamasco, but now I seem to have awakened in the Land of Oz."

"Some advice for you Dorothy. Don't ever trust a smiling munchkin." Frank said still on one knee. They both laughed, though Allison didn't know why. Frank rose to his feet and struck a more serious posture.

"So where did you move here from?" he asked.

"Chicago. Well, actually I'm from here originally."

"Oh, really?"

"Yep. Lamasco born and bred. So how about you?"

"New York City. Well, the burbs of Connecticut actually but I'm technically a New Yorker."

"I thought I detected an east coast accent. So what brings you here to the middle of nowhere? Must be the pharmaceutical business. You're with Mead Johnson, right?"

"No." He smiled.

"You're going to make me guess, aren't you?"

"That's right." He seemed to enjoy toying with her.

"Okay. You're a professor at Lamasco U. That's it! I guessed it, didn't I? So what do you teach? No, let me guess. Must be in the Humanities? I'm right, aren't I?"

"No."

Allison looked him over again. Marketing and sales had taught her to read people. He had the air of a college professor about him. Brainy. Perhaps he was a nerd at one time. Remnants of nerdiness still remained, traces left over from puberty, now barely discernable. But yet there was something about him that gave Allison second thoughts. Maybe he was too polished to be a professor, too sharp and aware of what was going on around him. Not absent minded enough. His clothes weren't rumpled enough. In fact they appeared to be neatly pressed. His yellow button down Oxford shirt was not only pressed but starched. His white shorts didn't have the dingy grey appearance of the typical bachelor who throws his whites in the wash with all the other colors. These shorts were white white. Bleach commercial white. *He must be gay. That's it! He's a gay professor.*

Sizing him up one last time she noticed his shoes. His shoes were the only thing that didn't fit. He wore an old beat up pair of topsiders. They were too worn to belong to a gay man. The stitching was beginning to rip at the toe and the leather laces were broken. *He's a preppie. Of course! Why didn't I see it before? Not gay, just a classy guy.* The words "dapper" and "debonair" sprang to mind. Old fashioned words. Like a Brill Cream commercial.

Allison hoped that maybe she was wrong and that he was gay. She couldn't be friends with a straight man this good looking. That was another interesting thing. He didn't seem that attractive last night, or even when he first approached her, but now a strange transformation was taking place before her very eyes. He became more attractive with each moment that he stood there. It was the dark hair and skin contrasting with those amazing blue eyes.

"C'mon. C'mon," he said in his thick New York accent.

"I'm thinking."

"I thought you were quick on your feet."

"I am." Allison laughed and blushed again. *My God, I've turned into a giggly school girl. I'm acting like such a dork. He must think I'm an idiot. Oh, well, what do I care what he thinks?* "Okay, so you're not a Humanities professor or you're not a professor period? Which is it?"

"I'm not a professor."

"Are you sure?" He laughed at the remark.

"I give. What in the heck are you and what brought you to the middle of nowhere?"

"My line of work. I own my own business."

"You're an entrepreneur?"

"A struggling entrepreneur at this point, but nonetheless."

"So now you're going to make me guess what business you're in?"

"Naw, I won't string you along anymore. It's market research. In the whole United States do you know where most new products are tested? Right here in Lamasco."

"Right, I've heard that. It's because we're so conservative. If a new product goes over here, it'll go over anywhere. That's why you moved here?"

"That and I've always had a somewhat romantic tie to the Hoosier state."

Oh, no! Now he's going to tell me his girlfriend lives here. Why should I care if his girlfriend lives here? Allison thought. "Ah, a romantic tie?"

"Yep, Notre Dame football."

His face broke into a slow dreamy smile, and he was all at once dazzling and beautiful to Allison, like a Greek god standing there smiling all his graces down upon her.

A little sigh accidentally escaped from the back of her throat and she felt her face blush again. Allison quickly cleared her throat in an attempt to regain her composure. "So, you like Notre Dame football?"

Frank only nodded and continued smiling, only this time more knowingly with a twinge of amusement, as if he'd seen right through her embarrassment.

"Well," Allison said, "it's too bad South Bend's at one end of the state and Lamasco's at the other."

"Yes, well, I still manage to make my annual pilgrimage every fall," Frank said. "What about you? Do you like sports? You're not going to tell me you're a Cubs fan are you?"

"Actually I am. I did live in Chicago, you know. Why? Is that a problem?"

"Oh, no! Just when I was starting to like you. Boo! Yankees all the way."

"Yankees! Well, I'm not sure about your moral fiber. Only Cubs fans have true character, you know".

"Oh, yeah?" He teasingly challenged her, piling on the New York accent for affect.

"Yeah! They know what it's like to be the underdog."

Together they laughed and bantered back and forth a bit until it became awkward again. But Allison was good at not letting a conversation go to that place. Much poise and confidence had come to this naturally shy girl from all the career training. She knew how to get a person talking about themselves and how to really take an interest; or at least fake like she had an interest. She had to admit sometimes she had to concentrate really hard in order to take an interest in what another was saying. But right now, here with Frank, taking an interest was no problem at all.

"What else is there around here to keep you from going crazy?" she asked him.

"Actually I like Lamasco. There are two universities, a theater, and best of all, an orchestra."

"I could tell from your music you must be a cultural kind of guy."

"So what about you, Allison? Do you enjoy the arts?"

"Well, it's been a while since I've been to a tractor pull."

He laughed deep and heartily from his gut. It was a rush, a high, surely better than any narcotic. *He remembered my name, and he laughed at my joke,* Allison thought. *Kent never laughs at my jokes.*

"So you're a big opera buff I take it? What was that I caught you singing along with?"

Verdi. La Donna e Mobile.

"Oh. I always knew it as Tra-La-La-Boom-Dee-A." Again his shoulders shook with laughter. "Let's see if I'm not too rusty on my Romance languages that means 'The Lady is...Moving? Changing?"

"Fickle. The Lady is Fickle," Frank said making eye contact and making her uncomfortable.

"Ah, I see. You know I lived and studied in Paris for a year and I took in my share of opera while I was there, but I could never listen to it without envisioning Bugs Bunny and Elmer Fudd."

"You're a very funny lady, Allison," he laughed. *He called me by my name again. We're practically intimate. Dale Carnegie was right.*

He began singing again in a clear tenor tone. "Welcome to my shop. Let me cut your mop. Let me shave your crop..."

"Daintily. Daintily," they both sang together, remembering the Bugs Bunny and Elmer Fudd cartoon. This time they laughed in unison, his deep thundering from the gut and her school girl twitter.

"I guess about as close as I come to being cultured is an appreciation for Gershwin. I love Gershwin!" Allison said.

"Of course! American in Paris. It's all about you."

"That's my favorite. My all time favorite."

"It's a remarkable piece of music."

"You know, actually you have a very beautiful voice," Allison said. "Where did you learn to sing like that?"

"My mother. She was an opera singer... from Italy. Very up and coming back in the fifties. If it hadn't been for her health she might've really gone somewhere with her career, but unfortunately she died of cancer. I was just ten at the time." His eyes blurred ever so slightly, making them even more beautiful.

"I'm so sorry. That must've been hard growing up without your mother."

"Yeah, life definitely took a downward turn after that. My Dad never really got over it."

"At least he loved her. That's more than I can say for my parents. They're divorced."

"I think that's harder on a kid than the death of a parent," he said and his look was so piercing it made Allison uncomfortable. It was too soon for this soul bearing.

"So is your dad still living?" Allison asked.

"Yeah, he lives out east."

"Is he Italian too?"

"Nah. One hundred percent WASP. That side of the family came over on the Mayflower...the Hamiltons, old Philadelphia family." Allison was intrigued by this strange combination of Italian heritage and old money from Philadelphia. There was something magical about this DNA mix. He was compellingly enchanting.

"My dad saw Mom sing at the Met one night, just a minor part but nevertheless, he saw her and instantly fell in love. Needless to say, his family did not approve. So he left Philadelphia, eloped with mother and together they moved to New York and had me and my brother."

"How romantic! I mean he must've really loved her to defy his family and all."

"Yeah," Frank said a little sadly as he reached back into the bucket of soapy water, pulling out a large sponge with one hand and retrieving the water hose with the other. She stood for a while and watched him. He went back to washing his car, all the while humming. His shirt sleeves were rolled up to the elbow. Allison watched the movement of his shoulders and forearms as he moved the sponge in circular motions across the car. Sweat poured off his forehead. He lifted his shirttail and wiped his face, revealing his stomach and a good portion of his upper torso. He was well-toned and had the right amount of body hair, not too much, not too little. She stood close enough to notice his scent. She detected the fragrance of cologne, mixed with the odor of sweat. She was surprised that she found it enticing, and not at all offensive. She imagined what it would be like to kiss him. Suddenly Allison realized she was just standing there wordlessly watching him, fantasizing about him as if in a trance and that this might just seem a little creepy to the casual observer.

"I better let you get back to your car. It's been nice talking to you."

"I can wash my car and talk too. Stick around and keep me company; that is unless you've got something else to do. I'm not holding you up, am I?"

"No, you're not holding me up." There was nowhere else she wanted to be, nothing else she wanted to be doing. She hoped he felt the same way. Excitement welled up within her, and she wanted to start running again, but instead she stood there smiling like how she imagined the Cheshire cat from Alice in Wonderland might do.

"Can I help?"

"You can be my bucket carrier."

"Pardon?"

"Just follow me around with the bucket and keep me company," he said with that piercing gaze and that boyish smile. Her stomach flip-flopped at the sight of that smile.

All right, that's it. I'm lusting after a man I just met, Allison thought. *I need to get out of here before I'm in big trouble.* She was all set to bid him a hasty farewell and jog off before he continued the conversation.

"So you lived in Paris, huh?"

"*Oui*, for a year. I minored in French. *Parlez vous Francais?*"

"*Oui ui. Je ne suis pas sure que je me rappelle beaucoup. Je n'ai pas beaucoup d'occasion de le parler.*" (Yes. I'm not sure I remember much. I don't have much opportunity to speak it).

"*Je pense que vous faites tres bien. Je suis bien impressionne. Peut-etre nous pouvons le pratiquer parler ensemble. Je n'ai pas beaucoup d'occasion de le parler non plus."* (I think you do quite well. I'm very impressed. Maybe we can practice speaking it together. I don't have much opportunity to speak it either.)

"I'd like that." He looked at her again with those eyes and Allison thought she would come completely undone.

Allison looked down before her attraction to him became too apparent and she said something stupid.

"So I never asked what you do," he said.

"Well, interestingly enough, my background is also in marketing but I'm kind of in transition right now. Tomorrow I start work at an outdoor advertising agency. It's a step down for me. Actually I'm a little apprehensive about the whole thing. It's going to be so different from the firm in Chicago where I came from."

"Don't let 'em walk all over you. All right," he said in a forthright manner. This statement meant more to Allison than, perhaps any of the other sweet things he had said thus far. She could tell he meant it. He had sensed somehow her fear of facing the ol' boys' network and all the chauvinism that accompanied it in the work place.

"Don't worry. I won't. And thank you for being concerned."

"You'll be all right. Someone like you doesn't stay down for long. I can tell."

"Oh, yeah, how can you tell?"

"You forget I'm in marketing too. I've observed your determination already."

"Thanks for the vote of confidence."

"So I take it you moved back to Lamasco because of your fiancé?" He said stating it like a question.

"You guessed it," she said looking away then glancing briefly back at Frank's face to see if there was any disappointment there. She remembered she had introduced Kent to him last night as her fiancé and she was now wishing she hadn't. *That's a terrible thought! You love Kent. You've just been away from him too long,* she told herself.

"So when are you getting married?"

"Well, we haven't exactly set a date yet. We're kind of waiting until I get settled in before we take on wedding plans."

"I see."

"It's a lot you know, moving back here. So do you have anyone special in your life?"

"No," he said working particularly hard to wipe clean the streaked glass of the windshield.

"Why is that?"

"I haven't met the right woman yet. Seems like all the good ones are taken."

"Hmmm. So how did you get interested in research?" Allison abruptly changed the subject.

"I've always been interested in statistics, how you can gather information and predict outcomes. Numbers are very meaningful. They bring order to chaos."

"Ech! I hated statistics. No offense."

"None taken."

"You were a math nerd in school, weren't you?"

"Tell me it doesn't still show. I've tried all my life to overcome it. I even got athletic in high school so I wouldn't be bullied by the jocks anymore."

"Well, I'll tell you a little secret. I was a nerd too. It takes one to know one."

"No way!"

"No, it's true. I was a little fat girl in grade school. I always got picked last for the kickball team."

"Ah yes, the kickball team. Responsible for countless hours of therapy to maladjusted nerds everywhere,"

He finished up his work with the car and Allison helped him gather his bucket and rags.

"Thanks for keeping me company," he said. Their eyes met again and Allison quickly looked down. She realized she was always the first to break the gaze.

"My pleasure. Nothing like commiserating with a fellow former nerd."

Suddenly there were no more words to be said. The two stood there in silence.

"So..."

"So..."

"Which apartment do you live in, Frank?"

"The one right across the hall from you."

"Oh."

"That's where I'm headed now."

"Me too. I mean, to my apartment."

"Shall we?"

Together they walked to the building, and though no words were spoken, Allison thought it seemed comfortable, almost familiar, walking alongside him. Frank held the door open for her. They walked up the stairs, Frank following close behind Allison. They lingered at their respective doors for a moment.

"*Au revoir* Allison. I enjoyed talking to you."
"*Moi aussi,* Frank. *Au revoir.*"

The sound of keys jingled in unison as they turned their doorknobs and opened their doors. Allison was back within the confines of her apartment, back with the unpacked boxes, the half a box of donuts, and the half-read paper. Everything was the same as when she left it, yet nothing was the same. She ran to the bathroom, flipped on the light, and looked at herself in the mirror.

"My God, I look horrible," she said out loud. Her dirty hair was pulled tightly back in a pony tail, and Allison thought it made her look like a skinned rabbit. Her makeup-free face looked red and blotchy, and staring back at her was a pimple just below the right corner of her mouth. She examined it more closely, a miniature volcano ready to erupt. Last night's sleeplessness showed in and around her eyes, which seemed colorless compared to his. *No wonder the female of the species is always plain beige or grey.* Her t-shirt was wet around the chest and under the arms. She lifted her arm and sniffed. "And I smell! Good! I hope he was really grossed out." She covered her face with her hands and turned away from the mirror.

Chapter 5

Allison awoke Monday morning feeling tense and hurried. About the most constructive thing she did was finding the band-aids for her blistered heels. It was her own fault for jogging without socks. They were in a box marked "bathroom". It was the only box she dug through and it was out of necessity. She didn't care about anything yesterday, not even the fact that Kent didn't call until nine o'clock at night.

Her navy pumps were in the bottom of the box and when she pulled them out they looked like they'd been run over by a truck. *It's too bad you can't iron leather,* she thought as she stuck them on her feet. *I would kill for a cup of coffee*, she thought looking at her boxes wondering which box her coffee maker was in. Her breakfast consisted of a stale donut and a swallow of juice from the bottle she purchased at Gasmart on the trip back to Lamasco. *I've got to get my life back in order.* Allison stood at the door, purse on shoulder, keys in hand, looking around her new apartment. *You're a professional, Allison. A professional.* She cleared her throat, straightened her shoulders, and headed out the door.

There was the door to Frank's apartment right across the hall from her. It was a strange feeling knowing this was the first thing she'd see every time she left her apartment. She wondered what time he left for work. *It's your first day on the job, Al. You have more important things to think about,* she told herself as she headed down the stairs. She opened the door into the bright sunlight. The humidity had dropped, leaving in its wake a clear blue sky and refreshingly cool air. Allison was glad. She'd been off work just long enough to forget how uncomfortable panty hose and suit jackets were in the stifling heat. She looked at the sky and thought it was lovely. Then she heard the music. It took a few moments for the melody to register.

It was Gershwin. "An American in Paris". The busy Parisian street sounds ringing through the early summer air of southern Indiana. She looked up and there stood Frank on his porch, smiling and watching her with his sliding glass door open and the music cascading out of his apartment. She was thrilled and moved all at the same time. This was better than coffee. He'd selected this piece of music just for her and waited to play it as soon as she stepped outside.

"Thank you," Allison called up to him.

"You're welcome. Knock 'em dead! And remember, hold your head up and don't take any flack," Frank called down to her, his eastern accent particularly thick but strangely endearing.

Allison smiled and waved.

Allison's first morning at work was spent meeting her fellow employees, discussing how she wanted her new office set up with the office manager, who was clearly the Jewish mother of the firm, and getting a key for the women's restroom; which proved to be the lengthiest portion of the morning, leaving the office manager in an irritable and frustrated state because there should have been an extra key but wasn't. Her afternoon was spent reading the Policies and Procedures manual and, finally, going over a few of the accounts that would be turned over to her. One of them was with the Indiana State Police, who presently had a billboard up that said, "Watch your speed. We are."

Allison met Kent for dinner downtown after work. They talked, laughed, and toasted their new life together. They discussed spending the night together but they were both tired and decided it would be better if they waited until the weekend. She drove home content.

Allison forgot about Frank until she opened the door to her building and found him standing on the other side with a big plastic trash bag slung over his shoulder.

"Frank!"

"Allison!"

"You startled me."

"Sorry. Just taking my trash out to the dumpster."

"Oh. Of course."

"So how was your first day of work?"

"Fine. Fine. I think it'll be... okay." Allison stood face to face with Frank. She came to his collarbone. She looked up at him and he looked down at her. Her mouth went dry and she realized how close she stood to him and quickly stepped out of the way. She was angry for a moment–angry that he would show up again so suddenly in her life and create all this confusion, just when things went so well with Kent. She quickly told herself how irrational it was to feel that way and that she might as well get used to bumping into him because he was her neighbor. *Smile and be neighborly, Al.*

"Hey, thanks for the music this morning. That was really sweet of you."

"I'm glad you liked it."

"I needed something to get me going, considering I had to leave for my first day of work without any coffee."

"You need coffee? I can loan you some."

"No, I have some. I just can't find my coffee maker. It's still packed away."

"It'll turn up eventually."

"Yeah."

"Hey," Frank said, his eyes lighting up, "I forgot to tell you we're having a cookout Friday night."

"Who is?"

"The Camelot residents. We have these little get-togethers every so often. You know, helps build community and all that good stuff. I hope you can come. Of course, your fiancé's invited too."

"Well, thank you. We'll try to make it."

"It'll be down by the clubhouse about six."

"Do I need to bring anything?"

"Nah."

"I don't mind. Really."

"I'll put you in touch with Barb and Sally. Have you met either one of them yet?"

"I don't think so."

"Barb lives down the hall from us and Sally lives downstairs."

"Okay then."

"Great. I'll see you later." With that, Frank quickly disappeared around the corner of the building as Allison watched in baffled silence.

The next morning she nearly tripped over something by her front door. She looked down and there was a box with a red bow stuck on top. She quickly opened it and inside was a coffee mug with the Cub's logo on it. Inside the mug was a note that read, "In case you haven't found your coffee maker yet... Stop by for a cup. Frank."

It wasn't so much the desire for caffeine that drove her across the hall as the desire to see her new neighbor. She told herself he was only being friendly. She wished he wouldn't be so friendly. By Friday, stopping by Frank's for a cup of coffee each morning had become a ritual, even though she found her coffee maker Tuesday night.

She met Barb and Sally that first week. It was a relief to meet some other women who lived in the building, though neither one was the type of person she thought she could become friends with. The two knocked on her door Wednesday evening and introduced themselves. They were a peculiar pair. They sat on her couch for nearly an hour. Sally talked incessantly and Barb dozed off from time to time. They reminded Allison of an old married couple who'd grown used to one another's annoying little ways.

Barb never said what her last name was. She was a medical resident at

Mercy Hospital. Originally from rural southern Indiana, she made it into IU medical school. Allison tried to strike up a conversation with her about IU, but she didn't seem interested. She was either very aloof or very depressed. Allison couldn't tell which.

Barb had large dark deep-set eyes which stared out of a gaunt face. She wore surgical greens and an exhausted look from having worked twenty-four straight hours. Smiling seemed unnatural for Barb, though she forced both corners of her mouth upward in something that faintly resembled a smile, the affect was odd and out of place, like a poorly fitting garment. She spoke mostly in monosyllabic words, certainly not due to a lack of intelligence, but rather from some great apathy that hung over her like a heavy drape. She didn't have to with Sally around. Sally did the talking for both of them.

Sally Buckner, on the other hand, was more than willing to talk about her alma mater–Purdue University. All the Purdue / IU rivalry was more than just fun and games to her. She was a third generation Boilermaker and proud of it. She was one of the Buckners of Buckner's Fine Dry Cleaning. She worked for the family business, which was fine, she said, but she found her creative outlet as a Mary Kay representative. She welcomed Allison by presenting her with lasagna (enough to feed eight people), and offering her a free facial. Sally also offered Barb's medical services free of charge if she ever got sick. Barb didn't reply.

Sally was short, a little overweight, and her face had all the glitz and none of the glamour of Las Vegas. Sally was battery-operated from her hot pink knit shirt, Lilly Pulitzer skirt with loud floral pattern, all the way down to her neon green espadrilles. But it wasn't just her clothing that glowed in the dark. Her face was positively florescent with her bright blue large framed glasses and her overdone makeup in the brightest shades imagined. She spoke quickly and nervously, and Allison believed she knew her entire life story by the time they departed from their visit. She was thirty-two, divorced, and childless. She was worried about her clock running out. She wanted a husband, a house, and a baby, but not necessarily in that order. She bemoaned the fact that she was still renting at her age. Allison wondered why and decided that Sally either had a spending problem or just hated the idea of being alone.

* * * * * * *

Storms had been predicted that Friday, but as the day progressed Friday evening turned out to be near perfect weather for the cookout: clear and mild, a little humid, but not unbearable.

Allison, Sally, and Barb sat at a pool side table under the shade of an open umbrella. The smell of food grilling floated through the air along with the sound of laughter, chattering voices, and above it all, Hall and Oates blasting from the clubhouse speakers. Sally wore a matching skirt and blouse, which Allison thought was a bit dressy for a cookout. Her hair was particularly big tonight, and so thick with hair spray that Allison thought it may crack. The colors of her face and matching outfit were bright enough to bring on a migraine. Barb was as subdued as Sally was overdone. She was not, however, wearing her surgical greens tonight. She wore a pale blue button down shirt, khaki pants, and a white doctor's jacket with her name tag on the collar. Her stethoscope hung around her neck. Allison wondered if she slept in some sort of medical garb.

"Are you working third shift again tonight, Barb?" Allison asked.

"Yes." Barb answered looking thoroughly bored. Allison had read somewhere in one of her "How To Sell People" books, that you have to ask open ended questions to the shy and introverted in order to draw them out. Allison made a mental note to ask more open ended questions to Barb and only closed ended questions, or better yet, no questions at all to Sally.

"When do you ever sleep?" Allison asked Barb.

"I don't." A two word reply, but still not enough to qualify as a conversation.

"She's serious," Sally interjected. "She doesn't sleep."

"I'm surprised our *Barbara* here has a bed. She only sleeps sitting up."

"I don't have a bed." Barb breathed out the words.

"That's right. It's just a mattress on the floor."

"Really?" Allison remarked, realizing too late that she had just set Sally up for a long soliloquy.

"Really. And it doesn't get much use either… for anything, if you get my drift. But we're trying to change all that. Aren't we Barb?"

"You're embarrassing me again, Sally."

"So. It's what I live for." Sally laughed and slapped Barb on the arm with the back of her hand. It was an annoying habit which always caught Barb off guard. This time it seemed like it would have knocked her over if she weren't sitting down.

"I'm not embarrassed. I'll honestly admit it. My mattress isn't getting enough use either," Sally said as she gulped down the last swallow of white wine from a plastic cup that was blotted with pink lipstick half-way around the rim. "Do you know any single men you can fix us up with, Allison?"

"The only ones I've met since I've moved back are Frank and Tim." Barb and Sally looked at each other and smiled.

"Neither one of us would mind Frank. He's such a sweetheart. Unfortunately he's saving himself for someone special. He told us that at one of our get-togethers. I think he had a little too much to drink that night.

Allison looked over at the other side of the pool by the clubhouse where the men stood, grilling burgers and chicken breasts, drinking beer and laughing loudly. She spotted Frank for the first time that evening. She felt her face automatically break into a smile. He wore a chef's apron and chef's hat, which made him look so corny that Allison chuckled. He had a spatula in one hand and a bottle of beer in the other. He was smiling and laughing with the guys. He looked right at Allison. It was as if he knew she was watching him. He acknowledged her with a smile and a lift of his beer bottle, as if to offer her a toast. Allison beamed. When she saw Sally was watching her, she stopped smiling and turned her attention back to the ladies.

As Sally continued to talk, Allison thought of Kent and discreetly looked at her watch. Six-thirty. She stole another quick glance at Frank. Kent wasn't due to arrive at the party until eight–had to stop by the farm to catch up on some things first. There was a part of her that wished he wouldn't come at all.

The young man that Allison remembered as Tim, the Totally Impossible Man, stood next to Frank. He was slightly shorter and fairer than Frank. He wore a pair of swim trunks and no shirt. He had a muscular build, and the look of a man who worked on developing those muscles in order to show them off. Allison suspected he may have a cocaine problem. He sniffled, pinched his nose a lot, and seemed perpetually wired.

"And then of course there's Tim," Sally said looking at Barb. They both rolled their eyes. "It's a shame his character doesn't match his looks. Oh, we all love Tim like a brother; it's just that he's the black sheep of our little Camelot family. Deep down he's nothing but a sleazeball. More wine?"

"Please," Allison replied lifting her cup.

Sally pulled her bottle of white wine out of a cooler and poured some for Allison. Sally offered some wine to Barb who stuck her hand over her cup. "Time to switch to caffeine."

"Oh, right." Sally pulled a can of Coke out of the cooler and handed it to Barb.

"What does Tim do for a living?" Allison said, realizing again too late that she'd just directed another open ended question to Sally.

"He's a lawyer. He's one of the Shultz of Shultz Law Firm."

"Oh. Of course."

"But poor ol' Tim. He's trying to break away from the family firm so he became a public defender."

"Public defender? He can't be all bad then."

"No. He just did it to piss his family off, and to see to it that his drug dealers don't end up behind bars." Then leaning over to Allison and lowering her voice, Sally whispered, "I live in the apartment right next to him. I hear it."

"Hear what?" Allison asked.

"The porno flicks He's got a VCR, you know. He was the first at Camelot to have one. Anyway, he watches these porno movies on his VCR, turns them up so loud the entire building can hear all the moaning and groaning. I bang on the wall sometimes to try to get him to turn it down. He never does."

"That's our Tim," Barb said with her feeble effort at a smile.

"Yep. What would we do without him?"

"He's a very faithful friend," Sally said. "If you're his friend he'd do anything for you. I believe he'd even give me some sperm if I asked for it. But in Tim's case I'd be concerned about damaged genes."

"Sperm?" Allison choked on her sip of wine.

Sally handed her some cocktail napkins. "I wouldn't have sex with him or anything. I'd be too afraid of getting a disease."

"You're talking about artificial insemination," Allison pondered aloud. "Are you serious?"

"Yes, but I've ruled Tim out as a candidate. Now Frank! There're some good genes there. Him I would have sex with. I asked him once, you know."

"Asked who what?" Allison felt flustered.

"I asked Frank to impregnate me," Sally said loudly.

"You're kidding! What did he say?"

"He said no. I assured him he wouldn't have to be responsible for anything, that I just needed his sperm. He told me he *wants* to be responsible for his kids when he has them. And he told me–get this–you're not going to believe how sweet this is, that he wants to be in love with the mother. Told me he wants to do it the conventional way. Wants to fall in love, get married, and then have kids. In that order. Says he couldn't stand the idea of a kid of his out there somewhere that he couldn't be a father to. Isn't that sweet?" Sally put her hand over her heart, fell back in her chair, and sighed. "They just don't make 'em like that anymore. The woman who gets Frank is going to be one lucky woman. It's too bad you're engaged. You're the first woman he's shown an interest in since I've known him. And I've known Frank for three years now."

"What!?" Allison didn't know if it was the wine or the conversation that was causing her face to feel so hot.

"That's enough, Sally. You've had too much to drink," Barb said. Allison could tell from Barb's words and stern look that Sally had just committed an indiscretion–something, Allison got the feeling, that Sally did a lot.

"Oh, I don't care," Sally poured herself some more wine. "You're the one who has to work tonight. Not me." Barb shook her head and put her finger up to her lips, giving Sally the signal to say no more.

"What?" This was one time Allison hoped Sally would talk

"Oh, Barb, stop shushing me. It's no big secret. Everyone knows about Frank's little crush on our new neighbor here."

"Frank has a crush on *me*?!" Allison leaned in and lowered her voice. She felt suddenly dizzy. Careful to hide her exhilaration, she bit the inside of her cheek to keep from smiling. "What makes you think that?"

"I was privy to one of Frank and Tim's conversations. Don't ask me why those two are friends but they are. Best friends. Anyway, Tim said to Frank that it was about time a decent looking woman moved into our building. Tim has a thing for you too, you know. Anyway, he was trying to convince me to convince Frank to hit on you. Said if Frank doesn't hurry up and do it then he will."

"You're kidding."

"Not at all. You should've seen Frank. He got all red and embarrassed. He said he couldn't do that because you're engaged. Tim said, 'Big deal. She ain't married yet.' Then Tim said, and I quote, 'She'll take one look at this and she'll dump the chump,' referring to himself, of course. He was clowning around like he always does saying stuff like, 'Allison baby. Dump the chump and hop on this'. All of a sudden Frank got really angry at Tim. Said he better not hit on you or he'd deck him. Said you were a good person, worthy of respect. Frank actually told Tim he'd kick his ass if he kept talking about you like you were a piece of meat. We were stunned. We'd never seen Frank like that before."

Allison tried hard to process all this information she'd just gleaned from Sally. Sally took a big gulp of wine and stared at Allison hard in the face.

"So do you know everything about everybody in the entire apartment complex, or just our building?" Allison asked without expression.

"She knows about everybody in the entire complex," Barb replied with her left eyelid twitching slightly.

"Not everybody. Only those worth knowing about. Thanks a lot Barb! You make me sound like a gossip." Barb didn't say anything to retract the alleged accusation.

The awkwardness of the moment got to Allison. "It turned out to be a nice evening, didn't it?" she finally said in desperation.

Tim approached them and said, "Hey Sally, you know you want me," he said putting his arms around her, puckering his lips up, and making a kissing noise.

"Oh, please!" Sally stuck her hand flat on his chest and firmly pushed him away.

Allison could tell she secretly enjoyed the attention.

"It's no use fighting it, baby. This thing is bigger than the two of us. Steal down the hall to my place tonight."

Sally reminded Allison of the cat in the Pepe le Peu cartoons as she struggled to free herself from Tim's embrace. "And wouldn't you just shit a brick if I did?"

"I'll leave the door unlocked for you," he said in a barely audible whisper, but mouthing the words so everyone could read his lips. Everyone who witnessed the silly comical scene laughed. Allison didn't know who enjoyed being center stage more—Tim or Sally. Tim finally let go of Sally and turned his gaze toward Allison.

Tim was not a bad looking man, Allison thought. He was quite good looking actually, funny, and charming. But he was a jerk. A quick-witted, smooth-talking, coke-snorting, cocktail-guzzling, skirt-chasing jerk

"I see the Camelot Welcome Wagon has gotten a hold of our new neighbor here," Tim said eyeing Allison up and down. "May I give you some advice?" he said standing uncomfortably close to her. "Don't believe a word these two tell you. You hang around these characters long enough and you won't know fact from fiction anymore."

"No, Tim. We've told her nothing but the facts," said Sally.

"Then I'm sure she knows what a virtuous guy I am."

Allison felt his hand tapping ever so slightly on her left shoulder. She looked at his hand, remembering that his arm was attached to that hand at the wrist. How or when his arm got around her shoulder she had no idea, but there it was. *Boy, is he ever smooth. I didn't even feel it.* She peeled his hand off her shoulder with the same disdain she had once peeled leeches off her arms and legs after swimming in an infested lake.

"Stick with me and I'll show you the ropes," Tim said still standing too close and seeming completely unfazed by the fact that Allison was inching away from him.

"Oh, really? What ropes are those?" Allison asked.

"The ones he uses to tie women to his bed post," Sally said.

"Oh, so you've seen these ropes, huh Sally?" Allison replied.

"Touché," Barb said with more expression than she'd had all night.

"Uh oh! Looks like we're busted Sally ol' girl," said Tim laughing a loud and raucous laugh. Barb made guffawing gestures with no noise coming out. Sally humphed, clucked, and rolled her eyes.

"Hey Frank," Tim called out above the party din to the other side of the pool. "She really is fast on her feet," he said pointing to Allison.

"Put you right in your place, didn't she Tim?" Frank hollered back.

"Whoa! She's not that fast."

Allison was distracted by hunger pains. She tried to figure out some way she could discreetly make her way over to the grill so she could be away from these three and closer to Frank and the food. Allison wanted a medium rare burger. She didn't care at this point if it was rare or just warmed halfway. She'd eaten steak tartare in France and survived. Allison watched in amazement as Frank handed his spatula to one of the other guys and walked over toward them.

So there they were, the five existing residents of Camelot building 3300 clustered around one another. Frank in his chef's hat and apron with his bottle of imported beer; Tim with his bulging muscles, no shirt, sniffly nose, and dented beer can, which he repeatedly pushed at with his thumb, making an annoying clicking noise; Sally with her plaster of Paris hair, bright colors, and big glasses; and Barb with her stethoscope, big tired eyes, and nails bit down to the quick. It was a strange family, but oddly one she felt herself becoming a part of whether she wanted to or not.

Chapter 6

Allison thought it peculiar that she felt comfortable around the residents of Camelot building 3300. Frank was the only one that she really liked. Wasn't that just like a family though?

Allison was estranged from her own family. She thought she had adopted Kent's family. That's what they kept telling her anyway. His mother would say, "Why you're family, Allison honey." She never felt like family around them. They were too nice, too normal. Kent assured her that they had skeletons in their closet too, and she knew that must be true. Yet she'd never seen them as anything but friendly, polite, and stable. She felt more comfortable around the blatantly flawed, and that's what this group was.

"I saw Louise showing the vacant apartment to some old guy today," Sally announced.

"That downstairs apartment is still vacant?" Barb asked.

"It has been for some time," Tim said.

"You don't suppose it's the history of the place, do you?" Sally said.

Allison watched as they all looked knowingly at one another.

"Don't go getting superstitious on us Sally," said Tim.

"What happened?" asked Allison.

They all looked around at one another knowingly.

"The last guy who lived there committed suicide," said Sally.

"That's horrible!" said Allison.

"He shot himself in the head last Christmas eve."

"It's been empty ever since?" Allison asked.

They all nodded.

"It makes you think," said Frank. "We were his neighbors."

"We tried to reach out to him, but the guy was a loner," said Tim.

"It really shook us up," said Sally. "That's why our building's so close. We all promised to look out for one another after that."

"And Sally takes that promise very seriously," said Tim. The comment brought smiles and a few low key chuckles, but the mood of building 3300 was now quite somber. Even Sally was quiet and thoughtful.

The bells from the nearby church rang out. Though the chimes competed with the sounds of the stereo and all the other hubbub, Allison heard the bells somewhere in her subconscious mind. She looked at her watch. Seven o'clock.

"Life can be so sad," said Sally. A strange moment of reverence followed in which the little crowd remained silent. Allison looked around at their faces and wondered if they were all secretly mourning.

"For whom the bell tolls," Allison said, but she didn't know why. A few more unbearable moments of silence followed. It was Tim who spoke this time.

"Uh, this is a party, guys. We're supposed to be having fun."

"I better go check on the food," said Frank. Allison guessed Frank to be in his mid to late twenties, but already she noticed worry lines around his brow. The thought of his former neighbor had completely transformed his cheerful countenance into one of deep woefulness. His eyes were now a deep, almost navy blue. His serious and sensitive nature became apparent to her at that moment. This must be the other side of Frank underneath all the surface lightheartedness, Allison thought and she admired him for it. He walked slowly, back to the grill.

Allison watched him until Tim put his arm around her shoulder once again and shook her out of her trance.

"C'mon, Allison," Tim slurred his words, "Let's go for a swim."

"I don't have my bathing suit on," she said, once again peeling his arm off her shoulder.

"That's okay. You can go change. I'll wait for you."

"Yeah, you just want to leer at her," said Sally to Tim.

"Better than leering at you, Sal."

"I think I'll pass on the swim invitation. Thanks anyway," said Allison.

"Suit yourself," said Tim, as he left the three women and promptly dove into the pool. They were standing close enough to get splashed by Tim's wake.

"Warn us next time," Sally yelled at him, clucking, harrumphing, rolling her eyes, and shaking her head as she surveyed her damp skirt.

A few other party goers clad in bathing suits jumped in the pool.

About forty-five minutes lapsed, in which everyone ate, talked, laughed, and drank some more. For Allison dinner was unsatisfying, coming too late on top of all that alcohol. She'd had more than her share tonight. Clouds appeared in the darkening sky and it had become more humid. The crowd had gotten louder and rowdier and so had the music.

Barb excused herself to go take a nap. She asked Sally to make sure she was up by ten-thirty so she could be at the hospital by eleven. Allison watched in bewilderment as Barb walked over to one of the lounge chairs, pushed the head back, and lay down. She appeared to be asleep within moments.

"Why didn't she go back to her apartment?" Allison asked.

"She didn't want to miss the party," Sally said.

"Yeah, but she's asleep."

"Hey Allison," a male voice called to her from the pool. Allison recognized it as belonging to Tim. "C'mon in. The water's fine."

"No, thank you," Allison called back as she searched the crowd for Frank.

"Ah, c'mon Allison."

"I already told you, I don't have my suit on."

"Would it make you feel more comfortable if I didn't have mine on either?"

"What?"

"Uh oh, Tim's in rare form. And it's not even eight o'clock yet," Sally said looking at her watch.

"Da da da..." Tim blurted out the tune to "The Stripper". Allison watched in horror as Tim pulled his bathing trunks off from inside the pool. He let out a loud whoop, pulled his wet swim trunks up out of the water and held them over his head. He swung them around and around lasso style, all the while whooping and hollering. Several of the other partygoers egged him on, whooping and hollering right along with him.

"Allison baby! This is for you." He flung the wet swim trunks through the air. Allison saw them flying toward her head and tried to duck. It was too late. The cold, wet suit hit her on the side of the head, leaving her stunned and dripping. The reaction from the crowd was mixed. Guffaws mingled with boos.

"Nice goin', Shultz," someone yelled.

"You really know how to impress the women, Shultz," another said laughing.

The stunned reaction was subsiding and in its place Allison felt angry and humiliated. She bent down and picked up the wet swim trunks which fell first to her shoulder then to the ground. She flung them with all the strength, might, and anger she could muster. They landed in the branches of a tree behind the clubhouse.

"Are you all right, honey?" Sally hovered and fussed over Allison.

"Fine. Just a little stunned," she said gritting her teeth.

"You're soaking wet. Somebody get us a towel. We need a towel over here," Sally hollered out. "You idiot!" Sally screamed at Tim.

"I was aiming for you, Sal," Tim hollered back. "Sorry Allison. Do you still love me?"

Allison ignored him, pretending not to hear.

"You know, you're sexy when you're wet." Tim said and Allison shot him a look of contempt. "But not as sexy as when you're mad."

M. Grace Bernardin

Frank emerged from the crowd with a towel which he placed around Allison's shoulders. His fingers touched the back of her neck where they lingered for just a moment. Allison shivered. She thanked him and began drying the wet side of her hair with the towel.

"Looks like our problem child really did it this time," Frank said to Sally. "How ya doin'?" he asked Allison in his New York accent, his concerned expression showing just the slightest glint of humor over the previous incident. Allison and Frank broke down and laughed at the same moment.

"We can laugh now," said Frank, "but it still won't stop me from kicking his ass."

"Hey, if nobody's gonna skinny-dip with me then I want my swim trunks back," Tim yelled.

"You moron! I oughta kick your ass, Schultz," Frank hollered back.

Allison was surprised to see how angry Frank got. He looked as if he was ready to dive in the pool and go after Tim. This was too much chivalry, she thought as her feminist sensibilities flared up.

"No, no, you don't need to kick anybody's ass," Allison said staving Frank off. "I've got a better idea for revenge."

"Oh, yeah! What's that?" Frank asked.

"Look where I tossed his swim trunks," she said pointing to the tree behind the clubhouse.

"Ah, ha! I think I follow you. You're devious, you know? But I like it!"

"Bring it on, Franky boy!" Tim hollered out. "You wanna fight, we'll do it. Just, uh, toss me my swim trunks first."

"Allow me the pleasure," Allison whispered to Frank just as he was getting ready to speak.

"Certainment," Frank said with a mischievous glint in his eye.

"C'mon, man. Somebody get my swim trunks."

"You'll have to come out here and get them yourself, Tim dearest," Allison said. "Of course you'll have to climb up that tree to retrieve them." All the partygoers laughed.

"Ah, c'mon guys!" Tim whined.

"If Tarzan can do it, then so can you. Of course Tarzan did have a loin cloth," Allison said.

"We won't look, Tim. We promise," Sally called out.

"You'd have to strain to see anything anyway," Frank said to Sally loud enough so Tim could hear.

"Very funny. C'mon guys! Have mercy. I gotta piss."

"You better not piss in the pool, Schultz," hollered one of the other swimmers.

"I'm gettin' out of here," yelled another one.

"Me too," yelled another as they all scurried out of the pool.

Amidst all the hilarity, the laughter, the loud music, and the thick cloud of intoxication which hung over the party goers, came a moment of silence and stillness which caught most everyone off guard. The stereo stopped in between tracks, and the crowd paused to inhale, simultaneously it seemed, in between laughter and conversation. The church bells from the nearby church sounded once again, like an alarm awakening everyone from a dream, but instead of jumping into action like one would do at the sound of a real alarm, they all just paused for a brief space of time. In that short-lived quiet moment nothing could be heard but the sound of the water lapping against the sides of the pool and the toll of the bells. And then it was over just as quickly as it had begun.

"Those bells are so damn loud," Sally snapped. "They drive me crazy!"

"Hey, turn some music on somebody," a partygoer yelled out.

"They chime on the quarter hour. Don't they?" Allison asked.

"What's that?" Frank asked, finally snapping back into reality.

"The church bells," said Allison.

"Yeah. Nobody around here needs an alarm clock. Just open your windows," said Sally.

"They wake me up in the middle of the night sometimes," said Frank.

"Wait," said Sally, her index finger raised in the air. "Listen! They're still pealing. Somebody just got married." Sally dramatically slapped her hand against her chest. "Oh! There's nothing more romantic than wedding bells. Don't you think, Allison?"

Allison smiled and said nothing. She wished the bells would stop ringing. Meanwhile Sally sidled up between Frank and Allison and began pushing the two of them together.

"I now pronounce you king and queen of Camelot," Sally said, her makeup and hair beginning to wilt from the humidity and wine. .

"Huh?" said Frank, bewildered.

"Oh c'mon, play along with me," Sally said, grabbing Frank by one arm and Allison by the other. "You may now kiss your queen," she said giving them both a forceful shove until they were standing nose to nose.

Allison didn't know why she did it. Maybe it was the alcohol, or maybe just an attempt to shock Sally. Maybe she just wanted to see Frank's reaction. It was an impulsive thing to do, but she did it all the same. She threw her arms around Frank's neck. She intended to kiss him on the cheek, but he turned his head, maybe accidentally, maybe not. Their lips met. He didn't pull away and neither did she until the cat calls coming from the other partygoers crept into Allison's consciousness. She realized what she was doing and backed away.

There stood Frank, gazing at her with those blue eyes as if she were the only person there.

"I'm sorry," Allison said to Frank.

"No need to apologize," Frank said almost in a whisper. He smiled at her. A smile, it seemed, that was intended only for her. She wished someone would say something, anything, to distract her from that on-looking smile. Even Sally was speechless.

Allison became aware of someone standing behind her, his hand firm on her shoulder. She turned around and there stood Kent.

"Kent!" Allison gasped. He didn't say anything but only gave her a feigned smile which she wasn't sure how to read. She worried about how long he had been there and how much he had seen. She didn't want to ask him for fear of arousing suspicion.

"Honey," Allison wrapped her arms around his waist and turned the charm on high. "I see you had no trouble finding the pool."

"None whatsoever. I just followed the sound of all the hoopin' and hollerin'. You seem to be enjoying yourself." Allison wondered what Kent was implying. His body was tense and rigid. She released him from her embrace.

The effects of the alcohol were wearing off fast, leaving her with a headache and a sense of agitation. She pinched her eyebrows together, trying to get rid of the headache and the accompanying worry and embarrassment. *I'm an engaged woman and I just kissed a man on the lips I haven't even known one week; in front of God and everyone. Did Kent see it too? How long was he standing there?* Panic hovered over Allison's head like one of the clouds in the ever darkening sky as she searched his face for answers. He was looking back at hers and she was sure he could read the guilt. It seemed everyone was looking at her waiting for her reaction.

"I want you to meet my new neighbors," Allison said with new found ease.

"Frank, this is Kent. Kent, this is my fiancé Frank – I mean, my fiancé Kent, Frank. *You idiot!* Allison said to herself as the nervous laugh ushered forth unimpeded.

"I believe we met the night Allison moved in," Frank said extending his hand graciously. "Glad you could make it."

Kent shook Frank's hand but said nothing, merely acknowledging him with a hard to read nod.

"And this is Sally. She lives in my building too." Allison put her arm around Sally and shook her with all the feigned chumminess she could rally, as if she were her very best friend. "And that's my other neighbor, Barb," she said pointing toward the lounge chair where the sleeping Barb, whom someone had tossed a towel over, was now curled up in the fetal position.

"And that's my other neighbor, Tim," she said pointing toward the pool, her voice losing momentum by now.

Suddenly everyone's attention turned back to the pool by the sound of Tim's voice, "Will somebody get me a goddamned towel? I've got to pee and I'm freezing my nuts off in here."

Everyone but Kent laughed at Tim and his predicament.

"Have mercy," Tim called out. "Will someone please toss me a fucking towel?"

"What's with him?" Kent asked.

"Your fiancé threw his swim trunks in a tree," Sally said.

"He threw them at me first. They hit me so I threw them in the tree. It's a long story."

"Nice night for the party. Don't you think?" Frank said directing the question to Kent.

"It was," Kent said with a pause, "but it's going to storm later."

"Nice meeting you again, Kent."

"You too." The two shook hands again. Kent was a little friendlier this time. Maybe because he knew Frank was leaving their company.

"C'mon, lets go see if we can torture Tim some more," Frank said to Sally.

"Sounds like fun," Sally replied.

Allison finally turned her attention back to Kent. "Wild party," he said wistfully. He had that familiar expression he used to get when he'd come visit her in Bloomington and then again in Chicago; as if he never fit in anywhere in her circle. She felt sad for Kent. And guilty.

Her mind was beset with worries. *What if he saw me kiss Frank? I don't want to lose him.* She missed him already, the thought of him being gone, being out of her life.

Yet she had made her decision. That's why she moved back to Lamasco. She would seal their commitment tonight.

They turned to one another and spoke each other's names at the same time. They spontaneously embraced. "I'm so sorry Kent."

"Sorry about what?" he said laughing and squeezing her tighter.

She looked hard into his eyes, but didn't see any indication that he knew what she was apologizing for.

"For being so wishy washy about what I want. You're what I want. Please know that I love you."

"I love you too."

They kissed. Here Allison was in the same spot where she kissed Frank just a few minutes prior to this. She held on tight to Kent, her arms around his neck. Over his shoulder she could see Frank and Sally standing at the opposite end of the pool, talking to Tim who was still stuck in the pool.

Frank glanced over at her. She thought she saw dejection on his face. She squeezed Kent tighter and closed her eyes so she wouldn't have to look at Frank anymore. *What's wrong with me? How can I be in love with Kent and still be so attracted to someone else? It's just a crush. An infatuation. The right combination of chemicals and hormones. That's all it is. Chemicals and hormones.* Allison remembered that she'd read in some women's magazine that your body chemistry dramatically changes every seven years. This was her seventh year with Kent. The seven year itch. She decided that's what was ailing her.

Allison kissed Kent again, this time long and deep. She realized she was making out with him in front of all these people, something she hadn't done since senior prom. She hoped it would rekindle some of those feelings she had for him back then, but all she could think about was Chemicals and Hormones. Chemicals and Hormones. Her mind wandered off back to her high school Chemistry class. She kissed Kent as fervently and passionately as she could, but all the while her mind was trying to remember the Periodic Table of the Elements and which conglomeration of molecules and atoms was shifting around in her brain causing this magnetic attraction to Frank. She tried to remember the abbreviation for the different elements and why potassium was "K". Was it "K"? She thought so anyway.

What was the first chemical reaction that human beings learned to produce and control? Answer: Fire. She was aware, even with her eyes closed that it was becoming darker. She heard the distant roll of thunder. She ended her kiss with Kent and opened her eyes in time to see a flash of lightning streak across the sky. Some of the party members began to disperse at the sound of thunder.

"I guess that's the end of this party," Allison said looking up at the ever darkening sky.

"That means we gotta go back to your place," Kent whispered into her ear as he tightened his embrace and kissed her softly on the temple.

Another bolt of lightning lit up the sky and a loud crash of thunder followed immediately.

"Holy shit! I'm gettin' outta here before I get electrocuted," Tim hollered out from the pool. The nude lawyer bolted out of the pool, his hands covering his genitals, as he streaked to the clubhouse as fast as he could amidst raindrops and laughter.

Allison looked around for Frank but didn't see him. She was relieved.

Chapter 7
September 1983

Everything moved a little slower outside her car window these days since Allison became a student of Defensive Driving School. She figured she'd slow it down a notch, if for no other reason than the ever-conscious knowledge that she was going to be a bride in June. Such a wonderful season to get married, but first she'd have to get through fall and winter. She observed the trees; all around the edge of leaves were beginning to splash with colors of reds and gold. Already the days were getting shorter and the nights cooler. Fall was coming and for Allison a certain sadness. Soon Kent wouldn't be around much as his time would be divided between work at the bank and work on the farm.

Kent was the only real friend she had in town since she moved back to Lamasco. They had been closer than ever this summer. They had reconnected and recommitted that night back in June after the cookout at Camelot. They became lovers again that night after such an awfully long time; and it was she, not Kent, who insisted on setting a wedding date before that night was over.

And so a date was set—June 1984—which at the time was a whole year away. Kent didn't really understand why it had to be so far off. Hadn't they been engaged long enough without having to wait another year? But Allison explained if they wanted the kind of wedding she'd always dreamed of then they would need a year to plan. The year would give them a chance to save some money and buy a house, and best of all; it would give them a chance to get reacquainted. They had such a lovely time doing so this summer, but soon it would be over, Kent would be absent, the air would be colder, and she would be stuck having to plan this wedding with no one but her mom.

Her mother's idea of a wedding reception was fried chicken and mashed potatoes in the church basement, which they would decorate themselves the night before. She imagined staying up all night with her mother blowing up balloons and taping twisted streamers of crepe paper onto paper table cloths. She imagined setting up metal folding chairs, while Kent and his buddies moved long rows of old beat up cafeteria tables together. She imagined the pale green tile and the smell of the church basement, which was a cross between disinfectant and decades of cooking odor that never went away, but lingered in the air along with the mildew.

Then after the dinner, when all the greasy fried food, tepid warm beer from a keg, and thickly iced wedding cake baked by Aunt Evelyn lay in their guts like a slab of lead, they would have their dance. All the female relatives would take their uncomfortable high heels off, put on thick white socks over their hose, and dance to a scratchy version of the Chicken Dance and the Hokey Pokey played by Uncle Herman because their Germanic frugality would not allow them to hire a real disc jockey.

Allison didn't want a disc jockey, not even a real one. She wanted a first-rate, class act band that could do justice to all types of dance music, from Big Band to disco. She didn't have the band yet but she did have the place, and it wasn't the church basement either. It was in the Gold Room of Lamasco's River Inn the nicest hotel in Lamasco.

Her parents had voiced their disapproval so Allison and Kent would have to pay for most of the wedding themselves. The money she planned on saving to go toward her and Kent's dream house was now going toward the wedding. This had triggered some arguments between the couple about starting off their marriage in debt. But Allison just had to have something looming ahead in the horizon to look toward; like the castle on the hill in the distance. So this dream of a beautiful wedding with all the plans that went into it was what would keep her going when the sadness of fall and bleakness of winter set in. She didn't want to think beyond the wedding day. Visions all faded to black after she and Kent ran to the limousine (which she intended to hire without her parent's or Kent's knowledge) amidst a shower of rose petals and excited cries from the mirthful wedding guests. There were no visions in her mind after that day, only a vague fall-like feeling which she managed to squelch by going back to thoughts of *the day*.

* * * * * * *

Allison turned her car into the entrance of Camelot and drove slowly down the long lane to the last building on the right. As the parking lot in the front of the building came into view, she was all at once surprised and infuriated to see motorcycles, about eight or ten of them, cluttering up the parking lot. The owners of these big bikes obviously didn't care that some of these parking spaces were clearly marked and numbered for the residents only, because there in her space, sat a motorcycle. A U-haul parked with the back-end facing the door, took up two spaces. There wasn't a single place to park on the front side of the building. Exasperated, she turned her car around and drove to the back of the building. Then she remembered Sally mentioning that a new tenant was finally moving into the vacant apartment downstairs, the cursed apartment where the previous tenant committed suicide. It had been vacant nearly nine months now. Sally tried to squeeze information out of Louise the landlady, but all she could get was the new tenant's gender and name. It was a woman by the name of Vicky.

Allison had been glad to hear it was another woman, and hoped maybe she could be friends with this one, but now that she'd seen the motorcycles out front she began to have her doubts. She parked her car in back and walked around to the front entrance of the building. As she approached, the blaring sound of hard rock music became louder and louder. *Whoever the new tenant is she wasted no time in setting up her stereo*, Allison thought. It certainly wasn't her type of music yet it struck a familiar cord: *Steppenwolf*. Her oldest brother had owned one of their albums when he went through his drug dabbling, hippie wanna-be days back in the early seventies.

The front door to the building was propped open allowing the deafening din, along with boisterous laughter, clouds of cigarette smoke, and the scuffling noise of people moving about to spill out into the autumn air. As she crossed the threshold, Allison's hope that this new tenant might be someone she could befriend grew dimmer and dimmer.

She was struck with a sudden homesickness for Chicago, Paris, and Bloomington. She had friends there, friends with whom she was rapidly losing touch. Would life in Lamasco always be like this for her? Would it always mean living with those who couldn't understand her, those with whom she merely shared a roof – even her own husband?

She thought she'd found a friend in Frank, but the attraction got in the way. Ever since the party last summer he'd been cold to her. Oh, he was friendly and polite enough, but it was a guarded friendliness, held in check by a deliberate aloofness and calculated distance.

Her throat grew tight again. Allison recognized this as a signal that she needed to cry. She hung her head. She needed to rush upstairs as quickly as possible, throw herself on her bed, and let it all out in one great gush of tears. Not that Allison was prone to self-pity; she despised it in others as well as herself. Either her remedies for depression weren't working or weren't available to her.

Her first urge when depression struck was to stuff some carbohydrate in her mouth, preferably a sweet and sugary one. She couldn't do that because she couldn't let herself get fat before the wedding. Her other remedy was exercise. Aerobics was out because now she lived in an upstairs apartment, and all that jumping around disturbed her neighbors beneath her. She couldn't afford to join a gym and it had been too rainy to jog.

The other remedy was positive thinking. And that just didn't work lately. She kept having the thought that maybe all this positive thinking was merely self-delusion, like Peter Pan with his happy thoughts and pixie dust—all he claimed one needed to defy gravity and fly. Or was that just another negative thought? A negative thought she would try to stave off with another positive thought. It became an exhausting mental exercise.

To hell with it, she thought fighting back the tears. She would look neither to the right nor to the left. She would run upstairs and have a good cry, then she would put on her sweats, go for a long jog, and think some more about the wedding.

A veritable road block stopped Allison as she crossed the threshold into the foyer of the building. It felt like she'd run into a wall, not a brick wall, but rather a padded wall which caused her to bounce back upon impact. Staring back at her was an endomorphic creature whose face stuck out from amidst sparsely strewn tufts of unkempt hair. *Aw shit! One of the big bike owners no doubt,* Allison thought as she backed off enough to observe the long scraggly beard and hair. A hairy gut protruded out from under the owner's black *Lynyrd Skynyrd* T-shirt. He resembled one of her childhood troll dolls.

"Excuse me," Allison said instinctively.

"Hey baby, you can bump into me any time." He laughed, and the smell of beer blasted forth from his mouth into Allison's face. She studied the image of a green naked lady tattooed on his arm.

Don't show your teeth when you laugh at him, Allison thought. *He'll think you're genuinely amused.* She pinched her lips together tight and let go a mocking little chuckle through her nose. Clearly he was on his way out and would require most of the door space in order to get out, so Allison scooted out of his way and backed into the corner of the wall.

"Beer break's over, you lazy sons-a-bitches," the fat little biker yelled into the open door of the apartment on his left. "Time to get back to work."

Before Allison had a chance to run up the stairs into the safety of her apartment, a flurry of uneven beards, dark sunglasses, leather jackets, thick boots, and colorful tattoos poured into the hallway. She stood in the corner with a look of disdain hidden beneath a taut unnatural smile. It was an expression that gave her confidence against these noisy and uncouth intruders. *Who are you kidding, Al? They know you're scared of them. You're clinging to the wall like a stupid vine.* Allison struck a big city tough girl pose as she wedged her way tighter into the corner. She felt in the pocket of her jacket for her keys. She made a fist around all of her keys except one, the work washroom key, because it was the oldest and rustiest and could probably do the most damage if used as a weapon. She maneuvered the key around in her hand until it was pointing outward, between her index and middle finger. She prepared herself to thrust it into the face of any biker who might mess with her. Then she noticed the chains sticking out of their jean pockets and prepared to scream instead.

Who the hell is moving in here? Allison thought as she waited for the derogatory remarks to pelt her like hailstones during a spring storm. Surprisingly, however, the bikers scarcely noticed her as they hurried outside like a football team charging their way out to the field. They had a job to do and they were on their way to do it.

They returned just as quickly as they left carrying boxes, furniture, and other odds and ends. In came a biker with a pile of unfolded clothes up to his nose: sweaters, jackets, old slacks, and blue jeans haphazardly stacked one on top of the other as if it was laundry day. Two more bikers came in carrying an old beat up sofa, one on either side. And finally the fat little troll biker came in carrying a rocking chair.

"Hey Eddie, careful! That's my most prized possession. Don't go bangin' it against the wall." The deep, raspy, but distinctively female voice hollered out the door to the troll biker.

The accent was southern, but not the genteel southern accent of the deep south that one might expect from a Louisiana belle at a cotillion. This was a southern accent that twanged more than drawled. It was back woodsy, rough, and completely without pretense. It went perfectly with the deep husky voice she'd heard holler out the door. Allison recognized the tones and inflections of that voice. She knew at once where it came from. Kentucky. Pure Kentucky. The river and a mile long bridge separated western Kentucky from southern Indiana, but to cross that bridge was to enter another world. To cross the bridge was to leave the Midwest behind and enter the South with all its' battle scars, ghosts, romance, and prejudice.

Allison's curiosity became stronger than her fear, as she edged her way out of the security of the corner where she'd been clinging. She wedged her way between the bikers, who were too busy coming and going to take much notice of her. She stuck her head in the door, tentatively at first. She saw her. There in the middle of the front room sat the woman on one of the boxes.

The first thing Allison noticed about her was her auburn hair, which fell just below her shoulders in a wild thick mass of tangled up curls. She was darker than the average red head, with skin more bronze than ivory, and Allison guessed that her eyes were probably brown. Judging from the voice she expected to see a rough, leathery, worldly worn face. Instead she gazed upon the profile of a flawless work of art: high prominent cheekbones, long straight nose, symmetrical heart shaped lips, and clearly defined jaw. Allison called to mind all the artists she'd studied while in Europe. The face of this strange woman embodied the beauty that they'd all tried so hard to depict. By the woman's tough masculine manner and the self-conscious way the thick mess of hair draped her face it was as if she was uncomfortable with her beauty and was trying to hide it.

She wore a black leather jacket, tight blue jeans and pointed toe boots.

She was long and thin, the kind of thin that never had to work at it. This was a woman who not only took the stairs instead of the elevator, but she took them two at a time.

Allison felt a twinge of envy. She'd read the fashion magazines all her life and had made herself literally sick trying to be beautiful. She'd poured over books and articles on how to present herself and improve herself, and here sat this woman, on a box, in an old pair of jeans, who had all the right raw material for class, beauty, and elegance. She probably didn't even know it, and even if she did, she probably didn't care. She was completely oblivious, as she sat there like a queen on her throne while all these tough men buzzed around her doing her bidding, mere drones flitting about the queen bee.

Allison got a good look at the man with whom the woman was speaking. He was squatting before her, causing him to look slightly up in order to be face to face with her. The man was dark skinned, smooth faced, with a long braid down his back. He wore a red T-shirt, blue jeans, cowboy boots, and was adorned with Native American jewelry of silver and turquoise, and what the jewelry didn't cover, tattoos did. They were oblivious to all the activity going on around them, intent in conversation, and there seemed to be some type of connection between them but they didn't appear to be lovers.

Allison, confident and self-assured, decided to walk right into the apartment and introduce herself. She stepped across the threshold of the apartment, clearing her throat all the while, partly to get the woman's attention and partly so she could project her voice over the loud music. The man with the long black braid was the first to notice her. He tapped the woman on the knee with the back of his hand and motioned toward Allison. The woman looked over at Allison and gave her a quick apathetic appraisal, then gestured to the man with the long braid who went over to the stereo and turned the volume way down. The woman didn't budge from her box as she took a pack of cigarettes and a lighter out of her jacket pocket. She ignored Allison as she nonchalantly went about the business of lighting her cigarette.

There was no turning back for Allison. She had been seen already, so there was nothing to do but walk right up to the woman and proceed with her usual greeting, a greeting she'd learned from observing top sales people, a greeting designed to show interest and put the other at ease.

"Hello." Allison beamed with confidence and vivacity as she held out her hand to the woman. "I'm Allison Brinkmeyer. I live upstairs." The woman remained seated, but condescended to shake her hand. As expected, her grip was firm. The woman looked her in the eye as she squeezed her hand. Allison was right about the eye color. They were a fiery hazel brown, and like real fire, they seemed to have the capacity to either warm or burn. Slowly the corners of the woman's mouth formed the slightest trace of a smile. It took Allison a moment to size up the smile. It seemed to be one of amusement mixed with a little admiration that this stranger should march right into her apartment unannounced. It may have been just a gutsy enough gesture to win the woman over. Her face relaxed and her smile broadened, exposing a somewhat crooked set of teeth, grown too close together with one overlapping another. Instead of detracting from her appearance, however, her imperfect smile only served to enhance her strange and exotic beauty.

"Vicky Dooley's the name," the woman said flipping her hair back from her face. Allison noticed at once the woman's long swan-like neck. Then she noticed a jagged scar about three inches in length on the woman's left cheek, just under the cheekbone and cutting back to the temple. All the more reason for her hair to drape her face, Allison thought. The scar stuck out like a glaring reminder to the world that in the midst of all this beauty, her life had not been an easy one. She took a long draw off her cigarette, inhaled deeply, and breathed out a perfect stream of smoke.

"This here's Chief Bobby." Vicky motioned to the man with the long braid who eyed Allison suspiciously.

"Nice to meet you, uh, Chief," said Allison shaking the man's enormous hand.

"Call me Bobby," he said smiling only slightly.

"Bobby's my kin. We're cousins."

"Second cousins." Chief Bobby spoke in a deep bass voice that commanded authority.

"Once it gets past first cousins I'm completely lost. I never could keep all that once and twice removed business straight," Allison twittered in her nervous cocktail party voice. They looked at her without laughing, though the woman's eyes laughed a little as she smiled her amused smile. "I mean I admire anyone who can," Allison said looking at Chief Bobby.

"My grandma on my mama's side, grandma Miner, was Shawnee. Now what kin was she to you again, Bobby?"

"My aunt."

"Just a couple wild injuns looking for our silver mine, ain't we Bobby?" Vicky said smiling her peculiar and crooked smile through a cloud of cigarette smoke.

"We'll find it yet," the Chief said smiling that slight smile which Allison guessed was as broad of a smile as his face would allow.

"Silver mines?" Allison was too intrigued not to ask what this meant.

"See, there was this group of Shawnee that come back to their original stomping grounds in Kentucky from the reservation out west around the late 1800's."

"Back in the 1760's," Bobby took over telling the story, "an Englishman by the name of Jonathan Swift is said to have worked some silver mines somewhere around Mud Lick Creek in Johnson County–that's Eastern Kentucky. Nobody knows for sure the exact location of these mines and so far nobody's found them. The legend goes that Swift used Shawnee laborers. A group of them led by a descendant of Chief Cornstalk returned to the area from the reservation out in Oklahoma to search for the mines in the 1870's. Eventually they migrated to western Kentucky. Only instead of silver mines it was coal mines. Vicky and I are descended from that group of Shawnee that came back."

"So we always talk about findin' our silver mine… you know, our fortune," Vicky said.

"Wow, great legacy," Allison said. "My background isn't nearly so colorful–just poor German farmers who came to the New World and ended up in Southern Indiana with all the other poor German farmers."

"The Shawnees are only on my mama's side. You'd think my Daddy's side would be the more interesting, but they're just a bunch of backwoods hillbillies." Allison laughed at Vicky's remark and her unpretentious way. It seemed her new neighbor was warming to her a little.

Since Allison first noticed Vicky, the bikers had been busily coming and going, transporting Vicky's belongings from the U-haul into her new home. Now they appeared to be wrapping up the job as one of them, covered with sweat and breathless, carried in a huge box.

"This here's the last of your stuff, Vick," the biker announced. The rest of them had gathered in the hall just outside the door.

"Thanks a lot, boys. I couldn't have done it without you all." she said somewhat coyly, as if to humor these silly men.

"They insist on helping," Vicky said to Allison barely above a whisper, as if she could read her thoughts. "Well, c'mon in, you know where the beer is," she hollered out to the men.

The room was suddenly alive with testosterone as the men rushed to the small kitchen and hovered by the light of the open refrigerator door, handing cans of cold beer out to each other. The men avoided eye contact with Allison and walked around her as if she wasn't there.

As one of them walked by he wolf whistled at her and said, "Hey blondie." Then he said "Hey Vicky, ain't you gonna introduce us to your new friend?" He smiled a grimy smile, while some of the other bikers chuckled.

"C'mon Trash, be nice," Vicky reprimanded him.

"I am being nice. I'm just asking who your new friend is?"

"This here's my new neighbor, Allison Brinkmeyer."

Allison was taken aback. The woman actually caught her name, not only her first name, but her last as well.

"Very good, Vicky Dooley. You remembered my name."

"And you remembered mine. I never forget a name or a face, though I might forget just how I know them."

"That's our Vicky, all right," Trash chuckled as he popped open his beer and took a slug.

"I never forget a face either, but I'm terrible with names," Allison said. "I had to take a class to teach me how to remember names."

"A class to learn you to remember names? I ain't ever heard of a class to teach you how to remember names."

"Oh, yes! You can take a class for just about anything these days."

"I fuckin' guess. Pardon my French."

"Don't worry, my French is worse than that." Allison chuckled at her own joke.

"You? No way. Now me, I got me a foul mouth. Bad habit. Suppose I could take a class to learn me to quit cussing?"

Though she was trying to be facetious, there was something half-way serious in the way she posed this question. Allison thought she recognized something of herself in the way the woman broke eye contact for just a moment, her eyes darting downward so that no one could see what was there for that heartbeat of a second. It was the same lack of satisfaction with herself that Allison saw every time she looked in the mirror. It was a desire for someone or something to come along and lift her out of herself and refine her, a miracle that might make her acceptable.

Chief Bobby was standing like a statue with his arms folded. He didn't seem to belong to the biker gang. His role appeared to be protector or bodyguard for Vicky.

"So, how did you remember my name?" Vicky asked Allison, taking another long draw off her cigarette, unaware of the long ash that drove Allison crazy with the desire to flick it.

"I thought of Queen Victoria."

"No shit?" Vicky laughed a sensual husky laugh that sounded as if it strained to break free from her lungs. A wheezy congested cough followed the laughter, which caused the ash to fall off Vicky's cigarette and onto the carpet.

"Are you all right?" Allison asked.

"Fuckin' bronchitis! Yeah, I'm fine. Need to quit smoking. I believe I could give up cussing easier. So what made you think of Queen Victoria? "

"Because you look like a queen sitting there on that box."

"Yeah, that's me all right! Queen of strong drinks, fast boys, and big talkin' bullshit," Vicky said as straight faced as can be. Allison laughed out loud. "So what are you queen of, Miss Allison?"

"I don't know about the strong drinks and fast boys part. Fast cars, maybe. And big talkin' bullshit most certainly. I could give you a run for your money on that one." Vicky smiled her crooked smile at Allison. "But still, you're the one with the queenly name."

"My name ain't Victoria though. Just plain ol' Vicky. Vicky with a 'y'. Vicky Lee to be exact. That's what's on my birth certificate. So how did you remember my last name?"

"I thought of that old song. 'Hang down your head Tom Dooley'," Allison half-sang, half-spoke the first line of the song.

"Hang down your head Tom Dooley. Hang down your head and cry," Vicky sang.

"Hang down your head Tom Dooley. Poor boy you're gonna die." Allison and Vicky sang together in unison.

"Yeah, I heard that one a time or two," Vicky said.

Chief Bobby had disappeared momentarily, but reappeared again with a brown glass ashtray which he stuck under Vicky's chin at the precise moment she was ready to scrunch out her cigarette.

"So what's your secret?" Allison asked. "How do you remember names so well?"

"I listen."

There was a brief silence between the two women, finally broken by the voice of one of the big bikers putting on his black leather jacket. "Hey Vicky. We're gonna take off."

"Thanks a heap, Jimmy." Vicky stood up for the first time. She was about six feet tall, all legs.

Vicky said her goodbyes to the bikers, and they all left with the same noisy burst of adrenaline with which they'd moved her things. After the last of the bikers was out the door, Vicky looked at Bobby, who looked back at her while he put on his jean jacket preparing to go. There was a definite kinship between these two as they seemed to communicate without words.

"Thanks Bobby. You didn't have to come, you know."

"Had to check out your new home," Bobby said.

"So does it pass the inspection?"

Chief Bobby gave a quick nod in response. Vicky embraced the strong man with the long braid. He was about as tall as her.

"Love you, bro," she said as she hugged him. Bobby's stone face showed a crack of tenderness though he spoke no words. "Bobby's my bro, you know. Only one I got," Vicky said to Allison as she slapped Bobby on the back. Bobby looked at Allison then back at Vicky as if to make sure everything was okay and that Vicky was comfortable being left with this stranger. Vicky gave him a nod. Unlike the bikers, Chief Bobby parted without a sound. The two women watched as he silently slipped out the door, giving only a slight wave of his big hand to signal his final farewell.

Allison knew she should go too, but she didn't want to go. She didn't want to be all alone in her apartment with nothing but her own self-pity.

"I need to get going myself," Allison said looking at her watch for no reason whatsoever, except that it was a habit of hers to check her watch upon arrival or departure from any given place. "It was nice meeting you Vicky Dooley."

"Nice meeting you too, Allison Brinkmeyer."

"Let me know if you need anything. I'm just upstairs in apartment 5."

Allison headed for the door and Vicky called after her. "Hey, you don't have to run off." Underneath the strong unwavering tones of Vicky's loud raspy voice was an almost desperate plea for companionship. Allison turned around.

"I know how it is living alone. Folks don't get to know their neighbors no more. Ain't no front porches in apartments."

"Nor even houses anymore for that matter," Allison added.

"Ain't it the truth," Vicky said, lighting another cigarette and walking over to the kitchen. "You look tired, girl. Have a seat. Can I fix you a drink?" she called out from the kitchen.

"No, thanks," Allison called back, taking a seat on the old beat up sofa.

"Mind if I fix myself a drink?"

"Not at all. It's your home."

"Yeah, it is, ain't it? Nicest home I ever had. Always wanted to live in a castle," said Vicky, emerging from the kitchen with a black coffee mug. She breathed out a stream of cigarette smoke and proudly surveyed the place with a broad smile and bright brown eyes. She grabbed hold of the rocking chair, and dragging it behind her, pulled it right up to the sofa next to Allison. She plopped in the rocker with all the grace and finesse of an adolescent boy. Allison got a strong whiff of whiskey as Vicky lifted the black coffee mug to her lips.

"Is that straight whiskey you're drinking?" Allison asked.

"Jack Daniels. Tennessee's finest. You sure you don't want some?"

"Brrrr. No, thank you! Way too strong for me. I'm getting a buzz just off the fumes. I'm a hopeless lightweight."

Vicky laughed her hoarse wheezy laugh. "I kinda figured you was. You like them sweet frozen, Easter egg colored drinks with the little umbrellas in 'em. Don't you? You'll drink a beer every so often. And you're trying hard to acquire a taste for fine wine, though secretly you'd just as soon have the cheap sweet stuff. But when you go out partying, it's a daiquiri or margarita every time."

"That's amazing! How did you know that about me."

"I'm a bartender. It's my job to know." Vicky took another gulp from her mug.

"Where do you work?"

"The lounge at Lamasco's River Inn. Been working there going on four months now. Nicest place I ever tended bar. Believe me I've worked some real dives in my time."

"That place has become quite the hot spot lately. I keep hearing about it." Allison said, recalling how the River Inn lounge had become the yuppie hangout of Lamasco. She tried to envision this hillbilly motorcycle mama from Kentucky in the midst of all those yuppies. "They have jazz bands there on the weekend."

"Yeah, that's the only down side of the job. I'm trying hard to acquire a taste for jazz. Same way you're trying to acquire a taste for fine wine. But like you, I still prefer the cheap stuff. Hell, I'm just an ol' country girl. Give me Elvis or Hank Williams Jr. any day. 'Course I like rock too. Janis Joplin. The Who. The Stones. All them ol' greats." Vicky rocked in her chair, and smoked and drank her whiskey contentedly.

"I'm talking your ear off. Ain't I?"

"I don't mind," said Allison. "Honestly."

"I do a lot of listening with my job. It's nice just to be able to talk."

"I do a lot of talking with my job, so it's nice just to be able to listen for a change."

"What do you do?"

"I'm in advertising."

"I could tell you some stories, girl. I seen it all. I heard it all. Bartenders are kinda like low rent psychiatrists. We listen to people's problems, advise them as best we can, and prescribe medication."

"I never thought of it like that. What an original outlook. Let me know next time you work. My fiancé and I'll stop by for a drink and some free counseling."

"Oh? You need it?"

"I was just kidding."

"I figured you was getting hitched." Allison gave Vicky a questioning look. "The ring," Vicky said in response, pointing to Allison's left hand. "So when's the wedding?"

"This June. As a matter of fact we're having our reception at your place. In the Gold Room. I'm sorry to say that's about all I've seen of the River Inn. I haven't been to the restaurant or lounge yet."

"Well, you and your honey just gotta come pay me a visit, now don't you?" Vicky said exhaling smoke through her nose and scrunching out her cigarette in the brown glass ashtray which sat on a box by the sofa. She stood up, lit another cigarette, and went into the kitchen for just a moment. She emerged with her bottle of Jack Daniels. "Sure I can't get you anything?" she asked, cigarette hanging from her mouth as she poured some more whiskey into her mug. She placed her bottle on the box by the ashtray, and sinking into the comfort and security of her old rocker, appeared to settle in for the evening.

"No, thank you," Allison said, her stomach beginning to ache with hunger. "You've been very hospitable, but I really need to go home and get something to eat," Allison said rising to her feet and collecting her purse.

"Is it suppertime already? What time is it anyway?"

"Ten 'til six," Allison said looking at her watch.

"Shit! I didn't reckon it was getting to be so late." Vicky quickly jumped up from the rocker. "I'd offer you something except all I got is a bag a chips. Sometimes I forget to eat."

"Maybe if I'd forget to eat I'd be as skinny as you," Allison said re-slinging her purse over her shoulder.

"But you ain't fat. You was, but you ain't no more. Except now you can't see yourself any other way."

"How did you know I used to be fat?"

"I just figured you couldn't have always been so good looking. You're too nice. Not stuck up like someone born and raised good looking might be."

"Thanks. I think."

"I meant it as a compliment."

"And I thought I knew people."

"You just learn them in my business," Vicky said taking another gulp from her mug. "You better go get you something to eat, girl."

"What about you?"

"Oh, I'll be all right. Got me a bag a barbeque potato chips. That oughta hold me over 'til morning."

"You've got to have something more than that."

"I'll be fine."

"Hey, I just remembered. I've got some lasagna. Do you like lasagna?"

"Sure. I'll eat just about anything that ain't still crawling or got something crawling on it."

"One of the girls who lives here made a ton of lasagna for me. Sally's her name. Believe me, you'll meet her soon enough. She lives down the hall from you. If I don't finish it up soon I'll just end up throwing it out. We can have it for dinner."

"That's awful kind of you. Sure I ain't imposing?"

"Not at all. You're saving me from having to eat alone. I hate to eat alone.

No, I'm the one who feels impertinent; barging in your apartment like this and just making myself at home."

" 'Impertinent'… don't tell me the definition. Let me look it up. As soon as I find my dictionary," Vicky said looking around at the boxes. "In the mean time let me write that down. I'm tryin' to educate myself–get a better vocabulary," Vicky said grabbing her purse off the kitchen counter and digging through it.

"Oh!" was all Allison could say at this sudden shifting of gears.

"Impertinent. Now how do you spell that?" she asked pen and paper in hand. "I-M-P…"

"I-M-P-E-R-T-I-N-E-N-T," Allison finished spelling the word.

"No, I hear what you're sayin' about hatin' to eat alone. That's why I just a soon munch on a bag of chips. I can't remember the last time I sat down to supper."

Vicky followed Allison upstairs to her apartment. Allison was right about Vicky. She bounded up the stairs two at a time, with a bag of chips in one hand and a bottle of Jack Daniels in the other. Despite Vicky's heavy smoking, Allison didn't detect the slightest hint of puffing or panting once she reached the top.

And so the two had dinner together. Vicky helped Allison chop up carrots, cut up, rinse, and dry a head of lettuce for salad, while the microwave oven radiated the frozen lasagna. Vicky was insistent that she contribute something to the dinner so she brought along her bag of chips, which they crushed into tiny crumbs and sprinkled over the top of the lasagna. The chips actually helped the lasagna, which wasn't exactly fresh and never quite made it past warmed. The two talked well into the night.

Vicky told Allison all about her life. How she grew up in rural Western Kentucky between two coal mining towns. How her mother died when Vicky was only a teenager. How it was the cigarettes and worry that killed her. She told her about her father, a mean alcoholic who died shortly after her twenty first birthday. He wanted to see her before he died but she refused to go. Now he visits her in her dreams, all sober and cleaned up, and asks her why she didn't come. She feels regret and sorrow in these dreams, until she wakes up, then she's angry all over again.

Vicky was an only child. The emptiness of no brothers and sisters threw a kind of pall over her childhood, as it also did for her mother who lost baby after baby to miscarriage. No brothers and sisters, but she did have her cousin Chief Bobby who was as good as any brother. The only problem was Bobby couldn't go home with her. He had his own home and his own set of problems there, just like Vicky.

She always thought if she had a brother or sister at home maybe she could laugh more about her Daddy. She would've had someone she could hide under the bed with when he was on a whuppin' rampage. Someone she could giggle with when he passed out in his lazy boy with his glass still firmly clutched in hand, his head tilted back, his mouth wide open, and that reverberating snore that you could hear from anywhere in the house. Someone she could make dares with about who could get the glass out of his hand without waking him up. Someone she could take whuppins for. Someone who could take whuppins for her.

Her paternal grandmother was the stabling influence of her life. She always knew just when to call or show up, just when things got really bad. She was a good Christian woman, always quoting the Bible and dragging Vicky along to church and holy roller prayer meetings. This grandmother outlived both her parents, dying about a year after her father. She still cries sometimes at night into her pillow for grief over the loss of her grandmother.

Vicky left late that night. Allison opened all her windows and the sliding glass door to the balcony, to air out her apartment from the cigarette smoke. Although the smoke was intense and Allison had grown unaccustomed to the smell during the past year, it reminded her of her college days and of the sorority house. The smell of smoke made her homesick for her friends. She fanned the smoky air with a thick magazine and laughed. She was surprised how much she enjoyed Vicky's company. She thought how completely different they looked standing side by side, yet their backgrounds were actually very similar. They both had unhappy childhoods. They were both teased in school, Vicky for being too skinny, Allison for being too fat. They both knew the rural life, the seasons of planting and harvest. It was the land, with all that space to run around in and dream that saved them both from going crazy. Yet here they both found themselves, years later in these tiny apartments, not far from where they both grew up, yet somehow a million miles apart.

Chapter 8

Sally's built in radar was well known around Camelot. It allowed her to detect movement out in the hall from within her apartment. Like some unseen burglar alarm, a footstep in either the upstairs or downstairs hall was all it took to trigger it. Once the radar was triggered, she'd poke her head out the door and do a quick inspection, first looking to the left then to the right. If there was someone she wanted to talk to out there, she'd step into the hallway and form an invisible gate in front of the unfortunate passerby, so they couldn't get around her no matter how hard they tried. This radar worked no matter where Sally was in her apartment. Even in the shower, Allison suspected, as she once came to the door in her robe with a towel wrapped around her head, water still dripping from her face. She wondered, in fact, if Sally's radar even worked while away from her apartment. Because of this, Allison tried to be vigilant whenever she descended the stairs of her upstairs apartment. She'd brace herself as she got to the bottom, scurrying around the corner past Sally's downstairs apartment as quickly as possible. But of course, she couldn't always have her guard up, and that's when Sally was most likely to catch you.

Allison was on her way to Vicky's place one September evening with a bottle of red wine in one hand and a loaf of French bread in the other. When her right foot stepped down on the second to last stair the door to Sally's apartment opened.

Damn! Allison thought as she looked up to see Sally standing there with her crazy Elton John glasses and her big hair forming a plaster helmet around her head.

"Hello, Sally." Allison was surprised at how lackluster her greeting sounded. Even for a Dale Carnegie graduate, she just couldn't feign enthusiasm and good cheer around Sally. It was too tiring and made her face muscles hurt.

"Allison dearest," Sally said her eyes wide and her head poked through the opening of the door like a snapping turtle straining to be released from its shell. "You wouldn't happen to be taking those goodies to our new neighbor, would you?" she said stepping out into the hallway, her oven mitted hands holding a large casserole dish covered in aluminum foil. "I just baked some lasagna for her."

"Oh, how nice. Well, yes, as a matter of fact, that's where I'm headed right now." She tried to step around Sally but it was no use; an invisible gate had gone up.

"What do you say we go together?"

"Oh, um, well. All right." What else could Allison say? Besides, maybe it was better this way. She might be able to steer Sally out of Vicky's apartment before midnight. They knew Vicky was home because they could hear her music, some country rock band hollering out proclamations of love over their steel guitars.

"I haven't met her yet, but I understand she's different," Sally said in a hushed voice so that Allison had to strain to hear her over the loud music. Allison looked away from Sally and focused her eyes down the hall toward Vicky's apartment. Just a few simple steps, yet she felt completely helpless to get there. Sally's short round body effectively blocked the hallway, causing Allison to feel claustrophobic.

The funny little woman blocking the hallway in her bright purple sweat suit with matching purple eye shadow looked like the grape from the Fruit of the Loom commercial only more formidable. Allison knew she would be trapped there indefinitely until she gave Sally the information she desired. She didn't want to get sucked into Sally's gossip game, but it was far too powerful of a vortex to resist.

"I heard she's different," Sally whispered. "That was Tim's impression of her anyway. You've met her. What do you think?" Allison had no idea how Sally knew.

"I like her. I guess she is a little different, but not in a bad way."

"Tim says she's rough; says she's pure Kentucky white trash."

"Not pure exactly. I think she has some Indian blood."

"Tim says she has a lot of biker friends."

"So?"

"So she doesn't sound like your typical Camelot resident."

"And what exactly is the typical Camelot resident?"

"College educated. You know…yuppie."

"Oh, c'mon, Sally! There really is no such thing as a real yuppie in Lamasco. Just a lot of wanna be yuppies."

"Oh? How do you figure that?"

"Young Urban Professionals? You can hardly consider Lamasco urban."

"I thought it stood for Young Upcoming Professionals."

"Whatever. Vicky is a professional. She's a bartender. She had to go to school to learn to be one."

"And just how does bartending school compare with college?"

"Well, bartending's both an art and a science. You have to know which ingredients to mix and how much. That's a science. Like chemistry. And yet getting the drink to taste just right, now that's an art. Not to mention you're dealing with people, so you have to know something about psychology. That's a social science. In fact she even knows a little something about the fine arts. Wine tasting for example. She told me herself she had to take a course on it. All in all I'd say she knows just about as much as us college educated folks."

"It figures you'd think that. You're an IU grad. You can probably major in bartending at your alma mater. In fact isn't that one of the tougher schools to get into at IU–the School of Bartending?"

"Oh, yeah, I thought they called Purdue folks 'boilermakers'."

"Very funny! Seriously though, I just hope she won't be a problem. She sure plays her stereo loud."

"Maybe it comes from working in bars."

"But she's not in a bar. She's in an apartment with neighbors. It's inconsiderate."

Sally had a point. Not that Vicky was the first person to play her stereo loud. Everyone did from time to time. Frank was one of the worst perpetrators, though his was usually classical music or opera. But Vicky's stereo went on the moment she entered the apartment and usually stayed on until she left. Even in the middle of the night when she returned home between three and four o'clock in the morning after River Inn's last call. Allison figured she probably turned it down a little to go to sleep, but it was still loud enough to hear out in the hall when she passed by her apartment in the morning.

"I guess we should say something to her about that." Hospitality and nosiness were all mixed together with Sally, but Allison felt strange about welcoming the new neighbor and scolding her at the same time. The imaginary sign read in Allison's mind: *Welcome to Camelot. Please accept these small tokens of our warmth and hospitality. By the way, no stereos or TVs after eleven p.m. Absolutely, positively no Hell's Angels on the premises. Thank you for your courtesy.* Allison blinked her eyes and refocused on Sally.

"So what else do you know about her?" Sally asked.

"Not much really." Allison shrugged, hoping Sally couldn't read the hesitancy in her tone. Sally seemed satisfied that she was not withholding any information. The invisible gate vanished, and once again, Allison was allowed to move. The two made their way down the hall to Vicky's door.

"You'd better knock," Sally said motioning to her oven mitted hands. Allison rapped her knuckles hard on the door so that Vicky could hear the knock above her music. The door opened wide and fast. The music filled the hall with its coarse romanticism. The rough hard sound that bounced off the walls between the vibrating bass and twanging strings contrasted with the lyrics, which Allison was always able to hear as separate and distinct from the music. The lead singer cried out words of heartbreak, longing, and the sweet pain of lost love. It distracted Allison who stood there stunned staring at Vicky. She was barefoot, clad in blue jeans and an oversized black Jack Daniels tee shirt. Her sleeves were rolled up with what appeared to be a pack of cigarettes tucked into the one sleeve. Allison noticed for the first time a tattoo on Vicky's upper left arm just below the protruding rectangular box. It was a heart with thorns wrapped around it and flames pouring forth from the top. A deep gash cut into the heart with a large drop of blood dripping out.

"Impertinent," Vicky blurted out, as Allison stared at the tattooed drop of blood as if it might actually roll down her arm. " 'Exceeding the limits of propriety or good manners. Ill bred. Disrespectful. Saucy.' Well, hell, Allison, I thought you was using that word in reference to you. Not me. Hi, nice to meet you. Vicky Dooley's the name," she said suddenly shifting her attention to Sally. She extended her hand toward her then quickly withdrew it upon observation of the oven mitts and the casserole dish.

"You must be the lasagna lady."

Allison winced at Vicky's remark.

"This is Sally," Allison interjected as quickly as possible. "She lives down the hall from you."

"Welcome Vicky. I hope you like lasagna," Sally's remark sounded more like a question than a statement.

"As I told our friend Allison, here, I like anything that ain't still twitching, or got something twitching on it." Sally's face curled up in disgust. "Thank you kindly," Vicky said reaching for the casserole dish.

"Careful. It's still hot." Sally cautioned.

"Hot don't bother me none," Vicky said taking the casserole dish from Sally's hands. "My hands are all calloused up. Bartenders use their hands every bit as much as auto mechanics. Most people don't realize that. Lots of grabbing and twisting in my line of work. And you gotta do it fast. Grab and twist. Grab and twist. That's all I do of a night. C'mon in." Sally looked at Allison and shrugged. They followed Vicky into her apartment.

"Mmm. This smells good," Vicky leaned her long straight nose over the aluminum foil of the casserole dish as she made her way into the kitchen.

"Excuse the stereo," Vicky hollered emerging from the kitchen, her long legs doing a quick jog over to the machine to turn the volume down. "My fuckin' ears are shot. Have a seat." The two dazed women merely stood there in response to Vicky's request.

"Looks like you're already settled in. I still had boxes in my living room for over a month after I moved in. And you have more stuff than me. A lot more stuff!" Allison said looking around at all the clutter. The kitchen table was covered with paper: stacks of envelopes, bills, newspapers scattered and strewn. A card table and a TV tray were set up in the middle of the living room, the tops of which were littered with more paper.

"Early American Yard Sale," Sally nudged Allison in the ribs, and said in a tone that may have been hushed for Sally, but wasn't for any other ordinary human being.

Their gawking had struck a nerve with Vicky, and Allison realized it. With all the finesse of James Dean, Vicky whipped out her pack of Marlboros, stuck a cigarette in her mouth, and defiantly struck a match. "So I'm a fuckin' pack rat. You got a problem with that?"

"None whatsoever," Sally blurted out.

"I'm sorry if we offended you somehow," Allison said apologizing more for Sally than for herself.

"No big deal," Vicky said letting it go with a wave of dismissal and exhalation of smoke.

Allison smiled sympathetically at Vicky and Sally laughed nervously.

"Have a seat y'all," she commanded more resolutely this time. "Make yourselves at home. I'll be back in a jiffy," she said her long legs and agile bare feet carrying her out of the room in one quick stride. "I got to go to the can," She hollered down the hall.

As soon as they heard the bathroom door close, Allison and Sally popped up again and resumed their snooping. The sight, smell, and feel of the place had the musty smell of mothballs mixed with cigarettes. A brightly colored afghan hung over the back of the old beat up sofa that was so worn that its stuffing hung out in places. Above the sofa hung a velvet painting of a Native American warrior wearing only a loin cloth and feather headdress. He stood with spear in hand poised for battle, war paint smeared across his cheeks as the wind blew back his long black hair.

"Nice Hummel collection," Sally chortled as Allison turned around to see a curio cabinet filled mostly with cheap souvenirs and mementos. Allison stepped closer to it to get a better look.

"My memoirs," Vicky said startling them both as she suddenly reappeared in the doorway. "It's okay, y'all can look," she said inhaling from her cigarette then popping her jaw three times fast, producing three perfect smoke rings.

Allison's eyes fell on an assortment of plates, cups, salt and pepper shakers from Graceland, Lookout Mountain, and Vegas. Elvis memorabilia lined the rows of the cabinets, along with small figurines of Indians, airplane bottles of booze, roach clips, a pipe, and a wilted corsage. There was also a picture of Vicky standing in front of the Grand Canyon, one of chief Bobby, and one of a kindly looking older lady.

"My grandma," Vicky said pointing to the picture. "She's gone, but I still got my memories and some of her memoirs."

"Memoirs? She wrote her memoirs?" Sally asked.

"No, you know, memoirs–treasures. That's her hope chest over there," Vicky said pointing to the antique treasure in the middle of the room which served as a coffee table. Allison thought it truly a beautiful piece of furniture, marred only slightly by the bumper sticker plastered on the side proclaiming, "Real Women Ride Harleys". On top was a pickle jar filled with matchbooks, and a brown glass ashtray piled high with cigarette butts and ashes. A bottle of beer sat on a cork coaster. Allison remembered from before that Vicky was careful about using the coasters. What a contradiction, she thought, that the same care that went into protecting the top of this extraordinary piece would allow a gummy and adhesive bumper sticker to be placed on the side. Everything in Vicky's world seemed to be in conflict. Her memoirs were neatly dusted yet her table tops were piled with junk. A burning cigarette hung precariously on the edge of the brown glass ashtray, threatening to burn a hole in the hope chest.

"Oh, I almost forgot. I got you a little house-warming gift too," said Allison, presenting Vicky with the bottle of wine and the loaf of French bread.

"Thank you, Allison Brinkmeyer. I was going to grab it out of your hands but I thought that might be impertinent." Allison watched as Vicky surveyed the bottle. She held it like someone who knew what they were talking about, carefully supporting the neck with one hand and the bottom with the other. "Merlot. A fine selection. A good year and a good brand. I'm proud of you, girl. I know you was wanting to buy that Boone's Farm instead," she said smiling at Allison, then looking at her quizzically she added, "How's come the French go and stick 'T' at the end of a word if they don't expect you to pronounce it?"

"Pardon me," Allison said in reply.

"As in Merlot. Made from a grape around the region of Bordeaux; or should I say Bordooks?"

"I understand you know something about wine tasting," Sally said.

"I ain't exactly an expert, but in my line of work you got to know a little something about the fruit of the vine."

"Could you give us a demonstration?" Sally asked.

"Allison here lived in France. I'm sure she knows more than I do."

"Not necessarily," said Allison.

"I didn't know you lived in France," said Sally.

"Just for a year. As an exchange student in college. But as Vicky knows, I never acquired a taste for the good stuff. Maybe you could give us a little crash course, Vicky."

"To tell you the truth, I was hoping to share this fine beverage with some neighborly folk. Wine is the one drink you should never drink alone. Just give it a few minutes to cool," Vicky said walking to the kitchen. Fifteen minutes in the refrigerator is about all it needs. Most folks think you got to serve these dry red wines at room temperature but that ain't the case. It's much better slightly chilled. Not as cold as the white stuff mind you, but still, slightly chilled. Somewhere between 60 to 65 degrees. Remember, it's supposed to be sitting in a dark cool cellar, but since most of us don't have a dark cool cellar, the refrigerator for ten to twenty minutes will do.

"Now you ladies know always to store wine on its side. You don't want that cork drying out on you. Cork dries out you got yourself a nice bottle of vinegar is all." Sally and Allison stood at the entrance of the kitchen watching Vicky, by the light of the refrigerator place the bottle carefully on its side.

Vicky turned to face the women. There was something about her presence that commanded such authority that it rendered even Sally silent. "Now as every good Frenchman knows, you got to have some bread and cheese with your wine."

Vicky presented the loaf of French bread to her guests. She raised it to her face and took in the aroma with great pleasure. "I'd say this here's a notch or two above a loaf of Wonder bread I might pick up at the A&P. Unfortunately, all I got in the way of cheese is this," she said opening the refrigerator and pulling out a package of American sliced cheese. "We got something for everybody. Something a little classy for you ladies," she said lifting the loaf of bread with one hand. "And something a little tacky for me." She lifted the package of American cheese with the other hand. "You all have a seat in the living room and I'll fix us up a little spread."

"Can we help?" Allison asked.

"No! Now go on and have a seat. Today's my day off. Can't hardly stand going a whole day without serving someone. I start sitting around too much. Start getting lazy. My feet start to wither."

Allison quickly complied, surrendering herself to the old beat up sofa, claiming a spot on the far right corner. "What do you mean your feet wither?" Allison called out.

"My grandpa used to say that. Not only do you get a fat ass from sitting around all the time, but your feet wither. Feet were meant to be stood upon, he'd say. Meant to carry you from place to place. You don't use your feet the way they was intended and the muscles start to go weak. But he also used to say, there's a time for sitting and a time for standing. It's time for me to stand and you to sit." Vicky directed her statement to Sally who remained standing by the entrance of the kitchen.

"Go on! Sit your donkey down," she commanded slightly irritated.

Sally reluctantly made her way over to the old beat up sofa, giving Allison a roll of the eyes, and a facial gesture which communicated her displeasure at Vicky for being told to sit. She perched on the opposite end of the sofa from Allison.

"This is a beautiful piece of furniture you've got here," Sally chirped, her fingertips roaming lightly across the surface of the hope chest. "You say it belonged to your grandma?"

"Yeah," Vicky called back from the kitchen in a wistful voice.

"What's inside?"

"I don't know. Granny never told me and I ain't ever looked."

"You've never looked inside?" Sally was incredulous.

"I don't feel quite right about it."

"But she left it to you. Didn't she?"

"I know it sounds crazy, but I just can't bear to open it." Vicky called back from the kitchen. "When granny died, it about tore me up to go through all her belongings. Whatever's in there, it's precious to her. I just ain't ready to look yet. I ain't over her passing yet. You get what I mean?"

Vicky emerged from the kitchen with the slices of bread and cheese neatly lined on a small meat platter. In the other hand she held three small plates. Allison recognized the china pattern at once. It was Blue Willow, the very old Blue Willow pattern. One could tell by the chips on the rims that the plates had a long life of use. Under her arm was a roll of paper towels.

"Your grandma's china?" Allison asked.

"Yeah." Vicky's hazel brown eyes faintly glistened with a grief still not entirely spent. "Granny was poor. She just had a few nice things. This little ol' set of china. The hope chest. A few odds and ends."

"Excuse the fancy napkins," Vicky said, tearing off a piece of paper towel for each woman. "Now this here's real butter. I just can't stand that artificial margarine shit. You won't find any diet pops or artificial sweeteners around here either. Nothing but real sugar. I'm telling you that artificial shit causes cancer. I'm fuckin' convinced. And no light beers or decaf coffee either," she said with her characteristic plop into her rocking chair. "If it ain't real, you won't find it here. Course I have to serve my customers light beer when they want it, but I warn them. You need that extra alcohol to kill off the germs."

"I'd say about five more minutes on that wine," Vicky said leaning forward. Allison automatically looked at her watch. Vicky didn't wear one. She was aware of time and how one moment slips into the other without needing a watch. "Go on, dig in. Have some bread and cheese. But just nibble. Don't fill up. You don't want your palate and gut all tuckered out before we taste that wine.

Allison observed how carefully Vicky watched the two women eat. She wiped her mouth in just the same fashion that Allison had done. She caught herself slouching for just a moment, but quickly corrected this. She scooted to the edge of the rocking chair, her posture perfect, her back as straight as a yardstick. It was Vicky's contradictions again, her commanding, take charge presence conflicting with her insecurities about who she was and where she came from.

"That wine should be about ready," she said rising to her feet and doing a short jog into the kitchen. Back out again Vicky came, as quickly as she had left, this time with three wine glasses in one hand, a corkscrew, and the bottle of wine in the other. She set the bottle, the corkscrew, and the glasses down for a moment; then grabbed a stack of cork coasters, which she placed quickly, with a flick of her wrist as if she was dealing cards, on her grandmother's hope chest.

"All right ladies, here we go." Vicky opened the bottle of wine with the speed and skill possessed only by one who does it frequently. She set the corkscrew, with the cork still on it, back on the table.

"Don't we get to sniff the cork?" Sally asked.

"Hell no! That's nothing but a bunch of Hollywood bullshit. Sniffing the cork ain't gonna tell you jack shit about the quality of the wine. What you need to sniff is the wine itself," Vicky said while pouring the deep red liquid into each glass. "Now you ladies know to always use a glass with a wider bowl for red wine. Keeps the bouquet from escaping all at once. And only fill the glass about a third the way full. Gotta leave room for swirling.

"Now before you do any sniffing there, Sally, you got to *look* at the wine and give it a little time to breathe." She tore off a block of paper towel and picked up her wine glass. "Careful to hold the glass by the stem. You don't want to get that wine too warm." She lifted the glass and held the block of paper towel behind it. "It helps if you got a white background." She studied the glass, not with an academic sort of intensity, but with more of a tender longing–the way a lover takes in the face of her beloved right before a kiss. "Beautiful shade of red, ain't it? Almost a ruby red." Sally and Allison lifted their glasses, picked up their blocks of paper towel, and "oohed" and "aahed" in agreement over the beautiful shade of red.

"What exactly does the color tell you about the wine?" asked Allison.

"The intensity of flavor. The age. The quality of the grapes for those that really know their stuff, but I ain't there yet. With a red wine the darker the color, the more mature the wine. You can really tell age by looking at the rim. Hmmm," Vicky said tilting the glass slightly and donning her most carefully studied look as she examined the wine."

"So can you tell how old it is?" asked Sally.

"I know exactly how old it is," Vicky replied. "Two years," she said turning her gaze from the wine to the ladies, while giving them her crooked but confident little smile.

"You can tell just by looking at the wine?" asked Sally.

"No. I read the date on the bottle."

"You kill me!" Sally let out a loud guffaw.

"Okay, so what next?" asked Sally.

"The next step is swirling." Vicky swirled her glass of wine first, then Sally and Allison followed.

"So why do we swirl?" asked Sally.

"We swirl for two reasons. It releases the bouquet and it allows you to check out the legs."

"Legs! Wine has legs?" Sally asked.

"Yes. Wine has legs," Vicky said studying the glass intently as she skillfully swirled the contents. "It's them little streams that run down the sides of the glass," she said peering inside. "See?"

"No," said Sally, furiously swirling with one hand and lifting her large glasses off her nose with the other, while straining to see the elusive legs.

"Hmm. I guess this is for the trained eye only," said Allison, also straining to see.

"You gotta give it a few seconds. The legs tell you how full bodied the wine is. This one here's got nice legs, "Vicky said, her mouth slowly forming a crooked and sensual smile.

"I see them," said Allison excitedly, watching the little drops run down the side of her glass.

"I give up," said Sally, big glasses perched on top of big hair. "So do I get to drink it now?"

"No!" said Vicky emphatically. "You don't just drink wine. You make love to it. So consider all this foreplay."

"Excuse me?" said Sally.

"Wine is like the grand lady of alcoholic beverages. So it ain't just slam, bam, thank you mam. Not when you're dealing with wine. You got to get to know your wine first. The next step is to smell it. Swirl it a little to release that bouquet then take in one deep whiff."

"Then do I get to drink it?" asked Sally.

"No, not yet."

"What, more foreplay?"

"You gotta kick back, close your eyes, and concentrate on the aroma. Alright ladies, ready? Close your eyes and take in one deep whiff." Holding their wine glasses over their noses, the three women inhaled deeply. "Okay, now sit back in your chair and tell me what you smell."

"Wine," said Sally.

"Ah, c'mon Sally! You can do better than that. I thought you had a creative side," said Allison.

"What's it smell like to you?" Sally asked.

"Fruit."

"Oh that's real creative! It's made from grapes. What do you expect?" quipped Sally.

"It's just my initial impression," Allison said, her eyes still closed, wondering if Vicky and Sally's eyes were open.

"Now ladies, don't go getting into a scrap." Allison opened her eyes after Vicky's remark. Sally's eyes were open but Vicky's were still closed. "Allison's right. You need time to accurately label the aroma. It takes practice. Wait a few more seconds and take another whiff if you need to."

Allison took another whiff, closed her eyes again, and thought about the wine. It was difficult to pin a label on the smell. She was too distracted by the memories it conjured up. It reminded her of Paris. It was a smell she might have smelled on the street while passing a sidewalk café. It made her happy. "I can't tell you exactly what it smells like, only how it makes me feel."

"Go for it," said Vicky.

"It makes me think of Paris. Everything was new to me there. New and exciting. I felt like I could move and breathe there. I felt alive." Allison opened her eyes for a brief moment. Both Vicky and Sally's eyes were closed, their heads leaning back in their chairs. She closed her eyes again.

"Did you miss home?" Sally asked after a long pause.

"Just a little at first. Perhaps if I'd been there longer I would have missed it more."

"It's funny. The smell makes you think of Paris, but it makes me think of my home down in Western Kentucky. I smell these little white and yellow flowers. I can't remember the name of them, but they're edible. Bobby and I used to eat them when we were kids."

"Alright I think I have an impression now," said Sally. "It smells like tea. Some type of herbal tea."

"Good. Very good," said Vicky, her voice softer, less harsh than usual. The spell was broken by the sound of Vicky's voice. Everyone opened their eyes.

"Now we get to taste the wine. But you gotta remember a few things first. You don't just drink and swallow. You got to savor it on your tongue for about sixty seconds. That very first taste is gonna be a shock to your taste buds, so give it about fifteen seconds or so just to sit on the tongue. Then you gotta slosh it around your mouth a little, and be sure to breathe in some air at the same time. Your sense of smell is very important when it comes to taste. Then you gotta ask yourself some questions. Like, does the fruit overpower the alcohol? Does the alcohol overpower the fruit, or is it a nice balance. Is it too bitter, too sweet, too dry, or just right? After you swallow, then you gotta determine the aftertaste. If it's a high quality wine, it'll leave a real nice, long aftertaste – one that'll kinda prepare you for the next taste."

"Before we taste, I'd like to propose a toast," Allison said, and they all raised their glasses in unison. "To our new neighbor, Vicky. May you live long and prosper. And if that doesn't work out, may you at least know love."

"Hear. Hear," said Sally.

Vicky's broad crooked smile let them know she was pleased. The three women clinked glasses then took their first taste. Allison and Vicky took an appropriately small sip, but Sally took a larger gulp. The swishing around in the mouth appeared to be something of an agony for Sally. To Allison's surprise, she thought she tasted a hint of chocolate. She closed her eyes, swallowed and, for the first time ever as a wine drinker, basked in the aftertaste. The spell was broken by the sound of Sally coughing and Vicky slapping her on the back.

"You okay?" Allison asked.

"Fine," Sally said as she strained to get the word out between a cough and a clear of the throat.

"What did you expect? You're only supposed to take a little sip," said Vicky.

"I thought I was at the dentist's for a moment there. I was waiting for someone to tell me to spit."

"Here's the situation with you, girl," Vicky said to Sally. "You really are a wine drinker, unlike Allison here who only likes them foo foo fruity drinks. You like wine because you got a problem with nervousness and wine makes you mellow. No other alcohol takes the edge off quite like wine."

"How did you know that?"

"She knows. Believe me, she knows," said Allison.

"The problem is you drink it too fast 'cause you're looking for that quick buzz. Now don't get me wrong. I can appreciate that. But you don't guzzle wine. Guzzling is for beer and whiskey, not wine. It ain't proper. You gotta learn to slow down. Take a small sip this time and breathe in through your nose," said Vicky.

"My overall impression," said Allison.

"Yes?" said Vicky.

"Elegant yet unpretentious," said Allison holding her glass up.

"Wait a minute. Let me write that word down," said Vicky hopping up and heading back to the kitchen to fetch her notebook.

"Unpre… What was that again?" Vicky said looking up from her pencil.

"Unpretentious," Allison repeated.

"U-N-P-R-E," Vicky looked to Allison for help with the spelling.

"T-E-N-T-I-O-U-S. She writes down words she doesn't know. Then looks them up later," Allison explained to Sally who was taking in a fresh sip of wine and concentrating very hard on going slowly lest Vicky scold her again.

"Go on, girls. Go on. Don't mind me," Vicky said, somewhat embarrassed, as she put down her notebook and pen. "Very good, Sally. You did much better this time. So what did you taste?"

"Tea. I still say tea. This herbal tea I used to drink in college. A sorority sister of mine used to make it when we'd stay up late to study."

"So maybe you're tasting some type of herb growing in the soil near them grapes," Vicky remarked.

"Believe it or not, I tasted chocolate," said Allison.

"I believe you. That's actually a common flavor that folks pick up in their wine. I, myself, have never tasted chocolate. I tasted soil. Tastes like the ground down around my home."

"You've tasted soil?" Sally asked

"Not intentionally. But I have fallen down in the dirt enough to get an idea what it tastes like." Allison smiled at the way Vicky said 'intentionally'. It reminded her of a kid trying to impress a grown up.

"We're drinking wine that tastes like Kentuckian dirt?"

"Sure as hell better than Hoosier dirt."

"You know what's funny?" said Allison taking another sip. "This wine reminds all of us of someplace other than here. Sally, it reminds you of your college days, drinking tea at Purdue. It reminds me of Paris. And Vicky, it reminds you of your home in Kentucky." She took another sip. "I'd say this wine also has a nostalgic quality to it."

"I know what 'nostalgic' means. It means homesick," Vicky said and the church bells down the street began to chime.

Chapter 9
November 1983

It was a quiet night at Camelot and quiet nights were becoming more of a rarity at 3300 Lancelot Lane. The stereo wars between Frank's classical and Vicky's rock were becoming increasingly more of a nuisance and Allison was beginning to wish she and Kent could find a house soon so she could move out before their wedding in June.

She grabbed the remote control and turned the TV on then went into the kitchen. *Screw the diet! Let them take a few more inches out of the wedding dress. I need something salty and crunchy!* Allison said as she rifled through every cabinet. The closest thing she could find to what she was craving was a box of Saltine crackers. Two of the cellophane wrapped stacks had been ripped open and not tightly secured closed again, leaving the remaining crackers very stale. Allison didn't care. She went back to the couch with her box of Saltines and went at it. And there on the screen in front of her eyes was Sally's face, as big and bright and startling as ever:

Come to Buckner's Dry Cleaning.
Serving the Tri-State for over fifty years.
Bring your dirty laundry to us.

And then the jingle:

Buckner's Buckner's Cleaners —friendly service you can trust.
Buckner's—bring your dirty laundry to us.

Allison had the Buckner's Dry Cleaning account at work and she'd seen Sally's gigantic face go up on billboards strategically located all around town. Even at work she couldn't get away from her Camelot neighbors.

Allison zoned out in front of the TV, finished off one stack of stale Saltines then decided she needed something sweet. She brought the gallon of chocolate chocolate chip ice cream and a large spoon back to the couch and alternated between salty and sweet several times before making it easy on herself and just crumpling the remainder of the crackers into the gallon of ice cream and eating them together. She fell asleep on the couch with the TV on. She felt a little ill and her last thought before drifting off to sleep was that she must be sure to run an extra mile the next day.

Time passed as only it can in sleep. Just how much time, she wasn't sure exactly, when suddenly she awoke with a start to the sound of breaking glass and male voices shouting obscenities outside her window. She took one disorienting scan around the darkened room with only the flashing of the television screen serving as a night light. The sound of motorcycles being revved up competed with the noise of the shouting men. The bass from Vicky's stereo vibrated up through the walls and melded with the hum of white noise from Allison's TV. She got up, flipped the light on, and opened the sliding glass door that led out to her balcony. A little fearful, Allison stuck her head out just enough to get a better listen. She heard Vicky call out from her downstairs apartment.

"You fuckheads! Take your argument somewhere else or I'm calling the cops!"

Then Frank's voice rang out from his apartment directly above Vicky. "Forget it! I'm the one calling the cops. And it'll be your ass on the line, Dooley, for allowing this crap to go on here. This used to be a respectable place to live until you moved in. Why don't you just go back to your trailer park where you belong?" he hollered out as two motorcycles noisily sped away.

"Fuck you!" Vicky yelled back.

"You'd die trying and I'd die laughing," Frank hollered.

"Yeah, you wish, Frankie boy!"

"Not really. I've never had a venereal disease and I certainly don't care to catch one now."

"Go fuck yourself. That's about all you're used to getting anyway. Ain't it?"

"There you go, spouting off your favorite word again! You know, only people who aren't intelligent enough to curse creatively resort to such childish obscenities as the "F" word," Frank hollered back.

There was a brief pause followed by a sudden blast as the volume on Vicky's stereo got louder. Moments later, some loud classical piece blasted forth from Frank's stereo. Allison thought she recognized it as the climax to the 1812 overture.

"Shut the hell up! Both of you," Tim hollered out of his downstairs apartment across from Vicky.

Allison, now angry rather than scared, stepped out onto the balcony and leaned against the grate. "For once I agree with Tim," she hollered out into the night. "Talk about childish!"

"Whose side are you on, Allison?" Frank hollered above the raging chorus and blasting cannons of the 1812 overture.

"Shut up Frank!" Allison yelled back, feeling a surge of resentment toward him. He'd been cold and snooty toward her ever since the cookout last June and it irked Allison to no end.

"You tell him, Allison," Vicky yelled.

"You know, Vicky, it would help if you didn't give him so much ammunition," Allison yelled.

Suddenly Sally became visible to all of them as she ran out the front door of building 3300, her robe fluttering behind her in the cold night air. She stood underneath the streetlight which lit their parking lot and screamed so hard that she shook. "Shut up! All of you! Just shut up!" There was silence as some lights from some of the nearby buildings went on. The church bells rang. They chimed twice–two o'clock in the morning.

"Meeting in the downstairs hallway in five minutes. Everyone be there, including you Vicky," Sally barked from the parking lot.

This wasn't the first late night hallway meeting. But it was the first one that Vicky had been invited to. Of course, Vicky was the reason they had the meetings in the first place. This was about the third or fourth, Allison figured as she tried to remember each of the futile middle of the night gatherings. They always started and ended the same way. Everyone would be awakened from their slumber by some disturbance that Vicky had created. She would then be confronted, usually by Frank, in which case she would tell him to "fuck off", as she stormed out of the apartment and sped off in her pick up truck. The rest of Camelot, building 3300 would then meet in the hallway, usually by Sally's door, and discuss what they should do about the "Vicky problem."

And so Allison got to observe all her neighbors in their nightwear. Tim was typically barefoot, clad in only a pair of boxers no matter how cold the weather was. Frank usually showed up looking like someone's dad in his plaid flannel robe, matching flannel pajamas, and tan leather slippers. Sally's unsprayed hair was calmer than usual, having been flattened out by her pillow, and her face wasn't caked with makeup. She always wore the most exquisite silky gowns, matching robes, and slippers with heels and pink puff balls on the toes. Barb wore her surgical greens and a pair of flip flops, looking the same in the middle of the night as she did during the day. Allison wore striped pajamas and a blue terry cloth robe to the first meeting, but Sally teased her and Frank, calling them Doris Day and Rock Hudson. Since then she dressed for the meetings, quickly throwing on a pair of jeans or sweats and an old sweat shirt.

Frank was spearheading the "evict Vicky campaign". He'd taken it upon himself to talk to Vicky, and attempted to delegate responsibilities to everyone else. Sally was in charge of carefully documenting the date, time, and nature of each disturbance. Tim was to check into possible legal recourse and to find out about Lamasco's noise ordinance. And they had all spoken with the landlady, Louise. As for Allison, she refused to do anything except defend Vicky.

"Why do you defend her?" Sally asked Allison later that night in the hallway. Allison was distracted for a moment by the pink feather boa-like collar on Sally's robe.

"Because everyone has the right to a fair trial. Isn't that right, Tim?"

Tim said nothing in reply. He simply stood there, arms crossed against his bare chest as he pinched his nose and sniffed.

"This isn't a trial, Allison," said Sally.

"Oh, yeah, then what is it? And where the hell is Frank?"

"I'm here," he hollered from the top of the stairs.

"We thought maybe you were going through the dumpster again looking for more evidence of a cat," Allison said, thinking about Frank's accusation that Vicky owned a cat. No pets were allowed at Camelot, yet Frank was convinced. He claimed he was allergic and could sense the cat every time he passed Vicky's door.

"I was calling the cops," he hollered, sounding like an irritated old man as he galloped down the stairs. Allison felt a sudden wave of heat ripple through her as Frank came into view. He just had on his plaid pajama bottoms, no top and no robe. The surprise at seeing Frank half naked from his broad perfectly formed shoulders all the way down to his hips, upon which rested the elastic band of his pajamas, nearly knocked the wind out of her. She felt suddenly ridiculous, as her mind conjured up images of screaming teenage girls watching Elvis or the Beatles. Had he looked at her and smiled in that moment, she might just have swooned. Fortunately there was no chance of that happening. She touched her cheeks to see if they really were as hot as they felt. *Stop it, Al. You're lusting after your nemesis. Remember you hate this man and love Kent. Don't look at his eyes. Don't!*

Allison looked instead at the clipboard he held in his hand. Frank wouldn't show up for a meeting without his clipboard. It was the perfect turn off. She focused hard on it and wondered what notes he might have jotted down.

"I see 'father knows best' forgot to dress for our little meeting," Allison said.

"It's hot in here! I'm burning up. Is anybody else hot?" Frank's agitation was apparent by his reddened face. He frantically fanned himself with the clipboard.

"I'm freezing," said Sally. "It's the middle of November."

"It's you, Frank. Your blood pressure is through the roof," said Barb. "Have you ever heard of a Type 'A' personality?"

"What are you talking about?" asked Frank impatiently.

"You. You're Type 'A'. Stroke material. You need to learn to relax," said Barb.

"Where the hell's Dooley?" said Frank, ignoring Barb's comment.

"You actually think she'd come?" said Barb.

"Did anybody see her leave?" asked Frank.

"No, and I would have seen her," said Sally.

Frank made his way down the hallway to Vicky's door in three quick purposeful strides. He pounded on the door and hollered, "Come out, Dooley. We know you're in there."

All the women called out to Frank to stop while Tim just laughed. All at once Frank stopped banging on the door, put his hand on his chest, and began a series of short labored breaths. He wheezed hard with each inhalation and his eyes grew wide and bulging with panic.

"You okay, buddy?" asked Tim approaching him with concern.

"Just take it easy, Frank," said Barb hurrying over to him.

"Oh my God, is he having a heart attack? I knew something like this would happen," said Sally.

"It's that damn cat. I can't breathe," said Frank gasping to catch his breath.

"Oh, c'mon, how can you have an allergic reaction through a door?" said Allison, who now wondered how she could have possibly been attracted to this man just moments before.

Tim and Barb walked him over to the steps. "I can walk by myself, thank you. I don't need your help," Frank said red in the face and wheezing.

"Just sit down," commanded Barb, sitting him on the steps. "Do you have an inhaler?"

"Take it easy, buddy," said Tim, also aiding him.

"Do I need to call 911?" asked Sally.

"I'm fine," said Frank. "I just need to get away from her door," he said, sitting on a step, his elbow propped on his knee and his head buried in his hand, his other hand still clutching the clipboard. "I know there's a cat in there."

"I've got some meds upstairs that might help," said Barb.

"I don't need anything."

"I do. What've you got?" asked Tim.

"Nothing that would help you," said Barb.

"C'mon guys, don't you think we got enough drug dealing going on around here?" said Sally.

"Exactly!" Frank said as he lifted his head and seemed suddenly better, despite a slight remaining wheeze. "I do think there's enough drug dealing going on around here. And I think that's one of the things we need to address." He stood up, pulled the pen out from the metal clip of his clipboard and began making notes. Allison strained her neck to get a look at the page that Frank so furiously scribbled on. He had a list of items. 1) Loud Stereo, 2) Early A.M. Disturbances, 3) Pets!, 4) Possible Illegal Activity. Under each item was at least a paragraph with certain words underlined. The most noted thing on the top of the page, however, were the large capital letters, all in red ink and underlined that spelled out the words–STAMP OUT V.D.!!!

"What makes you all so sure that Vicky's dealing drugs? Unless, of course, you've purchased some from her, Tim," said Allison.

"I wouldn't do Dooley's drugs. God knows what they're cut with," said Tim.

"Seedy looking characters coming and going at all hours of the night, staying for five minutes at the most then leaving. That's enough evidence for me," said Sally.

"Beyond a reasonable doubt?" asked Allison.

"In my mind," said Frank.

"In your mind, of course. In your mind it's guilty until proven innocent. But all you have to go on is some kind of vague hunch. Produce the evidence and I'll believe it," said Allison.

"This isn't a court of law, and she's not on trial," protested Frank.

"Listen to you hypocrites," Allison snapped. "Frank can play his stereo as loud as he likes as long as it's his music. And you, Tim, you can snort your coke and smoke your pot on the sly and that's okay, but let someone move in whom you suspect might be dealing drugs and you're all ready to throw her out on her ear."

"I'm not even going to humor such nonsense with a reply," said Frank, rolling his eyeballs at Allison.

"Look, I've got nothing against Vicky personally," Tim said. "I have no desire to see her slapped with drug charges. Hell, I'd probably end up defending her if she was. Whether she is or isn't dealing dope is completely beside the point. She probably is, but who gives a shit. I just want her out of this apartment complex for two very simple reasons. One, I'm tired of getting waked up in the middle of the night. I have a hard enough time sleeping as it is," he sniffed. "And two, I'm tired of bumping into my clients in the hallway. I'm not real comfortable with them knowing where I live."

"We're all short on sleep," said Barb, who looked as if she'd never known any other state of being. She yawned and it sent off a chain reaction.

"I thought by moving to a smaller town in the Midwest, I'd wouldn't have to deal with these kinds of problems anymore. This is the kind of crap you have to put up with in Manhattan," said Frank as he made his way down the hall and looked out the front door of the building. "Her truck's gone. She must've escaped through the balcony. She doesn't even have the guts to face us."

"You really expect her to walk head long into the lion's den? It's five to one here," said Allison.

"It is?" Frank glared at her. "I thought you were on her side."

"Why do you always take her side, Allison? You're standing in the middle of a freezing cold hallway at two a.m. when you could be snug and warm in your bed snoozing away. Why? Because of Vicky. Close the damn door, Frank. It's freezing," Sally barked down the hallway to Frank.

Allison wondered why she was defending Vicky. Hadn't there been too many mornings when she dragged into work tired and exhausted because of Vicky's stereo or her loud parties the night before? Hadn't she been suspicious herself of some of the scary strangers either coming or going from Vicky's? Deep down Allison was convinced that Vicky and Chief Bobby had some kind of shady operation going. She wasn't blind, and despite what everyone thought, she wasn't naïve either. She knew what was going on. So why did she always take Vicky's side?

They all stood there looking at Allison, just waiting for her reply. She quickly searched her mind but found no explanation there. The reason defied logic, because the answer was not in her mind, it was in her heart. She liked Vicky, plain and simple. Had Vicky been given some of the same opportunities that she'd had they might even be best friends. But Vicky hadn't had any opportunities and she hadn't been given any second chances. Not that she expected any. She set her own self up for failure, daring them all to kick her out because that's all she knew. And yet Allison couldn't forget that little reflection of herself she'd seen in Vicky–that part that wanted something better, wanted to raise herself up out of the dust heap. That's why Vicky went to work for a swanky club instead of just another dive. That's why she moved to the nicest apartments in town instead of just another roach-infested dump. So why was she ruining it all for herself? What was it in her that kept holding her back? And why did Allison feel so responsible for her?

A small voice deep down whispered again and again to Allison that Vicky's failure would be her failure too. If Vicky failed then all the Cinderellas of the world were condemned to remain in the pile of dust and ashes with never a hope of anything better. If Vicky failed then all the fairy tales were just that–fairy tales and nothing more.

"I guess I always take the side of the underdog. After all I'm a Cubs fan," she said glaring at Frank.

"So am I," said Tim. "That's why I'm a public defender. But this particular underdog's interfering with my sleep, and subsequently, my ability to effectively defend other underdogs."

"She needs a second chance. Haven't we all at some time in our lives?" Everyone paused for a moment and thought about it. She wondered what second chances they'd all been given in their lives.

"Second chance? If I'm not mistaken this is about her fourth or fifth chance," said Frank. Sally, Barb, and Tim all agreed.

"Not technically. It doesn't count as a second chance unless the person knows they're being given one. So far nobody's sat down and really talked to her about it," said Allison.

"Wait a minute. I've talked to her," protested Frank.

"You've threatened her and verbally attacked her. The rest of us have snubbed her and given her the cold shoulder in the hallway, including myself. Frank, you're in marketing. You of all people should know your don't insult someone before you try to persuade them."

"I'm not trying to sell her a product."

"It doesn't matter. It's the same thing. Don't you realize that if you put someone like Vicky on the defensive she'll do just the opposite of what you want her to do?"

"I say we talk to Louise again," said Barb.

"So far Louise hasn't done squat," said Sally.

"No kidding. Louise is great at dealing with maintenance issues. You got a burned out light bulb in the hallway or a roof leak and she's right on it, but people problems, forget it. Hell, she doesn't care–as long as you pay your rent on time and don't damage the property. Those are about the only two capital sins Vicky hasn't committed," said Tim.

"What about the 'no pets' policy? An animal can do a lot of damage to property," said Sally.

"She says she's talked to Vicky about it and she emphatically denies having any pets," said Barb.

"She's got a cat, and I will find evidence of it if it's the last thing I do. But until then, I've got a plan that I think will speak volumes to Louise," said Frank, forthrightly pulling a piece of paper out from under the top page of the clipboard. "A petition stating that unless Vicky Dooley is evicted we refuse to pay rent."

"Great. She'll evict us instead of her," said Barb.

"Well, you know I'm not going to sign it," said Allison.

"I figured as much, but it really doesn't matter. All we need is a majority." Frank scribbled away on the page then handed the paper, pen and clipboard to Sally who stood to his left. "What do you say? Does everyone besides Allison agree to sign it?"

Sally was thinking about it. Allison could tell by the way she hesitated. This was her one last opportunity to jump in and save Vicky's hide.

"I'm going to appeal to you all one last time. I say we give her one more chance, if she blows it, then I'll sign the petition too. Only this time let me talk to her. I think she'll listen to me," said Allison as calmly and convincingly as possible, being sure to go around the circle and look them each in the eye like how she'd learned to do in one of her books on selling. Frank's eyes were the last in the circle she looked at. She thought maybe he let his guard down just a little when she looked at him.

"Let's vote on it," said Frank. "All in favor of Allison's suggestion say 'aye'."

Barb, Sally, Tim, and Allison all said "aye".

"All opposed, 'nay'," said Frank, looking very defeated as he raised his hand and said "nay".

"All right, you win," said Frank to Allison. "But only for now."

"I'll talk to her as soon as possible," Allison assured everyone.

"Good. Let's all go back to bed. Meeting adjourned," said Frank tapping his pen twice on the clipboard like an imaginary gavel. Allison craned her neck to get one last look at what Frank wrote on his legal pad page. He'd doodled in red ink a circle containing the initials V.D. with a hard red line cutting through the encircled letters.

Barb, Frank, and Allison made their way upstairs in silence. Barb abruptly turned the corner at the top of the stairs and shuffled her way back to her corner apartment. Allison and Frank stood together at the top of the stairs, both hesitating to return to their respective apartments. Each one of them had something to say but was afraid to say it.

"I know what you're thinking," said Allison breaking the silence between them.

"You do, do you?"

"You think I'll be sorry. You think it'll be no time before I come running to you begging to sign that stupid petition. You're getting good and ready to gloat in my face, aren't you?"

"You think I'm a bastard, don't you? You see, I can read your thoughts too."

Allison said nothing as she turned the knob to her apartment and stepped across the threshold back into her own private world. Even as she did so, she sensed Frank still standing by his door out in the hall with a sad look on his face. She thought she heard him say something about second chances as she closed her door behind her.

Vicky

Chapter 10
February 2006

Vicky and some of the other drunks were bussed to the AA meeting from the shelter. It was one of the conditions for staying there–all drunks had to stay dry and attend AA meetings. The lead speaker was a Vietnam vet. He talked about a three day blackout where he woke up in a hotel room in Oklahoma City, having no idea how he got there. That's when he hit bottom.

"I'd rather hit the bottle than the bottom." Vicky mumbled in her not so discreet raspy whisper. "I'd rather have a bottle in front of me than a frontal lobotomy," she said a little louder. Two of the other drunks from the shelter looked over at her. One chuckled, the other glared. In a restless attempt to get comfortable, Vicky shifted around in her chair which sat in the back row of the meeting room. All the dry drunks from the shelter sat in the back. She felt annoyed towards that grungy grey bearded sober drunk up there behind the podium witnessing away. "Is that what sobriety does to you? Hell, he looks worse than I do," she said. The glaring drunk from the shelter shushed her. She halfway hoped she'd be heard closer toward the front, down where the big wheel sober drunks sat. Then maybe they'd throw her out of the meeting. Then she might just get thrown out of the shelter. Then she could go back under the expressway bridge where a buddy of hers lived during the winter. He'd share his booze with her.

"Now that's sharing. Like how they taught you in kindergarten," Vicky mumbled aloud, imaging her crony under the bridge handing her his bottle to take a sip. Well, maybe he'd share with her, if he had enough. "All these sober drunks wanna share is their experience, strength, and hope. "Experience, strength, and hope. Experience, strength, and hope," she said in a barely audible tone. She had too much experience. She guessed that's why she now had very little strength and virtually no hope. One of the clean drunks–not one from the shelter, but one who'd obviously been sober a while, looked over at her from the right row of chairs and smiled. They were all so disgustingly nice here.

Vicky pulled a crumpled pack of cigarettes out of her hip pocket. She pulled the last cigarette out and lit it. She inhaled deeply and the smoke hit her lungs. It was the briefest moment of comfort in an otherwise agitated world. She popped her jaw and blew out three perfect smoke rings. "I can still do something right," she said.

"Ain't nothing to do around here but smoke," Vicky said aloud to the conscientious dry drunk sitting next to her. Again he glared at her like a kid at school who keeps talking in class. Vicky looked at the clock. The Vietnam vet had been speaking for over twenty minutes.

Vicky coughed. And she coughed again.

The speaker paused and people turned to look. The nice lady with the kindly clean drunk smile moved behind Vicky, carefully ducking and creeping as discreetly as a cat, so as not to disturb the meeting. The lady touched her on the shoulder and offered her a Styrofoam cup of water. Vicky accepted it. "Cheers," she squeaked as she raised the cup to her lips. The water was very cold and made her front tooth ache. There was a hole where the other front tooth should've been. She touched her bare gum with her tongue. She couldn't remember how she lost the tooth or when exactly she lost it. She may be a drunk but she was still self-conscious about the missing tooth. She'd learned how to speak without showing the tooth and she covered her mouth when she laughed. Smiling without showing her teeth was unnatural for her so she tried not to smile much, which actually wasn't very hard since she didn't have much to smile about these days. Despite her aching tooth she finished the water. She didn't realize how thirsty she was.

"Are you all right?" asked the nice lady.

"Fine. Thanks," said Vicky, clearing her throat and inhaling deeply.

"Can I get you anything?" the nice lady asked.

"Could I bum a smoke?" The nice lady pulled a half pack of cigarettes out of her jacket pocket and handed them to her. Vicky fished one of the smokes out of the pack.

"No, take the pack," the smiling lady said. Her kindness made Vicky feel bad, like there was a price on those cigarettes. How nice could someone really be who gives cigarettes to a choking woman?

"Got a light?" Vicky said nudging the drunk to her left. He struck a match and held it in front of her. She tried to suppress the ever increasing urge to cough as she leaned forward to light the cigarette. She took a drag and exhaled the smoke as she leaned back straight in her chair.

Even as a dying drunk she was still careful to sit up straight. But she wasn't drunk now. She hadn't had a drink in about two and half weeks, not since the night the cops picked her up in the dumpster. When she left the hospital several days later after the hell of withdrawal, she went to the shelter where she'd been ever since. She knew she wouldn't stay sober though. That was the price she could never pay.

Vicky sat there smoking, becoming more quiet and thoughtful with each drag. She wasn't listening to the speaker. She was studying the twelve steps which were posted on the wall behind the podium. She'd been to so many AA meetings over the years; she knew the whole spiel by heart. There were times she took it seriously, but even then she couldn't stay sober. But it wasn't the first step that hung her up anymore. She was a drunk and she knew it. That stubborn wall of denial was finally gone. It hadn't collapsed all at once with one rush of revelation, but fell away brick by brick with every bitter failure–every job she got fired from until she could no longer get a job, every place she got thrown out of until she no longer had a place to go, every friend she ever lost until she no longer had anyone, and every stupid and regrettable thing she ever did for booze. She had no excuses, pretenses or defenses left. "I'm a drunk. I admit it." She had proclaimed again and again to would be AA sponsors, doctors, and social workers along the way.

She looked at step number two. "Came to believe that a Power greater than ourselves could restore us to sanity." This is what hung her up every time.

Vicky closed her eyes. She finally gave full reign to the memory that kept clamoring for her attention since she sat down at the meeting that night. She was twelve years old and she was sitting at another meeting. The seats were lined up in rows on the left and on the right with an aisle down the middle, just like they were tonight in this meeting room, only she wasn't sitting in the back row. She was sitting in the front row with her grandma.

* * * * * * *

The floor was the Kentucky earth, and the ceiling and walls were the canvas of an old tent that reverberated with the Word of God. The heat was from the humid July air of Western Kentucky. And behind the pulpit was a clean and scrubbed preacher man in a white starched shirt holding up the bible. She remembered him preaching: "'God so loved the world that He gave His only begotten Son, that whoever believeth on him will not die but will have eternal life.' And who is that only begotten son?"

"Jesus," the crowd in the tent called back.

"I can't hear you," the preacher man said, cocking an ear toward the congregation.

"Jesus," the people called back a little louder.

"Who's that again?" The preacher man said pacing back and forth, working the crowd with each dramatic flail of his arms.

"Jesus," the people called back again, this time in a loud fevered pitch.

"Yes. Jesus. The sweet sweet name of Jesus," he said softly, closing his eyes and swooning ever so slightly.

"Amen," someone called out from the congregation. Some of the folks started speaking in tongues. It didn't frighten Vicky like it might have some twelve year olds. She'd grown up hearing the strange babble of the Holy Spirit. She looked over at her grandma.

Vicky's grandma stood with arms outstretched, eyes closed, swaying back and forth, her lips moving, forming the words of some forgotten ancient language. Vicky knew the look. Grandma was filled with the Holy Spirit fire.

The murmuring continued as the preacher man continued his sermon. "Je-sus," he said with emphasis. "Give your life to Jesus. Come and be saved, poor sinners. Have the blessed assurance of eternal life. Oh, weary one, cast your burdens at the precious feet of Jesus." Vicky looked up. The preacher man looked right at her–looked her right in the eye. "He knows that burden you bear." And Vicky believed that preacher man was speaking directly to her. Sometimes it seemed when her Daddy was drunk and mean as a snake, hollering at her and whuppin' her black and blue, that there was an invisible someone else in the room, crying for her, comforting her, distracting her Daddy just when things got so bad she thought she couldn't take it anymore– right at that point when the tears were at the rims of her eyes and she couldn't bite down any harder on the strip of leather Bobby gave her, something or someone would stop him.

"Come and be saved," the preacher man's gaze turned from Vicky to the congregation at large. "It ain't too late. Jesus is calling you. Come up right now and profess Jesus Christ as your Lord and savior. Know peace. Know the promise of eternal life."

People began making their way up to the front. The first in line was a blond haired boy of about fifteen with long bangs hanging in his eyes. The preacher man put his hand on his head and said something to him. Vicky was scared. Her throat was dry and her heart started pounding. She didn't want to go up, but she knew she was supposed to.

"I got a word of wisdom from the Lord for you," her grandma turned to her and said. "It's time, Vicky Lee. He's calling to you. Don't you hear him knocking at the door of your heart?"

Vicky's grandma was spooky sometimes, the way she seemed to know what Vicky experienced in her deepest heart of hearts. Indeed she felt it– something prodding and compelling her out of her seat.

"Go on up," her grandma urged her.

And so Vicky got up, careful to walk back to the end of the line. She kept her head down and prayed all the way up–prayed that lightning wouldn't strike her. She did feel something like electric currents go through her when the preacher man placed his hands on her head and asked her to repeat the Jesus prayer. She opened her eyes. It wasn't lightning. She wasn't dead. She

Odd Numbers

was alive. She didn't fall to the floor in a Holy Spirit slaying, for which she was grateful. Everything was just as real to her as it was before, perhaps more so.

She scooted over her grandma and back to her seat, though she found it very hard to sit still. She wanted to run, shout, tell the world that she had been chained and shackled but now she was set free. So this is what hope feels like, she thought. "For all eternity," she said aloud. Her grandma hugged her. "Welcome to the family of God."

* * * * * * *

And so Vicky was saved, but from what she began to wonder. Things just got worse after that summer day at the tent revival when she accepted Jesus. Her Daddy got meaner and drunker. Her Mom got more quiet and worried, and her grandma got real nervous and teary-eyed all the time. It wasn't fun to visit grandma anymore. She lost a lot of weight and took up smoking again. She'd walk around her house, wringing her hands and crying, all the while praying aloud–"Jesus help. Jesus help," she'd pray. "My son, my son. What's to become of him? Heal him. Oh, heal him, sweet Jesus." And then she'd burst into tears and light another Pall Mall. She went through a box of Kleenex and two packs of cigarettes a day. She started burning supper or worse yet, feeding Vicky something out of a can. She didn't know what was worse–staying with grandma or Momma and Daddy.

She couldn't stay with her maternal grandparents, the Miners side. Her grandmommy was too sick, and her granddaddy, well, he had the same problem her Daddy had. His drinking bouts kind of came and went, unlike her Daddy who was drunk all the time. That made it trickier though, because you never knew, you just never knew when he'd go off on one of his binges. Her Momma didn't want Vicky around him, so she sent her off to live with her Grandma Dooley, her daddy's momma–was now driving the thirteen year old Vicky crazy with her endless pleas to Vicky to promise to stay in school and have nice Christian friends. She made her promise to get baptized and never to go down that road her Daddy took.

Vicky started feeling crazy scared all the time–that same feeling she felt when she climbed a tree and couldn't get back down. And angry! She was mad all the time. She knew if she ever unleashed that demon anger inside of her that someone would get hurt.

Grandma's prayers didn't help and Vicky's prayers certainly didn't help. Those Holy Ghost goose bumps she got when the preacher man put his hands on her head and said that prayer was just a mirage–like Santa Claus and all the other fairy tales. Grandma said if she'd just get baptized and recommit her life to Jesus it would all go away. Just like magic.

Prayers didn't help, but Vicky found something that did. She tasted her first drink of alcohol in that thirteenth year of life. It was a Falls City beer in the basement of Chief Bobby's house. That first sip made her gag when it hit the back of her tongue, but as it slid down her throat she felt the most enticing warmth float up to her head–better than the Holy Ghost goose bumps. By the time she finished that first beer the crazy scared feeling was completely gone. Not too long after she tried pot for the first time. Her teenage travails didn't seem nearly so dark and serious when she was stoned. It made her laugh at her grandma's hand wringing (as well as just about everything else), and even the burnt pork chops and canned carrots tasted good when she was high.

Within a year she tried just about every drug she could get her hands on–uppers, downers, whatever. She enjoyed them all but none so much as booze. She never forgot that warmth that seemed to settle everything in her brain with that very first swallow in Chief Bobby's basement. It was quickly replacing the comfort of her grandma's big arms which were slimmer now, and hung with skin that didn't know where to go since her weight loss. It was a whole other world with its own language, music, style of dress, and attitude. She and her companions brought their anger to this other world. There it was fueled through the loud strums of electric guitars and the voices of rebel poets screaming out their lyrics–all then sacrificed at the altar of oblivion. This was her secret underground world that no self-righteous adult could take away from her.

Her grandma, being the wise woman she was, saw the change brewing within Vicky long before Vicky perceived it herself. Vicky began doing something she'd never done before. She started lying to her grandma. Of course, it was no good. Her grandma knew she was lying and Vicky knew she wasn't fooling her any. She didn't think it possible for her grandma to produce any more tears from her reservoir, but she did and these new tears were for her. There was remorse in the beginning, but the more entrenched Vicky got in this secret world the more she convinced herself that it was all just harmless fun and that her grandma's tears were ridiculous. There were only two paths left to her–one of even greater deceit and one that demanded she break off ties with her grandma. She chose the latter.

Vicky moved back in with her parents shortly after her fifteenth birthday. All the fighting, screaming, and violence was a blur in Vicky's mind. It hurt too bad to remember. Her Dad calling her a slut, her calling him a hypocrite, and her mother's painful cough always echoing from the bedroom where she watched soap operas and slept. When they finally got Mama to go to the doctor it was too late. She was eaten up with the cancer. Less than five months later she was dead. Grandma hoped that this loss might bring Vicky and her son to their senses. She made Vicky promise to stay and take care of her

Daddy. She'd broken so many promises to her grandma she felt she owed it to her to at least keep this one.

But her mama's death just made matters worse between Vicky and her Daddy. With Mama gone there was no longer any buffer between the two of them. The fighting became vicious and often violent. However, Vicky could protect herself from her Daddy now since she was stronger than him. She could blacken his eye easier than he could blacken hers. And she had a ticket to freedom now too–Chief Bobby's used GTO. He gave her the car for free. He could afford a new car and then some from all the money he made selling drugs.

Vicky remembered her last fight with her Daddy and the final culmination of all that anger. Every detail played out in her mind. She heard the screen door slam behind her. She heard the engine of her GTO fire up. She tried to stop the memory before it got too far. But try though she might she could still hear the sound of her own scream, the brakes screech, the impact of the collision, the sensation of being hurled forward, the terrible sound of the broken glass, the pain and shock. She touched her left cheek and felt the scar. A terrible burden for a girl of seventeen. That's what everyone said.

She broke the last of her promises to her grandma shortly after that terrible day. She quit high school, left her Daddy, and moved in with her boyfriend. The few contacts she had with her Daddy after that were civil but cold. She was completely estranged from him when he died some four years later. Her grandma followed him to the grave the very next year.

The monotone voice of the Vietnam vet finally stopped droning and the sound of applause replaced it, bringing Vicky back to the present. The meeting closed as usual with everyone holding hands and saying the Lord's Prayer. Vicky couldn't bring herself to say the words.

A few people cleared out after the meeting but most hung around, refilled their coffee, and visited. It was like this after AA meetings–plenty of sipping, smoking, and mingling. It was like a cocktail party, except booze had been replaced with cigarettes. AA meetings were the only social gatherings she'd ever attended sober in her adult life. She hung with her little group from the shelter in the corner, all of them in their awkwardness, clinging to one another for security. There was always that fear that she'd see someone she knew–someone from her past who remembered her as Vicky the bartender. She spotted plenty of her old customers at these dreaded meetings, after all Lamasco was a small town. They'd notice what a pitiful old toothless wreck she'd become. Never mind that they were drunks too. Nobody had gotten as bad as she had.

She looked around the crowd anxiously trying to spot the sober drunk volunteer man who drove them to and from the shelter to the meetings. She spotted him sipping coffee and talking with a group of men. From the looks of it he wasn't ready to leave anytime soon. The room was beginning to clear out but this happy little cluster remained, oblivious to the thinning crowd. Everyone in her group began to express their impatience to leave, but the volunteer man didn't notice.

Vicky looked again. This group of men was certainly a strange potpourri of humanoids. But then it was always that way at AA meetings. "Doctor, lawyer, Indian chief," Vicky said aloud, cackling up a little bit of phlegm. Laughter rose from the group of men across the room but one laugh in particular cut through all the rest. It was loud, boisterous and very familiar to Vicky's ears. It hadn't changed over the years. The face that went with the laugh had changed, however. It had all the puffiness and lines around the eyes and mouth that came with hard living. Still she recognized it.

"Aw shit," Vicky said as the man's familiarity found his place in her memory. It was Tim Shultz from back in the Camelot days. She only lived there about a year and a half, but that was the longest she'd lived anywhere since she left her Mama and Daddy's home at the age of seventeen. Tim looked over in her direction. She didn't think he recognized her but then he turned and looked again. The wheels were turning in his mind. He'd figure it out eventually. That was it. That was the cue she'd been waiting for. It was just the excuse she needed to make her exit.

"I gotta go to the bathroom," Vicky said to the drunk standing next to her.

"Well, go on and go. You don't need my permission. We'll wait for you."

"Yeah. I'll be right back," she said.

She stepped out of the meeting room and into the hall, where the bathrooms and the front door were. She looked back just briefly to see if anyone was watching her. She bypassed the bathrooms and headed straight for the front door.

She stepped into the cold night air. The thought of spending the night trying to stay warm when she could walk right back inside like nothing ever happened vied with that compelling craving that kept her moving forward, further into the cold dark and farther away from the door and her two and a half weeks sobriety. She began her all too familiar monologue, the lie she always told herself.

"It's my right to be a drunk. America's a free country. Ain't nobody's business how I live or die. If I want to die a drunk it's my right. I'm living how I like. I don't care." Except deep down she did care. Still she kept telling herself this lie in hopes she might one day believe it, then at last she could drink without guilt and despair.

"It's my right. It's my right," Vicky cried out. By now she was running as far and fast as she could.

A few days passed since Vicky ran away from the meeting, Tim Shultz, and her sobriety. At nights she stayed in an abandoned warehouse in the old manufacturing section of Lamasco. Once alive and bustling with industry, it had now become a ghost town with its broken windows, uprooted rails, rotting crossties, and endless rust. It was there amongst the rubble and the faint haunting of dead dreams where Lamasco's homeless stayed during the cold winter months.

The old warehouse provided more protection from the elements than most places. It had a roof and four walls, though part of the ceiling was caved in. And you could always find a fire burning there just outside the big sliding warehouse doors by the abandoned railroad tracks and loading docks. Occasionally the cops came and cleared the place out, but folks always came back.

Vicky warmed her hands over the flames that licked out of the large industrial sized drum. She and her companion, Joe, were the only ones by the fire. Joe was one of the last of the hobos who hopped freights from town to town. He stole away on a blue and yellow L&N boxcar from somewhere up north and was trying to get as far south as he could before he froze to death.

Folks would go inside the warehouse, sleep for a while, then come out by the door and warm themselves by the fire. Whoever was out there at the time was responsible for keeping the fire going. She and Joe went out earlier that night, climbed a chain link fence and stole some pallets for firewood. Joe did the climbing and gathering while Vicky stood guard and stole swigs off his tall bottle of beer.

"I appreciate you helping me Joe. I can't climb no more. Oh, I can climb up I just can't get down," Vicky explained to Joe while he hurled pallets over the fence with loud accompanying groans.

She paid him back for doing the grunt work by sharing a bottle of whiskey and some fine weed. Together she and Joe stood by the fire passing the bottle and the joint back and forth.

"A first rate buzz and a first rate fire. Warm inside and out. It don't get much better than this," Vicky said.

"You got that right," said Joe holding his breath after taking a deep toke off the marijuana cigarette.

"I just wish I could sleep standing up so I could stay here by this fire all night. It's colder than a witches tit in a brass brassiere inside that warehouse," said Vicky wrapping a threadbare blanket tighter around her shivering shoulders. "Oh, well. Beats the hell outta sleeping in a dumpster. Last big snow we had I climbed in a dumpster and couldn't get back out again. If the cops hadn't found me I'd been a fuckin' popsicle by morning. A dead fuckin' popsicle." They laughed, coughed, and hacked, and Joe spit chunks of phlegm through his toothless mouth.

"You was lucky the cops found you. How did they find you anyways?"

"I don't know. I wondered that myself a time or two. I was laying in that pile of garbage just fixing to die. Thought for sure I'd be dead by morning. Then this squad car just drives up the alley where the dumpster was. Just like they knew I was there. Last thing I remember is the cops hauling my frozen ass outta that dumpster. Next thing I know I'm coming to in the hospital, shaking like a leaf, tubes sticking out of everywheres."

Joe nodded as if he understood.

"Winter's the best time to go dumpster hunting though, cause the smell ain't so bad. Never know what little treasures you'll find." Vicky coughed, all at once becoming quite pensive. "I miss my memoirs. My memoirs. My pictures. I got no memoirs left. Nothing but memories." She began sobbing.

"Memories is all any of us got left," Joe said, placing his hand on her back and trying to comfort her.

Vicky stared into the fire, mesmerized by the flame. "It was fire that took it all from me," Vicky said as she remembered.

All her memorabilia and pictures burnt up in the last real home she had–a run down little house near the river she rented about five years ago. She left the house with the stove on during one of her benders, just plain forgot to turn it off. With all the paper junk mail and memoirs set too close to the burner, it didn't take long to catch fire. Anyway, she thought that's how it happened. Nobody ever claimed to know for sure, but deep down she knew it was her own fault. She came home that night to a house in flames.

She lost everything but her grandma's hope chest. She sold it to an antique dealer about a year or so before the fire. She sold it, contents and all, and she never even opened it to find out what was inside. At least it was still out there somewhere. She dreamed one day she'd find it and buy it back.

"Of all the stupid things," Vicky said through sobs.

"What's that?" asked Joe.

"Nothing," Vicky said wiping her damp face with the filthy worn blanket she had wrapped around her shoulders. "Just remembering."

"Whatever it is it ain't worth remembering. Here, this'll help you forget," said Joe, passing the joint to her.

"Trouble is it ain't making me forget. It's making me remember," she said taking the joint anyway, holding it up to her lips and inhaling.

"Of all the stupid things," she said again shaking her head. She was drunk at the time she hocked that chest and needed the money fast. She had intended to get it back. She helped some of her buddies hoist the chest onto the back of a pick up truck and that was the last she ever saw of it. She didn't care at the time. Now all she had left of her grandma was the key to the hope chest; she wore the key on a chain around her neck. She touched it. It was still there. She often thought she might still have a home if she just had something of her grandma's left–something other than a key without a lock.

How she wished she had one of her grandma's quilts wrapped around her right now and not a dirty old blanket that wasn't even long enough to cover her frozen feet.

"You gotta let it go, Vicky," said toothless Joe. And remember, when you got nothing, you got nothing to worry about. Nothing tying you down or holding you back. IRS can't take nothing from you 'cause you ain't got nothing. You're free, lady." Joe said, holding the bottle of whiskey up to her lips. He poured a fair sized swig into her mouth and it flowed down her throat like liquid gold. She didn't even have to tell herself to swallow. She closed her eyes and basked in the warmth of the whiskey.

Her eyes were still closed when Joe suddenly grabbed her and began kissing her. His tongue nearly choked her and his face pressed so close to hers' that it felt like his large bulbous nose might bruise her cheek.

"Off of me, you old fool," Vicky said pushing him back. She picked up a wood slat off the wood pile ready to defend herself if need be. "I'm warning you, Joe."

"Whoa! No need getting huffy. I ain't ever forced myself on no woman before and I don't intend to start now. If you don't want me, you don't want me. 'Tain't nothin' I can do about it. 'Course, you don't know what you're missing." He smiled a great toothless grin at her.

"It ain't you, Joe," Vicky said dropping her guard along with the wood slat. "I just don't have no desire no more. Maybe I burnt myself out. The only time I ever fuck around anymore it's, you know, for money," Vicky said hanging her head. "So I guess you're keeping company with a whore tonight."

"'Tain't the first time," said Joe. "Shit, almost makes me wish I had some cash on hand."

"You're awful nice, Joe," said Vicky.

"What the hell," said Joe shrugging his shoulders. "To tell you the truth, I'm kinda relieved. I'm probably too wasted to get it up anyways." Together they laughed. He took a swig of whiskey and handed it to Vicky.

Vicky lay in the warehouse later that night curled up in the tightest ball her long legs could possibly allow her so that her blanket would cover her. She was remembering again. Not all of Vicky's memories were unbearable. Some were pleasingly painful and she loved to revisit them time and time again, like a scab you just can't help picking. She knew she shouldn't indulge in the past so much but those memories were all she had left. She nursed them, and babied them and held onto them like a miser. She enjoyed her memories most of all when she found them at the bottom of a bottle, all bittersweet and wrapped up in self-pity and tears.

"Frank the Fuckwad. Frank the Fuckwad," she cackled over and over again until the laughter became a sob. "Francis. My Francis. I've lost you."

"Hey, Dooley, people are trying to sleep around here," a voice hollered out to her from the darkened corner.

"Least I ain't hollering," Vicky screamed out all the louder.

"Shut up, Dooley! Or we're gonna throw your ass in the dumpster," another voice called out.

"My loud mouth's always getting me thrown outta places," she mumbled. "They all wanted to kick me outta Camelot. Banish me from the Round Table. Sir Francis Fuckwad wanted me out worst of all. Wish they had gotten me thrown out then and there." Vicky sat up and wrapped the blanket tightly around her shoulders. She couldn't sleep.

She went back outside by the fire. It was dying down so she threw a newspaper and some wood slats into the drum and poked around at the embers with a stick until she got the fire going again. She stared into the flames, remembering another fire. Not the one that burnt her last home down, but a pleasant cozy fire—one she could only dream of being by these days: the hearth of the great brick fireplace in the lounge of Lamasco's River Inn. The smell of wood burning and the warmth that only fire can produce was the same as what she now experienced, and in the hush of this cold winter night, only the occasional noise of a passing car might distract her from hearing the sounds of cool jazz and polite cocktail laughter. As long as she kept her eyes closed she could make herself believe she was back there.

Chapter 11
1983

Vicky stood before the fireplace poking at the logs with determined effort, hoping to resuscitate each fizzling spark and ember. The fireplace at Lamasco's River Inn was located on the west wall of the lounge where Vicky tended bar. The fireplace kept her sane and warm on long winter weeknights when customers were few and there was nothing else to do but wash bar glasses and wipe the bar down. The restaurant was known for its excellent cuisine, elegant ambiance, and awe-inspiring view of the Ohio River.

As she wiped off the large mahogany surface of the bar, she suddenly saw the reflection of a man on the shiny finished wood. He cleared his throat and lightly tapped a rolled up newspaper on the edge of the bar to get her attention. She looked up and there he stood smiling, all pressed and starched, clean shaven and smelling good, with his suit coat buttoned and not a hair out of place. Vicky quickly concluded that he was not from Lamasco. The men from Lamasco were easy to read, but not this man. His eyes were dark, almost navy blue, framed by black thick lashes.

He ordered a dry martini with Bombay gin. This distinguished him from other customers. Not many people under fifty drank martinis in this town. She made it extra dry and put two olives in it. After he got his drink he joined some businessmen at the table nearest the huge fireplace. Vicky had ample opportunity to watch him. He obviously enjoyed that martini, which gave Vicky unsurpassed satisfaction. She remembered the way he savored it and how he closed his eyes and inhaled deeply with each swallow. There was something very sexy about this man who took such pleasure in a simple drink. Before he left he stopped by the bar, complimented her on the drink, and stuck a ten dollar bill in her tip glass. A bartender doesn't forget that sort of thing.

Vicky saw him a few times at the lounge after that and she never forgot him. But the first time she saw him up close without a bar separating them was days after she moved into Camelot. She was on her way out to go to work one evening when the door to building 3300 opened before her hand reached the knob. There he stood under the front porch light, the wind blowing at the tails of his expensive suit coat, as he held the door open for her. He was taller than she remembered but it was him.

"Well, if it isn't Prince Charming," she said with her hand on her hip as if he were an old friend. "Where've you been?"

He had a bewildered look like an old man. It made Vicky laugh. The wind, filled with impending autumn chill, blew through the open door. Realizing she wasn't going to exit the building right away, he stepped across the threshold and pulled the door shut behind him.

"I'm sorry. Do I know you?"

"Dry martini. Bombay gin. Right?" Vicky stuck her hand out. "Vicky Dooley. I tend bar at the River Inn. I've waited on you before."

"Oh! I haven't been there recently." Recognition still had not dawned on him but he gave her an obligatory handshake all the same.

"I know. That's why I asked where you been. You know you once told me I make the best martinis you ever tasted. You toss that line out to all the lady bartenders or what?"

"No, I must have meant it," he said with a chuckle.

"So you remember my martinis but not me, is that it?"

"Come to think of it you do look a little familiar."

"A little familiar? I make the best martini you've ever had and all I am is 'a little familiar'? You know, most people remember me, especially men."

"My humble apologies. I assure you from now on I will." He said with sarcastic emphasis giving a kind of mock bow, then smiling politely without showing his teeth, he stepped aside and began to make his way through the hall and towards the stairs.

That was something she hadn't noticed about him before. Vicky didn't trust people who smiled without showing their teeth, unless they had good cause to, like her granddaddy whose teeth all rotted out of his head because he was too afraid to see a dentist. But that certainly wasn't the case with this guy. People who smiled without showing their teeth were hiding something. What was fucking Prince Charming trying to conceal? Vicky guessed it was boredom and impatience with this unexpected intrusion in his life–namely her. This only made Vicky want to irritate him all the more. She quickly maneuvered herself in front of him, successfully cutting him off before he reached the stairway that led to the upstairs apartments. She stood just inches from him, face to face and eye to eye, resolutely blocking his way.

"I don't believe I caught your name," she said.

"I don't believe I pitched it."

"Well?" Vicky said waiting for the pitch. He said nothing but merely held her gaze with that same smile that revealed no teeth and very little else except a smug sort of confidence.

"Have a good evening," he finally said with a polite nod that almost made

Vicky forget she was being snubbed. He reclaimed his hallway with a quick stride right past her, creating a breeze as cool as his demeanor.

Vicky thought nothing would have stopped him from getting up those stairs and away from her as quickly as possible, but curiously something did stop him. It was the sound of someone descending the stairs. Vicky had only met Allison a few times but already she recognized the light skipping trademark of her footsteps.

The countenance of this chilly Prince Charming completely changed when Allison came into view. A spontaneous smile broke across his face that not only showed his teeth, but ignited his brilliant blue eyes. It was as if he'd suddenly been plugged into an electric socket. Everything about him came to life. The transformation only lasted a few moments, however. As soon as Allison spotted Frank and greeted him with her usual friendly smile, he called on all the self-restraint he could muster and resumed his icy distance.

Vicky saw it. He was in love with Allison, didn't want to be, and was trying hard not to be. Vicky guessed it was because she was engaged to another man, but it was even more than that. He didn't think the feeling was mutual. He didn't think he stood a chance. He wasn't really as confident as he wanted everyone to think he was. That was it! It had to be. She did love him though. Vicky could tell. Allison blushed and her voice cracked when she greeted him. It was a dead give-away. She cleared her throat and touched her cheeks, as if to make the blushing subside. She regained her composure almost as quickly as he did.

Couldn't this man see that Allison was crazy about him? Couldn't Prince Charming put on his armor, mount his steed, and come after her in some selfless act of bravery–in one honest undying profession of love? He didn't even have to scale the walls of the castle to rescue this damsel in distress. All he had to do was walk across the hall. But there was a huge dragon to slay first and it was breathing its fiery breath on both of them. The dragon's name was fear.

"Frank, have you met our new neighbor, Vicky Dooley?" Allison inquired, seemingly pleased there was a third party there to distract them from each other.

"Yes, just now as a matter of fact."

"Vicky this is Frank Hamilton. King of Camelot."

"Nice to meet you, Frank," Vicky said with her own sarcasm and mocking bow.

"Nice meeting you too," he said with yet another obligatory handshake.

"Funny, you don't look like a Frank," Vicky said.

"Well, that's my name."

"Vicky moved in last week," Allison chirped a little nervously.

"Welcome," he said with that perfunctory smile.

"She tends bar at Lamasco's River Inn."

"So I've been told." He looked at his watch. "If you ladies will excuse me, I really must be going. I've had a very long day," he said acknowledging them both with a slight bow of his head which made it very clear that their meeting was at an end.

"My day's just beginning," Vicky called to him, but he was already halfway up the stairs.

"What's up his butt?" Vicky asked Allison as soon as they heard the door upstairs shut.

"Who knows? Don't take it personally. That's just Frank," said Allison putting a jacket on and pulling her golden locks out from under the collar. "Where are you headed?"

"The old salt mines. And you?"

"My fiancé's place. Must be weird going to work at night. I've only ever had day jobs before."

They were about to exit the building when the woeful sound of strings being played slowly and skillfully floated down the stairs and filled the hallway. The strange sound caused Vicky to pause. The music was foreign to her ears–not good, not bad, just unfamiliar.

"What the hell's that?"

"Frank's classical music," Allison said rolling her eyeballs.

"He sure plays it loud. Not that I got anything against loud music. I prefer it that way, but hell, we're talking about music by a bunch of old dead white guys. Don't get me wrong, some of my favorite music's by dead guys– Jim Morrison, Jimmie Hendrix, Buddy Holly, and of course the greatest of the great–the king himself. It's just that we're talking dead guys who've been dead over a hundred years. We're talking fucking Beethoven."

Allison smiled. Her toothy grin was warm and wonderful. There was something about that unrestrained smile that made Vicky decide she liked Allison.

Vicky looked long and hard at Allison's smiling face as they stepped out into the late evening dusk. "No wonder he loves you. You're fuckin' perfect."

"What are you talking about?"

"You. You're smart, kind, and pretty. You're like–Cinderella."

"Cinderella?"

"See here's the thing about Cinderella. She was destined to be a princess but she wasn't afraid to get down and dirty and clean out the fireplace and mop the floor and shit. Now me–I'm more like Sleeping Beauty. I ain't even awake yet. I won't be until Prince Charming finds me and plants a big ol' wet one on me."

"You've read too many romance novels, Vicky. Why do we give men such power over us anyway?" Allison said.

"Well, maybe it ain't a man exactly I'm waiting for. But something. Hell, I don't know what."

"So if I'm Cinderella and you're Sleeping Beauty, who's Sally?"

"Snow White. She just wants a house and a bunch a kids. Seven little gnomes she can cook and make beds for and shit."

"And Barb?"

"Well I've only met her once, but I'm guessing she *is* one of the little gnomes. Sleepy, I think."

White teeth flashed as Allison laughed, but as the laughter died down she became very solemn. "I don't know if my prince still loves me. I think I'm driving him crazy with the royal wedding plans."

"You mean your fiancé?"

"Who else?"

"I wasn't talking about him. I was talking about that Frank guy."

"Frank?"

"Yeah, he's got it bad for you."

"Oh, no, please don't tell me you've already been inundated with the rumors."

"Spell that word please," Vicky said pulling the small spiral notebook and pen out of her jean jacket pocket.

"Inundate. I-N-U-N-D-A-T-E."

"Thanks," said Vicky capping the pen, flipping the little notebook shut, and returning them to her pocket. "I ain't heard no rumors. I just call it as I see it, and the way I see it that guy's crazy about you."

"No," said Allison shaking her head emphatically.

"And what's more, you're crazy about him too."

"No, no, you got it all wrong."

"Maybe so, but I still say there's something between you too."

"Air. That's all that's between Frank and me. Just air. Now I will admit I found him a little attractive at first, but then I got to know him. Have you forgotten I'm in love with Kent and I'm going to marry him?"

Vicky still wasn't convinced but she set the argument aside for Allison's sake. They stood for a moment in silence and watched the sun setting over Camelot.

"Ain't it beautiful?" said Vicky with a sigh.

"Red sky at night, sailor's delight," said Allison.

"I love fall," Vicky exclaimed.

"I hate it. It's the only time of year I'm really sad" Allison said.

"Why's that?"

"I guess because the days are getting shorter and everything's getting ready to die."

"I think there's something beautiful about a thing just before it dies. I mean look at all them colors bursting forth. Why even this day is dying and look at that gorgeous sunset." Vicky looked at Allison. Her eyes were straight ahead, still on that sunset, and a smile was still on her face.

Allison always smiled, even while talking about things that were sad to her like falling leaves and short days. She was so careful to always look cheerful. It was the cheerleader in her.

"Oh! I gotta run," Allison said suddenly, taking a quick glance at her watch.

Vicky waved goodbye to Allison as they parted ways in the parking lot– Vicky to her pick up truck and Allison to her red Trans Am.

"Later," Allison shouted back to Vicky with an energetic wave, smiling all the while.

* * * * * * *

Vicky drove to work that evening thinking of Allison and how she was much too good for that stuck up Frank guy. She'd only known Allison a week, but already it felt like an old friendship, even though Allison was a cheerleader and Vicky was a hood.

She remembered their conversation that first night she moved into Camelot. They were in Allison's apartment preparing dinner – cutting up vegetables for salad and trying, mostly in vain, to defrost and reheat leftover lasagna that had been in Allison's freezer for three months.

"This lasagna still feels cool in the middle," Allison said cutting through the middle of the large casserole slab and touch testing it with her finger. "Let's try it again," she said handing the dish to Vicky.

"Maybe them new-fangled microwave ovens ain't all they're cracked up to be," said Vicky who was still learning about microwave ovens, and was about to learn the most important lesson. She stuck the casserole in the microwave with the knife still neatly tucked into the edge of the lasagna.

"Holy shit-fire!" she exclaimed as little sparks of lightening flared and crackled, and Allison practically dived across the room to open that microwave door and put an end to the high frequency electromagnetic eruption.

"Sorry! I done something wrong."

"No, my fault," Allison said removing the knife from the casserole and explaining to Vicky about microwaves and metal.

"I hope I didn't break it."

"Me too," Allison said placing the glass casserole dish back in the microwave and quickly pushing this button then that button with a synchronized beeping preceding the noise of a fan-like whir. They both breathed a sigh of relief which ended with laughter.

"I guess we can laugh now. I only moved in a few hours ago and I almost burn the place down," Vicky moved in closer to the microwave for a better look.

"Careful! Don't stare into the oven. I've heard the radiation may be bad for your eyes." Allison warned.

"If it's bad for my eyes then what the hell is it doing to my food?"

"Uh! I hadn't thought of that," said Allison, ignoring her own warning and joining Vicky in front of the microwave. "Well, look at it this way. It's nuking off all the germs."

The light inside the small oven went off followed by three just loud enough beeps. Allison took the lasagna out and touch tested it again. "I think this is about as warm as we're going to get it. Let's see how it tastes." With that she took a fork and cut a small corner off the casserole. She stuck the bite in her mouth.

"How is it?" Vicky asked

"It doesn't have much taste left. I think it's been in the freezer too long.

Vicky examined the casserole while munching away on a Dorito. She held the large plastic bag of chips in front of Allison's face. "Want one?"

"Sure." Allison reached in the bag, pulled out a chip and began munching as she reached into a cabinet and pulled out some plates. "Mmm," said Allison reaching in the bag again for another chip. "It's better than the lasagna."

"Hey, I got an idea. These Doritos here ought to spice up any meal. Let's sprinkle 'em over the lasagna. Maybe that'll help."

"It couldn't hurt," Allison agreed.

So they sprinkled Doritos on top of the lasagna. Vicky was so pleased she could contribute something to the meal. Then she helped Allison set a beautiful table, complete with wine glasses.

"It's too bad I don't have any wine," Allison said taking a can of Fresca out of her refrigerator. This is the closest thing I got. Want some?"

"What kinda soda pop is that? Ain't ever seen it before."

"It's Fresca. It's a diet drink. It's got kind of a citrus flavor to it."

"Shouldn't drink that shit. It's bad for you," Vicky said, pouring some Jack Daniels into her wine glass. "Mind if I smell it?"

"Not at all. Here." Allison handed her the can of Fresca.

Vicky sniffed it. "If you mixed this with a little bourbon and beer it might make a half way decent whiskey sour. The alcohol might kill off some of them bad chemicals they put in that diet shit." She reluctantly handed the can back to Allison. "Here. If you wind up with cancer don't say I didn't warn you."

Allison just smiled and poured the contents of the can into her wine glass. "I'd like to propose a toast," Allison said lifting her glass toward Vicky. "To my new neighbor and her new home. Cheers"

They clinked glasses. Vicky offered another toast. "To my new neighbor and new friend." Was it too soon to call her a friend, Vicky wondered as they lifted their glasses once again. Judging from the smile on Allison's face she guessed it was okay.

Vicky was right about the three month old lasagna. It was better with the crumbled Doritos on top. Allison said if they stretched their imagination a little it could even pass as a French dish – "old baked pasta amandine, no, aged twice baked pasta amandine" or something of that nature.

It wasn't until after dinner that Vicky really took some notice of Allison's place. Vicky noticed people much more so than her surroundings. She could tell you what someone wore on their first meeting, the location of each freckle, mole, and fine line on the face, and how nervous or peaceful they were just by looking at their hands. She could tell a lot about a person just by looking at their shoes. Allison's black leather pumps weren't scuffed or skinned at all, with just a slight crease where the toes ended and the arch began. At first seeing them she guessed either they were brand new or Allison was just one of those people who could keep a pair of shoes forever. By observing Allison walk she guessed the latter. She was so light on her feet that it seemed they hardly touched the ground, as she skimmed so quickly and thoughtlessly across the floor. She reminded Vicky of a rock skipping upon the surface of a lake. Unlike Vicky who was very hard on shoes and walked with such heavy footsteps that everyone knew when she was coming. Chief Bobby just hated taking her hunting, not because she wasn't a great shot but because she was way too noisy. She went barefoot as often as she could. Her feet felt confined and heavy with shoes on.

Vicky noticed things like shoes and hands and the way a person smiled or didn't. She could hear a person's emotions in the subtle tones of the voice that most other people couldn't hear. She could tell how much pain and hardness a person had known by a careful observation of the eyes, but when she left a room she usually couldn't tell what color the walls or carpet were.

Vicky was drawn to the tall bookshelf in the corner of the living room, with its framed photographs and plants and rows and rows of books. It was the only thing in the room she really spent much time observing. She looked at Allison's framed pictures first–Allison standing with her arms outstretched in front of the Eiffel Tower; Allison with her arms around Kent; Allison with her arms around several other girls, all of them pretty and smiling with their hair done up and makeup just right, wearing colorful evening gowns which showed off their tanned shoulders and arms.

"My sorority sisters at one of our big dances," Allison said as Vicky paused in front of the picture of the girls.

"Oh," said Vicky remembering the difference between them. Then her eyes went to the one picture from Allison's distant past–the old family picture–and this once again brought to mind some of the similarities between the two women. Though Allison was chubby with three older siblings and Vicky was skinny and an only child, the picture reminded Vicky of her own childhood and all the pain of growing up with parents who either hated each other or themselves.

"The fat little girl with glasses is me in the fifth grade," Allison said.

Vicky stood at the picture in brief memorial before moving on to Allison's plants on the top shelf. Compelled to touch anything green and living, Vicky gently handled one of the plants with leaves that hung down and draped over the books. She enjoyed the texture of the leaves between her thumb and forefinger.

"I ought to have you come water my plants for me. You're tall enough to reach. I have to get a stool out. Sometimes I neglect the poor things because it's just too much trouble."

Vicky's eyes moved down to the next shelf. She ran her finger across the books, reading each title as she went. The books on the upper shelf, at eye level with Vicky, had titles like *Thinking Your Way to Greatness, The Art of Selling, Keys to Success*. She pulled one large vinyl bound book off the shelf. It wasn't a book, but rather a series of cassette tapes.

"My motivational series," Allison said.

"Your what?"

"Motivational series. As in to motivate. That's M-O-T..."

"I know how to spell it. I even know what it means," Vicky said defensively.

"I'm sorry. I didn't mean to offend you."

"It's okay. Only reason I know that word is cause I used to see it all the time on my report cards–'Capable but lacks motivation'."

Allison laughed and Vicky laughed too but that old familiar pang of regret stabbed her in the heart. "Mind if I smoke?" Vicky asked with a cigarette already dangling from her lips and a book of matches already in her hand.

"No, it's fine."

"I dropped out of high school in my junior year. I was unmotivated," she said with emphasis. "And ...something bad happened to me," Vicky inadvertently touched the scar on her left cheek then caught herself and stopped. "I was in this really bad car wreck."

"Oh, no! What happened?"

Allison was listening attentively but Vicky couldn't go on. "I know I been talking your leg off all evening, but I just can't talk about that."

"That's okay."

"I always regretted quitting high school. I did go back and got my GED then I went to bartending school. Decided to get a job at a nice classy place and quit working in dives. That's when I got on at River Inn. I'd like to own my own place someday. That's my dream. I want to be something better than what I am."

"I understand," Allison nodded.

Of course what Vicky wouldn't tell Allison was that at one time she even vowed to give up the drug business. But she couldn't avoid the one person in her life who'd been there for her since her grandma died–Chief Bobby. Whenever she mentioned getting out of the business to Bobby he'd argue that she was doing the same thing legally by selling alcohol to people. She could never argue with that kind of logic. They were modern day bootleggers, he'd say, and Vicky thought there was something terribly daredevil and romantic about that. But it was more than that and more than her loyalty to Chief Bobby that kept drawing her back into the business. It was the money. Between the drug money and the tips she made at River Inn she not only made enough to live comfortably, but also enough to put aside for her own business someday and maybe even a little house out in the country with lots of land. Once she had enough money saved she would quit the drug business for once and for all. That was the argument she always made for herself even though the voice of her conscience told her it was wrong.

"Vicky? Earth to Vicky," Allison said, snapping Vicky out of her inner world.

"Sorry." Vicky drew her attention back to the books. Her eyes moved down to the next shelf. These were older books. Just from the touch and feel of the creased worn binding she liked these books better. *Wuthering Heights, Pride and Prejudice, A Tale of Two Cities, Jane Eyre,* and one that was vaguely familiar to Vicky– *The Sonnets of Shakespeare.*

"You sure got a lot of books."

"I love literature. Thought about majoring in it but then you can't make a living unless you teach," Allison said as Vicky pulled *The Sonnets of Shakespeare* off the shelf and began paging through it.

"Say, I remember this sonnet," Vicky said delighted at finding one she recognized from Mrs. Ambrose's Lit class her junior year. She recalled it so clearly because that was the time right before her accident, right before she dropped out of school.

"Which one is it?" Allison asked.

"Sonnet 29."

"Read it to me."

Vicky cleared her throat to read.

"When in disgrace with Fortune and men's eyes,
I all alone beweep my outcast state,
And trouble deaf heaven with my bootless cries,
And look upon myself and curse my fate,
Wishing me like to one more rich in hope,
Featured like him, like him with friends possessed,
Desiring this man's art, and that man's scope,
With what I most enjoy contented least;
Yet in these thoughts myself almost despising,
Haply I think on thee, and then my state,
Like to the lark at break of day arising
From sullen earth, sings hymns at heaven's gate;
For thy sweet love rememb'red such wealth brings,
That then I scorn to change my state with kings.

"Beautiful," said Allison looking misty eyed.

"I love romance," Vicky said holding the book to her chest.

"Me too."

"Guess that's why I moved here... to Camelot I mean. It reminded me of all them fairy tales."

"It's funny but I think I moved here for the same reason. It's the closest thing to a castle in heartland, USA. Of course, you have to ignore the fact that there's a cornfield on one side and a strip mall on the other."

"I'm glad I moved in when I did. I'd been told that as soon as an apartment comes available around here it gets snatched up right quick." Vicky said.

"It's a popular place to live." Allison said.

"Except my apartment. I heard it was vacated several months ago. Couldn't figure out why it didn't get snatched up right away like the others, until the first time I set foot in it. I knew right away something bad happened there. It must've spooked folks away. Damn near spooked me away. Did somebody get killed there or something?"

Allison grimaced at Vicky's question.

"You know, don't you?" Vicky persisted.

"Well, I've heard. I didn't live here at the time so I really don't know much."

"You can tell me."

"I heard it was a suicide."

"Did it happen in the apartment?"

"Yes. He shot himself."

"Oh, Lord, no," Vicky said shaking her head as her face dropped.

"I shouldn't have told you. Especially right after you moved in. So tragic, isn't it? How did you know something bad happened?"

"Just felt it. Anyways, I almost didn't move here 'cause there were no other vacant apartments. But then I got to thinking, this is my only chance to live in a castle. Just something about looking outside and seeing all them fancy towers takes away all the bad feelings. I wonder if it was a love affair gone wrong?"

"What?"

"The suicide."

"I don't know, but please try and forget I told you. It's your place now, Vicky, and you can change all of those bad memories and replace them with good ones. I know you will." Allison said smiling and seemingly trying to change the tone and direction of the conversation.

Vicky could see Allison's desperate desire to change the subject. She paged through the book of sonnets again then put it carefully back on the shelf. Her eyes began traveling again along the rows.

"Keep looking," Allison said.

"Vicky's eyes stopped at *Fairy Tales by Hans Christian Andersen*. She pulled the book off the shelf.

"I knew that one would catch your eye. Are you familiar with his stories?"

"Hell yeah! *The Ugly Duckling* is one of my favorites," Vicky said paging through the book until she found it.

"It's one of my favorites too," Allison said.

"It's my story too. Only I'm still waiting to become a swan."

"With a long neck like yours? What are you talking about?" Allison asked. "You are a swan."

Vicky said nothing in reply, but slowly put the book back on the shelf. None of the other books were familiar to her. She remembered the difference between her and Allison, the difference between the ignorant and the educated. Yet somehow there didn't seem to be much difference between the two of them at that moment.

As they stood there the church bells rang eight o'clock.

"You got a window open?"

Odd Numbers

"No. Why, are you chilly?"

"No, it ain't that. It's them church bells. Shit they're loud. Where do they come from?"

"The Catholic church down the street. They ring every quarter hour. Don't worry, you'll get used to them. I don't even hear them anymore."

"Do you believe in God?" Vicky asked after a somewhat long and thoughtful pause.

"I'm an agnostic, I suppose."

Vicky retrieved her little spiral notebook and pen from her pocket again.

"That's A-G-N-O-S-T-I-C. It means…"

"No, don't tell me. You got a dictionary around here I can borrow?"

Allison pulled her big red Webster's Dictionary off one of the bottom shelves and handed it to Vicky.

"Guess I'm gonna have to know the definition if we're to continue this conversation," Vicky said paging through the dictionary. Her eyes found the page and the word. "Says here," Vicky said with her finger pointing to the word. "A person who believes that the human mind cannot know whether or not there is a God or an ultimate cause, or anything beyond material phenomena." She struggled with the word "phenomena", but tried to pronounce it slowly, just like how it was spelled. Allison didn't correct her so she guessed she got it right. "So you ain't sure, huh?"

"That's right. What about you? Do you believe?"

"I'm afraid to believe and afraid not to believe. If there is a God I'm in deep trouble 'cause I've turned my back on him. He's gotta be pissed off at me. If there isn't a God, well then, shit, what is there?"

"So I guess we're in the same boat with all this uncertainty."

"I guess so." Vicky took a long drag off her cigarette.

"If there is a God," Allison pondered, "then he or she must be the brilliant master mind behind the universe, beyond that I can't even begin to comprehend."

"Do you think he knows you? Personally, I mean?"

"No. What about you?"

"I think he does." Vicky looked at Allison. She wasn't smiling. The look on Allison's face made Vicky think of that old gospel story she'd heard preached on in her grandma's church–the one about the rich man who went away sad because Jesus asked him to give up everything and follow him.

"But, hell, the way I figure it there must not be a God 'cause I'd of sure been struck by lightning by now."

Laughter and another gulp of whiskey eased the tension. Vicky convinced Allison to try some Jack Daniels with her Fresca. There was more laughter and even less tension after that. The hours and the conversation passed quickly until the bells struck midnight, startling Vicky back into reality. She apologized to Allison for wearing out her welcome and promptly left with a noisy gait down the stairs, a loud tromp in the downstairs hall, and a banging door.

Chapter 12
September–November 1983

You couldn't call it a love affair because Vicky knew the difference between lust and love. It wasn't exactly a one night stand because Vicky had slept with him on more than one occasion. She even spent a whole weekend with him once. The fuzzy term "relationship" didn't fit either because the only time they ever really related to one another was in bed. She couldn't even remember exactly how or when she'd met him except that he was one of Chief Bobby's oldest and most faithful customers.

She only knew she had a weakness for him. Mostly it was about sex. But for him it was also about free drugs and money. So Vicky tried her hardest to avoid him, but then she'd run into him somewhere, or he'd be broke and he'd call her and she'd give in and agree to see him. He had an irresistible charm that she could never walk away from. She'd see him and couldn't wait to get him alone, to undress him, to touch him all over, to smell his fragrance, and feel his skin against hers. So the result was always terrific sex.

Afterwards followed the inevitable sob story about how he was in between jobs and down on his luck. Then Vicky would want to kick herself as she emptied her wallet and watched him walk out the door with her money. She didn't mind him using her for sex–that was all right between two consenting adults with whom it was mutually understood were using one another. But to use someone for money–now that was wrong. And so every time she swore it would be the last time. Like this time. But he knew her weakness and he knew how to use it.

That night during the height of passion he breathlessly professed his love for her and made her promise never be angry at him again. She would have promised him anything at that point. In the aftermath of all this lovemaking he told her that his boss was an unfair son-of-a-bitch and that he fired him for no reason. Then came the big hit-up for money, after which he fell right to sleep, while Vicky stayed awake and tried to figure out some way she could make him mad enough so he would leave her alone forever.

She would have to be strong, that was for sure, because if she had sex with him again she would wind up giving him even more money. She set her internal alarm clock for early so she would be up, showered, and dressed before he awoke. And most important of all, she would be sure to remain completely sober and straight until after he left–nothing but black coffee. This would be the last time and that was that.

"Just a gigolo," she said, placing her hand on the sleeping man's back. Her water bed rocked gently as she turned on her side, away from him and toward the wall.

* * * * * * *

"This is it! I ain't gonna help you no more. Now get your clothes on and go," she said the following morning with unwavering resolve as she flung some money on the bed and turned to exit the room. He followed her out the bedroom door and into the hallway.

"But baby, you promised never to be mad at me again."

"I ain't mad, and just to prove it I threw in a little extra for cab fare."

"C'mon baby, don't make me take a cab. You can drive me home," he pleaded coming up behind her, wrapping his arms around her, and speaking the words softly and sensually so that his hot breath tickled the nape of Vicky's neck.

"You're a big boy. You can get your own self home." She felt his lips on the back of her neck and felt her resolve beginning to weaken.

"You shouldn't have gotten dressed so soon," he said nibbling on her ear lobe.

"You know I can't stand to hang out in my jammies. Makes me feel lazy," Vicky said as he held her tighter and hummed the tune of some popular song in her ear while rocking her back and forth.

"Come back to bed," he said unbuttoning the top buttons on her blouse. She closed her eyes and felt herself giving into the moment. Then all at once she heard that voice inside her head talking sense.

"No! It ain't gonna work this time," she said opening her eyes and unwrapping his arms from around her. "You got what you came for. Now go."

"But baby."

"Don't but baby me," she said as she began shoving him backward, through the short narrow hallway and into the living room. He kept arguing and she kept shoving until somehow she managed to maneuver him out the door, which she promptly slammed in his face and bolted behind him.

"But baby, my clothes," his muffled cry sounded from out in the hallway as he banged on the door. She suddenly realized she had pushed him out the door in nothing but his leopard skin bikini briefs. The ones he always wore when he was with her because she thought they were sexy.

"Shit!" Vicky said running back to the bedroom and grabbing the pile of clothes from on top of the bed. The cash she had flung at him was on top of the pile. "That's the only reason he's still calling me 'baby' and not 'bitch'.

Cause he ain't got my money in his hot little hand yet," she said running back to the door where he was still pounding and still calling out to her, though somewhat more irritably by now. She opened the door.

"Here's your fuckin' clothes," she said throwing the pile at him. "And don't forget *my* money," she said hurling the bills in his direction.

All at once she gasped in complete surprise as the figure of a man emerged in the hallway and stood behind her leopard skin bikini clad lover. It was Frank, standing there with his briefcase in hand all dressed for work. He wore an expensive suit and tie, wingtip shoes with tassels, and the most unpleasant scowl Vicky had ever seen. Her lover jumped in startled surprise and attempted to cover himself with the pile of clothes. The look on Frank's face made Vicky feel like she was in the presence of a preacher man. She felt her face redden with shame as Frank stared his disapproval back at her.

Vicky had only seen Frank a few times in the hallway since she moved to Camelot, yet there was something about him that made her feel uncomfortable, like a pin sticking somewhere in her clothing and she couldn't exact the location , she just knew it was there, pricking her, irritating her.

"Excuse us. Lovers' quarrel," Vicky said, grabbing her stunned lover by the arm, pulling him inside, and closing the door behind him. She took a long hard look at the young man's face. Had it been ten years ago she would have loved him, but too much had happened since then and it seemed a callous like blister was forming over her heart.

"Sorry baby," she said touching his cheek. "Get your clothes on and I'll drive you home."

* * * * * * *

Vicky's next encounter with Frank came a few days later. He appeared on her doorstep one Sunday evening in his plaid flannel robe and tan leather slippers and asked her in his controlled but obviously angry way to turn her music down. She stared at a bulging vein in his neck that looked like it was ready to pop while he informed her that he'd been knocking on her door for at least ten minutes before she even heard him.

"What about you? You play that high brow shit of yours loud enough. I'll turn my music down if you turn yours down."

"What exactly are you referring to?"

"That shit you were playing yesterday morning. It woke me up."

"Schubert is not shit."

"Neither are the Allman Brothers."

"There's a vast difference between playing classical music at a reasonable volume and…"

"It was too fuckin' loud."

Frank tightened his lips into that stern expression of disapproval that was becoming all too familiar to Vicky.

"There's a difference between me playing my stereo at ten o'clock on a Saturday morning and you cranking your volume to max on a Sunday night at eleven p.m."

"Listen pal, not everyone works nine to five around here. Friday night is my busiest night. I'm bustin' my hump for nearly twelve hours. Last call ain't 'til two a.m. By the time I finish cleaning up and closing up it's after three. All weekend's like that. I don't get a break 'til Sunday night. That's how I unwind," Vicky said raising her bottle of beer and gesturing back to the living room where the stereo was still blaring.

"It's inconsiderate as hell. But shall we discuss some of the other noises coming out of your apartment–noises that have also awakened me in the middle of the night?"

"Fuck you!"

"In your dreams."

The door across the hall opened and Tim stuck his head out. He was bare-chested and bare-foot, clad only in a grey pair of sweat pants. "Keep it down, guys!

Sally opened her door and strolled sleepily down the hall in her floral robe. "What's going on?"

Vicky realized she was outnumbered, so before anyone had a chance to answer, she slammed the door and bolted it. Frank's little pin prick was poking at her flesh again, irritating her, making her feel bad for no reason with his haughty hoity-toity attitude. She would have turned her stereo down if he had just asked nicely, but someone like Frank just couldn't do that. He had to use this little infraction as an opportunity to remind her of her ignorance and inferiority. All the people who ever thought they were better than Vicky came back to haunt her in the form of Frank.

That demon anger burned inside the pit of Vicky's stomach, causing her to clench her fists and grit her teeth. She thought about turning the volume on her stereo up louder, but then that might be pushing it too far, even for Vicky. She thought about acquiescing just to get Frank off her back, but then he'd win. She left the volume dial alone, leaving it at the same level. This would show Frank that she wasn't about to budge. She plopped in her rocker and began to feel very pleased with herself, when suddenly she heard vibrations come from the ceiling above her. Her initial thought was that it was an earthquake. She reached over to the volume dial and turned it down to get a better listen. It was Frank's classical music–some loud and fiery piece penetrating the floor boards and barging through her walls in a most unwelcome manner. The tune was familiar and Vicky thought maybe she recognized it from a salad dressing commercial. Then she heard more pounding coming from upstairs and an angry female voice which she thought she recognized as belonging to Allison. Soon Frank's stereo was silent. Vicky turned her stereo off too, partly because she wanted to hear Frank and Allison's conversation, and partly because she didn't want to make Allison mad. Allison was the only person she had any regard for in this God forsaken Camelot. She couldn't hear what they were saying, just their voices bantering back and forth–first Allison's then Frank's. They both sounded angry. The conversation ended with the slamming of doors.

The next day Louise the landlady paid a visit to Vicky. Louise was a middle age woman with a round friendly little face, and a penchant for pink and polyester. Vicky opened the door on Louise mid-knock. Louise's fist was raised in knocking position. Vicky observed her large callous knuckles which were the same chapped shade of pink as her slacks. The pant suit which clung to her in a most unflattering way, revealed a bulge of cellulite on either hip.

"Oh, hello," Louise said. Despite the friendly smile, Vicky knew why she was there. It was all right though. Vicky was not the least little bit intimidated by Louise. She could handle her as long as she didn't trespass on two particular counts–property damage and rent payment. Those were the two points she emphasized again and again when Vicky moved in.

"Well, hi there neighbor," Vicky said, pouring on the Kentucky accent. Louise was from Kentucky originally, in fact she and Vicky were from neighboring counties, but Louise had been a Hoosier so long she'd nearly lost her Kentucky twang. Vicky thought if she could remind Louise of something homey and familiar–something from her distant past, then maybe she'd have better luck with her.

"What a pleasant surprise. Come on in and make yourself at home." Louise stepped across the threshold of Vicky's place, as Vicky closed the door and motioned toward her couch. "Please excuse the mess," Vicky said rapidly moving about the living room, grabbing up stacks of junk mail and newspapers off the chairs, sofa, and hope chest. Louise's eyes scanned quickly over the clutter, moving to the walls and ceiling. She was examining the place for damage, no doubt. "What can I get you, darlin'?" Vicky's arms were full of paper which she tried to arrange in a neat stack on the kitchen counter top

"Oh, I can't stay, honey," she said. The term of endearment was a good indication to Vicky that her that defenses were down. Kentuckians either called you terrible names or sweet names, depending on your present standing.

"What can I do for you?"

"Well, this is not an easy matter for me to bring up. Normally, I tell tenants to work out their disagreements themselves. As long as tenants pay their rent on time and keep the place up, it's none of my business what they do with their time. I don't enjoy playing referee or babysitter. Y'all are grownups around here." *She said 'y'all'*, Vicky thought. She was reverting back to her Kentucky roots. Her defenses were dropping even more. "It's only when tenants can't work out their problems on their own that I intervene. So you understand I wouldn't be here if I hadn't been pressed." Vicky heard the subtle but distinct way she dragged her vowel sounds out a little more with each spoken word. She was beginning to talk Kentucky. Vicky had her right where she wanted her.

"Yes, I understand," Vicky said as sincerely as she could. "And I ain't gonna pretend I don't know why you're here. It concerns a little scrap I had with a neighbor upstairs. Right?"

"Yes, that's right." Louise looked almost embarrassed that she had to mention it. "You gotta keep the volume down on your stereo."

"Yes, ma'am."

"Like I say, I hate bringing it up but..." Vicky heard her dragging out those long "i" sounds and she wanted to smile but didn't dare. "It's my job, you understand."

"Oh, I understand. Ain't no hard feelings. I was wrong to have my music up so loud. Sometimes I just forget that I'm the only one in this here building who don't work your typical day shift. Thoughtless of me, ain't it?"

"To tell you the truth that neighbor of yours who's doing the most complaining," Louise said in a hushed tone. "I won't mention any names but I think we both know who I'm talking about–I've received complaints about *his* music being too loud a time or two. I'll tell you, those New York City folks really think they're something. Think they're better than everyone else. Think they can talk down to you just 'cause you're from the Midwest."

"Or the South," Vicky added.

"You got that right. What's he doing here anyway if he thinks we're all such dang hicks? Why doesn't he just go back to his precious New York where he belongs?" Vicky was doing a victory cry in her head. She knew she didn't have to say anything–just listen. Louise disliked the stuck up Prince Charming of Camelot just as much as she did.

"He thinks he's something, don't he?" Vicky finally said after she knew it was safe enough to speak her mind "You sure you can't stay for a short visit?"

"Why no, honey, you're very kind," she said looking at her watch. "But..."

"Well, hell's bells, lady. You gotta eat, don't you?" It's just about time for your lunch break, ain't it?"

"It's a little early yet."

"So take an early lunch. I make one hell of a Kentucky hot brown, course I don't have all the necessary ingredients right now, but I could fix you up a toasted BLT. I make the best, you know."

"Well, I suppose I could take an early lunch."

So Louise took an extended lunch break at Vicky's. Vicky made them sandwiches, chips, and coke. Louise mentioned that her nerves troubled her and that she suffered from chronic back pain. Vicky convinced her to take a little dash of rum in her coke–"just a dash". She propped pillows behind her back, insisted she put her feet up, and made a terrible fuss over her. By the time Louise left, Vicky knew all about the trials and tribulations of managing an apartment complex.

Those tenants with bad tempers were especially troublesome, not because of all the mean and evil things they did to others inside their apartments, but because of the inevitable damage to the property. She heard about the windows they'd broken, the full length mirrors on the back of the bedroom doors they'd cracked, and the drywall they'd stuck their fists threw. It seemed Louise didn't care if murder was committed in her apartments as long as the murderer didn't get blood on the carpet. Then there were those tenants who didn't know that body waste and toilet paper (in small quantities) were the only things that belonged getting flushed down a commode. Oh, the plumbing bills she'd been stuck with over the years! Then, of course, there were those tenants with children. It wasn't that Louise didn't like children. Why, she had children and grandchildren of her own, but children inevitably meant one thing–property damage. But she didn't have any control over that. People were going to have children and there wasn't much she could do about that. But, by God, she could control the little four legged critters with a strict no pet policy. Try though she might to enforce it, there were still those renegades who snuck animals in.

Temperatures dipped into the thirties on that exceptionally cold and frosty morning in late October. Vicky shivered from the unexpected cold as she stepped outside around three a.m. after closing the bar. She stopped to get gas and a pack of cigarettes on her way home. When she got back in her truck and started the engine, she was startled to hear a shrill screeching noise come from the engine. She turned the ignition off, grabbed a flashlight from under her seat, and stepped outside to take a look. Vicky popped the hood and spotted a pair of green glowing eyes staring back at her. The beam from the flashlight revealed a brown, black, and white striped animal curled up between the wires and coils in the engine. Vicky wasn't exactly sure what it was until it meowed loudly at her, as if scolding her for disturbing it.

"Good Lord in heaven, you poor little thing," Vicky said reaching into the hood and pulling the small creature out. "I almost killed you." She felt the cat shake and shiver as she held it against her. She thought of the cat's fate had she not turned the engine off. "I'm sorry. I'm so sorry," she said rocking the cat and rubbing her nose on its soft fur. "Forgive me," she whispered, but not to the cat this time. She stood there rocking the cat for some time until the emotions subsided.

"You must've crawled up there to get warm," she said holding the cat away from her body and examining it more thoroughly. "Looks like you're an ol' tom cat. " It bore no collar, so she assumed it was a stray. If not it was badly neglected judging from the extreme thinness of the creature. "Poor little thing. Poor little whiskers," she said lifting the feline up until she was face to face with the small creature and could feel its whiskers tickle her cheek. "I think that's what I'll call you–Little Whiskers. Ain't very original, I know. Guess I ought to try and find out if you belong to someone."

Vicky took the cat into the convenient mart and asked the man behind the counter if he knew if it belonged to anyone. The man said he'd seen the cat hanging around the place before and was pretty sure it was a stray. That's all Vicky needed to know. She took Whiskers home with her that night. Vicky wasn't sure if she'd keep the cat or not. She wasn't accustomed to thinking or planning too far into the future. She only knew that Whiskers needed a place to stay for the night, but her decision to keep the cat was forever sealed by morning.

Vicky laid towels down in the bathroom and was careful to close the toilet lid so Whiskers couldn't crawl in. She tried to ignore the constant meowing as she tossed restlessly in bed that night, but she soon found herself in the same state as a nervous mother with a fussy newborn. "Why fight it?" she said to the cat as she wrapped him in a blanket and plopped down in her rocker. She rocked him and sang lullabies to him and soon his anxious meowing became soft purring.

The moonlight shone in her window as she rocked and sang to Whiskers. How Vicky longed for a baby, but she feared that would never be. She believed she had the same curse as her mama. She'd already lost two babies to miscarriage. She felt certain that as the clock ticked closer and closer to her thirtieth birthday that her chances of becoming pregnant were quickly diminishing with each monthly cycle. She had the same heavy periods and gut-wrenching menstrual cramps as her mama. Still, she was never one to give in to sickness. She'd simply pop a couple percodan and wash them down with a shot of whiskey. That was usually enough so she could stand up straight and smile. If she could do that then she could still go about her business.

Vicky thought of her own mama while rocking and singing to Whiskers. Sometimes her mama would sit by her bed at night and sing to her when she was little. Once she told her that it was a miracle that Vicky was born at all–that she was the one and only baby of hers who made it, and that God must've had some reason for getting her here safely. But then she slowly began to lose her mom, long before she ever died. As her daddy got drunker and meaner, the roles reversed and Vicky had to become the mother when her mama became too down hearted to do much of anything but lay in bed and watch TV.

The orange-pink glow of sunrise shone through Vicky's window, pouring its light on her as she lay on the couch with the sleeping feline on her chest, both Vicky and Whiskers sleeping peacefully, breathing in unison. She woke up worrying about the cat, eager to get to the store for food and a litter box, and wondering how she could sneak him in and out of the apartment to take him to the vet for a check-up. She'd grown up with animals all around and waking up with a warm, furry, little creature next to her felt so natural. Now her apartment felt like home.

* * * * * * *

Once Frank figured out that Louise wasn't going to do anything about Vicky's music, a cold war was declared. She'd turn her music up and he'd turn his up even louder until she finally turned hers down. When that didn't work, he'd wait until she was asleep–and he always seemed to know just when that was–then he'd blast her out with the strange fiery sounds of his classical music. The truth that Vicky wouldn't admit to anyone, least of all herself, was that sometimes she turned her music down so she could hear his. It was different. It intrigued her. Sometimes when they weren't in the midst of a music war, she'd hear the sound of a piano or strings playing a woefully romantic melody, floating hypnotically down the stairs and through the hallway until it reached her ears. Sometimes she'd sit out on her patio so she could hear it better.

It was a couple weeks after Vicky adopted Whiskers that Frank showed up on her doorstep again wearing a perfectly starched white Polo shirt, khaki pants, and beat up loafers. His face didn't match the rest of him. He said nothing but merely stood there with an accusatory look as he wheezed in and out with the labored breathing of a dying man.

"Why if it isn't Camelot's own Prince Charming. What the hell's wrong with you?"

"Allergies. Pet hair allergies to be exact. That's what's wrong with me," he said coughing out the last few words into a white handkerchief with fancy lettering on it.

"You know, it would be nice if you spoke English for a change, then maybe I could understand what the hell you're talking about," Vicky said, knowing perfectly well what he was talking about. She hoped Whiskers wouldn't meow too loudly from inside the bathroom where she made sure he was hidden when she heard Frank knock on her door.

"I do speak English–the King's English which is why you don't understand me. But if you want me to speak in your vernacular, I will. You've got a fucking cat in here and I'm allergic to it. Is that plain enough for you?"

"Whoa, whoa, back up."

"What part didn't you understand?"

"I understood all of it except for one word–sounded like it started with a "V"."

"Vernacular?"

"That's it. Could you spell that for me," Vicky said pulling out her small spiral notebook and pen from her jean jacket pocket.

"Why, may I ask?"

"Because I like to look up new words in the dictionary."

"Look I didn't come here to give you a vocabulary lesson, so if you're trying to get me sidetracked forget it." He inhaled with a painful sounding wheeze and exhaled with a forceful cough into the fancy white handkerchief.

"So let me get this straight. You think I got a cat just because you got yourself a bad chest cold there."

"Listen, goddamnit!"

"Don't take the Lord's name in vain," Vicky said emphatically.

"Oh, that's rich coming from the original Miss Potty Mouth."

"I never take the Lord's name in vain."

"Maybe not, but I've heard you throw around the 'F' word and other charming little expletives."

"Ex-ple-tive. That's E-X..." Vicky began writing in her notebook.

"I don't believe this!"

"I don't understand why the 'F' word offends you so. The way I always understood it, it was New York City folks who invented that word. You know, all them pissed off taxi cab drivers hollering out their windows at one another, flipping the bird back and forth."

"All right, no more side tracking. Let's deal with the issue at hand. I don't have a chest cold. What I'm experiencing is an allergic reaction to cat dander. The only time I ever have these particular symptoms is when there's a cat nearby."

"So what makes you think *I* have a cat?"

"The symptoms are worse when I pass by your door."

"Oh, c'mon!"

"I know it's you. I can smell it on your clothes. You're covered in cat dander." Frank wheezed again into the handkerchief.

"Prove it!" Vicky slammed the door in his face.

Later that day she received a copy of the lease agreement stuck under her door. Highlighted in yellow were the words printed in bold type from the final paragraph–**Absolutely No Pets.** She knew what to expect next. It was all right though–she had her counter attack strategically planned. Her first step was to go to the store and buy all the necessary ingredients for Kentucky Burgoo. Of course you couldn't find squirrel at a city supermarket. If she had enough time she would have gone hunting with Chief Bobby and shot her one herself, but she would have to make do and substitute with chicken.

The next step was to call Chief Bobby and ask him to take Whiskers for a few days, just until the inevitable visit from Louise came and went. She arranged for Bobby to come over late at night so that no one would see him leave with the cat.

The next day Vicky dusted, mopped the kitchen and bathroom floor, vacuumed the carpet, then changed the sweeper bag and vacuumed again. "Cat dander, my ass," she said while running the vacuum a second time. "That chest cold of yours is going to clear right up, Frankie boy," she yelled up at the ceiling. "At least for a little while," she whispered and turned her attention back to the carpet. Then after every remnant of Whiskers had been cleaned, cleared, swept, and thrown away, Vicky sat down in her rocker and cried like a mother sending her child off to summer camp for the first time. She called Chief Bobby and made him put Whiskers on the phone so she could tell him Mommy loved him and would see him again in a few days.

"And Bobby, you make sure to keep them biker boys away from him. They'll torment him for sure," she gave Bobby this final instruction after reminding him to give Whiskers his worm pills.

After spending the day cleaning her apartment and most of the night working, Vicky was exhausted after closing the bar at midnight. Normally she didn't take amphetamines since she was already high energy. Most uppers made her heart palpitate and caused her to feel jittery and paranoid. She only took speed when she had to stay awake–like tonight. It was crucial that she get that Burgoo made. Day old Burgoo was the best and that's when she calculated Louise would be over. She popped the bright yellow capsule Bobby gave her and washed it down with a shot of tequila, just enough to take that jittery edge off, then stayed up all night cooking.

The aroma of the flavorful stew still filled her apartment when Louise showed up at her door the next day.

"Louise, darlin', what can I do for you?" Vicky said welcoming Louise into her apartment.

"I'm afraid this isn't a social call," Louise said, looking as if someone died.

"Please come in," Vicky said soberly, as she carefully ushered Louise across the threshold and closed the door behind her. "Don't tell me. You've been talking with our New York City friend again."

"Yes, but I'm afraid he isn't the only one who's issued complaints against you.

There've been several complaints and I've ignored them all, honey. You know my policy. Residents work out their problems themselves. But this recent complaint I just can't ignore. If it's true then it's a serious violation of the rules."

"I know all about his complaint, Louise, and it just ain't true. I don't have no cat."

"Are you telling me the truth, honey?"

"Yes!" Vicky said emphatically, with the strain of hurt feelings in her voice and on her brow. "How can you even think I'd lie about a thing like that?" She almost convinced herself. After all it wasn't a lie. She didn't have a cat *at present*, and the present was all that counted for Vicky. However, if Louise asked her if she'd *ever* had a cat then she'd have to cross her fingers behind her back while she lied and that would be more serious. Fortunately, Louise didn't ask her.

"You're welcome to take a look around," Vicky said. "If you find any evidence of a cat then I'll pack up and leave today."

"Honey, I'm not the law and I don't have a search warrant."

"I'm asking you to search my place. I'm begging you to search my place."

"That won't be necessary. I believe you."

Vicky's shoulders dropped as she exhaled a sigh of relief. "I love Camelot, Louise. This is the nicest place I ever lived. I just hate the thought of being exiled from here." This was the truth that slipped out, and Vicky wished the words had never left her mouth. She tried not to be too honest around people like Louise–people who could make trouble for her. She heard in Sunday school that the truth would set her free, but it only seemed to get her in trouble. "I mean, if I'm gonna get kicked out I hate to think it's on account of some high falutin', big city rich boy who's got himself a bad case of bronchitis, and decided I should take the blame for it just 'cause he don't like me."

"I know I shouldn't speak ill of my tenants, but I have to agree with you. He certainly has it in for you."

"Yeah, and I don't know why. I don't know what I ever did to him."

"Who knows? Maybe he's in love with you."

"Say what?"

"Well, now, I don't claim to understand men, but after two divorces I have learned a few things–most of them not very favorable of course. My first husband left me for a woman I thought he hated. He had nothing nice to say about her whatsoever. Course little did I know once he shut up and stopped bad mouthing her, he started sleeping with her. There's a fine line between love and hate. Someone said that anyways."

"I don't know about that, Louise."

"Well, who knows? My hat's off to anyone who can understand the male mind."

"To understand the male mind, you first have to understand it ain't located between their ears, but a little further south if you get what I'm saying."

"Amen to that, sister."

"Where are my manners? Sit down, Louise," Vicky said motioning toward the sofa. "Can we consider this a social visit now?"

"Why yes, honey. My goodness, something sure smells good," Louise said, her Kentucky twang having returned.

"This is such a coincidence that you would show up today. I just got a wild hair last night and decided to whip me up some Kentucky Burgoo. You know, I hardly ever cook anymore 'cause it just ain't no fun cooking for one, but the fact is I'm a great cook. My grandma taught me how, you know, but I'm afraid I'm getting out of practice living alone here and having a bag of chips and a pop every night for supper. I just had to cook something–you know, home made and hot. A girl's just gotta eat real food every so often or she'll go plumb crazy. So you'll join me for lunch?"

"I really shouldn't, but…"

"No buts now. You're gonna save me from eating alone and that's all there is to it." Vicky called out as she made her three sprint stride into the kitchen. "Now this ain't real Kentucky Burgoo, you know, 'cause it ain't got squirrel in it. I had to use chicken instead," she called over the din of the clanking spoons and bowls which she grabbed out of drawers and cupboards.

Vicky set a quick table and poured two cokes into tall glasses. She mixed some rum into both–a sizeable splash for Louise and her aching back since she figured the heavy stew would absorb the alcohol, then an even larger splash for her since she needed to come down from the speed.

"This is delicious," Louise praised Vicky in between bites of the hearty stew.

"Thank you, darlin'," Vicky said out of an unoccupied corner of her mouth. The other corner had a large piece of meat and some vegetables parked in it. The speed had left her with very little appetite. She commanded her jaws to chew as best they could and washed down the remnants with a gulp of rum and coke.

"You eat like a bird, honey. Of course so do I–a vulture, that is." She chortled into her napkin. "No wonder you stay so slim."

"You know how it is. You do all that tasting while you cook. You sit down to eat and you just ain't hungry no more. Most of the time I got the appetite of a bear waking up from hibernation."

"You sure you're taking care of yourself, honey?" Louise said with a sudden intent look of motherly concern.

Vicky didn't want to stoke the fires of those maternal feelings too much. She didn't want Louise stopping by to check on her unannounced and unexpected. "I've been taking care of myself for a long time, Louise. You don't need to worry about me none."

Later that afternoon, Vicky sent Louise on her way with a large Tupperware bowl of Burgoo, a full belly, and a slight buzz. She gave the rest to Allison and Sally along with the recipe–her grandma's recipe that called for squirrel.

It was ten days after Louise's visit before Vicky retrieved Whiskers from Chief Bobby. During those ten days she behaved herself, kept her stereo down, kept late night visitors to a minimum, and crept as lightly in and out of Camelot as her heavy feet allowed her. Whiskers' homecoming made her feel like celebrating. She celebrated and celebrated until October slipped into November and November nearly slipped away. She managed to escape banishment from Camelot despite repeated conflicts with her neighbors. Then one stormy mid-November night a streak of lightning flashed outside her window and sent a chill of paranoia up her spine, as if the very hand of God would find her out and smite her. She knew then her luck was about to take a turn for the worse. One small corner of her mind fought to reason with the larger part, which was clouded over as the outdoor skies from the effects of Columbian weed and Tennessee whiskey. "I'm just stoned," she reasoned aloud. Then with a great heaving sigh she got off the couch where she'd been glued for how long she didn't know, hypnotized by the rain pelting against her sliding glass door. Upon arising a sudden onslaught of the munchies besieged her. "I need to eat something." Vicky stood up, her bare feet feeling heavy, clumsy, and strange to her. A thousand little pins stuck her all throughout the heel and arch of her right foot. "Man, am I ever messed up," she said realizing her foot was asleep. She stomped her foot on the floor, shook it, and hobbled off to the kitchen.

"It stinks in here," Vicky said once inside the kitchen. She sniffed inside the refrigerator, in the sink near the garbage disposal, and in the pantry where she had some large trash bags stashed. "Whew! It's definitely coming from in here," she said her head in the pantry. "Time to empty the trash," Vicky said picking up two large trash bags.

That small corner of her brain that could still reason remembered that it was night, but that was all right, she'd taken her trash out at night before. The area behind building 3300 where the dumpster was located was well lit with flood lights. She carried the two large trash bags, one in either hand to balance herself, to the door. Suddenly a flash of lightning caused her to jump. The larger part of her mind, the part that was clouded over, had forgotten in just the short span of a few minutes that it was storming out.

"Shit! What am I thinking? I ain't going out there in this. But I can't put it back in the kitchen. It stinks too bad. What should I do, Whiskers?" She asked the green eyed, striped furry feline at her feet. Whiskers meowed in his careless aloof way, as if he was giving his opinion. She decided to put the trash bags out in the hall, just until the storm passed.

"Who cares if that garbage stinks up the place," she said returning to her kitchen with a can of Lysol which she scrupulously began spraying. "Fuckin' neighbors! Serves 'em right. Hope they all gag to death from the smell in their next little hallway meeting about me."

Vicky sat on the floor between her stereo speakers and listened to Led Zeppelin, ate a bag of chips and two Twinkies, watched the rain, finished off an unsmoked roach, drank a half glass of whiskey, thought about God, judgment, heaven, hell, eternity, and death until she fell asleep right there on the floor between the speakers. She didn't think about the trash bags again that night.

A loud banging roused her and it took her a few moments to get her bearings.

"Open up, Dooley! I know you're in there," came the all too familiar battle cry from behind her door.

"Ah shit! Not that fuckin' buzzard again," she said trying to decide if she should face him and square off, or simply slip out the patio door, into her pick up truck, and out of Camelot. It would be so easy to drive off, not returning until mid-morning. He'd have to leave for work soon and by the time he got home, she'd be at work.

"I-N-T-I-M-I-D-A-T-E. Intimidate. To make timid. To fill with fear," she said quietly to herself as she paced back and forth across her living room floor. "Implying the presence or operation of a fear-inspiring source that compels one to or keeps one from action. That's it! I ain't gonna let that son-of-a-bitch intimidate me no more," she said, her fists clenched and her jaw set. "Hold your horses, Frankie boy!" she hollered at the door.

"I've got all day," he gleefully hollered back.

Vicky wondered what he was up to this time. She did her three stride gallop into the bathroom and looked at her reflection in the mirror above the sink. The left side of her head revealed flattened auburn curls and a red pocked cheek from where the carpet had left its mark on her face. Remnants of yesterday's mascara was smeared under her bloodshot eyes. "Let the asshole wait," she said turning on the faucet and splashing cool water on her face. "I can't hear you. I'm freshening up," she sing-song'd back in response to Frank's persistent pounding. By the time she finished brushing her teeth and changing her shirt, Frank had stopped pounding. For one hopeful moment Vicky thought he might've left. The thought passed. Frank didn't give up that easily. He was still out there all right and he was up to something.

"Time to face the music—old dead guy music," Vicky said proceeding as bravely as she could to the door. "I am not intimidated. I am not intimidated."

Her rehearsed greeting was halted before she could even get the first syllable out. Instead of seeing Frank's face on the other side of the door she saw a flattened kitty litter bag. He was holding it—in front of his face. He lowered the bag to just under his chin, his eyes glowing with triumph. "Evidence, Miss Dooley. Exhibit A."

"What are you talking about?"

"Subconsciously you must've wanted to get caught. Sort of like the homicidal criminal who gets tired and sloppy and starts leaving clues behind."

"I ain't no criminal."

"Well, now, that's debatable, but entirely beside the point. You are, however, a liar and a pet owner."

"First you call me criminal then you call me a liar," she said with feigned indignation.

He just smiled at her. She hadn't seen him so happy since that time in the hall when he spotted Allison and let his guard down for a brief moment.

"You want to tell me what the hell's going on?" Vicky said, still a little befuddled and disoriented.

"I'd be delighted. I found your trash strewn all over the hallway this morning."

"You went through my trash? You sick bastard!"

"I didn't have to. It was all over the floor." Vicky remembered. A wave of heat moved from her bowels up to her head and broke in a sweat around her hairline. She swore she had the trash bags tied up, but maybe not. Maybe the ties came undone somehow.

"I should have left it there for Louise to see but I graciously cleaned up your mess for you."

"All right I admit it. I put my trash in the hallway last night because it was too stormy to take it out to the dumpster. I was going to take it out just as soon as it quit raining, but I guess I fell asleep," she said beginning to lose steam. "It could happen to anyone."

"So you admit that this bag came out of your garbage. Or are you going to try to lie your way out of it and claim you have no idea how it got there? Face it, Dooley, you're busted!"

"I admit it. It came out of my garbage. So what! That don't prove nothing, Mister Know-It-All. What you don't know is what I purchased it for. C'mon. I'll show you if you think you're so smart," she said regaining a nice head of steam. "Follow me." Vicky forcefully took Frank by the arm and led him to the door. He didn't resist. His skin was warm and she felt the veins and muscles around his wrist. She suddenly became very aware of Frank, not as the self-imposed ruler, the dictator of building 3300, her adversary, her nemesis, but as a man. She looked at him, her eyes quickly scanning his face until they came to a stop at his eyes. It was only a moment that she looked into them. She looked away and quickly continued leading him by the arm out the front door of the building.

"This ought to be good," Frank said with a sarcastic chuckle.

"Here." Vicky gave him one last tug then released his arm as they came to a stop in the parking lot in front of her pick up truck. "Look! Look under my truck. If you observe carefully you will note some kitty litter there on the ground. It's an old truck. It leaks oil. I use the stuff to absorb the oil. That's why I buy it. Any questions?"

"Yes, as a matter of fact. It says here on the bag that this is twenty-five pounds worth of kitty litter."

"So?"

"So what did you do with the other twenty-four pounds?"

"I ate it, shit head! What do you think I did with it? I just showed you what I use it for."

"Yeah, right, and you expect me to believe that? Though I will confess I find it your most inventive lie to date."

Vicky felt that demon anger burning and rising within her until it felt like it might blow her scalp right off the top of her head. She clenched her fists. "You fuck head!" she yelled in his face.

"You know, you really ought to come up with a more original curse than that. Please don't bore me with anymore of your vulgar epithets. That's E-P-I-T-H-E-T," Frank hollered at her as she turned her back to him and stomped back to the building with her long determined strides.

Chapter 13
November & December 1983

Vicky was all alone in her apartment waiting. She knew it was coming, but it really didn't matter. She'd known all along. Louise would be at her door serving eviction papers any time now. Perhaps she was even on her way at this exact moment. She tried to go about the business of her usual day–preparing her late breakfast which she usually ate around ten o'clock. She tried to focus her attention on the simple things–the sizzling pad of butter in the skillet, the egg cracking on the side of the pan, the clear liquid becoming white solid around the perfect yellow center.

She sat down to eat, scooping up bites of egg onto buttered toast. She couldn't really taste her food, and she only ate because it gave her comfort. Not the food so much as the very act of sitting at the table and going through the motions of partaking in a meal. It made her think of her grandma. Her grandma never neglected to feed her, even when Vicky was a troublesome teen and made her mad as a wet hen. Even then her grandma would still cook supper and insist Vicky sit down to table with her. Some of those suppers were taken in silence. Some they'd wind up arguing. Some ended in weeping or praying, and once even a laying on of hands. But now she ate alone and her grandma wasn't with her.

The morning crept at its tortoise-like pace while Vicky tried to keep herself busy. She figured Louise would show up around lunch time. But this time Vicky wouldn't try to persuade her with rum and food. She would be honest with Louise about the two a.m. rumble in the parking lot the other night between the biker boys. She wouldn't deny a thing if asked about any of the other middle of the night disturbances. She would tell her the whole truth this time. Who knows? She might even tell her about Whiskers. What the hell? Louise couldn't protect Vicky any longer. Not when all the others had gone to her with their complaints, as she was sure they had done about this most recent incident. It wasn't just Frank this time. Even Allison was at her wit's end. Vicky could tell by the way she barely acknowledged her greetings in the hallway and parking lot.

The inevitable knock upon her door was almost a relief. Soon it would be over. Vicky looked at her clock on the kitchen wall. Sure enough, it was twelve twenty. Right about when she estimated Louise would drop by. Vicky opened her door. She gasped out loud when instead of Louise, she saw Allison standing there before her.

"Allison! What are you doing here? I thought you'd be at work."

"I'm on my lunch break. May I come in?"

"Sure." Allison stepped inside and Vicky closed the door behind her.

"I really can't stay long. Twenty minutes max," she said looking at her watch. "But I just had to talk to you. I was afraid you'd be at work by the time I got home this evening. I made some chicken salad," she said holding up a Tupperware bowl in one hand and a loaf of bread in the other. "Can I make you a sandwich?"

"No, thanks."

"Mind if I make myself a sandwich?"

"You know where the kitchen is," Vicky said, her hand extended in that direction. She followed Allison into the kitchen. "What can I get you to drink?" Vicky inquired of Allison who'd already helped herself to a spoon and a plate.

"Just water."

"So… this little talk you just have to have with me–it's something serious, ain't it?" Vicky said reaching into the cabinet for a glass.

"Yes, it is." Allison stopped scooping chicken salad on the bread for a moment and gave Vicky a concerned look.

"It's about the other night, ain't it?" Allison nodded slowly with a slightly pained smile. "Quit looking at me like that. You remind me of a dang undertaker. And it's my funeral, right?"

"Could be."

"Look, I appreciate your coming here to warn me, but I already done figured it out. Louise is gonna kick my ass outta Camelot. I'm banished from the round table forever, ain't I?"

"Not necessarily. Nobody's gone to Louise yet, at least not anyone from this building."

"This building!? Those crazy ass fools probably did wake up the entire complex. I thought they'd settled their differences before they left my place. How was I to know they was gonna continue their little spat out in the parking lot? Crazy fools!" Vicky muttered with her head down.

"Little spat? I'd hardly call breaking beer bottles over one another's heads a little spat."

"They didn't bust 'em over each others' heads. Trash just got all pissed off and threw his bottle against the building then threatened to cut Jimmy's throat with the broken glass."

"I can't help it. My friends are trashy. They're rough and wild. They're screw ups… like me."

"You're not a screw up."

"Oh, yeah? Respectable people, like you, don't have friends who break beer bottles in parking lots at two o'clock in the morning then make death threats." Vicky's eyes burned with tears and her stomach knotted in anger. "Respectable people's neighbors don't have meetings about them in the middle of the night. Respectable people don't get laughed at. I've heard the wise cracks about Ellie Mae and her critters; and about Chief Bobby bein' my boyfriend because you know how them Kentuckians are about their cousins." Hot tears rolled down Vicky's cheeks and her voice quivered with each syllable she strained to utter.

Allison looked at Vicky with a sympathetic look.

"If you show me pity right now I swear I'll hate you for the rest of my life," Vicky yelled in between sobs.

Allison's head and shoulders dropped with one terrific sigh of resignation. The two women just stood there for a time–one sobbing, one seemingly paralyzed. Allison left the kitchen and returned moments later with a box of tissues she'd retrieved from the bathroom. She pulled several sheets out and handed the wad to Vicky. "Here, you're going to have to dry your own tears lest you think I'm taking pity on you and decide to hate me for the rest of your life." Allison smiled as Vicky accepted the wad of tissues.

"So what did you do?" Vicky asked. "Beg them to give me another chance?"

"I wouldn't say beg, but I did have to use my best salesmanship skills."

"Why? I don't deserve another chance."

"I know you don't."

"Then why?"

"I asked myself the same question. I guess it's precisely because you don't deserve it."

"Is this something you learned in college 'cause I ain't following your line of thinking?"

"Don't you see, Vicky? If you get evicted then *you* win… again"

"Whatever."

"You do this to yourself, don't you? You set yourself up to fail. Things are going along great for you then you do something to screw it all up. Why?"

"I told you, 'cause I'm a screw up."

"No, you're not. You wouldn't have a reputation as the best bartender in town if you were such a screw up."

"Big whup! Ain't nothing to tending bar," Vicky said lighting a cigarette and nonchalantly exhaling a stream of smoke along with the aftermath of a heaving sob.

"Maybe not, but no other bartender I know can remember a person's name six months after meeting them once. No other bartender can accurately guess what a person's favorite drink is nine times out of ten. And I've never met a bartender who can size up a person the way you can, or get them talking about their troubles only to get them smiling again all in less than ten minutes. I've watched you. You're incredible! Everyone knows Vicky Dooley. Everyone loves Vicky Dooley. You just need to learn how to use those people smarts once you step out from behind the bar."

"And you're just the one to teach me I suppose?"

"Somebody needs to," Allison said sternly, cutting her chicken salad sandwich diagonally with a fierce determination set firmly in her jaw. She picked up her plate and her glass of water and proceeded into the dining area where she sat her plate down with a firm but controlled clunk. "Coaster, please," she said still holding her glass of water.

"Hold your horses, I'm getting it." A moment later Vicky was at her elbow, placing a coaster on the table. Allison sat her glass on it.

"I don't have much time," Allison said checking her watch as she sat down. Vicky grabbed her brown glass ashtray and sat across from Allison with her cigarette. Allison took a bite off her sandwich, quickly chewed and swallowed, then took a drink of water. "Play by the rules, Vicky, or leave Camelot. It's as simple as that. If you screw up again all the residents of building 3300, myself included, will sign a petition stating that we won't pay our rent until you are evicted. And you won't be able to charm Louise out of that one. She'll throw you out on your ear, and I won't be there to bail you out."

"I'm so glad I have someone like you to save me from myself."

"Look, you have to decide what you want. If you want to blast your stereo and have your noisy visitors come and go at all hours of the night… fine. If you want to leave your trash out in the hall and have a cat…great. Move somewhere that'll let you do all that. It's no skin off my nose."

"I don't have no cat."

"Hang it up, Vicky. We aren't all as easily conned as Louise. I know you've got a cat. I've seen it sitting in your window." Vicky wondered if Allison was simply calling her bluff in an attempt to get her to confess. The two determined women glared at one another–one as immovably fixed in her position as the other. "It's white with brown and black stripes, isn't it?"

"All right, so I got a cat."

"Geez, Vicky, did you really think you'd get away with it?"

"It's a stupid rule. He ain't done no damage to this place. Hell, I got him declawed and fixed. There ain't no damage left for him to do. And cats are cleaner than humans you know. It's just a stupid rule and that's all there is to it."

"Louise is the one who makes the rules, Vicky, not you. Whether you think they're stupid or not, you still have to abide by them if you want to live here."

Allison looked at her watch. "I've got to go. You need to decide what you want," she said carrying her plate and glass into the kitchen.

"So do you."

"What are you talking about?"

"Kent. You're all over my ass for breaking the rules and maybe you're right. But sometimes it's just as dangerous to play it safe. I seen the two of you together. I know you don't love him no more."

"No, you don't know that," Allison said, as she placed the plate and glass in the kitchen sink nearly hard enough to break them. She quickly made her way to the door, stopping only briefly to retrieve her purse and coat from the chair where she'd laid them. "Oh, one more thing," She turned and said before exiting. "If you decide to stay, I know someone who will take your cat for you." Allison was gone a moment later, closing the door behind her with a finality that startled Vicky.

* * * * * * *

Vicky worked until midnight and didn't get to bed until after one. She set her internal alarm clock for early. It would have to be early if she wanted to catch Allison before she left for work. Her few hours sleep was the restless half-sleep of those who know they must get up early, but fear they will not. She rolled from one side of her waterbed to the other with strange dreams about Whiskers. She was looking for him in her dreams. Someone had taken him away. She would hear him meow. She would see the black tip of his tail disappear around a corner, but she couldn't get to him. Worst of all when she did find him he was in the middle of the street all flattened and bloodied, small fragments of tendon and bone barely holding his nearly detached head to his body. He was still alive, still meowing, and she tried to put him back together again, but she couldn't and she knew he would die all alone out there in the middle of the road. She returned to her pick up truck which was parked on the side of the road. She thought it was mud and dirt splattered all over the vehicle until she got closer. To her horror she discovered it was blood. She checked her tires. They were covered with blood. She was awakened by the sound of her own scream.

It was still dark when Vicky awoke, but from the looks of the navy blue sky her internal alarm clock told her it was close to dawn. She wrapped her blanket around her shoulders as she shivered in the frigid morning air and stumbled into the kitchen to check the time on the one and only clock she owned. It was six thirty-five. She stood there in her bare feet on the cold tile floor and listened to the clock tick tock the seconds away.

"I guess it's time I made a decision about my future," Vicky said aloud to herself as her cold fingers reached out from underneath the blanket to grab a pack of cigarettes off the kitchen counter. "I ain't used to planning for my future." She struck a match and lit the cigarette which dangled from her lips. Smiling at her thoughts, she sent a puff of smoke quickly into her lungs then quickly back out again. She huddled one last time in her blanket and generated as much warmth as she could, then with one quick tug and toss she discarded the heavy wool thing onto the back of her rocking chair. Her bare feet padded quickly along the cold kitchen floor as she moved about.

"My future. My silver mine. My own place. Vicky's Country Inn." Vicky chuckled, feeling self-conscious at the grandiosity of saying it aloud. She thought of the place made of logs, but with plenty of windows and doors to let light and air in. In clement weather the doors would always be open so that hospitality, old time country music, and the smell of fried chicken could flow out, letting folks know they were welcome. She saw the oaken bar in her mind which lovers would be free to scratch their initials on. She saw the stone fireplace with old iron skillets and kettles hanging about.

"My own home. My big ol' dream house, way out in the country with lots of land, and horses, and dogs, and cats, and wild flowers, and a vegetable garden, and kids running around..." Vicky paused. "And someone," she said, removing the lid from a can of ground coffee. She turned the sink faucet on and filled up her grandma's old percolator. "Like Allison says, I guess it's time I decide what I want," she said filling the metal basket of the percolator with scoops of coffee. She plugged the old percolator in and stood motionless with her thoughts silent, as if they were too personal to speak aloud, even to herself. The percolator bubbled. *What do I want? What do I want?*

I want to be smarter. I want to be better. I want to be loved. I want someone to look at me the way Frank looked at Allison that first time I saw them together. What would it be like to have someone look at me like that? What would it be like if Frank looked at me like that?

The mere suggestion caused Vicky to slap herself hard on the cheek. "Stop it, you stupid girl!" But her mind couldn't help wondering. She'd seen glimpses of something in Frank–something she couldn't explain, yet understood. She'd heard something when he spoke, something faint, far away, and distant. It was like the woeful moan of a ghost haunting a castle, forever pining away, never freeing itself from the chains it rattles in the middle of the night–something that longs to be freed yet if someone brave enough gets near, it only draws back in fear. But what if someone dared get close enough to touch the pitiful imprisoned thing? She wouldn't have to reach up very far to kiss him. Vicky closed her eyes and imagined it.

All of those things that make a woman love a man were real at that moment. The perfect balance of toughness and tenderness were in everything he did. The touch of his lips on hers, both soft and firm. His cheek against hers, both rough and warm. The feel of his arms, hard and solid to the touch held her in a tight embrace, yet his hands and fingertips touched lightly. It was gentleness. It was passion. It was the two together in perfect harmony.

The daydream ended abruptly when Whiskers appeared, seemingly out of nowhere as he so often did, rubbing up against her leg then planting himself on her bare feet. "Phew, you must be hard up Vicky ol' girl. Getting to be one horny ol' broad," she muttered as she reached down and picked up Whiskers. She held him close and said, "Whatever happens to you, just remember Mommy loves you and always will. I'm gonna see to it you get a decent home." She stroked him and kissed him then set him down in front of his food bowl. The coffee was ready so she poured herself a cup. Then with a sigh of determination, she commanded her legs to move out the door and up the stairs to Allison's place.

Vicky knocked hard on Allison's door. She waited, took a gulp of her coffee then knocked again. Vicky would persist until she spoke with her even if it meant waiting out in the hallway. She knocked hard one more time. "Allison. It's me, Vicky. I gotta talk to you!"

"Hold on a second. I'm coming," the muffled cry from behind the door called back.

"Sorry, I was in the shower," Allison said opening the door, a towel wrapped around her head and a terrycloth robe wrapped around her body. "What are you doing up so early?"

"Making sure I talk to you before you leave for work."

"Come on in." Allison politely stepped aside making room for her unexpected visitor.

"Say, I apologize if I came on a little strong yesterday."

"It's cool. I'm sorry for what I said about Kent. I had no right."

"Apology accepted."

"Listen I been thinking, you know, about what we talked about. And I think I–that is, I know I wanna stay."

"I'm glad."

"You sure about that?"

"Yes," Allison chuckled. "Despite everything you're the only person around here I actually like. Don't ask me why but I do."

"So, uh, there's the situation with Whiskers–my cat. I talked to my cousin Bobby last night. You remember Chief Bobby? He said if worse come to worse he'd take him for me, but he ain't really a cat lover, besides he's on the road a lot. I'd rather it be someone who'd love Whiskers–someone who could give him a real home. You mentioned you knew someone."

"Yes, a lady I work with. Her name's Grace."

"She a cat lover?"

"You bet! She has pictures of her cats on her desk where most people have pictures of their kids."

"That's a good sign. I'm guessing she's got more than one?"

"She had two but her oldest one died recently. Since then her other cat hasn't been eating. She took him to the vet and he said there's nothing wrong with him physically. It's just plain ol' grief. He needs a companion. I told her your situation. She said she'd take your cat–sight unseen."

"Is that right?"

"He'd be in good hands. Believe me, Vicky, I know this lady. She'll take good care of him."

"Okay then. I'll take your word for it. Tell her he's been fixed and his shots are up to date."

"I'll let her know."

"Tell her his name is Whiskers. I don't want her to go renaming him. I want her to call him by the name I gave him" Vicky felt a knot of sorrow forming in her throat and she didn't want to cry in front of Allison again. She still felt vulnerable from their last meeting. She swallowed back the tears, cleared her throat, and squared her shoulders.

"I'm sure she'd be very agreeable to anything you want. In fact she said you could come and visit anytime. She doesn't live far from here."

"No. When I say goodbye I say goodbye. He'll be her cat, not mine no more. I just ask that she honor my one request and continue to call him Whiskers."

"I'll make sure she knows."

"Can she take him today?"

"I'm sure she can, but don't you need more time to say goodbye?"

"I'd like to just get it over with. The longer I wait the harder it'll be."

"I understand."

"Stop by my place before you leave for work. I'll have him ready for you."

It was an hour later that Allison appeared on Vicky's door step.

"C'mon in. I got his stuff right here in this box," she said motioning to a cardboard box by the door filled with kitty litter, cat food, and various other items. Vicky bent down and pulled a gray furry fake mouse out of the box. She held it in her fist and wiggled it as she stuck it in Allison's face. Allison gasped and jumped back. Vicky laughed. "It looks real, don't it?"

"I thought it was," Allison said with her hand on her chest.

"This one's his favorite toy. I'm almost tempted to keep it as a memoir."

Vicky felt the emotions building up again in her chest and throat. "Pitiful, ain't it? A grown woman getting sentimental over a toy mouse."

"Maybe you should keep it."

"Naw, it'd just tear me up every time I saw it." She tossed the toy mouse back in the box. "Well, I guess I better go get him."

Vicky went back into her bedroom where Whiskers lay curled up sleeping on a vent, taking advantage of the heat it provided.

"No wonder it's always cold in here. You hog all the heat," she said squatting down and lifting him into her arms. "I'm gonna have to clean that vent out. It's probably all clogged up with hair. We wouldn't want any trace of cat dander floating through the Camelot air, now would we?" Vicky stood up and opened the door of her walk in closet. She stepped into the corner and felt around behind her suitcase and some stacked shoe boxes for the handle of Whiskers carry on cage. Her long arm reached down and retrieved it while the other arm clutched Whiskers tight.

"Be a good kitty and remember, always remember..." The knot in her throat choked off her words. She kissed Whiskers on the top of the head then quickly put him in the cage. She reached for her laundry basket in another corner of the closet, then after dumping some dirty clothes out on the floor, she placed the cage in the basket, carried it into the bathroom, grabbed several bath towels, and draped them over the cage.

Allison still stood by the door waiting patiently for Vicky when she returned to the living room with the laundry basket. "This is how I sneak him in and out of the building," Vicky said

Allison reached onto the laundry basket and pushed some of the towels away. Vicky looked away.

"Well, hello there, you cute little fellow," Allison cooed at Whiskers.

Vicky closed her eyes. "You'd think I was giving my kid away," she said with her back turned to Allison and Whiskers.

Only the sound of sniffling along with an occasional whistle from the north winter wind could be heard as they made their way through the parking lot and loaded up Allison's car. Vicky was not wearing a coat yet she hardly noticed the cold. She felt only numbness. "Remember, his name is Whiskers," she said finally breaking the silence.

"I'll remember. It'll be fun having an animal at work today. Grace will be ecstatic. But I just want to know one thing," Allison said. "What made you decide to stay?"

"I talked with Chief Bobby last night. Remember them silver mines I told you about that my Shawnee kin was always looking for. Well, Bobby says we gotta keep looking. Says there's something in our blood that just keeps driving us to look for something better. Says there's something better for me here in Camelot. I don't know what, but something. Does that make sense?"

"It does to me." With that Allison put her arms around Vicky who was somewhat taken aback by this unexpected gesture of friendship When Allison pulled away Vicky was weeping again.

"Don't be a stranger," Allison said descending into the driver's seat of her car. Vicky remained in the parking lot until Allison's car was out of sight.

* * * * * * *

Another Florida drug run. They seemed to follow one after another these days, Vicky thought as Chief Bobby explained to her that it was only for a while and that he would be back by Christmas.

"You better be, bro, 'cause you're the only family I got. Who the hell else I got to spend Christmas with?" Vicky said catching the pack of Marlboros he tossed to her from where he sat on her sofa. She stuck a cigarette in her mouth then threw the pack back to him.

"I'll be back by Christmas and I'll bring the snow with me," he laughed. Bobby's voice was unlike anyone else she ever knew. It was so deep that his vocal cords made a vibrating noise whenever he spoke or laughed.

"A white Christmas for Lamasco," Vicky said, cigarette hanging off her lip as she struggled to light a match, striking it again and again until the worn sulfur tip finally caught flame.

Vicky plopped into her rocker, reached for the bottle of Cutty Sark on grandma's hope chest and poured some into her glass of melting ice. "Want some more, Bobby?" she asked extending the bottle toward him. Bobby held up his glass and leaned in until it clinked against the tip of the bottle. "Damn fine scotch," Vicky said as she poured the yellow liquid into Bobby's glass. "Hey Bobby, I need to talk to you about something–kinda serious." Bobby gave her a nod and a look that told her to proceed.

"You know I gave Whiskers away? Well, that ain't the only change I gotta make. I can't do as many transactions around here no more. It's too suspicious having so many customers hanging around. I know it's the perfect cover and all. The cops watch you like a hawk, Bobby, whereas they never come around Camelot. Forget it that some of the biggest yuppie coke heads in the tri-state live in this complex. It's respectable. Too many of your customers ain't though, Bobby. They got reputations in this town. They got records a mile long. They make trouble for me, even more than I make for myself. You know the cops have already been called out here more than once on account of some of those retard dope heads. You see my point?"

Bobby nodded in his silent way. "Don't worry. I'll pick up the slack for you."

"Thanks Bobby. Say, did you ever wonder how we got into such a crummy business in the first place. And don't give me no shit about this being our silver mine we always done looked for. You know you don't believe that no more. Ain't no silver mines in prison. Don't you ever think about getting out of the business?"

"Yes. I'm thinking about it now. Remember you're not the only one with dreams. I got one too."

"You mean your dream about moving to Oklahoma to live with our people?" Bobby nodded and smiled his calm even smile. "So you can learn more about the Native ways and maybe even make a living as a storyteller or a medicine man–whatever."

"People do make livings teaching about the Native American life and history? Yep. That's the dream. You still have your dream?"

"The one about owning my own restaurant and bar and having a house out in the country with lots of land and animals? And of course living there with Prince Charming and about ten kids?"

"Your silver mine."

"Yeah. My silver mine."

"I give up looking for it here. Our people left the Ohio River Valley back in the 1820's. There's nothing left for us here now."

"No silver mines?"

"Not for me."

"So why don't you leave and go to Oklahoma? Leave and quit this crummy business. Why do you stay here?"

"Because of you. Like you say, we're the only family we got."

"Bobby, I ain't a kid no more. I can take care of myself."

"You could go to Oklahoma with me."

"Shit I ain't no Okie. I ain't no Shawnee squaw either. No offense, but I just ain't into the Indian ways like you are, Bobby. It just ain't as deep in my blood or something. I gotta stay and you gotta go. You gotta go and you gotta quit feeling so responsible for me. We're destined to go our separate ways, but you know you'll always be my only kin. My bro no matter where you go. So go on ahead and go. I give you my permission."

"I wish it was that easy."

"What's stopping you?"

"Debts. More than just money debts. You know what I mean."

"Don't go on this run, Bobby. I just got a bad feeling about it."

"This will be my last one."

"You mean it?"

"This run oughta square me with some folks. I'll just let everyone know I'm taking a little Christmas break when I get back, then I'll slip off to Oklahoma."

"You gotta promise to come visit once I move out there."

"I will. You gotta promise not to chicken out." Vicky walked Bobby to the door and hugged him. "Now, you better get your ass back here for Christmas."

"I said I'd be back."

"Why do I feel like this is the last time I'll ever see you?"

"'Cause you're saying goodbye to a different Bobby, maybe. I don't know."

Bobby turned around for a final wave as Vicky stood at the threshold of her apartment and watched him walk out the front door of the building.

The cold December air made Vicky shiver.

Chapter 14
December 1983

The full moon cast just enough light through Vicky's window for her to make out the image of Chief Bobby standing by her bed. He was trying to tell her something. But Bobby left for Florida over a week ago.

A few hours later Vicky awoke. The questions spun around and around in her head making her dizzier than any carnival ride. Was Bobby back from Florida? Did he not leave at all? He had a key so he certainly could have paid her a visit if he wanted to. But why would he do such a strange thing? Why would he sneak into her apartment in the middle of the night? Why would he return from Florida without calling her? Why hadn't she heard from him at all since he left town? Was it really him standing there by her bed? Or was it just a dream?

It couldn't have been a dream because no matter how real a dream may seem at the time, in the morning you know it was just a dream. In the morning all those middle of the night phantoms that tricked you into believing their absurdities and illogic show themselves for what they are. You laugh at them by the light of day. But this didn't seem unreal and absurd the way a dream would seem the next morning. Yet like a dream, Vicky remembered struggling and grappling to solve some problem during the entirety of the visitation. And like a dream, she couldn't remember what the problem was now that it was all over.

She had to talk to someone about it. Allison would think she was crazy, but then Vicky was beginning to wonder herself. She scuffled into the kitchen in her nearly worn out blue furry bedroom slippers, yawned, and stretched, and made conversation with herself.

"Man, if I didn't know any better I'd think I dropped acid and hallucinated the whole thing. Bobby was in my room. I know it. Maybe I finally done blew a cog. " Busying herself to drive the thoughts away, Vicky stood at the door of her refrigerator and wondered what to take to Allison's.

It was customary to show up at one another's place with food. Vicky smiled as she mused over this ancient female ritual that she thought perhaps came from their poor country girl roots. "Take care of your neighbors," Vicky's grandma would always say remembering the depression days. "If you got extra food take it to your neighbors. You never know if they've had to go without today. Do them a good turn. It'll come back to you."

Vicky selected some left-over baked ham wrapped in foil from the refrigerator and placed it in a grocery sack with a five pound bag of potatoes and a can of peas. "Sunday dinner," Vicky said as it suddenly occurred to her to check out her window to see if Allison's car was there. She looked out the window and there was her red trans am, but no sign of Kent's white pick up truck. "Good! She's home and she's alone." Kent hadn't been spending the nights as much lately, Vicky thought as the other part of her brain tried to figure out what would be the best Sunday brunch drink. Mimosas were good, and the sweetness might go nicely with the salty ham but she didn't have any champagne.

"Tomato juice, vodka, tobasco sauce," she said pulling bottles out of cabinets, deciding nothing could really top a Bloody Mary for Sunday. She stuck the bottles in the grocery sack and headed for the door. It was funny, Vicky thought, how she and Allison never called one another first–just showed up at each other's doors with food.

Allison seemed as happy to see Vicky at her door as Vicky was to be there. Vicky felt all those anxieties which so greatly disturbed her when she was alone quickly slip away with the distraction of friendly small talk. And so they found themselves where they always found themselves whenever they got together–in the kitchen. It never mattered if the other was hungry or not. They always sat down to table together even if only one ate. But today they were both hungry. And it was Sunday. And Vicky didn't have to go to work until later in the afternoon. It seemed like Christmas already as they laughed, and chatted, and placed the ham in the oven and peeled potatoes. The only sour note for Allison was the canned peas. Allison explained to Vicky that she never liked peas and, even as an adult when she forced herself to partake, she had to politely stifle the instinct to gag, all the while flashing back to her mother who made her sit at the table until she ate every last one of them.

"I think every adult's got a vegetable like that," Vicky said laughing. "Mine's Brussels sprouts."

"Really? I like Brussels sprouts."

"They taste like dirt."

"Yeah, but you thought that fine red wine I got for you tasted like dirt too. Kentucky dirt. Remember?"

"Brussels sprouts taste like Hoosier dirt. And there's a whole heap of difference twixt the two." Vicky said as they stood at the sink and peeled potatoes together.

In the midst of their good cheer, Vicky's grief and worry resurfaced for a moment like an unwelcome guest. Her grandma was gone and what if Bobby was gone too? The pensiveness must've shown on her face because Allison asked what was wrong.

"Oh, it's just that Christmas is coming," Vicky explained.

"Why don't you like Christmas?"

"I used to love it when Grandma was alive. It' just ain't the same since she died."

"Do you have any plans for Christmas?" Allison said, cutting a peeled potato into quarters on a small chopping board and throwing it into a large pot.

"I'll spend it with Bobby. He's the only family I got. What about you?"

"I have three Christmases—one with my mom, one with my dad, and one with Kent's family. And that's the only part about Christmas I don't like—the actual day. Too much tension. Too many sad memories of the way Christmases used to be before Mom and Dad split up. Of course, my parents despised each other long before they split up but they always managed to pull it together for Christmas. So it was nice. And then there's Kent's family."

"Too crazy?" Vicky asked pouring the tomato juice mix into a large pitcher.

"No, too sane," Allison said filling the pot of peeled potatoes with water. Vicky laughed hard. "See, I knew you'd understand."

"But you seem sane."

"Not like that I hope," Allison said. "See, theirs is a dull and uninteresting kind of sanity. Sanity can be a wonderful thing if it brings order and logic into your world—if it makes things make sense where they didn't before—if it makes everything clear and meaningful. That kind of sanity I'd welcome, but not their kind. Nobody can stick so much as a big toe out of the boundaries of their kind of sanity. Do you know what I mean?"

"Hell yeah! I been fighting against that kind of sanity all my life," Vicky said, shaking salt then pepper into the thick red mixture.

"Anyway, I love the part leading up to Christmas—the shopping, the carols, the cookie baking, the parties, the decorating. All of it reminds me of how it used to be. Then the actual day comes and I'm smacked back into reality," Allison said

"I don't mind Christmas day too much 'cause I know it's just about over with," Vicky sighed. "It's the build up I can't stand. Everybody talking about peace on earth, goodwill toward men, making room for Jesus—you know, all that happy horse shit. But yet everything goes on just the same—people hating each other, people killing each other, the rich getting richer, the poor getting poorer. Same ol' bullshit," Vicky said.

"Yeah, but you can dream during that time," Allison said. "What would it be like if all those things came true? And you can remember what all that magic was like when you were a kid and you believed all those things really were true. I see my nieces and nephews on Christmas day and I remember. And they make it all bearable. It's like magic."

"Yeah, the kids make it. If I had kids I think I might get that Christmas feeling back.

"Aw shoot! I forgot celery. You got any celery, Al?"

"Yes, I do," Allison said, opening the refrigerator and pulling out a bag from the crisper drawer.

"It ain't all slimy and brown now is it? I know how much you eat out, girl."

"No," Allison said in mock defensiveness as she held the bag of celery close to her chest. "I just bought it this week."

"I knew I could count on you to produce some rabbit food. Hand it over. A Bloody Mary just ain't a Bloody Mary without celery."

"Hey, you know what? We don't have to worry about a vegetable. We've got tomatoes and we've got celery with the Bloody Mary. No peas, no Brussles' sprouts."

* * * * * * *

So the two women found themselves together again at table, laughing, discussing, and eating. Vicky wondered how a left over half dried out ham, and an old sack of potatoes, most of which were starting to sprout, could taste so delicious. She guessed it was the company.

Allison had a half a Bloody Mary and said it was already going to her head. By that time Vicky had nearly finished off the remaining contents of the large pitcher. Despite the warmth and relaxation, Vicky still had not mentioned her real, dreamed, or imagined visitation from Chief Bobby. She felt too good–too happy. Bringing it up would just make her feel worried and sick again. She would wait until they rose from the table and moved back into the kitchen to do the dishes. In the meantime she would enjoy this blissful peaceful moment that came to her so freely and unexpectedly.

"Aaahhh," Allison sighed contentedly as she closed her eyes and leaned back in her chair, swirling the contents of her glass about. The contented look on her face matched Vicky's own inclination to loosen the belt around her tightening slacks. "Just the right combination of salty and spicy," Allison said raising her glass toward Vicky.

"Thank you darlin'"

"Now all we need is the sweet. It's Sunday–the perfect day for a sundae. I've got vanilla ice cream and chocolate syrup," Allison said moving uncomfortably out of her chair with a great groaning effort as she made her way back into the kitchen.

"Can I help you?" Vicky said standing up from her chair.

"No! Sit down," Allison ordered her from the kitchen.

"I ain't gonna argue with you today," Vicky said plopping back down into her seat.

"Of course the closest thing to heaven on earth is a little salty and crunchy mixed with a lot of chocolate," Allison said leaning against the door frame shaking a jar of peanuts. "Want a little whipped cream and peanuts on your sundae?"

"Naw, I'm a straight up sundae woman myself. Now if you wanna top off that fancy ass sundae of yours' just right, I got a jar of maraschino cherries back at my apartment. Want me to run downstairs and get it?"

"No, thanks. I'm not big on maraschino cherries."

Vicky was relieved. She didn't want to leave the comfort of Allison's place to revisit the ghostly loneliness that hung in the air of her own place. She looked around Allison's apartment which was usually fairly tidy and noticed the Christmas clutter–cardboard boxes of different shapes and sizes, strands of lights strung across the sofa, a wreath on an over stuffed chair, and a tall skinny tree in the corner all graced Allison's living room space as if they were supposed to be there, as if the clutter were strategically planned. If she could just stay at Allison's until she had to leave for work then she wouldn't have to face the chaotic clutter of her own place–clutter that had no object, purpose, or design.

"Would it be too tacky of me to invite myself to stay after dinner and help you decorate your tree?" Vicky called to Allison in the kitchen.

"Are you kidding? I'd love it." Allison said stepping into the dining area with a bowl of ice cream in either hand. "Kent's supposed to come over tonight and help me, but I know he won't be in the mood," she said with a sigh that she caught before it completely escaped. She quickly forced a smile in its place.

"I don't mean to impose," Vicky said pretending not to notice the stifled sigh and forced smile and all that it implied.

"It's all right, believe me. He's helping his parents put up their tree this afternoon. He will have had enough Christmas cheer for one day I'm sure."

Vicky watched the sparkle leave Allison's eyes as a dreary colorless shadow seemed to pass over her face. Allison looked down at her bowl of ice cream and the life returned once again to her visage. Vicky wanted to ask her about Kent and why she hadn't seen much of him around the apartments lately, and why Allison seemed so miserable whenever she spoke of him. Of course,

Vicky already knew the answer and she knew better than to ask the question. She thought how she and Allison were just alike really–alone and lonely.

"Please stay and help me decorate the tree," Allison said, placing the bowl of ice cream in front of Vicky. The thoughts traveled through Vicky's mind–Allison's tree and would she ever get around to putting one of her own up. She thought how sad it would be to take all her grandma's old Christmas ornaments out of the cardboard box marked "decorations" that was printed in her grandma's scrawling hand–the same cardboard box her grandma stored them in. The box was probably near as old as the decorations themselves. It even had water stains around the bottom corners where it got wet once when grandma's basement flooded. Then she thought why should she bother putting up a tree if Bobby never comes back? She wondered if she would spend Christmas alone.

"It's been fun having you here today," Allison said as her spoon dipped into the ice cream then returned quickly to her mouth where it lingered as if she were sucking on a lollipop. "Ever notice how we always eat when we get together?" The words were scarcely out of Allison's mouth when Vicky began to cry.

"I'll get the tissues," Allison said quickly scooting her chair back. "You don't have to talk about it if you don't want to," Allison said appearing at Vicky's side with a hand on her shoulder and box of tissues in her face.

"I gotta talk about it. That's why I came here."

"I'm listening."

"Go back to your seat and finish your ice cream. And quit looking at me like an undertaker," Vicky protested.

"Who can refuse an order like that?"

Vicky waited until Allison was settled in her seat, then with one great heaving sigh she began. "It's Bobby. I'm worried. I think he might be missing."

"Missing?"

"Yeah, he left for Florida over a week ago and I ain't heard from him since."

"What's he doing in Florida?"

"He's there on business. He travels a lot with his work."

"What business is he in?"

"He's–uh–self-employed. It's kinda hard to explain. But, anyhow, it's just not like him. I should've heard from him by now."

"Maybe he's just busy."

"No. He always checks in with me. You know Bobby and me. I'm his home base. Generally, I'd a heard from him at least three or four times by now. It's just plain weird. Something's wrong. I just know it." The dwindling effects of the Bloody Mary made Vicky feel particularly blue and gloomy. She wiped her nose and eyes and sat up straight clearing all the tears back down her throat. Only two things would make her feel better–to cry some more or drink some more. Of course she knew if she drank some more she most certainly would cry some more, but at least she wouldn't feel so weak and self conscious about the crying if she were drunk.

"You wouldn't by any chance have some brandy and crème de cacao, would you?" Vicky said stirring the melting ice cream around in her bowl. "I could mix it with some ice cream and make a Brandy Alexander."

"Sorry," Allison said shaking her head. "It really is too bad too, 'cause it sounds like my kind of drink."

"How about Kahlua and rum? I could make some Hummers."

"Actually I do have a bottle of Kahlua. No rum though. Sorry."

"It's okay. You get your Kahlua, I'll get my vodka, we'll mix it with this ice cream and make some White Russians. Gotta refresh my buzz a little if I'm gonna get through this story."

Vicky got up and began mixing, measuring, pouring, and stirring. She was on her feet. She was comfortable in this role. She was doing what she did best. So Vicky mixed drinks and Allison quickly scraped dishes and stuck them in the dishwasher. Vicky's drinks for herself were darker in color than Allison's–mostly Kahlua and vodka with just a teaspoon of ice cream to give them flavor. "More like a Brown Russian," Vicky said, handing the lighter colored drink to Allison. Only then did she feel together enough to continue her bizarre tale about Bobby's visitation.

"I saw him last night."

"Saw who?"

"Chief Bobby," Vicky said.

"Wait a minute, wait a minute. I thought you said he was missing–that you hadn't talked to him since he left for Florida."

"That's right."

"Then how could you have seen him last night?"

"I keep asking myself the same question."

"What are you saying, Vicky?"

"I'm saying I woke up in the middle of the night and he was standing in my room, by my bed, trying to tell me something, but I don't remember what."

"Sounds like you dreamt it."

"I don't think so."

"What makes you so sure?"

"Well, I ain't sure, but I don't think it was a dream 'cause it was too real. You know, not all fuzzy and weird-like, but like it was really happening. I know, you're thinking maybe I don't know the difference between a dream and real life. Maybe I ain't right in the head. That's what you're thinking."

"I didn't say a thing."

"This is me, man–Vicky Dooley. I may be ignorant, I may be wild as a March hare, but I ain't fuckin' crazy. And no–I wasn't under the influence of any hallucinogenic drugs either. At least not at the time."

"I believe you. It's just that some dreams can seem pretty real."

"Yeah, I guess so."

"Then there's always the possibility that it really was him. Could he have gotten into your apartment? Does he have a key?"

"Yeah, he does. But it just ain't like him to do something like that. It just ain't like him to show up in the middle of the night, tell me something while I'm half awake, then leave. Besides, if he was back from Florida, I'd know about it."

"Either you dreamt it or he really was there. There aren't any other possibilities. Are there?"

"Yes, actually there is one more possibility."

"What?"

"He's dead and his ghost came to visit me."

After a long pause where neither one of them knew what to say, Allison asked, "Don't you think if he were dead you would have heard something? You are, after all, his next of kin. Aren't you?"

Vicky only nodded as she sniffled into her tissues and tried to regain her composure.

"What if no one knows he's dead?" Vicky finally said, looking up through blurred eyes and dampened eyelashes.

"Oh, c'mon Vicky, someone would've found him."

"Like who?"

"I don't know – a hotel maid, a business partner, someone for crying out loud. It's not like he's off in the Himalayas. He's in Florida on business. Someone would've noticed he's missing and started asking questions. He probably just decided to play hookie and take a few days off."

"He wouldn't do that, not without telling me."

"Look, you have to have a body before you can declare someone dead. I learned that much from Perry Mason."

"Not if there ain't no body to be found. Not if he got fed to the gators."

"Alright, now you are talking crazy."

"Bobby has enemies. If somebody wanted to kill him and make sure his remains ain't ever found, they can do it. They never found Jimmy Hoffa's body and they never will."

"Vicky?" Allison sat up straight on the couch.
"Yeah."
"Never mind."

Vicky could tell by Allison's tone what kind of question she intended to ask. She intended to ask if Bobby was on the wrong side of the law, but she stopped herself because she already knew the answer. Vicky thought for a moment about divulging everything to Allison. It was a crazy thought and she dismissed it immediately. That shred of distrust and paranoia, that loyalty towards the others would never allow her to do such a thing. And so they looked at each other, both knowing what the other was thinking though they couldn't allow the conversation to go any further down its current path.

"You need to file a missing person report," Allison said suddenly.

"But that would involve the police." The unchecked words came out of Vicky's mouth before she had a chance to stop them.

"So? Look, if you want to find him you've got to involve the police." Allison paused. "Despite what the consequences might be for Bobby," She said looking Vicky straight in the eye.

Maybe he just decided to chuck it all and go to Oklahoma, she thought with some relief. *That's it! That must be it. But he wouldn't do that. He promised he'd be back for Christmas,* Vicky reminded herself once again. It had to be his ghost. He had returned from his swampy grave in Florida to warn her. He didn't want it to end for her the way it did for him.

"It was strange, Al, but I think he was trying to warn me about something."

"What about?" Allison's question came through like static on an AM radio, vying with all the other voices in her head.

"Look, it ain't like it's no big secret or nothing, but Bobby's been in trouble before. He warned me not to make the same mistakes he has. Then he told me goodbye, like it was goodbye forever." Vicky started sobbing again. She felt claustrophobic and thought she might panic again if she couldn't get up and move around.

"I'll make us some more drinks," Vicky said picking up the pitcher as she quickly rose from her chair. Vicky poured the remaining contents of the pitcher into Allison's glass then her own. "Let's decorate the tree, Al, after I refresh our drinks."

"I'll start with the lights," Allison said carefully gathering the strand of Christmas lights off the back of the sofa.

Once back in the kitchen, Vicky drank down her White Russian from the small highball glass in three large gulps. She opened the bottle of vodka and checked over her shoulder to make sure Allison wasn't standing behind her. She poured her highball glass full of straight vodka and drank it down quickly. She poured another glass and drank it down even faster then made another batch of White Russians. The warmth that finally hit her brain and bounced all up and down her was as welcome as the rays of the early summer sun on her face. She told herself that everything would be all right, that Bobby would be back for Christmas and that the whole thing was just a very vivid dream. She believed it–for the moment.

The White Russians became darker and darker as the afternoon wore on, and as the bottles of Kahlua and vodka got closer and closer to the bottom, the tree became fuller and fuller, and the Christmas sing along more and more absurd. Allison pulled out all her old Christmas records–everything from the dogs barking along to Jingle Bells to Pavorotti singing O Holy Night. The two women were sometimes boisterous, sometimes maudlin–the mood of the music always exaggerated by the alcohol.

"This one always gets to me," Vicky said throwing the last little bit of tinsel onto one of the upper branches. Then sitting cross legged on the floor, Vicky began to sing along with The Carpenter's rendition of "I'll be Home for Christmas".

"I'm an old rocker from way back when so I'm kinda ashamed to admit this, but I've always loved The Carpenters." Vicky said.

"Oh, me too! That deep rich alto voice of Karen Carpenter just speaks to me."

"You said a mouthful there, girl. Some of these new fangled female pop singers can't sing their way out of a wet paper sack. They all sound alike – got them damned wispy, breathy, wimpy-ass voices. Sound like little girls with a budding case of laryngitis. But not Karen. She sang like a real woman. Poor Karen.

"I know. It's so sad."

"Why do all the great ones have to die?"

"We're getting awfully morose around her. We're gonna have to put the barking dogs back on."

"Morose." Vicky pulled her spiral notebook out of her pocket. M-O-R-O-S-E."

"It means…"

"Don't tell me."

"Oh right. I forgot. You know, it's a good thing we're finished with this tree because I'm feeling a little tipsy," Allison said lying on the floor.

"All but the top," Vicky said. "You've gotta put an angel or a star up there."

"I don't have any Christmas tree toppers."

"Well, we gotta make one."

"What for? Look at the tree. It's too tall." Vicky's eyes roamed up the

Odd Numbers

sparse branches of evergreen all the way to the top where the tip was scrunched against the ceiling at a slight right angle. "Is that tree rotating or have I just had too many White Russians?" Allison asked.

"They quit being White Russians a while back. For the past hour you've been drinking Black Russians: straight vodka and Kahlua."

"Black Russians, White Russians, whatever," Allison said sitting up and grabbing her highball glass off the coffee table. "Here's to the Cold War." Allison raised her glass toward Vicky.

"Cheers."

So Allison and Vicky cut out a cardboard star and wrapped it in aluminum foil. Both of them giggled like pre-pubescent girls as Allison climbed up the step ladder to place the asymmetrical star atop the asymmetrical tree.

"Allison." A male voice suddenly startled them as they turned to see Kent who had let himself in the apartment, unbeknownst to them. His presence startled Allison so much, in fact, that she turned and fell off the step ladder landing on the floor with a loud crash.

"Shit!" Vicky said hurrying to Allison's side. Kent slowly made his way over to Allison too, but he seemed more perturbed than concerned.

"Are you okay?" Vicky asked. Allison looked up at Vicky who had a hold of her arm. They exploded in laughter.

"I'm fine. Just help me up," she said straining to get to her feet. Kent finally took a hold of Allison's other arm and together they pulled her to her feet.

"From the looks of things I'd say you're more than just fine. I'd say you're feeling no pain at all," Kent said. It was then that Vicky noticed how angry he was. His feigned smile failed to smooth out the stern fixed lines etched in his jaw and around his brow. His controlled tone of voice failed to cancel out the sarcasm that snuck through with every syllable. It was the look and sound of the very angry who try very hard not to look or sound very angry.

"Sorry love," Allison said throwing her arms around Kent and giving him a noisy wet kiss on the cheek. "Vicky and I've been sharing a little Christmas cheer. You remember Vicky–my neighbor. She tends bar at the River Inn?"

"Hi, Vicky," he grunted. "I see you two have been busy," he said looking at the tree.

"Yeah, we got you off the hook."

"Off the hook? What do you mean?" Kent asked.

"I just figured you wouldn't be in the mood after helping your parents decorate their tree."

"Maybe I wanted to help you decorate it."

"And maybe pigs are flying outside my window too. You never want to do anything half-way fun or frivolous anymore–at least not with me."

"Not now Allison," he said, the feigned smile finally leaving his face.

Vicky almost felt sorry for Kent in that moment. Kent wasn't a bad guy–just the wrong guy, and that was enough to make a bad guy out of a nice guy. Vicky could tell by the diminishing light that it was getting close to evening.

"What time's it getting to be anyway?" she asked. Kent and Allison both looked at their watches.

"Four twenty," Kent said.

"Time to drag my sorry self outta here. I gotta be at work at five," Vicky said, relieved that she'd managed to stay out of her haunted apartment all day.

Allison walked Vicky to the door where they spoke their parting words in a whisper so Kent wouldn't hear. Allison urged Vicky not to worry about Bobby anymore, but to file a missing person report as soon as possible and leave the matter in the authorities' hands. Vicky advised Allison not to go so hard on Kent. When Allison asked why, she said because he loves you. They said their goodbyes, each of them knowing they would not take the other's advice.

Chapter 15

Christmas Eve night Vicky was jolted awake by the sound of a gunshot, so close it sounded like it was being fired from inside her room. She jumped up and flipped the bedside light on before she had a chance to think whether or not that was the right thing to do. She saw nothing, just her bedroom with everything in its usual place. She heard nothing but the pounding of her own heart. She checked the drawer of her nightstand. Her handgun was there, cool to the touch and undisturbed.

She grabbed her flashlight off the bedside table and in one quick continuous movement rolled off the bed and onto the floor, flipped her grandma's quilt up and shined the flashlight under the bed. Nothing. Next she checked the closet. Wire hangers scraped noisily against the metal pole as Vicky pushed clothes back and shined the flashlight up and down hidden corners, all the while hollering threats at the unseen intruder. Nothing. She ran to the door, opened it stuck her head out in the hallway. Still nothing. She didn't see or hear anything peculiar. She felt a peculiarity, however, and it was all around her. She turned all the lights on hoping to dispel the fear that was causing her heart to beat up in her throat and her mouth to go dry.

"Bobby?" Vicky gasped, turning around suddenly as if someone was right behind her tapping her on the shoulder. "Is that you, Bobby? Is that you?" She inquired again and again of the invisible presence that hung in her apartment like thick stagnant air. "Were you trying to tell me you got shot? Is that it?" She heard no reply, nothing but the church bells down the street chime twelve times, followed by a long and loud pealing chorus, bidding worshipers to come to the midnight service.

Vicky had heard about the strange Catholic ritual of going to church in the middle of the night on Christmas. She read the sign on the church's marquis–something about "Oh, come let us adore Him. Join us this Christmas." Then it listed the Christmas Mass schedule, beginning with Midnight Mass. She wondered what it was like. She wondered if she should go and debated the question aloud while she paced back and forth in her living room between her hallway and the front door. Vicky did her best problem solving on her feet while pacing and talking to herself.

"I gotta get outta here! I gotta go somewhere. Where else am I gonna go at midnight on Christmas morning? Hell, grandma would think I'd done turned pagan going to a Catholic church. Then again, she might be happy to see me step foot inside any church. Besides, I think they're Christian. Sorta. Shit, I'm going. Better than hanging around the haunted castle," she said aloud to herself as she moved quickly down the hallway that led to her bedroom, grabbed a pair of jeans off the floor, pulled them on, and tucked her night shirt into them. She pulled a big sweater out of her dresser drawer and quickly put it on over the night shirt, the electricity from it causing strands of red curly hair to stand straight out. She opened another drawer and retrieved a pair of thick gray socks which she put on one foot at a time while hopping to the bathroom. Once in the bathroom she brushed her teeth, splashed her face, and wiped the remnants of the day's make up off from under her eyes. "I look like shit," she said looking in the mirror. "Who cares? Ain't nobody gonna know me there. Oh, yeah! Bet you see some of your customers. You know how them Catholics are. I believe they drink even more than the Baptists. I'll just sit in the back and keep my head down."

Vicky made two more stops before leaving–one to her corner kitchen cabinet to take a couple swigs off a pint of Jim Beam she'd opened an hour or so ago, and another to the front hall closet. She wrapped the red knit scarf her grandma had made for her years ago around her head and neck, put on her brown suede winter coat with the big fake lamb's wool collar which she pushed up around her ears, and pulled on an old pair of hiking boots she got back in high school. Her grandma thought they looked like Frankenstein monster's shoes.

She looked around the apartment one last time and sighed. She hadn't put a tree up. If she'd heard from Bobby she would have. Maybe the greenery, lights, and smell of pine would have cheered her heart. She regretted not putting one up. She turned and closed the door behind her.

Vicky walked to the church through slush and ice and melting snow, muttering all the while how odd it was that she was leaving her apartment in the middle of the night to go to church. She felt she was doing the right thing. The night air lifted her spirits a little. She involuntarily smiled upon entering the church as if she'd stepped from a black and white world into one of color and warmth and light. "Anyways, I'm outta that apartment," she said pulling the scarf off from around her neck as she stood in the warm vestibule of the church staring at an enormous tree.

"May I help you?" A middle aged man in a red coat with a Santa tie approached Vicky from the side. She saw from the puzzled expression on his face that he must've heard her talking to herself.

"Oh, sorry, I was just noticing your tree. Who are all them gifts for?" Vicky asked pointing to the brightly arrayed packages under the tree.

"The poor."

"Oh!"

"There're no seats left but there is standing room in the back," he whispered leading her into the church. Vicky realized that this must've been the man's job, and she thanked him, and explained to him that she was used to being on her feet and was actually more comfortable that way.

The choir was singing *Gloria in excelsis Deo*, and the priest was walking back and forth up front swinging around a large silver pot on a chain with smoke pouring out.

"What's that smoke?" Vicky asked the man in the red coat standing next to her by the door.

"It's incense."

"I didn't think they used that for church," she said with a chuckle, her only experience of incense had been to cover up the smell of marijuana. She looked around the church. It was so different from the little country church her grandmother took her to–larger and much more modern in architectural style. Had it not been for the Christmas decorations it would've seemed almost stark which surprised her for a Catholic church. She'd always heard Catholics had a lot of extras–statues and the like. Then in the right hand corner up front she spied the statues. It was a nativity scene, complete with a large stable and star on top, shepherds, St. Joseph, Mother Mary, and of course baby Jesus in the manger. She smiled at the scene and began to lose herself in the service.

Maybe it was the music or the sweet smell of the incense that made her wonder about the incarnate god come down to earth, and of course she had to admit to herself as the tears welled up in her throat and her eyes that she did still believe. "Help me, sweet Jesus," she muttered aloud. She looked up. There was one similarity between this church and her grandma's old country church. It was the ceiling, arching way up and up to heaven trying desperately to reach God. She was too grown up to do what she did as a kid–lay down on the floor and just stare up at that ceiling, so she knelt down instead, right there on the floor in the back of the church, and stared up until her neck ached and the tears blurred her vision. She buried her face in the red scarf and wept. When she left church it was snowing.

Vicky stayed in her apartment all Christmas day, even though she didn't have to. Allison had invited her to her mother's house for Christmas, and Eddie invited her to hang out with some of the biker boys at his place and party. She declined both invitations because this was the last twenty-four hours she had to hope for. Maybe Bobby would show up at her door, maybe he would call her on the phone. She had to keep vigil though it was painful to stay in that haunted apartment. Maybe he was waiting until Christmas day to reach her. Why? Who knows, but maybe he had some reason. If she hadn't heard from him by Christmas night then she'd know he was dead.

She told herself that maybe the sound of the gunshot and the eerie presence that filled the apartment had nothing to do with Bobby. Maybe it was an evil spirit from the bowels of hell sent to deceive her, to torture her, and frighten her, but she wasn't sure if she really believed that sort of thing. Her grandma used to cast out demons in the name of Jesus. Vicky wondered if she should try it but then decided it might be blasphemous for the unbaptized to attempt such a thing.

Vicky knew the only way to cope with staying in that apartment all day was to achieve some state of oblivion. So she curled up on the couch under her grandma's afghan with her best buddy, Jack Daniels, close by her side, a pack of Marlboros, her brown glass ashtray, and the remote control. She flipped the channels on her TV back and forth until she'd seen "A Christmas Carol" and "It's A Wonderful Life" lap themselves for about the third time. By about eight o'clock she knew Bobby was not coming. She looked out her window into the parking lot but no sign of Allison's car. She had to get out of that apartment. She threw on her coat and scarf, stuck in her pocket the pack of Marlboros along with her purple Bic lighter which was running low on fluid, and went outside to wait on the stoop of the front porch for Allison to return from all her family festivities.

When Allison finally arrived some fifteen or twenty minutes later, Vicky was hopping up and down trying to stay warm, but she wasn't going back inside that building unless another human being was with her.

Allison called out to Vicky as she approached the building. "Thank God you're here. I need a drink from someone who really knows how to fix one."

"And I need to fix a drink for someone who really needs it," Vicky called back.

"That would be me. Merry Christmas."

"Merry Christmas to you. Thank God it's almost over." The two women embraced. "C'mon let's get inside. I'm freezing my ass off," Vicky said through chattering teeth.

"So what are you doing standing out here on such a cold night anyway?"

"Waiting for you. I been stuck in that apartment all day. I was beginning to feel like a caged lion." So together they entered Camelot building 3300 and Vicky let out an involuntary sigh at the warmth.

"I told you that you should have come with me today."

"I couldn't leave."

"Did you hear from Bobby?"

"No." Vicky looked up slowly at the silent Allison who seemed to be trying to find the right words to say.

"So you're coming to my place, okay? Sounds like you could use a little change of scenery," Allison finally said.

"I was going to follow you whether you invited me or not. There's something wrong with my apartment."

"What!?"

"I'll explain later. Oh, shit! I forgot something. Wait here," Vicky said turning around halfway up the stairs to Allison's apartment. "I hate going back in there but I gotta. Wait for me."

Allison agreed to wait as Vicky ran back to her apartment, all the way back to her bedroom closet, and pulled a green and gold wrapped package with a gold bow out of a plastic department store bag. She stopped at her corner kitchen cabinet, grabbed a bottle of Irish whiskey, turned, opened the refrigerator, grabbed a can of whipped cream, and hurried out of the apartment, slamming the door behind her.

"This is for you," Vicky said handing the package to Allison as she met her halfway up the stairs in one giant bound.

"Vicky," Allison said as if she was scolding her.

"And *this* is for you too," Vicky said presenting the bottle of Irish whiskey. "You provide the coffee. I'll provide the alcohol."

"I love it," Allison said as Vicky charged up the stairs. "So what's wrong with your apartment?" "I'll tell you just as soon as we get inside your place," Vicky said in a whisper.

Vicky made sure Allison had closed the door completely before she told her. "I think Bobby's ghost is haunting my place."

"Not again."

"No, now wait a minute. Hear me out. I went home early from work last night, so I went to bed about ten. Around eleven thirty or so someone fired a gun off in my room. Woke me up, of course, and scared me shitless. This was no dream, Allison. I heard it. I looked all around my apartment but didn't see nothing suspicious. But, there was someone there with me, as real as you're standing here now. I couldn't see or hear no one, but I know someone was there."

"And?"

"I think it was Bobby trying to tell me he got shot."

Allison suddenly gasped, her eyes grew wide, and her face blanched.

"What?" Vicky said.

"It was Christmas eve a year ago that the previous tenant shot himself. I just remembered."

"Shit!" Vicky said dropping into a chair.

"Do you still feel like there's someone in your apartment?"

"I felt it all last night and today real strong, but as evening wore on I felt it less and less, like he was leaving. I thought maybe it was Bobby's spirit come to spend Christmas day with me like he said he'd do. But maybe it was someone else."

The mood became silent and somber as the space between the two women filled with a paralyzed sort of terror, like Ebenezer Scrooge afraid to pull back the bed curtain.

"Did you ever find out why he killed himself?" Vicky said finally.

"I heard Sally talking about it not long ago. She said it was drugs."

"Oh," Vicky said looking down, afraid that Allison could read her thoughts. Bobby came back to warn her once and now the previous tenant had returned from the grave to warn her also. But she wasn't alone now and she wasn't in her apartment. She was with a friend and she had a bottle of Irish whiskey and drinks to make. Soon coffee would be brewing and Karen Carpenter would be crooning Christmas carols and she would temporarily forget her troubles. And temporary forgetfulness was better than nothing.

Vicky made Irish Coffee that night and she and Allison exchanged gifts. Allison gave Vicky a new dictionary, noticing that the binding on her old one was coming unstitched and pages were falling out. Vicky gave Allison a gold angel for the top of her Christmas tree. Vicky slept on Allison's couch, and when she returned to her apartment the following morning the presence was gone. But like the ghosts of Christmas past, present, and yet to come, the warning lived on, causing an anxious paranoia to descend on Vicky's soul in the coming days just before the arrival of the New Year.

Every time the phone rang she feared it was the police calling to inform her that they had found Bobby's body and wanted her to come identify him, and, of course, also wanted to question her about his business dealings. She took different routes to work every day, continually looking in her rear view mirror, afraid someone was following her.

Her boss noticed the change in her and approached her about it one relatively quiet afternoon between Christmas and New Years. She was cleaning up a mess she made behind the bar at the time.

"You been spilling more lately, Vick. Breaking glasses too."

"So take it outta my paycheck," she said looking up at him from the floor where she was wiping up.

"I'm not worried about that, Vick. I am worried about you though."

"Yeah, sure," she said going right on with her cleaning, not even bothering to look up this time.

"You've even been edgy with the customers lately. That's not like you. What's going on?"

"I just gotta lot on my mind. It's personal."

"Well, whatever this personal matter is it's interfering with your job. Maybe you need some time off to work it out."

"I don't need no time off." She finally rose to her feet.

"You got some time coming. You haven't taken any vacation since you started."

"Maybe I'm saving those vacation days for something big."

"Like what?"

"I don't know yet," she said tossing the dishrag back and forth.

"You're a nervous wreck. Take a few days off."

"I don't need a few days off. I just need for you to quit being a mother hen."

"Take some vacation days, Vicky."

"Are you crazy? We got New Years coming up."

"Don't worry. I'll see to it we're covered. If I get in a pinch, I'll call you."

"For how long?"

"Just until after the New Year. Take a few days off and come back after the New Year. And bring back the old Vicky."

It was Saturday, New Years Eve. Vicky was so unaccustomed to being off work on a Saturday, particularly New Years Eve that she scarcely knew what to do with herself. She drove around that morning, visited some of the biker boys, drove around some more, thought about it, talked it over with herself, and finally made a decision. She went home and called Eddie.

"Eddie, I've made a decision. Get over here fast, but come by car, don't ride your Harley. I got something to give you." After she hung up she paced back and forth in her usual hallway spot and rehearsed what she would say when he arrived. This nagging agitation would not allow her to sit still even for a moment.

This was more than the usual nervousness Vicky was familiar with. This was a fear as deep as the fear of death itself mixed with dread and guilt. In a way she was glad to be inside and away from people. She felt certain that the guilt showed on her face. Indeed her boss had been right when he said this was not like her. The only thing that helped was alcohol.

She poured herself a shot of whiskey, then another. Finally the knock on the door came. Vicky opened the still bolted door a crack to make sure it was Eddie. She let the fat little biker in and asked him to stop and wait at the door. She checked out the patio window carefully and closed the drapes. "Did anyone see you come in?"

"Shit, I don't know. Why? You in some kinda trouble, Vick?"

"Let's hope not."

"You heard from Bobby?"

"Not a word," she said trying to light a cigarette with her purple Bic lighter. It sparked again and again but never fired. Her hands trembled with fear and frustration. "Fuck it!" she said throwing the lighter across the room.

"Calm down, girl," Eddie said, swiftly and casually producing a book of matches out of his hip pocket. "Look at you. You're shaking," he said lighting Vicky's cigarette. "You been nervous as a jack rabbit ever since Bobby disappeared. Hell, we're all worried, but this ain't no time to lose your head. You gotta stay cool. You gotta lay low."

"I'm gonna do better than lay low, Eddie. I'm gonna lay off."

"Lay off? What are you saying?"

"I'm saying I want out. Outta the business. That's why I asked you to come over." Vicky picked up a suitcase that sat on the floor between her sofa and her rocking chair. She handed it to Eddie. "Here, this is for you."

"You sending me on vacation, Vick?" The fat little biker said with a hoarse chuckle.

"The contents of that bag could send you on one hell of a nice vacation, Eddie. If that's what you want. I don't no more. I just wanna go home."

"You are home, ain't you? Shit, you ain't making no sense, girl."

"Look inside."

Eddie knelt on one knee, laid the suitcase flat on the floor, and unzipped it all the way around. "Towels?" He said looking up. "Whatcha got underneath the towels?"

"Look," Vicky said exhaling smoke out her nostrils. She watched him remove the neatly folded towels and watched his eyes grow wide with surprise. "Merry Christmas–a little late."

"Goddamn!"

"Don't take the Lord's name in vain."

"How much dope you got in here?" he said lifting a plastic bag containing miniscule purple pills. Vicky shrugged her shoulders trying to look as nonchalant as she could. "Dollars and cents worth? How much Vick?"

"Don't know. Don't care. Do what you want with it. Just get it outta here."

"How much of a cut you want?"

"None. Profit's a hundred percent yours. It's blood money as far as I'm concerned. It's what killed Bobby. I don't want no part of it no more. I would've flushed it all down the toilet, but how you gonna explain that much dope suddenly vanishing without a trace. Bobby's customers might start asking questions. Start thinking I turned narc or something if all at once I come up empty handed. This way I can just say I'm taking a break on account of Bobby disappearing and all. Wanna make sure the heat's entirely off before I make any false moves. You're taking over for me for a while. Time will pass and folks will forget I was ever a part of this business."

Eddie gave her one last look then zipped up the suitcase and rose to his feet. "You sure about this, Vick?"

"Yeah, I'm sure. And by the way—you can keep the suitcase. It belonged to Bobby."

Vicky walked Eddie to the door and looked carefully to the right then to the left down the hallway before addressing him. "Spread the word, Eddie. Spread the word. The heat's on me big time. Make sure you tell them. My porch light ain't gonna be on no more. Least not 'til things die down. Whatever you do, don't let on I'm out for good," she whispered. "Drive careful now, Eddie. This is one time in your life I'm begging you not to speed. You don't wanna get pulled over with that in your trunk," she said pointing to the suitcase, her voice disappearing into a throated whisper.

She dismissed Eddie with a forced smile and a playful smack to the upper arm then she closed the door ever so quietly behind him, slowly turning the knob until it latched, not wanting to make a noise, as if she feared waking someone. She tiptoed over to the patio window, still afraid of making too much noise and peeked out the drapes just long enough to watch Eddie pull out of the parking lot.

Vicky thought she would feel a sense of relief after unloading herself of such a heavy load, but instead she was still so afraid. She poured another shot of whiskey and found herself back at the worn pathway in the hall, pacing and talking to herself.

"The money, the money. What am I gonna do with the money?" She said stopping suddenly and smacking herself on the side of the head as if this would somehow set her brain to moving in the right direction. She made her way quickly down the hall and was in the back corner of her bedroom closet before she had time to think about it, back where she used to keep Whisker's pet taxi. Feeling around in the darkness behind boxes and into the shadows she retrieved the old dusty cracked cowboy boot without a mate. The boots had been Bobby's. He had to get rid of the mate because Vicky had thrown up in it so of course, it was never the same after that.

"You left them right by the bathroom door, Bobby. I didn't quite make it," Vicky said remembering with a shake of her head and a nasally noise that was a sort of half laugh, half cry. "You was so mad at me, Bobby. For an injun you sure thought highly of shoes. Couldn't run without them like me. Remember, Bobby. So you left me the mate." She wiped some of the dust off the boot with a sweater sleeve and tried to stave off thoughts that Bobby had once walked around in these boots, and not so long ago at that.

She reached deep inside the boot until her arm was nearly immersed up to the elbow, then turning the boot upside down, the palm of her free hand pounding against the side of the boot then the bottom just beneath the pointed toe–her other hand with grasping fingers worked quickly to loosen the contents. The folded and crumpled bills began to fall out on the floor. At last when she was satisfied that all the money was out she began counting, smoothing out one bill at a time as she did so.

"Six-thousand seven-hundred and forty dollars," Vicky said unfolding the last bill. "What am I gonna do with it? What am I gonna do with it? I can't keep it. It's blood money. I just can't keep it." She put the money back in the boot, shoved the boot back into the darkened corner making sure it was concealed, closed the closet door tightly, and went back to her pacing spot. "What am I gonna do? What am I gonna do?" She felt condemned to this path in the hallway until she got some kind of answer. All she heard were the church bells from down the street. "What time is it I wonder?" Vicky asked moving to the patio door to get a better listen. She stuck her ear against the cold glass. The chimes struck three. "Three o'clock. Three o'clock on a Saturday afternoon. New Year's Eve, no fucking less, and I ain't working. I gotta get outta this apartment before I go completely stark raving fucking nuts."

Vicky's coat was on and she was out breathing the cold winter air before she even had time to think about it. The cold was a relief to her. It reminded her she was alive as she saw the visible evidence of her breath upon exhaling. It woke her up and snapped her out of the dream world which had become such a nightmare of late. She found her feet treading the same path she had tread so early Christmas morning. She didn't know where else to go. She didn't know what else to do except follow the sound of the bells.

Chapter 16

Vicky stepped into the warmth of the church vestibule and found herself engulfed in a silence so complete and disturbing–so different from her experience at Midnight Mass. It was a silence that evoked only a whisper, even from the likes of Vicky who usually spoke loudly to everyone–even herself. She felt a little better, as if somehow she could claim sanctuary here.

"Here is the church. Here is the steeple. Open the door and where are the people?" Vicky mouthed the words of the children's rhyme in a low whisper. She walked past the rows of candles and the large holy water font and all those things which seemed so foreign to her. She pulled the heavy wooden door that led into the main part of the church. The silence and emptiness was even more pervasive in the worship space and it filled her with such an immediate awe that she involuntarily gasped.

The only light in the darkened space came from the late afternoon sun sending shafts of light through the stain glass windows. She sat down in one of the pews and unzipped her coat. "Now what do I do?" she said barely loud enough to hear herself. "Shit, I don't even know why I came here. It's New Year's Eve. I should be out partying." She thought for a moment about throwing her coat back on and bolting for the door. She felt so restless, so anxious. She stood up, put her coat on, and zipped it. A moment later she sat down again.

It was the silence, Vicky realized with a smile. That's what made her uncomfortable and made her want to leave. It was also the silence that wouldn't let her go. It was never silent at her place. The stereo or TV were always on. And, of course, it was never silent at work. She often longed for the quiet, but now that she had it she found it hard to take, like some awful tasting medicine–the kid in her squirmed away but the grown up in her knew she had to swallow it for her own good. She thought about it long and hard. She really didn't want to be at a party. She really didn't know where she wanted to be, but she thought maybe she was where she was supposed to be. She had to get some answers, and after all, didn't people go to church to get answers? It's what her grandma always said would answer her heart's riddle though she never really believed her.

Vicky unzipped her coat, and as she did she heard the heavy wooden door behind her open. She turned around to see a short, well dressed man in his late fifties enter the church. He settled in a pew on the other side of church and Vicky watched as he pulled a kneeling bench down, knelt upon it, and made the sign of the cross. Vicky didn't want to appear suspicious so she decided to do what he did. When she pulled the kneeler down it landed with a loud thud, which caused the man to glance over at her. She knelt down quickly. "There must be some trick to these kneeling things," she whispered into her cupped hands which were folded in front of her face just like the man's.

Vicky continued to observe the man. After a few minutes he got up, walked to the back of church and disappeared into a room, more like a closet door with a green light above it. The green light switched to red after a few seconds. She thought of Alice in Wonderland and the white rabbit disappearing into the rabbit hole.

She was puzzling over all this when, again, she heard the door from the vestibule into the central part of the church open behind her. Soon a plump, white-haired, grandmotherly looking lady made her way up the center aisle in a too tight vinyl coat that made noise with every movement she made. She knelt on one knee before entering a pew a few rows up from her. Vicky watched as she did the same thing as the man–kneeling, crossing herself, and praying. At least Vicky guessed she was praying.

Vicky heard another door open only this time it was not the heavy wooden door leading in from the vestibule. It was a much lighter door with somewhat of a squeak. Vicky looked around. It was the man exiting the little closet like door with the light above it. The light above the door was now green again. The man returned to the same area where he first knelt. He genuflected and knelt once more. Then the grandmotherly lady in the noisy vinyl coat made her way back to the broom closet. Vicky watched curiously as the green light, once again, turned to red moments after the woman entered the door.

"Well, I'll be a fucken' monkey's uncle," she whispered into her cupped hands, now far too curious to think about leaving. Vicky watched the door. She'd become adept at watching out of the corners of her eyes without moving her head much. It came from tending bar. She watched for customers coming up to the bar from all sides and kept mental tabs at how long they'd been waiting. It came from the drug business–always checking, always watching, always making sure you knew who was coming up from the sides and the back.

Soon the grandmother in the vinyl coat came out the door and carefully closed it so it barely squeaked this time. The light switched back to green. The woman made her trek back to her area of the church where she knelt down and prayed. Vicky felt a little more comfortable with the quiet now, and she soon realized that the fifteen minutes or so she'd been sitting in church just observing that something had happened to her. She wasn't so afraid anymore.

In fact, her old devil-may-care attitude was resurging. She looked back at the little door. "I guess there's only one way to find out," she whispered to herself.

Vicky got up and walked to the back of church, back to the little door with the strange little stop and go light above. There was a name on the door–Father Mudd. Vicky smiled, took a deep breath, and opened the door.

She walked into a darkened vestibule with a worn kneeler in front of a partition. She could hear the sound of someone moving around behind the partition. She heard him clear his throat and saw a black loafer sticking out. She wondered if she was supposed to kneel on the kneeler or what.

"Hello in there," she called.

"Yes," the man's voice called back.

"I'm not sure just what I'm supposed to do."

"Do you wish to go to confession privately or face to face?"

Confession. She'd heard the term before. She knew it was another strange Catholic ritual, like going to church in the middle of the night on Christmas Eve. Her grandma had a Catholic neighbor, a widow lady about the same age as her grandma by the name of Mabel Murphy. Grandma liked Mabel, they were friends of sorts, but she always worried about her–worried Mabel wasn't saved on account of her being a Catholic and all. "Them Catholics are given to idolatry," grandma would say. "They got some strange beliefs–believe they got to go confess their sins to a priest before they can be forgiven." She prayed every day that Mabel would be saved and she never missed an opportunity to witness to her too, though her efforts became fewer and further between when Mabel began to avoid her. Even still, this never stopped grandma from praying and worrying about Mabel.

So this is how Catholics do it, Vicky thought. They go to a little closet in the back of church and confess their sins. How appropriate that it be in a closet, Vicky thought. So many dirty little sins get hidden in closets, like Bobby's cowboy boot without a mate containing all that drug money.

"Hello. Are you still there?" Vicky heard the voice of the priest call to her from behind the partition.

"Yes, I'm sorry. What do I do again?"

"If you wish to confess privately you may kneel on the kneeler. If you prefer face-to-face then please step around the partition."

"I'm a face-to face kinda gal."

"Then step around the partition please."

Vicky's legs were trembling. She hadn't planned on this. She didn't know what she would say or do, but she felt it was too late to back out now. She commanded her shaky legs to move forward and step around the partition.

The man sat across from an empty chair where he motioned her to sit.

His face showed the first faint etchings of lines between the brows and around the mouth so characteristic of someone in their early forties. His hairline receded in such a way it was difficult to tell where the hair stopped and the forehead began. His hair was light brown and his skin washed out by the winter weather. His cool grey eyes met Vicky's with a disturbing lack of spark, and though his thin lips smiled at her as he gestured for her to be seated in the empty chair, his eyes were not smiling. Vicky didn't know if it was apathy or sadness which she perceived in the eyes. He was a thin man and very nervous from the looks of his long fingers with nails bit down to the quick.

Vicky had seen him before at River Inn. He drank scotch on the rocks, though he always requested it light on the rocks with a twist of lemon, and he liked to swirl the ice around in his glass in between gulps. And he was indeed a gulper, if Vicky's memory served her correctly. He could finish off eight ounces of scotch in about three large gulps. He usually sat at the bar, drank quickly, spoke to no one and ordered two or three drinks. He would leave then, always seemingly unaffected by the alcohol, his gaze and gait as clear and steady as when he walked in the bar. She had no idea he was a priest for he was always dressed just like anyone else, not like today, in his black pants, black shirt, white collar, and something like a long purple scarf draped over his shoulders and hanging down into his lap.

Vicky wondered if he recognized her too. He made no indication that he did and, for once, Vicky was too embarrassed to indicate that she recognized him. She sat in the chair across from him, thinking it best to remain silent and let him speak first. She would figure out something to say by then. He made the sign of the cross and muttered the words, "In the name of the Father, and the Son, and the Holy Spirit." He looked at her with his cool grey eyes and thin lipped smile of disinterest, waiting for a response. Vicky said nothing until she could stand it no more.

"This could become the stare off of the century," she said finally.

He smiled, a natural smile this time, and seemed a little amused and caught off guard. "Are you here for confession?"

"Not exactly. To tell you the truth I ain't even one of your fold–Catholic, I mean." He nodded as if he already knew. "Are you gonna throw me out?"

"No." He said it without hesitation, waiting again for her to respond.

"Guess you'd like to know why I'm here then?" Again he said nothing, acknowledging with a slight nod and giving only the faintest trace of a smile. "I ain't at all sure to tell you the truth. Except that I need to talk to someone." Vicky's guard was still up as she searched for something she could trust in the cool grey eyes of this stranger with whom she found herself face-to-face. "Is this confidential?" she blurted out.

"Absolutely. I'm bound by the seal of the Sacrament."

"Sounds serious."

"It is. Rest assured that anything you say here must remain here."

She took a deep breath and sized him up one more time. She thought she remembered her grandma telling her something Mabel Murphy had said about priests. When her grandma asked why they couldn't get married Mabel told her it was because they'd be too tempted to tell their wives everybody's sins. So confession had to be secret. Right? She still wasn't at all sure but she had to step out in trust–and faith.

"I have this problem," she began slowly. I have close to seven thousand dollars I got by illegal means. Drugs. My cousin is–was–a big-time wheeler dealer in the Lamasco area. He's been missing for several weeks. I think maybe he's dead." Vicky began crying. Father Mudd handed her a box of tissues that sat on a small table next to him. The box was full, new, and quite undisturbed until Vicky quickly pulled out several tissues from the top. Some dust flew up as she did so. No one had touched this box in a long time. She wiped her eyes and blew her nose and wondered why more people didn't cry in here like she was now. Vicky saw a spark of humanity in Father Mudd's tired grey eyes as he handed the tissues to her. Vicky told her story–the whole thing, including why she decided not to notify the police, how she desperately wanted out of the business, and how paranoid she'd been of late. Father Mudd listened mostly, interjecting a few questions here and there for clarification.

"So how exactly can I help you?" Father Mudd asked when she was finished.

"You can tell me what to do with the money. I can't keep it. It's blood money."

"That's a tough one. If it were stolen I'd to tell you to return it. But it's not exactly stolen, is it?" Vicky shook her head. "You've already told me you're getting out of the business, so you're on the right track. I don't know what to tell you about the money except you're right in not wanting to keep it. You have to give it away–to someone or some place where it will help people. I can't tell you where or who to give it to. You just have to pray about that."

Vicky nodded her head, satisfied with the answer and feeling some relief from the pressing anxiety that weighed on her so heavily over the past few weeks. She didn't want to leave. She felt safe in this little room with this stranger who would keep her secret. Just as she would keep his secret about the scotch, which she now knew after studying his face that he imbibed too much and far too frequently.

"I have a few more questions to ask, but I don't wanna hold you up or deprive someone else of a turn."

"They're not exactly beating the doors down to get in here."

"Oh, yeah?"

"Yeah. Not many people go to confession anymore, at least not around here. So what's on your mind?"

"Well, how exactly does this confession thing work anyway? I'm just curious."

"Actually the new term is the Sacrament of Reconciliation though most everyone around here still calls it confession. You're reconciling with God, making peace as it were. The person seeking forgiveness comes confesses their sins–all those thoughts, words, and deeds that have separated them from God and others. After that the penitent makes an Act of Contrition, a prayer stating that they're sorry for their sins with their whole heart, and that with the help of God's grace, they'll make a new start and make every effort to amend their life. Then the priest gives them absolution."

"Absolution?"

"Offers them God's forgiveness and releases them from their sins."

"You say that like you're reading it out of some textbook. Do you really believe it?" Vicky said, noticing the weariness had returned once again to his countenance.

"You're here to talk about yourself, not me."

"Right. So why go to a priest? I thought only God could forgive your sins."

"We believe He can and does forgive your sins the very moment you repent, but because we're human we need some tangible evidence of His forgiveness. We need to tell somebody."

"Like get it off your chest?"

"Precisely. And we need to hear from somebody that God has forgiven us. The priest represents Christ with skin on."

"You really believe it?"

"Yes. I do."

"Your name's Mudd, right?"

"Father Mudd. Yes." He smiled a smile suggesting that he no longer found the tiresome old reference to his name amusing.

"So tell me, Father Mudd, if I confess my sins will you give me absolution?"

"I can't. You're not a Catholic."

"What difference does that make if I'm really sorry?"

"Are you a baptized Christian?" The question was like a slap in Vicky's face. Suddenly she was no longer the one in charge with her needling and baiting. Now she was the vulnerable one.

"Not exactly," she said feeling her face drop and her voice take on a lower tone. "I got saved when I was thirteen, but I never got baptized."

"Why not?"

"I don't know. At first I believed real strong–after I got saved, I mean. But then things started going downhill in my life not long after that and I started to doubt. Started thinking the whole thing was just a mirage. I mean, sometimes it just seems too good to be true and life seems so hard. I don't know what I'm trying to say."

"It's all right. I think I know."

"But I just can't let go of the idea that it might be true–the whole thing about Jesus dying for our sins and rising again. Most of the time I go along not even thinking about it then all of a sudden something happens, like Bobby disappearing, and I get it stuck in my head again. Sometimes it's like he just won't let me be."

"I understand."

"I know you do. I can see it in your eyes. You're all dried up inside and confused, just like me. But I know, I know, I'm here to talk about me not you. Is my time up yet?"

"I don't know. Is it?"

"I asked you first."

"If you'd like to confess your sins I'd be happy to listen. I can't grant you absolution but I can pray with you."

"My sins! Are you kidding? Now I know you don't have enough time." She said with her usual brand of worldliness, but the truth was she was pleasantly surprised. He guessed just what she wanted–to unburden this heavy load onto some anonymous stranger who didn't know her and was too unconcerned to spread stories. It was the same reason people confessed to her behind the bar. How desperately she needed the favor returned.

"So where do I start? Do folks generally confess their worst sins first or do they start with the little everyday bad habit type sins and work their way up?"

"They usually stick the really bad sins in the middle sandwiched between the cotton balls."

"Cotton balls?"

"Yeah. Those sins they throw at me just to have something to throw, the ones that never shock or stun."

"The ones meant to buffer the really bad sins you mean?"

"Exactly. The cotton balls are always meant to buffer the really bad sins, even if they never get around to confessing those."

"Ah, ha," Vicky said giving this last statement some thought. "You mean some folks are just too chicken to get to the really bad ones?"

"Sometimes. And sometimes they're not even aware of what their really serious sins are."

"So all they've got to give you are cotton balls?"

"Something like that."

"Before you confess you have to examine your conscience, look within and see what faults you find there."

"I been doing a lot of that since Bobby disappeared. So what do you want first? Cotton balls or golf balls?"

"I don't think you'd be here if all you had to toss was cotton balls."

"You're right. Well, here goes," she said with a deep sigh. "I'm a liar and a cheat. When you live on the other side of the law, you just naturally learn to lie and cheat so as to save your ass, sorry Father, I mean backside. You get to where lying and cheating becomes so much a part of your life. Half the time I don't even realize I'm doing it. I might've told a half dozen lies today and I wouldn't even know it." Vicky stared at the floor and heard only the hum of the heat go on.

"Is there anything else?" he asked.

"I'm an idolator."

"Is that right?" He seemed slightly amused.

"You're shocked I know a word like 'idolator', ain't you?"

"I didn't say that."

"Yeah, but I seen it on your face. You didn't say it but you were thinking it."

"You have a chip on your shoulders."

"How would you know? You don't know me." Vicky said in a voice that quivered and stammered. That same old hurt, that same old sense of being mocked, laughed at hit her as it always did–unexpectedly from some seemingly harmless look or remark from another. Her eyes and nose began to smart with the stubborn sting of tears.

"I know because you're daring me to knock it off."

"So what's that got to do with anything?"

"We're talking about your sins, right?"

"So what sin am I guilty of? You tell me."

"Pride."

"Pride?"

"Yes, pride. One of the seven deadly sins."

"If I get rid of my pride then there's nothing there. I'm just an inch worm ready to get stepped on. You know what I think? I think it takes one to know one. I think you got pride too."

"Maybe so, but we're not here to talk about me."

"Yeah, and you interrupted my one sin to talk about another."

"Where were we?" He handed her a tissue. Vicky sniffled and dabbed the tears.

"Idolatry."

"Oh, yes. So what exactly is your idol?"

"The golden calf."

He looked confused.

"The almighty dollar. Money," she clarified. "Why else would I be in the drug business? It's great money and all tax free. But it ain't just the money. It's loyalty to Bobby. And something else. A thrill, a kick, the high you get from doing something dangerous, something bad. There's this excitement with being able to get away with it, being able to thumb your nose at all those respectable hypocrites out there. I've stolen and vandalized just for the hell of it, just to get that kick, that high from being bad. It feels good to be bad. I'm a rebel. I don't know if that's a sin or not."

"Only if you're one without a cause. Do you have a cause other than thumbing your nose at all the respectable people?"

"I guess not."

"Then you are guilty of pride?"

Vicky resisted the urge to make a comeback and thought about it. She guessed there was a sort of logic to his accusation of pride. She was, after all, a sort of reverse snob.

There was silence again between them at which time the heater clicked off and they were left with no hum, no white noise, no noise at all, only pure silence. "Anything else?"

"I got a vulgar mouth, but I don't take the Lord's name in vain. And I'm a drunkard." Father Mudd looked at the floor. She didn't want to talk about it anymore than he did.

"So what do you think so far? Golf balls or cotton balls? Vicky asked.

"Mmmm, more like ping pong balls."

"Well, how's this for a golf ball? I'm a harlot, a fornicator and an adulterer. Yeah, I've had sex with married men as well as single men. Just how many I couldn't say. I've even had sex with women. Don't get me wrong, I ain't a dyke. I much prefer men. And I only did it three times, the women I mean. The first time I was, well you know, wasted—and sorta curious what it would be like. The second time I was also wasted and lonely and no one else was around."

"And the third time?"

"I was just plain wasted."

"Are you sorry for your sexual sins?"

"Sorry," Vicky repeated the word back in a reflective whisper. "When I was younger, a teenager, I sometimes felt ashamed afterwards. I thought I'd really grown up when I quit feeling that shame. You know, thought I'd become a woman of the world. What a joke! Even those times when I thought it was really love, I look back on it now and I know it was nothing but feelings run wild. I look back on those great loves now and I can see we was just using each other for that high. You know that high where you feel so special, like a queen, like you're walking on air. That's the greatest high there is, better than booze, better than dope. But just like any high, once you get what you want you throw the bottle away, you burn the roach up until it's nothing but ash. It's the same with so-called love. You use someone to get high then you get rid of 'em. It's all so selfish really. Not like real love. Not that I would know what real love is, but I know it's more than just feelings run wild.

"I don't know if I answered your question or not. Heck, I don't know if I'm making any sense or not. But I guess what I'm trying to say is, yeah I'm sorry, sorry for what I've done, sorry I can't feel ashamed and embarrassed no more. I wish I could get that back. I wish I could be…I don't know."

"Innocent again?"

"That's it!"

"Your sexual sins seem to be an extension of all the others. You're driven by this recklessness, this need for excitement."

"I didn't know confession included a free head shrink session." There was silence again.

"There's something else, isn't there?"

"Yes. This one's a freaking bowling ball." The heater clicked back on. Vicky groaned inwardly at the thought of having to speak louder to be heard over the annoying drone. She made herself sit up straight and look him in the eye before she proceeded.

"It's the biggie. Thou shalt not kill."

He furrowed his brows into a sympathetic look designed to give her the courage to continue.

"You nailed it when you said I got this recklessness in me. But it's even worse than recklessness. It's something dark and hateful. I always knew if I ever let it go it would kill someone. I ain't talked about it since it happened. I've tried to put it behind me."

"Tell me," he said moving closer.

"When I was seventeen I had this bad accident." She touched the scar on her cheek and began to tell her story.

* * * * * * *

The fight with her father that precipitated the terrible incident had always been fuzzy in her mind after that day. So many of the fights all blurred together in her mind, but they all ended the same way–harsh words, accusations, slamming doors, and Vicky escaping from that house into her ticket to freedom—the used GTO Chief Bobby gave her. That terrible day was no different.

"I'm gonna kill that fucker," she said as she started her engine and turned the GTO around on the long gravel drive that led up to their house. It had been an unseasonably warm day in mid February as the late afternoon sun burnt off the last of its glory. Ordinarily Vicky loved this kind of day with its promise of spring, beckoning her outside and opening up her country girl eyes to the wonders all around. But Vicky didn't notice the day. She didn't notice much of anything when that demon anger got a hold of her. She didn't notice the trees in the woods by her house with their stark branches in silent waiting for the first light green buds to surface. She didn't notice the sound of the gravel under her wheels.

She turned off the drive onto the long country road without noticing the wide open land that was their neighbor's tobacco field with its brown earth waiting to be sown once again. Nor did she notice the neighbor's clothes line with its sheets and dungarees hung upon it for the first time since autumn departed. She didn't hear the birds chirping loudly as a noisy flock migrated back to their Kentucky home hoping for an early spring. She drove past the land and the farmhouses without turning her head once. Her eyes were fixed on the road ahead of her but even so she didn't see the road. Not really. She'd seen it all too many times. The only thing she noticed was the heat of her blood as it coursed through her veins, the pressure in her temples and the tightness in her jaw. She noticed the burning all through her that made her want to do something terrible with her hands—to hit, to strike, to render the same hurt she felt onto someone or something.

"I'd call the fucker a son-of-a-bitch except then I'd be insulting Granny. That fucker! That asshole!" She banged her hand against the steering wheel with each loud curse. She kept her eyes focused on the stop sign way off in the distance that marked the end of the old country road. There she would turn right and head into town where Bobby lived, over another hill and then a straight shot. She was close enough now to make out the spray painted initials "C.J" under the word STOP. Vicky knew most everyone in the area but she never figured out who C.J. was or who had spray painted the stop sign. As she approached the stop sign she realized how fast she was driving, as if she was late getting somewhere. The thought quickly crossed her mind that there was no need to hurry. She was only going to Bobby's house. She wasn't late.

"Take your foot off the gas, girl. Slow down. Smokey Bear's thick through here," she told herself as she braked at the stop sign. She was careful to switch on her right turn signal and look both ways before she turned onto the old two-lane state highway. She drove slowly and cautiously at first. Bored country kids with nothing better to do than drag race their hot rods down the highway had forced the cops to patrol this particular stretch of road. Two more miles and she would be in town.

The caution was short lived, however, and soon the demon anger surfaced again, causing her to forget about the cops. She accelerated. Her grip tightened on the steering wheel and her jaw clenched shut once again as curses escaped her throat and teeth in staccato-like bursts. Again she didn't notice the land, the old barns, farmhouses, and fields. She remained oblivious as she passed the gas station on the edge of town and the sign welcoming all those entering the small rural community. Something instinctual slowed her down a little as she entered town. But still, she didn't much notice the old courthouse or the public library or the storefronts or the parked cars or the people standing around outside the places of business, delighted to be outdoors on this unusually sunny and pleasant day in the middle of winter. She scarcely noticed the driving beat of the rock music that blared over her car stereo.

Vicky didn't notice the oncoming car that passed her. She didn't notice the little boy on the bike approaching her from her peripheral left immediately following the passing car. He crossed the street from the other side between two parked cars just as the oncoming car passed her, but she couldn't see him until it was too late. (That's what the police report said).

The sound and feel of a thud turned the demon anger into a sudden and stark terror. In a second the bike was under her car, the boy was on her hood, and blood was everywhere. Her immediate instinct–to swerve to the right as if trying to back track and avoid what just happened. Her foot fumbled for the brake, finding the pedal she pushed down hard. But to her complete and utter horror it was not the brake at all but the gas that her foot landed on. She was on the curb in a moment, smashing into the metal pole of the street sign at the corner of Main and Providence. The pole bent in half and came crashing through her windshield. Glass broke and then a searing pain on the left side of her face as the metal street sign bearing the name of Providence slashed her cheek. At last she came to a stop from the impact of the sign and her foot finally reaching the brake.

The next thing she remembered she was being placed on a stretcher, staring up at the bright blue sky and wondering if she was dead. She felt something liquid and warm on her face. She touched the area and examined her fingers; she gasped at the sight of her own blood. She felt it oozing out all over–on her cheeks and forehead from splintered glass embedded in the flesh and the deep gash left by the metal street sign.

"Relax," a paramedic said leaning over her as he wrapped a blanket tightly around her. She'd been warm, almost hot, all day from the unexpected change in weather, but now she felt a violent iciness surge through her veins and she shook uncontrollably. She heard the paramedics say something about blood pressure and respiration.

"I–I," she struggled to get words out.

"Shhh. Don't talk," the paramedic said.

"But there was a boy on a bike. I hit him. Oh, my God, I hit him."

"Shhh. Relax."

"Is he okay? Please tell me he's okay."

"He's on his way to the hospital right now. Don't worry."

"So he'll be okay then? Right?"

"You concentrate on you right now."

"Me? What's wrong with me? Am I dying?" She felt herself slip away as everything around her faded into a swirling black.

"Hang in there, now. Stay with us," the paramedic said. She was vaguely aware of being confined, strapped onto a stretcher and lifted. "What's her name again?" she heard him ask someone.

"Vicky. Vicky Dooley," an unfamiliar voice replied.

"Stay awake, Vicky. Stay awake. Can you hear me, Vicky?"

Vicky looked at Father Mudd through eyes too blurred too see. All the years of anguish, pain, and regret–all the going back over it in her mind and replaying it–if only, could have, should have–all those years of trying to keep it down and keep it to herself came out in great heaving sobs. Father Mudd scooted his chair closer to her until their knees touched. He offered her the unused dusty tissue box. She pulled off several sheets and buried her face in her hands. Father Mudd said nothing until she composed herself enough to speak, until there was nothing left but a few aftershocks and an occasional sniffle.

"When did you find out about the boy on the bike?"

"The next day from my grandma. I spent the night in the hospital. They had to dig the glass out of my face and stitch me up. I was in pain and shock but still I kept asking about him. All the doctors and nurses just kept telling me not to worry. He died that night in the hospital. Imagine that, under the same roof as me. Funny, I was up most of the night. I knew they couldn't save him." She wiped her eyes and blew her nose.

"His name was Joey. His Daddy called him little Joe. He was only nine years old. He'd be nineteen if he were alive today."

"Were you under the influence at the time of the accident?"

"No, I was stone-cold sober. No drugs, no alcohol in my system. They tested me all right to make sure."

"Were you speeding?"

"That's a good question. See, there was this whole investigation that went on afterwards. I could've been charged with manslaughter. But it could never be proved that I was speeding. Personally, it seemed like I was speeding, like I had to have been or I could have stopped in time. But the witnesses, and there were plenty of them standing around on the street, gave mixed reports. The only thing that they all agreed on was that my car radio was turned up too loud. In the end it was decided that it was an unavoidable accident because of how it happened. They said that my vision was obstructed since he crossed from the other side of the street between two parked cars at the same time that oncoming car passed me. They said even going the legal speed limit I couldn't have seen him in time to stop."

"So why do you still blame yourself?"

"Don't you see?" she blurted out "I *was* driving too fast. I know I was. I hit the gas instead of the brake."

"Yes, but you told me that was after you already hit him."

"It don't matter. I wasn't paying attention to what I was doing. I would've seen him on the other side of the street if I'd been paying attention and I would've slowed way down. My mind wasn't on my driving. It was on hateful things, terrible things, wishing my father was dead. So instead I killed this innocent little boy."

"I wonder if you blame your father as much as you do yourself."

"Damn right I blame him. Nobody could get me as angry as he could. You know he never came to see me that night in the hospital. I only saw him one time after that. It was when I went home to get my things. I moved out right after that and moved in with my boyfriend. You know what he said to me? He said 'I knew you'd do something stupid like this some day'. Here I am wishing I was dead instead of that little boy and that's all he says to me."

"You never saw him after that?"

"No, he died when I was twenty-one. Grandma said he wanted to see me there at the last. She said he wanted to make peace with me. I didn't really want to believe her 'cause I was still so pissed off at him. I never even went to his funeral. I think it just about broke my grandma's heart. She died a year later."

"Do you regret it?"

"Sometimes I do, sometimes I don't. Right now I do. But then when I get to thinking about all the mean things he did to me, how he never once said he was sorry, and then all of a sudden on his death bed he wants to apologize and expects me to write the whole thing off. It was just too late. Just too damn late."

"Surely you've heard 'forgive us our trespasses as we forgive those who trespass against us'. "

"From the Lord's Prayer. Yeah, I've heard it."

"Do you want to forgive him?"

"Yes. Maybe I won't tomorrow, but today I do."

"Willingness. That's the first step. Then, of course, there's someone else you must forgive."

"Myself, right? Yeah, yeah, I know."

"Why do you have such a hard time forgiving yourself?"

"Because it's still there with me."

"What is?"

"That demon anger, that recklessness, rebel without a cause, whatever you call it. For crying out loud, I sell drugs."

"*Sold* drugs."

"Okay. *Sold* drugs. It don't matter. I could be responsible for other people's deaths. I tend bar for a living. I've let people leave the place drunker than skunks knowing full well they're gonna get behind the wheel of a car. Hell, I've driven home so drunk myself I don't even remember it the next morning. You know there been mornings I've had to run out to check my truck and make sure there's no blood or dents on it. It's horrible. I hate it. I already done killed one person, you'd think I'd never do stupid stuff like that ever again. So why do I keep doing it? Why?"

Father Mudd's brows furrowed once again, but this time not in a sympathetic look designed to encourage gut spilling. His eyes seemed focused somewhere way beyond her as if he saw his own reflection on a distant wall.

"The worst part of it is that God sees me."

"Are you afraid God will punish you?"

"It ain't so much that as the fact that he's gone, just plain gone. It's like he's way far away watching me from some other world and I don't know what he thinks because I can't reach him. I can't get to him. He's gone and he'll never come back to where I am. I can't get him back. I just can't get him back." Vicky felt herself succumb to a defeated tearlessness that left her with only sighs and a crushing gravity that pulled her down into the chair.

"I just wish I knew if you believed. Tell me, please. Do you?" Vicky pleaded in a tired voice strained from sobbing.

"I used to believe. Fervently. It's why I became a priest. Well, at least partially why I became a priest. I had mixed motives, some right, some wrong, though at the time I didn't know that. But that's beside the point. I can't exactly say I don't believe anymore. I just have more doubt than faith."

"What happened?"

"How does it ever happen? How did it happen to you?"

"Life just nibbled away at me. You know, like I said before, after a while it just seems too good to be true."

"And that's how it happened to me."

"You know what I wish for you? I wish you believed again. Do you want to believe again?" Vicky asked.

"Yes."

"Willingness. That's the first step. Someone told me that once."

"You know what I wish for you?"

"This oughta be good."

"I wish you'd get baptized."

A strange hope stirred inside Vicky and the crushing weight began to lift off her shoulders. She smiled and sat up straighter.

"Could you baptize me?"

"Yes."

"Today?"

"No, not today. I'd want you to come back and talk to me more about this."

"Ah, c'mon Father Mudd," Vicky whined like a kid begging for a treat.

"I want you to be sure you know what you're doing first."

"But you believe right now, or at least you want to believe, you have willingness, whatever. If I come back you might not believe again and then it won't take."

"It would still take. It doesn't so much matter what I believe as what you believe. It's the grace of the sacrament."

"Whatever. I just wanna know that it's another believer dunking me in the water."

"But don't you see? It might help me to believe again, that is if I help you to believe again. We could walk through it together," said Father Mudd.

"Okay, so if you won't baptize me today could you at least give me abso.. abso..?"

"Absolution?"

"That's it," Vicky said, her notepad and pen already in hand writing down the letters. "That's A-B-S-O-L-U.."

"T-I-O-N." Father Mudd waited patiently for her to write down the word, and he seemed to lack curiosity as to just why she was writing it down. She finished and put the notepad and pen back in her coat pocket.

"So will you give me absolution?"

"No, I can't do that. I already told you."

"Please, please give me absolution. I need to know that I'm forgiven."

"I'll pray with you."

"Please, Father, please." Vicky began to cry again, and as the tears ran down her cheeks in unrestrained torrents, she scooted off the chair and fell to her knees. "I gotta know I'm forgiven. I've been carrying this terrible thing around with me for ten years. Please, please give me absolution. I beg you. I'm kneeling at your feet. I'm begging you." Father Mudd handed her a wad of tissues before her eyes and nose dripped onto his black loafers. As she wiped her face and stared at the black loafers she felt his hands on her head.

She was catapulted back in time as she remembered the preacher man who placed his hands on her head when she was thirteen years old back at the tent revival where she got saved. The same warmth went through her. He bent closer to her face and she could smell the faintest trace of whiskey on his breath. He said the words in a hushed voice just barely above the sound of a whisper.

"God, the Father of mercies, through the death and resurrection of his Son has reconciled the world to himself and sent the Holy Spirit among us for the forgiveness of sins. Through the ministry of the Church may God give you pardon and peace, and I absolve you from your sins in the name of the Father, and of the Son, and of the Holy Spirit. Amen."

"Was that it? Am I forgiven?"

"Yes."

"Thank you. Thank you, Father." Father Mudd bent down and helped Vicky to her feet. He stood with her and as they rose they found themselves looking eye to eye. He was the exact height she was.

"What is your name?"

"Vicky."

"Vicky. Call the parish office Monday and make an appointment to see me. Our number's in the book. We'll see what we can do about getting you baptized. Consider that your penance."

"My what?"

"Your penance."

"Could you spell that please?" Vicky said taking out her notepad and pen from her coat pocket.

"P-E-N-A-N-C-E." It means…"

"Don't tell me. I'll look it up when I get home."

"The Lord has freed you from your sins, Vicky. Go in peace."

"Free." Vicky exhaled the word slowly in a half whisper, letting its sound and meaning permeate her. "Thank you."

"Thank you," Father Mudd said.

Vicky turned without another word and walked out the door.

Chapter 17
The New Year: 1984

Vicky stopped by the River Inn that New Year's Eve. She didn't even need a drink to celebrate the New Year. Her boss let her stay and work that night since the New Year's Eve crowd was larger than he expected. She called cabs for the big drinkers and paid the fare out of her own pocket. And so she was back to work.

January spilt out one day into the next as Vicky experienced her New Year with a strange bitter-sweetness. She stopped worrying about Bobby and began grieving for him; just as surely as if his body had been found, cleaned up, dressed in the one blue suit he owned, laid out, eulogized, memorialized, and buried. She had laid him to rest in her mind; it was the only way she could go on.

She moved about with a cautious sort of gait at first, like someone recovering from a long illness or a prisoner released from years in a dark dank dungeon whose eyes are not yet accustomed to the light. She permanently turned off her porch light. Eddie must've gotten the word out because no angry customers came looking for her. She made excuses not to see her friends and acquaintances. She had to make a complete break from her old life. She didn't know why exactly, but for something. She moved slower these days, but she thought perhaps her footsteps were a little lighter.

It was a day in late January when she retrieved her notepad and pen out of her coat pocket to write down a new word. There were the words "absolution" and "penance" on the page before her eyes. Vicky remembered with an exasperated sigh at herself. She still hadn't made an appointment with Fr. Mudd and she still had nearly seven thousand dollars stuffed in a boot in the corner of her closet. She grabbed the new dictionary that Allison had given her and looked up the word "penance". She skipped over the definition that said something about "confession", "sacrament", and "self-mortification." It all sounded like it came straight out of Father Mudd's text book. Her eyes moved quickly to the definition that said, "A penalty for wrongdoing: discipline, correction." That she understood.

Father Mudd had given her two penances really–to give the blood money away to help others and to see him again about getting baptized. She remembered the somewhat crude wooden box in the back of church with the words painted in black, "Poor Box." There was a slot in the top of the box large enough for coins and a few folded bills. She laughed to herself at

Odd Numbers

the thought of trying to discreetly put six-thousand seven-hundred and forty dollars into that box. Yet, that's where she wanted it to go. Bobby could never really rest in peace until she accomplished that task.

* * * * * * *

Vicky clutched the manila envelope containing six-thousand seven-hundred and forty dollars close to her chest as she walked against the bitter January wind which stung her face with every step. She wondered what people in the passing cars would think if they knew this pedestrian had that much money on her person. She clutched the envelope tighter and only occasionally loosened her grip between gusts of heavy wind to check the zipper on her purse. She was sure to zip it only halfway so she could easily pull out her 38 special if needed. Normally Vicky didn't carry her gun with her, but she didn't dare venture out with this much cash and not have some kind of protection. She stuck her hand through the opening of her purse and touched the handle of gun. Secure in the knowledge that it was still there and easy to get to, she went back to the business of guarding the manila envelope; its biggest threat presently the wind which blew at a free corner.

Her eyes watered and her nose ran by the time she reached the two story brick house next door to the church. She didn't dare reach into her purse to retrieve some tissues. She passed the sign that read "Parish Office" and hiked against that fierce wind up the path to the front door. She rang the doorbell, checked the handle of her gun one more time, and zipped her purse.

A short, stout woman in scuffed up pumps, a stretched out cardigan sweater that accentuated her matronly manner; and an unflattering mid-length skirt, answered the door. Her hair was dyed a deep dark brown to cover the fifty-something grays. The hair color was too dark for the rosy complexion and large apple cheeks. Her smile was pleasant and friendly and she had a merry little voice like an elf.

"May I help you?" The woman asked.

"Yes, I'm here to see Father Mudd."

"Father Mudd's not here right now."

Vicky said nothing but simply stood there trying to figure out what her next move would be. She hadn't even thought about the possibility that he might not be there.

"Did you have an appointment scheduled?"

"Kind of, but not exactly," Vicky said remembering how the professional and overly educated like to know exactly when you plan to show up. Where she was from, you never called first, you just dropped in. If it was a bad time you left or just hung around until it was a good time. Her grandma always said that's what olden time parlors were for, for waiting until you could be received by your host.

Vicky looked around the woman into the warmth of the foyer. The woman picked up on Vicky's cue.

"Please come in. You must be freezing." Vicky stepped across the threshold and the woman closed the door behind her.

"Thank you."

"Is there anything I can help you with?"

"When will Father Mudd be back?"

"He's out of town. He's not expected back for several weeks."

"Several weeks!"

"Would you like to speak to Father Frisbee?"

"Who's that?"

"Our associate pastor. He's in charge while Father Mudd's gone."

"No," Vicky said, her voice lowered and her shoulders dropped. The realization that Father Mudd was gone caused her spirit to sink all the way down to her feet and out onto the hard wood floor. "Father Mudd said I should call and make an appointment to see him. That was a few weeks ago."

"Oh. You just missed him actually. He just left town three days ago."

"Shoot. I should have called first."

"So what can I do for you? I'd be happy to let Father Mudd know you were here, but as I said he won't be back for several weeks and I have no way of getting a message to him before then. If it's something urgent Father Frisbee can speak with you."

"No, it's not urgent and, no, I don't wanna talk to no one else. Where is Father Mudd anyway?"

"I'm surprised you don't know. I thought everyone in the diocese knew by now." The woman dropped her voice along with her professional stance and took on the demeanor of the neighbor lady leaning over the fencepost, just dying to share the latest gossip. "Alcohol treatment," she whispered.

"Come again?" Vicky said leaning in closer.

"His problem...his drinking problem finally got the best of him."

"Well, we all got our bad habits. So do you know when he gets back?"

"I think it's a four week program, but to tell you the truth," she said lowering her voice once again to a whisper, "I don't think he'll be back here. I bet you a dollar to a hole in a donut the Bishop reassigns him. Betcha he sticks him out in the boondocks where he can't embarrass him anymore."

Vicky wondered what the final act of embarrassment was that got him sent off. Or maybe it was his decision to go on his own. She wondered if he knew he was going already when she talked to him. She knew she could easily get all the details with just minimal encouragement, but it really didn't matter and she didn't really want to know. There was nothing to say and only one thing left to do.

"I'm guessin' you're the secretary around here?" Vicky asked.

"That is one of the many hats I wear, yes."

"Then I guess I oughta give you this," Vicky said reluctantly releasing the manila envelope marked 'For the Poor' in black marker on the front. "It's a donation. For the poor."

"Why thank you."

"Please don't open it now."

"Certainly."

"You'll see to it they get it now, won't you? The poor, I mean."

"Yes, I'll give it to our St. Vincent de Paul Society."

"What's that?"

"It's an organization that serves the poor."

"Oh, right. You won't lose it now, will you?"

"Why no. I never lose anything."

"You're sure you won't forget?"

"Of course not. I'll put it in my in-box where I'll be sure to see it. Don't worry. So whom shall I say is making this donation?" The woman cleared her throat and asked.

"No name," Vicky said shaking her head and her hands at the same time. "I wish to remain anonymous."

"I understand. Well, thank you very much, dear. And don't worry. I'll see to it your gift gets to St. Vincent de Paul," she said as she stepped toward Vicky, her extended hand leading her toward the door. Vicky thanked the lady and left. She wanted to hide in the bushes and spy through a window to see how she would react once she opened that manila envelope. Gauging what little she'd observed from the woman she guessed the envelope would be open within thirty seconds of her exit.

The wind was to Vicky's back on the way home moving her along at a quick and steady pace. She felt so many things. She felt relieved of a great burden, yet she was disappointed. She felt assured that she had done the right thing, yet she was frustrated. It was the disappointment and frustration of an uncompleted quest.

"Now you can rest in peace, Bobby," she said aloud. "But I can't. Not yet, anyhow."

* * * * * * *

Vicky left work around midnight on that cold crisp Tuesday night in late January. The night was dotted with stars that nearly shouted out at Vicky from the sky as she walked to her truck after closing up the bar for the night. She had to stop in spite of the cold and just look up. She looked up and all around until she was dizzy. She wished she were in a grassy field somewhere way out in the country, far away from all the light pollution, lying on the ground just looking up. She hadn't felt such a perfect awe in a long time. "Wow!" was all she could say as she turned this way and that until the sky twirled right along with her. She stopped twirling for a moment and in that stillness was aware of a sudden sadness. It was a longing, a craving so intense she ached. Something was missing. She only had to think about it for a moment to realize what it was. It was a lover.

"Can't look at the stars alone. Gotta have a strong pair of arms you can lean back in, like an easy chair. Gotta feel him swaying back and forth saying, 'wow, would you look at that?' Gotta feel his cheek against yours and his breath in your ear."

"Well, Vicky ol' girl, it ain't gonna happen tonight. This ol' gal's going home and going to bed. Alone," Vicky said as she unlocked her car door. She looked up one last time. She sighed and then shivered as she caught sight of a celestial body shooting through the sky then disappearing along with all her cloudy-headed dreams into that vast ocean of shimmering black velvet. She would never forget the stars that night.

Just fifteen minutes later, the sighs and the longing and the awe were replaced by real life with its frustrations and irritations and trivial inconveniences. "Damnit, son-of-a-bitch, where are my fucking keys," Vicky blurted in a curt whisper so as not to wake her neighbors as she knelt in front of the door of her apartment and dumped the contents of her purse onto the floor. "Shit," she blurt whispered again remembering her New Year's resolution not to cuss and how she'd just broken it several times in succession. She shook the leather bag and onto the floor fell a red hair pick, her wallet, her checkbook, a tube of lipstick, two tampons, a peppermint wrapped in cellophane that had been there for who knows how long, a broken cigarette, the purple Bic lighter which by now was completely out of fluid, three pennies covered with lint and pieces of tobacco, an expired coupon for barbequed chips, and the keys to her truck. But no apartment keys. She separated all the items out and shook her purse upside down one more time as bits of tobacco and a crumpled bank receipt floated out. She checked her pockets one more time. Empty.

"Aw hang!" Vicky said as she banged the palm of her hand against her forehead trying to think what could have happened to the keys. It was such a routine, such a ritual that she hardly thought about it. She couldn't remember doing it, but she always locked the door behind her and dropped her apartment key in her purse. Had she done it differently this afternoon when she left her apartment? The door only locked from the outside with a key so she had to have locked it. But where were the keys? All these thoughts jogged around her brain as she picked up the items on the floor and put them back in her purse one at a time.

She wished she was back in the country where nobody locked up their homes. She could be half-way to bed by now. It was too late to wake up Louise. "What about Sally? She's usually up at all hours," Vicky thought aloud. She walked carefully, almost apologetically to Sally's door. She knocked then put her ear against the door to listen. There were no lights on and no sign of life inside. Then she remembered that Sally was away on a singles Caribbean cruise.

She had two choices. She could sleep in the hallway or she could go to Allison's. If she slept in the hallway the neighbors would see her in the morning and Frank would probably be the first to trip over her. So she headed upstairs to Allison's apartment. As she stood at Allison's door prepared to knock, that's when she heard it.

It was music floating softly across the hall from Frank's apartment, the tinkling sound of a piano turned down low. Her knuckles were less than an inch from Allison's door but she didn't knock, she stopped and stood perfectly still. She held her breath and closed her eyes so she could get a better listen. It was slow and lovely and yet sad. She thought she heard in it that same longing she had felt when she looked up at the stars earlier that night. Every note that flowed into the next enchanted her and compelled her to listen. She moved closer to the sound until she was fixed in the corner between the wall and Frank's door. Her back and legs were tired so she slid down the wall until she was sitting on the floor.

She closed her eyes and lost herself in the music. The melody picked up a little and changed to a slightly more cheerful, almost childlike and playful mood, though the tempo behind it remained slow and steady. Her mind and her memory traveled back to a scene that matched the music. She was a kid back in Kentucky running across the fields with Bobby and climbing trees. Vicky's mind picture gradually metamorphosed from a memory into the strangeness of a dream as she floated into a deeper state of unconsciousness though all the while still aware of the music with its earlier theme of sadness and longing returning once again to the melody.

Deeper and deeper into a tunnel of sleep she floated, then swirled, slowly at first then faster and faster until finally she was falling and about to crash into the bottom of the abyss. Her body jerked with a unexpected violence. Her hand went out to brace her fall and smacked hard against Frank's door. Her heart pounded and her hand stung. She heard the sudden commotion of footsteps and a male voice expressing outrage. The door opened and Vicky fell across the threshold of Frank's place. The first thing she saw were his bare feet, up far closer than she ever wished to see them–large and manly with visible black hairs on the toes and prominent arches. Her eyes traveled upward and she couldn't help but notice what a formidable presence he was, despite the plaid flannel pajamas. There he stood staring down at her and there she lay staring up at him.

Chapter 18

"What the hell is going on?" Frank demanded from his lofty standing position.

"I ain't ever seen nobody yell and whisper at the same time, but I'll be danged if you didn't just do it," Vicky responded from her lowly position on the floor.

"What!?" he said, a shadow of confusion spreading across his face, mixing with the shock and outrage.

"Sorry, guess I'm still half asleep," Vicky said, beginning to stand up. In a moment Frank's hand was extended toward her. She looked at him and was surprised that he seemed concerned about helping her get off the floor. She grasped his hand. It was large and strong and warm. He effortlessly pulled her to her feet. So now they stood face to face. Vicky had never seen anyone as young as him look so stern.

"What were you doing on the floor in front of my apartment?"

"Sleeping."

"What the hell were you doing sleeping on the floor in front of my apartment?"

"Better watch it. That whisper yell of yours is turning more yell and less whisper. Gotta be considerate of the neighbors you know," Vicky said lowering her voice all the more.

"Just cut the crap and tell me what's going on."

"If you just calm down I'll explain everything. Shoot, you're as uptight as a long tailed cat in a room full of rocking chairs. Oops sorry, forgot you don't like cats." Frank rolled his eyes and crossed his arms.

"Don't worry I wasn't planning on burglarizing you. Believe me, you ain't got nothing I want," she said, her eyes scanning him from head to toe. "So here it is, the truth, the whole truth, and nothing but the truth. So help me, God." Vicky raised her right hand.

"A statement you've heard many times in court, no doubt."

"I locked myself out of my apartment. Lost my...keys," she said as she caught herself almost cussing. "So I decided to go to Allison's place to see if I could crash there. I was just about to knock on her door when I heard your music." Vicky felt suddenly embarrassed at the thought of telling him it was his music that had drawn her to his door, so much so that she was unable to meet his eyes.

"I...I liked it. I mean, it was unusual so I wanted to get a better listen. I sat down in the corner over there and I guess I must've fallen asleep. I had one of them falling dreams. You know the kind where you jerk right before you hit bottom." She raised her eyes to his for a second and it seemed his face had softened a little.

"I guess I must've fallen against your door. And that's the whole truth. So help me, God," Vicky looked him in the eyes so he could see for himself she was telling the truth.

"I guess I must be crazy but I believe you."

"It's about time. Sorry if I woke you up."

"You didn't. I couldn't sleep. That's why I had my music on."

"Oh. Well, it worked for me. I guess I'll just head across the hall now to Allison's."

"No, wait! No sense waking Allison. You can use my phone to call a locksmith."

"Well, thanks, Frank," Vicky said with a mix of surprise and sarcasm.

Frank directed Vicky to his phone and handed her his phone book. After Vicky finished the call to the locksmith she thanked him and headed to the door, her eyes focused straight ahead, neither looking to the right or the left.

"Where are you going?" Frank said as she got to the door.

"Downstairs to wait for the locksmith."

"Where do you plan on waiting?"

"In the hallway. I'm sure it won't be too long."

"You can wait here if you like."

"Are you kidding me?"

"It beats sitting in a drafty hallway."

Vicky looked at him in disbelief. Something she said had disarmed him. When was the last time she saw him without that firm set jaw and those furrowed brows? Ah, yes. It was that time she caught him off guard looking at Allison. What was it that softened that brow and turned the fire in his eyes down to a warm blue flame that made her want to draw near? He was ready to shoot her down and something caused him to lay his weapon aside. Of course, Vicky thought, it was the mention of his music.

"It's all right. I've had my rabies shot," Frank said.

"You sure about this? I don't want you to do something you might regret in the morning." To Vicky's astonishment Frank smiled, broad enough to show his teeth.

"Well, all right then," Vicky said moving away from the door and back into the living room. This time she looked around the apartment. The first thing she saw was rows and rows of bookshelves, all of them filled. Framed photographs sat here and there on the ledges of the bookshelves, mostly older ones in black and white of ancestors long past. She looked at the walls and her eyes caught sight of a large painting of mallard ducks rising over a marsh on a hazy morning. Everything was so neat and orderly, so tidy with everything in its place. She was the only thing out of place. "I shouldn't be here," she said, afraid to take one step further.

"Don't worry about it. I can't sleep anyway so it's not like you're keeping me up. Here, I'll put on some more music. Have a seat. If you're tired go ahead and lie down," he said motioning toward the plaid couch that looked as if it had never been sat on. "I'll keep a lookout for the locksmith. You want a blanket?"

"How come you're being so nice to me all of sudden? It ain't like you, Frank."

"Oh, yeah? I can be a very nice guy when I want to. Besides, I heard you went through a rough time over the holidays. I heard about your cousin. I'm sorry."

"Thanks," Vicky said, a twinge of pain grabbing her in the chest at the thought of Bobby. "So I guess you been talking to Allison. She must've told you to be nice to me."

"So what if she did?"

"That explains it. Bet she told you to give me one last chance."

"Something like that."

"Uh-huh."

"So maybe you could give *me* another chance. I told you I can be a very nice guy."

"So can Dr. Jekyll when the full moon ain't out."

"You're in luck. No full moon tonight, just a black sky with brilliant stars."

"So you saw the stars too?"

"I always observe the stars. Astronomy's my hobby."

"They're beautiful tonight. Don't you think?"

"Yes. Beautiful." Frank looked away for a moment in which he seemed suddenly shy and self-conscious.

"Can I take your coat?" Frank asked. Vicky unzipped her jacket, thinking it all a strange dream. In a moment Frank was behind her, helping her off with it. "Make yourself at home. Have a seat," Frank said as he walked over to the front hall closet and hung her coat on a hanger.

"I'm afraid I'll break something or mess it up," Vicky said, slipping off her black flat heel shoes she always wore to work. She took one look at the carpet and didn't want to get it dirty.

"Don't be ridiculous." Vicky put her shoes neatly by the door and headed toward the navy, tan, and green plaid couch. She looked at the books on the bookshelves on her way over. They were the only things that seemed to be worn in the whole place. Her eyes scanned the shelves that were eye level. Some titles were familiar, The Three Musketeers, King Arthur and the Knights of the Round Table, The Hunchback of Notre Dame, Tale of Two Cities. The shelves higher up contained books on mathematics, statistics, and yes, astronomy.

Every book seemed worn as if there was something in them he needed, something he had to visit time and time again–adventure, danger, mystery, and heroism, but also logic and order from the math books, problems with solutions in a universe that made sense. Despite the neatness of the place, it had a very strong manly presence. Even the painting of the mallard ducks suggested more the conquest of the hunter than the mere beauty of a nature scene. The place smelled male, like the very faint fragrance of some type of musk or cologne mixed with coffee. It was an appealing fragrance that would mark its memory forever in Vicky's mind. Yet something was missing from Frank's place, those little touches of life one sees in a woman's place–the plants, the souvenirs, the candid photographs stuck with magnets to the refrigerator, the place of comfort–perhaps in the corner where a rocking chair might be. There were no living things, no place for comfort, and no room for sentiment, yet the place cried out for these things.

Frank had disappeared into another room while Vicky was looking around. She decided to give the couch a try, but it was no use, there was no lounging on it. Not that it wasn't comfortable, just that she was in Frank's place and she could tell there wasn't much relaxing done here. Still she tried. It felt good to get off her feet and rest her back.

Frank appeared around the corner with a suddenness that gave Vicky a start. He was carrying a neatly folded plaid blanket and a pillow which he handed to her. "Here," he said.

"You really like plaid, don't you?" she said looking at the neatly folded blanket. Frank smiled his shy, self conscious smile, and Vicky thought he looked almost boyish in that moment. "I don't wanna get too comfortable and, you know, miss the locksmith."

"Don't worry, I told you I'd keep an eye out for him," he said scooting his chair at an angle so he could see out the sliding glass door into the parking lot.

"Do you mind if I smoke?"

"No," he said and handed her a beautiful crystal ashtray off the coffee table. "Just watch the ashes."

"This thing weighs a ton."

"Its lead crystal,"

"Of course it is," she said as Frank pulled a book of matches out of a worn but beautiful maroon leather case on the coffee table.

"Are you sure it's okay if I flick my ashes in this thing?"

"It's what it was designed for," he said with match book in hand awaiting her to fish a cigarette out of her purse.

"Have you ever used it before?"

"Occasionally I smoke a cigar."

Vicky produced the cigarette and before she had a chance to draw it to her lips, Frank was there before her face with the lit match. Vicky stuck the end of the cigarette in the flame and inhaled.

"You feel weird being here, don't you?" Frank said, shaking the matchstick out to extinguish the flame.

"Let's face it, Frank, it is pretty weird." Vicky said exhaling a stream of smoke.

"Yes, it is." He said it in such a way it made her laugh. They both laughed and Vicky noticed how handsome he truly was. She'd noticed it before at those off guard candid moments at the lounge when he laughed with some of his friends, and of course when she'd seen him look at Allison. "I'll put some music on if you like."

"I'd like that."

"Let's see, I believe it was Chopin that caused you to fall head long into my door." He went over to the stereo and took the record off the turntable. "Yep, my old buddy Fred."

"Who?"

"Frederic Chopin, the dead guy who composed this music. He lived around the 1830's. He was born in Poland but moved to France as a young man. He never returned to Poland but he remained Polish through and through. You can hear his love for his native country in much of his music. The traditional folk music of Poland inspired many of his waltzes and mazurkas.

"I'm sorry, I'm boring you," he said looking back over his shoulder from the stereo as the piano music softly filled the room.

"No, you ain't. I mean, no, it isn't boring," Vicky said catching her incorrect English. "Not to me anyway. It's funny you mentioned he missed his country. I could tell the guy who wrote that music was homesick. I could hear it. It made me a little homesick. It made me think about my cousin, made me think about when we was kids." Frank had seated himself in a navy blue upholstered easy chair across from the sofa. He said nothing in response.

"I can relate to...Spell his name for me, will you," Vicky said, pulling her notepad and pen out of her sweater pocket.

"C-H-O-P-I-N."

Vicky repeated the letters after him. "I may be an ignorant country girl but I know it ain't pronounced 'Chop- In' like how it looks. Could you pronounce it for me again?" Frank pronounced the name with a bemused smile on his face. Vicky wrote down the phonetic spelling next to Chopin's name. Sho-Pan.

"I can relate to Chopin. Here I am living in Indiana but I'll always be a Kentuckian at heart. I guess that's why I like this music so much."

"How did you come to live here?"

"My work. I applied to all the upscale restaurants and clubs in the tri-state area, plus some in Louisville and it finally came down to the River Inn. I also got an offer, a better offer actually, from a Country Club in Louisville, but Bobby had already settled here in Lamasco so this is where I decided to come. He's the only family I got, or had I guess I should say."

"Again, I'm very sorry for your loss," he said in a very formal manner as he looked at the floor, seemingly uncomfortable with her grief. "So why did you want to work somewhere upscale particularly?"

"Why, does that surprise you?"

"No, no. Just curious," he said defensively.

"I got tired of working in dives. I want to run my own place someday. It's my dream really, so I wanted to learn as much as I could about the business, you know, the correct way to do things."

"Good for you."

"You really mean it?" Vicky said exhaling a stream of smoke, wondering if he was being sincere or merely condescending.

"Yes, I do. You said it was your dream. I don't think we just have dreams by chance. I think we have them for a reason, because that's what we're meant to do."

"You surprise me, Frank. I'd have thought you'd be more cynical than that."

"Me cynical? I told you I'm a very nice guy. Besides, it's simply a matter of reason. For example, my brother can build anything with his hands, whereas I'm terrible at building things. I have no ability, no aptitude whatsoever. Fortunately, I have no desire to build things. We're born with a natural desire and aptitude to do certain things. That's what we were designed to do."

"By God, you mean."

"Yes, I believe that. We each have some purpose."

"So that's why we got these dreams, huh? To spur us on, right, so we'll fulfill our purpose."

"That's it."

"I hope you're right because I really want to believe you."

"So you don't believe that, huh?"

"I don't know. I think some dreams are all wrong. We only want what we want for ourselves and screw everybody else."

"That's strange because I wouldn't guess you to be cynical."

"Really?"

"Really."

"Well, ain't we all just a mystery." He smiled and chuckled softly. "What's so funny?"

"You are. You're so right. We are indeed a mystery. Human beings."

"So tell me, how did you end up here in Lamasco, Indiana? And what's your dream?"

"Like you, I came here to work."

"Why in tarnation did you, a New York City boy, come to the middle of nowhere to work? I mean, Lamasco's a big city for me, but for you, man, it's gotta be Hicksville."

"This is Middle America. Its Midwestern towns like Lamasco where we find out what the average American wants. That's why I started up my market research firm here."

"You mean you got your own business?"

"Yes."

"Wow, your own place. That's exactly what I want. Who'd have ever thought you and I have something in common. So how's your place doing?"

"We're struggling. I guess that's why I don't sleep too well at night. I worry about things–how I can cut overhead costs, how I can continue to pay my skeletal staff all of whom work so hard and get so little in return, how I can keep from going under just one more month, how I can make something out of nothing here."

"So that's what I have to look forward to when I have my own place?"

"Yep, that's it."

"So what exactly do you do?"

"Market research. We find out what consumers want and need in terms of products and services."

"How do you do that?"

"We ask questions, conduct surveys mostly, and then we use statistical analysis on the data to tell us what we need to know."

"So how is that your dream?"

"Statistics is something of a passion of mine. People don't realize how exciting numbers can be. Numbers can help reveal facts, predict future trends, unlock human mysteries. Everything's mathematical–time, space, even the human body."

"It's weird but I kinda know what you mean. I don't know numbers or math but I do know people. One thing I've observed in my line of work is that you gotta look out for the odd numbers."

"Odd numbers?"

"By that I mean the odd numbered parties, especially parties of one and three. You got a party of one sitting at the bar all by themselves, it's my job to figure out why that person is there alone. Sometimes it's just because that person's waiting on a friend. I can always tell 'cause if they have to wait any amount of time they usually start looking around, watching the doors, checking their watch. It's my job to put them at ease until the other party arrives. Once that other person gets there, they relax. It's strange, even if they don't have to wait long; the waiting party is never quite comfortable until that second person shows up.

"Then there are those who come alone but hope not to leave alone if you get my meaning, then finally those that come alone and plan on leaving alone. You gotta keep a special eye on them last types because they're most likely to leave drunk."

"I'm sorry. Now I'm afraid I'm boring you," Vicky said.

"Not at all, I find it fascinating. So why is this last type most likely to leave drunk?"

"Cause they're there to get drunk. They just split with their boyfriend, girlfriend, wife, husband, whatever. They just lost their job, or else they can't stand the pressures from the job they do have. They got money problems, relationship problems, loneliness, stress, guilt, you name it. My job is to listen, help if I can, but most of all to make sure they don't drive home too crocked.

"Then you got your parties of three. Now not always, mind you, but a lot of times you got someone feeling left out when you got a party of three. Two out of the three are gonna hit it off and one person's gonna be standing out in the cold. You see it sometimes with parties of five too.

"Of course the fights are always between two people–lovers, husbands, wives, co-workers, rivals, you name it. Now we don't have a bouncer at River Inn because it's a classy place so most fights don't come to blows, but we do have occasional raised voices. I'm the one who gets to play referee. So you see that third party ain't always bad. Sometimes they're there to make peace. Anyhow, you might see fights and factions with even numbered parties, but it's with the odd numbers that you see loneliness. That's why I gotta look out for my odd numbered folks. Hospitality is what' it's all about. That's why I want my own place. A place where everybody feels welcome–no one's left out. That's my dream. It's too much to hope that the world will ever be that way, but maybe we can make little places in the world where all are welcome, even the odd numbers."

"Vicky."

"Yeah."

"I'm sorry if I've made you feel like an odd number at Camelot. Is it too late to say 'welcome'?"

"No, Frank, it's not too late, but I hope you don't think I was fishing around for an apology. That's not why I said what I said. I mean, hell, we're all odd numbers here at Camelot. When you're single you're automatically an odd number in a paired off world."

"We're not odd numbers right now."

"No, we're not." It was perhaps the first time they looked each other straight in the eye without anger and bitterness between them. It was just for a moment lost in time until it became awkward and self-conscious. "I'm sorry. Here I go shooting off at the mouth again. I got way sidetracked. It's one of my many bad habits. So, um, how did you decide on market research as your dream?"

"I love statistics, I have a good business mind, and I've always wanted to build something from nothing. Be independent, be my own boss."

"You said a mouthful there. So tell me, how do you conduct these surveys?"

"We have many different methods, but we've found the most effective and least intrusive is to stop people in public places where they might be shopping for example and simply ask for a moment of their time."

"Wait a minute! Are you one of them clowns that follow me around the mall trying to get me to try out different sugar-free gums?"

"That probably was one of my clowns, yes. I hope you didn't feel too harassed."

"Naw, he was probably the one who felt harassed. I told him to f-off, pardon my French."

"Uh-oh!"

"Sorry I didn't know he worked for you. If I'd known that I probably would've been a whole lot meaner," she said and Frank laughed.

"It's good to see you smile," Vicky said.

"It's good to smile. I guess I haven't smiled much lately."

There was silence between them. They both turned their gaze away from each other. The music floated between them with all of its sweetness and feeling as Vicky realized it was the song she had first heard that had brought her to Frank's door.

"This is it! This is the song that was playing when I fell against your door. What's the name of it?"

"It's Chopin's Berceuse. I believe that's French for lullaby."

They chuckled at the irony of it all then got caught up in the music again.

Vicky reclined spreading the blanket out over her. The sofa seemed more comfortable this time. Frank laid his head back on the easy chair.

It was the last song on the record. There was the sound of the needle crackling just before it lifted off the record then the sound of the turntable clicking off, then silence. Vicky heard only the ticking of a wooden framed clock with a large gilded face sitting on the book shelf. Frank's breathing was slow and steady. His head was back on the easy chair so she couldn't see his face and couldn't tell if he was asleep or not.

Some time passed, maybe several minutes, maybe just a few moments when Frank finally spoke. "Did you ever notice how loud the silence is?"

"Is it because you can hear your own thoughts?"

"I think so. Silence is never really empty though, like the number zero. Most people think zero signifies nothing but the fact is zero is the point at which all other numbers originate."

"You're blowing my mind, Frank. I'm sitting here thinking about silence and the number zero and how it all adds up to something really."

"You want me to change the subject?"

"No, I think it's interesting. I just ain't–sorry–I'm *not* used to having these kinds of conversations when I'm straight. You sure you ain't been smoking dope, Frank?"

"No," he said with a laugh. "I'm not stoned, just sleep deprived, which can also produce a state of semi-psychosis."

"Go ahead. Continue your thought," Vicky said relaxing more on the couch, as she pulled the blanket up over her shoulder and the pillow tight around her ears.

"Silence is important, even in music. Pauses are notated in music. It changes the whole feeling of a piece of music to place a pause in at certain place."

"Like zero, right? You stick a zero at the end of a number and it changes it."

"Precisely. Did you know music is mathematical? It's made up of patterns and rhythms. Recent research suggests that mathematical abilities and musical abilities come from the same part of the brain."

"I knew it."

"Knew what?"

"You got another dream, don't you?"

"What do you mean?"

"Oh, I know you're working on your dream building up your business and all, but I can't help feeling you got another dream buried deep down inside you. It's got something to do with music, don't it? I mean, doesn't it?"

"You're incredibly insightful."

Odd Numbers

"It don't take a rocket scientist to figure it out. It's what you love most. Or it seems like it anyway. Tell me about this other dream. Tell me how you lost it."

"My mother was an opera singer. That's where I get my love of music. She always said I had the gift of music. I started taking piano lessons when I was four."

"You play the piano?"

"I used to. Oh, if I'm in someone's home and they have a piano, I'll sit down and tinker a little, but not like I used to. I wanted to be a concert pianist. My mother encouraged me, but she died when I was ten."

"How hard that must've been. I don't think you ever get over losing a mama at an early age. I was seventeen when my mama died. It was cancer. All the cigarettes and worry, I guess."

"My mother died of cancer, too."

"So is that when you gave up music? Was your daddy against the idea?"

"No. In fact he pushed me with my music, pushed me hard. He was that way with everything, sports, academics, you name it. I came in third in this very prestigious piano competition when I was fifteen years old. Third place wasn't good enough for him." Frank looked down at the floor for some time, and Vicky didn't know what to say. There was a noisy silence between them until Frank looked up with questioning eyes and said, "Why am I telling you this?"

"Because I asked how you lost your dream. I'm listening. Please go on."

"There really isn't much more to tell. I knew I could never be number one after that. I started crumbling under the pressure and soon my piano playing started to deteriorate as a result. Sometimes I think my father was almost relieved when I got out of music. He knew I'd have more security as a businessman, and in a strange way, I think the music reminded him too much of mother.

"It's all right, I'm happy doing what I'm doing. It's just that, as you so eloquently put it, there's still this other dream buried deep inside. It really doesn't matter though. What can I do about it now?"

"Well, you don't have to be a concert piano player, but you should be making music if that's a dream you got. Buy yourself a piano. Check the classified ads. I'm sure you could find one fairly reasonable. You could rearrange the furniture a little and find room for it. You could take lessons again. Give recitals. You wouldn't have the pressure this time around. You'd be calling the shots, not your old man."

"You've inspired me, Vicky."

"I'm glad."

"What about you? How can we get your dream jump started?"

"It takes money to jump start a dream like mine. I had some money saved, but I… lost it."

"Don't worry about that. You can get financial backing. You just need to know who to talk to. You need to find out as much about business as you can. Take some courses at the university."

"You mean college?"

"Why not?"

"I never was much of a student. I dropped out of high school. I eventually went back and got my GED, but college, I don't know about that."

"Look, I can tell just from talking to you tonight that you're smart. You don't have to let past failures intimidate you either, you know. You can start all over without all those pressures."

"You really think I'm smart?"

"I know you are."

"Huh, me intelligent? Well, I'll be!" Vicky was feeling something she hadn't felt in a long time, or at least hadn't allowed herself to feel…vulnerable and a little embarrassed. "Where is that locksmith?" she said walking over to the window and looking out.

"It does seem to be taking a while," he said then after a pause he got up and excused himself. Vicky thought he was going to the bathroom at first but instead he went to the kitchen. She heard him clinking around in there, all very familiar noises to her. She smiled as she realized what he was doing. He returned with two wine glasses about one quarter of the way filled with red wine. Frank handed her a glass and sat down next to her on the sofa.

"Since we have to wait, we might as well do something to pass the time. A toast," he said, raising his glass to her. "To our dreams, the ones we've lost and the ones we've found."

"Cheers," Vicky said, clinking her glass to his. They both took a drink of wine and Vicky was surprised how quickly one small drink went to her head. "What time is it?" she asked, realizing suddenly that she was very tired. Frank swallowed a drink of wine and looked at the clock on the bookshelf.

"Almost two-thirty."

"Where is that locksmith?"

"Let me call them. I'll see what's taking them so long," Frank said.

"You don't have to do that. I'll call them."

"No, no, you sit right there and make yourself comfortable. I'll handle this."

"Suit yourself," Vicky said taking another drink of wine, lighting another cigarette and reclining on the couch.

She heard Frank go in the kitchen and make the phone call. Agitation rose in his voice as he spoke, letting the dispatcher know how long she had been waiting. He referred to her as "his friend" and this made Vicky smile.

"Forget it! Just forget it! Just cancel the call," he said finally into the phone before slamming the receiver down. "Damn incompetents!"

"My hero," Vicky whispered softly to herself before he came back in the room.

"They had three other calls to make before yours and only one guy on duty. I took the liberty of telling them to forget it. I hope that's all right with you. It's already almost three o'clock in the morning and Louise is usually up by six. I figure you'll have better luck just waiting 'til then. That is if you don't mind sleeping on my couch."

"I don't mind."

"I'll set the alarm for six. We've got to get some sleep. Drink up," Frank said raising his glass.

"I'll drink to that." Together they finished their wine. "Thank you. The wine is excellent. A very good Burgundy."

"Why, yes. You know your wine."

"It's my job," she said handing him her empty glass.

"I'm taking you with me next time I shop for wine." Frank rose to his feet and carried both wine glasses carefully by the stems back to the kitchen.

Vicky lay down on the sofa. As she lay there she noticed a statue on the end table. She picked it up and examined it. The figure of the long robed man with the funny haircut seemed familiar to her. Her grandma's neighbor, Mabel Murphy, had a similar statue in her front yard. With Mabel's statue, chipmunks, rabbits, and other small animals encircled his feet. With this statue, the barefoot man's arms were outstretched in prayer and a small bird was perched on his right shoulder. Was it Jesus? He bore the same wounds in his hands and feet.

"I see you found St. Francis," Frank said, entering the room from the kitchen.

"Who?"

"St. Francis of Assisi. My patron saint. I was named after him."

"So your real name's Francis?"

"Yes."

"No wonder the name Frank never seemed to fit you. You're Francis. Mind if I call you Francis?"

"The last person to call me Francis was my mother."

"Is that a bad thing?"

"No, no, it's a good thing."

"Good, then I'll call you Francis." Frank smiled. Vicky thought how much she'd changed her mind about his smile. She'd noticed that he only showed his teeth when he was very amused, and either laughing, or on the verge of laughing. The rest of the time he smiled softly without showing his teeth. This wasn't the cold, calculated smile she'd seen before, but tender, boyish, and almost shy.

"You know, I thought maybe this was Jesus with a bad haircut," Vicky said, holding the statue up. "Look, he's got marks in his hands and feet."

"Ah, yes. The stigmata."

"What's that?"

"Legend has it that sometimes very holy people will receive the wounds of Christ in their flesh."

"The wounds of Christ?"

"That's what I said."

"Is it true?"

"Francis is a saint."

"Are you Catholic?"

"I used to be. My mother was Catholic. She raised me and my brother to be Catholic. After she died we fell away from it. Occasionally I still go to Mass."

"Have you been to confession lately?"

"What?"

"I was talking to a friend about it lately," Vicky said remembering Father Mudd. "You oughta try it. That is, if you haven't been lately. They say it's good for the soul."

"I haven't been to confession since I was twelve."

"So tell me about St. Francis."

"He was from Assisi, Italy. He lived in the Middle Ages around the late twelfth, early thirteenth century. He came from a prosperous family and he enjoyed a privileged life, lived it up with his friends, did a lot of drinking and carousing."

"Sounds like my kind of guy."

"Yes, but he changed. He had this conversion as a young man. He gave away all his worldly possessions, including the clothes on his back which he piled up in the middle of the town square and his own father disowned him."

"So then what?"

"He heard God telling him to rebuild his church. He had this band of followers that grew they took a vow of poverty and went around helping the poor and needy. He had a special love for the poor. One day he saw a leper walking down the road and he was so overcome with compassion for the man that he ran up to him and embraced him. As he did, the leper changed into the figure of Jesus.

"Francis also had a particular love for nature and animals which is why he's so often depicted with animals. He's the patron saint of animals."

"Wait a minute," Vicky laughed. "You mean to tell me you of all people were named after the patron saint of animals, a guy who can't be anywhere near an animal without hacking, sneezing, and gasping for air?"

"Hey, I love animals. It's their dander I hate. Especially cats and that cat of yours was the worst. Admit it you had a cat didn't you?"

"I exercise my right to remain silent."

"You had a cat and according to my calculations you got rid of it approximately one month ago." Frank got up from his chair and began rummaging through some notebooks on the bottom shelf of his book shelf. "Ah, here it is," he said pulling out a navy blue three ring binder. "Look." He flipped the notebook open and went over to the sofa to show Vicky. He pointed to a chart neatly plotted out on graph paper. On the top of the paper in red ink was marked 'Allergy Flare Ups, 1983'.

"What's this?" Vicky asked sitting up.

"I charted the severity of my allergy reactions last year. Look, notice the sharp rise during the months of November and the early parts of December," he said pointing to a red line. "Then notice here around mid-December it gradually begins to decline," Frank said following the red line with the tip of a pencil to illustrate.

"How very interesting. You know what I think?"

"What?"

"I think you need to get out more."

"No, no, no, you're trying to change the subject," Frank said slamming the notebook shut with one hand and sitting down on the sofa next to her. She felt nervous sitting so close to him and when she looked at his face she couldn't help but smile. He smiled back with a boyish mirthful grin that made his blue eyes sparkle and his whole face light up.

"No, you need to get out more, Francis, darlin', I'm concerned about you. You keep a chart on everything? How many more charts you got down there on that shelf?"

"You know what I can't figure?" Frank said changing the subject. "I can't figure why you didn't leave Camelot and just tell us all to go to hell. Why did you decide to stay?"

"To piss you off. Did it work?" Frank grabbed a throw pillow off the corner of the sofa and playfully smacked her in the face with it. "Don't hurt St. Francis," she said clutching the statue to her chest as she wrestled the pillow away from him and smacked him back in the face.

"I always knew we'd fight again, Vicky, but never in my wildest dreams did I ever think it would be a pillow fight."

"You're feeling that wine, Francis honey."

"With no sleep and very little to eat all day, you're quite right. Let's get some sleep." Frank stood up, yawned and stretched.

"Is it all right if I sleep with Francis–St. Francis I mean?" Vicky asked holding up the statue.

"Sure, if it makes you feel better."

"Did your mother give you the statue?"

"Yes."

"Nice," Vicky said looking at the statue. You're nice, Francis. I mean, it's nice of you to let me stay here tonight. I just wish I knew what I did with those…keys."

"You should be holding on to St. Anthony, not St. Francis."

"What's that?"

"St. Anthony of Padua. My little brother was named after him. He's the patron saint of lost objects. My mother used to swear by him. If anything in our home was ever lost she prayed to him and invariably it would be found. 'Tony, Tony, turn around. Something's lost and must be found.' That was the little invocation she'd say. She claimed he never failed."

"Oh, well, goodnight, Vicky," he said with a yawn and a stretch.

"Goodnight Francis. See you in a couple hours." Francis smiled and disappeared around the corner. With a start and a gasp, Vicky suddenly remembered.

Chapter 19

"Francis, my keys, I think I might know where they are!" Vicky called out to Frank who came running around the corner, his eyes so wide he looked comical and it made Vicky blast out a laugh, not only at his expression but at the excitement of her own discovery. "That prayer to St. Anthony–I think it worked.

"When I was driving home from work I had my purse on the seat next to me like I always do. I grabbed a cigarette out so it was open. Well, I turned this corner kinda fast, my purse tipped over and everything spilt out onto the floor. I thought I got everything back in my purse, but you know I was driving and trying to grab stuff off the floor at the same time. I'll bet that's where my keys are. I bet they're on the floor of my truck. I'm gonna go look for them," Vicky said, throwing off the plaid blanket and rising to her feet.

"Wait, I'll come with you. Let me get a flashlight. It's dark out there." Frank hurried down the hall then hurried back again a moment later with tan leather bedroom slippers on his feet and a large flashlight with a long black handle in his hand. Vicky let go a laugh once again at the sight of him. It was his wide-eyed serious expression and his quick sure steps to the front hall closet with such purposefulness. It reminded her of some soldier going off to war in an old movie

"I bet you was a boy scout."

"Absolutely . Always be prepared," Frank said, setting his flashlight down for a moment then taking her coat off its hanger. He held the coat open and off to the side, shaking it just a little. The image made Vicky think of a matador taunting a mad bull to come charging after his red cloak. "Shall we go?" Vicky laughed at the sight of him. He smiled a curious smile at her laughter and Vicky thought he must know that his seriousness and uprightness was a source of great amusement and fun poking for others.

"You remind me of Dudley Doright," she said as she walked over to Frank and let him help her with her coat.

"Come, Nell, I have come to rescue you from that dastardly villain, Snidley Whiplash."

"You still got your jammies on, Dudley. It's cold out there. It's going on three o'clock in the morning. Why don't you just sit tight? If I don't find my keys I'll come back up here. How's that?"

"I want to help," he said, straightening the collar on her jacket. He pulled a mass of tangled hair out of the back of her collar and his fingertips inadvertently touched the back of her neck. A chill ran through Vicky and she instantly reacted by squaring her shoulders back in resistance. "I can help myself," she said, backing away as she zipped her jacket.

"I know you can," he said putting on his khaki colored trench coat and tying the belt around his waist without bothering with the buttons. "I didn't say I *had* to help you, I said I *want* to help you."

At that moment Vicky understood instinctively what made Frank tick, deep down inside underneath the mathematical mind and the lost dream of his music and his manners and his good breeding. He wanted to help. She thought about it. Wasn't it that very characteristic that separated a bad man from a good man? Could a man ever really be good, could he ever really learn how to love until he could do that?

What about Bobby? Was it an ever-increasing feeling that he was a hindrance not a help that drove him away into some unknown exile? Did he walk into his own death because he felt it was too late to turn back? Did he die at his own hand?

What about her father? His desire to help was continually stifled by a lack of employment. He tried to drown out that desire with booze but it never really worked. And was it that same stifled desire in Francis that caused him to look so sad at times and read those books about chivalry that lined his bookcase time and time again. Was he the true Prince of Camelot born strangely out of time, finding himself so lost in the 1980's?

And so she would let him help. A man of Frank's caliber never desired to help her. She was too rough, too strong, too scarred, she thought touching the scar on her cheek and becoming aware of it for the first time that evening. She hadn't felt self-conscious about her scar in a long time, but she did now. She was standing under an overhead light and he was standing so close to her smiling that enigmatic smile. She turned her scarred cheek away from him as they walked out Frank's door, he of course, standing aside to allow her to exit first.

They walked out of Camelot Building 3300 together. She noticed that his stride was long and purposeful, deliberate but not particularly fast. There was no hesitation, no tentativeness about him. He knew where he was going and why he was going there. Vicky felt nervous for the first time that evening. Maybe it was just the change in environment, being alone with him outside in the middle of the night. Funny, she thought, how she wasn't that nervous in his apartment.

"Please excuse my truck," she said stammering. "It's dirty as all get out. Let's see here, I reckon we oughta check the floor on the passenger's side first," she chattered nervously as she led him toward her truck.

"Did you ever get that oil leak fixed?" he said with a slightly wry tone. Vicky remembered the last time she had dragged him out to her truck. It was to prove to him the half-truth that (some of) the kitty litter was used to absorb an oil leak.

"Oh, that. No, I still got that problem," she said, hoping he wouldn't shine his flashlight underneath her truck in search of kitty litter.

"You really should get it looked at," he said. Vicky opened the passenger door to her truck. "You mean you don't lock your truck at night?"

"Why should I?" Vicky said as Frank shone the flashlight on various papers, fast food cups, and empty cigarette packs that littered the truck floor. "If anyone wants to steal what's in this truck they're welcome to it. Of course," Vicky said, embarrassed by the look of shock on Frank's face, "there could be valuables buried underneath this junk for all I know."

Vicky began rummaging through the debris while Frank stood just behind her shining the flashlight strategically over her shoulder as she searched. Some instinctive pull seemed to guide her hand under the seat. She reached back as far as she could until her fingers touched something metal. She knew immediately from the feel that it was her keys.

"I found them," Vicky said victoriously pulling the jingling metal objects out from under the seat and holding them up so Frank could see. "Thank you Saint Anthony," she said, kissing the keys.

"*Bravissimo Antonio*," Frank said with an excited cry. He threw his arms around Vicky in a giant bear hug that caused her to gasp for breath.

What a contradiction he was, Vicky thought. This man of decorum, so thoughtful and purposeful in his actions and speech could startle her so suddenly with this impulsive act of exuberance. Vicky backed away from Frank's embrace and stumbled just slightly as she did.

"You all right?" Frank said grasping her arm so she wouldn't fall.

"I'm fine. You just caught me a little off guard there is all," Vicky said, aware again of the scar on her cheek which she felt certain the beam from Frank's flashlight had revealed to him. She turned her face away.

"So what other keys do you have on that key ring if you don't mind me asking?" he said becoming his serious thoughtful self again.

"The keys to work, the keys to Chief Bobby's house," she said with a moment of worry as she wondered for the first time since his disappearance what she should do with his belongings. "And the keys to my apartment."

"You know you really ought to consolidate. You need to put all those keys on one key chain along with the key to your truck."

"Why? So when I lose them again I won't be able to start my truck or get into my apartment?"

"If they were all together you wouldn't have lost them in the first place. It's a matter of efficiency."

"You sure like to give advice, don't you?"

"There's always a better way to do things."

"Well, if you must know it's 'cause my Uncle Louie had so many keys on his key chain that the weight from it caused something to trigger in his car's ignition, and it finally got to where he could start his old Dodge without keys. I ain't lying neither. He could just turn the ignition, no keys required, and his car would start right up."

"Hmmm," was all Frank said, looking very skeptical. "Well, I suppose we better head back," he said, tightening his upper torso against the cold. Vicky hadn't really noticed the cold until now. Frank shone the beam of the flashlight straight ahead of them as they made their way back. He took her arm. At first the gesture reminded her of someone helping an old person, someone injured and not so sure-footed, or perhaps someone with poor eyesight. Her fist instinct was to yank her arm away and make some remark about not being an old lady, but then she remembered his need to help, and although she was uncomfortable she let him guide her.

"Wait a minute," he said suddenly stopping. He turned his flashlight off and looked up. "Look," was all he said. There was the same black velvet sky alight with stars that Vicky had gazed at in awe just a few short hours earlier. He audibly gasped at the sight.

"Beautiful," Vicky said. "All I know is the big dipper, though I'm never quite sure where to look for it."

"You'll find it in the northern sky," he said, and with that he placed his hands on her shoulders and gently turned her to the right. "Let your eyes adjust. Now look where I'm pointing. Can you see the bowl?" Vicky followed the tip of his finger up into the sky and watched as he traced the bowl, then the handle.

"I see it."

"It's so clear tonight you can even see the Little Dipper. Look for the two stars on the outer edge of the Big Dipper's bowl. See?" he said tracing again with his finger. Vicky found them in the sky. "Then you trace an imaginary line between those two stars and extend it straight out beyond the bowl until you run right into that bright star there. See it?"

"I see it."

"That's Polaris, the North Star. Polaris is the anchor in the night sky; it is considered true north because it doesn't move during the course of the night. Sailors and travelers have always used it as a compass.

"Now look to the south." He gently steered her by the shoulders and situated his face so close to hers' that they were nearly cheek to cheek. "There it is," he said pointing, "the brightest constellation of the winter sky–Orion, the Hunter. At least the ancient Greeks thought it looked like a hunter holding up a shield. Now find his belt. See those three bright stars right in a row?"

"Yeah, I see them."

"That's Orion's Belt. And that bright star underneath his belt is Rigel. That marks Orion's foot. Now take a look to the Northwest." He turned her and pointed. "See that bright star? That's Aldebaran. One of the brightest starts in the sky."

"Wow, I see it," Vicky said following the tip of his finger as it traced along the vast darkness of the sky.

"That's the bull's eye in the constellation Taurus. Now if we look to the West of the bull's eye we should see a cluster of seven stars," he said searching, seemingly lost for a moment. "There it is. That's Pleiades, the seven daughters of Atlas. Only six are visible to the naked eye. The seventh daughter is lost. Zeus condemned him to carry the earth and turned his daughters into stars."

"I guess I don't want to get Zeus hacked off," Vicky laughed.

They stood in silence and looked up for a while. Vicky felt the cold after a few moments. Her shivering became uncontrollable and she sniffled repeatedly to prevent her nose from running. "You got a tissue?"

"Here," Frank said handing her a neatly folded white handkerchief with a navy monogram beautifully and meticulously stitched near one of the corners. "Don't worry, it's clean."

"You just happened to have one in your jammies?" She asked while wiping her nose.

"In my coat pocket. I have allergies."

"Yeah, I know all about your allergies. Thanks for the hankie. I'll wash it and get it back to you."

"Don't worry about it. You can keep it."

"You sure? This is a nice handkerchief."

"I've got plenty." Vicky blew her nose and put the handkerchief in her pocket.

"Let's go in before you freeze to death," Frank said, his hand resting protectively between her shoulder blades. She realized it was part of that helping instinct so she walked along with him, following the beam of his flashlight which he so conscientiously shone before them, in spite of the fact that the street light in the parking lot was plenty bright enough to light their way. He held the door open for her and Vicky welcomed the warmth with a sigh of relief as they stepped into it. Fatigue rushed over her and her legs felt suddenly heavy as she commanded them forward a few short paces to the door of her apartment.

"Well, here we are," Vicky said. "Thanks for everything."

"You're welcome."

"Sorry I kept you up half the night. I hope you won't be too tired tomorrow."

"I'll be fine. What about you?"

"I don't go into work until four tomorrow so I get to sleep in."

"Think of me as I'm slumped over my desk," he said with a smile.

"Well, thanks again. It's been a very interesting night."

"That it has."

They stood there for a moment in silent awkwardness and Vicky wondered just how to express her gratitude and just how she might bid him goodnight. He lingered, seemingly waiting for her to initiate the farewell. She wanted to embrace him; after all he had already hugged her. Surely it would be all right, but still something held her back from doing so. For all Vicky's bravado, she couldn't approach a man like Frank, at least not while she was sober. She raised her left hand to cover her scarred cheek and extended her other hand for him to shake. "Good night, Francis."

He took her hand firmly in his, but instead of shaking it, he raised it to his lips and kissed it. "Goodnight Vicky."

Vicky's thoughts whizzed speedily along while her heart didn't know what to feel, her hands didn't know what to do, and her feet wanted to run away and carry her outside into the open air. But she had to turn around and calmly unlock her door like she always did when she came home.

Normally very dexterous, Vicky found herself fumbling with the keys as she clumsily unlocked the door. Frank continued to stand there though at a distance. "You can go now," Vicky said. Her face, already warm with embarrassment, grew suddenly hotter as she wondered why she had said such a stupid thing.

To her surprise, Frank laughed at the remark. "I'm just making sure you get in all right."

The doorknob turned, Vicky hastily pulled the keys out of the lock, opened the door, and quickly stepped in immediately closing the door behind her. "Vicky, old gal," she said to herself, head leaning against the door in shame. "You're such a fool. I can't believe you said such a stupid thing. He was being a gentleman, but you don't know a gentleman when you see one."

* * * * * * *

The album had been shoved under the door and Vicky discovered it the following morning around ten shortly after she woke up. She spied it on the floor yet it didn't register at first what it could be until she was right up on it.

She felt elated as she read the attached note handwritten on stationary that read:

From the Desk of Francis C. Hamilton.

Dear Vickie,

Here is a collection of Chopin's most well known works. I thought you might like to borrow it. I can tape it for you if you like.

I Remain,
Francis

So this is what his handwriting looks like, Vicky thought, her eyes absorbing each carefully marked ink stroke and her memory recording every word on the page. She could tell he had made every effort to make this distinctively masculine hand, with its thin slanting letters, as neat as he could. It was somewhat surprising to see that his handwriting was not as neat as she thought it would be. She ran her fingers over the page and ink and smiled at the way he misspelled her name and the formal way he signed off. "He signed it 'Francis'," she said aloud. She raised the paper to her face and inhaled. It smelled like him.

Vicky went immediately over to the stereo and put the record on. The music was just background noise that morning as she tried with great effort to go about her day. Her thoughts were scattered and disorganized and her morning ritual took much longer than usual. "I must really be tired," she said to herself time again as she struggled to organize her thoughts and move from one activity to the next.

Despite her lack of sleep, however, she never felt sleepy; not once all day. Instead she was infused with the most optimistic exuberance. Her scatterbrained state remained but did not cause her great concern. She kept looking forward to something though she didn't know what. Then she remembered the record and thought, yes that was it. She wanted to sit down and really listen to it without distractions. She would do it when she got home from work. She would turn it way down low and lay between the speakers.

When she arrived home the first thing she did as she stepped out of her truck was to look up, directly above her apartment to the second floor of building 3300. His lights were out. She didn't want to see him again empty handed. She wanted to give him some sort of a gift as a gesture of thanks, but what? She looked up at the stars. It was another clear night and she found the Big Dipper and Polaris with just a little effort. She found Orion's belt and what she thought was Aldebaren. She smiled as she thought of the perfect gift.

She played the first side of the Chopin record and at first, it didn't resonate with her soul the way she thought it might. She read the titles of each track on the back of the album cover. She played the second side and found the Prelude subtitled Raindrop to be pretty, sweet, and a little sad just like the first Chopin piece she heard outside Frank's door. But what really moved her was the Nocturne No. 1. It triggered something deep in her heart that no piece of music had ever touched in her before–a longing for something she couldn't quite get to. Something that was there just around the corner of every note, but then it would elude her. It spoke to her of something in her own heart that she could never quite get to. Her eyes blurred with tears and her arms became a mass of gooseflesh. She played the nocturne a second time and fell asleep in between the speakers.

The following day Vicky ran into Sally out in the hall. Vicky noticed some extra weight clinging to Sally's short frame. She reminded Vicky of a balloon in the bright red blouse she wore, floating way up high, filled with helium like her squeaky little voice. Vicky walked right into her like one walking into balloons suddenly let off a surprise party.

"Surprise. I'm back." Sally's presence filled up the hallway like that large balloon held up to the face which you can't see around and clings to you with static electricity.

"Why, hello, Sally. When did you get back from your cruise?"

"Late last night," Sally said excitedly and Vicky could see she was dying to tell her all about it.

"You gotta tell me all about that cruise someday real soon, but right now I'm late for work," Vicky said with a forceful shove to the clinging balloon leaving sparks of static in its place.

The big red balloon floated back around in front of Vicky, blocking her passage out the door of building 3300. Sally cleared her throat as if there was something else even more important than the cruise she was trying to get at. Sally was only this vigilant when there was gossip brewing.

Vicky quickly searched her mind but could think of no transgressions on her part, nothing that might have conjured up the Spirit of Sally Past. Yet here she was, back, with attitude.

"So what did I do this time, Sally?"

Sally slapped her hand to her chest as if in great shock and dismay. "Nothing. Why would you have done something?"

"Because you're in my face."

"Whatever," Sally said shrugging her shoulders as if she had no idea what

Vicky was talking about. "I just wanted to tell you I heard your music playing last night when I came in and…"

"So what about it? Was it too loud for you, Sal?" Vicky said interrupting.

"No, not at all, it's just that… well, I liked it."

"Thank you. Can I go now?"

"It's kind of a different style of music for you, isn't it?"

"Maybe I'm changing my style," Vicky said, picking her defenses right back up again where she'd nearly dropped them. "Maybe you ought to try changing your style too." Vicky started to walk away but Sally was right on her. The balloon, only having lost a little air, continued to cling to her.

"Almost sounded like something Frank would play."

"Well, as a matter of fact it was Francis who loaned me the album you heard."

"*Francis?*"

"That's his name."

"Since when did you and *Francis* become chums?"

"I'd love to continue this conversation, Sally, but I really must go or I'll be late for work." Vicky turned her back to Sally with a smile of victory. She could almost hear the rush of air leaking rapidly out of the large red balloon.

A few nights passed before Vicky arrived home from work to find Frank's light on. She almost wished it wasn't. The thought of visiting him again made her nervous. "Have I ever felt nervous around a guy before?" Vicky asked herself. She thought about it. She searched her memory. "Never," she answered her own question as honestly as she could. "This ain't like me. Where's your guts, girl?" she muttered to herself as she walked into the building. "Of course I don't have to visit him," she argued with herself. "You had an excuse to barge in on him in the middle of the night last time. Ain't got no excuse this time. But I gotta return his record and I gotta give him his thank you gift. Just leave them at his door. Don't disturb him none."

Vicky went to her apartment and quickly retrieved the Chopin album and her thank you gift which she had wrapped and made a bow for. She stewed over just what to write on the attached thank you card. She finally decided on the following.

Dear Francis,

Thank you for loaning me Chopin's Greatest Hits. I had to listen to it a few times through before I got it. But when I finally got it, I loved it. Especially the Nocturne number 1. Would you tape it for me? I would appreciate it. Please accept this token of thanks for your kindness and hospitality.

Later,
Vicky

She fluffed out the bow on the package and left her apartment, quietly closing the door behind her. Something told her to be as quiet as possible, not just because it was well past midnight but because she felt strangely secretive, like a child stealing a sweet right before supper. There was some forbidden pleasure in this early A.M. visit to Frank.

Vicky made her way down the hall when she noticed Sally's light was on and her door was ever so slightly ajar. She tiptoed swiftly around the corner and up the stairs, looking back only once. No sign of Sally though the light was still on and the door still ajar. "Nosey bitch!" she muttered.

"He's up. You know he's up," she continued to argue with herself all the way up the stairs. "What's the big deal anyway? It's the '80's, man. He ain't gonna think you're forward. He's *not* gonna think you're forward," she corrected herself. "Watch that hickabilly talk around Francis. Gotta quit talking like an ignoramus.

"Francis won't care," she argued back to herself in a whisper as she stood at his door, the silence of the dimly lit hallway feeding her anxiety. "Maybe he left his light on so I'd see it and I'd come visit him. Yeah, right! Get over yourself, Vicky, ol' gal. I wonder what grandma would suggest? A fine lady doesn't just knock on a gentleman's door in the middle of the night, that's what she'd say. Shit! Why am I acting so weird, anyway? What's with me?"

Vicky decided on a compromise. She would knock softly, ever so softly on his door. If he didn't answer she would leave the gift and the album and go. If he did answer, that meant he really wanted to see her.

Her knuckles wrapped lightly on the door while her heart pounded hard and fast. She was ready to leave the album and the gift and go when she heard the sound of footsteps moving toward the door. "Be cool, Vicky, be cool," she told herself.

The door opened and there he stood, wearing a warm navy blue robe with the collar up almost to his ears and his tan leather slippers. "We've got to stop meeting like this," he said so dryly that for a brief moment Vicky wondered if he was serious. His face broke into a smile and she smiled too. The pent up tension needing sudden release caused Vicky's smile to turn into an uncontrollable giggle. Frank quickly motioned her inside.

"I hope I didn't disturb you," Vicky said once the giggling subsided.

"Not at all; as a matter of fact I was hoping you'd see my light on and drop by."

"You were?"

"Yeah, I could use the company. I can't sleep."

"Again? What are we going to do about you, Francis?"

"I don't know. You're the expert."

"What do you mean by that? I'm boring? I put people to sleep?"

"Hardly! No, what I meant is you're a bartender. It's you're job to help people relax. So what do you recommend?"

"A two by four."

"What goes in that?"

"No, I mean a slab of wood across the skull."

"Literally?"

"Brings about a state of unconsciousness every time."

"I thought you meant a drink," Frank laughed.

"No, but that is a great name for one. I oughta come up with something."

"So what did you think?" he said, pointing to the Chopin album in her hand.

"I liked it very much. Of course I had to listen to it a few times for my ears to adjust. You know what I mean?"

"Yes, I do. I like the way you put it, the part about your ears adjusting. That's so true, especially with new types of music you're not used to listening to."

"Let me help you with your coat," Frank offered.

"No, I really can't stay. I just wanted to give you this," she said handing him the album and the gift.

"What for?"

"Just a little thank you gift, you know," Vicky stammered, "for the other night."

"Thank you. That's very thoughtful of you but completely unnecessary," He opened the front hall closet and placed the gift up on a shelf, which nearly broke Vicky's heart with disappointment.

"Well, ain't you gonna open it?"

"Absolutely, I just wanted to help you off with your coat first." He was behind her in a moment, his fingers gripped around the collar of her coat, ready to remove the wrap from her shoulders.

"But I really can't stay." Vicky pulled her coat around her.

"Can't or don't want to?"

"No, it's not that I don't want to." Vicky turned to face him. His look was one of complete earnest.

"Then stay."

"All right. As long as you put it that way I guess I can't refuse."

This time the wrap slipped easily off her shoulders into his hands. Frank hung Vicky's coat up then retrieved her gift off the closet shelf where he had placed it. He examined the neatly wrapped package with the yellow bow. He said nothing but only smiled that pleased little boy smile for a moment before making his way over to his desk, which stood just to the side of his bookshelves. He pulled out a fancy looking letter opener with an ivory handle from a maroon leather cup filled with pens and pencils and such. He opened the envelope which contained her thank you note with the fancy letter opener.

"I just rip my mail open," Vicky said, immediately wishing she hadn't.

Frank's eyes quickly scanned the note. He laughed like she'd never seen him laugh before. Vicky's spirit dropped and heat rushed to her face as she wondered what she'd done wrong. She'd looked up "especially" and "appreciate" in the dictionary to make sure they were spelled correctly. She had her boss check the note to make sure grammar and punctuation were correct. What could it be?

"What's so funny?"

"Chopin's Greatest Hits," Frank said gleefully.

Vicky thought. It said, Chopin–Masterpiece Selections, on the album cover. She took it to mean his greatest hits.

Frank must've noticed the look of chagrin on Vicky's face and set about at once to put her at ease. "No, no, that's great. They *are* his greatest hits. I've just never heard that term used for classical music before."

"I'm so ignorant."

"No, you're not. You're refreshing."

"So is a bottle of pop, but that don't make it very smart, *doesn't* make it very smart. See there I go using incorrect English again. I'm trying to improve my speech."

"You're one of a kind, Vicky."

"You too, Francis. I never met anybody who signed a letter 'I remain' before. Of course you remain. You wouldn't be here if you didn't," Vicky said quickly pulling out of her morose self-consciousness and throwing the banter right back at him. Frank smiled.

He opened her present so slowly it nearly drove Vicky wild with impatience. She watched as he seemingly in slow motion pulled the scotch tape off, careful not to rip the wrapping paper. "You planning on saving that and using it again? I had an aunt, Bobby's mother in fact, she had this problem–couldn't get rid of anything. She'd rewrap presents in used wrapping paper. It drove her crazy at Christmas to see us kids tearing into them presents. 'Don't rip

Odd Numbers

it, don't rip it,' she'd holler at us. You can't believe the junk we found in her basement when she died. Anyway, she'd approve of the way you're opening that gift."

Frank just smiled as he pulled the flat package out of the paper. He scrutinized it closely, his eyes moving back and forth over the letters on the paper label. Vicky thought it best to tell him what it was before he got too confused. "I decided to give you the stars—glow in the dark stars, that is. You stick them on your ceiling. Here, let me show you," Vicky said in a sudden rush of enthusiasm. She slipped her shoes off and stuck her hand out to receive the package. Frank obediently handed it to her. "Follow me," she said as she jogged down the short hall to Frank's bedroom. She flipped the light on and hopped up on his bed.

"Don't worry, it ain't a real gluey substance so it won't damage the plaster none," she said ripping open the plastic package and pulling out the contents. "It's just a very light adhesive, just enough to stick. Here feel for yourself," she said, unpeeling the back of one of the stars and holding it out for Frank to touch.

"It's all right, I believe you." Frank said.

She was so excited about showing Frank the finished product that she nearly forgot he was in the room watching her as she stood on his bed, peeled the back off the stars, stretched as far as her long limbs allowed her, and began sticking the star shaped pieces of plastic to his ceiling. After affixing about several stars, she stopped to give her outstretched arm a break and to see his reaction. Vicky, who was so good at reading people, did not know how to read the expression on his face except to say that it was something akin to shock. She gasped at the realization that she may have offended him by her impulsive actions.

"I'm sorry, Francis," she said stepping down from off his bed.

"What?" he said, looking even more confused.

"I'm outta line, ain't I? Come on admit it. I barge into your private boudoir and force my tacky-ass gift on you. That's what you're thinking, right?"

"Boudoir? Isn't that a *lady's* private chambers?"

"Well, how should I know? I'm ignorant and tacky."

"Oh, geez, I stuck my foot in my mouth again."

"Don't worry, I'll get my stars off your ceiling in no time then I'll be on my merry, tacky little way," she said hopping up on the bed again.

"Wait! Please give me a chance to explain before you jump to the worst possible conclusion?"

Vicky looked at Frank again. She searched his face as he stammered in frustration to get his meaning across. "I love the gift. I never received anything so unique."

"*Unique?* Is that's a polite way of saying tacky?"

"No, that's not true. I keep saying the wrong thing. Maybe it's better if I don't speak at all. Vicky, I'm speechless."

She saw it. Or thought she saw it there in his eyes. He wasn't shocked at her so much, as himself. Could it possibly be, Vicky wondered, that what she saw (and was now seeing) on his face as he looked at her was desire, and his own disbelief and shock over that desire? Maybe, but probably not. Frank would never desire someone like her, but then she realized that she was in his bedroom, standing on his bed in her stocking feet and all the connotations that might occur in a man's mind. Men are very weak creatures where sex is concerned, Vicky thought, and no one knew that better than her.

She quickly stepped off the bed again. "You really mean it? You really like the stars? 'Cause if you don't, I can have them down in a jiffy. No big deal. Different strokes for different folks. It's really no big deal."

"I really like the stars. Please give them to me. I'll finish the rest," he said taking the package from her hand.

"Sorry about this mess I made on your bed," she said picking up the debris from the stars and the package in which they came and crumpling them up in her hand. "Were you ever in the service?"

"No, why?"

"Looks like you could bounce a quarter off this bed. That is before I jumped on it and got it all messed up."

"Vicky."

She squeezed the crumpled paper in her hands. The sound of his voice speaking her name made her feel weak and she didn't like that feeling. "Gotta waste basket?" she asked before he could get a word out.

"Over there," he said pointing to the corner of the room. Vicky threw the waste away then turned, crossed her arms, and looked at him defensively. "What do you want?" she said, doubt and suspicion furrowing her brow at the persistent thought that he was merely being condescending about the gift.

"I want to look at the stars with you," he said as he reached over to the wall and flipped off the light switch. It only took a second for Vicky's eyes to adjust in the darkened room and the stars on the ceiling to glow forth.

"Wow," Frank said, "they're different sizes."

"Yeah, and some are brighter than others. Just like the real thing," Vicky said, beginning to believe in his sincerity but still uncertain as to whether or not she should.

She was aware of him moving closer to her in the dark until he was right next to her. He bent down slightly until, again, they were practically cheek to cheek like the other night when they stood outside and looked up at the real stars. He only had about an inch and a half to stoop because of Vicky's height. He put his hand on her back.

"Look there's Aldebaran," he said pointing.

"Well, I'll be. And there's Orion's belt."

They stood in silence and looked up at the glow in the dark stars. Vicky felt excited, nervous, weak, and most of all, angry at herself for feeling those things. She wished she was a little buzzed, not drunk enough to do something stupid, just a little buzzed so she wouldn't feel so jittery. She wanted to put her hand on his back too, like it was nothing really, like she could play this game as well as he.

More self-reproach at her inability to relax around a man like Frank if she wasn't relating to him as a customer, wasn't fixing him drinks or cracking jokes, but just standing there with him in a dark room, staring at the ceiling with nothing but a tense silence between them. Finally she just did it. She put her hand on his back and at that moment their pose evolved into a kind of half hug, one pulling the other closer until each had an arm draped around the other's shoulder. This closeness to Frank pulled all the defensiveness and doubt right out of her, though she kept trying to grasp them back with the fingers of her mind, to clutch them and return them securely to the prison of her heart. But instead she felt them evaporate through every nerve ending of skin that was warmed by Frank's touch. She wanted to put her head on his shoulder, to be completely and forever vulnerable. She dared not, though, thinking this was enough, in fact, almost too much.

"Want to look at the real stars again, only this time through a telescope," Frank said.

"You have a telescope? Well, of course you do," Vicky said answering her own question. "Where is it?"

Frank reached around her and flipped on the wall switch. They both squinted and blinked from the harsh reality of the sudden bright light, and of course, their embrace ended. "It's in my closet right now. I'm ashamed to say I haven't used it in a while. I was thinking about setting it up on the patio. We'd get the best view that way. But I don't know; it depends on if you mind freezing your kuester off again."

"I don't mind if you don't mind."

They set up the telescope on Frank's patio and bundled up in coats, hats, and gloves. But Frank had to set the stage before they could actually look through the telescope. He poured some brandy for both of them, Vicky herself recommending brandy and a little warm milk as the very best thing for cold and insomnia. Frank couldn't go for the warm milk so they drank their brandy straight.

He brought his tape player outside and played the music 'the planets' by Gustav Holz, which consisted of a piece of music depicting each planet (with the exception of Pluto which had not yet been discovered when Holz wrote the music). The music had to be playing and they had to toast with their brandy before Vicky finally got to look through the telescope. It was the first time for her. She kept expressing awe, while Frank kept expressing disappointment over the ever increasing light pollution which made their viewing less than optimal. He said it was getting as bad as New York City. Vicky suggested they pack up the telescope one evening and drive out to the country. Frank liked the idea. And so they looked at the stars until they could bear the cold no longer.

"Between the cold and the brandy I'm plum tuckered out," Vicky said with a yawn upon entering the warmth of Frank's apartment through his sliding glass patio door. She figured it wasn't just the cold and the brandy but her nerves that had worn her out as well, and she was grateful for the sudden onslaught of sleepiness. It made her care less about Frank and her doubts, leaving her with a welcome relief from the self-consciousness that plagued her all night. Her only thought right now was to satisfy this need for rest.

"You gonna be able to sleep now, Francis?" Vicky said with another yawn which infected him and she noticed his terribly blue eyes were watery and a little droopy after the yawn.

"At least I have something to stare at if I can't."

"That's right, you get to sleep under the stars tonight."

"There's a song about stars on the ceiling, one of the Big Bands, Glen Miller, I think. Something like, 'Why do I have the feeling there are stars on my ceiling? I know why and so do you.'" Frank sang the line. "Anyway it's a love song. I wish I could remember the rest."

"You gotta great singing voice, Francis. Gotta do something about that musical talent."

"You're right. Speaking of music, remember I asked you to listen carefully and pick out which of Gustav Holz' planets was your favorite. You didn't tell me."

"I think it was Jupiter; the real happy one. Part of it was real pretty, like a hymn almost. I think it was Jupiter anyhow."

"The one that goes like this?" Frank hummed a few bars.

"That's it."

"Bless your heart, Vicky, Jupiter's my favorite too," Frank said approaching her suddenly, grasping her face between his hands, and giving her a loud noisy kiss on the forehead.

"Thank you for another interesting evening," Vicky said, unable to look at Frank who was still holding her face in his hands. She wondered if he could feel the scar on her left cheek

"And thank you for the stars. I'd like to give you something in return," he said, at last releasing her face from his grasp and backing away slightly. "Come for dinner. Believe it or not I'm a pretty good cook."

"All right. I'll make some Brandy Alexanders for desert. No warm milk, I promise; just a little crème de cocoa, half and half, and a little nutmeg."

"I'll supply the Brandy. When's a good time for you?"

"Is midnight too late for supper?"

"That seems to be the only time we can synchronize our schedules, doesn't it?"

"I'm guessing we oughta make it a little earlier in the evening. That way I get to see you in something other than your P.J.'s. Let me check my work schedule for next week and I'll give you a holler."

"Great. Go home and get some rest," he said retrieving her coat and purse and seeing her to the door.

Vicky had no trouble falling asleep that night, but she didn't stay asleep. Anticipation of something wonderful kept waking her up.

Chapter 20

Frank opened a cabinet above the stove and pulled out a metal colander which he placed in the sink, humming along with the opera music he'd turned way down low when Vicky knocked on the door, just low enough to be heard subliminally. "Stand aside, this is hot," he said, potholder in hand as he carefully moved the pot from the stove to the sink and poured the steaming noodles into the colander.

"I thought all bachelors used tennis rackets to drain their spaghetti."

"You mean like in the movie The Apartment with Jack Lemmon and Shirley Maclaine? Great film!"

"I guess that's where I got the idea. It was some black and white movie I seen on the late late show one night when I was half asleep. Sorry, I mean, I *saw* on the late late show."

"Well, not only do I not use a tennis racket to drain my pasta, I make my own sauce," he said returning to the stove and stirring another pot with a long handled wooden spoon.

"You mean it ain't Ragu or Prego or something out of a can?"

"Tell me if this tastes like something out of a can?" he said, his hand held under the tip of the wooden spoon which was coated with the thick red sauce. He gently blew the heat off then turned and offered the sample to Vicky. It was strange, him feeding her like this, Vicky thought as she sucked the dollop off the tip of the spoon.

"It's very good. You're quite a cook. For a guy, I mean."

"Not really. I just follow my mother's recipes," he said filling up two fine china plates with spaghetti and sauce.

"So she was the good cook then?"

"Outstanding," he said carrying the plates to the table.

"Her recipes and her music, two things your mama left you. She died too soon didn't she?"

Frank said nothing, only nodded a little sadly to her from the dining room, but the spark and warmth that were in his eyes when he greeted her disappeared for only a second, returning as quickly as they had vanished. "Shall we eat?" Frank said smiling as he motioned Vicky to the dining room table.

The table was set with silver, two crystal goblets, one large and one small at each place setting, and fancy linen napkins folded neatly like the ones at

Odd Numbers

River Inn. A crystal carafe of wine, a large bowl filled with salad, and a tray of bread sat waiting there. He held her chair for her, unfolded the napkin and placed it in her lap.

"Well, ain't you just Prince Charming in person?!"

"Mmmm. This is delicious," Vicky said as she placed another bite of spaghetti in her mouth. "Are you sure you don't have a jar of Ragu stashed back there in the corner where I can't see it?"

"So you doubt Prince Charming can cook as well as slay dragons?"

"A man who can cook and slay dragons is just too darn good to be true. And like my grandma always told me, if a deal seems too good to be true it probably is."

"All right, so I never slew a dragon."

"I knew it." There was an awkward lull in the conversation, and Vicky didn't know what to do except raise her wine glass to Frank and say something about the fine dinner and his excellent culinary skills. He touched his glass to hers and gave her that searching scrutinizing look that always made her nervous.

"Francis."

"Yes."

"I have something to ask you."

"I'm listening."

"I want to learn. Could you help me?" Vicky's tongue was all tied up with her thoughts.

"What exactly is it you want to learn?"

"I want to learn about the finer things."

"The finer things?"

"Yeah, you know, high class things, like…"

"Like which fork to use?" Frank said lifting his small salad fork and spearing a piece of lettuce. Vicky nodded. Her face felt warm from the wine and from sudden self consciousness. She followed Frank's lead, picked up the small fork closest to her plate.

"When in Francis' place, do as Francis does," Vicky said taking a bite of salad. It was vinegary and sour in a delicious way, and like the wine, it sent a pleasurable chill shooting through her jaw bone.

"I assume this is for your restaurant business someday?"

Vicky nodded as she chewed a mouth full of salad.

"I have The New Emily Post's Book of Etiquette by her daughter, Elizabeth Post, if you'd like to borrow it. It's over there on my bookshelf somewhere. I'll look for it after dinner," Frank said.

"Thank you, I appreciate that. But I want to learn more than just what's proper and what ain't, I mean, what's not. See, it's that kinda thing. How I speak. I wanna better my mind."

"Go to college, Vicky."

"The thought terrifies me."

"Start out slow. Take one class and go from there."

"What about you? Will you take those piano lessons?"

"I will if you enroll for a class at the University."

"Are you for real?"

"Absolutely."

"Wait a minute. Don't say it unless you really mean it."

"I don't say things I don't mean. So, is it a deal or isn't it?" he said extending his hand.

"It's a deal." Vicky grasped his hand and gave it a firm shake. "Even though the thought of it scares the living tar outta me."

"I can't imagine you being scared of anything."

"I'm a good faker."

"Well, then you can fake your way right into that classroom on the first day and start from there. You just have to do it, Vicky. I'll help in any way I can. I'll go with you and help you get registered. I'll even walk you to the classroom your first day and see you off at the door if that's what it takes."

"Just like a mama on the first day of Kindergarten."

"Right. I'll pack your lunch make sure you have all your new supplies together."

"Will you make sure my shoes are shined and will you give my nose a good blow at the door?"

"Sure. Well, maybe not the nose blowing part." Frank's bemused look caused Vicky to laugh.

"It's just an early memory. My first day of kindergarten I was so scared and crying so hard. I remember my mama dropping me off at the door, bending down and making me blow my runny nose into her handkerchief. 'Keep your chin up, Vicky Lee. Be my brave little injun.'"

"And I can remind you again to be brave."

"You'd do that for me?"

"If that's what it takes."

"But why? Why do you give a rat's ass if I go to college or not?" Vicky searched Frank's face, and as she did so there was that strange hope again. That hope which she had so flippantly discarded earlier that evening before she arrived when she told herself they could never be anything more than friends. That hope like an old worn out scrap of clothing beyond repair and too raggedy to even give away because, Lord knows, who would want it; that same hope Vicky found herself searching through the trash piles of her heart for because she might just have left something valuable in one of the pockets. She was surprised at how easily she found it, how readily she retrieved it from the refuse, and how willingly she put it back on again. She certainly didn't want it so why couldn't she part from it? She could hide the old tattered garment, her shameful hope, from everyone. But not herself.

Frank didn't answer her question. By not answering he had answered. Vicky thought so anyway. She thought she saw a glint of something in that cryptic smile, something that flashed for a moment in his eyes and then was gone.

They finished dinner, cleared the table and chatted freely while Vicky made Brandy Alexanders; so freely, in fact, that she nearly forgot who she was with. They talked about college classes and piano lessons. They talked about cold weather. They talked about stars and planets and what type of telescope Vicky ought to purchase.

"Speaking of which," Frank said during the course of their conversation. "Have a look at my bedroom ceiling. Go ahead, I'll finish up here," he said above the sound of running water and the clank of metal pots which he tossed into the sudsy sink.

Vicky left him behind in the kitchen and made her way with great haste and excitement down the short narrow hall to the room at the end. She opened the door to the already darkened room and closed it quickly behind her shutting out all remaining light from the hallway. Since she had last been there, Frank had completed the task of placing the glow in the dark stars all over the ceiling from one corner to the other so now it seemed to Vicky that it truly did resemble the night sky. She stood there alone in the quiet and darkness with only the slight green glow from the stars and the red light from a digital bedside clock.

She heard the record fill the space outside the darkened room with its music, so strange and exciting to Vicky. A sense of mystery and awe, a feeling of anticipation, and warmth from the wine all mingled together and culminated in an audible sigh of contentment. But like most of Vicky's pleasurable and peaceful moments it didn't last long. A thought, a worry overshadowed her. The wine hadn't fogged Vicky's mind so completely, however, that she forgot who she was with that evening, whose darkened room she stood inside and just who it was who waited outside for her. It was idle chit chat they made all evening, simply small talk. Eventually they would run out of things to say because of who they were.

She decided then and there she should leave. She would make up some excuse. She would tell him thank you very much for the dinner and would go back downstairs to her apartment where she belonged. She would give up this silly hope, so wretchedly shameful to her. She didn't want it. She would give it up once and for all.

On her way out the door she ran headlong into Frank and they both gasped in startled surprise then broke into laughter. *We still have something in common,* she thought. *We're both human beings. It jolts us to bump into someone in the dark, even if we know who that someone is.* It was the commonality of their humanity that they laughed at as they stood between the darkened bedroom and the lit hallway. It seemed in that moment that they would always have something to talk about, but Vicky knew that thought was only a trick of the wine and the music. She bit down so hard on her lower lip it hurt. She was resolved. She'd move if she had to. Move somewhere where she could have a cat.

"So what do you think?" Frank said looking up at the ceiling.

"I was just admiring it. No telescope needed for these stars."

"No telescope needed. See, I told you I didn't think they were tacky," he said turning his eyes from the ceiling to her. She could see in the dim half-light that strange expression on his face that she wasn't sure how to read, yet sometimes it seemed to be desire. All her usual ability to read others was gone with Frank. She was never sure what she saw in him. She knew she had to leave before her defenses dissolved anymore.

"Francis, I..."

"Come with me," he said interrupting her as he placed his hands on her shoulders, turned her around, and steered her down the hall.

"Where are we going?"

"You'll see." He continued to walk her into the living room until they stopped in front of the most comfortable seat in the house, a plaid soft cushioned armchair, where he handed her the open album cover containing the English translation of the libretto to *La Boheme*. He squatted down next to her chair.

"We're right here," Frank said pointing to a line of text. "It's just a little way into the first act," he whispered as if they were watching the live performance

"It's a little confusing trying to follow along in English when they're singing in Italian.

"And it's even more confusing when you think that the story takes place in Paris, France."

"As opposed to Paris, Kentucky."

"Exactly, so really they should be speaking in French, not Italian." Frank smiled a certain smile she had come to recognize one of amusement. They read on together in silence, his hand again on her shoulder. After a time, Vicky began to get used to the pace, rhythm, and timing of the operatic voices as she read along in English with the occasional aid of Frank's pointing index finger.

A scene sprang to life in her mind. It was her own self Vicky saw, only smaller and frailer, dressed in olden time clothes swooning as her candle and her key fall out of her hand and onto the floor. Rudolfo touches Mimi's hand in the dark as together they look for her lost key. Rudolfo sweetly tells Mimi how cold her little hand is in his. He tells her about himself. Vicky's eyes skipped ahead of the music across the pages of the libretto. Mimi is telling Rudolfo about herself. She's a poor girl. She makes flowers and sells them. She's a sad girl it seems and she has a secret sickness. She coughs. Mimi and Rudolfo are falling in love, so quickly, right there in Rudolfo's small flat.

Vicky stood up suddenly. It was either that or sink deeper and deeper into the comfortable plaid chair. "I have to go."

"Now?"

"Yes, now."

"But why?"

"I just can't hack it anymore. No offense, but this music's really getting on my nerves."

"I thought you liked it."

"I did at first, but not anymore."

"I can put something else on."

"No, it's okay, maybe some other time. I gotta go. Dinner was great. Really. You're a wonderful cook." With quick deliberate steps, Vicky hurried to the door.

"Vicky what's wrong?"

"Nothing."

"But your crème de cocoa …"

"You can have it."

Vicky let herself out with just one quick glance back at Frank. The look on his face was as confused as her thoughts.

* * * * * * *

A couple of days later Vicky paced up and down the little hallway of her apartment, talking to herself, trying to figure out just what to do about the Frank problem. "Son of a bitch," she called him. "Snake in the grass," she blurted out. "What's his gig, anyway? He ain't for real. He can't be. Does he mean to make a fool of me?" She tried to work it all out in her brain in quick logical steps like the restless stride that moved her back and forth down the hall. "And then there's my other problem: too many people know where I live. I can't have ex-customers hunting me down," she said, remembering how two of them had shown up at her door earlier this week, angry that she had nothing to sell them, accusing her of turning narc, and pissed that they had to drive across town to Eddie's. She managed to get rid of them without too much of a scene, but what about next time? If she moved no one would ever find her again, not if she didn't tell anyone.

She'd move on. It's what she always did. Maybe she'd find a little house out in the country and she'd get a big dog with lots of room for the both of them. She didn't need Camelot any more with its' fake towers and turrets and its' empty promises of happily ever after. "It's settled. I'm moving!" She grabbed the newspaper off the kitchen counter and hurriedly paged through it until she got to the classified section and scanned the print until her eyes landed on the words "houses for rent". She grabbed the pen she always kept in her pants pocket and circled the bold lettered words.

She just got paid, and tips from yesterday's Super Bowl party at River Inn nearly made up for a month of lousy business and meager tips. She had plenty to put down a deposit on a new place. She was on her way. She grabbed her keys off the kitchen table, her purse and coat out of the front hall closet, opened her door, and stopped. There he was.

Had it been anyone at her door at that exact moment she would have been startled but even more so with him; the surprise of it all mingled with the effect his presence always had on her. She felt control slip away as her face flooded with an uncomfortable heat. All she managed to get out was a gasp.

"I see you're all ready to go," he said. She flashbacked to another time she had seen him at her door, disgruntled, angry, holding a kitty litter bag in front of her face.

"Francis, what are you doing here?"

"Being spontaneous," he said taking hold of her arm and draping it through his until their arms were locked, escort style. "Of course, Emily Post does advise against dropping in on a person unless you call first, but sometimes instinct overrules propriety."

"What are you talking about?" Vicky said trying to gather her wits about her and not act so confounded.

"I'm talking about taking you to the University to enroll you for some classes," he said walking her closer to the door of the building. "The new semester's a couple of weeks underway already but you can still audit." He was leading her out the door of building 3300, out into the chill of the midwinter day. "I thought if I didn't come see you today, then it would be too late."

"What did you say?" Vicky said stunned at the thought that he somehow read her mind and knew of her plans to move.

"I said if I didn't come see you today I feared it would be too late."

"Too late for what?"

"To get you enrolled for classes." He was moving so fast Vicky felt like he was dragging her. She walked faster and faster to keep up with his pace.

"Francis, leave me alone," she protested, pulling back on his arm and creating enough resistance to stop him. "I have something else to do today." She unlocked her arm from his with an abruptness that matched her words.

"I know: enroll in college."

"Why aren't you at work?" Vicky spoke tersely as she, once again, yanked her arm out from his.

"Since Monday's your day off, I took off work. I'm my own boss. I can do that if I like."

"Are you crazy?"

"What other time could we ever synchronize our schedules? The registration office isn't open at midnight when we usually get together. Seriously, what else do you have that's so pressing today? I know you don't have to work, so what is it?"

"I don't like the fact that you think you can just barge into my life and take over." The words were scarcely out of her mouth when swiftly and skillfully, without her realizing it, he slipped the newspaper section she held onto out of her hand.

"What's this? The classified ads," he said looking at the paper. "What are you looking for, Vicky?"

"None of your fucking business," she said grabbing the newspaper back. "You just made me break my New Year's resolution not to cuss. Fuck you. There I broke it again."

"I know how to break you of that habit. I'll charge you a quarter every time you cuss. It seems the "F" word is a particular problem for you."

"At least I don't take God's name in vain."

"You owe me fifty cents."

"What right do you have?" Indignation pounded at Vicky's temples and pooled in burning tears at the brims of her eyes.

"Houses for Rent?" he asked. "I saw the newspaper."

"You bastard!"

"I won't charge you a quarter for that since I have it coming." He was backing off and backing down. Vicky could see it in his stance and hear it in his tone of voice. "You're right," he continued. "I shouldn't have barged into your life this morning. I shouldn't have snatched the newspaper away from you. I'm sorry. But do you mind telling me why you're looking for a house to rent?"

"Why is it any of your business?"

"Because we're friends and I like having you as a neighbor. Maybe I don't want you to leave Camelot."

Vicky dug through her wallet and pulled out a dollar bill. "Here," she said waving the dollar bill in front of his face. "Just take it."

"Why? I'm not taking your money."

"You said I owe you fifty cents. Just take the dollar and let me buy myself two more cuss words."

"I was only kidding about that."

"Take it before I owe you more," she yelled at him.

"All right, all right" he said, his hands raised in defeat as he took the dollar from her.

"You fucking son of a bitch! You do everything you can to turn me out of this place my first few months here and now suddenly you're my best friend. What gives?"

"I thought bygones were bygones. I said I was sorry. You forgave me. Remember?"

"I thought I forgave you. But now I just wonder," she said eyeing him suspiciously. "What made you up and change your mind about me so quick?"

"I got to know you, and in doing so I discovered I'd misjudged you."

"Yeah, right! Sometimes I wonder if all this nicey-nice business is just a front and you're waiting to trip me up so you can get me kicked out of Camelot for once and for all."

"You really believe that?"

"I don't know what to believe."

"Fine." Frank set his jaw firmly against Vicky. His posture became tense and rigid and his face taut and crimson in color. Vicky had seen Frank angry before but not like this. This was not a cold disdainful contempt like the other times; this was a volcanic eruption held in check; a hot violent fury, the kind that can only discharge itself by hitting, or at least that's how her father always discharged it. As Vicky watched Frank during those slow passing moments she could see the restraint wrestling with the anger, one over the other, each struggling to overcome. Vicky stood motionless, waiting for the successor to emerge while Frank waged his inner battle in silence. She could fight back and she was prepared to.

Restraint finally won out. He said nothing, he did nothing. He turned and silently walked away. Men only got that crazy mad when they were deeply wounded. She saw it in the bars, she'd seen it in lovers, and of course, she saw it with her father many times. Vicky realized as she watched him walk away that what she'd just witnessed was too good to be an act. He really was crazy mad.

"I hurt him. He must really care," she muttered, smiling at the thought, but only for a moment. Then she got scared. "Oh, no, I really did hurt him. Vicky you ding dang idiot. You blew it."

"Francis," she called out to him. "Francis, come back."

He stopped for a moment, as if thinking about it. Then he continued walking. "Grandma would tell me never to run after a man. Don't make a fool of yourself, girl. I'm sorry, grandma, I'm already a fool." Vicky ran until she breathlessly caught up with him at the door of building 3300.

"Francis wait," she grasped his arm. He turned around and looked at her coolly. She could see some of the anger had spent itself just in the short walk across the parking lot. "I'm sorry. I was wrong. You really are for real. Aren't you?" He said nothing but his expression softened as soon as he met her eyes. "It's just it don't, sorry, doesn't make sense to me why you should care."

"It doesn't make sense to me either, but I do."

"I won't doubt you again."

"Good," Frank said with a smile. Vicky willingly gave him her arm this time and he placed it through his.

"Know what? I got a great idea. Let's go to the University and get me enrolled in some classes," Vicky said catching a sparkle in the corner of his eye as he tilted back his head in laughter.

"Introduction to Literature and Art History," Vicky said, looking over the yellow copy she'd received at the registrar's office. She and Frank sat together on a small, functional, and not terribly comfortable vinyl love seat in the hallway of the administrative building right outside the office where she had registered. All around college students were coming and going, walking rapidly down the hallway with books and backpacks, their faces weary yet young, with a dim hope shining beneath the surface. They were all going somewhere in their faded jeans, their worn sweatshirts and tee shirts bearing various signets and designs, their ski jackets, and dirty hair under caps or pulled back from their faces. There was purpose in the quick steps they took. They all knew where they were going. But Vicky felt lost, lost and a little envious as she watched them go by. She may have had a few years on these young passersby but their brains were brighter, sharper, and more focused.

Frank must've seen the wistfulness on her face because he touched her on the shoulder and shook her ever so slightly in what Vicky recognized as a masculine attempt at comfort. "Hey, you're every bit as smart as these young punks who think they know everything." Vicky smiled at Frank's perceptiveness. "C'mon let's go to the bookstore."

"You mean I got to spend more money."

"I offered to help you out, but you wouldn't let me. I'm going to buy your books and I don't want any argument. After all, I'm the one who got you into this."

"I ain't gonna argue with you this time. Man, is it ever expensive! There goes my idea for a little house out in the country and a big dog to go with it."

"So that's what you were looking for. Too bad! Guess you're stuck at Camelot."

"This better be worth it."

"It is. Just trust me on this one," Frank said as they finally made it down the long hall of the old building and out the door. They jogged at the same pace down the steps that led up to the administration building. Upon their descent they found themselves immersed into the fast moving traffic of the campus which contrasted so sharply with the old stone buildings, tall trees, and old fashioned looking lampposts dimly shedding fluorescent pink light against the white midwinter sky. Vicky noted the different looks people bore and the different way they moved and carried themselves, unlike people from Lamasco or anywhere in the area. Two dark skinned people passed quickly by speaking another language.

"I hope you know where you're going," Vicky said.

"I have a rough idea. Just follow me."

"So you're serious about your offer to buy my books, 'cause you don't have to, you know."

"I'm serious."

"Phew, what a relief! Hell, I'm not proud. Oops," Vicky said quickly slapping her hand over her mouth. "Does 'hell' count as a cuss word?"

"You're really serious about this quarter a cuss word business, aren't you?"

"How else am I gonna break myself of this habit?"

"Personally, I think it's a great idea. After all I did come up with it. In fact I think I should charge interest." Vicky glanced over at Frank just long enough to give him a playfully reproving look. It was then that she realized they were holding hands. Somehow it happened and she wasn't sure how or when exactly. She didn't know who took whose hand first or if it had been mutual, but there they were with their hands clasped together, swinging their arms to and fro, like a couple of kids at recess.

"So how much do I owe you?"

"Let's see," Frank said, leading her off to the right down a lovely tree lined pathway that led to an open area with a statue in the center and buildings all around. "Seventy-five cents, I believe."

"Wait a minute. I bought two words, remember?"

"I know. I'm not counting those. You said one in the car on the way over here."

"That was because of your driving. You pulled in front of a car."

"Then there were two choice expletives in the registrar's office."

"When I saw how much it costs just to audit a class."

"The other time was reading over the course description."

"No, I just mispronounced that Russian guy's name."

"Dostoyevsky? Nice try, Vicky, but I don't think so. So that's three; I'll cut you some slack this time, but don't let it slip again."

"What about you? You cussed when you pulled in front of that guy and almost hit him."

"I didn't pull in front of him. He didn't yield for me."

"Doesn't matter."

"All right then you only owe me fifty cents."

"Okay, I got one question. What about when you're really in pain; like say you hit your thumb with a hammer? There're just no other words you can say at a time like that."

"I suppose we could have certain dispensations, for moments of extreme duress. But then again if we start making exceptions where will it ever end?"

"You're right. No exceptions. We'll just have to come up with another word that works."

Vicky felt glad to be there with Frank, holding his hand. She could imagine the solitary feeling of rushing about a busy place like this all by herself. After all, there was no loneliness like the loneliness she felt in a crowd. So often she wanted to reach out and touch people, physically, to stop them, to talk to them and see if they were real and not just pieces of her imagination, to enter into their world for just a moment, and in so doing, break out of the solitude of her own. It's just what she did as a kid, stopped people on the street, sometimes bumping into them on purpose. She'd strike up a conversation with anyone. Grandma said she never knew a stranger and it was true until she got old enough to figure out that it scared most people to have their worlds intruded upon. So she learned to control that impulse, and it left her with an uneasy feeling of being all stuck inside herself. But she didn't feel lonely now, not with Frank's palm pressed against hers and their fingers locked. His hand was colder than hers at first but now it was the same temperature.

"Here we are at the quadrangle. This is the center of the campus. I think that's the bookstore right over there," he said pointing to one of the buildings. They stopped for a moment but were still holding hands. "Who's that?" Vicky asked pointing to the bronze statue of the man in olden time clothes reading a book.

"The founder of the University I believe."

"I wish I had a look like that," Vicky said noticing the way his brow furrowed, not with worry but with intent as he pondered the words on the page of the bronze book which he held in his hand. "When I was a kid at school my brain just never stayed with me long enough to get what I was reading. Teachers said I was smart but I never believed them. How can you believe you're smart when you read the words but you just don't get it. I wanna get it. I wanna look like him."

Frank squeezed her hand and they both stood there in silence for a while. Vicky sensed Frank gazing at her out of the corner of his eye. She turned to meet his gaze. He swung her hand in his and said, "I hope you don't ever look like that guy," Frank said.

Upon entering the University bookstore Vicky was overcome by a hot wave of embarrassment, as if everyone, Frank included, could see her inadequacy.

"Look at all those books I gotta read before I look like that guy," Vicky said. Frank laughed but Vicky wanted to cry.

Vicky made Frank go to the music store after they left to check on piano lessons. After all it was their deal. "Man, who dusts around here? This place flippin' shines," Vicky said upon entering the store as her eyes beheld beautifully polished shades of black, brown, and tan pianos in all styles, each reflecting the light of crystal chandeliers which hung helter-skelter from the ceiling.

"May I help you?" a man in a dark suit asked approaching them.

"Yes," Vicky said as she pointed to Frank, "he's here for piano lessons." The man broadened his smile and lifted his eyebrows in what seemed to Vicky a feigned interest. She guessed he'd been carefully groomed to be nice to all the customers, even the annoying ones.

"Well, not now actually." Frank corrected Vicky's outburst. "What the lady means is that I'd like to find out about getting lessons. Can you recommend someone?"

"Why yes, I know of an excellent teacher. Let me get her card."

As soon as the man turned his back, Vicky grabbed Frank by the arm and led him to a grand piano in the center of the room. "You gotta play this one. I gotta hear you play, Francis."

The man came back with a business card which he handed to Frank. Frank thanked the man and examined the card.

"Is there anything else I can help you with?"

"No, thank you, we're just looking."

"Let me know if I can be of any help." The salesman walked off and occupied himself with looking busy; repositioning piano benches and music sheets, dusting off corners with a big white dust rag he produced from his suit coat pocket. All the while his attention was covertly focused on them.

"You promised. Remember?" Vicky said in a half whisper.

"You hold up your end of the bargain. I'll hold up mine," he said in mock defense pulling the card away from Vicky when she tried to look at it.

"Ask him. Ask him if you can play," Vicky pleaded in hushed tones tugging at Frank's sleeve while motioning toward a piano. "Ah-hem," Vicky cleared her throat. "Excuse me, sir. May he sample one of your pianos?"

"Certainly."

"He knows everything there is to know about music. Actually I don't really think he needs lessons, just a refresher course. Why, he could probably teach."

"Vicky!"

"Can he play that one over there?" Vicky asked, pointing to the shiny black grand piano in the center of the room.

"No, no. This one will be fine," Frank said settling himself at a lesser instrument closer to the corner of the room. How handsome and dignified Frank looked sitting up so straight as he scooted the bench in.

"Ah, see, I picked a lucky piano," he said, a sudden smile of surprise spreading across his face as he spied the sheet music before him. "Debussy's Claire de Lune. It was the piece I played in my last recital."

"Let's hear it, hot shot." With that Frank took a deep breath, locked his fingers together and stretched them until Vicky heard them crack. He carefully positioned his fingers on the keys and began to play.

The sound of his playing transported Vicky into that same world of sweet ecstasy she visited briefly outside his door on the night their friendship began. She moved carefully and quietly over to him and sat down slowly, with great decorum and restraint so as not to disturb him, on the corner of the piano bench. It didn't seem to bother him, her being there. At that moment Vicky was oblivious to everything but Frank. She watched his fingers move back and forth over the keyboard, she was so closely aware of his breathing that it seemed she was breathing right along with him. Most notable of all was his face, filled with an expressiveness Vicky had never seen. She'd seen him jovial and outgoing, with that intelligent good humor and wit. She'd seen him thoughtful and good mannered, ever the gentleman. And she'd seen his darker side; stern, intolerant, and angry. But she'd never seen this before; tenderness with a subdued passion just barely peeking out every now and then. It was something akin to love, she guessed, all of these emotions she read on his face. She wanted to put her arms around him, to rest her head on his shoulder but she knew it would disturb his playing. When he finished he turned and looked at her, and for a moment it was just the two of them inhabiting the planet all alone and undisturbed. The brief spell was quickly broken by the sound of the salesman's applause.

"Bravo," the salesman shouted and Vicky joined in with the applause adding the sound of cheers and whistles.

"See you weren't as rusty as you thought you'd be. Did it all come back to you like riding a bike?"

"Actually yes," Frank said with surprise.

"Sir, may I honestly say that I don't know if you need lessons. It seems to me you've already had sufficient training. I think your skills are more advanced than what the instructor I recommended is accustomed to working with. Perhaps you need to work with someone more advanced. You say it's been years since you played?"

"I play maybe once a year, when I go home to visit family. My father has an old baby grand which belonged to his father."

"You need to play more. You have a real gift," the salesman said.

"It's what I keep telling him," Vicky said. "And I never even heard him 'til today, but I knew it. I just knew it."

"Well," Frank said, hesitating, as he stood up and pulled the business card out of his wallet. "I'd still like to give this instructor a call, if for no other reason than to have a chance to play on a weekly basis."

"You know with your ability you really ought to own one," the salesman said with a gleam in his eye as if his fruitless day may suddenly pay off after all.

"I really can't afford one right now. Thank you anyway." Frank smiled politely and zipped his jacket with certain finality, to let the salesman know their conversation had come to a close. He then took hold of Vicky's elbow and tried to steer her away. "We really need to go," Frank said to her with raised eyebrows and a tense smile. "Goodbye and thank you." Frank put his arm around Vicky's shoulder and hurried her toward the door.

"We'll be back," Vicky called out to the salesman.

"Boy, you are one expensive date," Frank said as soon as they got outside. The sun peeked out from behind the winter clouds as they walked at a slower pace making their trek toward Frank's car and their next destination, wherever that might be.

"Do you have any idea how much one of those things costs?" Frank asked, his arm no longer around Vicky's shoulder but tight against his body, his hands in his pocket. It seemed to Vicky he was feeling the cold more intently than she was.

"Francis darling, it's an investment, like my education."

"No, it's *not* the same thing."

"If I'd known that I wouldn't have let you buy my books."

"Nonsense, Vicky that was my pleasure. I can afford a few books. I just can't afford a piano right now."

"I know, but still it doesn't seem fair somehow."

"What do you mean?"

Vicky didn't reply right away. She waited until they got to Frank's car, so they wouldn't be moving, so she could turn and face Frank, so she could look at him eye to eye, human to human, soul to soul.

Ever the gentleman, Frank escorted Vicky to the passenger side of his car.

"You helped me out with my investment," she turned and said to him before his hand could reach the door handle. "I just wish there was some way I could help you out with yours."

"Forget it," he said opening the car door. "A cad like me needs to do something nice for someone else every now and then. How else am I going to redeem myself?"

"You already have. But then again maybe you haven't. Don't stop trying anyhow. You just don't have to try that hard." She playfully elbowed him in the ribs and it made him laugh.

Vicky took one step into the car and immediately Frank was assisting her.

"I'm not an invalid, you know," Vicky protested as Frank made sure she didn't bump her head getting in. He pulled the shoulder strap over her and pushed the metal buckle into its sheath with a click. Vicky was uncomfortable with this sudden and unexpected closeness of proximity.

Frank smiled and quickly kissed her on her scarred cheek on his way out. The kiss stunned her. She touched her cheek as if she'd just received a wound.

Chapter 21

It was hot in the little apartment from all the cooking; the biscuits baking in the oven and the chicken frying in the skillet, which Vicky turned over one piece at a time with a pair of metal tongs. She turned the heat down on the burner and wiped the sweat from her brow, examined the corn and the green beans on the back burner and gave them a quick stir with a long handled wooden spoon.

"Phew, it's hot in here," Vicky said as she reached into a drawer just off side of the stove for her potato masher. Indeed, it was one of the first warm days of spring. A welcome breeze blew in through the screen door that led out to Vicky's patio and brought with it the distinct smell of spring with its fresh air, rain, and faint fragrance of honeysuckle. So much was changing; the earth, the weather, and Vicky. "Our blood's still gotta thin out before we become accustomed to the heat again."

"Thin out? This is something your grandmother told you, isn't it?" Frank said, stepping behind Vicky as she pushed the potato masher into the hot steaming pot.

"You're getting to know me, Francis."

"So what did Grandma say?"

"Grandma said your blood thickens up in the winter to help you stay warm. Now I don't know if that's a scientific medical fact but it makes sense. Don't you think?"

"Who am I to argue with Grandma's medical knowledge? Her whiskey and honey mixture fixed me up just fine when I had bronchitis."

"Fixed you up just fine now, did it? You know, you're starting to talk like me."

"And you're starting to talk like me."

"Yes, King's English and all that rot," Vicky said in a mock British accent. "Anyhow, the whiskey and honey mixture was just a standby really. Grandma always said the best cure for a cough was bark from a black gum or wild cherry tree."

"I'll remember that next time I have a cough. Instead of going to the drugstore I'll go to the park and peel some bark off a tree. So what do you do with this bark; chew it, smoke it, what?"

"You boil it in water and drink it, you ignoramus." Vicky said carelessly grabbing a dishtowel and opening the oven door. She pulled the rack out and lifted the biscuits, only half aware that the worn through material of the dishtowel served as a poor protection from the hot pan.

"Mmm, those smell good. Careful, you'll burn yourself. Don't you have any oven mitts around here?"

"Naw, why should I? Don't need them. Oh, that's another thing about Grandma, she cured burns."

"Of course she did."

"Actually she'd take offense if I said it was her did the healing. She claimed it was the Lord, she was just a vessel used to draw the fire out."

"Draw the fire out?"

"Right. This one time, I guess I was around seven or eight, I was at grandma's house and she was ironing some clothes. I was running through the house being silly; grandma warned me to settle down but you know I was just a stupid kid. I tripped over the iron cord, fell to the ground, and this piping hot iron lands smack on my bare leg."

"Ouch!"

"So grandma runs over to me, grabs the burnt leg, holds it up in the air and commences quoting bible verses. All the while she's just a blowing on the burn. Says she's got to blow the fire out 'cause it's still burning inside the skin. Says she's gotta get it out before it burns all the way down to the bone. I can see her kneeling there beside me, frantic, just a prayin' and a blowin, prayin' and a blowin, then all at once she lets go my leg, breathes this big sigh of relief, and starts thanking and praising the Lord for the healing. Sure enough, my leg stops hurting right at that instant. "

"You're kidding!"

"I swear by my grandma's grave."

"Move over Mayo Clinic. So then what happened?"

"After that she put a little talcum powder on the burn. A few days later it dries up and peels off, never even left a scar. Anyhow Grandma said the devil was mad about my healing 'cause the Lord done it – sorry – did it – so he was gonna try and get me back somehow with fire. But she said not to fear 'cause the Lord would be my protection. Since then I never burnt myself. Even if I touch the hot handle of a pot or pan, it's like I got a callous right there protecting me, like some kind of protective shield clinging to the outer layer of my skin. I know it sounds weird. Unbelievable really, but true. You think I'm crazy, don't you, or at least ignorant and superstitious?"

"Vicky, since I met you I don't know what to believe."

"I mean here I am reading the likes of Charlotte Bronte, Charles Dickens, and all them and I'm really starting to get it and enjoy it and yet a part of me is still so ignorant."

"You're not ignorant and neither was your grandma. Obviously she knew something we don't if she could cure a burn by blowing on it and quoting bible verses."

"So you do believe me?"

"Yes, Vicky, I'm learning to believe things I can't explain."

"And I'm learning to find a reason for things I believe. I don't know, I think my brain's changing. I think it's from all the reading," Vicky said, picking up a chicken leg with the tongs, examining it then placing it back in the bubbling grease.

"Speaking of which, how's Great Expectations coming along?"

"Better. I only had to reread like maybe three or four paragraphs this last chapter. I didn't have my usual trouble, you know, reading a whole page then wondering what the heck I just read."

"Good. So you're getting it?"

"I'm getting it. I think I'm getting smarter. At first I thought how am I gonna relate to this English dude who lived a hundred and fifty years ago. And the language is so different, you know, at first I had to reread a lot, but now I'm getting used to it, I'm getting into it. It's like I'm inside Pip's head and I totally relate to him."

"Oh, yeah? How so?"

"He's an orphan. All he's really got in life is Joe, kinda like me and Bobby. I felt like him a lot growing up. And how about that crazy Miss Havisham and all the nutty head games she's playing at poor old Pip's expense. But the thing about Pip is he's so alone."

"He's an odd number."

"Yes, he's an odd number. And I'm the only one privileged enough to get inside his head and hear his thoughts; just me, well and any ol' person who happens to pick up the book and read it. And the thing is, by getting to know Pip and Jane Eyre and all them other folk I thought I wouldn't have a thing in common with, I'm understanding myself better and I'm figuring out that we're all more alike than we think. And I feel less like an odd number. Maybe we wouldn't be so lonesome if we would just pour out our hearts and souls and share our stories with one another instead of walking around like we all got corn cobs stuck up our backsides and it hurts too dang much to smile at our fellow man."

Frank laughed as he reached for her and drew her into his arms. Vicky was taken by surprise at first until she got caught up in the laughter and began laughing too. She squeezed him tight and remembered how somewhere she'd heard, maybe from her grandma, that you could always tell how in love a couple was by how much they laughed when they were together.

The embrace lasted longer than any other, even after the laughter subsided. It ended all at once and somewhat awkwardly, and Vicky thought it a shame that after her lengthy discourse on the benefits of opening up the heart and mind to others, she couldn't let Frank know how much she loved him. No matter, she thought while Frank set the table in silence and she nervously hummed and whistled while stirring the contents of pots, placing chicken pieces on blocks of paper towels, sprinkling flour in the pan drippings, and stirring in milk to make gravy. No matter. She loved her Francis in private and was content to do so. She feared to expose such a love was to jinx it somehow.

"Dinner's ready. Now this is how we do it in the country," Vicky said placing all the serving bowls and plates on the table. "It's called self-service."

"You gotta observe country hospitality. You don't grab, you pass. And your guest gets the first pick. Francis darlin'," she said passing him the plate of chicken.

"Thank you. This all looks delicious: an authentic country meal."

"About as authentic as you're gonna get these days. For truly authentic it'd have to be game I killed and skinned myself, and instead of plain ol' corn, maybe hominy."

"What is hominy anyway?"

"Hulled corn with the shit boiled out of it."

"Hmmm. Maybe it was just your description of it, but somehow that doesn't sound too appetizing. By the way, you owe me a quarter."

Vicky winced, then without a word she reached into her jeans pocket and retrieved the coin and put it on Frank's placemat. Frank handed her the plate of chicken with a bemused smile. She handed him the bowel of mashed potatoes and the gravy boat. "Mr. Perfect," Vicky said sticking her tongue out at him. "Your curse words oughta be worth fifty cents 'cause they're worse than mine. Least I don't take God's name in vain."

Frank heaped mashed potatoes onto his plate with a big grin. "So tell me."

"You're changing the subject."

"You're right. So tell me," he said, pouring gravy over his potatoes then reaching for the corn, "have you actually killed, skinned, and cooked your own game?"

"Well, heck yeah, city slicker! My Daddy used to take me hunting and fishing. It was the only time we ever really got along. I think he wished he had a son instead of me. Anyways, the first time I killed something I cried my eyes out. I remember it was a squirrel. I couldn't look at it afterwards. I sure as heck couldn't eat it. It was funny, you'd think my Dad would be all tough and Mr. Macho about it, but he was actually pretty cool. Said he cried the first time too. Said it's all right if you kill for food. If you just kill for the fun and sport of it, it's *not* right. Anyhow, Bobby told me some of the American Indians used to ask forgiveness from the animals after killing them, explaining to them that they needed the food for their family. When I learned that I felt a little better about it. Now fishing never bothered me quite so bad. I don't know why. Maybe it's because fish are cold blooded creatures. But to kill something warm blooded. It's just…" Vicky touched the scar on her cheek. "I don't know."

"Vicky, how did you get that scar on your cheek?" He had seen her touch it. She wasn't even aware that she had.

"Barroom brawl," she said, picking up the chicken breast she had placed on her plate and taking a large bite, large enough to occupy her mouth for a while why she considered just how far she would elaborate on this fib. "See, I was working at this really divey redneck joint…"

"Don't lie to me."

"Sorry. It just sounds more adventurous than to say I got it in a car accident."

"What happened?"

"I had a run-in with providence."

"Excuse me?"

"Providence–that was the name of the street. I hit a street sign." She said it nonchalantly then turned her attention to her plate and began working fork and knife together to create a large mound of corn kernels. She quickly put the forkful into her mouth. She would eat slowly. She would try to count to forty and make the bite last that long. She looked at him and shrugged like it was nothing.

"How?"

"I was trying to avoid this kid on a bike who pulled in front of me. I went up on the curb and hit this sign. It bent in half and came crashing through my windshield. It was pretty fierce. There was bits and pieces of glass all over my face, but what left this here scar was from the sign itself not the glass. It cut me. Damn near cut my head off. Oops, there goes another quarter," she said retrieving the small spiral notebook from her pocket. "That's twenty-five cents for the 'D' word," she said writing in her notebook, her head bent down so that her hair fell strategically in front of her face. She shaded her eyes with her hand as she doodled in her notebook, pretending she was writing something. She didn't want Frank to see her crying. Her jaws ached and her eyes burned as she swallowed back tears. 'Help me,' she wrote on the small page. Then she remembered she'd been forgiven. She scribbled some stars and a crescent moon and wondered if it really took. She believed it had. She believed. So why couldn't she tell him?

"Are you crying?" He reached across the table and pulled her hand away from her eyes. "Vicky, look at me."

What a relief. He guessed something was wrong. She wouldn't have to stifle her tears. She could tell him the truth.

"That kid on the bike... I hit him and killed him."

Frank got out of his seat and walked over to her. He handed her his monogrammed handkerchief and put his hand on her shoulder. He remained silent while she sobbed. Vicky knew he was thinking of something to say to make it all right. She knew it was a male anomaly, this problem of not knowing how to handle tears. Male bartenders were better at it. She figured it was because there was a bar between them and the crier, and they could do something, either give them a drink or cut them off. But Vicky was a woman and she knew what most criers needed were a kind word and a touch, even the sloppy, drunken, self-pitying ones. Of course when they sobered up most of them needed a good swift kick in the ass, but there was usually something behind the tears, something only love could heal.

Vicky stood up and threw her arms around Frank's neck. She only hesitated doing so for a moment. After all seeing someone cry was much the same as seeing them vomit; what with all of the shame, vulnerability, and humanity exposed. She didn't care. What did she have to lose? She cried out all the details. How she'd fought with her Dad before she got behind the wheel, how she didn't see the kid until it was too late, how she feared she was driving too fast though she was never charged with anything; and how they were in the same hospital that night, she and the boy, only she pulled through and he didn't. Frank shushed her and rocked her and petted her hair as she dampened his neck and the front of his shirt with her tears.

"You're soaked," Vicky said as the tears subsided.

"I guess I don't mind as long as it's just tears, not snot."

Frank smiled and Vicky couldn't help but smile at the sight of him. They both sighed deeply at the same time.

"What we need around here is a little music," Frank said changing the tone.

"So what is it today?" Vicky asked through sniffles as she blotted her eyes with the handkerchief.

"Let's see, we've covered baroque, classical, romanticism, impressionism..."

"Neo-romanticism, modern, movie soundtracks..."

"And a strange potpourri of pop and rock..."

"Ain't it the truth? Everything from Erik Satie to Eric Clapton."

"Ah yes, Clapton, the greatest guitarist of our time."

"You pick."

"I didn't bring anything. It's your place, you pick."

"I can't decide. You know my album collection as well as I do, give me some ideas."

"Well, it seems to me that music is like wine. It should always go with your meal. Bearing that in mind I think something more on the country side is what we need."

"I know. Johnny Cash." Vicky said as her heart lightened, filling up with a cleansing sense of calm, hopefulness, and starting anew which sometimes follows the release of tears.

"Seems like the logical choice to me."

"My favorite Johnny Cash song is," she said, pulling out the desired album, its cover beginning to fade and wear. *"Man in Black."*

"I don't know that one."

"Listen to the words," she said carefully placing the needle on the correct track.

Vicky danced around the living room as she sang along with the record, stumbling over some of the lyrics which came back to her in fits and starts.

> *Well, we're doin' mighty fine I do suppose,*
> *In our streak of lightnin' cars and fancy clothes,*
> *But just so we're reminded of the ones who are held back,*
> *Up front there oughtta be a man in black.*
>
> *But 'til we start to make a move to make a few things right,*
> *You'll never see me wear a suit of white.*
> *Oh, I'd love to wear a rainbow everyday*
> *and tell the world that everything's okay,*
> *But I'll try to carry off a little darkness on my back,*
> *'till things are brighter I'm the man in black.*

"Don't you see, Francis darlin', Vicky said in a flash of insight as soon as the song ended. "Johnny Cash and Charles Dickens are just the same. They're both storytellers and they both care about the poor and downtrodden."

"A connection I would have never made. Please join me. I miss your company at the table," Frank said taking a sip of beer from a glass mug.

Vicky frosted the mugs in the freezer before Francis arrived. She explained to him that you had to drink beer with fried chicken, not wine. She looked at her plate of half-eaten food and decided she was no longer interested in the food, just the beer. So she joined Frank at the table, picked at her food, and tried not to gulp her beer too fast, but the brew flowed down her throat ever so smoothly, washing clean all the tears that had past.

So together they sat, Vicky and her Francis. She laughed at the sensual way he ate and the yummy noises he no longer tried to stifle. He noticed she wasn't eating and scolded her for gulping her beer on a virtually empty stomach. "You've got to make room for that homemade apple pie you slaved over all day."

"I ain't that interested in my own cooking," she said taking another slug of beer.

"Take it easy," he scolded again. Vicky shrugged it off, but after the meal when Frank excused himself to go to the bathroom, she downed two shots of whiskey and opened another bottle of beer which she quickly pushed to the corner of the kitchen counter and threw a dishtowel over as soon as she heard him come out of the bathroom. She began rinsing off dishes, wiping off the counter and singing along with Johnny Cash as he crooned 'Sunday Morning Coming Down', all so nonchalantly, hoping he wouldn't suspect.

He walked right up to her and stood close. He said nothing, just looked at her very seriously and touched her scarred cheek. He caressed the scarred area tenderly and it felt so good Vicky closed her eyes and basked in the warmth of his quiet touch.

"I wish I could take it away," Frank said suddenly.

"It's ugly, ain't it?"

"No, Vicky, nothing about you is ugly, even the scar. It's just that I wish you didn't have to be reminded every time you look in the mirror."

"Most of the time I don't take notice of it. Heck, I'm so used to seeing it there it's just another part of my face, like my nose or my mouth. It's not like I walk around thinking about the accident all the time. Most times I don't. But still, it's always there, gnawing around at my gut. It's just not something you ever lay to rest."

"Is that why you drink so much?"

"Don't start in on me, Francis. I don't drink anymore than anybody else." Vicky said defensively backing away from him.

"Sorry my mistake. Leave it to me to spoil a tender moment. How can I get it back?"

"Easy. Touch me again, look in my eyes, say them sweet words you're so famous for."

"Vicky let me take that scar away from you," he said, gently clasping her shoulders and pulling her toward him. "Maybe I could kiss it away."

He pulled her close and started kissing her scarred cheek over and over again. It was a moment suspended in sheer bliss as their arms wrapped tightly around each other. Tears filled Vicky eyes again only this time not tears of sorrow, but tears of utter and profound joy, almost something akin to shock. Indeed, there was this feeling of disbelief, as if this moment wasn't really happening to her. A tear escaped out of the corner of her eye and he kissed it. Her legs felt as if they would give out from under her, and she thought if she wasn't holding on to him so tightly she wouldn't have been able to stand but would have fallen limply to the floor like a rag doll. Their lips found each others' so easily and naturally. Vicky both hoped for and dreaded that moment since the night she first came to his apartment, and now here it was, their arms locked around each other, their lips pressed and melded together. The kiss could have gone on forever it seemed, never completely spending itself, always finding more fuel to ignite it. It was the single most ecstatic moment of Vicky's life up to that point, until it ended quite abruptly.

Like all magic spells it was broken, suddenly, intrusively, and cruelly by the world outside. A clock striking twelve, the prick of a finger on a spinning wheel, the stubbing of a toe, the ring of a telephone, the beep of an alarm clock, all those things that demand we wake up and look harsh reality in the face. This time it was a knock on the door. It started them both with a sudden jolt.

"Don't get it, Vicky," Frank whispered into her ear as he kissed it.

"I got to Francis. Whoever it is knows I'm here. I got my stereo playing and I done filled up the hallway with my cooking odors. They're gonna keep trying until they get me. It might be Allison. Maybe she needs something." Vicky broke loose from their embrace. She was strangely relieved for the knock on the door.

"You've become too good of a neighbor," Frank said, folding his arms with a wry smile.

There stood Sally at Vicky's door in her electric pink and neon green floral print culottes and matching top with glow in the dark flat heeled slipper type shoes on her wide little feet. Her hair was big and her face was bright. She held in each hand a bottle of red wine.

"Vicky," Sally said sounding like she was in a panic.

"Hey, Sally. What can I do for you?"

"I hope I'm not catching you at a bad time, but I'm absolutely desperate. I'm going to this swank dinner party and I need to know which wine to bring."

Vicky deliberated quickly in her mind whether she should take a look at the bottles right there while Sally stood at the door, give her a rapid fire opinion, and send her on her way or should she invite her in? Why not invite her in? If she was too hurried with her, it would only make Sally suspicious, and besides, what did she have to hide anyway?

"C'mon in," Vicky said stepping aside.

"Thanks so much. Really, I hope you don't mind. Well, hello Frank, what are you doing here?" She said coyly as if she already knew.

"Vicky treated me to an authentic country meal complete with homemade apple pie."

"Is that the delicious smell I keep smelling?"

"I'd offer you some but I know you're on your way to that dinner party and I don't want to keep you."

"So what do you think?" Sally said holding the two bottles out for Vicky to see.

"Do you know what they're having for dinner?"

Sally proceeded to tell her what the dinner menu was as Vicky studied the two bottles of wine.

"This California cabernet here is the one. We serve this at River Inn. It's a little fruity and a little nutty in flavor. Tastes like a cross between plums and sunflower seeds."

"Plums and sunflower seeds?"

"Yeah, it's wonderful. Real subtle. Flows down like that first sip of water on a hot day. Never makes your mouth pucker like some dry reds. It's not going to overwhelm the palate but rather accent all them, sorry, all *those* flavors," Vicky said catching her grammatical error. She was much more likely to catch herself speaking incorrect English when her guard was up, and it definitely was up right now.

"Of course this is just my opinion. Either one's an excellent choice when you get right down to it. You can take both of them and sample them right before dinner. Make sure you swirl and sniff first."

"That's our Vicky. She knows her wines," Frank said.

"She certainly does," said Sally.

Vicky wondered what was going through Frank's mind now that Sally was here. She looked at him and realized he looked a little different, slightly more crumpled, less polished, hair and demeanor less in place, almost a little disoriented. She liked the look and she loved him this way. She wondered if it showed, the fact that they'd been kissing. Was her face chaffed from razor burn, was her hair messed up, and did she have that glazed dopey far away look? Sally had to know and how did Frank feel about her knowing? Vicky didn't care if she knew. She didn't care if the whole world knew, but the question was did her Francis care if others knew. She hoped he didn't but she feared he might. She would observe him and see.

"I hope I haven't intruded on a private little wine tasting party for two," Sally said coyly, with eyebrows raised so as to leave little doubt about the innuendo behind her statement. Vicky said nothing. She would see how Frank responded.

"Nonsense Sal, I was just leaving. I'll walk you to the door."

"Please don't leave on my account," said Sally.

"No, I need to get going before I stuff myself with anymore fattening food. I think I'll go home and coil up in a big ball like a boa constrictor that just swallowed an elephant. Maybe I'll be able to move by tomorrow. Vicky, could you roll me to the door please?"

"I'll try," Vicky said playing along.

"Well, at least you don't look like a boa constrictor that just swallowed an elephant," Sally said looking at her midriff and shaking her head.

"Now no self-deprecating on my watch, Sally old girl, you're as lovely as ever."

"I may be lovely, but I'm still fat."

"Not fat, merely voluptuous," Frank said.

"Yeah, right, well I guess it's time to go get more voluptuous," Sally said with a sigh. "Here Vicky, you can have this other bottle of wine."

"That's not necessary."

"Please take it, for all your trouble."

"It wasn't any trouble. Are you sure?"

"Positive. Now take it."

"Thanks Sally, that's awful generous of you," Vicky said taking the bottle of wine.

"And thank you for all your help."

"And thank you for a wonderful dinner," Frank said affectedly as he took Vicky's hand and kissed it. It was a kiss for show, carefully contrived not to show any real feelings. They said their goodbyes and Frank walked Sally to the door. Vicky had her answer.

Of course he would be back after Sally left. What would she tell him? She stuck four ice cubes in a highball glass and poured some Jack Daniels over it. She drank it down quickly, crunched the ice cubes then poured another glass, and another, and another. Would the liquor make her weak or strong? "Please be strong, Vicky, you fool. Please be strong. I won't be his private little whore that he can just tuck away and hide in a corner."

The inevitable knock on the door came, startling Vicky as she paced back and forth rehearsing her speech. She paused a moment, took one last swig out of her glass of whiskey, crunched an ice cube in half and reminded herself that she was angry at Frank. He was too embarrassed to let Sally know the truth about them. Too embarrassed to put his arm around her and say to Sally, "Yes, as a matter of fact you were disturbing something." He was too embarrassed to let anyone know. He was embarrassed of her.

She clenched her fists, gritted her teeth, and grunted. She had to work herself into this state of anger. It was her only defense. Anger had always been her ally and protection, except when she let it burn out of control. Would it be possible to keep that anger, yet still keep it in check with all the alcohol floating around in her brain, confusing and exaggerating her emotions?

"Keep him at arms length. Keep him at arms length. Don't let him kiss you again," she told herself. She slowly opened the door.

"Come in," she said coldly avoiding his gaze.

"Were you talking to someone?" Frank asked.

"Myself. I do that when I'm trying to work things out in my head," Vicky said as she closed the door behind him.

"Vicky," Frank said laughing. "You are one of a kind, you know that? Come here." He took her in his arms and began kissing her face.

"I knew you'd be back."

"Of course I'm back. We have unfinished business. Now where were we before we were so rudely interrupted?"

With one gigantic force of the will, Vicky pushed Frank away. "Stop kissing me."

"What's wrong? It's me, Francis. Remember me?"

"All I can say is God bless Sally. When she knocked on that door she knocked some sense into me."

"What are you talking about?"

"Don't come any closer. Don't look at me like that."

"Like what?"

"You got that horny guy look. You done had it all evening. I know that look. I've seen it before."

Frank laughed.

"Stop mocking me," Vicky snapped.

"All right, I admit it. I like you, Vicky, I like you a lot. I find you very desirable. I thought you felt the same way."

"I do, Francis. Ain't no use in lying to you about it." The confused look on his face made her feel almost sorry for him.

"Then what's wrong?"

"I can't be mad at you, at least not for long. Why is that?"

"Were you mad at me?"

"Yes."

"Why?" He blurted, the frustration causing his face to redden.

"Think about it, Francis. You're the intelligent one, the sensible one. It don't make sense. It just don't make sense, the two of us together. I'm sorry, it *doesn't* make sense. Look at us. We're two totally different people from two totally different worlds. I don't fit in your world and you don't fit in mine. Oh, you'd be a prize catch for me, but unfortunately it would never be that way for you."

"That's not true."

"I might be kind of a novelty at first but time would wear on and you'd grow ashamed of me, the redneck girlfriend with the bad English and tacky taste."

"I don't think of you like that."

"That was your first impression."

"It's changed."

"Maybe, but first impressions die hard."

"Do you have such little faith in me?"

"Francis, we're both grown ups. You know as well as I do sex changes things between people. We let this thing go where it's heading and it'll ruin what we got. Don't ask me how I know, I just know. It'll never work 'cause you're you and I'm me. It'll have to end eventually and when it does it'll end how these things usually end; with us being bitter enemies instead of friends. And I can't stand that thought, Francis. I just can't stand that thought."

Vicky could no longer see Frank from the blur of tears in her eyes. She felt suddenly dizzy and weak and her eyes attempted to focus on two Franks instead of one. "Shit, I'm crocked," she said leaning against the wall.

"Vicky," he said approaching her.

"Don't touch me."

"Don't worry. I'm not in the habit of taking advantage of ladies who've had too much to drink. Good grief, I've never seen booze hit somebody so fast before," he said putting his arm around her and walking her to the couch. "Will you even remember this conversation tomorrow morning?"

"Hell yes."

"Sleep it off. We'll talk about it tomorrow." The whiskey was causing her head to spin and she was feeling suddenly too drunk to argue with him. He sat her on the couch, propped up all the throw pillows, and helped her lay down.

"Oh, you're already barefoot," he said examining her feet to see if there were any shoes to remove. He pulled the afghan off the back of the couch and spread it over her. "I'll be right back," he said hurrying out of the room. He returned a little while later with a tall glass of water and the small trash can from Vicky's bathroom.

"I don't need that trash can, Francis. I ain't gonna puke."

"Purely precautionary," he said sitting the small can down next to her.

"I ain't gonna puke. What's the matter, don't you think I can hold my liquor?"

"That's the problem, Vicky. You hold it a little too well. If I drank as much as you did tonight I'd be in the hospital getting my stomach pumped. Here, drink this," he said helping her sit up and handing her the glass of water.

"I didn't drink anymore than you did."

"Oh, yeah, then what is that bottle of Jack Daniels and glass with melted ice doing sitting on the kitchen counter? I saw it when I went back to get your water."

"Shit!"

"How much did you drink between the time I walked Sally to her car and came back here?"

"None of your beeswax."

"Drink your water. It won't make you sober but it will help your hangover." Vicky took several large swallows from the water glass.

"Easy there! Not so much at once." Frank gently took the water glass away from her

"I've taken care of a lot of people when they was drunk, but nobody's taken care of me. Why are you being so nice to me?"

"Why do you think?"

"You must have something up your sleeve."

"Why do you always believe the worst of me?" Frank walked to the kitchen and returned shortly with a damp dishrag. He squatted before the couch where Vicky lay and blotted her face. The cool dampness felt good against her skin.

"You really do care don't you?"

"Yes!" he said somewhat crossly, as if he was irritated that she had to ask.

"I won't doubt you again. You know I'm crazy about you, Francis. You sure you don't want to take advantage of me in my drunken condition. You could, you know."

"There you go, expecting the worst of me again. Besides, nobody would dare try to take advantage of you, Vicky. You'd deck 'em."

"Damn straight I would." Vicky wanted to say more, but she couldn't get her tongue to work properly.

"Just remember, Vicky, whatever happens between us…" He paused.

"Remember what?"

"Nothing. Hey, I want you to know I heard everything you said back there before you collapsed to the floor."

"I didn't collapse to the floor."

"That's because I caught you first."

"My fucking hero. How many quarters is that?"

"I lost track," he said dabbing the washcloth on her forehead and cheek. "Like I was saying, I heard you. Every word you said. As far as I'm concerned you're the boss lady. You call the shots. You want us to just be friends, we'll just be friends."

"We are still friends? Aren't we?"

"I think so. He looked at her for a moment as if there was something else he wanted to say. "Goodnight Vicky. Please take better care of yourself."

Vicky woke up the next morning with the most terrible sense of dread. She rolled over and tried to go back to sleep again, hoping somehow it would go away. She had the sense she had done something wrong and whatever it was she didn't want to face it. She closed her eyes, pulled the afghan over her head but sleep would not return. She'd done something wrong all right, she knew the feeling. She just couldn't remember what. The last thing she remembered was the kiss. Oh, what a kiss it was! How could she ever forget? Then somehow things went wrong. There was something about Sally. After that everything was fuzzy.

She didn't think she and Frank made love because she was on the couch by herself and fully clothed. It was something she said or did–something to drive Frank away. The sudden smell of vomit filled her nostrils and made her gag. It was in her hair, on her clothes, and some on the carpet. Thankfully, she only found a small remnant of it on the couch. Most of it had made it into the trashcan which had miraculously made its way from the bathroom to the side of the couch, as if some guardian angel had placed it there.

"Shit, did Francis see me puke? Worse yet, did I puke on him?" The thought catapulted her into a sitting position, but not for long, as the room swung around making her dizzy and causing her to fall back onto the throw pillows. She would have to go to work later that day. She would have to clean up and pull herself together. Her head throbbed, her mouth was dry, and her hands shook. "Gotta get up, gotta help myself, gotta get aspirin, water, a little hair of the dog. Gotta call Francis, gotta apologize to him, though I have no idea what for. Just know I gotta. But first I gotta check the truck."

Vicky wrapped the afghan over her head and shoulders so as to hide the remnants of dried vomit. She ran out into the parking lot. Her truck was in the same spot. That was a good sign. She walked around the vehicle carefully, checking it for dents, scratches, and blood. She checked the inside. Everything seemed to be right where it was the last time she recalled driving it, which was when she came home from the grocery store the previous day. "Well, that's a relief, anyways." She said. She ran quickly back into building 3300, her grandma's old afghan trailing behind her, knocking out the chill from the cool spring morning.

Chapter 22

"All right Francis, tell me what happened last night?" Vicky inquired of Frank over the phone.

"What, no cordial greeting, no exchange of pleasantries, just 'tell me what happened last night, Francis'?"

"I called to apologize," Vicky replied, "but maybe you need to apologize to me first."

"What for?" Frank asked.

"Did we?"

"Did we what?"

"What do you think?" Vicky's voice was shaky.

"Don't you remember?"

"Francis, did I hurt you?" Vicky asked as she held her breath and waited for his reply.

"I'll say! I got scratch marks all over my back. You little hellcat, you!"

"You're kidding me? Right?"

"I'm having way too much fun at your expense. Yeah, I'm kidding you. Nothing happened. Just a kiss."

"Yes, I remember that," Vicky said nonchalantly as she cleared her throat which felt like she was gargling sand. "Okay then, now to get to the reason for this call. Like I said, I called to apologize."

"For what?"

"I have no idea. I thought maybe you could tell me. I just know I did something wrong."

"Vicky!"

"I probably don't want to know, do I? Send me the cleaning bill if I puked on you. Well, anyhow, I'm sorry for whatever it was. And I want you to know I'm on the wagon." *Just as soon as I cure this hangover,* she thought as she placed two white tablets under her tongue and washed them down with some bourbon, then quickly popping a small yellow capsule in her mouth she gulped down the last little bit of brown liquid from the highball glass. The alcohol was to quell the anxiety and numb the discomfort. The aspirin were for the headache. The amphetamine was to counteract the effects of the alcohol and give her a boost of energy so she'd be able to work later that day.

"Do you remember our conversation?" Frank asked

"No, but I do remember being mad at you–not entirely sure why. I didn't try and slug you, did I?" Vicky said pouring a half a glass of bourbon. She figured with the speed she could afford to have another glass.

"No, Vick," he said sounding amused.

"You sure?"

"I'm sure. You were pretty hacked off though. I think if you'd had your wits about you, you would have tried to slug me."

"Sorry."

"It's okay, it didn't last long. Actually, you were fairly reasonable, for a drunk that is."

"How's that?"

"You really don't remember, do you?"

"No."

"You gave me a very logical argument as to why we should remain just friends."

"What did I say?"

"That it would never work out because our backgrounds are so different."

"And what did you say?"

"That I respect your wishes and I don't want to do anything to hurt you or our friendship."

"And that was it?"

"Well, then you collapsed to the floor and I, with great effort mind you, managed to get you up and get you over to the couch."

"'With great effort?' What do you mean by that? I wasn't belligerent was I?"

"No, you were heavy."

"Excuse me."

"Not fat, heavy. Dead weight, heavy. I had to practically carry you."

"Oh. All right then," Vicky said clearing her throat in closure. "That's all I wanted to know. Catch you later." She abruptly hung up the phone and got ready to go to work.

Vicky turned a new leaf after that day, like she always did, like she'd done so many times before. Each time she started off hopeful. This time it was no alcohol for an indefinite period of time and all around cleaner living. Allison had started her on the cleaner living kick. She'd taken to arising every morning at five thirty and jogging with Allison at six. She took mid morning naps on days she had to work. She went to bed early on days she didn't work. And she started taking vitamins at the urging of Allison who was now selling vitamin and supplemental nutritional products on the side.

"The soil's not what it used to be," Allison would tell her as they jogged together on those cool spring mornings in early May. "And I should know. I grew up on a farm. The produce just isn't the same as what it used to be. It's been depleted of its nutritional value by all the insecticides and herbicides. We have to have vitamins to supplement what we're not getting in our food." Allison would say between audible yet unstrained and even breaths.

"You sure that's not all a ruse by the vitamin manufacturers." Vicky would say between labored and sometimes painful gasps for air.

"I've got research from some very credible sources if you'd like to take a look at some of it."

"No, thanks, I'll take your word for it. I'm trying to get through Melville for my Lit class without falling asleep. Throw some research papers on top of that and I may just slip into a coma. How some guy could get so whacked out over a whale, I'll never know."

"How many times have I told you not to make me laugh while I'm jogging? It hurts."

"Oh, yeah, you don't seem to be in any pain at all."

"Well, neither do you."

"You mean you can't hear my lungs rattle from here?"

"You've got to quit smoking Vicky. What an incredible athlete you'd be if you'd just give up those cancer sticks."

"I gave up booze and I've cut back to a pack a day. What more do you want?"

"Look at you Vicky, you outrun me every time."

"It's 'cause my legs are longer than yours. I'm naturally fast. Always have been. But you, Allison, you're the long distance runner. You're the one with endurance. I start out fast and furious then burn out. But you just keep going, like one of them little battery operated bunnies with the drums."

"A sprint runner and a long distance runner. The tortoise and the hare. What a great team we are. Speaking of teams, what's new with you and Frank."

"Ah, it's getting harder to talk," Vicky said between gasps for air. "I was hoping you could do the talking and I could do the listening."

"Sorry, you don't get off that easy."

"There's not much to tell. We're good friends; that's all."

"Just how good of friends are you?"

"Hey, don't believe everything Sally tells you."

"I was just kidding."

"Hey man, can we walk now? I'm hurtin' for certain."

"Sure," Allison said effortlessly easing back to a walking pace. Vicky stopped abruptly, stooped over with her hands on her knees, coughed, hacked and spat as she tried to catch her breath.

"Sorry, this isn't very ladylike."

"Sometimes you just gotta do what you gotta do. Are you okay?" Allison patted her on the back.

"Never felt better," Vicky said pulling a handkerchief out of her shorts pocket and coughing hard into it. "Much better. Nothing more satisfying than bringing up a good loogie."

"You know, I never would have pegged you as the handkerchief type."

"What would you peg me as? The sleeve and shirt tale type?"

"Gross! Funny but gross. Say, that sure is a fancy looking handkerchief you got there!" Allison said teasingly, her eyes moving in on the corner of the linen material in Vicky's hand.

"Well, I ain't gonna hand it to you. I got some sense of decorum, you know," Vicky said pleased she got to use her new word of the week.

"Good, I don't particularly care to handle it. But it is a very nice handkerchief. And whose initials are those on that monogram? Did I see an "F" and a big fancy "H" in the middle?"

"All right, so it's Francis'."

"You know I love giving you a hard time, but you also know you can talk to me. I'm not going to go around spreading rumors like Sally. That's not me. I don't break confidences."

"I trust you, girl. It's just that honestly there's nothing to tell. We're friends. That's all there is to it. That's all there can ever be to it."

"You look sad when you say that."

"I'll be honest with you. I'm crazy about him. Its nuts, isn't it? Who'd have ever thought?"

"It is pretty crazy, considering how the two of you started off. So why can't it ever be?"

They walked past the church and Vicky wondered how Father Mudd was doing. A sweet morning breeze touched her cheek. She looked at the field across the street with its tiny green sprouts just breaking through the soil. By mid summer Camelot would be a different place, much quieter, as the corn stalks would grow tall enough to muffle the sound of traffic from River Road. Next to the church another strip mall was being built and soon the noise from the construction crew would break through the quiet of this early morning serenity.

"I'm not sure he'd ever love me as much as I love him," Vicky replied, finally coming up with an answer to Allison's question. "He kissed me once but we'd both had a little too much to drink and you know how that goes. Oh, I think he gets a kick out of me and all, and there's no question he's a little attracted to me but I think that's only 'cause we're so different. You know that old saying about opposites attract. Besides men have always reacted to me like that. I must give off some kind of scent or something."

"Vicky! Well, you are gorgeous, you know. I just wish you'd let me talk you into cutting your hair," Allison said lifting a tangled mess of auburn curls from her shoulder. "You have such a pretty face but no one can see it with all that hair hanging in front of it. I know you're self-conscious about the scar, but…anyhow, go ahead about Frank, you were saying…"

"Where were we?"

"Something about giving off a scent."

"Oh, yeah. Men just naturally flirt with me. I'm not bragging or anything it's just always been that way. I don't take it seriously. Flirting is one thing, love is another. So Francis flirts with me. So what? But the thing is we're friends," Vicky said, hanging on to that word "friends" desperately as if it was a precious, rare, and highly coveted treasure. She clutched the unseen thing that was Francis friendship to her chest. "I don't want to lose that."

"What makes you think you would?"

"If we get, you know… involved, it'd change everything. One thing I've learned in my twenty-seven years, you best be mighty careful before you make that leap from friends to lovers. You can go there but you can't ever go back again. No way back from lovers to friends, no matter what anybody tells you. The way I see it there's no sense in us becoming lovers because there's no future in it. It's doomed. It'd end eventually, once he found him a suitable bride, then I'd become nothing more than an embarrassing little memory. His wild fling with the white trash girl. And I couldn't stand it, Allison, 'cause I love him too much."

"What makes you so sure he's not in love with you too? What makes you think he wouldn't consider you a suitable bride?"

"C'mon!"

"So your backgrounds are different. His own parents came from very different backgrounds. So why couldn't it work?"

"I don't want to think about it Allison. If I do I'll get my hopes up. I refuse to do that. I'm just going to enjoy what I have while I have it. Nobody but you and I know I love Francis, nobody else needs to know, including Francis."

"Okay, supposing everything you say is true. Supposing, he does find a 'suitable bride' as you call it. Then what happens to your friendship?"

"It would change things of course. We could never be as close as we are now, but at least we could still be friends without all that hangdog embarrassment between us."

"You know you might find someone else before he does."

"I don't think so."

"Why do you say that?"

"Cause I never had it so bad for anyone before. It just ain't, sorry, *isn't* gonna wear off anytime soon."

"What makes you so sure?"

"Girl, once you've had filet mignon it's kinda hard to go back to spam. Lord almighty, I'm a fool. Listen to me go on like I ain't got a lick of sense. But enough about my love life, what about you and Kent? You're gonna be an old married lady soon. Too bad in a way. Here I've gotten used to us jogging of a morning and now you're gonna move out. You mailed your invitations yet?"

"I hope to finish addressing the last of the envelopes tonight."

"You said that last week. Kinda dragging your feet, ain't ya? The wedding's what?"

"Five weeks away."

"I'm looking forward to it myself, especially the reception. It'll be switch for me being on the other side of the bar at River Inn. I told my boss I'll quit if they don't treat you right."

"Thanks for all your help with the reception plans. I couldn't have done it without you."

"Think nothing of it."

"It's time to head back," Allison said looking at her watch. Together the two turned around and faced the looming turrets of Camelot. Vicky squinted just like Allison instructed her to do. The first time she saw Allison do it she asked if there was something wrong with her eyes. She said she always squinted when viewing Camelot from a distance. She tuned out the strip mall on the one side and the cornfield on the other and imagined she was in some far distant place and time. She imagined it was a real castle. But only Vicky was squinting today. When she looked at Allison she saw her eyes wide open with no imagined world of romance and adventure before her, only the stark reality of an apartment complex in the midst of suburban sprawl that was infecting everything, even Allison's beloved Midwest.

"All right, Allison, I've been totally honest with you. Now it's you're turn."

"What?"

"You know darn good and well what. You just aren't acting like a bride to be or how a bride to be oughta act at any rate."

"Just how is a bride to be supposed to act?"

"Excited, nervous, you know, upbeat. You're supposed to be… happy. Don't give me that old song and dance about the wedding plans just stressing you out so bad. The fact is I know happy when I see it and you ain't happy."

Allison's eyes welled up with tears and she looked at her for the first time with total candor. "I just wish I loved Kent the way you love Frank."

"We're a pair, ain't we? I'm in love with a man I can't marry and you're gonna marry a man you can't love."

"It's not that I don't love him, it's just…"

"Allison, quit trying to make something right in your mind that just isn't right in your heart."

"I believe they call that rationalization."

" 'Rationalization.' Shoot, I don't have my notebook with me. Oh, well, it's like you're trying to talk yourself into loving this dude just so you can go through with the wedding. But you aren't married yet, Allison. You don't have to go through with it."

"What am I supposed to do?" Allison cried, covering her hands with her face. "The invitations are supposed to go out tomorrow."

"They ain't out yet. If you don't love him, don't marry him. You ain't doing either one of you a favor. Don't you think he deserves to find someone who loves him, I mean really loves him?"

"I never thought of it that way. I just don't understand what happened. I used to love him, back in the beginning."

"You were a kid then. You didn't know shit from shinola. No offense, most teenagers don't. You grew up. You changed. Both of you did."

"You think I should end it? You really think I should end it? Oh, my gosh! It'll kill him. He'll hate me."

"You ain't that special, Allison. He'll get over it. Better to end it now then five, ten years down the road with a couple of kids and a house you gotta split up and a mean ol' divorce lawyer breathing down your neck for every last penny. Then he really will hate you. Think about it. All right?"

They were silent for a while as they entered the drive into Camelot.

"How late are you working tonight?" Allison asked her eyes focused straight ahead.

"Eleven. Why?"

"Come see me when you get home."

"Kinda late for you ain't it? I don't think I've ever seen your lights on when I get home at night."

"Tonight they will be. I'm going to tell him it's over."

"You sure now? Don't just do this 'cause I think you oughta?"

"I'm not. I've wanted to end it for the longest time. I'm just such a coward. You're the first person who's given me permission to do it. I've tried to talk to other people about it but everyone keeps telling me it's just prenuptial jitters.

"Oh, my gosh, I'm actually going to do this. I'm scared to death! But at the same time I already feel free. Promise you'll come see me."

"I'll be there, friend. And don't worry, it'll be all right. My grandma always said it's senseless to worry. Everything comes out in the wash."

When Vicky arrived home that night Sally's door was wide open with the light on. Often times it was open or just slightly ajar, and always a light was on. Whatever the reason for this odd habit, whether it gave her a sense of security or a feeling of control, Sally knew when people came and went. There was no way up the stairs without passing her apartment. She knew when Vicky went upstairs to visit Frank and when he came downstairs to visit her. Vicky didn't care, but she cared that possibly Frank cared. She feared that Sally's speculations and rumors might run Frank off. But tonight she wasn't going upstairs to see Frank.

Vicky knocked on Allison's door and, to her surprise, Sally answered. Of course Sally already knew about Allison's break up with Kent and had come to comfort her. Sally stood at the door like a sentinel, the perfect barricade between Allison and any intrusion from the outside world.

Vicky craned her neck to see around Sally. There she spied Allison sitting at her dining room table with her head down, her shoulders shaking, a box of tissues at her elbow, several of them used and scattered about the table top like the debris from some natural disaster, the aftershock of which left her with silent sobs and barely audible sniffles.

"I'm guessing she went through with it," Vicky said.

"You guessed right."

"Is she all right?" Vicky asked.

"As good as can be expected under the circumstances."

"I'm glad you were here for her, Sal," Vicky said meaning it quite sincerely. She thought how Sally's nosiness had paid off in this situation. Allison needed someone with her and Sally, the interfering matriarch of Camelot Apartments, could also be the concerned and comforting mother presence when called upon. Vicky actually felt a kinship with Sally at this moment.

"C'mon in," Sally said stepping aside and allowing Vicky to enter. "Here, let me take that," Sally said taking the large brown grocery sack out of Vicky's arms.

"Just a little something to ease the pain," Vicky said as she handed Sally the sack. Sally looked inside and smiled.

Vicky went over to Allison, squatted at her side where she was seated and placed her hand gently on Allison's back.

"Hey, are you okay?" she said gently. When Allison didn't even raise her head she decided to try a different approach. "Congratulations, you're a free woman," Vicky said slapping her on the back. Allison laughed a little in the midst of her sniffles.

"Yeah, I did it," Allison said finally lifting her head to reveal two bloodshot eyes and a damp face.

"Look at it this way; you don't have to address those envelopes now. I can make you laugh, can't I? After all, we're not jogging."

"And how about those thank you notes you don't have to write," Sally said.

"Thank you, ladies. Thanks for helping me put things in perspective," Allison said smiling. It was the best kind of smile, Vicky thought, the kind she'd often seen at the bar, a smile that finally sees the humor behind the suffering and can laugh about it somehow, someway. It was the only thing that made heartbreak bearable and it was a miracle of sorts–a gift from the gods for the price of tears. Laughter in place of pain, better than any analgesic or even narcotic.

"See, you just gotta laugh, Al. Let it all out. That's it!" Vicky said as Allison laughed then snorted then cried, laughter turning to sobs, turning back to laughter again, all mixed together with tears.

"The best part of it is I can quit my diet now," Sally said.

"So can I," Allison said.

"I have just the thing for those not worried about their weight," Vicky said standing up.

"I put it on the kitchen counter," Sally said motioning to the brown grocery sack.

Vicky retrieved the sack and set it on the dining room table. "An economy size bag of chips," she said pulling the bag out of the sack and laying it before Allison as if it was precious loot. "Sour cream and onion dip." She said lifting a pint size plastic container from the bag. "And a little something to wash it down with." Vicky lifted a large bottle containing greenish, yellow liquid from the sack. "Sweet and Sour mix," Vicky said presenting the bottle. Allison had already ripped open the bag of chips. Reaching once more into the grocery sack, Vicky pulled out two bottles. "Tequila and Triple Sec," she said placing the two bottles down at the same time with a slight but deliberate bang.

"Oooh, looks like we're going to have a party," Sally said snapping her fingers, wiggling her hips, and la-la-ing along to the tune of "Tequila".

"And…" Vicky said reaching into the bag, "just a little beer to give it that touch of something extra." She pulled out a single bottle of beer. "And of course, what would margueritas be without lime and salt." Vicky dipped into the bag one last time and pulled out two limes and a small baggie of salt. "I know they're your favorite," she said smiling at Allison. "Now if you'll just loan me your blender and some ice I'll get to work. But I must tell you

I'm strictly bartender tonight. I can't join you. I'm on the wagon for the present."

"Whatever for?" Sally asked.

"Clean out my system from all them poisons. It's Allison's doing really," Vicky said gathering up her bottles and bringing them over to the kitchen counter. "She's got me on this cleaner living kick, got me taking all these vitamins." With that she withdrew a cigarette from her purse, lit it, and inhaled deeply.

"But you're still smoking?" Sally replied.

"Yeah, well, you gotta have some vice," Vicky said burying her face in the cabinet above the stove where she retrieved Allison's blender.

"Yeah, but smoking will kill you. It seems to me the healthier choice, if you're going to give something up for health reasons that is, would be to give up the cigarettes."

"I tell her that all the time," Allison said her voice hoarse and strained with tears.

Vicky hid her face in that cabinet for a moment longer than necessary so that Sally wouldn't see. She feared she might read something in her expression, that somehow she might see in her eyes the horror of waking up in the morning with absolutely no memory and that feeling of stark panic. Strange, but that awful feeling that came with the morning after a binge was the exact same feeling she awoke with morning after morning for several months after the car accident. It was sickness, shock, remorse, and dread all rolled into one giant knot in her stomach making her want to hide under the covers and not face anyone.

Would Sally be able to look underneath the surface into that great lurking terror which Vicky managed to keep hidden most times, the terror that somehow those demons of anger and recklessness would be unleashed if she lost control again. She remembered how she ran out and examined the pick up truck that morning.

"Hey, one vice at a time," Vicky said. "Besides, it's only temporary. Just long enough to get the poisons out." How silly it was that she was afraid to let Sally see her face. She shrugged it off.

"I don't want anything to drink, Vicky. Thanks anyway, but I just want to have a clear head right now," Allison called out to Vicky in a tearful voice.

"Well, I don't want to drink alone so you may as well not bother," said Sally.

"Not a problem," Vicky said with a sense of relief. She put the mixer back in the cabinet and stuck all of her bottles and things back in the grocery sack.

"What I really want is something chocolate," Allison said crunching on a chip. "I've got salty I just need sweet to go along with it." She took another chip out of the bag and stuck it in the white creamy dip.

"I've got some brownie mix back at my place," Sally said.

"Go get it," Allison and Vicky said in unison.

"Maybe we shouldn't," said Sally.

"It's all right, Sally ol' girl. I'm gonna get your butt up at six a.m. and you're gonna jog with us."

"Six a.m.! You two jog at six a.m.!?" Sally exclaimed.

"Amazing you don't know about it. But then I guess that isn't within your watch hours, is it?" Vicky asked.

"What are you talking about?" Sally said indignantly with her dwarf-like hands on her hips.

"It's about the only time your door's closed and a light ain't on. If somebody wants to do something in private around here they gotta do it between the hours of three and eight a.m.," Vicky said.

"Not true!" protested Sally.

"Seriously, Sally, how many hours of sleep do you get a night? It can't be more than four or five. No wonder you're so manic. You're sleep deprived." said Allison.

"Yeah, you're like a kid–afraid you'll miss out on something if you go to sleep," Vicky said.

Sally did what she always did when she was stymied–clucked her tongue and humphed. "I'm going to get the brownie mix now. Keep me informed on any new developments that might occur while I'm gone."

"You got it. We wouldn't want you to be in the dark, Sal," said Allison as she exited. "And close the door behind you. Not everybody keeps their doors open around here."

"That's right. Were you raised in a barn, girl?" Vicky called out. Allison forced a sad little laugh

"Everything's going to be okay, isn't it?" Allison asked with that look of worry returning to her brow. "He'll forgive me someday, won't he?"

Vicky nodded slowly and reassuringly then she put her arms around Allison. "Everything's going to be just fine. You'll see. Kent will find someone who's crazy about him and he'll forget. And as for you, you'll have a wedding someday and it will be wonderful because you'll be marrying someone you're crazy mad in love with. You'll wear that beautiful dress and it'll be the happiest day of you life. You'll find the right guy soon. He's waiting out there somewhere just like you, waiting and searching. Everything's gonna be okay, darlin', you'll see," Vicky said rocking her friend back and forth and shushing away her tears.

"Yoo hoo!" The voice of Sally rang out just moments later as she barged through Allison's door without a knock. "I got it," She said holding up the box of brownie mix with one hand and sounding somewhat winded. "I hope one of you has eggs."

"I got eggs," Allison said.

"Terrific," Sally said with her wide, purple shadowed eyes, accentuated by the big frames of her glasses. "Let's bake some brownies."

They baked brownies together that night. They laughed a little, talked a little, Allison cried a lot, and they all ate too much. Vicky thought this is what women do for each other. They feed each other.

Chapter 23

She found the note under her door that morning.

> *Come see me tonight after you get off work.*
> *I've got something to show you.*
>
> Love, Francis.

Sally's door was ajar and her light was on when Vicky arrived home from work close to midnight. "Not again," Vicky mumbled aloud in frustration. Things had been pleasantly quiet around Camelot building 3300 lately. Rumors about Frank and Vicky had died down. The focus was on Allison and her break up with Kent just five weeks before their scheduled wedding date. But now Allison was getting on with her life and Sally would soon need something new to gossip about.

The question in Vicky's mind was how to get to Frank's place without walking past Sally's door? There had to be some alternate route. It seemed the answer was right there, right on the cusp of being realized, something so obvious, but what? There had to be some way to get to his place from the outside, some way to climb up.

"What's wrong with these modern apartment buildings," Vicky said aloud to the wall as if someone might just emerge from behind it and answer the question, "how come they don't put fire escapes on the outside anymore? It would solve my problem in a heart beat." Her mind quickly raced through all possibilities until at last she stumbled upon the one so perfectly apparent, so serendipitous that she believed it had been placed right there for her and her purpose alone.

"The workmen's ladders!" The moment of awareness came with a rush of mischievous excitement that for Vicky was one of the most delicious natural highs. "Don't get too excited. Don't get too excited," she coached herself in a low voice as she unlocked her door.

Building 3300 was one of the many buildings in the Camelot complex undergoing roof repairs from recent storm damage. She knew the workmen usually left some of their things there overnight and she thought she saw a ladder by the light of the side floodlight when she came up the walk that night.

She entered her apartment and made sure to close the door behind her with a loud enough bang so that Sally would think she was in for the night. She threw her purse on the sofa then quietly crept out her sliding glass patio door into the coolness of the June night, bright with a full moon and alive with the sound of buzzing insects. She turned the corner and walked around the side of the building. Sure enough, there was a perfect aluminum ladder lying in the grass. "Yes!" she shouted aloud, then realizing she shouted a little too loudly, she quickly covered her mouth so as not to expose the clandestine operation she was about to carry out.

She carried the ladder to the other side of the building by Frank's place. The most difficult thing was remaining quiet. *Sally has ears like a cat,* Vicky thought as she gingerly set up the ladder and locked it into place in front of Frank's window. Her only fear as she slowly ascended each step was that someone might spy her with the brightness of the full moon shining on her like a searchlight.

She reached the top in a short span of time, and with all her tomboy agility climbed over the balcony railing. Frank's light was on and she could hear piano music playing. The sliding glass door was open as she figured it would be on this beautiful night. She stood for a moment just taking in the beauty of the whole scene: the moon, the piano music drifting into the night air, and the breeze blowing at Frank's curtains through the screen.

Carefully she slid open the screen door, pushed aside the curtains, and stepped into Frank's apartment. She heard a thump like a piece of furniture falling to the ground.

"Who's there," the terror stricken voice of Frank called out into the darkness.

"It's just me Francis darlin'–your friendly neighborhood cat burglar." Vicky said emerging from behind the curtains.

"Holy shit!"

"Watch it, you owe me a quarter."

"Holy excrement!"

"Too late. Did I scare you?"

"You knocked ten years off my life," Frank said dramatically clutching his heart, taking deep even breaths through his nose and exhaling noisily through his mouth.

"You know, you oughta be more careful about keeping your doors locked."

"Vicky, I don't know what question to ask first. What, why, how, when and where did you come from?"

"I just borrowed one of the workmen's ladders and climbed up. They just leave their stuff lying around on the lawn, you know. Why don't they put fire escapes on the outside of buildings anymore? It would make my job so much easier."

"Why, may I ask, would you do something so inane?" Frank said, his arms flailing everywhere like they always did when he got excited.

"Inane. You know you've used that word on me before. 'Devoid of meaning, Empty. Meaningless. Pointless.' But to get back to your question, I did it so I wouldn't have to walk past Sally's place. Her door's wide open and she's just a waitin' in there like a fox in a holler."

"Since when do you care what people think, especially Sally?"

"Since never! You know I don't give a rat's patootie what anyone thinks. Shoot, when the only reputation you ever had is a bad one, you got nothing to lose. But you, now you Francis got a lot to lose.

"Don't you see, it ain't–sorry–it isn't me I'm worried about, it's you. I don't want anyone going around ruining your reputation with a bunch of stupid rumors."

"What stupid rumors?" Frank asked.

"You know! You don't want them saying you're fucking the trailer trash, now do you?"

"I'm sorry I asked. You owe me a quarter," Frank said, his face blushing with embarrassment.

"I guess that makes us even," Vicky said, delighted that she had shocked him. "So, what did you want me to see?"

"I can't believe you haven't noticed it yet," Frank said.

"Noticed what?" Vicky asked.

"Noticed this," he said stepping aside and gesturing to a beautiful black shiny upright piano. "You scared me so bad when you barged through my window I knocked the bench over. You're lucky it didn't break," he said lifting the bench carefully off the floor and surveying the damage.

"Oh, Francis, it's beautiful! Is it okay? Is the bench all right? Are you all right? Did you fall too?"

"I'm fine, the bench is fine. Don't worry," Frank said calming her with his low soft voice and a gesture of his hand.

"When did you get it?" Vicky asked, a little embarrassed she hadn't noticed it right away, but then when she was around Francis she was so often oblivious to everything but him.

"It was delivered yesterday. Are you surprised?"

"Heck yeah, I'm surprised. I didn't think you'd actually do it. Oh, Francie boy, I'm so proud of you!" She excitedly gave him a quick and rather awkward hug.

"Can you play it for me, Francis? The one you played in the music store?"

"*Claire de Lune?*" Francis said, lifting the lid of the bench to look for the music.

"Yes, that's it! Meaning the light of the moon in French. Composed by Debussy. I'm getting good, ain't I?" Vicky asked with a grin. Frank looked up at her from where he knelt on the floor rifling through sheet music and merely smiled his bemused smile.

"Ah ha! Here it is!" he said pulling out the music. "*Claire de Lune* by Claude Debussy. What an appropriate song for tonight. By the way, did you see the moon?" Frank said situating himself on the bench and scooting it under the piano.

"Did I ever? It was so bright I was spooked it might blow my cover when I was climbing up here. Definitely not a good night for breaking and entering."

Frank laughed then began playing the familiar tune that Vicky fell in love with when she first heard it in the music store. His jovial mood quickly changed as he focused on the music before him and lost himself in the solemn beauty of the melody. Vicky quietly scooted next to him on the piano bench, watching Frank's fingers move up and down the keys and studying the expressions of passion and poignancy which shadowed across his face.

"Beautiful," Vicky said applauding as soon as Frank finished playing. "You've been practicing it just for me, haven't you?"

"Actually, yes."

"Does it bother you when I sit next to you? I mean, does it disturb your playing?" Vicky asked.

"You always disturb me when you sit next to me," Frank replied.

"Not like that, Francis darlin'. You know what I mean."

"Yes, I know what you mean, and no, it doesn't bother me. In fact I like it. It inspires me."

"Inspires you? How do you mean?" Vicky asked.

"I don't know how to explain it. You ask tough questions, you know that? Did you hear what I was playing when you broke into my apartment?" Frank said, abruptly changing the subject.

"Yes, it was beautiful. I had to stand on your balcony and just listen, like I was in some romantic dream. I had no idea it was coming from a live piano. I thought it was an album. What was it? I know I've heard it before. It sounded familiar."

"It was a variation from Rachmaninoff's Rhapsody on a Theme of Paganini. You remember me playing that Rachmaninoff album for you?"

"Rachmaninoff. Right. Last of the twentieth century romantics. Tall fellow, gaunt face, bony fingers just perfect for piano playing. Defected from Russia," Vicky said, proud of herself that she remembered all the details.

"Very good!"

"You like those Russian composers, don't you?"

"Definitely something about them. Speaking of which, did you get chance to listen to Tchaikovsky's *Swan Lake*?"

"Yes, I loved it. Sorry I haven't returned it. I couldn't figure out a way to climb up the ladder with the darn thing in tow. Unless of course I held it in my teeth and I didn't think you'd want me slobbering all over one of your albums. Please tape it for me," Vicky said.

"Of course," Frank agreed.

"How many albums have you taped for me now?" Vicky asked lighting a cigarette.

"I don't know. Enough to where it would qualify as an official pastime. It's become my hobby you know, about all I do in my spare time. I don't watch nearly so much baseball anymore and I've practically given up golf. I just tape albums for you," Frank said, as he lightly played the Rachmaninoff piece.

"Are you complaining?" Vicky asked leaning against the piano so she could be face to face with Frank.

"No, I rather enjoy it," Frank said with a smile. "Making music for others, even if it's just taping an album, is never a waste of time."

"Now you have a new pastime," she said pointing to the piano.

"Yes, I do. I'm glad you talked me into it," Frank said with a smile and a look that made Vicky's insides feel all at once suspended. Only Frank could do that, move her with just a glance, making her feel like a balloon filled with helium, like just one clip of the string that held her to earth and she would completely defy gravity. It always happened when she was around Frank, yet it always took her by surprise, as if each time was the first. She held his gaze for what seemed like too long, long enough for her face to redden. Vicky never remembered blushing until she met Frank, and it baffled her. She quickly strode over to his coffee table where she flicked the ash from her cigarette into Frank's lead crystal ashtray.

"So you golf? I never knew that," Vicky said, realizing how little she really knew about this man. There was a whole other side to him, a side that existed during the day, a side that his co-workers and those he socialized with knew but that he kept hidden from her.

"I love golf. You never knew that?" he said puzzled as he continued to play the piano lightly. It was as if the thought had never occurred to him that there was so much of his life that Vicky was not a part of.

"Where do you play?" Vicky asked as she bent over the coffee table and picked up a framed picture of Frank with his brother. She examined the picture as if there was some hidden clue there that might help her understand more about his world.

"Wherever I get a chance," he said, more just playing random notes over and over again than any actual piece.

"Where's your favorite golf course?" She asked trying to imagine herself there with him, riding about in the cart on a perfect early summer day before the southern Indiana heat becomes too intense.

"You mean around here?"

"I guess so," Vicky said, erasing the mental image of the two of them in the golf cart with an imaginary eraser and blowing away the eraser dust. It seemed too silly to even be a fantasy.

"That would have to be the Lamasco Country Club. I'd like to become a member. Maybe next year I'll make enough to join."

How funny, Vicky thought, he aspired to join the Country Club and she aspired to work there.

"What about you?" Frank asked. "What are your hobbies?"

"Bowling and motorcycling. I sold my motorcycle right before I moved into Camelot though 'cause I needed the money. I used to ride Bobby's, but..." A catch in her throat caused Vicky to stop.

"I'm sorry," he stopped playing and turned around on the bench to face Vicky who was still standing by the coffee table.

"For what?" Vicky said flippantly, not wanting those emotions to surface again.

"For your loss."

"It's okay. Life has to go on, you know," she said shrugging off the sudden sadness. "What were we talking about? Oh, yeah, hobbies. Anyhow, I had to quit my bowling league 'cause it just got to be too much with work and classes. You know, I'm signed up for American Lit during the first summer session. 'From Hawthorne to Hemingway', that's what the course description says. I've already got some of the books. I've flipped through them you know and..."

"Vicky, I hate how you do that," Frank said, turning back around on the piano bench and resuming his playing, only this time slightly harder and more deliberate.

"What?"

"How you start a book in the middle. How you read the last page first."

"I can't help myself. I always go back and read it from the start all the way through."

"But doesn't it ruin it for you–knowing the ending?"

"Most times the endings don't make much sense until I've read the beginning and the middle."

"Then why do you do it?"

"I don't know, to get a feel for where I'm going. I told you I can't help it. It's like a… what's the word–a compulsion. But anyhow I think I know who my favorite writer's gonna be."

"Don't tell me, let me guess. Mark Twain," Frank said without missing a chord of the tune he was playing.

"How did you guess?" Vicky asked dumbfounded.

"Because you are the female version of Huck Finn."

"Why, Francis, you know me better than I thought," Vicky said. Frank smiled.

He retrieved some more music books from inside the piano bench and began flipping through them. "Let's see, I know it's in here somewhere. Ah ha! Here it is," he said pulling out the sheet of music he'd been looking for in the pile. "Beethoven's Moonlight Sonata. What a perfect song for tonight. You have to sit next to me for this one, Vicky."

"Needing my inspiration, are you? All right, scoot over. So tell me about this one."

Frank played softly as he told her about Ludwig von Beethoven's Moonlight Sonata and how he'd dedicated the piece to a Countess he loved who jilted him for someone more socially acceptable. Vicky recalled the composer's ninth symphony which Frank taped for her and how moved she was to learn he was almost completely deaf when he wrote it.

After Frank finished playing the adagio movement, Vicky put her head on his shoulder and her arm around his back. Together the two just sat there in silence until Frank put his head against hers'.

"He must've really loved her. Poor dude must've been really heartbroken when she dumped him for that rich count."

"Poor Ludwig was never too lucky in love. He had another great love in his life. He composed several letters to her and referred to her as his 'immortal beloved'. Nobody knows for sure who she was."

All of this was too much for Vicky–the music, the moonlight, the June night air, all this talk of romance, and the proximity of Frank's body as they sat on the piano bench with their arms around each other. She felt the steady rise and fall of his breathing and smelled his cologne, a fragrance which was now on her and would stay with her all night, driving her half mad with longing.

"I have to go," Vicky said disentangling herself from Frank's embrace and scooting off the piano bench.

"So soon?"

"It's getting late and you know Allison's gonna be banging on my door at six o'clock wanting to go jogging."

"Let me walk you to the door," Frank said, rising to his feet.

"I'm not going out the door," Vicky said.

"You're not?"

"No, I'm going out the same way I came in."

"Vicky, that's crazy," Frank said, his arms once again flailing in frustration.

"You know, if someone tied your hands together I don't believe you could talk," Vicky said pulling aside the curtain to his patio door and sliding open the screen.

"Do you want to kill yourself? There are easier ways to do it." Frank said following her out onto the patio.

"I didn't hurt myself coming up so what makes you think I'm going to hurt myself going down?"

"Why are you so stubborn?"

"That vein in your neck is starting to pop out, Francis darlin'," Vicky said approaching the railing.

"Don't," Frank said reaching out quickly and grasping Vicky by the arm.

Vicky's first instinct was one of indignation. It always was when she thought someone was trying to tell her what to do. She pulled her arm away from his grasp and in one sudden act of defiance, climbed over the railing and onto the first wrung of the ladder. "I climbed trees a heck of a lot higher than this when I was a kid," she said to Frank through the railing.

Vicky's right foot tried to descend to the second wrung of the ladder, but she hesitated as a sudden uncertainty came over her. At that moment she remembered her childhood and that same foot grappling for a branch beneath her with Bobby looking down from a higher branch. Only this time it was the face of Francis above her. She froze. Fear and panic overtook her as another memory surfaced.

* * * * * *

She was just a kid, maybe ten or eleven. Her father was in a drunken rage over something she'd done, or not done, or possibly nothing at all. She never knew what set those rages off when he was drunk, she only knew she was the brunt of them. He'd taken his belt off and she knew what that meant. When he was really mad, like now, he'd wrap the end of the belt around his fist so he could hit her with the buckle end. He chased her through the house. Her mom used to try to stop him but she'd given up. She would become strangely quiet and absent when he was like this.

He knew all of her usual hiding places so it was no use trying those, and he was fast. She couldn't get around him and out the door. He'd catch up to her. He always did. Still, she had this belief that if she could just get out of the house and into the open air of the Kentucky countryside she would be all right. It was her one hope of escape. She figured out if she left the window unlocked in her bedroom she could get out of the house quickly.

She ran to the upstairs of the old farm house, all the while her father was close behind her, shouting obscenities and whipping at her with the belt. She tried to close her bedroom door but he wedged his foot in before she could shut it all the way. She knew not to struggle. He was too strong for her. And if she fought with all her might and injured him (which she sometimes did when defending herself) then he'd be even madder. The only thing to do was to get out that window and up on the roof as soon as possible. The open air was her friend, and even if he followed her out onto the roof she had the advantage of size and age which would allow her to slide down the guttering downspout quicker than he could. If she could just get to the ground before him, she could run and find a place to hide.

Vicky's actions, her father's actions, all blurred together at that moment—him crashing through her bedroom door, her running on top of her bed over to the window and opening it just in time to crawl out before he could grab her. She did it. She made it out the window and up to the roof, but she wasn't out of harm's way yet. She had to carefully and quickly make it over to the downspout so she could slide down.

The roof was too slanted to stand or walk on, plus the newly fallen October leaves which covered the roof made it treacherously slick. The most she could do was scoot. She scooted down near the edge of the roof and ever so cautiously rolled onto her stomach, letting herself drop until her hands clasped the guttering. It was scary, but not as scary as her daddy when he was drunk. There she was hanging from the roof of her house. She told herself not to look down. As long as she didn't look down she could do this. She'd always been good at the monkey bars and this was no different. She began working her way across the guttering over to the down spout.

Her escape plan was working out perfectly. There was no sign of her father out on the roof. She figured he was trying to get his nerve up. Vicky inched her way down the guttering. In a moment she would be at the down spout, slide down, and be on the ground. She could run and hide in the woods or climb a tree and stay there until he sobered up, then he would probably have no recollection of the incident.

Suddenly she heard her father's voice angrily calling out to her. But where was he? The voice didn't come from above her, it came from below her. He was on the ground standing there waiting for her. He outsmarted her. He simply stepped outside knowing she would have to come down sooner or later. Why didn't she think of it? She couldn't hang from the guttering forever and it was too dangerous to try and climb back onto the roof. She made it to the down spout where she hugged tightly to the top, afraid to slide down.

"That's right, you stupid brat, you can't hang there all day," her father yelled at her from the ground as he snapped his belt. "I'm gonna whup your butt so hard, your climbing days will be gone for good."

She'd never felt so trapped before. Of course she had to come down and face the inevitable, but that moment that she hung there clinging to the top of the downspout seemed an eternity, with no way up and the worst of alternatives waiting on the ground.

She climbed trees only twice after that. Both times she froze in fear at the top the same way she froze while clinging to the downspout. The first time she stayed up there until she finally got her nerve up to jump. The second time Bobby helped her down.

* * * * * * *

"Vicky, what's wrong?" Frank's voice called her back to her present reality. There he was leaning over the railing. If she hadn't been so afraid she might have been touched by Frank's look of concern that pinched his brows together in that intent fixed expression of helplessness.

"I can't move," Vicky said, hearing the sound of her own voice trembling.

"What do you mean you can't move?"

"I mean I'm paralyzed. I can't move. I forgot this happens to me. I can get up but I can't get back down again. I'm just so scared to go down. I know it's crazy, but I… I just…got scared all of a sudden." Despite the chill of the evening, Vicky felt sweat break out around her scalp line and under her arms.

"Vicky, hang on and whatever you do, don't look down," Frank said, his voice sounding less nervous and more in command. How could she let go? Her knuckles bulged from the tightness of her grip.

"Don't leave me," Vicky said afraid he might come and get her, and then she wouldn't have the security of seeing his face.

"I'm not leaving. I'm not going anywhere," he said sounding much calmer and even brave. "Can you climb back up?" He asked.

"No, I'm stuck. My legs won't move at all," she said. The only thing she felt safe moving was her head, which she turned a little to the side. All at once a fiercely demonic urge overtook her to look down, an urge totally contrary to logic and against anything she truly wanted to do, yet she couldn't help it. She obeyed the strange compulsion to look down and was seized with an even greater terror.

"Don't Vicky, don't look down. Look up. Look at me." The reassuring command of his voice was the only safety net she had. She turned her head and looked at him. Something serene, almost supernatural had taken over Frank's countenance. He was courageous and confident, tender and strong, everything heroic in that moment as he reached over the railing and took hold of her arms.

"I've got you. I won't let you fall." Frank said. She did indeed feel that he had a secure grasp on her.

"Now what?" Vicky asked her voice still tremulous. Much to her surprise he laughed and his laugh infected her enough to where she was able to squeak out a little chuckle though she wasn't sure why.

"Oh, Vicky, even when you're in perilous danger you're wonderful." Frank leaned over the railing and kissed her on the mouth.

"What was that for?" Vicky asked dumbfounded.

"Courage. And because you look so beautiful there in the moonlight."

The kiss had deliciously romantic overtones but this wasn't the time or the place to rehash their mutual decision to remain just friends. All she could say was, "Thank you." She wasn't sure what she was thanking him for. She guessed it was the kiss and the courage he tried to impart to her through it. It worked, for she did somehow feel a new calm and strength.

"All right, just tell me what I need to do to get out of this fix and I'll do it," she said trusting him entirely.

"Just look at me, Vicky. Keep looking at me. In a minute or so I'm going to let go of you and you're going to climb down that ladder and you're going to be just fine."

"Okay, okay," Vicky nodded. "And you promise you won't go anywhere. You'll stay right there where I can see you."

"I promise. All right, now you tell me when you're ready for me to let go," Frank said.

"Are your arms asleep yet? They gotta hurt hanging over the railing like that."

"Let's not worry about my arms. They're fine. Let's concentrate on your legs and how to get them moving again," Frank said.

"Just keep talking to me Francis. Talk to me like nothing's wrong, nothing whatever in this world, like we're just sitting in your living room having a conversation."

"All right, all right, let me think, conversation topics. You pick a topic."

"Tell me the story of *Swan Lake*," Vicky said.

"Now?"

"Yes, now."

"All right, if you think it will help. But don't you already know the story? Didn't you read the insert in the album cover?"

"I know that Odette dies," Vicky said.

"You read the end first, didn't you?"

"Well, yes, but then I did go on to read the whole thing."

"Then you know the story," Frank said.

"I just want to hear you tell it."

"All right then. Just don't get too lost in the story, start thinking you're a swan and try to flap your wings," Frank said.

"Francis, you're so silly," she said, like someone with a toothache, trying very hard to act normal in public, laughing at a joke, all the while preoccupied with the pain.

"*Swan Lake*, let's see, how to begin. Once upon a time in a far away and distant land there lived a prince, Prince Sigfried was his name. Now Prince Sigfried had finally come of age and all the royal court was eager for him to marry and produce an heir for the kingdom, none however, were more eager than his mother, the queen. She decided to give fate a little push; after all, she knew her son Prince Sigfried had no real interest in finding a bride just yet. So the queen decided to have a ball and invite all the royal maidens from all the surrounding kingdoms; the express purpose of which was for her son to select a bride."

"Now wait a minute, they don't have the ball just yet. It starts out with Sigfried's eighteenth birthday party," Vicky interrupted.

"See, you know this story better than I do," Frank said.

"Yeah, but you tell it better than me," Vicky said, finding in their bantering a fleeting feeling of normalcy, allowing her to forget her predicament for a second or two.

"Okay, right right, they don't have the ball yet but it's in the works. It's to take place very soon."

"The night after next," Vicky reminded him.

"Right, and at the end of this ball he must announce who, of all these lovely maidens, he has decided to marry."

"One day to plan a ball. Seems kind of soon, doesn't it?" Vicky asked, wanting to forget she was standing on top of a ladder, trying to conquer a childhood fear so she could climb down.

"Yes, it does, but that's how things happen in fairy tales," Frank said.

"Oh, right. Continue," Vicky said, noting that sparkle of liveliness in Frank's eyes that seemed nothing out of the ordinary when he was recounting a story. It helped her to forget her fears for a miniscule of a moment.

"So anyway, Sigfried decides to celebrate his birthday by going hunting with his buddies. A sort of medieval bachelor party if you will."

"What's with these dudes anyway? It's night and they decide to go hunting?" Vicky conjectured.

"More like dusk actually, but they've been drinking, so you know, it seemed like a good idea at the time."

"You sure these guys weren't from Kentucky?"

"Ah yes, the Kingdom of Kaintuck, I believe they may have been. So anyway, Sigfried and his royal young friends go hunting. Sigfried, however, breaks away from the others and rides off in pursuit of this flock of swans he sees on a lake. In the process he gets separated from his hunting buddies. He spies this one swan in particular and for some reason he's captivated by it. He watches this graceful creature glide about the lake for a while and decides that that's the bird he wants to take home that night. He raises his bow and arrow and he's just about to shoot it when suddenly this amazing transformation takes place. Before his very eyes the swan changes into a beautiful maiden. Naturally Sigfried is awestruck. He approaches the maiden who reveals to him that she is the Princess Odette and that the wicked Von Roth Bart had cast an evil spell on her whereby she is a swan by day and transforms back into a woman by night. Only a promise of true and eternal love can break the spell."

"Why did Von Roth Bart cast the spell in the first place? I didn't read anything in the notes that answered that question and it's been driving me crazy," Vicky asked.

"Who knows? Some political conflict with Odette's father probably."

"That makes sense. Ol' Von Roth Bart probably got his nose bent out of shape 'cause he didn't get promoted to kingdom wizard or something like that."

"He does seem a bit like the power crazed type, does he not? So anyway," Frank continued, seeming excited about the telling of this tale. "Sigfried falls madly in love with Odette and promises that he'll announce his marriage to her at the ball the next night."

"Like you said, things happen fast in fairy tales," Vicky said.

"Yeah, no kidding," Frank chuckled. "Okay, so where were we?"

"At the ball."

"Right. So poor old Sigfried has to go to the ball and dance with all these women he's not the least little bit interested in. But that's all right because he's floating on air. He's so in love with Odette, he's just biding his time until midnight when he can make the announcement that he's going to marry her. When all at once in strolls this mysterious stranger–the beautiful Princess Odeille, daughter of the wicked Von Roth Bart. Von Roth Bart has cast yet another evil spell, this time over Prince Sigfried so that he mistakes Odeille for Odette."

"Likely story. I think it's Sigfried's version."

"Ah, so you think Sigfried was really a cad? Huh, kind of makes the story more interesting actually. So anyhow, whatever his reasons, the effects of a wicked spell or a surge of hormones brought about by Odeille's charms, Sigfried professes his eternal undying love to Odeille and announces before all the ball attendants his intentions to make Odeille his bride.

"Suddenly, he hears something at the window. He looks up and there by the light of the moon he sees a swan desperately beating its wings against the window. Tragically, but too late for poor Odette he realizes he's been tricked."

"You don't have to tell me the rest," Vicky said, thinking sadly about the demise of the poor cursed swan woman for whom a promise of eternal love never came.

"That's right, you read the ending first."

"It's kind of a downer, isn't it?" Vicky said.

"Oh, well, makes for a great ballet. And the music's spectacular. So now that you're thoroughly depressed, what else can I do for you?" Frank said.

"Give me a good push," Vicky said and together they laughed.

The laughter subsided leaving in its wake only quiet between the two, and Vicky silently calling forth all the resolve she could.

"I think I'm ready now," she said after a while and Frank seemed to understand.

"Are you sure?"

"I'm sure. You can let go," Vicky said, still scared, her heart pounding, her mouth a bit dry, but no longer terrorized, rather feeling like her normal self and even a little foolish that this whole thing had happened to her.

"All right," Frank said giving the professor like nod he always gave before giving instructions. "Go slowly. Take it one wrung at a time. Keep looking up. Look at me and no swan dives."

"Don't worry, I won't be flapping my wings against your patio window any time soon."

"Good," Frank said and they both laughed, the laughter culminating in another kiss. This time it was humor, joy, and a natural affection that Frank imparted to her. It was enough. He let go of her arms, straightened up and spoke one word–"Go".

Out of sheer will Vicky commanded her left knee to bend until she felt her right foot land securely on the next wrung down. She had done it. She had taken that first step. The rest would be easier.

"You're doing it, Vicky, you're doing it," Frank exhorted her from above.

"Keep looking at me. That's it," he said as she took another step down, this one easier than the last.

In moments she had descended the ladder and was safely on the ground.

"You did it!" Frank cheered and whistled and it occurred to Vicky that he didn't seem to care if anyone heard him. "Wait there. I'm coming down," Frank said. She was surprised to see how quickly and nimbly he climbed over the railing and descended the ladder. As soon as Frank made it down, Vicky realized her hands were shaking. She broke down in sobs. Frank put his arms around her and shushed her.

"What's wrong with me? I'm such a fool. I don't know what's wrong with me."

"I believe its called aftershock," Frank said. "It's all right."

"No, it's not. I'm embarrassed. Besides my cousin Bobby, you're the only person who's seen me act like such a weak fool. How's come every time I'm around you I make a fool of myself? I get drunk, I get stuck on ladders, I snivel and cry like a dern baby. If I ever have the misfortune of wetting my pants, you'd probably show up right then and there."

"Gosh, I hope not," Frank said chuckling. "Listen." He took her face in his hands. "I'm just glad I was there for you. And it's not because you're weak or can't take care of yourself. It's because… you trust me. You let me be a hero tonight, and it's not everyday a guy gets to be a hero. Does that sound arrogant? Maybe I'm being the fool now."

"No, I get what you're saying."

Frank lifted a handkerchief out of his pocket, blotted her eyes then placed the linen material over her nose so she could blow. Vicky took the handkerchief from him.

"You even blow my nose for me." She wiped her face and put the handkerchief in her pocket. "I'd like to be strong for someone too; like you, maybe."

"Don't worry; you'll get your chance. That's the way it goes, you know."

"The way what goes?" Vicky asked.

"Friendship. Love," he said nonchalantly

"Did you say the 'L' word?"

"The 'L' word? Yes, I guess I did."

"Would you say it again?" Vicky asked.

"I love you."

"I love you too," Vicky said, feeling far too sober and vulnerable to look him in the eye. Frank touched Vicky's chin and gently directed her head up until her eyes looked at him. That was all it took. Once again they were locked in an embrace and joined together by a mutual kiss, a kiss initiated by both of them with all the passion and fervor that comes from full moons. How delightful it was to be kissed like this and be completely sober. The delight, however, soon gave way to the fears as Vicky stopped the kiss abruptly.

"Wait a minute, we said we weren't going to do this!" she said.

"Do what, for crying out loud?! An occasional kiss at your door under the moonlight–how can that be wrong?" Frank said, his hands gesturing dramatically, his voice intent. "It doesn't have to be about sex. That's not what I'm after here. You were right when you said sex complicates things," Frank said.

"I said that?"

"Yes, you said that."

"That was pretty smart of me," Vicky said.

"I told you you were a sensible drunk."

"But if we're more than just friends, but less than lovers, then what are we exactly?"

"Who knows? Who cares? Why do we have to define it? Why can't we just let it be?"

"Because I'm a woman. I gotta know where I stand."

"All right," Frank said, taking her hand in his and holding it against his heart. "You are about to embark on a romance–an old fashioned romance. The destination of which is unknown."

"An old fashioned romance. I like that. It's crazy, isn't it though, really? The two of us together," Vicky said, pressing her free hand hard against her head as if to keep it from spinning. She had never entered into a relationship like this before and it was all so strange and wonderful.

"It is crazy. That's what makes it so exciting."

"We won't worry about where it's going or where it all will end?" Vicky asked.

"We won't worry. We'll just take it one day at a time. It'll be what it'll be and we won't care what anyone says or thinks."

"You really mean it, Francis?"

"I mean it. No more hiding. No more sneaking around after midnight and stealing workmen's ladders…"

"I didn't steal it. I borrowed it."

"Sorry. No more borrowing workmen's ladders so that you don't have to walk past Sally's door. Promise me you won't ever do that again," he said taking her face in his hands and drawing close enough for their foreheads to touch. "Promise me," he asked her again.

"I promise. And do you promise me that you won't care what other people think about us?" Vicky asked.

"I promise. I'm tired of hiding my feelings for you." Vicky could tell by looking in his eyes that he meant it, at least for now. Who knows if he would still mean it a year from now, but that didn't matter. They agreed not to worry about the future. It was what it was for now and that was more than she'd ever hoped for. They sealed the promise with another kiss.

"This is too weird," Vicky said shaking her head in disbelief. "I never thought I'd be going steady with an ivy leaguer."

"That's right we're going steady. We need a porch swing and a pitcher of lemonade. And a ring," he said taking his college ring from the University of Pennsylvania off his finger. "You could wrap it in yarn," Frank suggested.

"Or wear it on a chain around my neck," Vicky said pulling out the gold chain she always wore out from under her shirt. "I'll wear it here right next to the key from my grandma's hope chest," she said showing him the small key that hung from the chain. In a moment she was unclasping the chain from around her neck and placing Frank's ring on it.

"So for our first official date I think we ought to go bowling," Frank said, clasping the gold chain back around the back of Vicky's neck as she held her hair up for him.

"Can we go to the symphony or ballet?" Vicky asked.

"Most certainly, I'll buy Philharmonic season tickets for us," Frank said.

"I don't have a motorcycle anymore but we could go horse back riding together. We both love horses, Francis. It's something we have in common," Vicky said.

"We could go to baseball games," Frank said.

"And play golf, though I've never held a club."

"It's all right, I could get you lessons."

"We'll dine out together, Francis, at the most elegant restaurants."

"And the greasiest spoons," Frank added.

They giggled like a couple of wound up kids in between noisy kisses.

"Let me ask you something, Francis."

"Anything" he said, holding her close and looking into her eyes.

"What would you have done if I freaked out and started to fall off that ladder?"

"I would have done a swan dive over that railing and caught you."

"My hero," Vicky said in her best southern drawl. "So when do I get to save your life?"

"You already have," he said.

They walked with their arms around each other back into the building. When they reached Vicky's door, Frank called down the hall, "Hey Sally, get a load of this." Vicky shushed him but he took her in his arms, bent her over backwards and kissed her. Together they giggled as they said their goodnights.

Chapter 24

It couldn't exactly be called a love affair, and certainly not the more modern term: relationship. A strange enigma for the 1980's because it didn't involve sex. They were, as Vicky once said, more than friends and less than lovers. It was what it was and Vicky guessed it was just what Frank had first dubbed it–an old fashioned romance. One in which Frank took his role as gentleman very seriously, complete with flowers, mushy greeting cards, cologne, and chairs held for her on dinner dates.

Whatever it was between Frank and Vicky it was now out in the open and everyone had an opinion. This atypical romance had a peculiar effect on the female residents of Camelot building 3300. It seemed to Vicky that if the single girls' quest for romance couldn't be found personally, it could at least be satisfied vicariously. The girls of building 3300 seemed giddy and starry-eyed about the whole thing. Sally gave Vicky free samples of Mary Kay products. Allison dragged her around to stores to outfit her in the most stylish and upscale of clothing. Even reserved and quiet Barb came out of her apartment more often to socialize with the other girls and when she did she had a certain spark about her that was normally lacking. It was as if they were all a little in love right along with Vicky.

And so August spilled into September, and that first week of the month flirted with fall, blowing the haze and heat away for a day or so only to return again by weeks' end. Vicky was alive with the exhilarating feeling of autumn coming on. It was a wonderful time of the year to be in love. She breathed in hope and anticipation of something magical with the ever cooling air and clearing skies. The third weekend of the month would be the opening of the Lamasco Philharmonic season. The opening night concert featured Mozart's Symphony Number 25 and Rachmaninoff's Third Piano Concerto with a guest pianist to accompany the orchestra.

This was Vicky's debut of sorts, and a most unconventional and unexpected debutante she made. She had a little over a week to prepare. So she recruited the aid of Allison who decided to take a vacation day (from the honeymoon she never had) specifically for the purpose of helping Vicky find a dress.

* * * * * * *

"Oh, good Lord!" Vicky said looking in the full length mirror of the department store dressing room. She was trying on evening gowns with Allison and an intrusive saleslady with grey hair, a grey suit, and rich lady horn rimmed glasses attached to a gold chain which she had an annoying way of perching on the end of her nose to examine the merchandise then taking them off again, she would stick the tip of the earpiece in her mouth and bite on it while she zipped and hooked up dresses.

"By the way that wasn't a blaspheme I just uttered. It was a prayer," Vicky said as the saleslady fussed with the hunter green dress while she bit the earpiece of her glasses and scrutinized Vicky's reflection in the mirror.

"A prayer for what?" Allison asked.

"Mercy! All I need is a pair of gossamer wings and a wand," she said looking at the big puffy sleeves and wide full skirt.

"And maybe a diamond tiara," Allison added.

"Well, you never know until you try them on dear," the tall, slender, grey saleslady with the bit-up glasses said in a condescending tone.

"Okay, I think we can all agree that this dress doesn't work," Allison said, and the saleslady agreed as she chewed on her glasses while unzipping and helping Vicky step out of the puffy sleeved gown into a black dress with rhinestones.

Vicky was very pleased with the effect of the black rhinestone dress. It was more sophisticated than the other. She loved the idea of sparkling, light reflecting off light, leaving a shimmering blur in the eyes of all she passed. "I like it," Vicky said.

"I don't know," said the saleslady perching the glasses back on the end of her nose. "It doesn't fit right, and besides it's too Oscars' night, too glitzy."

"Hey, I'm a glitzy kind of gal. If Dolly Parton can get away with glitz then so can I," Vicky said.

"There's nothing wrong with glitz my dear if it's the proper occasion, but it's simply not suitable for the opening night of the Philharmonic. Absolutely too many rhinestones," she said her small brown eyes roving up and down from behind the glasses. "You need something more stayed, more elegant."

"But I'm not the stayed and elegant type," Vicky protested feeling a little resentful that this woman had taken over her shopping spree.

"Not stayed perhaps, but any woman can be elegant, particularly if she has your natural good looks and a designer gown like this," the saleslady said holding up a burgundy gown. Vicky looked at the price tag on the gown.

"I'm sorry, grandma, I should've let you teach me how to sew," Vicky said looking up to the ceiling. She continued to express her enthusiasm for the black rhinestone dress while the saleslady counteracted with comments about how the neckline was all wrong and how it simply didn't drape right across the collarbone and just didn't fit properly in the shoulders.

Finally Allison convinced the saleslady to go back on the floor and bring back more dresses to try on.

"Thanks for getting rid of her," Vicky said. "That woman was on my last nerve."

"I figured we needed a little break from her. So would you tell me what's going on? Why won't you try on any of the dresses I picked out for you?"

"Because I like the black rhinestone dress and I think that's the one I should get."

"But the saleslady's right about it. It doesn't fit you right. It's not flattering. With your long neck and shoulders you need to try on one of these," Allison said, referring to some of the untouched strapless gowns that hung on a nearby hook.

"I can't show off my shoulders and arms," Vicky said. "It's this," Vicky said pointing to her upper left arm just below her shoulder.

The tattoo had been there so long she didn't often think about it. It was one of the samples shown in the tattoo parlor where she'd had it done. Vicky thought it was different and she'd never seen anything like it. A bleeding heart with thorns wove around it and flames shooting out of the top. She thought it was a good interpretation of how her heart felt sometimes–all stabbed and wounded yet burning with some relentless fire. How surprised she was to see that same heart revealed through the transparent chest wall of Jesus, depicted in a strange portrait which hung in Frank's hall just outside his bathroom.

"What's this?" she asked him the first time she saw it.

"It's a portrait of the Sacred Heart of Jesus. It was my mother's."

Should she tell him or not, Vicky wondered at the time. This was in the winter, shortly after their friendship began. She figured if they remained friends through the warmer months he would certainly see her bare arm at some point.

"Hey Francis, let me show you something," Vicky said peeling off her sweater and pushing up the sleeve of her tee shirt.

Frank examined her arm. "Well, I'll be…"

"Watch it! You can't cuss around Jesus' Sacred Heart," Vicky quickly interrupted.

"No, I guess not," Frank said in astonishment as he held Vicky's arm and examined it, then looked at the picture. "Where did you get this?"

"It was one of the samples at a tattoo parlor."

"You're kidding me." He looked at her. "You're not kidding me."

"I bet you've never been friends with a girl who had a tattoo of Jesus' Sacred Heart before."

"I've never been friends with a girl who had a tattoo period. Come to think of it, I've never been friends with a guy who had a tattoo."

"Figures!"

The warmer months had come and were soon departing, and Frank often teased Vicky about her Sacred Heart of Jesus tattoo when she wore sleeveless clothing. She smiled as she thought about the origin of her strange tattoo. Allison asked her about it saying she'd often wondered if the bleeding heart had any significance, so Vicky told her the story.

"So there you have it, I can't very well show up at a classy affair like the Philharmonic with Jesus' bloody heart etched onto my arm," Vicky said to Allison turning her attention back to the mirror.

"You can wear a nice shawl or something. It'll probably be cool in the evening anyway."

"I don't know."

"Look, you can't pick a dress based on whether or not a tattoo shows. It's the eighties, Vicky. More and more women are getting them. I predict by the year 2000 it'll perfectly acceptable, even fashionable for a lady to have a tattoo."

"I like the black rhinestone dress," Vicky said with finality as she pulled the dress over her head and grabbed her shirt and jeans off the hook.

"Wait. Just try on one more… for me. Then I'll quit bugging you," Allison said holding a shiny gold gown before Vicky.

"We're just getting ideas. Right?" said Vicky.

"Right. This is the grand finale. Then you decide if you want to get the black rhinestones or hit some of the second hand bridal shops."

"I better hurry, before Miss La-de Dah gets back here with another whole armful of dresses," Vicky said quickly pulling the gold charmeuse dress over her head.

There were no zippers or hooks on this one, just a sash in the back. The neckline was cut low in a "V" shape. The sash gathered at the sides along the rib cage and in the front center just under the "V", with the bodice rising up into straps, much like the sash, which gathered at the shoulders. The skirt hung straight down from the ribcage for what seemed to be miles.

Vicky felt the silky fabric of the skirt brush against her legs as it naturally draped into place, the hem falling to her ankles. Allison loosely tied the sash, pulling the bodice snug around her ribs. She stepped back to get a better look in the mirror. The two women simultaneously gasped as they looked at Vicky's reflection.

"Look at you! You're gorgeous!" Allison said.

"For once you're right," said Vicky in amazement.

"Hey, I was right about the fairy princess dress. But this…who would've thought? It didn't look like much on the hanger."

"There's just one drawback," Vicky said looking at the price tag. It was the most expensive of the five dresses she tried on. "Well, two, actually," she said looking at the tattoo on her bare left arm.

"Stop worrying about Jesus' bloody heart," Allison said.

"Jesus' Sacred Heart," Vicky corrected her.

"Jesus' Sacred Bloody Heart. It goes with gold."

"Keep talking, Allison."

"Well, it's shiny, it's perfectly acceptable to wear something shiny with a tattoo."

"All right you talked me into it. I'm sorry, Grandma. I'm weak and vain."

"She forgives you."

The saleslady came back about that time and was quite thrilled to see the finished product. She used words like "fabulous", "divine", and "goddess" to describe Vicky in the gold charmeuse gown

* * * * * * *

"If nothing else, I'm glad we went shopping for your sake," Vicky said to Allison after they returned to Camelot later that day and sat at Vicky's place drinking coffee.

"For my sake?"

"Yeah, it cheered you up."

"Guess you noticed I've been a little down lately."

"Fall?" Vicky asked.

"Fall," Allison confirmed.

"And…"

"And the realization that it's really over with Kent. It's taken three months but I'm finally out of denial. Summer tricked me into thinking that everything was okay. It's all that sunlight and those long days. It fooled me into thinking there was something new for me–a new start–hope. But soon the leaves will be dropping off those trees and with it mold and spores will burrow into my sinuses making me sneeze and my head feel like a swollen balloon, and then the days will get shorter and I'll be alone in the evenings in a dark apartment with this nagging ache and this need for someone, and ugh, I hate it. Why can't I just be alone and be happy?"

"You don't hate me, do ya?" Vicky said.

"Why would I hate you?"

"You know, now I've got someone and you're alone, and because that someone is Francis, and well, I always thought maybe you two would get together."

"Who? Frank and me? Don't be ridiculous, Vicky! I'm happy for you. It gives me hope, like if true love can happen to you it can happen to me too. Anyway, I don't have to watch schmaltzy movies or read racy novels to get my romance fix, I just come see you and borrow some of that romantic energy.

"It's what we poor women need, you know," Allison continued taking another sip of coffee. "Although, every self-help book and article in Cosmo tells me I'm not supposed to have that need. I'm supposed to rise above it all and find validation outside a man. Of course one article tells me that and the next one tells me how to find his erogenous zones or how to achieve orgasm every time. Have as much sex as you want but, careful now, don't fall in love. Forget this foolish country girl notion of love. Like Tina Turner says, 'what's love got to do with it?' I guess I just haven't evolved to that psycho-spiritual level yet. Ugh, what a weakling I am!"

"Weakling? You're stronger than me! I rely on you for so much, Al. In fact, if I could ask you just one more favor before you go."

"If I can help I will," Allison said with a sad smile.

"Well, it seems to me I have the right dress, the right shoes, the right handbag, and the right look, but I still don't have the right style. My grandma always said I walk like a truck driver. Could you teach me how to walk like a lady?"

Allison leapt over to where Vicky stood, hugged her hard and fast, then stepping back she bowed her head humbly and placed her hand over her heart. "Allison's Charm School at your service. I am honored.

"Let's see, we need a book, a *big* book," Allison said, her countenance beginning to brighten. "What's the biggest book you own?"

"What do we need a book for?" Vicky asked bewildered.

"Your dictionary, that's it! The one I got you for Christmas."

"I thought you were teaching me to walk, not talk."

"I *am* teaching you to walk," Allison said and then donning a French accent, along with a melodramatic tone and hand gestures, she continued. "You must trust me–your teacher. Madame Allison knows the secrets to beauty and charm," then turning the French accent off, she said, "now get the damn dictionary."

"All right then," Vicky said complying as she walked toward her small book shelf.

"Now put the book on your head," Allison said as soon as Vicky retrieved the book.

"Madame Allison says," Allison said again donning the fake French accent. "put the book on your head and walk across the room without letting it fall to the floor. Beauty does not come without a price, without sacrifice. Now, let us see," Allison said in the phony accent, putting her hand to her chin, as she observed Vicky walk. "You have excellent posture. You stand straight and tall like an oak tree."

"My grandma told me not to slouch."

"Yes, but something is still wrong," Allison said with the fake French accent.

"I'll tell you what's wrong," Vicky said catching the thick heavy book as it toppled off her head. "No one walks like this. Not unless you got a broken neck and you can't move your head from side to side. You gotta move like you're wading thorough a pool of molasses to pull it off. Heck, I've never seen you move that slow, girl."

"Yes, yes, you're right of course. When one moves too quickly one is out of balance. Balance is the key here; to be centered, to move in harmony with one's surroundings. All living creatures move toward such a one, are drawn to the soul in complete balance," Allison said in her French accent.

"Would you quit talking like Pepé le Pew."

"Okay, it's me again," Allison said resuming her normal voice. "Honestly though, it is all about balance. I get to moving too fast and my pace throws me off balance. Some people's postures throw them off. But you, I can't figure out what it is that throws you off. Try it again."

So Vicky put the dictionary back on her head and began walking, all the while aware of Allison's scrutinizing gaze.

"Ah ha! I have it," Allison said all at once, startling Vicky as she steadied the book back on her head. "It's your feet. They hit the ground too hard."

"I've always had heavy footsteps. It's why I chose to live on the ground level. I used to live in an upstairs apartment and the neighbors below me complained. Said it sounded like the ceiling was going to cave in when I walked around. I've always been hard on shoes. It's why I don't like to wear them."

"Yes, yes, and your stride is too long."

"That's because I have long legs," Vicky said.

"Yes, but it's something else," Allison said as she stopped to ponder it.

Vicky pondered the question too. Sometimes she felt as if gravity held her too bound to the earth. Never leaving the ground for long, she was destined to come crashing back down, despite her fears of descending from those great heights. But she wanted to rise above it all, to fly effortlessly with just the slightest movement of her arms like how she'd done in dreams. She wanted to float and wondered what it would feel like to be weightless. But that was all just a dream. Her feet were firmly planted on the earth, the hide of her feet were rough and calloused. She remained locked to the ground with all of its harsh realities: the dirt, the dust, and the soil. That made her who she was, but, oh, if she could just fly, just once.

"Try floating," Allison said almost as if she'd read Vicky's thoughts. "Close your eyes."

"Now you want me to walk around with this heavy thing on my head *and* my eyes closed?"

"Try it," Allison said. "Forget about the book on your head. Focus on your feet. Let your feet skim lightly across the floor," Allison said.

Vicky looked on disbelievingly. "Just humor me, all right."

And so Vicky closed her eyes. "Think light. Think light," she said to herself as she began to move. After a while it seemed it was not her feet that she needed to focus on, but rather her chest. With her eyes closed she could imagine a string tied about her sternum and threaded through her chest wall lifting her shoulders back even further and pulling her up and up, lifting her feet up with each step. She imagined it nearly lifting her off the ground. Suddenly the weight was gone from her head.

"That's it! That's it!" Allison said. Vicky opened her eyes and Allison had removed the book from her head. "Keep going, keep going. Feel how your feet just glide like a figure skater on ice. What was it Peter Pan said? Think happy thoughts. That's the key to flying. Just think happy thoughts and you lift right off the ground."

Vicky thought about it as she walked ever so lightly, her stocking feet skidding across the top of the carpeting. She realized the heaviness wasn't in her feet at all. It was in her heart. And truthfully, when she thought of her Francis, she felt lighter. Perhaps she already walked like a lady when he was near.

"You're floating. You're really floating, Vicky," Allison said her cheerful optimism exuding with every syllable she uttered.

"It doesn't come naturally. I don't know if I can keep it up all evening, though. It's tiring," Vicky said skidding across the floor.

"The control top hose and the high heels will help," Allison said.

"That's right, I gotta get all dolled up, don't I? You know I never get dressed up, not like that anyhow. I don't know which I hate worse, high heels or panty hose."

"They were invented by a misogynist, you know," Allison said.

"A what?"

"Here," Allison said handing her the dictionary. "That's M-I-S-O-G-Y-N-I-S-T."

Vicky flipped open the dictionary and went to sit in her rocker as she looked the word up. She wrote the definition in her notebook.

"You don't have to try so hard Vicky," Allison said. "There's really nothing wrong with the way you walk. It's really all about attitude, and you've got plenty."

"Yeah. All bad."

Chapter 25

A single red carnation boutonniere is what Vicky selected for Frank to wear in the lapel of his suit coat. She opened the white cardboard box in which it came several times just to see it there, freshly cut from the florist and placed so delicately in a small cellophane bag, folded over at the top and held shut with a white pearl straight pin. Carefully she would place it back in the refrigerator, only to take it out again a little while later for another peak. The effect upon Vicky of seeing that single red carnation was as magical as if fairy hands had cut the flower itself and placed it in that box.

Tonight was the night, and she was so restless all she could do was pace, smoke, and check the boutonniere. She never knew what to do with nervousness, even the kind she was feeling now, the good kind of nervous excitement in anticipation of something wonderful. She wished she had a little alcohol to quell her jittery gut but she hadn't kept liquor in her home since the last time she got drunk. She'd gotten rid of all of it and had faithfully abstained since then. She toyed with the idea of running down to the liquor store.

"It's not like I'm gonna get drunk," Vicky told herself as she paced and smoked. "Just a drink to take the edge off." But some unknown fear caused her to hesitate. Maybe it was the spirit of her grandmother. "Fool!" she said stopping in her tracks and smacking herself on the side of the head. "You can't let anything screw up this day.

When Allison, Sally, and Barb arrived they descended on her apartment without as much as a knock.

"Yoo hoo, anybody home!" came a high-pitched, yodel-like holler from Sally.

"We're here," Allison called, and in they stormed like a regiment of military troops with their duffle bags over their shoulders.

"You better not be doing anything to break your nails," Sally said, observing Vicky moving furniture and running her vacuum cleaner.

"Well, if I'm supposed to be queen for a day then this place better look like I got a maid. Besides, Stepmother says I can't go to the ball unless I finish my chores," Vicky said.

"Well, I'm your fairy godmother and I have just relinquished you from your chores," said Allison as she took the vacuum cleaner and put it away.

"What's with y'all anyway, you fixing to move in?" Vicky said eyeing a pink duffle bag marked "Mary Kay" which Sally had over her shoulder.

"Our work tools," Allison said setting her canvas bag on the kitchen counter, reaching in, and pulling out a hair dryer with one hand and a curling iron which she flicked open and shut with the other. "Since you refused to go to the beauty salon, the beauty salon has come to you."

"Our Vicky feels it's silly and frivolous to spend that kind of money on herself," said Allison.

"Haven't you ever been to the beauty salon, Vicky," asked Sally.

"Well, sure. I'm not that big a hick. I used to go to the Clip 'n Curl in Providence with my Grandma. She got her hair permed and set there. But see, everybody knew everybody there. All the beauticians were neighbors and friends, just like y'all. A stranger can't know how to make you look good. Oh, sure, they can make you look like some model in a magazine, but they can't make you look like you."

"Allison's going to do your hair and I'm doing your nails and makeup," Sally said placing the pink bag marked "Mary Kay" on the dining room table.

"And just what the heck is your role, Doctor Barb," Vicky said to Barb.

"Whatever you need me to do," said Barb.

"I know, Doc, you could write me a prescription for a strong sedative," Vicky said, half-joking.

"Sorry Vicky," said Barb. "I can't do that, but I can give you a massage. Nurses give patients massages before surgery. It helps relax them," said Barb.

"Surgery?" Vicky said.

Barb gave Vicky a neck and shoulder massage as she sat at a chair in her kitchen with a towel wrapped around her wet head. Barb didn't realize it but she was doing more for Vicky than Allison and Sally with all their rushing around and chatting and setting up. She was glad that Barb had a role. Vicky could see so clearly how out of place the plain and pragmatic Barb was in the feminine world. She wondered if she was the only one who could tell that everything about Barb tended toward the masculine. It wasn't terribly blatant but it was there and she wondered if Barb had figured out just who she was yet.

Vicky could relate to Barb in some ways. She often felt more at home in the masculine world, even though the very core of her being was feminine with this insatiable desire to nest and this quest for beauty. It was the perversion of that instinct that Vicky detested, that caused her to run away from the world of women. And yet here she was submitting to this makeover.

Allison plugged in the blow dryer then reached into her bag for a large rounded brush. The thought returned again to Vicky. Why was she going through all this silliness? She felt it was wrong somehow–vain and shallow. She had to let them know and she had to do it now.

"Wait!" Vicky hollered as Allison removed the damp towel from Vicky's head and began to brush her hair. Vicky shooed Allison's hand away and rose to her feet.

"What's wrong, Vicky?" Allison asked.

"Why are ya'll so into this?" Vicky said rising quickly to her feet. "Why is it so dag-nabbed important for y'all to do this stupid make-over?"

"This is our gift to you. Just accept it," Allison said with such sincerity that it took Vicky completely off her guard.

"I accept it," said Vicky.

"Now, let me do something with your hair before it dries on its own and frizzes up," Allison said, as she finally rose to her feet.

"Hey Al, you was gonna cut my hair, I mean…" Vicky said, her tongue stammering to correct herself as her brain sought the proper grammatical conjugation. "You were planning on cutting my hair, weren't you?" asked Vicky.

"I was just planning on trimming the ends," said Allison pulling a pair of scissors out of her bag.

"Why don't you just go ahead and cut it. Get rid of this bad perm for once and for all," said Vicky.

"Are you serious?" asked Barb.

"You're kidding," said Sally.

"No, I'm not kidding. Cut it all off," said Vicky.

"Wait a minute, wait a minute!" said Allison. "Let me get this straight. You want me to cut your hair *short?*"

"I don't know about *short* short, but definitely something different," said Vicky. "You're always saying I need to get the hair off my face. I'm gonna show off this scar of mine with pride."

"All right, but I'm not to be held responsible if I do a hack job."

"You won't do a hack job. I've got faith in you."

A magazine picture of a starlet (one whose hairstyle Allison thought particularly perfect to show off Vicky's features and long neck) was the aid and inspiration for the haircut. So Allison clipped Vicky's hair slowly and painstakingly, frequently pausing to look at the magazine picture and get advice from Barb whose eye seemed to be quite good in assessing the correct angles and equal lengths of things. Sally did her nails, fingers and toes, while

Barb straightened up her apartment and floated in and out of the kitchen giving opinions.

During the midst of all this, Vicky was affected by the most profound emotion–gratitude, yes, but something even more. She didn't fight the tears that welled up because she wanted to let them know, wanted to tell them some way, but couldn't find words. Sometimes tears are the only means to communicate.

Sally stopped filing Vicky's nails and looked up.

Allison quickly grabbed a hand mirror off the kitchen counter and held it in front of Vicky. "I think you look great."

Vicky tried to focus through the blur of tears. The image of three faces, startling in their contrast, appeared before Vicky. Her eyes darted to the pretty and ever-concerned face of Allison on her left to the comical face of Sally on her right (whose attempts at reassurance made her look even more comical) to the reflection of her own face in the hand mirror, dead center between the other two. Her face appeared stark, exposed, almost embarrassing in its candor. Her lashes and all around her eyes were damp with tears, her reddened nose more prominent than usual, and her eyes seemed larger with the shorter hair. And then there was the scar, which one might've thought more noticeable with the hair no longer there to hide it, but strangely, by the simple fact of it being so plain and exposed, the eyes disregarded it and were drawn away from it back to the focal point–her hazelnut brown eyes.

"My Lord, my eyes look enormous!" Vicky's voice cracked and wailed as she put her hand over her face and sobbed silently.

."You have beautiful eyes, Vicky. You can see them now," said Allison. "They're not hidden. Oh God, she hates me! I made her look like Marty Feldman. Vicky, I'm so sorry. Please don't cry."

"That's not why I'm crying. It's…it's because y'all are so nice, so…so good to me," Vicky said and broke down in sobs. Sally handed her tissue after tissue.

"I've never been…" Vicky paused and wiped her eyes and blew her nose, all the while trying to retrieve just the right word to describe this act of love. "Lavished… that's it! I've never been lavished before. Just put that mirror away and don't show me my face again until you're finished."

"Just for the record, you do not look like Marty Feldman," said Sally

"Shall we continue lavishing?" Allison asked.

"Lavish away," Vicky replied.

The hair at last was finished and together Allison, Sally, and Barb all gathered around her forming a semi circle. They were smiling. These were sincere smiles that broke upon their faces quite spontaneously. A good sign, Vicky thought, but then she never doubted.

Allison smiled a mixture of pride and surprise. "Before I let you look in the mirror Vicky, I have to warn you. It's a change, a real change."

"That's what I wanted," Vicky said. "Now let me see."

Allison held the mirror in front of Vicky's face. She was indeed all face with the different layers brushed back on the sides, just a wisp of auburn bangs sweeping across her forehead and auburn fringe adorning the back of her long neck. It was the same old features but brighter and more alive. Vicky wondered if it was the hairstyle or all the lavishing that made her look so lit up.

"Thank you," Vicky said rising to her feet and putting her arms around Allison

"Thank you for trusting me," Allison said.

"All right," said Sally breaking the mood, "when I start making up your face there'll be no more crying, so you might as well get it all out now."

The trick would be getting the women to leave before Frank got there, Vicky thought as she changed into her gown with this one blissful moment of privacy she had in her bedroom. Allison and Sally brought cameras and they wanted pictures of her in her gown so they refused to leave until she got dressed. Vicky stepped out of her bedroom and into the living room to the flashing of cameras.

"Now listen ladies, I don't mean to be rude, but you gotta hurry it up. I don't want you hiding in the closet or hanging around the hallways when Francis arrives," Vicky said.

"Vicky, how do you feel?" Allison asked beaming.

"I feel downright beautiful. I'll never be able to thank you enough, but there's just one thing."

"What?" they all asked looking anxious.

"I need an honest opinion," Vicky said turning to the side, revealing her tattoo. "What do you think?"

"Don't worry about the tattoo," Allison said, seeming exasperated that she would even bring it up.

"Mind if I take a closer look?" Barb asked. Vicky gave her permission. Barb held Vicky's arm and examined the tattoo as only a health professional might. "Hmm, interesting depiction of a myocardial infarction." Vicky glared at her. "Well, that's my interpretation of it anyway, but then I'm not much on art."

"She wasn't asking for your artistic interpretation of it," Allison said. "She's self-conscious about being seen in an evening gown with a tattoo on her arm."

"I wouldn't worry about it," said Sally. "The colors work with your dress and your makeup."

"Well, now ain't that comforting," Vicky said facetiously. "I gotta drawing of a heart attack etched onto my arm, but the colors work. I think I'll just put that shawl around my shoulders right now and forget about it. You got it for me, Allison?"

"Right here," Allison replied, pulling out a neatly folded gold block of material from her bag. "And don't let me forget your evening bag while I'm at it," she said retrieving a small gold beaded purse.

"What the…? Girl, what have you done?" Vicky said in astonishment. "I thought you were loaning me your black shawl and evening bag."

"I was. But then the more I got to thinking about it, the more I thought you really should be arrayed all in gold."

"How much did it set you back?"

"It's a gift. Just accept it."

Frank stood at Vicky's door just minutes after the ladies left. He wore a classic black tuxedo with black tie and cummerbund, a fancy white starched shirt with gold and black studs, cuff links to match, and black shiny shoes with just the slightest hint of a crease on the toe, as if they'd only been worn once or twice before. He held in his hand a dozen long stemmed red roses. And then there was his face–all clean shaven and smelling good.

Open and unguarded, he stood there. At the sight of her his face broke into a smile so broad it covered half his face, showing off the deeply etched dimples in those manly cheeks and causing his navy blue eyes to sparkle with lively exuberance. Everything about him, his smile, those eyes, the sound of his voice greeting her, the scent of his cologne, those hands so notably strong which had played the piano and caressed her cheek and now held roses, his presence, his very soul; all of these things that made up Francis swirled around her in that moment until Vicky felt as if her heart did a sudden quarter turn.

"Be still my beating heart," Vicky said catching her breath and slapping her hand upon her chest.

They did what they so often did in those awkward unspeakable moments– they laughed. Laughter was their secret language, releasing all those pent up feelings, foolish, as lovers so often are to the casual observer.

"I do declare, I never thought I'd see Prince Charming in the flesh standing right here at my door with roses," Vicky said. "They're beautiful."

"Of course. They match the recipient," Frank said handing her the roses. Vicky accepted them, cradled them in her arms like an infant, and buried her face in them taking in the fragrance.

"Come in," she said, stepping back and allowing Frank to cross the threshold of her apartment. Frank closed the door behind them and stood as close to Vicky as one person can get to another without physically touching.

"Your hair," he said smiling and running his hand lightly over the side of her head.

"It's a big change, isn't it? You like it?"

"Oh, yeah! Mostly I like you," he said in a soft voice.

Feeling suddenly embarrassed and vulnerable, as only Frank could make her feel, she cleared her throat as if to clear away the discomfort of that intimate moment. She quickly walked away, busying herself in the kitchen with cutting the stems of the roses and filling with water the crystal vase which Frank had given her to hold all the flowers he'd bestowed on her.

"Who cut your hair? Allison or Sally?" Frank asked.

"Allison, but how did you know it was one of them?" Vicky said placing one rose at a time into the vase.

"Our dear Sally isn't one to keep a secret."

"Thanks a lot, Sally!" Vicky said letting go a chuckle. "I never would have thought anybody would make such a fuss over me like that in a million years," Vicky said, separating the roses, one from another until they were just right in the vase. "If any of my biker buddies found out I played live Barbie doll to a bunch of giddy girls, they'd never let me live it down." Vicky thought about how little she saw of her old friends these days, but decided in that instant not to pause too long on that thought lest she begin to feel morose.

"Your secret's safe with me," Frank said.

"Yeah, you probably love it. All these women going to all this trouble just so your date could look her best," Vicky said.

"I admit, I'm honored."

"You better be. I did it for you."

"Come here," Frank said, and they walked toward each other until at last they were in each others' arms. They kissed long and carelessly.

"Oh, Vicky, this is what I wanted to do the moment I saw you there at the door–just grab you and kiss you. But I was holding roses and I didn't want to snag your dress on a thorn." They kissed again.

"Sally went to all this trouble to get my face just so, now you're gonna have it all smudged off by the time we walk out the door. And don't get too near my hair," Vicky said as he kissed her neck and his hand traveled near the back of her head. "You get your hand stuck in that snarled up mess of plaster and cement and you won't ever get it out again." They laughed while kissing–bestowing their merriment upon one another through the breath of their laughter, little fragments of joy exhaled and taken in through the mouth, passed on from one to the other like good medicine.

"I've never laughed so much in my life as I have these past few months with you," Frank said.

"Me too," said Vicky. "I'll make a deal with you. The day we quit laughing and start making each other cry instead, it's time to call it quits. Agreed?"

"Agreed," Frank said and kissed her again. "Thank you, Vicky."

"For what, Francis darlin'?"

"For looking so lovely." He took a step back and still holding onto her hands, he stretched out her arms as if to get a better, more full-length look at her. "Look at you."

"Look at you!" Vicky said right back at him. "You really like the hair?"

"If I didn't would I be attacking you like this?" he said pulling her to him once again and kissing her neck.

"You're a guy. I could be bald as a billiard ball and you'd still attack me. Come on, this is a serious question. I need to know if I oughta keep it short or grow it back out again."

"It doesn't matter to me. I like it both ways. It's you I like."

"Answered like a true guy. Anyway, the girls like it. Sally says it shows off my face more."

"That's it! That's what's so different about you," Frank said in a moment of epiphany.

"That and the fact I generally don't walk around in evening gowns and heels."

"No, it's your face. You can see it."

"It's right there in front of you, ain't it? You know it's weird, I keep going to brush my hair back, and there's no hair there to brush back. I feel a little freer, lighter, like I told the ladies. The only problem is I think maybe it draws attention to my scar."

"Your scar," Frank said touching the scarred cheek lightly and tenderly.

"Maybe I could get that plastic surgery you talked about."

"I don't notice the scar. Only you."

"You're sweet, Francis," Vicky said kissing the palm of his hand. Then looking at his wrist watch she said, "We better get going. Don't you have dinner reservations somewhere?"

"Indeed I do."

"Oh, I almost forgot something," Vicky said going to the refrigerator for the boutonniere. She snatched the white cardboard box and hurried back to Frank as quickly as the long dress and high heels would allow her.

"This is for you," she said presenting him with the box. She watched his face carefully as he opened it. "I hope you don't think it's too foolish or immature. Tonight is the high school prom I never had." Frank looked up at her, his brows knit together in an expression of poignancy.

"Thank you," he said in a voice so low and tender it was almost inaudible. "I'm truly touched. Would you put it on me?"

"I would be most honored," Vicky said with a smile. She pinned the stem onto the lapel amid barbs and bantering about being careful not to stick him with it.

"Shall we go?" Frank said after she had finished. "Do you have a wrap? It's chilly out," Frank said.

"A wrap? I bet I haven't heard that word since my first grade teacher, Miss Sweeny. We always had to have a wrap when we went outside for recess." Vicky said grabbing her gold shawl off the back of her rocker. She started to put it on but Frank was there at her shoulder in a moment spreading the silky material over her bare shoulders.

"I can dress myself, Francis honey."

"Why must we have this discussion every time?" said Frank.

"I know, I know, it's the gentlemanly thing to do–hold the door open, hold the chair, help the damsel in distress with her wrap. But still, how did this particular custom get started? Like someone might hurt themselves putting their coat on? What're you gonna do? Dislocate a shoulder or something?"

"I think it started back when women wore so much clothing they could hardly move. You know, they were on the verge of fainting all the time, so they required all this extra assistance. Then it just stuck," Frank said.

"Hmm, makes sense. Right now I feel like I could use one of them pageboys from the fairy tale picture books to hold my train so I don't trip over my dress going up and down steps." Watch out for me."

"I won't take my eyes off of you." Frank smiled.

Vicky switched off the light, closed the door to her apartment and locked it. Frank held the door to the apartment building open for her as they stepped out into the cool evening air.

The September sun shone in the western sky, lower in the horizon with the ever shortening days of autumn.

Chapter 26

Anxiety settled in Vicky's gut as the old Victory Theater loomed larger than life before them with each approaching step. The Victory Theater–the oldest movie theater in the heart of downtown Lamasco had been recently restored in an attempt to bring some life and culture into a dying downtown. The Philharmonic concerts where held in this beautiful old structure which seemed both daunting and mysterious to Vicky. She adjusted her shawl around her shoulders, making sure it covered her Sacred Heart tattoo. She concentrated on gliding and walking like a lady as they made their way through the front door and stopped just outside the old box office to hand their tickets to an usher. Vicky looked around at all the ladies. She was relieved to see many dressed as formally as her. It was something she worried about, but Frank told her not to worry, that many of the who's who would be coming from a fancy benefit gala to kick off the season. The only ones who weren't dressed up were the bohemians, but even in their studied carelessness, they emitted a certain pretension. Vicky was the only one of her kind there. An occasional customer from River Inn recognized her and waved, smiled, or said hello as they waded through the crowd; and she couldn't decide if that made her feel better or worse. It was good to be acknowledged but embarrassing to think there were those that knew her true identity and might be judging her for being there tonight. Frank must've picked up on her thoughts and gave her hand, which he'd been holding onto tightly, a quick squeeze. "Don't worry, Vicky, you're the most beautiful woman here," he whispered.

It seemed a long walk halfway up the aisle on the left side of the theater, but at long last they were at their seats, bringing to Vicky some comfort and security in the fact that she could now just relax, sit next to her Francis with the house lights down dim and enjoy the music. It was the first time Vicky actually looked at her surroundings, the first moment since they entered the building which she was free enough from the burden of self-consciousness to really observe where she was.

The Victorian décor transported her to another world, the reds and golds laced with intricate designs on the walls and ceiling, the heavy red velvet curtain on the stage, the candelabras on the wall, the balcony seats up and all around the theater where people mulled about. All of this was enhanced by the sound of the orchestra tuning their instruments, filling Vicky with a strange anticipation. As she looked all around she made a conscious effort not to gape, gasp, or exclaim though she was swept up by awe at her surroundings. She imagined she was in another time, another world, another place, and began to let go some of the anxiety.

She read in the program about the lives of Mozart and Rachmaninoff and what was going on at the time they composed the music she would be hearing tonight. Their lives and their art were so often marked with hardship and conflict, and this knowledge filled Vicky with a strange hope.

Finally it was time for the concert to begin. The house lights dimmed, the orchestra members stopped their tuning, and a hush fell over the audience. The first violinist came out on stage and everyone applauded as he took a bow. Then out came the maestro who bowed, shook the first violinist's hand, and raised his baton inaugurating the evening's performance with the Overture from Bernsteins' Candide.

It was a piece Vicky was unfamiliar with, but it was joyful, energetic, and fresh to the ears. With elation she experienced Mozart's symphony as alive and filled with the optimism and enthusiasm that is Mozart's signature.

What really moved Vicky was the second half of the concert— Rachmaninoff's Third Piano Concerto. The pianist was a Russian man, a Soviet defector, no less. Frank told her it was one of the most difficult piano pieces to master and there are few alive that can handle the Rock 3, as it is affectionately called by those who know and love his music.

They were fortunate enough to have a good view of his hands from where they sat but not as good a view of his face which the other side of the house would have more of an opportunity to appreciate. Just like in the first part of the concert with the Mozart symphony, she was startled into a new awareness of the music with hearing it new, fresh, and live. It was not just the sounds but the visuals as well; watching the orchestra, the conductor, and most of all, the pianist with his skilled fingers moving up and down the keys. She could tell the music affected him from the way his body moved in rhythm to the various chords and from profile glimpses of his face showing at times profound emotion.

And what of those emotions, Vicky pondered. Surely this artist was connected somehow to the heart of Sergey Rachmaninoff himself, being a Russian in a strange land and perhaps longing for certain things about his homeland that he had to leave behind forever.

The piece started out with something deep, dark, and Russian. At least to Vicky it sounded like what she pictured Russia to be from her limited knowledge and scant memories of high school history classes. She wished she'd paid more attention in school, but nonetheless, her mind conjured up images of exiled Bolsheviks in Siberia dressed in heavy winter garb trudging through the snow, and braving all sorts of hardships. There was something persevering and disciplined about this opening, something of the human spirit that would continue to trudge forward despite a cold wind blowing in one's face. It was struggle at its deepest core that Vicky heard and felt in this beautiful music. And then a change came about, like something hopeful and light blowing in, finding long awaited release from this struggle, a prisoner glimpsing at freedom; but never for long as the theme of struggle returned again and again with the sound of heart-wrenching melancholy, fighting not to surface, but in the end unable to restrain itself.

The second movement was pure longing, like she'd heard before in some of Rachmaninoff's other music. It was longing never quite quenched though the subject kept coming close, resolution was right there within reach but never grasped, leaving in its wake such deep sadness, relieved only by a few brief moments of humor. At times it was tragic. At other times, funny. It was the longing and homesickness of the stranger in a strange land who can never go back except in mind and memory.

Though she'd heard the recorded version, there was something quite distinctive about hearing it live that triggered all her emotions—every little bit of longing, melancholy, homesickness, and struggle she'd ever felt. Frank saw the emotion she was trying so hard not to show and he handed her his handkerchief. She covered her face with it and wept silently, wanting only to compose herself. Frank squeezed her hand but it only made her cry more and she wondered why.

The third movement began with a quick start, snapping everyone out of the dream world they had lapsed into during the second movement. It was here that all eyes were on the pianist hands as he pounded out the dramatic notes with powerful intensity, floating in and out of that dreamlike world, coming back to reality with that harsh reawakening, all of the various themes and emotions finally rising to such a height, achieving something of a resolution, then ending abruptly.

The audience erupted into applause and everyone sprang to their feet for a standing ovation. Shouts of "bravo" and even whistles were heard, which surprised Vicky, thinking it beneath the dignity of the classical concert-going set to do such a thing as whistle. Frank turned to the teary-eyed Vicky and said, "Are you all right?"

"Are you kidding? I'm exhausted. That was so chock full of feeling."

"It was indeed sublime," said Frank.

"Sublime and majestic," said Vicky through the applause. "I feel like I just watched someone live and die, like I felt everything he ever felt, like I got so attached to this person then suddenly without warning he up and had a heart attack and died. Now he's gone."

"I think he's going to play an encore," Frank said.

"I don't think I can take anymore," Vicky said, returning to her seat with the rest of the audience.

The Russian pianist played Rachmaninoff's Prelude in E-flat Major for an encore.

No emotion had gone unfelt, no experience of pain or joy that wasn't relived in that short span of a little less than an hour.

After the concert they were invited to a reception to meet the pianist. It was held in the hotel right next to the theater. This was a chain hotel, the largest in Lamasco, different from River Inn in both size and style; the establishment where many conferences, conventions, and other large gatherings were held.

Vicky and Frank arrived and, uncertain where to go, they consulted the front desk clerk who told them the reception was to be held in Ballroom "A".

"A ballroom!" Vicky said in surprise. "All right Prince Charming, I knew a concert was part of the gig but I didn't know I was going to a ball."

"I'm full of surprises," said Frank, giving her his arm.

"Hold onto me, Francis," Vicky said taking a hold of his arm as they made their way down the hallway. "Prop me up if I start to faint."

"You're not the fainting type, honey. Don't be so nervous. My friends will love you."

"Is my tattoo showing?" Vicky said adjusting her shawl. "How's my face? Do I have mascara underneath my eyes?"

"You're lovely."

This would be the most difficult part of the evening to get through. In her anxious imaginings she was kicking her uncomfortable high heeled shoes off her feet and up in the air, letting them land helter skelter (it didn't matter where she'd never wear them again), and lifting the skirt of her gown to run in her stocking feet as fast as she could out of this place. It was an impulse, a wild imagining. She blinked and swallowed hard to make it go away.

"Okay, here goes," said Vicky, inhaling deeply and exhaling slowly as they entered the room.

They went over to the bar. Vicky ordered a coke and Frank ordered a scotch which he would mostly swirl around in the glass, suck on the ice cubes, and generally nurse all evening, driving Vicky thoroughly crazy at the prospect of wasting such a good drink. As they made their way through the crowd they spotted a small group of five men standing in a semi-circle near one end of the room. "There they are," Frank said pointing them out and leading Vicky in that direction.

Frank introduced them all to Vicky. She shook their hands, chit chatted with them about the concert, and asked them prompting questions designed to get them talking about themselves. She hoped to take the focus off herself and seemed to be doing just fine for the first few minutes until she noticed one of the men studying her face in a quizzical manner.

"You look familiar. Where do I know you from?" he said.

"You've probably seen Vicky at the River Inn. She tends bar there," said Frank, seeming fairly unruffled. Vicky loved him for it. She squared her shoulders, stood up straight, looked the man who had inquired about her in the eye, and inwardly coached herself to smile at him, and smile confidently. Her cover was blown. Oh, well! Now all she wanted to do was hop behind the bar with the other bartender and have the security of that barrier between her and these socially elite young men.

"Of course, that Vicky," said another one of the men, recognizing her also. Already two of the men were looking at her in a different way, and she could guess what they were thinking judging from the glances they gave Frank.

"I was wondering how long it would take you to recognize me, boys. I recognized both of you," she said to the two men.

"You recognize me?" said one of them.

She glanced at Frank as if to get permission to proceed. He smiled in his amused way and at that moment she thought he might even be proud of the way she could hold her own. "Vicky never forgets a drink order. Tell him Vicky," said Frank.

"Tanqeray martini on the rocks with two olives. Or a Heineken. But I see they didn't have your brand of beer," she said motioning to his plastic cup.

"That's astonishing! Where did you find her Frank?"

"We met at a Menza Club meeting," said Frank, and Vicky gave him a discreet look in which she tried to communicate her desperation in not knowing what he was talking about.

"Vicky's been a member of Menza Club since she was a kid, but I almost wasn't admitted. My I.Q. was right at the cut off point–140. I'm definitely one of the duller members, but not Vicky. Of course, she downplays it because she doesn't want anyone to know she's a genius. It embarrasses her."

"Please, Francis, did you have to go and tell everyone?"

"A club for geniuses? Nice try, Frank," said one of the men and they all began laughing.

"Did you realize Francis is one of the greatest mathematical geniuses currently alive? Go ahead, Francis, explain that quadratic equation to them, the one we were discussing before we came across these very broad minded and interesting gentlemen. Of course, you may have to write it down for them, no offense."

"Now you're embarrassing me," Frank said.

Odd Numbers

"You shouldn't be so modest, darlin'. Did you know our Francis here can do the Rubik's cube? He solved it the first time he tried. No kidding! Of course it took him a little while. How long did it take you," said Vicky?

"The first time? Roughly seven minutes," said Frank.

"Now he can do it in under two."

The men just laughed, though a couple of them showed signs of discomfort, as if they were trying to discern if Frank and Vicky were for real.

"You all laugh, but I'd like to see you try and get all those colors lined up, without cheating and peeling the little stickers off that is."

"Isn't she wonderful?" Frank said giving her a hug. "I met her and I thought there goes my perfect correlation coefficient."

"So Miss Dooley," said the most intimidating looking of the men. "What's a genius like you doing tending bar at the River Inn?"

"Well, a girl's got to make a living while she works on her doctoral dissertation," Frank said jumping in, much to Vicky's relief, to answer the question for her. Vicky smiled and nodded.

"What's your dissertation on?" One of the men asked her.

"Correlation coefficients and the Rubik's cube. It's very complicated but if you truly understand the concept you can crack the Rubik's cube, and nearly any other code," Vicky said with her hand on her hip, daring any of them to call her a liar.

"In fact here's the equation," Frank said. He took a cocktail napkin and scribbled upon it some sort of long equation with the letters a, b, and z, and plenty of brackets and parenthesis.

"You remembered it Francis. How sweet of you," Vicky said taking the cocktail napkin and throwing her arms around him.

"You know I'd never forget any of your equations, love. Especially given the fact that it took you over a year to come up with it," said Frank giving her a quick kiss on the lips.

"So I take it, Miss Dooley, you can do the Rubik's cube also," said the intimidating looking man with a glint of amused superiority in his eyes.

"Let's get this straight, my name is not Miss Dooley. It's Vicky. And no, I cannot do the Rubik's cube. Not without peeling off the little stickers or tearing the dang thing apart," Vicky said letting herself slip into her true form. Some of the men chuckled.

"Of course I know the equation. I came up with it," she said quickly catching herself. "But that's somewhat different from actually doing it. That's why Francis and I make such a great team. I come up with the equations and he applies them."

"Really?" said the man intent on challenging her instead of playing along.

"If you figured out the mathematical equation to crack the so called code, then why is it you can't do the Rubik's cube?"

"Because I have what's called Low Frustration Tolerance," Vicky said thinking of the symptom she saw listed most often in her Abnormal Psychology textbook in the chapter they were currently studying on Behavior Disorders. It was the best Vicky could come up with at a moment's notice. She shot the intimidating man an even more intimidating glance, daring him to question her any further.

"Sometimes she flies into these rages, especially when she's being unnecessarily challenged," said Frank. "I'm sorry, hon, should I not have said anything?"

"It's all right, Francis. It's best they know. There's a fine line between genius and madwoman. Sometimes I just cross that line," she said with a wicked smile.

"All right you two, I think you've flung enough bullshit around here for one evening," said the skeptic.

"That's right, the jig is up," said another.

"All right if you must know the truth, I'm a high school drop out with a GED," she said in perfect English with a slight air of haughtiness. There were chuckles from the men, some of nervousness and some of disbelief. "I'm not working on a doctoral dissertation but I am working on a Bachelor's degree from the University."

She looked at Frank. He wore that cool unruffled expression that made it impossible to know what he was thinking. He certainly wasn't the type of man to ever blush, no matter how embarrassed he got. Vicky didn't know what else to do but continue.

"I do suffer from Low Frustration Tolerance though which causes me to throw things like Rubik's Cubes against walls. I've never been much for book knowledge but I do know people, and from the looks of it Mr. Brooks," she said addressing the most outspoken man in the group, "you're on about your third vodka tonic. If memory serves me correctly that's about your limit, isn't it? After that you start to sweat and become belligerent."

"Touché," said one of the friendlier looking men with a chuckle, and the other men began razzing him. "You sure pegged ol' Brooksie here," said another one of the men, slapping him on the back and they all laughed in relief, except for Brooks.

"What are you getting your degree in, Vicky?" asked the friendly man, who seemed to be trying to ease ill feelings.

"I haven't declared a major yet but it will most likely be Business Management. I hope to have my own place someday, restaurant and bar, that is."

"Really I'd think it would be Psychology judging from the way you seem to understand people," said the friendly man.

No. I enjoy taking Psychology classes because I enjoy observing human behavior, I do so much of it in my job, you know, but I got no desire to fix anybody. That's way too big of a job for me—even more frustrating than the Rubik's cube. By the way, Francis really can do the Rubik's cube. It's all mathematical, right Francis?"

"She's on a roll!" Frank said, presenting Vicky with an outstretched hand and physically standing back to let her have the floor.

"Like I was saying…" said Vicky.

"See, what did I tell you?" said Frank.

"See the problem is there just is no mathematical equation to fix people. We're all a bunch of broken Rubik's cubes and just when we think we got one row all perfectly lined up, you find you just messed up the other row that took you even longer to get all lined up perfect than the one you just completed. No, I just wanna serve folks a drink and a good meal and help them forget their troubles for a little while. Maybe that's as close as we'll ever come to fixing them."

The men all reacted differently to what Vicky said. People always did. They would draw their own conclusions about her: either a simpleton or a sage.

"What business classes are you taking now?" Another man asked.

"Economics 101."

"Oh, so tell me what you think of President Regan's policies."

"Not much!" Vicky said.

"Vicky's a dyed-in-the-wool Democrat," said Frank.

"The trickle down theory looks great on paper but it just doesn't work in real life. It doesn't matter how many benefits you give the big businesses, if the guys at the top are greedy then they'll see to it nothing's gonna trickle down."

"You Democrats just don't get it about capitalism and how it works," said Mr. Brooks. "Greed, as you call it, isn't always such a bad thing. When a business owner wants to attract more business you call it greed. Yet, how does he do it? By offering a better product or service and lowering his prices. This forces the competition to lower their prices too. Everyone wins—consumer and business owner."

"What about the poor grunts working for Mr. Capitalist Nice Guy? In the process of cutting all those costs he's cut pay wages and laid off workers left and right."

"No, your labor unions will never let that happen." said Brooks.

"Damn straight!"

"I was being facetious. Most of your labor leaders are nothing but a bunch of thugs who beat the crap out of the poor worker who doesn't pay his union dues on time. Talk about greed!"

"Nobody is immune from greed. It exists everywhere. It just seems to me that it's always the ones that have more that are most likely to want more. Corrupt labor leaders included. It's the same principle as a spoiled kid with too many toys. He ain't–excuse me–he will never be satisfied with what he has."

"You go ahead and study your economics," said Brooks condescendingly. "But just wait until you own your own business someday. That's your dream, right?" Vicky nodded. "It's the American dream, and it's only the free enterprise system that allows you the opportunity to do that."

"Hey I got nothing against the free enterprise system, just these big businesses ruled by greed and trying to force the little guy outta business–the same guy who's trying to offer a better product or service for a lower price," said Vicky, feeling her heart beat faster and something inside her burn.

"That's what I love about this woman," said Frank coming to her rescue. "We don't always agree but she's her own person."

"And she's obviously not afraid to tell you what she thinks," said the friendly man with a polite chuckle.

"Exactly!" said Frank, affectionately drawing her to his side.

Vicky rested in his embrace, hoping to gain just a small dose of strength and comfort from the feel of his arm around her. She never loved Francis more than at this moment. Yet she could tell these other men didn't see her in the same way Francis did, even the ones who were trying to be polite. They saw through the veneer of the expensive gown and the newly acquired way of walking and talking. They saw her for what she really was. Not that she cared what they thought, but would Francis care once their love began to wither?

"So I take it you're not voting to re-elect Mr. Regan in the upcoming election," said the friendly man chuckling in an attempt to steer the conversation to a more agreeable level.

"No, can't say I am. Mondale-Ferraro all the way."

Some of the men chuckled and the others groaned.

"How could anyone vote for Mondale?" Brooks asked.

"Because he has enough sense to pick a woman for a running mate. Now there's a thinking man! You know if we had more women in politics there would be fewer wars; just some fiercely heated debates about once a month." Even Brooks laughed at Vicky's little joke. If she couldn't get people to take her seriously she could always get them to laugh.

"Look who's headed our way," said one of the men suddenly and with a tone of surprise as he motioned behind Vicky and Frank. Vicky turned around. The guest pianist and a well dressed middle-aged woman were coming right towards them.

"Well, if it isn't our Rusky friend and the president of our board," said Brooks as if they were coming just to see him.

"Hello everyone," said the woman who approached the group first with the Russian pianist standing a modest two paces behind her.

"You all know Marge Kaplan, President of the Philharmonic," said Brooks who had taken upon himself the duty of doing the introductions.

"Nice to meet you. Nice to meet you," she said quickly, going around the circle shaking hands. Her small sweaty palm squeezed Vicky's hand tightly but very briefly, her eyes scanning faces, not really looking but more gathering information as she anxiously moved onto the next person in the circle.

"And this gentleman needs no introduction," said Marge Kaplan motioning toward the pianist. "May I present our esteemed guest artist, Nikolay Michailovich."

"Yes, we met already," said Brooks extending his most pretentious smile and firmest handshake to the Russian gentleman. The pianist, who stood so erect, did a quick funny sort of half bow. In turn, all the other gentlemen from the group shook hands with him and commented on the skill and beauty with which he played. He thanked each person graciously with a quick yet humble bow of deference. Frank was the last person in the group to be introduced to him. It seemed that Nikolay Michailovich planned to end these introductions with Vicky so that he might focus all his attention on her.

"And who is this beautiful lady that I have been secretly admiring all night?" Nikolay said in his Russian accent.

"This is my girlfriend, Miss Vicky Dooley," Frank said. It sounded to Vicky as if he had emphasized the word "girlfriend", and suddenly he stood closer to her with his arm around her waist.

"Mr. Michailovich insisted on meeting you my dear," said Marge to Vicky.

"I saw you from across the room like a ... how do you say? Like a vision of light from the heavens, like an angel," Nikolay said, ignoring Frank's posture of possessiveness. All Vicky could do was smile, and smile radiantly.

"An angel? Yeah, that's me all right," said Vicky as Nikolay kissed her hand, his lips lingering on her knuckles.

"Oh, please sir," said Vicky. "I should be the one to kiss your hands." She took both his hands in hers' and examined them. She was overcome with awe at the thought that such an ordinary looking pair of hands could produce such beautiful music. Her eyes welled up with tears as she lifted his hands to her lips and kissed them. Emotion overtook her and all she could say was, "Thank you. Your playing made me so happy."

"And standing here in your presence has made me so happy," said Nikolay beaming.

"We're all overcome with happiness tonight," said Frank, edging himself ever so slightly between Vicky and Nikolay. "Tell me Mr. Mikhailovich…"

"Call me Nikolay."

"Nikolay. How old were you when you started playing?" Frank said.

"I was four years old when I began playing the piano," said Nikolay.

"Ah yes, I've heard all great concert pianist begin playing before the age of eight," said Frank.

"Francis here started young. How old were you Francis?" Vicky said.

"I was six, but unfortunately I quit playing as a young man."

"I never knew you played the piano," said one of the men to Frank.

"He's taken it up again," said Vicky.

"Yes, and Vicky was my inspiration in doing so," said Frank.

"Yes, I can see that this is a woman who would inspire," said Nikolay.

"Speaking of inspiration," said Frank, "I've never heard Rachmaninoff played with so much emotion before. Does the fact that he's a fellow Russian influence the way you play his work?"

"Most definitely," Nikolay said modestly.

"Do you miss your homeland, Nikolay, the way that Sergei Rachmaninoff did? Sometimes his music sounds like homesickness to me," said Vicky.

"You are perceptive as well as beautiful," said Nikolay. "I think I miss a Russia I never knew. But perhaps it will be one day again."

"Someday Communism will fall, and I believe we'll live to see that day," said Brooks.

"Yes. Perhaps soon," said Nikolay a little wistfully, then turning his attention back to Vicky he said, "Tell me, Vicky, do you play an instrument?"

"No, only the radio and a little air guitar from time to time but I don't think that counts."

"Delightful," he said.

"It's been a great honor meeting you, Nikolay, but we really must be going," said Frank extending his hand.

"I will never forget this evening, Nikolay," said Vicky.

"And I shall never forget you," said Nikolay, giving her one last look before kissing her hand in a final farewell gesture.

Frank and Vicky said goodbye to Frank's friends and departed.

"Francis! How come you're in such an all fire hurry to leave?" Vicky said as he led her hastily by the hand through the crowded room. "Give a poor gal in high heels a break," she said jogging slightly to keep up with him. Finally they made it through the room and out into the hallway. "Now will you talk to me?" she said, yanking on his arm to slow him down.

"I thought I better hurry up and run off with you before Nikolay did," said Frank.

"Why Francis, you're jealous! How sweet. But you know how ridiculous it is. What a pair we'd make; Nicky and Vicky, the runaway ex-comie and part injun hillbilly. I really see that one working out!"

Frank stopped and laughed then taking Vicky into his arms, he kissed her on the bridge of the nose.

"Well, at least Nikolay was impressed with me. I wish I could say as much for the American men."

"They liked you. You know what Jameson said?"

"Jameson—he's the one who normally drinks Heineken but had to settle for Bud Light. Right?"

"I guess. He said, and I quote, 'I like her. It takes one hell of a person to put Brooks in his place'. And you know what else he said?"

"Do tell."

"He referred to you as a southern belle."

"A southern belle? Why Rhett, I do declare! I need a mint julep."

"So you see, Scarlet, you truly were the belle of the ball."

"What about those that know I'm just a hick in disguise? Like Brooks?"

"To hell with Brooks."

"You mean it Francis?"

"I mean it," he said in earnest.

"That's all I needed to know."

Frank stopped and, once again, held her face his hands. "Look, what do I have to do to pound it into your brain? I don't care what anyone else thinks about you. I love you." He continued to hold her face in his hands and look into her eyes, as if he was trying to transmit all the sincerity in his heart to her, as if he meant to drive out any doubt once and for all.

"Best night of my life. Brooks and all," Vicky said to Frank as they tarried by the doorstep of her apartment.

"Best night of my life too." Frank said; then he kissed her, a little more passionately than had been of late. The usual kiss at the doorstep since they began their courtship had been somewhat restrained, followed by abrupt and awkward goodbyes. Frank was trying to be the gentleman. But if this romance were to ever go further than goodnight kisses at the door Vicky would have to be the one to initiate it.

"Goodnight," he said, only not so abruptly or awkwardly this time. They lingered in silence, remaining in one another's arms for a time until Frank, in what seemed to be one sudden and great act of the will, broke the embrace and departed. Vicky watched him walk down the hall, past Sally's door, around the corner and up the stairs. She crossed the threshold of her apartment and closed the door behind her. The latch clicked with the sound of finality, leaving in its wake a deathly quiet. Nothing moved inside her apartment, not even the air. It was a stagnant silence, not the silence of restfulness and peace, but the silence of emptiness, dull and lonesome, driving her mad like it always did. She would be left alone tonight to pace the hall between her bedroom and living room.

Sometimes she paced it seemed just to move the air around and bring life and movement to this small square footage of space she called her home. Restlessness, loneliness, and emptiness all swirled around together in her gut, one overlapping the other. She lit a cigarette and opened her sliding glass door to let some night air blow in through the screen. If she could just get some air into the apartment, some life from the outside world then maybe she wouldn't feel so closed in and alone. She stepped out onto the patio and looked up at the stars, trying to find all the constellations she'd learned from Frank. She looked up again, this time just as high as Frank's place. His light was on.

Vicky knocked on Frank's door still clad in her gold gown, but now in her stocking feet as she had to take the uncomfortable gilded high heels off. Frank answered the door. He'd taken off his coat and tie and unbuttoned the top button of his formal shirt. He too had taken his shoes off and had on his tan leather slippers. Vicky chuckled.

"You're laughing at my slippers, aren't you? If they were good enough for Fred McMurray, they're good enough for me," said Frank with a smile.

"Whatever you say. Father knows best," said Vicky.

"Are you going to stand out there and make fun of me or are you going to come in?"

"Well, I don't know. Was that an invitation to enter?"

"Come in, Vicky," Frank said with a smile.

"I hope I'm not disturbing you," Vicky said changing the tone to a more serious one as soon as Frank closed the door behind them. "I had to walk past Sally's place, but you know what, I didn't even care. By the way her door was closed and her light was out." Frank said nothing but just stood there waiting, it seemed, for an explanation from her as to why she was there. He stood with his arms crossed guarding the entrance to the living room, and even though Vicky was inside his apartment, she'd not yet received full permission to enter his abode. He was on guard, holding everything in check. He'd transformed from his more emotional Italian side to his guarded English gentleman. He waited in silence for a word from her. Vicky, in turn, stood in the midst of this silence, not really knowing what to say.

"Why are you here, Vicky?" Frank finally broke the silence.

"I think you know," Vicky said finally looking him in the eye. "I know what I said earlier about keeping this whole thing on the straight and narrow. I know I've been insecure and afraid, afraid of things ending badly, but I promise I won't be anymore. I won't hold any ties to you. I won't expect anything from you. When it's time I'll walk away. I promise."

"What are you saying?"

"I'm saying that I need to be close to you." The realization of what she was proposing struck her with a harsh suddenness. She wanted to take it back.

"I don't know what I'm saying," she said, ashamed, casting her eyes downward. "If you want me to go I will."

"Don't go," Frank said and all guardedness completely dropped at that moment. He took her in his arms and kissed her, this time without restraint. At last this was the kiss that would not end until it had been completely spent. He led her silently by the hand into his bedroom.

In a moment Vicky was seated at the foot of Frank's bed where he'd asked her to wait. Wait for what, she wondered? And then she realized her sweet Francis was setting the mood as he searched through his cassette tapes muttering to himself about finding just the right selection of music. "Ah yes, Romantic Piano Classics by the various masters," he said as he put the cassette into the tape deck by his bed and the sound of Schumann's music filled the room.

"Don't go anywhere," Frank said, playfully slapping her thigh and kissing her quickly on the mouth before he scurried out of the room. Vicky watched, as nervous as a virgin, while Frank hurried in and out of the bedroom with candles he collected from around the apartment. He arrayed them on his dresser and night stand lighting each one, turning off lamps and flipping off the overhead light switch as he traveled around the room. When he finished he bade her wait just a moment longer. He turned the light on in his walk in closet then disappeared behind the door, leaving it slightly ajar, just enough to shed a shaft of light into the darkened room.

He returned moments later in a short black robe with ornate gold designs curling up and around like the tail of a fire breathing dragon.

"What in tarnation have you got on?" Vicky said letting go a laugh.

"Why? Don't you think it's sexy? It's a gift from my grandmother. She brought it back from her trip to China a few years ago. She said all men have to have a fancy robe like this when they visit the opium dens."

"Good. No wardrobe is complete without an opium smoking robe. Your grandma, huh?"

"She was never quite right when she returned from her trip to Asia. My father suspected she had a minor stroke while abroad. Personally, I think she may have visited some of those opium dens," Frank said in his droll way that Vicky loved and always caused her to laugh.

"But since I've never been to China and I've never visited an opium den I've been saving it for some sort of special occasion." Frank lay down on the bed next to where Vicky sat. He took her hand and kissed it. "You're trembling," he said examining her hand.

Vicky reclined next to Frank and put her arm around him she realized he too was trembling.

"Francis, I'm nervous."

"I know. So am I."

"I know. Since I've been with you it seems like I got my innocence back. I feel like this is my first time again, only scarier, because tonight I'm sober."

"Good. I want you to remember this night."

"I'll never forget this night."

They lay there on their sides one facing the other, taking in every detail of each other's facial features and the way the flickering candle light danced in one another's eyes. Frank took her hand once again and placed it on his bare chest just above his heart.

"Hear that?" he said and Vicky felt the vibration strongly pulsate through her fingertips. "You're the cause of that incessant pounding and don't you forget it. You're the only one who's ever made it beat like that." Her hand roamed up his chest and across the width of his shoulders. By now the loosely tied sash of his silky robe had come undone and she gazed upon him in the beauty of his manly nakedness and her own heart felt as if it would pound out of her chest. The sound of their breathing and a piano piece by Liszt filled the room.

He pulled her to him and they kissed. All the longing, all the pent up feelings no longer held back but expressed in each kiss, each touch, each word of love proclaimed, each new discovery of desire, each sigh and shiver of pleasure. They made love for the first time that night underneath the stars on Frank's ceiling.

Chapter 27
December 1984

Dear Francis,
December 22, 1984

I'll never forget 1984. Well, we almost made it a year. It was January when we first became friends. Remember that night I lost my keys and you found me asleep outside your door step? I hope you'll remember that and laugh and not think about the bad times here lately.

Vicky put her pen down and paused for a moment wondering what more to say. She stared blankly at her slanted narrow cursive hand which scrawled across the page in blotted blue ink, looking more like a man's handwriting than a woman's. She just stared at the page, transfixed as people so often become with mental fatigue and lethargy, her eyes too lazy to refocus. When her eyes did focus again it was on the Christmas tree in the corner. She put it up this year trying to make up for last Christmas when she hadn't decorated. She remembered the previous Christmas with all its good (the fun she had with Allison, starting her new life, and finally finding some peace over her long ago accident) and all its bad (the disappearance of Bobby). The lights on the tree blinked on and off and she wondered why she'd bothered to put it up.

This would have been their first Christmas together, she and Frank. She would have gone out east with him to meet his family; his demanding father whose love he was still futilely trying to earn; his younger brother Tony, named after the patron saint of lost objects and who himself was lost as he frittered away years of college with his drinking and underachievement, and now the family fortune; his eccentric and demented grandmother from Philadelphia old money, the one who brought the opium smoking robe back from China.

None of his mother's family would be there, a fact which he grieved. They all lived in Italy and he'd only seen them twice; once when he was about seven and they went to Europe to visit them, and the last time, at his mother's funeral.

Vicky was going to Connecticut with Frank for the holidays; it was a given, until the day before they were scheduled to leave. She picked up her pen and resumed writing.

I know my decision not to go with you out east was a surprise.

Her pen stopped on the page, thinking how that wasn't exactly true. Frank really didn't seem surprised at all when she told him. He seemed resigned, yes resigned, that's how he came across, a passive acceptance of the inevitable as he sat hunched over on her couch, his elbows on his knees, his hands folded. Frank often hunched and slouched when he was unhappy. He looked at her with his blue Frank Sinatra eyes and she could see the sad resignation there. He said nothing. He only nodded. And did she detect a little relief as well in that sigh of resignation that he exhaled as he pushed on his knees to raise his tired defeated self off the couch?

Did he know what that meant–her not going out east with him for the holidays? Did he know that this was the end for them? Or did he believe what Vicky said–that they just needed some space from one another, some time and distance to think things over.

Or maybe you weren't surprised. Maybe you were relieved. Anyway, it doesn't really matter. The point is when you get this letter I will be gone. I plan to move out tomorrow. Please don't try to look for me.

Why did she write that? She didn't want to say that, it sounded so melodramatic, and besides she really didn't mean it. Part of her hoped he would look for her. She couldn't cross it out though because that would only make it look worse. Let him read into it what he wants.

I know it may seem a little hasty but I want to end it before it gets too complicated.

Writing a letter like this was easier now that she completed a year of college (or nearly). She didn't even have to look up the word 'complicated' to check the spelling. She knew it was right. She had Frank to thank for that. She planned to continue her education, or at least she thought she did. She'd enrolled for the upcoming semester at the University. She must be sure to thank Frank for that. Not only had he encouraged her in her education but he also helped her with the tuition. She would promise to pay him back.

> *I'll always be grateful for all you've done for me. I promise to pay you back for the tuition you helped me with. I will get that degree and have my own restaurant some day, and I will be a better person for getting an education, like you always say, more able to think things through and more able to appreciate truth and beauty. So thank you.*

Vicky thought about what she'd just written. But wasn't that the very thing which was driving them apart. She was the ignorant hick he was trying to make over. Wouldn't he always know that deep down? He had to remake her into the image of a woman he could love and she was more than willing to let him in the beginning. Wasn't it just like that play she read in that elective she took: Introduction to Theater? What was the name of it? Oh, yes, Pygmalion. She was embarrassed when she read it. She was Eliza Doolittle and he was Professor Henry Higgins. He knew her true identity. He shaped her and formed her.

She looked again at what she'd written. *Grateful?* Sure she was grateful, grateful to her old buddy, Francis, whose help she had asked for. But he was no longer her old buddy, he had become her lover and now she resented him for trying to make her over. She had become his project, at times his obsession. If she was going to make it through college it would have to be on her own, without all this prompting and prodding from him.

How could she be grateful on the one hand and resentful on the other? It didn't make sense. She thought and thought and tried to reckon it, but it just didn't make sense. Maybe she would be able to figure it out after she completed the Critical Thinking class she was signed up for next semester. Now she wanted to scratch out all that part about being grateful and write, "You son of a bitch! Who do you think you are? Now I'm obligated to you. Now I owe you money. Aren't you so fucking noble? So magnanimous? That's right. Thanks to you, I know a word like 'magnanimous'. Well, aren't you special? Helping the poor ignorant country girl? Now you can claim her as your little prize, now that you've completely changed her and made her into your perfect little marble statue. But before I can become a work of art, a statue, a perfect fucking sculpture, first you gotta take the heart of me. Statues don't have hearts!" She muttered it to herself, but of course she wouldn't write it. If it's one thing she learned from the high society, it's to keep things civilized. Real honest feelings were not to be dealt with openly. What would Emily Post say? It might offend. Of course, it was acceptable to be snide or sardonic, disdainful or condescending, but always with a smile on your face. One must never ever be just out and out pissed off.

I'm sorry I embarrassed you in front of your friends. I guess I shouldn't have drank so much the night of that party.

She stopped and thought a moment. Was the correct conjugation drank or drunk? Who cares anyway, she thought. If it's wrong it only goes to show that once an ignoramus always an ignoramus. Her mind went back to that night. Or at least what she remembered of that night. Just a week ago, it was the incident that finally sealed their fate.

* * * * * * *

The Christmas party was given by one of the most prestigious and popular young men in Lamasco. He was the son of a third generation family owned and operated Lamasco business. The dashing young host was all the more celebrated for the fact that he had survived the demise of his family's manufacturing firm which, like so many manufacturers, had come upon hard times, leaving his father and uncles with few options but to sell the company to a national firm. The old Lamasco plant was promptly shut down and a new one opened in Mexico where cheaper labor could be found.

The shut down of the plant was a great shock and heartache to the family.

There were many sons and daughters in the same position who left for the bigger cities after family businesses were lost, but he stayed in Lamasco and started up a wholesale medical supply company, which for now, was doing well.

Frank was explaining the history of the host on their way to the party that night. He met him playing golf. They talked about how sad it was to drive through certain sections of town where old manufacturing companies had been and thrived for years, only to see them deserted. They talked about the economic effect it had had on Lamasco.

Vicky thought about how sad it was particularly for the laboring man and woman who had few options. They couldn't just uproot, go to a big city, and find another job. They didn't have an education or anything to fall back on. They'd lost everything, even their reason to hope. She'd seen it with her own father. All they had to fall back on was day to day survival and the periodic escape from it which they found in TV, bars, drinking, gambling, and drugs. The drug business was thriving in the wake of the plant closures.

Frank drove cautiously through an intersection, slick with a thin layer of freshly fallen snow. It had been flurrying off and on all afternoon and just since they got in the car the flakes had become larger and were now beginning to accumulate on the ground. They were approaching the downtown area and passing through a poor rundown section of town. Yet just blocks away was their destination, where the beautiful newly renovated historic homes sat like sentinels overlooking the river. Here in the oldest section of town was the diverse contrast of the classes virtually bumping up against each together.

Everyone who was anyone in Lamasco was at the party. The expensive cars were lined up and down the old brick covered street. They had to park more than a block away and walk across the bumpy surface of bricks, all the more treacherous from the slippery layer of snow. Frank had a hold of her elbow, the way he always did when assisting her, and Vicky protested the way she always did when he helped her, complaining all the while that she was not an invalid.

"I got cold feet," Vicky said as they approached the old Victorian red brick house, beautifully decorated with greenery, wreaths, red velvet bows and white lights.

"What do you expect? You're walking across snow," said Frank.

"Not that kind of cold feet."

"Are you ever going to stop being nervous at these social gatherings? You know you have nothing to worry about."

"I know. I just wish I could mix drinks or pass out hors d'oeuvres or something. Maybe they'll let me help in the kitchen. I'll offer."

"Vicky!" Frank said as if he was scolding a child. "They'll be plenty of people here you know. Tim and Sally are going to be here. You don't have to hang out with the kitchen staff."

They were greeted at the door by the hostess, the young host's new bride, a stylishly attractive though not beautiful Junior Leaguer and import from the suburbs of Chicago that he brought back from college. They did indeed have hired help at the party, and the first one to greet them was an acquaintance of Vicky's, a young black woman who worked at the River Inn.

"Hey LaVonna," Vicky greeted her as she approached them to get their drink order. "I see you're doing a little moonlighting."

"Vicky girl! What are you doing here?"

Vicky motioned to Frank. "LaVonna, this is Francis."

"This is the one I heard so much about?" La Vonna said, giving Vicky a knowing smile and a wink.

"This is the one," Vicky said, then turning to Frank. "Francis, I'd like you to meet LaVonna. We work together at the River Inn."

"Nice to meet you, LaVonna," Frank said in his stiff and formal way.

"Nice to meet you, Francis," she said holding her tray of drinks a little higher and giving Vicky a nod of approval. "What can I get you to drink?"

"I'll have a vodka martini," said Frank.

"I'll have a double Jack Daniels on the rocks. Make it light on the rocks, La Vonna."

"You're drinking tonight?" Frank said to Vicky with a look of surprise.

"No, I'm just going to swish the ice around in the glass like how you do," Vicky said with a smile, thinking she had earned a drink at long last. She had remained sober for months, worked fulltime, took twelve credit hours, made it through finals, and got all A's, a fact of which she was so very proud.

"If you think it will help those cold feet," he whispered sweetly, intertwining his fingers with hers and giving the back of her hand a quick kiss. "Come here I want you to meet some people," he said dragging her off.

The first part of the evening went so well. The bourbon certainly helped her confidence. Conversing freely with the party guests, she was charming and funny. She sensed Frank's pride in her. To this group of people she was something new, different from all the other girls, fresh, filling each room she entered with that charge of energy, peculiar to Vicky alone. They liked her.

Naturally, she didn't remain at Frank's side the entire evening. It was expected that any girl who was anybody would not cling to her date's side at such an event but would mingle. It was the difference between moxie and mousy. She went looking for Sally and found her. She met her circle of friends and kept them all entertained as she and Sally began recounting Camelot stories.

She met up with Tim. He and his circle of friends invited her into the den which was a small room with a door on the other side of the stairs. She remembered Tim telling her it used to be the kitchen back in the 1800's. They closed the door, passed around a joint, and snorted some lines of coke. She thanked them all profusely for letting her party with them. She had some more drinks, drink after drink. She had to take the edge off since the marijuana and cocaine had left her somewhat anxious and paranoid.

The next thing she remembered she was back in the kitchen talking to LaVonna and the rest of the kitchen staff. Frank came looking for her. He seemed angry. That was all she could remember, just a vague memory of his anger. It seemed he was angry that she wasn't out mingling with the guests instead she was hiding back in the kitchen talking to the kitchen staff. That was it; he used the word "hiding". She told him she wasn't hiding and that she could talk to whomever she wanted to talk to.

She remembered nothing else except the vague uneasy feeling she had the next morning when she woke up in her apartment alone. She was all too familiar with that feeling. Like Pinocchio's Jiminy Cricket, that little inner voice always told her she had done something wrong. She consulted Sally before anyone else. She begged her to tell her the truth. Sally told her she had gotten into a fight with Brooks about labor unions. The host had gotten into it to, saying that it was the labor unions that drove his family business under with their ever increasing demands. It was because of the labor unions, the host contended, that American businesses were moving to Mexico. She insulted the host, saying that for a fine private school, college educated man he certainly wasn't very smart in the ways of the world.

Sally downplayed the incident which worried Vicky all the more. Sally never downplayed anything; on the contrary, she hyped most things. Where there was no juice in a story she added it, yet she kept telling Vicky that it was no big deal; that everyone drinks too much at those parties. Still Vicky wondered why rich girls could get drunk and giggle and somehow manage to not make a scene.

> *You know I never meant to hurt anybody. I wish we could've talked about it, but maybe you were right when you said it wouldn't do any good. You've been different toward me ever since then. You say nothing is wrong but we both know that just isn't true. You're too much of a gentleman to step down. You feel obligated. I'll make it easy for you and end it now.*

Vicky reflected a little wistfully on that morning back in September after they first made love. It was just a little over three months ago, yet it seemed an eternity since they awoke naked in one another's arms, making love again with enough of the early morning light creeping through the blinds to reveal any flaws. Flaws weren't noticed that morning; all imperfections were fearlessly revealed and found worthy of acceptance, leaving them completely vulnerable, entirely spent, blissfully themselves as they lay in one another's embrace, catching their breath in the afterglow. She remembered their conversation that morning.

"You said last night you would walk away when it was over," Frank said.

"I meant it," said Vicky.

"It doesn't have to be over."

"Well, not now anyway."

"Not ever."

"What are you saying, Francis?"

"I'm saying I think we can make it."

"Don't say it if you don't mean it, honey."

"I mean it," he laughed as if some shocking revelation had just taken him off guard. "I really mean it! I think we can make it work."

She remembered how they spent the remainder of that morning, laughing and talking as if they had some private joke, all their conversation an offhanded way of planning their future together.

"Would you be willing to get allergy shots for our animals? I understand you can get those now. I can't have a big house out in the country without critters."

"What about kids? How many?"

"How many do you want?"

"How many do you want?"

"As many as I can have. Wonder what they'll be like."

"Some strange breed of human, never before or since seen."

Then they laughed and kissed and made love again. They did a lot of laughing in those days. Vicky smiled so much her cheeks hurt by the end of the day. It seemed so long ago. How could things change so much in just three months?

> *What were we thinking, Francis? Some things in this world just don't change. You plus me will never equal any kind of equation that makes sense. But one thing in this world will never change. I will always love you.*

There were tears in her eyes as she wrote this. She grabbed the handkerchief sitting there on the table with Frank's monogram stitched meticulously in navy blue thread. She wiped her tears and blew her nose and resumed writing.

I know I'll never find anyone like you.

She nearly wrote 'thank you for loving me' then realized how stupid that would sound. Still she meant it. He glimpsed passed her exterior into the deepest part of her soul for a brief period and found it worthy of love. Gratitude was as near as she could come to finding a word to pin on how she felt. There was that word again. Grateful. She looked it up in the dictionary. It came from the Latin, *gratus*, meaning pleasing. But it was such an inadequate word. Gratitude conjured up images of charity cases and feelings of obligation. That's how she felt now but not in the beginning. Now she was grateful to him, indebted to him. It was big of him to take a chance on her, to delude himself into believing for a short period, but of course he had finally come to his senses. Sadness mixed with anger, loss, love, resentment, and self-pity mingled together in her tears.

She put her head down on the table and sobbed. After a while, after she had composed herself she picked up her pen again and wrote through blurred eyes.

I know you'll find someone who's right for you. I wish you happiness.

"No, you don't," she said aloud to herself. "You hope he'll suffer without you."

She looked at what she wrote and thought she certainly had learned how to be civilized, how to hide her true feelings and say just the right thing. Her education was complete.

Love Always, Vicky

That part she meant. Despite everything, she meant it. She read over the letter one more time. She folded the paper and put it in an envelope. Sadly and somewhat ceremoniously she removed the silver chain from around her neck, undid the clasp and took Frank's college ring off. Now there was only the key to her grandma's hope chest on the chain.

"Well, grandma," she said looking at the key. "I hoped." She looked at the hope chest. "I was thinking maybe I could finally open it and look inside once I was properly betrothed, that it would be proper and acceptable to do it then." She thought about opening it just out of sheer curiosity but then thought it would only make her sad to see those things her grandma had intended for a bride.

"I can still hope," she said then wondered what she had to hope in now. She couldn't go back to her old life. She'd tried getting together with her old friends and found herself struggling for something to talk about. She had changed. They knew it and resented her for it. She was stuck between two worlds and she didn't fit into either. She would have to make her own world and some new friends. She thought of the adults she'd met in college, the ones who'd gone back. They were sort of in the same place she was. They would be her new friends. That was it! She would continue her education. She would throw herself into that. She would be disciplined and steadfast. She was training her brain to slow down and take in new information. It was getting easier for her. After all, didn't she enjoy the challenge? She looked at the key to grandma's chest and smiled. "I can still hope."

Vicky put Frank's ring in the envelope with the letter. She re-clasped the silver chain which bore the hope chest key and put it back over head. She would walk out of Camelot tomorrow and when she did she would do it with hope.

Allison

Chapter 28
December 1984

Allison made some hot chocolate, slipped out of her work clothes, into her grey sweats and pink fuzzy slippers, put on The Carpenters' Christmas album, and set about wrapping Christmas presents for the evening. Her thoughts were on her future, her new life, which she planned would begin after the holidays. She had copies of her new resume professionally printed and ready to go. After the New Year she would blanket the metropolitan Midwestern cities with that new resume—Indianapolis, St. Louis, Cincinnati, and of course Chicago, which was top of her list, but it really didn't matter as long as she could leave Lamasco far behind her. After over six months of convalescing from the break-up with Kent she was well enough to finally get up from her metaphorical sickbed and move around. If she didn't do it soon she would develop psychological bedsores.

She sat on the floor spreading out the wrapping paper, folding it around a box until the design of green holly with red berries covered it, then satisfied with the measurement, she began cutting the paper. As she folded and taped she realized she was content for the first time in ages. Perhaps she would bake some cookies tonight, or better yet, perhaps she could invite the Camelot 3300 girls to come over and bake with her. Sally would be able to join her and Barb if she wasn't working, but she hadn't seen much of Vicky lately. She and Frank were getting serious. In fact, she'd heard a rumor from Sally, who'd heard from Tim, who'd heard directly from Frank that he bought her an engagement ring. He was going to propose to her over Christmas. But then a strange thing happened. Frank left town, presumably to visit his family out east for the holidays, but Vicky stayed behind. Maybe things weren't going so well between them after all. She must be sure to ask Sally what was going on.

Allison's mind flitted easily from one thought to the next while her fingers struggled to make a neat fold out of a particularly obstinate and uneven corner of wrapping paper. A loud knock on the door interrupted the rhythm of her activities with a sudden and startling jolt. It only took a second to register that it must be Vicky. She knew each neighbor's distinctive knock by now. Vicky's was three loud very succinct knuckle wrapping bangs. *Looks like I get to find out from Vicky in person about Frank. I hope it's not bad news,* Allison thought as she hopped over a roll of wrapping paper on her way to the door.

"Vicky! I was just thinking about you," Allison said upon opening the door. The look on Vicky's face instantly alerted her that something was wrong.

"My God, you look horrible. Come in." She quickly closed the door behind them and embraced Vicky who broke into sobs. "You and Frank broke up, didn't you?" Vicky sobbed out a muffled cry in the affirmative. "Tell me what happened."

"I can't stay long," Vicky said, backing away from Allison as she tried to compose herself with one gigantic sigh. She blotted her damp face with a handkerchief. "I have to finish packing."

"Packing!? Where are you going?"

"I'm leaving Camelot."

"For good?"

Vicky nodded. "I move out tomorrow."

"Tomorrow! Wait a minute. Wait a minute. Don't you think this is a little hasty? Don't you think you ought to wait until after the holidays?"

"When it's time to move on, it's time to move on. No sense delaying it."

"Sit down and tell me what happened," Allison pleaded.

And so Vicky did.

"I'm surprised you didn't hear from Sally about my little faux pas, as they say, at the Christmas party. She and Tim were there you know," Vicky said after relating the story.

"I haven't seen much of Sally lately. This is such a shock!"

"I have to leave Camelot and I have to leave as soon as possible. Please understand."

"I'll try, but what about Frank? How are you going to break the news to him?"

"I wrote him a letter and stuck it under his door. I know it's the coward's way out, and I reckon I'm a little ashamed 'cause I never was one to take the coward's way out, but I just can't tell him face to face."

"Afraid you'll change your mind if you have to look at him?"

"No, I'm afraid he won't do anything to try to change my mind. He won't fight for me. He'll just accept it like the perfect gentleman he is. And I can't handle that, Allison. I just can't handle it."

"How do you know he won't fight for you? Give him a chance. You can't give up so easily. It's not like you. So you had a disagreement. So what? That's just part of being in a relationship. You can't just go throw in the towel like this. Talk to him about it. You can work it out."

"No, you don't understand. It was over before it even began. I knew it too but still I let myself walk into it like a damn fool. And you know what's weird about it? It was the new Vicky who walked in blindly. It's like something the old Vicky would've done; just jump right in and live for the moment, not worry about the future. But the new Vicky, she's got a head on her shoulders, she thinks and plans. She looks before she leaps. So why did I do it?"

"Because there is no thinking and planning with love," Allison offered the only explanation she could come up.

"You said a mouthful there, girl. I'll tell you why I did it. Because I started to believe. And do you know why I let myself believe? Because he believed. That is he used to believe until he let doubt creep in. See, it didn't happen overnight, Allison, and it's not on account of just one fight. It's been building. I felt it coming for well over a month now. I saw doubt poking at him like a tag or a pin that you get stuck in your clothes somewhere and you just can't find the exact location. He didn't say anything, but I saw it. Everyday he grew a little colder, a little farther away, a little more irritated and impatient with my ways. But being a gentleman he feels obligated. He figures he's gotta make it work. Sure it's noble of him, but the thing is deep down I'm not what he really wants. He feels trapped. He's thinking the only way he can make it work and still hold his head up is to change me into someone I can never be.

"It was great at first, for a time, for a season. Call it a fling, a part time love, a romance, whatever. But for keeps?" Vicky just shook her head. Allison began to understand what she was saying. If anyone was being noble, it was Vicky.

"The fact is I ain't ever gonna be... excuse me," Vicky said catching herself, stopping herself, and then proceeding to reiterate in a slow, succinct manner in which she carefully enunciated every word. "The fact is I will never be what he wants or needs. We both know there's no future for us but he won't end it so I have to. I have to save face for both of us.

"I hate what love does. It makes you believe the impossible. Ah hell, I said enough on the topic," Vicky concluded with a dismissive wave of her hand, a gesture that Allison observed time and again when Vicky was ready to move on to another subject.

"Your mind's made up, isn't it?" Allison said and Vicky nodded.

"But I couldn't leave without saying goodbye to you. You've been a real friend to me. Like a sister. You're the only one I really trust here at Camelot."

Allison was moved by Vicky's words and touched by the realization that here was the only real friend she'd known since she moved back to Lamasco. Her eyes welled up with tears and a familiar melancholia settled upon her. It was like the feeling she had when her parents divorced. It was the death of a dream; the breaking up of a family.

All of Camelot was in on the making over of Vicky and it had bonded them in some strange way. What a true Cinderella story it would have been if things had worked out for Vicky and Frank. But the two lovers weren't the only ones who believed. Allison believed. They'd all been seduced into believing. But, of course it wasn't meant to be, just like her parents ever loving one another was never meant to be. And so dreams died and fairy tales weren't real, and again, it was time to grow up.

"I feel so old," Allison said.

"What's that?" Vicky asked, seeming only mildly curious as to the cryptic meaning of Allison's statement.

"Nothing," Allison said snapping herself out of her fairy tale world and back into reality where people survive heartbreak and go on with forced smiles on their faces, replying 'fine' when asked the question 'how are you?' But that was never who she was around Vicky. She was always authentic with her.

"God, I'm going to miss you," Allison said then throwing her arms around Vicky, the two women wept. But like always with Vicky, tears somehow metamorphosed into laughter when they each simultaneously broke to blow their noses at the same time, and Vicky made a comment about not getting snot in one another's hair despite rumors that it made a good conditioner.

"That's right! I forgot you're not the handkerchief type. You're the sleeve type," Allison said and they laughed.

"Well, can I at least help you pack?" Allison asked.

"I really don't have that much more to pack. But I do need to get my tree down and my Christmas stuff put away. You could help with that."

"Sure. It may be the only time in my life I get to take a tree down before Christmas. Only you, Vicky, Only you!"

"It was about this time last year that I helped you put your tree up," Vicky said with a dreamy, far away look in her eyes, as if she was remembering twenty years back and not just one.

"I remember. We drank White Russians and listened to the Carpenters' Christmas."

"Wanna do it again. I can make the White Russians."

"I'll get my Carpenters' Christmas album."

Allison had three White Russians, which she requested very white, heavy on the cream, virtually albino. Still the heavy cream hadn't wiped out the effects of the alcohol entirely; and at the first sensation of lightheadedness and limp limbs, Allison put a stop to the drinking, informing Vicky that she would be of no use to her if she continued. Vicky drank Black Russians, one right after another, until finally she was just pouring straight vodka into a glass and downing it. Other than a slight slur of speech she seemed unaffected by the alcohol. Allison had seen her drink heavily before but never with such urgency, as if she was desperately trying to satiate some unquenchable thirst. She thought about saying something to her but decided against it. After all, Allison reasoned, Vicky's heart was broken. Didn't she have the right to get stone cold drunk if she wanted?

After they got the decorations down, Allison decided to stay and help Vicky finish packing. At last she understood how Vicky could move from one home to another (as had been her pattern) so quickly. Allison watched in horror as she indiscriminately turned drawers upside down and scraped every item out of cabinets into boxes without wrapping things or going through them first. She felt compelled to help her organize so she introduced her to the three pile method–the give away pile, the throw away pile, and the keep pile. She soon realized, however, why this concept of moving was so radically new for Vicky.

She got teary eyed over nearly every memoir (as Vicky called them) that Allison attempted to sort through. It was like going through a trash heap as Allison rifled through old worn out socks with holes, disposable lighters long run out of fluid, expired coupons, ancient to-do lists, empty matchbooks with unknown phone numbers written in them, and seemingly endless stacks of junk mail. Each worthless item had a story and she simply couldn't part with her memoirs. Allison realized just how drunk Vicky was somewhere between the slurred words, uttered in mawkishly tremulous tones, and the hillbilly vernacular which she automatically reverted back to. Finally Allison gave up. The three pile method would never work for Vicky. It's just who she was, Allison figured, as she resigned herself to helping Vicky with her method of haphazardly piling whatever she could into unmarked boxes.

Their parting that evening was bittersweet. Allison left Vicky at the door waving and calling out a slurred and weepy farewell over and over again until she turned the corner and made her way back up the stairs to her apartment. She wondered how many so called memoirs from Camelot Vicky would drag into her new life and if she would take them out of drawers in future drunken states and weep over them. Allison paused at the top of the stairs and thought of Vicky with all her peculiarities–her tee shirts proclaiming the names of every event she'd ever attended, every place she'd ever been, every icon she'd ever believed in; some of these shirts over sized and some far too tight; her blue jean shorts with the legs cut off unevenly; her beaded Indian moccasins or cowboy boots and the way you could always hear her coming down the hall with those distinct heavy footsteps; her twangy, nasaly, scratchy voice singing some popular song and always making whatever it was sound country; and her dangling silver jewelry that clinked with every movement. Allison smiled, already beginning to miss her. They vowed to keep in touch but Allison knew it would never be the same.

Vicky left Camelot the same way she came, with her biker buddies in loud and noisy droves hustling in and out with boxes, piling them as haphazardly as Vicky had packed them onto her pick up truck. And then she was gone. For once Vicky's timing was right though. She left just before Christmas so Camelot didn't have a chance to feel the vacuity which her absence left behind until after the New Year. The residents settled into post holiday normalcy that first week of 1985 with a deep pall falling over building 3300, as if someone had just died. They moved slower, more quietly and spoke in hushed tones, as if out of respect for the dead. There was something else too. They were all waiting in anxious anticipation for Frank's return.

Frank returned to Camelot the same way he left, quietly without notice or fanfare. No one could say for sure just when he arrived back except that they knew he was back because his car returned to the same parking space on the side of the building where he always parked. It was as if he sneaked back in. Maybe he knew, Allison thought. She listened carefully for signs of life. After all this was her self imposed assignment; to gather information and report back to Sally. But there was more to it than that.

The thought that Allison kept pushing away since Vicky left was becoming more persistent. Frank was free now and so was she. She told herself it was wrong to think that. Vicky was her friend. It was against her code of ethics to move in on another man before the corpse was entirely cold, particularly a friend's ex. There was an unspoken statute of limitation among honorable women, but for just how long was never clear. How long did he need?

This was the thought which she tried to keep captive in the recesses of her mind. But it continually broke free from its chains like a frightful monster, barging its way into her consciousness. She would scold it and whip it and take it back to its dungeon, but she could never tame it nor could she keep it constrained for long.

"We're just friends. We're just friends," she told herself that day she finally couldn't take it anymore and knocked on his door. She knew he was home because of the usual signs of life; his music, the trace of a light escaping from the crack under his door, the sound of water running. She had seen and heard these signs of life for weeks, but she hadn't seen Frank. He seemed to know just when to slip in and out of the apartment without being seen. He even managed to elude Sally. It was obvious he didn't want to be seen. Too bad for him, Allison thought, because the excuse she needed to knock upon his door had finally presented itself.

She held on tightly to the stack of old albums, bracing them under her chin, trying not to think about the fact that the cardboard corners were cutting into her forearms leaving indentation marks in her skin. She was relieved she only had to walk across the hall with this heavy, cumbersome cargo. She told herself to be careful lest she drop or damage any of the valuable musical memorabilia. She commanded her arm muscles to keep a firm and secure grasp on the precious loot; for this stack which she bore was her long sought after treasure, her redemption, her second chance.

Realizing there was no way to be free of the burdensome load long enough to knock, Allison maneuvered slightly to the side and bumped her hip three times against Frank's door. She would try her foot or perhaps her elbow next if he didn't hear her. She thought she detected the sound of him moving ever so slowly. She heard him cough, or clear his throat. It seemed that it was the cough of someone disinterested, like the coughs one hears in audiences when the performance has gone on too long. She tried her foot this time, kicking the door with the side of her padded running shoe, hard enough to get his attention but not so hard to cause damage to either door or foot. He called out an irritated "just a moment" and it seemed his movements slowed down even more, signaling her that he was in no great hurry to see who was on the other side of that door.

Allison rearranged the stack in her arms, getting a better grip on them and bracing them once again under her chin. Frank finally opened the door. There he stood before her so different looking that she quickly had to conceal her shock. His face was gaunt and his clothes hung on him. His skin had an ashen tone and dark etchings encircled his eyes. Those eyes seemed duller, more grey than the deep blue she remembered. He appeared to be clean and his hair was groomed though he had about a two days growth of beard.

"Happy New Year," Allison chirped wondering why she'd said such an idiotically cheerful thing to a man in the throes of depression.

"Hello Allison, how are you?" Frank replied in a bland voice, forcing a sort of half smile.

If she didn't know any better she would have thought he was sick and she couldn't help blurting out, "I'm fine, but how are you. You don't look so good."

"Thank you for your candor," he said in the same bland tone.

"I, uh, have something for you," she said presenting the stack of albums. Frank looked at the stack and said nothing. "They're heavy. May I come in?"

"Oh, of course, I apologize. Here let me take those," he said snapping out of his trance-like state and going automatically into gentleman mode as he carefully lifted the stack from Allison's arms.

"Those are for you," she said.

"You're giving these to me?" Frank said, baffled as he began to flip through the stack. "Where did you get them?"

"At a yard sale. They belonged to this lady's father who passed away. He was a big classical music buff. I think she said he taught music or something. Anyway, I thought of you when I saw them. She sold me the entire collection for three dollars."

"You're kidding? You got these for me?"

"It was only three dollars," Allison said, though the truth was she would have paid much more, seeing in this musty smelling old stack a priceless opportunity to edge her way into Frank's life. "I realize you probably have some of them already, but I..."

"Look at this," he said flipping through the records. "Dvorak's New World Symphony, Respighi's Pines of Rome..." A spark of life returned to his eyes and for a moment he looked like himself again. "Ah, here's Gershwin–Rhapsody in Blue and An American in Paris. You're a big Gershwin fan. You should have this," he said holding the album out and raising his eyes to look at her. There they were those eyes of his again with some of their former color and luster temporarily restored; the same eyes which looked straight at Allison this very moment, seemingly seeing her for the first time since she'd arrived at his door. He remembered she liked Gershwin. He actually remembered, Allison thought. She was moved by his glance and it took her by surprise.

"No, I couldn't really," Allison stammered in reply to his offer to take the album.

"Why? Do you have it already?"

"No, but..."

"No buts about it. Go on take it. I already have it."

"That's right. I remember you played it for me once."

"I did?" Frank said.

Allison remembered with what might have seemed to others to be a nostalgic smile; the smile of the old, wise and sad. It was only a year and a half ago when he played Gershwin for her yet so much had happened in that span of time it felt like she was an old woman remembering decades back.

"Don't you remember? It was right after I moved in. Right after we met. You played American in Paris out your window one morning when I was walking to my car. I think it was my first day of work. I'll never forget that." It was true, Allison had never forgotten it, nor would she. It was the single most romantic thing anyone had ever done for her.

"I did that?"

"Yes, you did that."

"That was nice of me." The wry smile, which just moments ago she thought she'd never see again, returned to his face.

"Yes, it was. It's good to see you smile."

"Here, take it," he said handing her the album.

"Thank you," Allison said accepting it. Frank continued to flip through the stack.

"Oh, I love this one, Schubert's Unfinished Symphony. Look at this; it's still got the plastic on it. It looks like it's never been played."

"I noticed that about a lot of them. They're in good shape, aren't they?"

He set the stack down on his dining room table and removed one of the records from its cover. "Unbelievable," he said examining the record under the light. "Not a scratch on it. Some of these are real collector's items. I can't believe you only paid three dollars for the whole stack."

"Well, you know what they say? One man's junk is another man's treasure."

"How can I ever thank you?" he said in earnest.

"I'll think of something," Allison said. They stood there smiling at one another and for a moment they connected, the same way they did just those few times when they first met. It was a short lived moment however; for it seemed that as soon as Frank realized what he was doing, he drew back. The color, light, and life left his face again, evaporating as quickly as it had emerged.

"Well, thank you. It was nice of you to think of me. I owe you one," Frank said forcing the saddest smile she had ever seen, so sad in fact it looked like his face muscles had to have ached to hold it in place.

"You don't owe me anything. I was glad to do it."

Allison didn't know what to do at that point but she felt she had to do or say something; something to make it better for him. For a moment she thought it would be better just to leave, but then how could she? He looked so desolate. Was there nothing more irresistible to a woman than a vulnerable man? Not a weak man, but a strong man, who for whatever reason, lets his defenses slip for just a moment. That was what Frank had done. She had no reason to leave so soon. Why should she? So she could go back across the hall, close the door, and retreat into the solitude that inevitably followed.

"Speaking of music, I notice you've been playing a lot of Bach lately," Allison said, grasping for something to keep the conversation going.

"You mean the disco queen of the Midwest knows Bach when she hears him?"

"You know Frank, you're a terrible snob. You know that, don't you? Yes, as a matter of fact I do know Bach when I hear him. I took Music Appreciation in college." An awkward pause followed.

"I'm sorry. I didn't mean to be a jerk. So tell me do you like Bach?"

"He's okay. But, I mean I could learn to like him. So why do you like him?" Allison said, attempting to delay her departure as long as possible..

"Baroque music and Bach in particular is the thing to listen to when you need structure and order in your life."

"You don't say," Allison said.

Frank responded to this glib remark with one single abrupt nod of his head which ended the conversation. More awkward silence came between them in which Frank stood with his arms crossed staring at the floor. Allison didn't know what to do so she stared down at the floor too. This was the first time she'd been to Frank's when she didn't notice the grooves of a freshly vacuumed carpet.

"Well, thank you very much for the albums. I appreciate your thoughtfulness," he said all at once sounding like a standard thank you note which one might send to an individual one barely knows. So Allison had the choice. She could pick up on his cue to depart and leave him all alone in his self pity or she could get honest.

"So tell me, Frank, truthfully, how are you doing? And don't you dare say 'fine' because we both know that's not true."

"Really?" he said disdainfully.

"There's too much evidence to the contrary. You've been listening to Bach, you need order and structure, you haven't vacuumed, you haven't shaved, and no offense but the Don Johnson look just isn't you. And…"

"And what?"

"You're slouching. I've observed you do that when you're not a hundred percent. It's obvious you're depressed." Frank gave a nonchalant shrug of his left shoulder. "Don't you shrug at me!"

"Excuse me, did I shrug?"

"You most certainly did."

"And what exactly is the problem with shrugging?"

"It's a defensive gesture intended to dismiss what was just said."

"Still the authority on pop psychology I see."

"Don't go getting snide and uppity and east coast with me. That's just another defense mechanism. And don't dismiss me. You're depressed. Okay!? Just admit it. It's perfectly natural after a break up. I know you don't want to talk about it and I don't want to make you uncomfortable, but I can't just stand here and pretend that nothing's happened. I miss her too, you know." Allison noticed a slight crack in the armor at the inevitable mention of Vicky. His smug superior smile evaporated and the sad pitiful face returned He raised his eyes to her and Allison could see the pain behind those deep blue pools. He spoke in a voice that conveyed desperate pleading.

"Please tell me, have you heard from her?"

"Not since the night before she left."

"Do you know where she's staying?"

"She planned on staying with some friends until she found a place of her own. I have no idea who the friends are or where they live."

"I tried to find her you know," said Frank. "I went to the River Inn looking for her. She doesn't work there anymore."

"She quit her job?" Allison said in surprise.

"No. She was fired."

"What? Are you sure?"

"Yes, I'm afraid so. I wasn't about to give up until I got an answer from somebody. One of the waiters finally leveled with me. He said she missed work several days and when she finally came in she was so drunk she could hardly stand up. A friend of mine who regularly frequents the place verified the story. He's not one to gossip so I feel certain it must be true."

"Oh, no!" Allison felt as if every organ in her body suddenly drooped, dragging her spirits right along with them into a sinking quagmire of futility and helplessness.

"What can we do?" Allison said wondering why she always felt responsible for Vicky as if she were a sister or a family member who kept blowing it, the perennial black sheep, someone whom she ought to give up on but hadn't quite yet.

"I've asked around but no one knows where she is," Frank said. "I have no idea where to find her. Unless she makes contact with me... or you, I guess there's nothing we can do."

"Except let go," Allison said as much for her own benefit as for his.

"I don't know how," Frank said and it was the most honest moment Allison ever had with Frank. Perhaps it was the most honest moment he had ever had with anyone. He seemed to be pleading with those eyes of his for some kind of help.

"May I sit down?" Allison asked.

"Yes, of course. I apologize for my lack of decorum."

"Don't apologize, Frank," Allison said, and as they made their way to the living room she noticed he'd been sleeping on the couch. His sheets, blankets, and pillows lay there giving the room a disarrayed look so totally uncharacteristic of Frank. Allison wondered if perhaps it was too soon for him to sleep in the same bed he shared with Vicky not so long ago.

For a moment she thought about her father who moved to the couch when he and his mother began to have problems. A man sleeping on the couch was always a sign of a love gone wrong. It made her feel that old familiar sadness again.

Frank quickly rolled up the bedding, tossed the pillow behind the couch and apologized for the mess. Allison sat in one of the wing back chairs. Frank propped up and patted down the couch cushions, then finally satisfied with their neatness he dropped into the midst of the comfortable furnishing with a heavy sigh.

"Excuse me, you were saying?" Frank said furrowing his brows into such a weary expression it seemed he was too exhausted to even try and remember where their conversation last left off.

"That you have to let go, Frank."

With great effort Frank moved to the edge of the seat, propped his elbows on his knees, put his head in his hands and said, "How could I be so stupid? How could I honestly believe that it would ever work between us? We're just too different I guess. Talk about your doomed love affairs. I...I just thought in the beginning that it really didn't matter... the way she is I mean. I thought once people got to know her like I did, once they got past that back woods hillbilly front she puts up, that they would see her for what she truly is, that they would see her the way I saw her."

"Did it matter to you that much that they didn't?"

"Yes," Frank said looking her directly in the eye. "I hate to admit it, but yes. What kind of hypocrite am I? I told her it didn't matter. I thought it didn't matter."

"You were lying to yourself, Frank, because you wanted it to work so badly."

"I can't stop thinking about her or worrying about her. God, I hope she's all right."

"Me too," Allison said. "Let me just ask you one question. If you did find her would you try and work it out. Could you ever accept that she is the way she is and just resign yourself to what others think about her?"

"If she could accept it and not have such a chip on her shoulders then maybe. I don't know. You know she started working on that degree. She's determined to get this education and it seems like since she started college some of the rough edges have smoothed out. Most of my friends liked her."

"Most, but not all?"

"No, not all. And unfortunately Vicky's so insecure about her background it didn't take much to set her off; a look, an off hand remark, a bit of a cold shoulder from someone and she'd take it to heart and fly off the handle. You know how Vicky is. It's bad enough when she's sober but when she's had something to drink it's even worse. Did you hear about the Christmas party?" Frank said looking up briefly then burying his head in his hands once again.

"Yes, unfortunately I heard about it."

"She embarrassed the hell out of me. It's like she's looking for a fight, looking to stir things up if they get a little dull. She does it to herself, you know. Nobody can shoot themselves in the foot quite like she can. If she could just stop looking for trouble where there isn't any. If she could just…be content, be more secure…"

"Be more like how you want her to be?" Allison interrupted. "She is who she is, Frank, and we just have to accept it. You can't change her."

"Is that what I've been trying to do? Change her?"

"I don't know. Maybe. I know I just finally had to accept that Kent is the way he is and that we want different things out of life. It's hard."

"By the way, how are you doing?" Frank asked, mustering up a sympathetic smile.

"Better."

"I'm sorry. I've been so absorbed with myself I forgot you just went through the same thing not too long ago. It must have been especially hard for you. You two were together for… how long?"

"Eight years. Since we were sophomores in high school."

"And here I am feeling sorry for myself. Vicky and I weren't even together a year."

"I don't know, in some ways I think I may have had it a little easier than you. Kent and I were away from each other through so much of our relationship that we'd really grown apart. I fell out of love with him a long time ago. It was like kicking an old habit, like smoking. It was tough but now I'd never go back. Whereas you and Vicky…you were still so much in love." Allison looked at Frank. His eyes were diverted from her, but she could tell from the slight reddening of his nose and the way the corners of his downward turned mouth quivered ever so slightly that he was about to cry.

"You really did love her, didn't you?" Frank held his hand up making a halting gesture as if imploring her to stop talking about it. It had become too intense, too personal and Allison could tell by the sudden tension in his body that it was taking all of his strength to restrain himself from breaking down and sobbing. "It's okay, Frank let it go."

Frank took his handkerchief from his pocket, did a quick blot of his eyes, blew his nose, and blinked hard several times then with one deliberate purposeful gesture, he put his handkerchief back in his pocket, sat up straight and pulled himself together. He looked at Allison with glazed eyes that seemed like a dam holding back a deluge as he forced a pathetic smile. "I'm okay," he said with feigned reassurance.

"You don't have to break down and ball in front of me or anything, but it is important to cry about it. Not now necessarily, but at some point in time when you're alone. Breaking up with Kent taught me the importance of grieving. You gotta grieve. It's the only way you ever move on. Before Kent I didn't do sad. I didn't watch sad movies and I didn't listen to sad songs."

"Why not?" Frank asked to her surprise.

"Because I hate feeling sad. I guess I just had enough of it growing up what with being the fat little girl in school and my parents fighting all the time. I know, I know, poor me! We all had tragic childhoods to some degree or another. But anyway at some point I just decided that I wouldn't dwell on things that bring me down anymore. I decided I'd be an optimist and think only positive thoughts, which is good except that when you suffer a loss you have to let yourself feel all those miserable feelings. I read a book on the subject.

"See, you have all these poisonous toxins that build up in your body from stress and loss. Those toxins are released through tears. You have to get them out of your body or they'll turn into cancer. I mean I know you're a guy and everything and it's not exactly real macho but you've got to get rid of those toxins. You'll feel so much better once you do.

"Now if you're not accustomed to crying, which was my problem because I was so used to suppressing it, then you have to set the scene. So what you need to do is put on the saddest music you have and just wallow in it. Ball your eyes out. Feel the pain then move on."

"How do you know when it's time to move on?"

"That's a good question. The book I read never dealt with that. I guess it's different for everyone. But the important thing is that when it's time to move on, you move on. And don't look back. No listening to the radio because they're too many love songs. Get out of your apartment as soon as possible and whatever you do, don't drink alone."

"I rarely listen to the radio except for NPR."

"Figures."

"And I don't drink alone unless you count a glass of wine with dinner."

"No, that's fine, unless of course you polish off the whole bottle."

"So I should be fine then."

"Except for the fact that you never leave your apartment."

"I leave my apartment."

"To go to work, that's about it. That doesn't count and you know it."

"But I can't get out of my apartment until I've wallowed and gotten rid of all my toxins."

"Right, right. So you got any sad music you can start wallowing in."

"Yep, I saw one in that stack you got me. Barber's Adagio for Strings."

"Is it sad?"

"It'll rip your heart out."

"In that case I better go. I don't do sad anymore."

"Wait a minute, wait a minute! I thought you could do sad since you and your former fiancé broke up."

"Ah, but I've moved on. I've let go."

"You sure about that?"

One look at Frank's face and Allison felt certain she had. "Yes, I'm sure."

"Well, I guess I better get to wallowing then," Frank said as he slowly rose to his feet.

"Time for me to go," Allison said also rising to her feet. "Make sure you go through that stack and get that sad album out."

"I will and don't forget your Gershwin," Frank said. Together they walked toward the door and Frank stopped at the dining room table to flip through the stack of albums. "Just to prove how sincere I am about flushing these toxins out of my system," he said, his fingers moving rapidly through the stack as the muffled sound of cardboard slapping against cardboard accompanied his quick movements. "Here it is," Frank said holding the album he'd been speaking of up for Allison to see.

The cover showed a faded color photo of a conductor from the waist up; older, stout, dignified, in white tie and tails with baton raised and eyes closed; an intent expression of dramatic angst on his face and sweat glistening on his forehead as he led the orchestra who faded into the background of the picture. Some difficult to pronounce Slavic names adorned the cover along with the photo.

"I'm putting this on as soon as you leave," Frank said.

"You'll say anything to get rid of me. That's okay, I can take a hint," Allison said standing once again at his door.

"Thank you, Allison. Sincerely, thank you for everything. I'll get through this."

"I know you will. It just hurts like hell."

"Yes, it does," he said looking down, the color and light completely gone from his face.

"I care about you, you know. You were my first friend when I moved to Camelot," Allison said. "When you're ready to move on and get out of this apartment, I'll be there for you." Frank nodded with a slight bewildered smile as if he really didn't know how to take that comment. That was good. She would leave him with that thought.

Chapter 29
Spring 1985

It was time for Frank to move on. That's what Allison decided anyway, and what better way to move on than on his feet. He skipped down the stairs that Saturday morning in spring and this was an altogether new thing, a sign that he was coming back to life. The thoroughly depressed don't skip down stairs, Allison thought. The thoroughly depressed have a hard time with stairs, both going up and coming down. They hang onto banisters, she thought, and are either overly deliberate in their every little movement or, if they're the more self-destructive type, they're not careful at all and trip going up or miscalculate and fall coming down. But only those not burdened by troubling thoughts are free enough to skip down the stairs. He wasn't slouching anymore either. Of course, one can't slouch and skip at the same time. The two simply don't go together. His feet had become lighter and more agile, more able to take him places he'd never been. Ah yes, Allison thought, what better way to move on than on his feet.

She would ask him and she would ask him today. It was time. She would watch his reaction carefully and listen with more than just her ears to his answer. If he said no then she would be the one to move on. She would accept the job offer from Eli Lilly in Indianapolis. It was, after all, too good to pass up. That's what she used to think. But if he said yes she would leave it all behind, decline the job offer, call off the job search entirely, give up the idea of moving, give up everything, all her hopes and plans for a more urbane and cosmopolitan life, and settle in Lamasco. Ah, but it wouldn't be settling this time, like how it was with Kent. It would be like coming home, truly, for the first time. She would change her mindset and she would change it gladly. She would become a big fish in a small pond and that would be more than all right if she could be in the same pond with Frank.

Lamasco seemed different now because it's where Frank lived. Lamasco is where his burgeoning business flourished and was beginning to get noticed. Lamasco is where he planned to stay. The budding trees and the old brick houses on all the old familiar streets that she passed every day on her way to work had been somehow transformed, enchanted, wrought with strange beauty and mystery because these were the same houses, trees, and streets that he passed. The same streetlights that lit her way home at night were the very same ones that guided his destination. And Camelot…Camelot had become a magical realm where everyday she might get a glimpse of the reclusive prince.

So when she happened to spy him skipping down the stairs of their apartment building that Saturday morning she knew it was time. Her future rested upon his answer.

"Frank, Frank," she called out, skipping down the stairs after him. He turned around, greeted her, and smiled. This was an excellent sign. It was a natural smile, a sincere smile. His shoulders didn't hunch in dread at the sound of her voice, he didn't look at his watch or pretend he was in a terrible hurry, he didn't cross his arms the way he so often did when he didn't want to be bothered. His body posture was open. She almost thought she could greet him with a hug but then decided that might be pushing it.

"Remember all those albums I got you a few months back?" Allison said, feeling herself automatically slip into that coy flirtatious mode. Of course he remembered. She received a thank you note from him written on engraved stationary with his name on the top of the ivory note card. It was all very formal until the last line which read, "Thanks for making me smile again. I owe you one."

"Of course I remember. I play them all the time. I hope they haven't been keeping you up nights."

"Not at all, not at all. I notice you're not playing Bach anymore."

"That's right. I'm back to my old favorites–the Romantic composers."

"That's promising. Well, uh, remember how you said you owe me one for selflessly getting you all those wonderful albums which you yourself said were collectors items."

"You mean that stack you paid three bucks for at a garage sale?"

"The very one."

"Uh, oh! I knew I should've never said anything," Frank said shaking his head with a mock look of exasperation. At that moment Allison was struck by his attractiveness; the deeply etched dimples in his cheeks, the fine angular jaw, the throat which can only belong to a man with its prominent Adam's apple, and of course his eyes which gleamed with his own special brand of humor.

"So what do you need?" Frank asked in mocking playful annoyance.

"A dance partner."

"Hmm," he said tapping his index finger to his lips in a quizzical sort of manner.

"I signed up for ballroom dancing and I need a partner. It's on Tuesday nights starting week after next, which I happen to know is a good night for you."

"Oh, you do, do you?"

"Yeah, Monday night is Monday night football and Wednesdays are racquetball. You work late on Tuesday, Thursday, and Friday but the way I figure it won't kill you to knock off one night. By the way, I'm glad to see you getting out of that apartment and playing racquetball again."

"How do you know all this about me?"

"I'm your neighbor. I live right across the hall in case you hadn't noticed. I got eyes and ears."

"You're getting to be like Sally. You're the one who needs to get out of your apartment more, not me"

"Precisely, that's why I thought I'd take up ballroom dancing. So are you in or are you out?"

"What makes you think I can dance?"

"Well, you're musical. I hear you in there banging on that piano. You have to have some sense of rhythm. Doesn't that come with the territory?"

"Not necessarily."

"Not to worry, even those with two left feet excel in the Arthur Murray School of Dance; or so I'm told."

"I don't know, Allison. I need to think about it," he said with a chuckle of merriment in his voice and a definite spark in his eye. This was all very promising. He just needed a little pushing.

"Oh, c'mon, Frank, this is the perfect pastime for you."

"Oh, yeah? How do you figure?

"Because you're the old fuddy duddy type. And I say that with the highest regard and admiration." All the while Frank was chuckling and Allison delighted in his amusement. "See the average '80's man is far too cool to even consider such a wholesome activity."

"So what I hear you saying is I'm uncool."

"Not at all. You were just born forty years too late. You're before cool. You're beyond cool actually. You're…" She searched her mind for the right adjective but all she could think of was 'sexy' and 'wonderful' and words she wouldn't dare say to him yet. "You're timeless," she said her mind stumbling upon the perfect word to describe Frank's appeal.

"Well, thank you, what a relief. I was afraid there for a moment you were going to tell me I'm the cat's pajamas or some such thing."

"I'm serious, Frank, you're a real gentleman, like Carey Grant or Gregory Peck. You're dashing, debonair, perfect for ballroom dancing."

"Buttering me up for the kill, I see." He exhaled a sigh of resignation and Allison knew at that moment she had won. "All right, I'll do it."

Allison wanted to jump up in the air, do a rah-rah cheer, and cartwheel down the hall. She wanted to throw her arms around him and give him a big kiss. She didn't however. She restrained herself and said rather coolly, "Thank you, Frank. That's all I needed. Have a lovely day," she turned quickly around and ran back upstairs.

"I'll be seeing you, Allison," he said in his old fashioned way, but she didn't dare turn around and let him see how she was gushing for him.

Allison and Frank glided so beautifully, so effortlessly to the sound of Glenn Miller's *String of Pearls* that Allison almost forgot they were at the American Legion dancing on an old squeaky wooden dance floor in a smoke filled room with circa 1950's décor. Even the waitresses with their staunchly sprayed, piled high hairdos and the old crony of a bartender with his toupee who actually said "What'll it be?" seemed frozen in time from some bygone era. The band consisted of a five piece combo made up of WWII veterans. They called themselves the Buccaneers, which was inspired by a love of the adventuring spirit that the five musicians shared. Frank loved to make cracks about Errol Flynn, and swashbuckling, and needing Geritol to carry off a pillage or plunder job and Allison would laugh at the obvious irony of the band's name; for here they were in their antiquated black tuxedos with American flag pins in their lapels, their graying thinning hair, their wrinkled freckled hands that still played those instruments so skillfully, and their serene smiles which bespoke a placid wisdom unique only to the aging. Allison enjoyed the music, dancing, and laughing so much that she almost forgot she and Frank were the only ones under sixty in the place.

They'd become quite good, the two of them together. They'd learned the basic waltz, the foxtrot, the rumba, the cha-cha, even the jitterbug. The American Legion was the only place you could go to dance to Big Band era music. It was their private little joke, the fact that they came here on Saturday nights. They laughed about it as much as they looked forward to it.

"Oh, good, here comes Peggy," Allison said as the song ended and everyone applauded. Peggy was the vocalist for the Buccaneers. She was married to Jim the clarinet player. Jim loved to tell the story of how they met in Vegas shortly after the war. Peggy was a young showgirl of twenty-three with plenty of promise, and when Jim caught her solo song and dance act he fell for her right then and there. One got the impression that Peggy was one of those people who still saw herself as twenty-three and somehow tuned out all the evidence to the contrary each time she looked in a mirror. Was it vanity or absence of vanity, Allison often wondered, and would she be just like Peggy when she got older? But despite the bleach white blond hair scooped up in back, the tanned leathery skin which had seen far too much exposure to the sun, the false eyelashes, and full figure frame poured into a powder blue evening gown, Peggy still had the voice of a twenty-three year old. Her voice rang out melodic, pure, and smooth when she sang the more sentimental pieces; but she could just as well belt out a more bluesy number, raw and drenched with youthful emotion without missing a beat of her ever moving shoulders.

"And now please welcome my lovely bride, Peggy," Jim said stepping up to the microphone. Peggy thanked the applauding audience in a manner so modest she almost seemed to be blushing.

The lights went down low and Peggy said in a smooth, sexy, honey coated voice, "We're going to slow down the pace here a little bit so grab hold of your sweetheart and squeeze tighter." The band began playing and Peggy began crooning some long forgotten sentimental love song.

Frank had been making wise cracks most of the evening while he and Allison laughed and bantered with one another. Their focus had mostly been on their dance steps with Frank resorting to his annoying habit of counting–1-2-3, 1-2-3–as well as warning Allison before he did any tricky dance moves– "All right, I'm going to spin you around now," he'd say and Allison would laugh and remind him that she could anticipate his moves and follow his lead without him having to warn her every time.

"All right, Al, I'm going to move you across the floor. Long strides back. That's it!"

"You're doing it again, Frank," Allison said.

"Well, I don't want to step on your toes."

"You know what your problem is? You're too afraid of making a mistake."

"One-Two-Three. One-Two-Three."

"And stop counting, for Pete's sake. Just relax."

"Relax and shut up!" Frank said, teasingly reproving himself.

"Well…yeah." Allison said.

"Message received," said Frank with a smile.

An older couple sidled up to the two of them, a short cheerful looking lady in a pearl necklace with penciled on eyebrows and her bespectacled husband who tried to disguise his baldness with a bad comb-over. "Excuse me honey, I couldn't help overhearing." Allison got a whiff of freshly done salon hair that had been over sprayed. It made her think of her mother and all ladies from that generation who got their hair done every week.

"We've been married almost forty years and he still gives instructions while we're dancing. He'll never change, so it's no use trying," the short, cheerful, older lady said.

"Thanks for the tip," said Allison.

"It's so nice to see young people here," the lady said touching her arm and her charm bracelet jangled as she did so.

"It's so nice to be here," said Allison politely.

"Where else in town can you go to hear this kind of music and dance?" said Frank.

"There used to be lots of places," said the bespectacled man with a look of sad nostalgia. "Lots of wonderful orchestras. It's a different world now."

"Remember the Trocadero?" his wife said and they gazed at each other dreamily.

"How could I forget the Troc? It's where I proposed to you."

"Oh, that's so sweet," said Allison.

"You have a wonderful thing together that the two of you can always share," said the lady, her bracelet clinking as her hand patted Allison's arm. Allison's mind went over the words the lady had just spoken in an attempt to decipher their meaning.

"What's that?" Allison asked.

"Dancing," the lady said.

"That's right," said her husband. "Whatever problems you have in your marriage, you can work them out on the dance floor."

"Well, thank you very much sir. We'll certainly remember that," said Frank. Then turning to Allison he said out of the corner of his mouth so only she could hear, "To the side," he instructed and together they waltzed away from the older couple.

"Enjoy your evening," said the short lady as her husband whisked her away in the opposite direction with a knowing smile.

"Should we have told them we aren't married?" asked Allison as soon as they were out of ear shot.

"Why? They would have been at our elbow all evening extolling the virtues of married life, you know, trying to get us together. I sometimes think older people believe it's their responsibility to get young people married off," said Frank.

"Now Frank, they were sweet," said Allison.

"I know. I wasn't trying to be unkind; it's just that I didn't come here to talk to them all evening."

"Why did you come here Frank?"

"To be with you. To dance with you," said Frank.

"To whisper verbal dance instructions in my ear all evening long."

"That's right," said Frank with a smile. Just then the song ended and everyone applauded. Another song began and the melody captured Allison's attention. It was familiar, but it wasn't until Peggy began crooning in her honey smooth voice that Allison recognized it.

"At last my love has come along

*My lonely days are over
And life is like a song..."*

"I love this song," said Allison.

"And no one can sing it quite like Peggy," said Frank facetiously.

Allison was only half conscious until the song was halfway through that she was singing along in a low voice just barely above the audible range.

"My heart was wrapped in clover the night I looked at you."

Embarrassed, Allison looked up at Frank to see his reaction. He smiled an awkward smile. She realized this was the longest she and Frank had gone all evening without saying a word to one other. She wondered if it was due to nervousness that they talked so much while dancing.

"It's okay, keep singing. I like it," Frank said. Allison continued and it seemed that Frank was tightening his embrace around her. She drew in closer to him until her chin was on his shoulder and her nose was against his neck.

"Now brace yourself," he said suddenly, resuming his instructor stance.

"Uh oh, here we go again! You're not going to dip me, are you? I hate when you do that, Frank."

"No, I'm going to kiss you."

Frank kissed her smack on the lips. It didn't last but a few seconds and it was far too quick and unexpected to do much of anything for Allison except cause her to lose her footing temporarily. She pulled back and looked into his eyes for a brief moment. She could see that he was falling in love with her and that the kiss was a test of sorts. She wasn't really sure up until this point if his feelings for her were mutual or if he was just a friend. She thought she caught glimpses of some hidden fire at times, but she was never sure and she didn't know how to broach the subject so she just kept avoiding it, hoping upon hope that somehow he would initiate it. He had.

Now it was her turn. She kissed him this time, only it wasn't quick and unexpected. It was long, purposeful, ardent, filled with promise and declarations of love yet unspoken. This time Allison felt it. "I'm sorry," she said after it was over, a part of her fearing she may have pushed too far.

"Why do you always apologize when you kiss me? If you recall this isn't the first time you've kissed me. Remember the cookout a couple years ago?"

"That's right. What was that? Sally was clowning around and pronounced us man and wife or something."

"Yep. And you kissed me."

"And Kent walked up right afterwards. I always wondered whether he saw us or not. I guess I don't have to worry about that now."

"No. you don't have to worry about that now," Frank said and they kissed again. *He has moved on,* Allison thought in her bliss. *But then maybe it's too soon. It's what I've hoped for but maybe there hasn't been enough time for him. It's June, let's see, only six months since Vicky left. It's been over a year for me, but what about Frank? Is he really ready so soon? It doesn't matter. It doesn't matter. It was meant to be this way right from the start. Oh, my God, what bliss, what joy! I'm so happy I could just die.* Allison cast all doubt aside at that moment and forgot everything, including the fact that she was in a room surrounded by people. She and Frank kissed and danced and gazed into one another's eyes and kissed and danced some more.

Peggy ended her song and everyone applauded, shaking her and Frank out of their private reverie.

"You see what this old music does for people," Peggy said and Allison realized she was talking about them. Loud applause erupted, along with a few hoots, hollers, and whistles. These older couples seemed to be enjoying the amorous attentions of the two nearly as much as they did.

"Uh oh! Busted!" Frank said and they both blushed and laughed with embarrassment.

"This next song is for you two young love birds out there," Peggy said. She sang "Hello Young Lovers" from *The King and I*.

Unfortunately Frank had bucket seats in his car so Allison wasn't able to snuggle close to him, but they did hold hands and kiss at stop lights.

"What exactly happened tonight?" Allison asked.

"What do you mean?"

"On the dance floor. Between us."

"I don't know but whatever it was I like it," said Frank.

"I haven't made out in public since high school," said Allison. "Oddly enough it was also at a dance. I remember it was in the gym and some song by Bread was playing, *Baby-I'm-A-Want-You,* I think it was."

"And you were slow dancing?"

"No, I was on the bleachers actually. Kent wasn't much of a dancer. But it's funny how you remember things. It felt the same as it did tonight."

"Except the onlookers were a little older this time around," said Frank and they laughed. "Oh, well, they probably got a much bigger thrill out of it. Actually I don't think I've ever made out in public. This is a first for me."

"Well, of course, Frank. You're far too distinguished to succumb to such a vulgar and public display. So what made you do it?"

"It was Peggy's voice. It cast some kind of spell over me."

"Seriously, what's happening between us?"

Without a word Frank pulled into the darkened parking lot of a strip mall, stopped the car, and turned off the engine.

"What's this, we're parking? I haven't done this since high school either," said Allison.

"We're going to talk," said Frank turning toward her.

"Really?" said Allison, surprised by this unexpected candor.

"Sure. I can be a sensitive 80's kind of guy when the situation calls for it. I know that women need to talk about things, to dialogue, to…oh, what's the new buzz word you women use?" He snapped his fingers in an attempt to jar his brain into remembering.

"Process?" said Allison.

"Process, yes that's it."

"You women!?"

"What's that?"

"You referred to my gender as 'you women'."

"Well, what should I say? You chicks? I don't think that would go over very well."

"*You men* need to try processing things for a change."

"We do. We just don't do it out loud. But for your sake, I'll try."

"How big of you to condescend to my weak womanly level."

"Why do we always bicker, Allison?"

"We're not bickering, we're processing."

"Okay, okay. Enough processing this subject. Let's move on to the next item on the agenda. You start," Frank said.

"The agenda?" Allison said half teasingly, but also half seriously for she got the impression that Frank was viewing this whole thing sort of like a board meeting. Each person was to report and hopefully some kind of consensus would be reached. "Okay, so where exactly do I start?" asked Allison, somewhat discombobulated.

"You compared this whole thing between us tonight to the time back in high school with Kent on the bleachers when you made out to Bread. You said, and I quote, 'it felt the same as it did tonight.' What exactly did you mean by that?" asked Frank.

"Okay, here goes," said Allison with a sigh. "I meant I was falling in love for the first time back there in high school and I haven't felt that way since. Until tonight with you on the dance floor. I was suddenly this foolish seventeen year old again and I didn't care who knew how I felt. And now I'm just a little afraid that I've said too much because maybe you don't feel the same way and it was all just Peggy's voice and the music and the dim lights, and what I saw in your eyes was nothing really, just my own imagination, just my own wishful thinking."

"Take off your seat belt." Frank was unfastening his seat belt as he spoke.

"What?"

"I know we've got a gear shift in between us to maneuver around, but if we're going to talk seriously about this then you've just got to be in my arms." At last she understood his meaning and in one gigantic flurry of awkward movements, the two had scooted next to one another until they were embracing. The discomfort of having only half their backsides seated and the other half suspended somewhere in mid-air, not to mention the problem of the obtrusive gear shift which seemed to be lodged against Frank's tailbone, seemed only a trifle for a pair of lovers who simply had to be close to one another. Frank kissed her.

"Look in my eyes again," he said and Allison did. "What you see there is not your imagination. You want to know something? I was prepared to be completely cavalier about this whole thing tonight because I was afraid you wouldn't feel the same."

"And what is it you feel, Frank. Is it real or are you simply on the rebound from Vicky? Are you just latching onto me in a desperate attempt to forget her? See, I manipulated this whole thing, the ballroom dance classes I mean, just to get close to you."

"I know," he said with a smile. "And I went along willingly."

"I'm afraid I pushed it. I'm afraid it's too soon."

"You're just afraid Allison. And so am I. We don't know what the future holds. I know it's sudden, but don't you see, we've got a lot of lost time to make up for. This is the way it should have been right from the start. I loved you the first time I saw you but what could I do? You were engaged to another man. If I had any idea you didn't love him anymore I would've been at your door night and day, but I had no way of knowing that. I had to forget you, to force you out of my mind. Then Vicky came along..."

"But you did love her. You said so yourself."

"Well, sure I did, but that was different."

"How so?"

"I knew deep down it had no real chance of working out though I tried to convince myself differently. But this–this could work."

"Do you still love her?"

"I don't know," Frank said seeming confused and frustrated. "I suppose if I saw her again I would still have some feelings. What about you and Kent? I could ask the same thing about you two."

"I already told you. I fell out of love with him a long time ago."

"Then there's no problem the way I see it."

"You really think it could work?" Allison said, thinking it all too good to be true.

"I don't see why not. I mean look at the way we bicker. If you're going to spend the rest of your life with someone you've got to be able to bicker with them."

"We don't bicker, we process."

"Process. Exactly."

"And we dance together," Allison said.

"There you go," said Frank. "Resolved."

"Resolved," Allison agreed. "Shall we shake on it?" They shook hands then kissed.

"Can we move back into our seats now?" Allison asked.

"I'm not sure I can," said Frank. "I think the gear shift may have done permanent nerve damage," he said lifting his legs back around with a groan as he awkwardly scooted back into the driver's seat.

It wasn't until they pulled into the parking lot of Camelot that Allison realized what Frank had actually said… 'If you're going to spend the rest of your life with someone you have to be able to bicker with them.' *The rest of your life,* she thought. *The rest of my life. The rest of our lives.*

The two lovers were silent, their arms around each other as they walked slowly, dreamily into building 3300. Allison realized that she was comfortable with the silence. Whenever there was silence between her and Kent it was because there was nothing to share. But this was different. This was a silence that didn't need words because there was so much to share and no hurry to share it. They would have time. They had the rest of their lives.

They entered the apartment building and passed by the first two doors. The door on their left, Tim's apartment, was dark and quiet since it was Saturday night and still too early for him to be in. To their right was Vicky's old apartment, vacant, still and lifeless. It had been occupied for a short time since Vicky moved out less than six month ago by a pharmaceutical rep; one of those modern American professionals, busy with work, traveling his territory, always on the go, and seldom at home. He moved out very suddenly after just a couple of months. That particular corner of the building seemed to be cursed or haunted and Allison wondered what ghosts might've drove out the previous tenant. Allison and Frank simultaneously picked up their pace as they passed by and looked straight ahead, just as if this were some uneven spot on the ground that one stumbles over every day until the self is finally trained to step over it; the unconscious mind always prepared for its coming while the feet and the will automatically take over.

They passed Sally's door and it too was strangely silent, dark, and locked up tight as she was presently away, floating through the Caribbean on yet another singles' cruise. Sally's absence made one stop and wonder if perhaps a light were burnt out in the hallway. The corner by the stairs seemed so dim, owing to the absence of light from her living room which typically flooded the hall through her almost always ajar door.

"Hey Sally, wake up," said Frank pausing to bang on her door. "You're missing out on some good gossip here."

"That's right. Sally's out of town," said Allison with a chuckle. "No wonder this place is so quiet."

They kissed right there by the stairs in front of Sally's door.

"That's something I never thought I'd do," said Allison after the kiss.

"It's been a night for firsts," said Frank and together, arms wrapped around each other, they resumed their walk upstairs.

They arrived in the small space of hallway between their two doors with its dim light overhead and gazed down the darkened hall to Barb's apartment. No sign of life there either.

"It's so quiet here tonight," said Allison in a whisper. "We're the only ones in the building."

"Why are we whispering?" said Frank in a whisper.

"I don't know," said Allison, still whispering. "I suppose we could yell if we wanted to. Why don't we?"

"What's that?"

"Make some noise. Like this…**wahoo!**" Allison hollered in her best cheerleader form. "C'mon Frank, give it a try. It's very therapeutic. Oh, c'mon, don't be a stick in the mud. Give us your best rebel yell."

"All right, here goes." Frank smacked his lips together, stretched out his arms to give his knuckles a good crack, and took a deep breath as if this was an exercise that required the utmost concentration. With a look of great intensity he let out an enormous rebel yell. "**Yeehaw!**" he shouted and together they giggled as if they were doing something terribly naughty.

"That was strangely satisfying," said Frank resuming a whisper.

"I don't know," said Allison looking around. "I'm just afraid someone we haven't accounted for is going to poke their head out of a door and start yelling at us.

"You know, it feels so strange, the two of us being together here like this. It's like we're an old married couple and we're back home from an evening out. The sitter's left and the kids are asleep. I'm sorry, was that a presumptuous thing to say?" Frank shook his head with a tender smile that put Allison's insecurities at ease. He drew her again into his arms and kissed her.

"Now what do we do?" Frank said. What to do, indeed. It was as if they didn't dare budge from this spot in the center of the hallway. It was their sanctuary. This small space of floor right here in the hallway between their two apartments seemed suddenly sacred, consecrated, as if they were suspended in time right there on that spot as they clung to one another.

"I think we both turn around and go into our respective apartments. I know I don't want to. I'm afraid once I step out of this spot the spell will be broken. But we have to break it. We have to go back to our own worlds and think about things."

"I'll tell you what; this will be our spot," Frank said. "Right here in the hallway. Let me see what time it is," he said looking at his wrist watch. Allison looked at her watch too. It was two minutes until twelve o'clock.

"It's almost midnight," Allison said.

"I have seven 'till," said Frank and they held their wrists out together, comparing times.

"My watch always runs fast," said Allison.

"Of course, that's because it's attached to your wrist," Frank said. "We'll just say midnight. Close enough. Let's meet back here tomorrow night at midnight."

"Right here?"

"Yes, in this exact spot. Our spot."

"And then what?" asked Allison still puzzled by his suggestion.

"I don't know," said Frank, and then looking her in the eyes he said. "Let's turn around, step into our dwellings, close our doors behind us and think about things as you so aptly put it."

"Then meet back here tomorrow at midnight?" Frank nodded with that tender smile of his. They kissed, turned around, and approached their doors with the sound of keys jangling, knobs turning, and the finality of doors closing behind them.

* * * * * * *

At 12:00 A.M. the following night they opened their doors at the exact same moment and stepped into their hallowed space.

"I thought I would get here first," Allison whispered.

"I knew you'd think that so I arrived five minutes early."

"You're not early; you're right on time," said Allison looking at her watch.

"I beg to differ," said Frank. "I am on the correct time. If you keep living your life five minutes fast you'll soon be into tomorrow and you'll miss out on today."

"Are we processing again?" said Allison. Frank crossed his arms and teasingly smirked. Allison noticed he was wearing his plaid flannel robe and tan leather slippers, and the effect of him standing there with that expression on his face in a robe that should belong to a much older man made her laugh out loud.

"Shhh," Frank said trying to stifle his own laughter.

"That's right. We're not the only ones in the building tonight."

"Correct. No rebel yelling and no cheering," whispered Frank. A moment of silence followed in which they stood in their sacred space simply gazing at one another. It was only a moment and they were in each others' arms, kissing with an urgency that surprised Allison and seemed to surprise Frank as well.

"I feel like cheering and yelling," Allison whispered directly into Frank's ear.

"Me too," said Frank, rocking her back and forth in his arms.

"Now what do we do?" said Allison. Frank let go of her and stepped back. He reached in the pocket of his robe and pulled out a small box. Allison recognized it as a jewelry box. She quickly put her hand to her mouth in an attempt to cover the gasp of surprise which escaped from her lips. Frank opened the box and dropped to one knee. *"He's going to ask me to marry him,"* she knew at once.

"Will you marry me, Allison? I know this is sudden and you don't have to answer right away, but I just had to ask you tonight. Too much time has slipped away from us already. I don't want to waste anymore time because we don't know how much time we have. Anyway, just tell me you'll at least think about it."

Allison stood in stunned silence staring at the diamond ring. How did he get a ring so quickly she wondered? Did he go out and buy it today? Of course it was always possible, but then another thought occurred to her.

"Forgive me, Frank but I just have to ask you this. Did you buy that ring for Vicky?"

Frank rose to his feet and his face blanched. He popped the lid to the box shut and stuck it back in his robe pocket. "Yes, I did," he said hanging his head. "How did you know?"

"I just had a hunch."

"She never wore it, Allison. She never even saw it. I originally bought it with the intention of giving it to her for Christmas. She never knew anything about it. Please believe me."

"I do, but what do you expect me to say, Frank? These things mean something to a woman. I look at that ring and I just can't help thinking I'm your second pick."

"I guess that was a pretty thoughtless thing for me to do, huh? Offer you a ring of engagement intended for another woman. But you've got to believe me, I'm over her. See, I really believe this ring," he said patting his hip pocket where the bulge from the jewelry box could be seen, "was intended for you all along. I just didn't know it at the time." He dropped again to one knee and looked up at her. "Please forgive this stupid fool of a man who would never consider you anything but his first choice."

"I do forgive you, Frank," she said and her eyes blurred with tears. How could she possibly say no? "And I don't need any time to consider your offer. My answer is yes. Yes, Frank, I will marry you." Allison's face felt as if it would split open with glee. She thought this is what a marriage proposal should be like. Never had she experienced this kind of exuberance with Kent. How could she say no?

"I'll return the ring and let you pick out one of your own. We'll do it together," he said still on his knees as he took hold of her hand and kissed it.

"Let me see it again," Allison said. Frank took the ring out of his pocket and popped open the lid. Allison took the box from him and examined the ring. "It's beautiful. I don't see any need to get another one because this is exactly the kind of ring I would want." Allison thought the ring looked as if it fit her style much more so than Vicky's, and wondered if Frank was right when he said perhaps the ring was intended for her all along. Perhaps some cosmic force truly does exist which controls and guides the destiny of us all, she thought. Some force of pure energy that not even the physicists could ever contain or fully understand. Perhaps this was meant to be her ring all along.

"Put it on my finger, Frank," she said handing the box back to him. "I don't want to waste anymore time either. I don't want to wait to wear this ring."

"I'm speechless," was all he said as he put the ring on her finger and Allison noticed tears also brimming in his eyes. He put the ring on her finger, rose to his feet and kissed her.

"Well, I guess I'll have to wait to wear it," Allison said wiggling the ring around on her finger. "It's too big. It'll have to be resized. Here, let me put it back in the box. I don't want it to slip off my hand."

"Let's meet tomorrow for lunch and then swing by the jewelry store where we can have it refitted," Frank said. Allison handed the box to him and he, in turn, handed it back to her. "It's yours now. Don't forget that." he said and together the two lovers kissed there in their sacred space in the middle of the hall as all of time came to a sudden stop.

Chapter 30
December 1985

Mildred Diefendorf lived next door to the Brinkmeyer farm ever since Allison could remember. She sold eggs to their family, the surrounding farms, and in town. She had a little ritual when she came around to sell her eggs. She'd give a perfunctory knock on the back door of the Brinkmeyer's house, wait a second or two, then just turn the door knob (since it was always unlocked anyway) and walk in with her basket draped over her arm. She'd call out "egg lady" and Allison's mother would say, "Mildred is that you?" Of course she knew it was her. And why Mildred didn't just announce herself as "Mildred" instead of "egg lady", Allison never knew. Then after the egg transaction had been made she would sit down to coffee with Allison's mother and fill her in on all the neighborhood gossip.

She was in some ways, Allison thought, the old German version of Sally. Their personalities and styles were different, but the basic spirit was the same. True, Mildred wasn't modern and forward thinking like Sally; nor jovial and boisterous like Sally. Mildred was sullen and chronically irritated and didn't have a fun bone in her body. Still, like Sally, Mildred Diefendorf had a talent for finding out your business, your deepest secrets, your vulnerabilities and embarrassments and dangling them over your head with an invisible string. She was the all knowing neighbor. Like Sally, Mildred had a knack for getting you to a place so close to despising her, only to turn it around and do something kind and endearing. Then when you're all set to forgive and give a second chance, she'd revert back and do something just awful, making you hate her anew. And thus it was when Mildred Diefendorf announced she wanted to give a bridal shower for Allison because, of course, she'd always been like a second daughter to her.

The day of the bridal shower in September of that year, an incongruous hodge-podge of assorted women descended upon the old farm house in one great hen symposium. They were all there, all the important women from Allison's life. Everyone from the backward country cousins with their ten years gone out of style clothes and hair, and Grandma Brinkmeyer whose poorly fitting dentures clinked and clanked around in her mouth and slipped each time she pronounced a word with "th" in it (but at least she wore them that day), to her sorority sisters and new found friends from the Junior League and Museum Guild.

It was here at Mildred's house, amid the white bread egg salad, ham salad, and chicken salad sandwiches with the crusts cut off, and the red Kool Aide, orange juice, and seven up punch concoction, all pretty in Mildred's big silver punchbowl with orange slices floating on top and served up with a silver ladle by Allison's mother and sister Paula; it was here that Mildred let her thoughts be known about the stupidity of having a December wedding. It was too close to Christmas, she said, and you never could count on the weather. What if it snowed? What if there was a blizzard, for crying out loud? Remember the blizzard of 78?

By the end of her long diatribe, Allison's mother was in agreement with Mildred and they both spent the remainder of the shower trying to convince the bride-to-be to bump the wedding up to October, just one month away. Allison tried to explain that there was no way they could have the wedding so soon. Allison's mother, fueled on by Mildred, said by gosh if she'd just agree to have the reception in the church basement and let Uncle Herbert spin records and all of them decorate it real nice instead of having this fancy-schmancy show at the Lamasco Country Club. Didn't she know how hurt Uncle Herbert was that she'd hired some band instead? Who was she trying to impress anyway? And then grandma Brinkmeyer kept saying "eh, what's that?" and then they'd repeat themselves in their loud voices that nobody could miss, not even her Junior League or Museum Guild friends, and grandma Brinkmeyer would say, "Well, I never heard such a thing," and her dentures would slip when she'd say "thing" and up would go the hand trying to conceal the faulty fitting upper plate and discreetly shove them back into place. The more egg salad Grandma Brinkmeyer consumed, the worse the "th" slippage problem became.

It's not that Allison and Frank wanted a December wedding, originally they'd scheduled it for September but three months just wasn't enough time to plan the kind of wedding they wanted. So they backed it off to October, then November, then finally the first week in December. Allison quickly adjusted her thinking and decided she would make the most out of a December wedding. It was, after all, her favorite time of year. And so the wedding would be adorned with all things Christmas; holly and mistletoe, shades of deep burgundy red, forests greens, velvet bows, golden baubles, and snow white satin beset with sparkling crystals. Secretly she hoped it would snow. Not enough to paralyze the Southern Indiana town (which really didn't take much), just enough to coat the streets maybe, just enough to create that childlike stir of excitement and anticipation of Christmas, just enough to make the day a bit more magical.

It did not snow that day, a fact which Mildred Diefendorf and her mother were quick to point out to her and told her she ought to be doggone thankful. Other things didn't go exactly as planned either, but no matter. Allison remembered what the minister told her and Frank the night before at the rehearsal. He said that as long as the bride, the groom, two witnesses, and someone to perform the ceremony are present you will still get married. Everything else can go wrong but that is all you need in God's eyes to have a successful wedding day.

She made a bargain with God that morning after throwing up from a combination of anxiety, red wine and rich food from the night before. After all she was already on her knees. She figured she might as well pray, even if it was in front of a toilet. She chuckled at the thought that many people must utter prayers in this very position, on their knees in front of the toilet. Prayers like, "God, let me live" or "God, let me die" depending on the condition of the sufferer.

"Dear God," she began slowly trying to remember how to pray. She hadn't done so since her high school youth group days. Then it occurred to her that she might be bothering the Almighty. "I'm sorry to bother you because I know you have much bigger things to contend with, what with famines, earthquakes, poverty, wars, and violence, but if I could trouble you just this once, and you know I never do, but just this once… Please get Frank, the Reverend, and let's see… at least two witnesses, though it might be asking for a miracle to get Frank's brother Tony there, and Sally, and, of course, me–get us all to the church on time–and don't let me worry about anything else. Thank you, God. Amen."

And there they all were and she was in the back of church with her father getting ready to walk down the aisle. There was Frank standing at the foot of the sanctuary waiting for her. She remembered one other thing the minister had told her and Frank. He told them to try to remember the day because it goes by in such a blinding blur. So there she stood in the back of church, holding on to her father's arm, taking deep breaths, recording each moment as a freeze frame in her memory.

She wanted to remember everything, the expression on her father's face and what he said to her right before they started down the aisle. "You ready, missy?"

"You can't call me that anymore," she whispered to him. "You'll have to call me missus-y now." Her father actually laughed at her bad joke. He walked her down the aisle in the same manner in which he drove, cautiously and at a maddeningly slow pace, tugging gently at her arm every time she began walking too fast. She thought she saw emotion welling up in his eyes as he kissed her goodbye and presented her to Frank; not quite tears for his proud stubborn Germanic heritage would not allow for that, but something akin to tears. That's when she started crying.

Then came the moment she and Frank stood before one another to exchange vows and rings. She had the same feeling as when they met in that small space of hallway between their two apartments in Camelot. Time was suspended and all her senses heightened. She wept through much of the ceremony until there was nothing left of the wadded up ball of Kleenexes she clutched in a sweaty fist along with the stem of her bouquet. She stuck the damp sinewy fragments of the tissue into the wrists of her long sleeves. Frank handed her his neatly ironed, perfectly folded monogrammed handkerchief out of the pocket of his day coat. Wedding guests must've noticed this thoughtful gesture because a few "ahs" arose from some of the female members of the congregation who were particularly touched. Allison looked at the white linen cloth with the delicate navy threaded monogram, afraid to soil it with her tears, snot and mascara. *I'm messing up his handkerchief and I'm about to mess up his life,* she thought. She attempted to convey her thoughts to Frank with a funny expression. She could tell by the silent chuckle that rippled through him that he got the message.

The minister pronounced them man and wife. They kissed. The congregation applauded. Sally, whom she and Frank had decided upon as the only illogically logical choice for their maid of honor, touched Allison lightly on the arm and handed her the bouquet which she held for her during the exchange of vows and rings. Sally's brightly colored eyes and cheeks shone with tears, but still her thickly coated mascara stayed stiffly in place with ne'er a smudge or streak. They turned and walked arm and arm down the aisle, husband and wife, and Allison now knew what married people meant when they talked about the blinding blur of the wedding day. Time had been graciously suspended for them for just that brief moment and now it was over. It had ended so quickly. Time would start up again and continue to move forward at its ever accelerating rate.

They arrived at the Lamasco Country Club and Sally was waiting for them at the door to whisk Allison off to some discreet corner to hook up her long train and detach the cathedral length veil. Sally then nervously herded all straggling guests into the main reception hall, being certain all the while to keep Frank and Allison out of sight until that moment when she motioned to them in covert whispers to make their grand entrance. Frank's brother announced their arrival via microphone, introducing them as Mr. and Mrs. Francis Hamilton.

The sight of so many loved ones there to greet them with smiles and applause was almost an overload of joy for Allison who didn't exactly know how to cope with such exhilaration. A waiter stood by the door with a smile on his face and a tray filled with glasses of champagne. "Congratulations," he said to her and Frank as he offered them a glass. They toasted each other, locked arms and drank from the glasses. Allison, typically not a big drinker, gulped the sweet bubbly liquid down quickly. She just had to come down from all this euphoria if she was to make it through this reception without becoming miserably tongue tied or paralyzed.

The club was decorated beautifully for Christmas with a tall skinny slightly crooked but thoroughly alive evergreen in the corner of the entrance hall, decorated with all manner of bows and streamers, shiny ornaments, some delicate some gaudy, but all of them working together to create an affect of an old fashioned Christmas. It filled the hallway with the fragrance of pine, triggering in all who lingered there a sweet sad nostalgia of Christmas past. Above every doorway hung mistletoe, and greenery gathered at the ends with red velvet bows draped the door frames. Fresh holly encircling candles served as centerpieces; more holly with its festive red berries encircled glass hurricane lamps at either end of the cake table. Everything so perfect, the tables set with silver for the sit down dinner, linen cloths and napkins folded crown style and sitting upright atop china plates; two glasses at each setting, a large goblet for water and a wine glass. A string quartet played Vivaldi while the guests mulled around during the cocktail hour. Of course no one else but the Buccaneers would do for the dance which would follow dinner.

The expense of such an event was exorbitant. In the beginning Frank and his family insisted on picking up the greater part of the expense. They were encouraged to back off on their offer because this had wounded the pride of Allison's dad, who in turn insisted that he was the father of the bride and, by gosh, he would pay all of it; all the while trying to talk Allison out of all this high class expensive folderol. Allison's mother said it wasn't a question of expense because "that tight fisted old Dutchman" could surely afford it. "Why, he has more money stashed in a sock in the basement than most people will ever see in an entire lifetime," Allison's mother would say. It wasn't a question of the money it was a matter of all this extravagant waste. How could Allison ever make her parents, who had never been to Paris, possibly understand that beauty and refinement is never a waste of money? She could never make them see how important it was to her that her guests not have to sit on metal folding chairs and eat with plastic utensils off of paper plates in the church basement.

Because of hurt pride her father put up half the expense but simply would not nor could not bring himself to pay more than this. So the fact that Frank and family picked up the other half was a source of embarrassment to

Allison's father who seemed so hangdog during the meeting of the parents and the night before at the rehearsal dinner.

Although much to Allison's happy surprise, today proved different. Mr. Brinkmeyer was in high spirits and even joked around some with Frank's father before the ceremony. There all the parents stood together, laughing, and applauding. The meeting of two worlds and nothing like a wedding to bring those two worlds together. What joy, Allison thought.

Allison had one and a half glasses of champagne. She had to abandon the second glass after two or three sips, placing it back on the tray of a waiter who bustled busily by. Combined with all the emotions and the empty stomach, one and a half glasses were all it took to dull her previously heightened senses. Sally helped organize the bridal party together into a receiving line in the back of the room. Then the real blinding blur of the day commenced with a barrage of faces and smiles, handshakes and hugs, congratulations and compliments, words of wisdom and advise, all moving along quickly one person to the next–dear old friends, distant and obscure relatives, veritable strangers having to introduce themselves as the bride and groom grappled for their names.

Allison was glad she'd imbibed in a little champagne because she was just numb enough to not be bothered by her feet, which she was vaguely aware were throbbing and beginning to swell in her high heels.

"How are your feet holding out?" She said out of the corner of her mouth to the bevy of bridesmaids that stood in line to her right.

"Beauty is torture," said Sally, who stood directly to her right.

"Well, I've had enough of this torture," said Allison's big sister Paula. She lifted up the hem of her long burgundy velvet gown to reveal stocking feet, her dyed to match pumps off to the side and slightly askew. She reached into the U shaped neckline of her gown and pulled out a pair of white cotton footies.

"Oh, please tell me you didn't have those stuffed down your dress during the ceremony," said Allison.

"You mean you didn't notice I was particularly buxom today?" said Paula.

"I thought maybe you got a boob job just for the occasion," Sally quipped back

"You're kidding me, right? You're not really going to put those on, are you? Not this time?" said Allison.

"Why not? You are going to have a dance, aren't you? You don't expect me to dance in my stocking feet? I'll ruin my panty hose. I paid enough money for these stupid hose. You made me get the most expensive brand. I'm not about to wear them once and run holes in them."

"Excuse me, darling," said Frank who stood to her left. "You remember Mrs. Jones, don't you?" he said drawing her attention to the regal looking lady before him.

"Why, yes. Hello Mrs. Jones. Thank you so much for coming."

"Lovely wedding, my dear. I wish you every happiness," she said with that restrained smile which only the socially elite of a gone by era can pull off.

"Thank you," Allison said, bowing her head slightly. She found herself just naturally bowing her head to some of these older rich people. Mrs. Jones moved down the line to Sally.

"We got extra footies," Paula called from down the line to Allison as she hopped around on one foot while putting on her sock. "You want some? Oh, come on, Allison, don't be so stuck up."

"Oh, all right, why not? After all it is a Brinkmeyer family tradition," Allison said, the effects of the champagne making her feel more farm girl than social aristocrat. She stepped out of her uncomfortable shoes. Her sister tossed her a pair of white rolled up footies from down the line. It just missed skimming the top of Mrs. Jones newly dressed hair as Allison reached up and caught it. She steadied herself on Frank's shoulder as she put her socks on.

"Hello, Mr. Jones. How good to see you again. Excuse me for a moment," Allison said to Mrs. Jones' husband as she pulled the heel of the footie in place. Seeing that the dignified Mr. Jones had observed what she was doing and not pausing too long to consider social protocol, Allison felt compelled, either by the champagne or the baffled look on Mr. Jones' face, to explain to him what she was doing. "It's a Brinkmeyer tradition. All us women take our shoes off and put on socks at weddings–you know, for the dance." She glanced at Frank who looked a little worried until Mr. Jones showed his approval by laughing heartily and making some comment to Frank about what a delightful and spirited young bride he had.

"Why, thank you, Mr. Jones. How sweet of you to say that. Thank you for coming," she said in an affected manner as she extended her hand, which he took and kissed. Everything was going so wonderfully, so beautifully. That's what Allison was thinking at that moment. She was thinking that she needn't worry again about these aristocrats and how she might fit in. She had won them over. And that's when it happened.

Like any sudden unexpected event, it produced that terrible inevitable surge of adrenaline that Allison would always relive to some degree each time she remembered. There was Vicky standing right there in front of them. Allison thought it strange that every time she recalled this incident the first thing she remembered thinking was how nice Vicky looked; or rather, how nice she would have looked had she not been so obviously drunk. She noticed the nice dress and shoes, the accessories that matched, the purse, the earrings and necklace–stylish and tasteful. Her hair and makeup had probably looked very nice when she started out, before the alcohol gave it that disheveled look of drooping disarray. She hadn't just thrown something on. This outfit had been carefully planned and thought out in advance. But where did she come from and what was she doing here? She certainly wasn't on the guest list.

"Why, Frank and Allison, my dear old friends," she said with an undertone of viciousness in her voice.

"What are you doing here, Vicky?" Frank said. His countenance quickly transformed from joyful to shocked disbelief to the tautness of a restrained outrage. Allison hated seeing him that way. She hated what was happening. She wished she could push a button, somewhere, somehow and make it stop. But she couldn't stop it. She could only brace herself for whatever catastrophe would inevitably follow; like someone right before that moment of impact in a fall or accident. She could tense every muscle; she could cry out for help; she could close her eyes, but she couldn't stop this pending collision with calamity.

"What am I doing here?" Vicky repeated her voice coarse and saturated with the effects of liquor. "Well, Francis darlin', you know I wouldn't miss this happy occasion for the world? Why I'm just as happy for you two as a pig in shit! I couldn't wait in line to see you. I had to hightail it right up here. Right here and now, I did. Of course, I had to push a couple of rich old geezers out of the way to get to y'all but I made it."

Allison was vaguely aware of some sort of commotion occurring just out of her peripheral field of vision immediately before she saw Vicky. She then realized Vicky had in fact cut through the receiving line and probably did push some people out of the way. There was a low murmur of discontent mixed with alarm coming from some of the wedding guests who waited in line just behind Vicky. Allison's head was reeling. What should they do? Should they politely ask her to leave or staunchly and firmly throw her out? But what then if she should become angry and make a scene–an even bigger scene than the one she was already beginning to create? She didn't have an answer and from the look on Frank's face, neither did he.

"You just can't imagine how overjoyed I was to see the engagement announcement in the paper," Vicky continued. "I thought, I can hardly wait, but for some reason I never got an invitation. Imagine that! I know it must've been an oversight or mix up of some kind. I'm sure you'd want me to come. Why, if you didn't want all your friends to come celebrate you wouldn't have made such a big fuss about it and had your name splashed all over the social page like you did. But then Allison couldn't do it any other way. Could you, honey?

"Well, you finally made it into the big league. Finally hooked you a big fish this time, didn't ya Allie ol' girl? Of course, you still need a little work on refining them social graces. I saw you take your shoes off and put them socks on there a minute ago. You can take the girl outta the country but you just can't take the country outta the girl, now can ya? Frank here oughta be able to help you with that. He's an expert at making a silk purse out of a sow's ear. Ain't ya, Frank? He'll teach you everything you need to know about being a lady. You might wanna start by taking them socks off and putting your shoes back on. You just gotta learn how to smile and be charming in spite of your aching feet. If you wanna be a really good rich lady you gotta learn how to hide your feelings. You gotta learn how to be a real phony. But then you're a fast learner, Allison, I'm sure you'll catch on. I never could quite get it, myself, so Frank had to pass me over for a better student. Right Frank? But then again, Frank didn't teach me everything. I taught him a thing or two. Didn't I Francis, honey? Let me give you a few little pointers about what he likes in bed."

"All right that's enough, Vicky," Frank interrupted tersely. "I'm going to tell you this as politely as I can. Please leave. You were not invited. If you will not leave of your own free will I will see to it that you are escorted out," Frank said with the utmost civility and restraint.

"Escorted? Ain't it funny how you can make the worst possible thing sound so proper? Still throwing your weight around, I see. Still trying to get me kicked outta places where I don't belong. Remember when you tried to get me kicked outta Camelot?"

In the meantime, Tim, who was one of the groomsmen, and Sally both stepped out of their places in the receiving line and situated themselves on either side of Vicky. They stood there like sentries, each of them waiting for a signal from either Frank or Allison to take Vicky by the arm and bodily remove her.

"Well, well, if it isn't the old Camelot gang! We got everyone here but Barb. Where is that ugly ol' dyke anyway?"

"C'mon Vicky, let's get some fresh air," said Tim who had taken a hold of Vicky's arm.

"Would you like me to drive you home, honey?" said Sally, her voice surprisingly tender with concern.

"Get your fucking hands off of me," Vicky said wrestling her arms away from their grasps. Then almost as quickly as she lost her composure she regained it again. "Forgive me, I owe you each a quarter," she said in a sickly sweet tone with a forced smile so pathetic as to evoke pity and disgust in equal portions.

"I'll go," she said squaring her shoulders and regaining what little dignity was left. "No need to show me to the door. I believe I can find it myself," she said, overly conscious of enunciating each word just so. Sally and Tim let go of her. She began to move toward the door, her head held high, her steps overly deliberate in some distorted effort to restore her wounded pride.

Allison and Frank grabbed one another's hands and squeezed tight, and Allison began to feel the first slight wave of relief, like one beginning to awaken from a nightmare and realizing all the terror just experienced moments before was over a mere shadow, a vapor and nothing real at all. After all, only a few guests had taken notice of the unpleasant disruption and had already chalked it off as the antics of a party guest who'd had a little too much to drink. You had to expect something like this at such social occasions. There was always someone who couldn't hold their liquor. Frank was making apologies to the people in line behind Vicky. It was all right. They were smoothing it over. All's well that end's well, Allison thought.

"We better not let her drive home like this," Sally said to them.

"Sally's right, you know," Tim said to Allison and Frank. "If she leaves here and drives her car into a ditch, you could be liable."

"Do whatever you have to do," said Frank.

Sally and Tim hurried off toward Vicky who was still making her way toward the foyer in that drunken manner of pseudo dignity. They reached her just before she exited the large dining area.

Allison watched as much as she was able in between guests who continued to greet her. She saw from across the room as Sally and Tim approached Vicky and spoke to her in hushed tones of discretion. She couldn't make out the words but she could tell from their manner and gesture that they were trying to reason with her. It was the voice of reason trying to break through like static on a too distant radio station, a voice which most drunks can't tune into. She watched as Sally and Tim reached out to Vicky with hands intended to help. She watched as Vicky pushed them away. She saw all too clearly what was happening in that awful moment. Sally and Tim's condescension had added another gash to Vicky's already wounded pride. She watched helplessly as the events of the next few moments unfolded before her in slow motion. She found herself back in the bad dream again, afflicted with that common paralysis which so often accompanies nightmares.

Vicky pushed Tim and Sally away. Because of her drunken state it was more like a shooing than a shove, not nearly forcefully enough to actually drive them back, but enough to draw attention. Then came the awful angry and inebriated wail of Vicky's voice crying out loudly over the din of the string quartet and the chit chat of the party guests. Suddenly everyone was aware of the upheaval taking place in this small area of the room.

"Fuck you! You never gave a shit about what happened to me when I was your neighbor, so now you're suddenly concerned!?" Sally approached her with that marked look of concern and said something. Vicky responded by giving Sally a sloppy shove. Then she turned, grabbed an abandoned glass of champagne from a nearby table, pulled a vacant chair recklessly around and stood on top of it. She stuck two fingers in her mouth and let out a shrill whistle.

"Attention everybody!" she yelled out, and to Allison and Frank's horror, she did indeed have everyone's attention even the string quartet who had stopped playing. "I'd like to propose a toast to the bride and groom," she said raising the champagne glass as she swayed to and fro on top of the chair. "To Allison and Frank, my favorite ex-friend and my favorite ex-lover. You're still my favorites, even though you went behind my back and deceived me and ditched me for each another. Even though Allison, you're a bossy bitch, and Frank, you're a lousy lay…"

"All right, that's enough, Vicky." The insult was quickly interrupted by Tim, but not quickly enough. The words still made it out, leaving Allison stunned like a swift unexpected slap across the face. Tim reached up to take Vicky's arm in his grasp. He put his other arm around her waist and practically lifted her off the chair. She was just drunk enough to come down without much effort on Tim's part, but not before she got one final dig in. She downed the champagne and hurled the empty glass across the room. It crashed against the wall with a nerve pinching shatter that went all through Allison in that awful moment. Then another loud crash was heard as Vicky pulled a tablecloth off a nearby table, sending silverware, china plates, and glasses crashing to the ground. Allison strained to see what was going on at the other end of the room but was shielded by well meaning bridal party members and guests who suddenly emerged with looks of concern and offers of false reassurances. As far as she could tell Vicky was being forcibly removed. Another loud din from out in the foyer caused the crowd to jump with alarm as a steady murmur of shocked exclamations rippled through the room. The next few minutes were indeed a blinding blur as Frank attempted to make his way toward the door but was restrained by some of the groomsmen. Frank's brother, Tony, who seemed suddenly sober, ran out to investigate. He returned a short time later at which point Allison was only vaguely aware of her mother, sister, and Mildred Diefendorf hovering about her, shushing her, and patting her hands. Tony carefully closed the great double doors that led out into the foyer behind him in an obvious attempt to shield remaining bridal party members and guests from whatever it was that was going on out there. Suddenly he had a microphone in his hand and he was making an announcement.

"It's all right, everyone. The situation's being taken care of. There's nothing to worry about. It seems that one of the guests just had a little too much to drink. Let's resume our celebration," Tony said with a smile befitting the polished politician who is quite expert at smoothing over a crisis in the public's eye.

The string quartet resumed playing Mozart's *Eine Kleine Nachtmusik* which made Allison feel even more nervous and dizzy than she already did. Her mother, Paula, and Mildred seeing her state of shock and dismay, led her as quickly as possible out of the reception hall and into the ladies room where Allison could have some space to collect herself. Guests, out of polite pity, stepped aside and said nothing, mostly just ignoring her as she was led away from the crowd. Once they got her back to the ladies lounge and seated her in a comfortable chair, Sally who'd returned from the frontline appeared on the scene with a glass of champagne which she tried to coax Allison to drink.

"No, I don't want it," Allison protested as her mother blotted her damp cheeks with a tissue and Paula rubbed her shoulders. "It will just make me emotional and cry even more."

"This is one time I'm insisting you drink, dear," her mother said. So Allison took the glass, held her breath and downed the champagne as she would a vile tasting but necessary medicine. Someone handed her a glass of water, which felt cool, refreshing, and somehow quieting as she swallowed it.

"You get all your crying out, honey, and I'll redo your makeup," Sally said, her bright, wide, almost comical face much closer to Allison's (in true Sally fashion) than what propriety allows. "It's all over and we can laugh about it now."

"I don't know, dear. It may be a little soon for that," said Allison's mother.

"Are you sure it's all right? Are the guests all right? Was anyone hurt?" Allison asked.

The women jumped in with reassurances of, "Everyone's fine. No one was hurt, etc…"

"All right, enough, you've got to tell me what happened out in the hallway. What was that horrible crash we heard? Where is Vicky now? Come on Sally you have to tell me. Please," she begged as she squeezed Sally's hand with an insistence that would not let go until she acquiesced. Sally looked to Allison's mother for permission to speak. She shook her head at Sally in silent disapproval.

"Okay, if you must know," Sally proceeded despite the lack of consent from all of Allison's female relatives. "Vicky knocked over the Christmas tree."

"Oh, my God," said Allison with a sensation of sickness rising from her feet to the top of her head. "I think I'm going to throw up." Mildred said, "shh dear," and patted her hand. Allison's mother stuck a cold rag on the back of her neck and Paula and Sally discussed among themselves which of them should go out and fetch another glass of champagne for the ailing victim.

"I don't want anymore champagne, and Mom get that cold cloth off of me. And Mildred…" Allison pulled her hand away from Mildred. "Please stop that!" She shot Mildred an angry glance. She wanted to slap her as hard as she could with the same hand she'd been patting. For some reason she wanted to take it all out on poor Mildred, as if the whole thing were somehow her fault. For one insane moment Allison wished Mildred had her basket of eggs draped over her wrist so she could grab it and smash it over her head. It was a short lived moment. She caught herself and apologized, first to Mildred then to the other ladies.

"It's all right, it's all right. Perfectly understandable," the chorus of reassurance and ready forgiveness rang out.

"It really is all right," Sally, who had stuck her head out a moment ago to inquire about damage control. "They're cleaning the mess up right now. Most of the guests have no idea what happened out there. The doors to the foyer are closed. When they open them again no one will see a thing."

"Including no Christmas tree," Allison said.

"Don't worry, they can prop what's left of it up in the corner. No one will ever suspect a thing. We'll just keep those doors closed and no one will know what's going on out there. Unless of course there's a fire between now and then and everyone suddenly has to clear out. Oh, well, people will just have to mind all the branches on the floor and be sure to step over them."

"Well, one thing's for sure, nobody's going to forget this wedding any time soon," Paula said. "Believe me, honey, the guests are lapping up so much booze at that open bar they won't remember a thing about this tomorrow."

"Oh, please don't tell me that," said Allison. "That's all I need is the dread fear of somebody else hopping up on a table to make another inappropriate toast."

"Let's hope we have no more ugly scenes. Your father's ready to go home and get his rifle," said Allison's mother. "But you know, honey, something good has actually come out of all this. Your father and Phil Hamilton have become allies. They're standing by the front door smoking cigars and drinking brandy and discussing what they oughta do about this whole thing."

"Dad's drinking brandy?"

"Well, no, he's drinking beer actually. But you should've seen them, puffing on those cigars and discussing whether or not they should call in the National Guard to surround the parking lot. "

"Nothing like a crisis to bring people together," said Sally. "You got your Southern Indiana hoosiers, then all of Frank's family; the Philadelphia blue bloods, the Connecticut suburban set, and some of Frank's Italian relatives to really jazz things up a bit. Everyone's suddenly friends with everyone else. I wager this goes down as the funnest wedding this town has ever seen."

"What about Vicky?" Allison looked at Sally in earnest and the room hung with sudden heaviness.

"Don't worry sweetie, Vicky's been taken care of," said Sally.

"What does that mean?" said Allison.

"The management was able to keep her restrained until the police got here," Sally said reluctantly.

"The police? You mean the police were here?"

"Don't worry, they didn't have their sirens on or anything. You didn't know they were here and neither did anyone else."

Allison buried her head in her hands. She had such fond feelings for Vicky. Vicky was her first real friend after she moved back to Lamasco. She was her true friend. Allison was always the first to defend Vicky when everyone else put her down. But now as she sat there with her head in her hands, taking in the events of the day, the only thing she could feel toward Vicky was hatred. Vicky knew good and well that she and Frank never deceived her. It was Vicky who chose to break up with Frank and leave Camelot. She was the one who left and cut herself off from everyone, and it wasn't until six months later that she and Frank got together. So how could she stand up there and make herself out to be the poor pitiful victim? How could she willfully and contemptuously humiliate them like that? The fact that she was drunk and might regret the whole thing tomorrow was no excuse. But then that was always Vicky's excuse. The more she thought about it the more she burned inside with a sensation like a flame, flickering up from her solar plexus straight through her esophagus and stopping at a deep smoldering knot in her throat, then burning back down again. She hated Vicky.

"Listen honey," her mother said, gently removing Allison's hands from her face then turning her chin toward her so she could look her in the eye. "Forget about what happened out there. Remember what this day is really all about. Remember what happened at the church. You married the man you love. You're married now."

"That's right. Reverend Whitman told us last night not to worry about anything that might go wrong today. He said that all we needed was the bride and groom, two witnesses, and someone to preside and we'd still married, no matter what else went wrong," said Allison.

"Reverend Whitman is right. It's not really about today, sweetheart. It's about what happens after today. I wish somehow your father and I had managed to remember that." Allison's mother gave a quick look around at the other women and they stepped away; all except Paula, whose hand her mother grabbed as she began to walk away, beckoning her back, inviting her in on the conversation.

"Listen up girls," she continued. "Marriage is not one long smooth road. Paula, you've been married a few years. You're learning." Paula nodded.

"Mom, I know that. I'm not sixteen anymore. But what does that have to do with anything?" Allison said.

"Just hear me out. There are plenty of bumps along the way in married life, lots of hardships, and you've got to work them out together. If you don't you'll end up like your Dad and me, and believe me you don't want to go through a divorce if you don't have to. So what I'm trying to say is you start today. You smooth this little bump in the road out together. Work it out together. Go to Frank. Somehow you've got to have a little time alone together to talk about this and get it all worked out before you leave. Don't leave here tonight with this still weighing on you. Work it all out. Then you can leave here today happy."

Allison looked through her tears into her mother's eyes, which also brimmed with tears. She saw all the pain and all the truth there and she loved her mother at that moment, despite all the conflict they'd ever had, she loved her as she'd never loved her before. She embraced her. Soon her sister Paula fell into the embrace also and together the three of them lingered for a time with their arms around each other.

It was all arranged, Frank and Allison would meet back in the coat check room so no one would see them and have a private meeting to talk about what happened. They had to go through the foyer to get to the coat check room, but it was all right, they almost had the mess cleaned up by then. Frank and Allison watched as some of the clean up crew, consisting of the club management and wait staff, as well as a few of the heartier bridal party members, attempted to get the tree back into its stand. Then they all set about trimming what was left of the ornaments and tinsel. They shooed the bride and groom away before they had a chance to offer help. So off Frank and Allison went, hand in hand to the coat check room like two children who'd been reprimanded for being in the way.

For once Allison didn't mind being in a small claustrophobic space. It felt like the only safe place to be right now. They went back toward the corner, back into the small space as far as they could without actually being in the coats. Allison touched the long sleeve of a beautiful brown mink full length coat. She didn't know why exactly. She wasn't one to handle something that belonged to somebody else without their permission. She ran the soft fur against her cheek. It smelled like expensive French perfume and somehow it made all her cares evaporate for a moment.

"Do you want me to get you one like that?" Frank said, shaking Allison out of her reverie.

"What? I don't know. Someday maybe."

"I don't know why I asked that. It was kind of a stupid thing to say at a time like this. Guess I'm just avoiding the real heart of the matter here."

"And I don't know why I'm standing here fondling another woman's coat. Same reason I guess." At that moment they embrace each other fast and hard. "I will not cry again. I will not cry again." Allison's words came out muffled as she spoke them into his chest.

"I'm sorry, Allison. I'm so sorry."

"I don't know why you should be apologizing. It's not your fault." Even as Allison spoke these words she understood full well why he apologized; and if she lingered on that thought too long it might ignite that flame of anger again. It wasn't logical for him to shoulder any of the blame, yet somehow part of the responsibility did fall to him. She understood why he and Vicky became lovers, even encouraged it. The love affair occurred before, while she and Kent were still together. So why was she suddenly jealous?

"Just tell me you don't love her anymore."

"I can't believe you're even asking that. Good God, Allison it's our wedding day! I took vows with you, not her. "

"I know, but sometimes I can't help think you were just on the rebound from her when we got together. It was so soon afterward. It's only been a year since the two of you broke up. Now here you are married. Don't you think that's soon? Are you sure I wasn't just some handy way of getting over her?"

"That's not true," Frank said with that firm set jaw and serious expression that signaled anger.

"Please don't get mad, Frank. We can't fight on the first day of our marriage. I just have to ask you one more question. Promise you won't get mad. I just have to know and then I'll drop the whole thing completely. I'll never bring it up again. I promise."

"Shoot."

"Did you really love her, or were you just using her?" Allison regretted asking it as soon as the words left her mouth. It was a no win question. If he said he really did love her then she would always wonder if something still remained. If he said he was just using her then she could never really respect or trust him. "I'm sorry it was a stupid question. You don't have to answer it. Forget I ever asked it."

"I thought I already answered that question back when we first started. I thought we resolved this one. But just to recap I'll answer it again."

"You don't have to," Allison said.

"Look, I'm not afraid to answer the question. I was infatuated with her. I thought I was in love with her. I realize now it wasn't really love."

"So what about you and Kent?" Frank said. "I could ask the same thing about you. You were with him a lot longer than I was with Vicky. Were you on the rebound from him?"

"You know the answer to that. You know I was over him ages before we actually broke up. I was just too chicken to end it. I'm sorry. Now I'm the one apologizing. There I go, making a mountain out of a mole hill again. This is so asinine. I can't believe we're having this conversation on our wedding day. Are we a couple of idiots or what?" With that one comment, Allison had successfully turned the tide of their dialogue. They now stood there in this small room against the backdrop of all these coats which smelled like the cold outdoors of winter, both of them conscious of their frailties and the frailties of the other. The relief of finally standing so honest before one another with no pretenses left caused them both to drop their tensed up shoulders and exhale a great mutual sigh of amusement which turned into laughter as they stood there and shook their head at themselves and one another.

"Hey, speaking of Kent, he's in there right now. He's waiting for us to come back so he can propose a toast," said Frank.

"Very funny! You are kidding, right?"

"God, I hope so." And together they laughed, embraced and kissed one another.

"I'm sorry," said Frank.

"I'm sorry, too."

"So I guess we've had our first fight," said Frank holding her tight.

"We weren't fighting. We were processing."

"Right. Processing."

Just then Sally stuck her head around the corner. Her face looked comical and alarmed and it startled the couple then made them laugh.

"Are you two about ready?" Sally said. "They've been holding dinner for you. If we don't eat soon we're going to have some really drunk people on our hands."

"Oh, no, we don't need anymore of that," said Frank.

"Shall I tell them you're coming?" asked Sally.

"Well, what do you think?" said Frank turning to Allison. "Are we ready to go out there and brave the crowd?"

"I'm ready…except," said Allison staring down at her feet which she was aware felt a little too snug, warm, and comfortable. There were her white cotton footies peaking out from under her gown. "Where are my shoes? I took them off in the receiving line. Sally, do you know where my shoes are?"

"I have no idea. Don't worry, we'll look for them later. C'mon guys, hurry up!"

"All right then, let's go," Allison said slipping her hand into Frank's. Sally scurried off ahead of them to throw open the double doors which had been closed since the incident occurred.

"Oh, my God," said Allison as they stepped out into the foyer. "It's Charlie Brown's Christmas tree." They both laughed at the sight of the skinny evergreen which now looked even skinnier and seemed to have shrunk in stature. It was much more sparse and bare since most of the ornaments were either damaged or broken. It looked as if it had been decorated haphazardly, by a child perhaps who lost interest halfway through the project. Oddly, however, the tree was no longer crooked in the stand but now stood erect in all its awkward starkness.

Sally, Tim, and Frank's brother Tony stood right at the entrance of the reception hall. "All right, let's try this again," said Tony into the microphone. "Presenting Mr. and Mrs. Frank Hamilton."

All the guests were standing at their chairs ready to be seated for dinner. Everyone applauded vigorously, with all their hearts, as if they were welcoming back refugees or perhaps heroes returning home from a war. What a difference from the first time they entered the room and were presented as man and wife. The battle weary bride and groom looked at one another. "Déjà vu," Allison said and they kissed.

The remainder of the reception was indeed a blinding blur, but happily, one without further incident. Frank whispered dance instructions to Allison during their first dance as husband and wife. "One-two-three, one-two-three. All right Al, long strides back." All the guests were awed by their dancing abilities.

Allison's shoes were never found. It snowed later that evening, just a little, just flurries, just enough to wash away what had been and restore lost faith.

2006

Chapter 31
November 2006
Vicky

The November wind sent brown leaves skidding across grey concrete, scraping as they went. Vicky's ear was close enough to the ground to hear the scraping noise. The sky above was the same light grey color as the concrete below, or at least it had been until just now when Vicky became aware of the light around her growing dimmer. She turned her head slightly, trying to look up at the sky but her neck hurt so she only got as far as the back of the bus stop bench where she lay. She was face to face with Carrie Cameron and Joe Duff from the WIKY Carrie and Joe morning show, whose pictures alongside the radio call letters, were plastered all in red and black on the back of the corner bench. Carrie was smiling big, and a juvenile urge to black out one of her teeth with a marker overtook Vicky as she cackled and muttered, "Then she'd look like me."

She was aware of what was going on today and these clear moments were her worst. "Fool, fuck-up, failure," she muttered aloud to herself. The one good thing about being a drunk was that she had lost all self-consciousness. She could lie on a park bench in the middle of downtown Lamasco with matted hair and dirty smelly old clothes as she talked to herself and not care what other people thought. It was freeing in a way, to have lost her pride. There were moments when she was aware, truly aware of someone's eyes on her. She'd turn to meet the eyes of the passerby but a glance was all she ever got. Just a glance, just long enough to see the disdain, or fear, the discomfort, or pity; but then the stranger on the street would turn quickly and awkwardly away again, lest the gaze be held any longer. The only thing she cared about in those moments was evoking enough pity to get a handout.

The diminishing light made her wonder what time it was. The only way she had of knowing came from the clock on the old courthouse. She forgot to count how many times it chimed on the hour when last it chimed. She felt a raindrop hit her hand, then another hit a wisp of hair on the side of her head very near her ear. It rolled down her face. "Tears from my ears," she said. Then another raindrop, then another; Vicky watched them hit the concrete one after another through the break between the back of the bus stop bench and its seat, until they were falling in rapid succession, dampening the brown leaves on the ground. The wind blew again but this time the leaves were too wet to blow away and instead clung stubbornly to the sidewalk. Vicky shivered. She pulled the soggy sweater she was wearing tighter.

Vicky remembered that cold November day when her grandmother died. She clutched the only thing she had left of her grandmother, the key to her hope chest on the chain around her neck. Thoughts of her grandma still made Vicky cry. Her tears fell sideways across the bridge of her nose and down her temples, mixing with the rain as she lay there on that bus stop bench in the fetal position. Perhaps today was even the anniversary of her grandma's death, she couldn't be for certain, but at any rate it was close. And Vicky wondered, what of all those who had nothing to live for during the upcoming Christmas holidays and nothing to come back to life for in the spring? What of all those countless number? Now she knew how they felt because she was one of them. "Another winter ahead. Lord have mercy on my soul," she said to the unresponsive and still smiling gigantic face of Carrie Cameron.

The bells in the old courthouse began to chime. One-two-three-four-five. Five o'clock. A few people filing out of office buildings at the stroke of five passed by the bench like specters. It was time to sit up and try to beg some money. She had resorted to a cardboard sign lately which read, "Homeless. Please help. God bless you." One of the transients at the center who'd spent a good deal of time in Chicago said you did better if you employed a sense of humor. He had a sign that said, "Why lie? I need a beer." He soon found out that that kind of sense of humor worked better in the big cities than here in Lamasco, where people tended not to appreciate it.

One by one the people emerged from the buildings and passed by her bench. She looked at her cardboard sign under the bench. She wondered if she'd written her message with a permanent marker. She didn't know for sure. If not the letters were likely to run in the rain. Oh, well, it didn't matter anyhow, she thought as she held her sign up and didn't even bother to check if the rain was causing her letters to run.

People walked past her, going out of their way not to look. She had heard it tell somewhere, who knows where, perhaps her grandma, that when people go out of their way to ignore you, they really ain't ignoring you at all. Who cares, she thought, if one, just one poor sucker would only look on her with pity and give her some money.

Some people with umbrellas came and stood around the bus stop bench. She could tell they wanted to sit down. She scooted over but nobody wanted to sit next to her. The bench was wet by now, giving the waiting people even less incentive to sit down. But still they were perturbed, as if somehow her presence there was a reminder of all the things that went wrong in their lives that day. It was so like Lamasco folks to hold her in silent contempt rather than to say anything to her about hogging the bench. It was just their way, and the way of most Midwesterners to seethe inside instead of openly confronting the matter. Oh, well, this was her bench, so screw them! "Screw them all!" she muttered out loud, just loud enough that someone might hear her, but not too loud so they would definitely hear her.

And then it hit her. All at once a realization descended upon her in a moment of clarity stronger than anything she'd felt in a long time, and she saw the foolishness of it all. Why was she doing this? Here she was begging for just enough money to get some booze and maybe a bite of food. It wasn't so much the degradation of it all (although it was that too) as it was the futility. She needed booze to survive as much if not more than she needed a morsel of food. So what if she got enough money to get these things? She'd just have to go back out again tomorrow and do the same. And for what? It didn't matter anymore. It was getting too hard, just too hard to scrounge up enough money to survive from day to day. She didn't have the energy to do it anymore.

"Not another winter. I just can't make it through another winter," she muttered standing up. "Look here," she said nudging a depressed looking woman standing next to the bench. "There's a dry corner right there on the bench. Have a seat. Go ahead. I ain't got cooties." Then placing the cardboard sign over her head to keep the rain off she turned to the little cluster of people standing there at the bus and said, "Don't worry, I'm leaving. I can take a fucking hint! So long Carrie. See you later, Joe," she said to the enormous smiling faces on the back of the bus stop bench. "I've enjoyed our time together. It ain't everyday a gal gets to share a bench with radio personalities. You might even say we slept together. Thanks for the memories. You're a fucking inspiration," she hollered out as she turned the corner and headed down Fifth Street.

Vicky walked; she just kept walking, quickly as she had not walked for a long time. A new surge of energy carrying her forward, taking long quick strides like she used to. This sudden clarity, this epiphany had opened her eyes. It was all so clear. She knew what she had to do. And so she walked on with the cardboard sign still over her head to keep the rain away. She realized she didn't need it anymore. It didn't matter. She tossed the sign on the front steps of the old courthouse. She had to find the perfect place. She would know it when she saw it; a blind corner, an intersection slick with leaves and cold fallen rain. It was almost the perfect time as the twilight hour descended with the ever darkening sky. She'd heard that dusk was the worst time for drivers, with visibility being at its lowest.

"Time to shut down, Grandma. Time to shut down completely." She passed the old Lutheran church, the oldest Protestant church in town. It was the church where Frank and Allison were married. Vicky remembered that day, and the year that preceded it.

M. Grace Bernardin

* * * * * * *

It had been a hard year, that year of 1985. It started off after the break up with Francis, after she left Camelot with her memoirs and memories, and a small modicum of hope that she might make a new start; hopes that she could throw herself into her college classes, get an education, make friends who would be good for her, find a house out in the country to rent and maybe buy one day. She tried, tried to go on, tried to put it all behind her. But it hurt. It hurt too much. So she drank. She alternated between booze and cocaine. She was staying with Eddie so there was an endless supply of drugs. She came into work all strung out on coke one day and snapped at a customer. Then she got caught drinking on the job that same day; something she never would've thought she'd do. She was just trying to come down from the cocaine, trying to take the edge off. She was instantly fired. Less than a week later she was charged with driving under the influence. Her driver's license was revoked. She was placed on house arrest and court ordered to go to AA meetings. Eddie was just too paranoid to allow her to stay at his place any longer; what with probation officers showing up at any given time of day. She left with no job and no place to go, so she moved into a women's half-way house.

It had been a good move at the time. She got her hope back for a time. She got a job and made new friends. She took the bus and walked a lot. She felt healthy. She wrestled with sobriety. She wrestled with those twelve steps, never quite sure where her higher power stood with her or where she stood with her higher power. But she was able to grasp hold of something, something that kept her going and kept her sober one day at a time. She thought about getting baptized. She just thought about it. That was all. She stayed sober that time nearly six months, not her longest stint, one time she made it almost a year.

Then came the day she saw the engagement announcement in the paper. Frank and Allison were to be married in three months. All the hurt and disappointment came back, only this time with a sense of betrayal too. The man she loved and her best friend had taken up with one another. How could they do this to her? Her AA sponsor warned her against such emotional setbacks. She struggled between letting go of the pain and hanging on to the pain. She went back and forth.

Vicky's sponsor told her not to be alone the day of the wedding. She advised her to go to meetings and to be with other people from the program on that day. She could have. Her sponsor called her that day and left a message on her answering machine. Vicky was home at the time but she never picked up. She knew her sponsor would advise her against going anywhere near the church that day. But she just had to. She didn't know why. She knew it wasn't right, that it was just some twisted fragment of bad feeling that would feed her sickness, like someone compelled to pick the scab off a wound. It wasn't right but she couldn't help herself. She just had to see for herself. That's what she told herself; that if she saw them walk out the front door of that church all dressed in their bridal attire then she would know it was real. Then she could cry a little, curse a little, but then she could move on.

She got a pair of binoculars and parked in the bank parking lot across the street. She saw the limos parked out front. She saw the guests go in. She heard the bells chime. She waited. And then she saw them. Allison dressed like a bride, radiant and more beautiful than Vicky ever remembered her. And her Francis in a tuxedo, so handsome it hurt to look at him. They looked happy. They seemed oblivious to the cold December wind that blew at them as they skipped merrily together, arm in arm, down the front steps of the church. So now she'd seen it for herself. So now she could move on.

Only she didn't really want to move on. She wanted to wallow in it. She wanted to make them hurt as badly as she did. She knew it was stinkin' thinkin', as they called it in the program, but she didn't care.

She stopped at the liquor store and bought a bottle of Jack Daniels. She would just have one drink. She would wait until she got home. She would resist the urge to open it and take a swig in the car. After all, she just got her license back, she certainly didn't want to blow it and lose it again. Just one drink after she got home, just enough to take the edge off all these hurtful emotions. It wouldn't count against her sobriety if she just had one. She figured you had to get drunk for it to really count. And she wasn't going to get drunk. A half a glass, that's all, she thought. She figured that's all it would take since it had been so long since she drank. Two or three sips was all it would take. No one would have to know. That's all she'd need to take the edge off, just two or three sips. She would put the bottle somewhere inconvenient to get to so she wouldn't be tempted to drink more. She would put it in the bushes outside. She wouldn't want to go out there in the cold. But then if it got really cold it might freeze. She'd give it away. That was it! Maybe to the older gentleman down the hall. One of her neighbors would take it. If worse came to worse, she'd put it in her grandma's hope chest and bury the key outside.

She went home, poured herself a drink and took out the newspaper clipping of the engagement announcement from a drawer by her bedside table. Her sponsor told her to rip it up, destroy it, get rid of it. She couldn't help it though. She got some perverse pleasure out of taking it out of that drawer and re-reading it, her eyes carefully going over Allison's picture with her perfectly cut and coiffed hair and her strand of pearls hanging down over the front of a simple but elegant top in the shade of something light and pastel. It said the reception was going to be held at the Lamasco Country Club. Just one more glass of bourbon, just one more wouldn't count.

The next thing she knew she was laying out her nicest clothes, clothes she'd worn to a recent wedding. She did her hair and put on makeup. Just one more glass before she left. She was still sober enough to drive.

She woke up in jail the next morning, her memory of the previous day, sparse and fragmented; but her whereabouts and the heavy feeling in her gut told her she'd done something horribly wrong. She didn't want to know. Wait a minute! She did want to know one thing. Had she killed anybody? Did she hit anyone with her car? No, to her relief she hadn't done that. She had been charged with public intoxication and disorderly conduct. The cops told her she'd knocked over a Christmas tree at Lamasco Country Club. She had no memory of it but it sounded like something she'd do. A part of her wished she'd done something worse. Not killed anyone, of course, but something bad enough for them to lock her up and throw away the key. Then maybe she could be saved from herself.

Eddie posted bail and she was released until her court appearance. It was the first of many overnights in jail and trips to the courthouse, the first of many tries at sobriety; soon to be followed by numerous trips to rehab, and countless visits to the hospital for that ailment or this injury. Later (after she burnt the last house she lived in to the ground) would follow an endless blur of crashing with strangers, staying at shelters and eating at soup kitchens.

* * * * * * *

She stood in front of the Lutheran church and remembered. The sign on the church marquis read: *If God seems distant, who moved?*

"Okay, God. So blame it on me. I moved. You didn't exactly do anything to make me wanna stay," Vicky said, the rebuttal coming from some corner of her brain that the alcohol had not yet absorbed. It was a cry from the old Vicky, locked between blaming a God who she hoped might rescue her but never did, and blaming herself for being so weak as to need rescuing.

Perhaps this was the perfect place, in front of a church that had shut her out, a church where she dare not enter because she wasn't invited. It represented every church to her. It certainly was the perfect spot as far as that goes, but the traffic wasn't nearly fast enough on this short city block between two stoplights. Drivers didn't have a chance to get up much speed between the one intersection and the next. No, she would need to go to the highway. That's the perfect place, she mused–nameless, faceless, no personality, nothing but billboards. Carrie and Joe can witness the whole thing as they look on and smile. The highway–how perfect! It's where people abandon dogs they don't want, she thought as she walked faster and faster, heading in the direction of the highway. By the time she reached the entrance ramp she was drenched from the cold rain and was trembling so bad, she had shaken herself numb. She was numb inside and out, as if nature itself had mercifully administered an anesthetic. But strangely she had this strength, this surge of energy to move her tired old legs up that entrance ramp. If only she had this kind of energy when she had the will to live then perhaps she wouldn't be such a fool, a fuck up, and a failure. A car heading up the entrance ramp honked and swerved. Normally, Vicky would have flipped them off, but what was the point?

She made it on to the highway and walked a little ways on the shoulder trying to get up the nerve to do what she had to do. She was too safe, too safe walking along the wide shoulder there. She walked up a way to where the shoulder narrowed. That was good. It was scarier there, too scary. She was surprised there was any part of her left that still wanted to live. She clung near the guard rail. She couldn't bring herself to do it. The guard rail was too much of a security, to have it right there, a safe haven to lean against, even the name, "guard rail" conjured up false feelings of safety from the potential plunge into the abyss. Ah, but if she stood on it then perhaps it wouldn't feel so safe. She couldn't be leaning or sitting. She had to take an active stance. Her legs felt stronger than they had in a long time. She compelled those legs to stand up, strong but shaky. It was a great thought but could she, an old sick drunk, balance herself on top of a guard rail? She used to be a strong coordinated girl. It would be like walking across the sturdy branch of a tree, something she did all the time as a kid before her fear of heights took over. She stepped up on the guard rail, still squatting, trying to get her balance, her arms moving to and fro trying to steady herself, then grasping back hold of the guard rail again. Slowly she stood up, surprised that she could do it, her arms circling backward then forward in an attempt to maintain her balance. Horns honked. Funny, she thought, they notice me now. Strangely, she found she did better with her eyes closed.

In that moment, her life moved quickly before her closed eyes like old family movies. Stuck in the tree with Bobby's hand reaching out to her; on that ladder outside Francis' window with his hands holding onto her. But now there was nobody there to help her down, nobody there to talk her down. She had to jump. It was the only way down.

She was on the roof of her childhood home, nothing but her father waiting below, screaming in rage, ready to beat the hell out of her. She was standing at the edge of the creek that ran through Bobby's property, the place where she learned to swim as a kid. She was getting ready to dive for the first time.

M. Grace Bernardin

"Remember it's shallow. Be sure to dive out. Dive out." She would do a belly flop and it would sting as the water slapped her stomach. Just one small slap to the skin; it's all she'd feel. She could move her legs this time. They weren't paralyzed like before. She could move them. She did, like a swan diving into a lake, crashing into a window in the middle of a dark night.

Chapter 32
November, 2006
Allison

"It sure is a nasty day, isn't it? I guess winter's really on its way, huh?"

No reply, just sullen silence staring straight ahead; a vain attempt at conversation with her fifteen year old son, Alex. It was so infrequent that she ever had him alone, pinned down, restrained so to speak, in such a way that he couldn't walk away, couldn't leave the room. And this was the one time he was not allowed the use of his cell phone or ipod so there was nothing attached to his head to tune out the sound of her voice; not now, not while he was driving. This was the last little bit of control Allison had with Alex, in this his fifteenth year of life, before he got his license but while he still had only a driver's permit, making it necessary for her to be right there with him in the front seat when he drove. This was the closest in proximity that she could get to him. He had to hear what she said during those driving excursions even if he chose not to listen, like now. But still, maybe something she said would soak into his skin like a sponge tossed onto a puddle, maybe something would reach him and come to realization at some later date.

The boy's large awkward hands gripped the steering wheel, hands grown nearly to man size but somehow out of place at the end of those still gangly arms; his adolescent brain having not yet fully coordinated the use of those hands yet. All the same, the hands reminded her of Frank's hands and a pang of sadness stabbed her in the heart.

"Alex, your hands should be at ten o'clock and two o'clock."

"Not anymore," he said with a contemptuous sneer. "Shows how much you know. Your hands have to be at nine and three because of the airbags. If your hands are at ten and two and the air bag deploys, this is what'll happen," he said throwing his hands straight up to illustrate.

"For God's sake, get your hands back on the wheel," Allison said grabbing at the steering wheel.

"Chill out, Mom," Alex said with a nonchalant smirk and a quick glance at her out of the corner of his eye. Of course he had learned so well from his father how to make her look like the hysterical one. Everyone says that adolescence is easier with boys, she thought. But she wasn't sure. With girls you fight; that's what they say (whoever "they" are). And indeed, Allison could see the beginnings, just a foreshadowing really, of that subtle breaking away process with Kristen who was now just a couple months from her ninth birthday. She had always been their little diva and was becoming more and more so, but at least Allison always knew what was going on in her head even if it was all exaggerated and overly dramatized. At least with Kristen the conflict was overt. And then there were her boys.

Matthew was eighteen, a freshman at Notre Dame, away at college. He had slipped away so silently and imperceptibly, like a wisp of a cloud dissipating into the air on a windy spring day. She hardly noticed it. All that hurt and pain was locked up inside somewhere but he kept it down by being the perfect child, now the perfect young man.

And Alex, their little Alexander Hamilton, their born leader. When she and Frank were together it was a battle of the wills between Frank and Alex; a harsh word spoken here, a terse word volleyed back, a push, a shove, a backhand across the face in response to the smart mouth, fierce grunts accompanied by fists slammed against hard objects, quick and hasty exits from the room, followed by sullen and brooding silence. That sullen and brooding silence carried over since she and Frank separated ten months ago. It was what she lived with now on those weeks that Alex was with her; angry wordlessness, arms crossed, eyes continually looking away, when he did look at her from above his long dark bangs, it was a look like daggers.

The worst part of it all with Alex was the pervasive joylessness. The infectious laughter was gone, the reckless exhilaration that sometimes got on her nerves was gone and now she missed it. Over and above this sad picture of adolescent angst, Alex dragged around with him an all encompassing wet blanket of apathy that pressed upon him and weighed him down. It seemed to Allison that he could shake it off so easily if he wanted to. A quick thrust of the shoulders and a fling of the arms and the dreadful wet blanket would be off. That's how easy it would be for him to snap himself out of it. But he didn't want to. He wanted to drag the awful thing around with him because it was his security. It made everything more bearable to just not care.

And there wasn't anything Allison could do, not really. Wasn't it just that way as kids grew up? You had to relinquish the driver's seat to them, but you still had to be there right in front, watching their every move, monitoring their speed, pushing on the imaginary brake, giving advice at every turn.

"Head the front of the vehicle toward the curb," she said on a too sharp left turn. "And slow down, for crying out loud!"

"You're a fine one to talk. How many speeding tickets have you got, Mom?"

"Exactly my point! I don't want you to have to learn the hard way like I did."

"You still haven't learned your lesson, Mom. You still speed."

"I know what you're trying to do, trying to make me out to be the hypocrite again. I'm not going there, all right. I'm not entering the dance of destruction. Do you understand?"

"Cut the therapy talk, Mom," he said with a contemptuous roll of the eyes. "It's a bunch of crap."

"Oh, right, that's right, you're beyond therapy now. Nobody can tell you anything. And you're not taking your medication anymore; or at least not the prescribed medication that might actually help you. I wonder what you are taking."

"I thought you weren't going to enter the dance of destruction," he said with that victorious smirk just like his father.

"Well, if I just knew what to talk to you about…" this sudden blurt of honesty escaped from her lips with a sigh of defeat. Anything but this angry brooding silence, she thought.

"If we could talk about something more interesting than the fucking weather!"

"Watch your mouth, young man!"

"Oh, like you don't cuss!"

"When have you heard me cuss?"

"When you and Dad fight. I've heard plenty of four letter words fly outta your mouth. I oughta tape you next time." This time his voice was raised in bitterness.

"Your father and I don't fight anymore."

"Yeah, right!"

"We don't fight. We've reconciled our differences since we finally decided to go our separate ways," Allison said, unable to actually say the word "divorce" to Alex. Would she forever refer to it as "going our separate ways".

The divorce wasn't final yet. She and Frank had finally decided to file after nearly nine months of separation, both of them agreeing this perpetual state of limbo had gone on long enough. It had been good for them to call it quits, she thought as she took a deep breath to calm herself. Allison hoped Alex would see the logic in what she said to him about her and his dad getting along better now that they didn't have to live together. It was true, after all. Wasn't it? They didn't fight anymore. Did they? She searched her memory and couldn't think of a single incident since the separation. Except for the one time, when it was his weekend with the kids and he let Kristen go on two sleepovers in a row then sent her back Sunday night exhausted and out of sorts, so much so that she couldn't wake her in time for school on Monday morning. She thought of a few other incidents, but she wasn't that angry, was she?

Her heart ached. She was losing her son, as she knew one day she would, but not like this. The painful desire to reconnect with the little boy she loved so much but never quite understood took over.

"Why won't you talk to me?" she asked in earnest.

"I told you. Because all you can talk about is the weather, how wet and cold it is; or me and my problems and how I should live my life and drive the damn car."

"I was only trying to help," said Allison, her sense of defeat growing.

"Well, you're not helping. Therapy doesn't help worth shit, and neither does the stupid ass medicine, so just get off my ass!"

"Hey, I told you once already to watch the mouth! I've had it with your lack of respect! You owe me respect."

"Whatever." His voice cracked with a screeching whine, adolescence mixed with contempt. He turned the radio on, tuned it to his channel and turned it up all in one swift movement. The sound of rap music filled the car.

"Turn it down this instant or I will ground you. And don't think you can sweet talk your father out of it when you go to visit him this weekend. Despite what you think there are some things we agree on, and this loud crap music while you're driving is one of them." Alex had acquiesced and turned the music down before the words were entirely out of her mouth. Allison realized she was yelling. It was back to the brooding sullen silence and staring straight ahead. "I will not enter into the dance. I will not enter into the dance," she mouthed the words inaudibly to herself and took a deep breath. After she'd had all the silence she could stand, she decided she'd try again, only this time she'd stick to safe small talk.

"How's basketball season going, sweetie?" She grasped for something with which they might connect.

"Fine."

"I'm sorry I missed that first game. I…" Allison stopped herself. Frank had taken charge of all the kids' sports activities. He knew he had an in there with the kids that she didn't have and he used it to his full advantage. He was sure not to get the schedule to her until just this week. And Alex was spending more time at his Dad's so she knew less and less of the boy's activities. She bit back on her resentment.

"There was a little mix up with the schedule." Allison caught herself.

"It's okay," said Alex.

She had lost control and spoken her mind about Frank in front of the kids far too often and she made a pact with herself that she wouldn't do it again. Though she knew he did it about her all the time. She wouldn't stoop to his level of nastiness, she thought and the thought filled her with a fleeting feeling of pride and victory.

"I'm going to do all I can to make it to this game, though you know I'm going to be a little late. I have to go pick up Kristie from dance class."

"Whatever," he said wearing that blanket of apathy like a royal robe.

There was a time that he would have cared if she made it to his games or not, but Allison believed he truly didn't care anymore. Was it all just a teenage phase that he would eventually outgrow, or was he permanently jaded? Would he ever come back, she wondered.

"Okay, this is where you merge onto the highway. Be careful now."

"I know how to merge, Mom," he said flipping on the turn signal, checking the rear view and side view mirrors, getting over into the far right lane, yielding as he approached the entrance ramp. All of his movements surprisingly smooth.

"You forgot to check your blind spot."

"Huh!?"

"Your blind spot. There's a blind spot in your peripheral field of vision. After you check your mirrors you're supposed to turn your head slightly and do a quick check in the direction of the lane you wish to change into." Allison knew it all by heart after all the defensive driving classes.

"I know what the blind spot is and I did check it."

"No, you didn't."

"Whatever."

"You're going a little fast. Slow it up," she said as Alex drove up the entrance ramp that led to the highway. "Check and see what's coming. Its rush hour, you know. People are tired. They just want to get home."

"Like you can really even call it 'rush hour'. This is Lamasco, Mom. Not L.A."

"I said slow up. This is not one of your game system games." Allison clutched the door handle and stepped on the imaginary brake. He merged onto the highway in front of an SUV that honked at him.

"My God, Alex, you could've gotten us killed."

"You're the one who doesn't know how to merge. That dude's supposed to let me in. You just have to call the other guy's bluff."

"Now you sound like your father."

"And what could be worse than that, Mom?" the boy said with angry sarcasm. "You're always criticizing him… and me."

"I know I'm overly critical, Al, and I know I'm nagging you." She said these words and yet there was something beyond mere nit picking and fault finding this time. She was tense, terribly tense. Some instinctual sense of dread compelled her to want to grab the wheel away from him. But how to get your kids to listen to your message when you truly have an important, maybe even urgent one to give them. Somehow deep in the marrow of her Germanic upbringing she believed that children never really received the message or took it seriously unless it was delivered with zealous authority. It had to be drummed into their heads and repeated time and time again with strict and unwavering command. And it had to be spoken loudly. If you said it nicely in a normal tone of voice, they wouldn't really hear you. How ridiculous to think that way because they tuned her out all the same, just like she did her parents. So, as she learned in therapy, she would try to state things differently, with more concern and respect, with more objectivity.

"I'm not going to nag you anymore. I'm just going to say this one thing and then I'll shut up. The road is just wet enough to be slick. It's when it's like this that you're most likely to skid." Maybe she should tell him that she was speeding once in weather just like this, had to slam on the brakes, skidded, and hit another car. Then again he might use that knowledge against her like how Frank always did. He had learned well from his father.

"Also, it's getting dark. Many accidents occur at dusk."

"I thought you were just going to say the one thing and then shut up."

"Are you telling me to shut up? Are you being disrespectful?"

"I was just repeating what you said. Forget it!"

Allison remembered that someone in an emotional state is much more likely to have an accident. She saw Alex grip the wheel tighter as he inadvertently pushed down on the gas. She figured she better back off.

She was distracted for a moment by a billboard advertising a local jewelry store. The focal point was a diamond choker on a woman's long lovely neck. Also notable was the gracefully prominent jaw line and chin, the head turned at a slight angle, the light colored hair pulled back revealing a diamond earring. The woman's lustrous sensual red lips and just the tip of her nose were the only visible facial features. Allison wanted to be that lady–beautiful, rich, glamorous, and yes… vain, but who gives a damn, she thought. She wanted to be somewhere exotic adorned with diamonds instead of here in southern Indiana in the cold drizzle of late November in a minivan driven by a surly teenager.

The moment of reverie vanished suddenly and reality thrust upon her with the flash of red brake lights and the sound of screeching tires. Her body was forced forward as she slammed on the imaginary brakes. Her arms flailing; her right hand clutching the door handle, her left arm reaching over to Alex, trying to protect him somehow. She instinctually leaned her body to the left, toward her son. All of this occurring instantaneously, yet there was her other self, watching from behind her shoulder, observing the whole thing in slow motion, unable to stop it.

Then something large suddenly and seemingly out of nowhere blew up in front of her, obstructing her view, pushing her back with a force stronger than anything she'd ever experienced. For a moment she thought she was dying and this was the entrance to the tunnel with the light at the end that she'd always heard about. She thought she heard herself scream then an expletive blurted out in utter fear by Alex; the force of impact, the crashing sound of steel and breaking glass. And then it was all over. The large object deflated, and only then did she realize it was the air bag.

A surreal stillness and silence followed as Allison noticed a powdery, smoke-like substance in the air all around and the smell of something burning. She could see but it didn't seem like she could hear. It was too quiet. Her neck was stiff but still she managed to turn her head in Alex's direction. He looked dead and she thought she saw blood. She tried to move but couldn't. It hurt too badly. She felt sore and stiff all over. Her face stung. It felt like a bad sunburn. It was far too quiet. In a fit of desperation and panic she called out for Alex. She asked him to squeeze her hand if he could hear her. She could barely hear herself talk, her voice coming through all fuzzy and muffled like someone speaking from inside a tunnel. She felt his fingers faintly and feebly wrap around her hand.

"Can you squeeze a little harder, honey?" Allison pleaded. She had to know that he was all right.

"It wasn't my fault, Mom," she barely heard him say as if he was now the one standing in the tunnel. Relief rushed over her. He was conscious and able to speak to her. He was squeezing her hand now.

"Are you hurt?"

"I think my nose is bleeding."

Poor Alex, he always got nosebleeds—chronic sinus and allergy problems. Grab some tissues. Pinch the bridge of the nose. Put a cold rag on the back of his neck. Poor Alex! Give him some Singular. Always something. Always something with the ear, nose, and throat. Ear tubes. Tonsillectomy. Strep throat religiously every March.

"Where are the tissues?" Allison said feeling around for the box, then realizing it was in the back seat. The soreness, stiffness, and trauma wouldn't allow her to reach back to get the tissue box though she tried.

"Don't worry, Mom, I'll use my shirt. It's already a mess." Allison looked over at Alex. The front of his light grey sweat shirt was covered with blood.

"Pinch the bridge of your nose."

"It hurts."

Allison said nothing, not wanting to alarm him but she wondered if his nose was broken.

"Oh, baby," she muttered. She wanted to help him but all she could do was turn her body at enough of an angle to see him. The sight of the blood and her son in such a fragile state sent a sympathy pain shooting all through her body. Allison felt faint, her mind going this way and that; like the alpha state right before one falls into sleep, only not so pleasant; a slipping away, a dying, dizzying, nauseous feeling. She must've muttered something unintelligible to Alex, because his voice came through loud and clear for the first time, bringing her back into reality.

"I wrecked the car, Mom. I hit the car in front of us. It wasn't my fault. I tried to stop."

"I know, Al"

"I'm just not lucky Mom. I try. I try." And then he was crying, angry and slamming his fist against the door. "Matt could've stopped in time."

Poor Alex! Always the one getting carted off to the emergency room with broken bones and stitches. He took the brunt for all of them. He was the more than willing scapegoat

"It wasn't your fault, Alex. It's why they call them accidents. Do you know how many wrecks I've had? By the way, how are your arms?"

"Okay, I guess."

"Can you move them?" Allison realized she could turn her head and move a bit more easily now though she was still sore and stiff. Both of them were only now able to assess the damage from the impact of the airbags. She watched as he moved his arms up and down and side to side.

"Yeah, I think my arms are okay. I don't know about the rest of me though," Alex said.

"Thank God. For once I can honestly say it was a good thing you didn't listen to me."

"What do you mean?"

"You're hands were at nine o'clock and three o'clock."

He chuckled a little and so did Allison. The moment of release was short lived. It hurt to laugh. It hurt to breathe. Only then did Allison realize just how sore her side was. And as for Alex, his short lived laughter quickly dissolved into a fit of angry and anxious sobbing. "Dad's gonna kill me. My insurance rates will go up. I'll never get my license."

"We have to call your Dad and tell him."

"No! Don't!"

"We have to. He's going to be waiting for you at the gym and you're not going to be there. He's got to know. Where's my cell phone?" She said searching for her purse which had been on the seat next to her but was now on the floor. She snatched her purse up and frantically felt in the front pocket for her cell phone. It was there, right where she had put it. The security of the small familiar object brought a flood of much needed relief. At that moment the blue lights of several squad cars flashed by them. Sirens squealed and then came an ambulance with its horrible squall of urgency. It was then that Allison realized this was a serious accident, possibly fatal, involving more than just themselves and the car in front of them.

"Shit!" Alex exclaimed. "I'm sorry, Mom. I cussed."

"It's understandable under the circumstances." Allison thought how ironic that Alex would apologize for cussing at a time like this.

"The car behind us hit us too," he said looking in the rear view mirror then straining to look around the SUV in front of them. "It's a pile-up."

The police officers at the scene, the paramedics who rode in the ambulance and some of the other injured who waited in the emergency room with Allison and Alex contributed bits of information about the accident. It was a five car pile-up and they were car number three. They heard that some crazy drunk woman staggering along the highway decided to hop up on the guard rail and do a swan dive onto the highway. Car number one slammed on the brakes in an attempt to avoid hitting her, setting off the domino chain reaction. According to all reports the woman had survived and was still conscious when brought to the emergency room. It was speculated she would most likely fare better than most due to the fact that she was intoxicated at the time. An indiscreet emergency room nurse responsible for check in vented her frustrations about drunks and all the harm and havoc they heap upon others through their recklessness; while they usually get off remarkably easy due to the looseness, limberness, and complete lack of muscle tension brought about by alcohol.

Frank met them at the emergency room with his usual frantic expenditure of alarm and misdirected concern. He was not the presence of strength and security Allison had hoped he would be; not for herself of course, she had long since given up looking to Frank for that, but she had hoped for Alex's sake he could be more of an example of quiet courage. There are certain things which only a man can adequately impart to a boy Alex's age, and as much as Allison tried she could only reach him just so far and no further. What little strength and comfort she could impart was being hindered by her own bodily injuries–pain on her right side which hurt every time she took a breath, pain in her right eye and a stinging sensation as if she'd been slapped repeatedly all over her face, apparently caused by an allergic reaction to the powder in the air bag. She knew she would have one beauty of a shiner in that right eye which she could feel swelling shut.

Most of her injuries, soreness, and stiffness were on the right side of the body since she was leaning to the left when the airbags deployed. She was told by one of the emergency room nurses that injuries caused by airbags can be greatly reduced if you are positioned properly. Yeah, right! Try telling that to a mother whose only instinct at the moment of impact is to protect her child. When Mattie and Alex were big enough to finally ride in the front seat, her instinct was always to throw an arm across them if she had to suddenly step on the brakes. And so it was still. And so it would always be. She leaned toward Alex but it didn't help. Nothing she could do could protect him.

They waited in an alcove, hung with curtains on all four sides, both of them on gurneys, Alex with his head elevated and an ice pack over his nose. Frank insisted that Alex recount the details of the accident over and over again, each question fired at him sounding more and more accusatory, as if he was trying to find some error the boy had made and some way it could have been corrected.

"Stop interrogating him, Frank. What's done is done," Allison said with some difficulty, each word uttered causing her to hurt.

"I'm not interrogating him. I just want him to think about what happened and how it could be avoided next time."

She wanted to scream at him that this wasn't what the boy needed right now. She wanted to shake him and make him understand that maybe no amount of caution can protect us from all calamities and collisions. But she couldn't do that because she was in pain and injured and Alex didn't need to see his parents arguing right now. She paused and thought about it. Maybe it was a lesson she needed to learn. Maybe we have less control than we think. Maybe the tragic and unforeseen is destined to crash in upon you despite all your best efforts. Frank continued his interrogation while Allison mouthed the words silently to herself. "I will not enter the dance of destruction. I will not enter the dance." *Hell, I'm too beat up and tired to enter the dance,* she thought trying to tune out Frank and Alex.

Over and above the sound of Alex's voice trying to convince his father that he wasn't driving too fast and wasn't riding the guy in front's bumper, came the sound of another voice. It was the sound of a woman's voice, loud and confused, incoherent, whining, and either drunk or insane; possibly both. It was coming from the alcove next to them. Alex suddenly became quiet, and Frank finally ceased his interrogation of the poor boy. The voice had caught their attention too. How could it not? Other voices were heard as well; voices of medical personnel, more than one, at least two, maybe three. All of these other voices blended and blurred together, some male, some female, some calming and reassuring, trying to quiet the upset woman; other voices were firm and strict, reprimanding, as if speaking to a child, giving brief terse instructions, trying to bring the woman back into reality.

"Hold still. You know we're not going to hurt you."

"Oh, oh," the woman pitifully moaned like some injured animal. Then suddenly she changed tones and shifted from pathetic to agitated. "Get that thing away from me. What is that thing? You trying to poison me?"

"It's an IV, Vicky. You've seen these things before. We need to get some nutrients in you."

"I don't need no damn nutrients."

"Have you looked in a mirror lately? You're half starved to death," said an authoritative sounding male voice.

"Last time I looked in a mirror I didn't look starved to death. I looked fat, looked like I was getting a big ol' beer gut on me."

"That beer gut you're talking about is an enlarged spleen. You're malnourished; severely malnourished."

"Don't stick me with that thing. I don't got no veins no more. They all done collapsed. I don't need no nutrients and fluids."

"Could you help me here a second? Nancy, could you come over here and help me find a vein?"

"Just let me go. Why won't you let me go?"

"Because you're hurt and you need someone to look after you. You haven't done a very good job taking care of yourself, you know."

"So you think it's your job to take care of me? C'mon man, just let me go."

"We don't want a repeat of what just happened. That was a pretty foolish stunt you pulled out there, Vicky. You're just lucky you didn't kill yourself, let alone anybody else," said the authoritative man.

"Did I kill somebody? Ah shit, tell me I didn't kill nobody! I was trying to kill myself, not nobody else."

"Calm down, Vicky. Shhh, everything's all right. That's a good girl. Calm down. Hold still."

"What a fuck up! I can't even kill myself. Here lies Vicky Lee Dooley. We had to bury her alive 'cause she wouldn't die. Oh, well, one thing's for sure. I'll be well preserved."

"That's for sure! They won't need to embalm you, Vicky." The medical staff laughed right along with the woman at the macabre joke.

Allison's eyes met Frank. There was nothing but a curtain separating them from the voice. The voice was recognizable still, though layered underneath years of sickness and abuse. Frank heard it too. They both heard that unmistakable voice declare herself as Vicky Lee Dooley. He'd heard it all right. There was unspoken acknowledgement in his eyes. It was there for just a second and then he looked away. They simultaneously turned their attention to Alex. Despite the ice pack, which covered most of his face, Allison could see in his eyes a deliberate effort to appear stoic and unscathed. Poor Alex! He only tried that hard to be cool when he was really suffering.

The curtain to the alcove was suddenly pulled back with a quick purposeful shove that caused them all to start. A tall tired looking, slouched shouldered doctor of about fifty entered carrying x-rays under his arm. He explained to them that Allison had a broken rib. There was too much swelling to x-ray Alex's nose but the doctor could tell by examining it that it was broken. They were to be admitted to the hospital over night. Though they protested, the doctor explained they needed to be monitored and observed to rule out the possibility of other internal injuries. Poor Alex would have to have his nose packed and set. The doctor said it was a bad break and there was strong possibility they would have to do surgery after the swelling went down.

Vicky had crashed into her world again, stirring it up, unsettling things. Wasn't it just like her? Poor Vicky! What happened to her? What happened to all of them? This was the last thought Allison had before the narcotic they gave her for pain began to cloud her mind and senses and send her drifting into a much needed sleep.

Chapter 33
Vicky

"Vicky, we're going to ask you some questions. Okay?"

"Okay," Vicky said. She knew it was her voice answering the pretty blonde nurse with marble blue eyes, but it didn't sound like her own voice. It sounded tremulous and faint, like a scared mouse trying to squeak but unable to get the noise out. She wanted to tell the nurse she knew about these questions, they'd been asked of her before, about ten months ago when she was last hospitalized. She wanted to tell her that, just for the sake of small talk, just because chit chat had always been a comfort to her, always eased the disquiet inside her mind and helped her forget about herself. But Vicky couldn't make chit chat right now. The utterance of words was too difficult. Her vocal chords, right along with the rest of her insides, were shaking beyond control.

"First question," said the nurse. "When was your last drink?"

"I…d-d-don't remember," Vicky said, the words straining through the earthquake in her larynx. The pretty blond nurse with the blue marble eyes said something to the nurse standing at her side, an overweight young woman with greasy brown hair pulled back tightly in a ponytail. It seemed from this second nurse's tentative and uncertain way that she was some sort of nurse in training under the tutelage of the pretty blond. She heard the blond nurse say something about Vicky's blood alcohol level when she was admitted, something about it being high for a normal person but not necessarily for someone like Vicky, something about bracing herself for what could happen the closer the BAL gets to zero. Something about contusions and injuries from the accident and how that will complicate things even more.

"You had something to drink before your accident. Do you remember?" the nurse said in a too loud voice with a patronizing tone as if she was speaking to a naughty child. Vicky wanted to tell her she didn't have to yell, that she wasn't deaf and she wasn't retarded.

"Yes, be-fore the accident. S-s-see, you knew the answer. You d-d-didn't need to ask m-me."

The blond nurse said something to the overweight nurse. Vicky caught the word "agitated."

"I c-can hear b-better than you think I c-c-can."

"All right then," she said with a condescending little chuckle. "Let's just move on to this next set of questions. All right, answer these questions on a scale from zero to seven. Zero being not a problem at all and seven being the worst possible. Are you ready?"

Vicky nodded her head and squeaked out something in the affirmative to indicate she understood. "Now this first question I might be able to answer for you too," she said with her annoying little chuckle and that sickly sweet, pseudo concern. She gave Vicky a reassuring pat on her arm. Her fingers were cold. She remembered the cold fingers taking her pulse before. She was liking Blondie less and less and she would have given her a piece of her mind had she not felt so bad.

"Now I know you had some nausea and vomiting since you were admitted."

"Why d-d-don't you just take the f-f-fucking test for me."

"It's all right, Vicky." Tap, tap went the cold fingers on Vicky's arm. "Do you feel sick to your stomach now? Zero being no nausea."

"If I stay here w-w-with y-you l-long enough, I'm sure I'll v-v-vomit again."

How does one explain that everything from the inside out felt dizzy, scary, shaky, and sickening? The nurse looked less pretty to her than she did when Vicky first saw her. When she moved closer to Vicky she looked a little distorted, like the way someone looks through the peep hole of a door. "Are your eyes r-r-really that b-b-blue?" Vicky asked, backing off from her, feeling a little horror from those startlingly blue eyes.

"You've discovered my secret," she said cheerfully. "I'm wearing tinted contacts."

Vicky thought how she looked a little like one of the pod people from some B horror movie she'd seen once–all aliens with abnormally colored eyes. Her hair was pulled back in a tight pony tail too. Just like the fat, scared, dirty-haired brunette nurse. It hurt Vicky's head to see that hair pulled back so tight. It made her look mean, like a wet rat with its fur slicked and its mean little features twitching and inhuman. Blondie was quickly evolving from annoying to downright sinister right before Vicky's eyes.

"Back to the question," Blondie said, the tone and cadence of her voice insincere and supercilious in all its' nasally shrillness. "Do you feel sick to your stomach?"

"I feel s-s-sick all over," Vicky blurted out. She began crying, then sat up and tried to get out of bed. "Just l-l-let me g-g-go. I have to g-g-get out of here. I have to move. Get th-this thing off of me! I'm plugged into the f-f-fucking wall." Vicky yanked at her IV tube.

Suddenly there was an entourage of hospital staff in the room. "Vicky, Vicky," they were all saying and too many hands were touching her and it felt like pin pricks. An authoritative female voice rose above the rest.

"It's all right. Let her move if she needs to move," then turning to Vicky, a kindly looking, middle aged woman with a nondescript face but a reassuring voice, said. "Would it help if you walked back and forth?"

"You mean p-p-pace? It's always helped me to pace."

"Would you mind if I pace with you?" She actually waited for her to answer and Vicky was beginning to believe she had found a friend. Vicky nodded. "I'll walk with you and help you with this apparatus here." She wheeled the IV along as she walked with Vicky. She put her hand on Vicky's shoulder. Her hand set something to crawling up and down Vicky's arm and she flinched and pulled away from the kind woman's touch.

"I'm s-s-sorry."

"It's all right. I'm sure your skin does feel a little sensitive right now. Is it burning, itching, or pins and needles?"

"All of the above," Vicky said trying to shake off the sensation. I d-d-don't got no b-b-bugs on me, d-d-do I? I mean, I know I g-g-got no bugs on m-m-me? That's c-c-crazzy. I d-d-don't got no b-b-bugs on me, d-d-do I?" Vicky said examining her arm.

"Does it look like they're bugs on you?"

"No, b-b-but it feels like it. You d-d-don't suppose they're some under my s-s-skin?"

"No, honey, it just feels that way." Then the kind nurse turned her attention to Blondie and Fatty who were in the corner of the room. Blondie was holding a clipboard with all the questions. "Tactile disturbance—give her a four."

They got to one end of the small hospital room. The kind older nurse helped her turn around while holding onto the IV pole. "Let me see your hand, Vicky. Hold your hand out for me. That's it." Vicky obeyed like a frightened little child as she raised a clutching claw like hand. She thought of the man with the withered hand in the Bible, the one that Jesus cured. She didn't know why. She looked at the shaking little claw and thought how useless and unproductive her hands had been for so long.

"Open your hand and spread your fingers out for me," the nurse said. Vicky obeyed though with great difficulty. Her fingers felt so stiff and she felt strangely ashamed to have someone observe her hand so closely. As if someone could see all the bad deeds spent and all the good deeds wasted with that, her dominant right hand, which she now held out with fingers extended for all to see.

"I'm s-s-sorry I'm s-s-so sh-shaky," she said trying futilely to make her hand obey her silent signals and commands to hold still. "It's p-p-pretty b-b-bad, isn't it?"

435

The nurse smiled and nodded. "The shakes don't get much worse than what you've got right now. Give her a seven under tremors and a five under sweats," she said to Blondie and Fatty.

"M-m-maybe if I do this," Vicky said holding her forearm with her other hand in a useless attempt to stop the shaking.

"It's all right, that shakiness is your central nervous system's reaction to no alcohol. You're sweating pretty profusely too. Would a damp wash cloth help you feel better?" Vicky nodded and the kind nurse gave an order to Fatty to get a damp washcloth.

"What about nausea? You were pretty sick when you left the emergency room. Do you feel sick to your stomach again?"

"B-b-before you brought it up, I was okay, but n-n-now that you're ask-askin' me to think about it… I d-d-don't w-w-want to think about it. I'm t-tired of p-puking. I d-don't want to puke again b-but now you got me thinkin' about it. Why did you have to b-b-bring it up?" A wave of nausea hit her as she tried to assess just how nauseous she was. She began dry heaving. She was handed a pale yellow plastic dish. As she coughed and vomited up water and mucous the kind nurse patted her forehead and the back of her neck with the damp cloth. She held up four fingers to Fatty and Blondie, signaling Vicky's score under the nausea and vomiting category.

"Please t-t-take this," Vicky said handing the nurse the pale yellow dish. She wanted to throw the yellow dish across the room. She wanted to scream and throw a tantrum. Tears and snot ran down her face. The nurse blotted her cheeks and wiped her nose with the damp cloth. "I'm okay now? C-c-can we walk again. I n-n-need to w-walk." They resumed their short pace from one end of the hospital room to the other.

"Do you feel nervous?"

"Hell yeah!"

"Just from observing I'd say on a scale from zero to seven, you're a five or a six. Does that sound right?" Vicky nodded. "Do you feel panicky?"

"I'm just s-s-scared, real s-scared."

"Give her a six under anxiety."

"Why do you n-n-need to ask me all these questions? And why z-z-zero to s-seven? Why seven? It's an odd number. Who the h-h-hell ever heard of a f-f-fucking scale from zero to seven? Who c-c-came up with this s-s-stupid ass s-survey for dr-drunks anyway?"

"I don't know," the nurse said with a curious chuckle. "I've often wondered that myself."

"Seven is supposed to be the n-n-number for p-p-perfection in the b-b-bible. That's w-w-what m-m-my g-grandma t-t-told me."

"I believe you're right," said the kind nurse as they turned around, the two of them along with the IV pole, making their trek back to the other side of the room.

"S-so if I score a s-sev-ven on every q-q-question d-d-does that make m-m-me a p-p-perfect d-drunk?"

The nurse laughed out loud. "How you can still have a sense of humor is beyond me. You hang onto that, honey. You hang onto that."

"Hang onto that. I'll hang onto that," she said clutching the nurse's arm as if it was some concrete representation of her sense of humor. "I'm hurting you. I don't mean to hurt you," she said releasing her grip. Did I br-break your arm? It felt like I broke your arm just then when I grabbed you. I d-don't know my own strength. Sorry."

"You didn't hurt me Vicky. I'm a tough old bird. If it helps you to squeeze my arm, go ahead. Hang in there! Just a few more questions then we'll be able to give you some medication. The questions help us to know just how much medication you need. We don't want to give you too much or too little.

"I just wanna drink. I just wanna f-f-fucking d-drink. It's all I c-c-can think about right n-n-now," Vicky blurted out in tears of desperation.

"I know, honey. I know," the nurse said patting her forehead and cheeks with the damp cool cloth. "Hang in there. Hang onto my arm. I'll make it quick. I promise."

The questions began to run together. "Are you more aware of sounds around you? Are they harsh? Do they frighten you? Does the light hurt your eyes? Does your head hurt? Does it feel like you have a band around it? Are you seeing things you know aren't there?" She tried to fib about the swirling grey cyclone in the corner of the room, the one that so often came to life when she went without booze too long, the one that threatened to suck her up and consume her and destroy everything in its' wake. She tried to ignore Fatty and Blondie who stood in the corner with the cyclone, just waiting to unleash it in her direction because they thought it might be funny to see a poor drunk get eaten by a figment of her own imagination. She tried not to look at how tight their ponytails were because it made her head hurt. She had to ask the nice nurse if someone had pulled her hair back tight like that too and would they please undo it because it was giving her a headache.

"I'm f-f-flunking. I'm not doing well? Am I? A p-p-perfect s-s-seven hundred. Seven thousand."

"Do you know what day it is?"

"It's Monday. No, Tuesday. Hell, I don't know."

"What about the date and the year?"

"It's November, 2006. Never thought I'd make it this long. November 20 or 21."

"Yes, very good! It's Monday, November 20. You're doing better than me. I usually never know the date."

"It's Thanksgiving this week. Right?"

"Correct! You're doing very well. What's two plus two?"

"Four."

"Four plus four?"

"Eight. And eight plus eight is sixteen."

"Very good! How about two plus three?"

"Five."

"Three plus four?"

"C-c-can I use my f-f-fingers? Just k-kidding. It's s-s-seven. Please don't m-m-move up to d-decimals and f-fractions. I s-s-suck at Math. Drunk or s-s-sober."

The kind nurse laughed and told her to hang onto her sense of humor. Vicky gripped her arm tighter. The nurse told her she sucked at Math too, and not to worry, she got a perfect score, a zero, under the orientation category. And then Vicky was confused and argued that zero was a bad score and seven was a perfect score. The nurse reminded her that a lower score was better, and Vicky had to think about it until she got it again, at which time she pleaded with the nurse not to up her score because she was confused about the scoring. The kind nurse assured her she wouldn't do anything to up her score anymore, since it was already pretty high. She liked the way this nurse was honest with her and didn't talk down to her.

Medication was quickly ordered and administered. The kind nurse had to leave but told her she'd check in on her and would be there to give the zero to seven test for drunks again in an hour. She watched as the kind nurse left and she wanted to cry. It felt the same as the first day of kindergarten when she watched her mother leave her there all alone at school; all alone with a strange teacher, only this time she was all alone with Fatty and Blondie.

She wanted to yell at the two nurses in the corner of the room, talking and laughing like two mean girls from school who were probably talking and laughing about her. She wanted to yell but the medication was taking effect. The rough edge around all those excitable emotions was sloughing off a bit and she had less of an impulse to yell. She cried instead.

The next thing she remembered was being awakened, not that she was startled awake exactly but something in the room shifted suddenly, like the air had been stirred up by a quick movement, and all at once Vicky was aware of a presence. She knew that some time had passed but just how much she wasn't sure. She opened her eyes and there stood a doctor in a white coat with a file under his arm. He introduced himself without a smile but she didn't catch his name.

The doctor was tall and thin with tufts of silvery gray hair sticking up on top of his head. He had a dictatorial, superior sort of nature which was evidenced when he immediately began spouting off orders and scolding Blondie and Fatty. He was someone whose bad side you wouldn't want to be on. But Vicky was glad he was there. He was just who she needed to put Blondie and Fatty in their place.

Maybe it was her half dazed state that made her more acutely aware of people around her. She had an intuition about this doctor—a feeling that he was brilliant, a born doctor, perhaps a little frustrated to be stuck in this backward town and backward hospital with people who were not naturally as gifted as him and whose incompetence he had to endure. He began to examine Vicky at which time Fatty quickly fled with the excuse that she had to go to the bathroom and that she would be right back.

The doctor examined her stomach, prodding and kneading with a kind of certainty that seemed he was getting information directly from his fingertips up to his brain. Her stomach was so tender that had she not been so sedated she would have been screaming in pain at even the lightest touch. A moan of discomfort was all that escaped her lips. He examined her chest and the palms of her hands, pulled her eyelids down and carefully looked at her eyes, all the while muttering in harsh tones, though not necessarily directed at her. He grumbled about varicose veins, her swollen stomach, and the hue of her skin, and for "Chrissake, any…" he almost said the word idiot but caught himself and changed it to something more professional sounding, "anyone with a limited medical knowledge can see she's in the latter stages of cirrhosis."

Although she wasn't quite sure he saw her as human, more like a knowledgeable mechanic looking at the engine of a car, she respected this doctor. She respected him because he took up for her and didn't talk down to her. He would be her ally, not a tender one like the kind nurse, but one who would fight for her nonetheless. Most people didn't think she was worth the fight anymore and, who knows, they were probably right, Vicky thought.

The doctor began ranting to Blondie about getting her off the IV immediately. "She's got too much water in her blood and tissues as it is. You're overtaxing her heart with all these fluids."

"I didn't order it, doctor. The ER doctor on call must've thought it necessary. What I mean is," Blondie said pleading for his understanding. "She was vomiting quite a bit when she was admitted. She was dehydrated."

"Well, she's not anymore. Remove the IV. She can take liquids orally."

Vicky heard the doctor's monologue come through in waves. She heard the part about the latter stages of cirrhosis and somewhere in her brain she grasped what that meant. Perhaps she would have been alarmed had she not been so dopey from the medication. She didn't really feel anything except a dim hope that she wouldn't suffer too much before she died. She heard the part about taking liquids orally and she wanted to make a joke about it, wanted to say something about that's what got her into all this trouble in the first place. She tried but it felt like she had a sweater over her tongue and she couldn't get the words out.

"And we've got to change her meds," she heard the doctor say. "She's over sedated. Look at this blood pressure–seventy over forty. Her liver's too damaged to metabolize the Librium. We need something shorter acting. If her score is still high next time we give her the CIWA I'm ordering Lorazepam. And look at this," he said thumping the file to indicate another area where they had messed up. "She has a history of seizures with alcohol withdrawal. She has a score of forty-five on the CIWA before she gets anything to help her? What's that all about? What in God's name were you people waiting for? She was already beginning withdrawal in the ER!"

"But she didn't have a seizure, doctor."

"You're just damn lucky," he interrupted before she could even finish her sentence. "She was probably just minutes away from one. Plus you add the trauma from the accident…"

The doctors' voice began to fade away and Vicky wanted to ask him why he even cared. Then she wondered if he really did care or was it just his job, which he obviously took a lot of pride in? Was keeping this poor pitiful mass of flesh and bones alive and semi comfortable simply a reflection of his own medical expertise? Was it about her or was it really about him? And why should it be about her anyway, Vicky reasoned?

She still reasoned. Somewhere in her foggy, clouded, damaged brain there was still some streak of cognitive light that came on every now and then and caused her to try to sort things out, to resolve matters, to make order of all the scrambled jigsaw puzzle pieces of her life. These moments were becoming fewer and farther between, but when they occurred everything was clear, lucid, terribly illuminated, and excruciatingly painful. These were rare sober moments and not particularly pleasant ones for Vicky.

"Why should anything be about me? That's part of my problem. I thought all along it was. Fool. Fuck up. Failure." Vicky muttered in a whisper, but the haze of sedation wouldn't let the thought go any further and it seemed as if thick black drapes like theater curtains were closing in front of her eyes. Her eyelids felt as if they were coated with lead and soon there was nothing before her but black.

Vicky heard voices conversing in hushed tones. She couldn't keep her eyes open long enough to see who it was. It was nurses and they were talking about her. She strained to listen but the conversation kept coming in waves like someone changing a radio dial from one station to the next. "They said in the ER it didn't seem like she'd undergone any trauma…covered in bruises, gashes, scrapes…bleeding like…conscious…still walking around…couldn't get her to lie down…loud…cracking jokes…perfectly oriented…knew where she was…severe withdrawal…still oriented…a little nervous and shaky…you or me…dead…why?…all these other people injured…nobody killed…thank God…others…pain…off work…months of physical therapy…totaled cars…walks out of here…like nothing…back on the streets…back at it…drinking again…strong constitution…should be dead by now…maybe better off.

Vicky was somewhere familiar, in a large room with light all around her, natural sunlight, streaming through windows in rays filled with thousands of dust particles dreamily floating about. It was a place she knew from long ago, childhood, perhaps even infancy. There was something about where she stood in this room, something about the space and shape of the room that filled her with some strange old familiarity, some bitter sweet longing for something distant and far away, something long past and forgotten.

She was facing either east or west because the sun was right there in front of her, low on the horizon, either setting or rising, she couldn't tell which. But then it occurred to her, it had to be setting. Only the evening sun on its way down could fill her with that kind of nostalgia. The light around her became clearer and objects slowly came into focus as she became aware of her surroundings.

She was at the River Inn again tending bar. She was doing what she did best, filling people up; filling up their glasses with perfectly shaped, crystal clear pieces of ice that clinked in the most melodious way when dropped into the bottom. She was pouring her magical potions over the ice, some clear, some pale gold, some caramel brown. She filled up wine glasses with deep bowls and long elegant stems. She poured deep red and purple liquids. She mixed up her potions, she shook them, she stirred them, she knew exactly how much was just enough for each person. She was careful, not too much of her magic potions, just enough to make them laugh or cry or talk or whatever it was they needed to do.

And then the people she was serving came into view. She handed them their drinks and they handed her their money. But they were paying her for more than just the drinks. They were paying her for the stories and jokes she told, and the ones they told that she laughed at. They were paying her for the problems she listened to, the counsel she gave, the ledges she talked them off of, even the fights she talked them out of. Her bosses always said you didn't much need a bouncer when Vicky was around 'cause she could stop a fight. She even made one particularly troublesome customer go stand in the corner with his face to the wall until he cooled off like some bad little school boy. And he did it because Vicky told him to.

She wanted everyone to feel that warmth and comfort that comes with that first gulp of booze as it trickles down your throat. She wanted everyone to stop being afraid; afraid to cry, afraid to laugh too loudly, afraid to talk to someone, afraid of being silly, or being rejected, or afraid to try because you might fail. Most of all she didn't want them to be afraid of each other. She wanted to fill everyone up with comfort, warmth, friendship, humor, the ability to laugh at their hardships, and just enough rest and release to go back and face those hardships the next day.

She wanted to fill them up with good food and a place to belong. She wanted to cook for people. She wanted to feed people. She wanted to hear their stories. She didn't want anyone to be left out. She wanted to take in anyone who had ever felt like an orphan. She wanted her own place. Vicky's Country Inn. And people would come from all over.

It was a dream that had long ago died but now it was alive again as she stood in this bright room, elevated above the city streets where you could look out and see the setting sun sinking into the Ohio River below. Every dream she ever had, every hope she ever knew was alive again in this place with the sound of clinking glass and laughter. She could even fly if she wanted. She could get off the ground where she'd always been stuck, and fly. All she had to do was spread her arms and start flapping. Why hadn't she figured it out before? She wanted to tell everyone how easy it was to fly, because certainly it was the best kept secret. She'd show them! That's what she'd do. She'd start flapping her arms and take off and everyone would be amazed.

Next thing she knew she was flying, out the window and over the river. She never felt so free. She never felt so alive, so elated, so exhilarated. Then it occurred to her that she must be careful not to get too close to the sun because then she'd burn, like the guy in the Greek myth. Who was it? She'd studied the story in one of her college classes. Icarus. The name came to her with little effort and stuck in her head as she flew. Icarus. Icarus.

She didn't have to worry about getting too close to the sun though because she was already above it. The sun was going lower as she was going higher. But still, she was getting hot and sweaty, and she noticed it was getting harder to flap. Her wings were starting to melt, she thought, and her confidence right along with it. She didn't want to fall into the river so she flapped as hard as she could toward the rocky shore. Each flap was becoming more strenuous as she descended quickly. She braced herself for the impact. She just barely made it over to the shore before crashing into the rocks. She landed hard but it didn't hurt, only startled her and she felt herself jerk.

It was an ugly place to be, there on the rocky shores of the river. It was littered with broken glass, beer cans, fast food wrappers, and cigarette butts. All around was the waste and negligence of those who tried to fly but would never leave the earth. Then suddenly there was her Dad standing right there in front of her. She was confused because she thought he was dead. So what was he doing here? Her heart sank. She thought she would never have to worry about fighting with him again. On the day they buried him she thought all that screaming, hollering, name calling, and slapping around would never occur again. She could lay it all to rest along with her Dad. She could put it behind her and try to find some peace, maybe even remember a few good things, like the times he took her fishing and hunting. Now here he was and he looked mad.

He hollered at her, called her a "show off" and who did she think she was trying to fly. He accused her of not really flying–he said it was just a trick to make everyone think she could fly. He struck her but she was so angry she didn't even feel the blow. She struck him back. She called him a stupid drunk and told him she was sick of him putting her down all the time. He said she was a fine one to talk. He accused her of being so drunk she could hardly stand up. He came at her again but she got to him first and pushed him with all her might. He fell against a rock and dashed his head. He lay there bleeding. Vicky felt a mix of horror and pity. She wondered if she was drunk. She was dizzy and seeing double. She must've sneaked some drinks back at the bar. She was so good at sneaking drinks even she didn't know when she did it. Her knees buckled and she fell on the rocks. Her Dad looked at her. He had a big gash on his forehead and blood dripping into his eyes but he was still conscious. Still conscious and still mean as a snake. "See, I told ya," he said. "You're so drunk you can't stand up." She realized he was right. He always was.

Chapter 34

Vicky felt someone touch her arm, gently but with purpose. Were they trying to help her up?

"Are you all right?" She heard a strange voice ask. She opened her eyes for a fragment of a second, just enough to make out the figure of a man, a priest or minister of some kind dressed in black with a white collar.

"I didn't mean to get drunk again. I didn't want to. I'm sorry." Vicky blurted out and she could hear the tremulous sound of her own voice.

"You're not drunk. You just had a bad dream."

"I'm not drunk?"

"No," she heard the man of God say.

Vicky blinked hard a few times but her eyes kept snapping shut again, she struggled to wake up lest she return to that awful dream. She unknowingly held her hand out so that whoever was there could help pull her up off these rocks. "Help me," she heard herself say in that shaky desperate voice. His hand clasped hers'. It was warm and strong.

"How can I help you?" the man of God's voice asked.

"Help me stay awake."

"Maybe if you sit up," he said and pushed the button on her bed. She heard the mechanical noise and felt herself elevating. He helped her scoot back and moved her pillow out from under her head, repositioning it around her mid-back. All this shifting around succeeded in awakening her. Her eyes took in her surroundings and she remembered.

"You look a little overheated," the man of God said, and Vicky realized she was indeed drenched in sweat. "Can I get you a damp cloth or some water?"

"No, I'm fine. My wings just melted a little, that's all."

"Oh?"

"Got a little too close to the sun."

"Ah! Sounds like Icarus."

"It's what I was dreaming about. The first part of the dream was great. I was flying. Did you ever fly in your dreams, Reverend?"

"It's been a long time, but yes, I believe I have once or twice. You can have some pretty strange dreams when you're going through what you've been through," the man of God said. There was something about the way he said it that made Vicky think he might know what he was talking about. He looked familiar but she couldn't place him.

"How long have I been here?"

"You were admitted three days ago. Do you remember anything?"

"Yeah, I remember some. But, my Lord, three days! Time flies when you're having DT's." The man of God said nothing in response but simply smiled enigmatically.

"So how bad was I? Did I have to be restrained? Did I have a seizure? Was I puking up pea soup like some crazy possessed woman? Is that why they called you in? Are you the exorcist?" Again he said nothing, just smiled in that strange perplexing way as if he had some secret. "Hell, I don't know why I'm asking you. You're just the Reverend. You wouldn't know the gory medical details, would ya?"

"Mind if I sit down?" he asked, pulling up a chair as he spoke.

"Go ahead, hunker down."

"As a matter of fact I do know a few of the gory medical details. I was in here to see you before, you know."

"You were?"

"You called for me. You said you had to get right with God and you asked for someone to pray with you."

"Huh! Don't remember that one. Okay, so tell me the gory details."

"You didn't have a seizure and you didn't have to be restrained. They managed to stave off the worst of the withdrawal with the medication. The big trouble was getting the medication right. They gave you the wrong kind and got you a little overmedicated at first."

"Yeah, I know. My liver ain't metabolizing the Librium. You had to switch me over to… something or other."

"Apparently you do remember some things."

"I remember some crazy doctor rushing in here like his hair was on fire. He looked like his hair was on fire anyhow. It was stickin' straight up on top of his head. Kinda like a cross between Billy Idol and Einstein."

"Dr. Anton," the Reverend said looking amused. "He's a little high strung but he knows what he's doing."

"Three days, huh? Just call me Rip Van flipping Winkle. Was I asleep most of the time?"

"Not really. Just after that first round of Librium you were out pretty cold for a few hours. You were up again after a while, a little nervous and shaky; some mild hallucinations."

"Mild hallucinations? What could be mild about seeing something that ain't there? That's sounds pretty serious to me. So what did I see?"

"The angel of death. That's what prompted you to send for me."

"The angel of death, huh? And that was mild? Shit, I'd hate to see one of my severe hallucinations."

"Well, I say mild," he said with a slightly amused chuckle, "because you knew you were hallucinating. The whole time you knew where you were and what was going on around you."

"Angel of death," Vicky said pensively. "Hmm, probably just one of them mean ass nurses. Some of them could pass for the angel of death."

"I have to agree," he said and for the first time he laughed beyond just a polite little chuckle.

"Did I take that crazy zero to seven test for drunks again?"

"I believe so."

"Did I do better?"

"I think you had a lower score each time if that's what you mean."

"Each time? I only remember the first time. I was a wreck. I had this really sweet nurse. She let me pace the room. She wiped sweat, snot, and puke off my face with a cool rag. That was the only time I felt a little better–was when she put that rag on my forehead and the back of my neck and talked to me in that soft low voice. She said she'd be back. I don't remember her coming back. I think I'd remember." Vicky felt a little wistful. She wanted to find out who the nurse was, but then with a sigh she thought it really didn't matter. She was only a nurse. She was only doing her job. She did it well, but it was just a job.

"So did you pray with me while the angel of death was in here hoverin' over my bed?" Vicky asked thinking how familiar this man of God seemed to her. There was something about the way he moved his head when he spoke and how he tended to smile more out of the left corner of his mouth. His voice triggered some memory in her. This was someone she recognized from long ago. She was recalling the same person only younger.

"Yes, I prayed with you."

"Maybe that's why you look familiar. I wish I could remember."

"Your memory will come back."

"You seem to know a lot about this kind of thing. You're like me. You're a drunk too, aren't ya?" she found herself saying, not really stopping to think how he might react to the impertinence of such a question. Somehow she just knew.

"Yes, I am," he replied. "I've been sober eighteen years."

"What's your name?"

"Oh, I'm sorry. Didn't I tell you? I'm Father Mudd, the chaplain here at Mercy Hospital."

Vicky's memory riveted back some twenty something years ago to the time when, out of sheer ignorance and curiosity, she stumbled into the darkened confessional booth in the back of Holy Spirit Church where she'd gone to pray at a time of desperate searching in her life. And there was a much younger Father Mudd to whom she poured out her heart and soul and confessed with copious tears every terrible thing she'd ever done. She recalled how she smelled whiskey on his breath and how he seemed disheartened and unbelieving, almost bitter. She had more faith in what he was doing than he did. Yet he spoke of forgiveness and she begged him to say the words of forgiveness–what was it called–absolution? He told her he couldn't do that because she wasn't Catholic. She knelt at his feet and wept until finally he acquiesced. She remembered how he placed his hands on her head and pronounced her free of all that guilt. He forgave her for all the terrible things she'd ever done, though none of them were against him personally. He forgave her–and it was like God forgiving her. God forgave her through this tired, depressed, whiskey guzzling man. She felt forgiven when she left there, and somehow it gave her the strength and resolve to start anew, to change for a time.

Of course it didn't last. It never did. But she remembered. She asked him to baptize her that strange, cold, late afternoon around Christmas. He asked her to come back and talk to him about it some more. She waited too long she guessed because when she did return he was gone. Shipped off to rehab she was told.

"Father Mudd. Of course! I never forget a face."

"Have we met before?"

"You don't remember me, do ya? But then why should you? It was a long time ago; long around '83, '84."

Vicky told him the story, including the part about asking him to baptize her. She saw no evidence of realization dawning upon him as she recounted the details of their previous meeting. She frequently stopped and said, "Remember?" But he'd just apologize and shake his head. He appeared to be trying, almost straining to recall, like someone carefully going through the files in a filing cabinet again and again.

"You still don't remember me, do ya?"

"Please don't take it personally, Vicky. Sometimes I believe God protects the people I minister to by helping me forget their confessions."

"Yeah, well, mine wasn't your run of the mill confession. You know, you'd been drinking at the time. I know 'cause I smelled it on you. Maybe you were more shit-faced than you seemed. We drunks are good at that you know; looking sober when we ain't. Maybe you had a blackout."

"Maybe," was all he said shrugging his shoulders.

Vicky was hurt. She understood why he wouldn't recognize her after all those years. The alcohol had caused so much damage and disfigurement to her appearance. It had aged her well beyond her years. Still she thought certainly he would remember once she refreshed his memory. After all, how often does a priest have a non-Catholic stumble into confession and proceed to tell their life story?

"Maybe you do remember only you're thinking I couldn't possibly be the same person you're recalling. You're remembering some tall long legged red head with big hazel eyes and high cheekbones and a full set of teeth in her mouth instead of holes here and there. You're remembering someone young and strong; someone feisty with plenty of fight still left in her."

As Vicky spoke these word she realized she was sober—not drunk and not in the throes of withdrawal, or at least the worst of the withdrawal had subsided. She thought it interesting because she never felt good anymore; hadn't felt truly good in years. She didn't drink to feel good anymore. She drank simply not to feel at all. She couldn't remember what normal felt like. The last time she felt normal was for a brief period of about two and a half weeks last winter, following the time of her last hospitalization and withdrawal.

She wasn't impressed with normal. Everything was too real, too solid, too concrete, and too unmovable. Perhaps seeing something that wasn't actually there like the angel of death or the grey cyclone dust monster in the corner was actually preferable to all this reality. Time moved too slowly in the normal world, and every feeling and sensation experienced seemed heavy, crushing and oppressive. In this normal sober world it seemed that death was the only freedom from this long dark tunnel that one had to trudge through endlessly with never any light on the other side. In a word it all seemed hopeless. She turned her head away from Father Mudd as she felt the tears brimming in her eyes.

"I know that person is still in there; that tall red head ballsy enough to walk into a confession and pour out her guts to a total stranger," Father Mudd said, interrupting her thoughts.

"So what if that person is still in there? She couldn't have been that great. You didn't even remember her. So what the hell are you trying to say, anyway?"

"I'm saying you've got more fight in you than you know."

"Spare me the pep talk, reverend. I'm tired of fighting. That's why I did what I did."

"I don't buy it. You throw yourself in front of a lane of fast moving traffic at rush hour on the highway and you walk away still conscious with only minor injuries. Lucky for you the driver of that first car you caused to wreck saw you hop up on the guard rail and position yourself for a swan dive. He had quick enough reflexes to slam on the brakes, but still, you manage to collide with his front right bumper, get tossed several feet into the air, and land on concrete. You know what I see in that act?"

"I don't really care."

"I see lots of drama. Plenty of desperation and crying out for help. Plenty of futility, but underneath it all, some tiny little spark of hope. Underneath it all, a will to live."

"What are you talking about?"

"You know what you did after you landed on that hard concrete? You got up. You actually stood up on your own and tried to walk away. This is not someone who has no fight left in them. This is not some poor pitiful victim of life's tragic mishaps. This is someone strong and tough. This is a survivor."

"Who you calling a victim? I ain't no victim."

"I know you're not but you like to play the part. It gives you an excuse to drink. It gives you an excuse to run from reality and escape life's challenges. It gives you an excuse to keep yourself down, to hate yourself and kill yourself. Though you've chosen the slow painful method of suicide. Poor me, poor me..."

"Pour me another drink." Vicky and Father Mudd said this last line in unison.

"I heard it all before so spare me the sobriety pep talk," Vicky said.

"You know, victim-hood doesn't suit you," said Father Mudd. A nurse entered the room on the heels of his words.

"Hello," the nurse said, an all too cheerful and out of sync voice erupting awkwardly on this all too real world. "Just need to get your vitals," she said pulling out her equipment from the deep pocket of the colorful jacket that nurses wear nowadays. This one was particularly annoying. It had smiley stick people holding colorful balloons.

"Hello, Father Mudd. Happy Thanksgiving," she said running the digital thermometer across Vicky's forehead for a reading. The nurse listened to Vicky's chest, took her pulse and blood pressure while exchanging pleasantries with Father Mudd.

"So how are things?" Father Mudd asked the nurse as he motioned to Vicky. Vicky found that these nurses never told you what your vitals were unless you asked. And Vicky didn't ask because she didn't care.

"Everything looks good," the nurse said addressing Father Mudd and not her. If they did give you any information at all it was usually very vague and general, chock full of words like "fine" or "not so good".

"How's her blood pressure?"

"Good. Climbing back up there–ninety-five over sixty-five." The nurse left the room.

"Happy Thanksgiving," Vicky said sarcastically as the nurse made her exit. "So it's Thanksgiving today?" she said to Father Mudd. "You gonna preach me a sermon about all I have to be thankful for?"

"No, I'm through preaching."

"Excuse the poor pitiful victim while she has a good cry," Vicky said and rolled onto her side, away from Father Mudd and toward the wall. She sobbed and sobbed, unable to stop it, for what seemed like a long time. She thought for sure Father Mudd would leave but she knew he was still in the room. After a while he lightly touched her shoulder and, without a word, handed her some tissues. She wiped her face and got enough control of her emotions to roll back over and face him. He said nothing but only gave her a sympathetic look, the one she'd seen so often from social workers, counselors, and do-gooder volunteers in soup kitchen and shelters.

"Do they teach you that look in priest school? Do they set you in front of mirrors and say 'okay, boys, on the count of three knit your eyebrows together and pretend you're about to cry right along with your client?' "

She didn't know why but she really didn't want Father Mudd to leave and she thought maybe he sensed this. She just didn't want to be left alone. And so he didn't leave. He simply sat there waiting for her to retaliate with more sarcasm; waiting for her to give him an opening; waiting for some enlightenment; waiting for something, God knows what and Father Mudd probably didn't know himself.

"Why are you still here?" Vicky asked.

"Do you want me to leave?"

"I really don't care what you do."

"Perhaps it's better if I leave and come back later."

He put his hands on his thighs and pushed himself up from his seat with a tired sigh. Vicky noticed his hands. They looked less aged than his face. They looked the same as she remembered–strong, vital; almost rugged. They were steadier now than they had been.

"Father, you was right when you said I still got fight left in me." The priest stopped his trek toward the door and slowly turned around. He resumed his seat in the chair next to Vicky's bed.

"Go on," he prompted her.

"I got plenty of fight left. But I'm afraid..." Fr. Mudd said nothing. He had a way with silence; a way that broke through the awkwardness that two virtual strangers feel when alone in a room together with nothing to say. Vicky found his silence comforting. This was something about him that hadn't changed. Even with whiskey on his breath his silence was restful, in no hurry, waiting patiently for the other to share. He was of that rare breed of humans known as a good listener.

"I'm afraid to let all that fight out because it hurts people."

"Hurts people?"

"It destroys everything it touches," Vicky was sobbing again. "Opportunities, friendship, love, homes, even lives. I told you about this before when I went to confession but you don't remember so I might as well tell you again. I got in a fight with my Dad when I was seventeen, stormed outta the house, got in my car and drove. I was pissed off, reckless, going too fast. I hit a little boy on a bike and killed him. That's how I got this," she said touching the scar on her cheek. "Now do you remember me?"

"Yes. Now I do," Father Mudd said in his cool way, not gasping in startled recognition the way some people might have, but nonetheless, Vicky could see the final realization of who she was in his eyes.

"And you know what, Reverend? I got off Scot free. No one could prove I was speeding; or so I was told. My grandma had some pull in that little town. No charges were pressed."

"But you were forgiven."

"I thought I was–for a while. But then it kept coming back to me that I hadn't paid the price for it."

"So that's why you're killing yourself?"

Vicky heard his words though he said them in a low voice and a reflective sort of tone with his eyes fixed on some spot in mid-air and not on her, as if he was speaking more to himself.

"Maybe the price has already been paid," Father Mudd said looking at her this time.

"By who?"

"Whoever it is that keeps that spark of hope alive inside you and keeps fighting for you when you say you have no fight left."

"My Higher Power?" Vicky said as facetiously as she knew how.

"Maybe?"

"Yeah, right. I've heard it before, rev."

"Vicky, you asked me once to baptize you. Now I'm asking you. Do you want to be baptized?"

Vicky hesitated. For a moment she wondered if she should. And then she thought what difference would it make? Her mind quickly ran through all the people in her life she'd known who'd been baptized and were horrible human beings. It was just another one of her grandmother's superstitions.

"Get outta here, priest!" Vicky angrily lashed out at him.

"Just think about it," Father Mudd said completely unfazed as he stood up to leave.

"Don't you have a date with a little altar boy somewhere?"

This was the first time Vicky noticed a little chink in the armor of his cool façade. He spun back around on his heels. "I have spoken respectfully to you. You owe me the same courtesy."

"Ooh, I must've hit a nerve. What's wrong? A little too close to the truth?"

"I've done some pretty despicable things in my day but I'm not a pedophile."

"How do you know, rev? You're a drunk right? We drunks don't remember what we do when we're on a bender. What's wrong, rev? I thought you wanted to see a little fight in me again."

"I'm leaving now, but I want you to know you haven't succeeded in driving me away completely like I suspect you have most everyone else," he said regaining his composure. "I'm not giving up on you."

"Not giving up on me? What can you do for me? Besides baptize me!"

"I can forgive you for the verbal abuse and I can pray for you."

"You do that, reverend!" Vicky hollered out as he exited the room. "Holier-than-thou sack of shit!" she muttered as she rolled over to face the wall. She felt terrible and she didn't know what to do but cry and go back to sleep.

* * * * * * *

"Vicky," she heard the voice call her name just barely above a whisper. It was a man's voice. He said it again, this time a bit louder and clearer. It wasn't Father Mudd. She felt certain it wasn't him. She opened her eyes but saw no one; yet she knew someone was there standing behind the curtain which draped around her hospital bed. Certainly it wasn't a doctor or nurse or lab technician come to draw her blood. They would have yanked that curtain back without a moment's hesitation and commenced to poking and prodding as readily as a bullfrog takes to hopping. Perhaps it was a social worker who had come to talk about what they should do with her next. But no, any hospital personnel wouldn't have waited behind the curtain like this, so tentative and uncertain, so afraid of poking their head around the corner of the curtain lest they disturb her rest. Maybe it was some church volunteer here to do an act of charity for the poor alcoholic patient with no family, friends and no other visitors. Vicky exhaled a huff of contempt out through her nostrils for whoever it was disturbing her sleep and her only chance to escape this wretched reality. "Who is it?"

"It's Frank Hamilton, Vicky. Do you remember me?" the voice called tentatively from behind the curtain.

"Francis?"

"Yes. Francis. You don't have to see me if you don't want to. I just wanted you to know I heard you were here and if there's anything I can do to help…"

Before he could get the words out, Vicky reached over and pulled the curtain back. "Francis!" was all she could say as a new set of tears brimmed in her eyes. Yes, he was older but still so handsome and even more dignified with his salt and pepper hair. A rush of startled surprise raced through Vicky as strange old feelings resurfaced. Just the very sight of him was enough for that bitter-sweet pang of love to knot her stomach the same way it did over twenty years ago. Vicky was stunned, not only by the fact that he was there but by the unexpected reaction it stirred in her. She was still human, still alive, and could still feel something besides sick and depressed.

She was so caught off guard by Frank's presence that she almost forgot herself, almost reacted like the old impulsive Vicky who never held anything back, almost hopped out of bed and threw her arms around him. But then she remembered who she was, who he was, where she was, and the time, distance, and difference between them. She quickly covered her face with her hands.

"Oh, God, Francis! Don't look at me. I'm so ashamed. I'm so ugly."

"Would you rather I leave?" he said, ever the gentleman, wanting to be considerate, wanting to do the proper and gracious thing.

Vicky removed her hands from her face and made herself look at him. "What do you want to do, Francis?" She wanted to see his reaction. If he tried too hard to be polite then she'd know that he was uncomfortable and she'd throw him out herself.

"I want to stay," he said. He shook his head and tears came to his eyes. He pulled out a white linen handkerchief from his pocket, and as he unfolded it Vicky saw the finely stitched navy thread bearing his monogram.

"I see you still use those things. I think I still have one somewhere," she said trying to make light.

"Francis, for God's sake, don't pity me. I got enough of that around here; priests, nurses, social workers, candy stripers, the fucking cleaning lady; hell, I even pity myself. And you know what? It makes me sick. I hate all this pity. I guess I've gotten used to being a charity case, but oh, God, not from you! I don't want to be your charity case! I'm disgusted enough with myself but when you come in here with that look on your face, and pull out your hankie, and ask if you can do anything to help me; I just can't handle it."

"I don't pity you, Vicky. I'm angry at you," he said raising his voice. "I'm pissed off! How could you do this to yourself?"

She lowered her eyes from his gaze which was now searing into her. She had no reply for him other than to change the subject. "So how did you know I was here?"

"Allison and my son were in the accident."

"What accident?"

"The one you caused when you dove into traffic."

"Oh, God, tell me they're all right. Tell me they're not hurt bad."

"They're going to be fine. Allison broke a rib and, Alex, that's our fifteen year old son, he broke his nose. After the swelling goes down he'll have to have surgery to move the cartilage back into place, but he's going to be fine. Of course, he's pretty shook up. He was the one driving. He just got his permit."

"Were they the one's that hit me?" Vicky said startled and aghast.

"No, they were three cars back. You caused a five car pile-up, you know."

"I know. I'm sorry. I'm so sorry. I didn't mean to hurt anyone."

"What the hell did you think would happen, Vicky?"

"I was trying to kill myself, not no one else, I mean not anyone else," she said remembering herself, remembering her grammar, covering her mouth, remembering her toothless mouth and ugly face.

"And why? Why like that? So that some poor sucker would have to live the rest of his life with the hell of knowing he killed someone? You of all people, Vicky! You of all people. Why?"

"Okay, so it was stupid!" Vicky yelled. "It was stupid, and reckless, and thoughtless, and selfish just like everything else I've ever done. And I'd take it all back and make it up to everyone if I could. And I can see that now because I'm sober. I'm sober," she said, her hysterical tears dying down to a whimper. "I just can't seem to stay that way. I just can't get used to being sober. It's miserable. Of course, getting drunk and high ain't no fun anymore either, so I thought I'd try death. Stupid, ain't it? Just plain stupid!"

"Look, I didn't come here to make you feel worse. I just…" Frank blotted his eyes with the handkerchief and returned it to his pocket. "I just had to see you; had to offer help, somehow, some way, though I don't exactly know what I could do or how I could help. And it's not because I think of you as a charity case. It's just when you find out an old friend is in trouble, you feel like you need to do something."

"And how does Allison feel about you helping me?"

"I don't know. We split up."

"What?"

"We separated about ten months ago. It's not final yet but we're in the process of a divorce."

"Oh. I'm sorry," Vicky said. She could see the pain in those blue eyes that were still so expressive and she really was sorry. She didn't know she could still feel for someone else but she did and in a strange way it felt good, this connection. She could see in his face that this was a pain as deep and profound as her own addiction and the dregs to where it had brought her.

"I'm sorry about what I did at your wedding. Can you ever forgive me for that?"

"It's all water under the bridge as far as I'm concerned," Frank said with a shrug.

"Do you think Allison's forgiven me?"

"I don't know. We haven't talked about it in years. We haven't talked about much of anything in years."

"Pull up a chair, Francis," Vicky said, "if you can spare just a few more minutes, that is."

"Sure," Francis said in a soft low voice, and then he smiled at her as he pulled the chair up to her bedside. It was that same slight, subtle, tranquil smile that seldom showed any teeth; a smile both pleasing and sad at the same time. It completely disarmed her. Any bitterness she felt for him seemed to dissipate into the air like a vapor at the sight of his smile.

"Shit, I just can't stay mad at you," Vicky said laughing and crying at the same time.

"Why would you be mad at me, Vicky?"

"Because you broke my heart."

"*I* broke *your* heart? You're the one who left me. I didn't leave you."

"Yeah, but it was only a matter of time. I only did it first so you wouldn't have to. Figured it was easier on both of us that way. I mean, look at us Francis. Look at you! Look how handsome you still are. Look at that expensive suit you got on. And I see your shoes are still polished and your fingernails still perfectly trimmed. You're rich. You're successful. A businessman well respected, on this board and that committee–yeah, I read about you from time to time in the paper, either the business section or the social page. You're the kinda guy who raises money to help people like me.

"Now look at me. I'm a hopeless alcoholic. I got no home, no friends, no family, nothing. I pissed everything away. I don't even got my looks no more. I look twenty years older than you. Tell me how we would've ever made it together. Ain't no way. I spared us both a lot of heartache and you know it."

"Things didn't have to turn out this way for you Vicky."

"You think if I'd stayed with you this wouldn't have happened. I'm a drunk. I would've been a drunk no matter what. Booze is the one thing I loved more than you. But hell, even if I never touched another drop again we still wouldn't have made it. You're a blue blood, Francis, and I'm nothing but white trash."

"Maybe so. But there was something there. Something brought us together."

"Don't look at me like that Francis." Vicky turned her head and wept. He took her hand but only for a moment, and after giving it a reassuring pat, released it. She turned back around to face him.

He was holding back tears too. And yes, she could see it was for her, but it was for more than just that. It was for all the losses, disappointments, and heartbreaks along the way.

"Well, we still got one thing in common," Vicky said.

"What's that?"

"We're both miserable." And with that they laughed through their tears.

"Tell me about your kids," Vicky asked. "You got any pictures?"

Frank pulled out his wallet and let her look at his pictures, pointing out each of his children along the way and telling her about each one of them; their ages, where they were in school, their interests, and their personality quirks. Vicky could see that this made him happy. For a moment he forgot himself and his troubles and so did she. She noticed the coloring, facial features, and expressions of each one. She saw how much Matthew, their oldest, looked like Allison; how much their daughter looked like Frank, and how much Alex, their middle son seemed to be a combination of the two, though something in his expression was decidedly Frank's. These were the progeny of two people she loved so much, this was the future they would leave behind and she wondered as she looked at their smiling faces, just how broken they must be.

"You send that boy to me," Vicky said pointing to a picture of Alex. "I'll straighten his ass out. I'll tell him he better start minding you and his mama and stay in school or he'll end up like me."

"Who knows? Maybe it'd work. We've tried everything else," Frank said with a chuckle.

"I see you still got a few pictures of Allison in here."

"Yeah, well, she is the mother of my children."

"She's still as pretty as ever. Even prettier, I think. You still love her don't you?"

"I suppose so."

"Ain't no supposing about it. You still love her. I can see it on your face. Why'd you split up?"

"It's long and complicated. We've had problems for a long time."

"Oh," was all Vicky could say, seeing the pain and fatigue in his countenance, a fatigue so enervating that he didn't seem to have the strength to say anymore on the topic. Vicky could certainly understand that kind of fatigue

Their visit seemed to be coming to a close, with little or no real resolution and nothing much more to be said. But Vicky noticed the presence of two desires in her heart. She hadn't desired anything but alcohol in so long and now that that was gone she desired nothing; nothing that is, except maybe death which she was still too afraid of to want wholeheartedly.

Yet here it was two things to hope for: she wanted to see Allison and ask her forgiveness, and she wanted Frank to see something in her that he could still love. She knew the latter was impossible and she quickly dismissed the thought as soon as it entered her head. He had done the nice thing by coming to the hospital to see her, but it was all out of obligation and charity. But then she realized that that was all right. It didn't really matter if he had ever loved her or not. What mattered was that the desire to love and be loved were still there at some tiny molecular level within her being. It was just a spark, but it was there and it was igniting something like hope. She smiled in spite of herself, in spite of her self-consciousness.

"Thanks for coming, Francis. It was real nice of you. I just got one thing to ask before you leave."

"What's that?"

"Tell Allison I want to see her. I don't know how much longer I'll be here and I have no idea where I'm going once I get out, but I want to see her. Will you tell her that?"

"Sure." Frank reached inside his suit pocket, pulled out a pen and a small pad of paper and began writing on it. "In case they discharge you before I get a chance to talk to her, I'm going to give you her number and mine as well." He scribbled down the numbers and ripped the small piece of paper out of the note pad.

"I'll call you later this evening and see how you're doing," Frank said handing her the note.

"That ain't necessary."

"I know," he said putting his pen and the small pad of paper back inside his suit coat pocket. Then he did something surprising. He squatted down on his haunches by her bedside until he was eye level with her. "Goodbye, Vicky," he said looking her in the eye. He stroked her hair and he kissed her on her scarred cheek, his lips lingering there for sometime before completing the kiss.

Vicky was incredulous over this act. He had risked contamination by touching and even kissing the leprous creature. When he stood up his eyes glistened with emotion.

"Thank you, Francis," was all she could mutter.

He turned and was gone.

Chapter 35
Allison

She had an image of Adam being formed by the dust of the earth like in the book of Genesis. God's hands scooped up bits of dry dirt, moistening it with his own saliva, molding and sculpting it until it began to take form. Then he breathed on the creation and the clay figure turned to flesh, as animation filled its once lifeless form. Then she saw God's large hand over the man, putting him in a deep sleep, opening up his side, the first surgery you might say; only there was no violence. In fact, it was so tender no blood was even shed. He simply waved his hand and a flap of skin obediently opened up and folded back of its own accord. Then gently and carefully the large hand reached in and removed a rib. She watched with the unquestioning nonchalance of a dreamer as the skillful hands of God took that rib and formed Eve.

And then she felt pain which began to draw her out of the dream and into the semi-conscious world of the not quite awake, yet no longer asleep. She reached an arm across the bed hoping to awaken Frank, and then she slowly became conscious and realized Frank was gone. He'd been gone for nearly ten months but she still sometimes woke up thinking he was there beside her.

Another surge of pain. At first Allison thought she was having a heart attack, but then she realized the pain was on her right side. She was told to lie on this side, the side with the broken rib, so that the lung on the uninjured side could do more of the work getting air in and out; but the pressure on that wounded site was enough to cause pain that would awaken her. Some nights she would roll onto the uninjured side to relieve the pressure, but then it hurt every time she breathed. She was sure to wake herself up every hour to take a deep breath and cough, something prescribed by her physician to ensure that she would not suffer pneumonia or a partial collapse of the lungs. Sometimes she woke up frightened, struggling for air, certain that she could feel her lungs collapsing. She could visualize them deflating in her mind like two big beach balls that somebody let the air out of, slowly sinking until they were a flat wrinkled mass of plastic. She tried to go without the pain medication, and during the day she could, but not at night. Ultimately it was Tylenol with codeine that granted her a brief merciful reprieve from the pain, anxiety and lack of sleep.

She looked at the clock–2:57 AM, her usual middle of the night awakening time. Only this morning she couldn't afford to take any Tylenol with codeine because it would knock her out and it would be too difficult to get up again in just a few hours. It was Monday morning and she had to get the kids off to school. They were back with her this week. Frank took them last week to help her out after the accident. But now she had to get back to her life and back to her job. She couldn't afford to take any more sick days, especially not now, not while she was still new and still on this learning curve with the job. There was only one way she could forget about the pain and the unbidden thoughts of air being squished out of old rubber, maroon basketballs that caused her to clutch her chest and obsess about breathing. She had to get up and move around. There was something else she had to do today, she had to go visit Vicky in the hospital.

Frank confirmed what she already knew, that it was none other than Vicky Lee Dooley who caused the accident, and that she was very sick, in the hospital, maybe dying, and that she asked to see her. Ever since then she felt compelled by some unknown force, something unfinished, some sense that if there was such a thing as fate, that it must be required of her to go see Vicky. And so it was with great apprehension and dread that she would do it, but do it, she must.

Allison moved slowly and painfully through the hospital lobby. She held on tight to the small spider plant she bought for Vicky and tried not to look at her distorted reflection in the shiny metallic helium balloon that was tied around the plastic planter. Her upbringing had taught her that one should never show up empty handed when visiting someone, be it in their home or the hospital. It was the thoughtful thing to do, but in this case, maybe it was something more than that. Maybe by the mere fact of offering Vicky something tangible, something pleasant, she could put some kind of buffer between them, some sort of guilt offering into which Allison could place all the years of silent resentment towards Vicky and all the helplessness she now felt over her inability to do anything to change the situation.

She had a hard time deciding what to get Vicky. What exactly do you get for someone who no longer has anything and no place in which to take anything? And then she remembered. Allison knew something that Vicky had no way of knowing… the whereabouts of one remaining possession which had once belonged to Vicky. Only Allison and one other person knew about it.

She traveled back in her memory, back to Camelot, back to Vicky's small corner apartment on the ground floor of building 3300. She could see the rocking chair, the worn sofa with the afghan her grandma had made thrown over the back, the velvet painting that hung on the wall of the Native American warrior who looked like Mr. Universe, and in the middle of it all, the cedar hope chest. There it was in her memory, the hope chest, atop of it was a large glass ashtray with a still smoldering cigarette perched on the side. Next to that sat those coasters, the ones made from the cork-like material with beer ads embossed upon them. The old cork coasters sat there like dutiful friends, catching the condensation of melting ice from glasses half filled with brown watered down liquid. The rocking chair swayed slightly back and forth as if someone had just gotten out of it. There was the scene so clear in her mind, yet the chairs were empty, the room desolate, like an abandoned ghost town. But there in the center was that hope chest which now belonged to Sally.

* * * * * * *

    The timing of Sally's phone call some nine and a half months ago seemed an odd coincidence at the time. Allison really hadn't kept in touch with Sally, though they still sent each other Christmas cards and ran into one another from time to time at social events. Sally never married again and never had the children that she so hoped for, but she had done well for herself in the community. She sold the family dry cleaning business and got her real estate license. Allison was accustomed to seeing Sally's larger than life, caricature-like face on signs in front of people's yards. She chuckled to herself sometimes when she passed those signs, thinking how perfect it was that Sally was in the business of going in and out of people's homes. But everyone knew Sally and respected her for her community and civic contributions.
    How strange it was, Allison thought in retrospect, that nine months ago she would receive that call from Sally out of the clear blue. She always wondered if Sally's busy-body-ness gave her some sort of psychic edge whereby she intuitively knew when something was about to happen. At the time she wondered if somehow Sally knew that she and Frank were in the process of separating. But how could she know that? Not even the kids knew it at the time. They thought their Dad was away on a business trip that week and had no idea he was in town staying in a hotel, looking for another place to live. His clothes and most of his belongings were still at the house. Tim was the only person who knew because he was their lawyer. But that was confidential. Surely Tim hadn't said anything to Sally.
    That was another strange thing; Tim was back in their lives again. They bumped into him that night after the symphony. Then what about later that night? There was the encounter with the drunken woman begging for money out in the cold as she and Frank walked to their car. The woman who deep down Allison knew was Vicky, but at the time she tried to rationalize that it couldn't be; just someone who reminded her of Vicky. The Camelot she and Frank knew was crumbling, but at the same time all of the original people from their fairy tale Camelot were resurfacing.

She remembered that phone call and how after chatting with Sally for a while, Allison was satisfied that she knew nothing about her and Frank planning to split. Sally said she hadn't seen Tim or anybody from the old Camelot days in the longest time, "but here's the thing of it," Sally said in her half whisper just like she'd always done when she wanted to inspire curiosity in another. And then she went on to tell her she'd been antiquing, her new hobby, and she ran across Vicky's hope chest in an antique shop.

"It was unmistakably hers," Sally said. "You remember? The one she used as a coffee table?" Sally had said.

"Yes, I remember."

"I swear it still has the ring on it from the one time Tim sat his glass down without a coaster. Remember? She had us all over for dinner I guess in an attempt to kiss up so we'd quit complaining about her to Louise."

"Louise! That was the landlady's name. I was trying to think of it not long ago and I couldn't recall it to save my life."

"Remember that night? Remember how much wine we drank? That girl really knew her wine."

"Huh?" Allison had said. For a moment Sally's voice was only background noise whose words had no real meaning. She was remembering the scene, and she was thinking about the drunken woman she'd seen on the street, wondering if it could be, if it could really be…

"Remember how pissed off she got at Tim for setting that glass down without a coaster? It was so crazy! She was so anally retentive about that damn hope chest. The rest of her apartment was like a pigsty, but she kept that thing cleared of clutter and dusted, treated it like crowned jewels. Poor Vicky! It was the only thing of value she owned. It really is a beautiful piece of furniture."

"It had sentimental value too. It was her grandmother's. Her great-grandfather made it for her grandmother as a wedding gift."

"That's right! I remember. Wasn't she almost superstitious about it? Like she thought bad luck would befall her if she opened it?"

"Somehow she felt she didn't have the right. Her grandmother kept some things in there. Vicky never knew what exactly. She thought that maybe they were intended to be wedding gifts for her someday. I can't imagine her ever parting with it. Are you sure it's Vicky's?"

"I'm positive. It's got traces of some kind of gummy, sticky substance right on the side where she had that stupid bumper sticker. Remember the one?"

"Real Women Ride Harleys," they both said in unison and then they chuckled. It was a sad chuckle; the kind that ends with a sigh, the kind that leaves questions hanging in the air after it's over, the kind that occurs when remembering something funny about someone who's died.

"I never could figure out how she could be so picky about setting a glass down on it without a coaster, yet she goes and puts a bumper sticker on the side."

"That's Vicky for you."

"But here's the thing," Sally said again in that gossipy hushed tone. "There's still stuff in it."

"What? Are you sure about that?"

"Most definitely. The antique dealer told me, plus you can feel it in there shifting around when you lift it. It's not completely full or anything and I'm fairly certain it's nothing hard or breakable. It's like cloth or material, maybe sheets or blankets, something like that."

"Why would an antique dealer sell a chest that still has someone's personal belongings in it?"

"He said it came that way. It's still locked and he never got a key. I asked him who he bought it from. He said he bought it from another dealer. He said he has no way of knowing who the original owner is but whoever it was they must've given him permission to sell it, contents and all. He said he had a locksmith try and open it, but the lock was too old and it couldn't be done without breaking it or damaging it somehow. He said he didn't want to do that because it was such a beautiful, well crafted piece of furniture; said ultimately that should be the buyer's decision, whether or not they wanted to break the lock and replace it with something new."

"Oh, my gosh! This is all so weird," Allison said thinking of the drunken woman on the streets and wondering if it really could be Vicky.

"So anyway, my question is do you have any idea what ever happened to Vicky?"

Allison did a quick debate in her mind as to whether or not she should tell Sally about the drunken woman on the street that she and Frank encountered a few weeks back. She decided not to since it probably wasn't Vicky anyway. "I have no idea. I haven't seen her since my wedding; and you know how that went." Allison replied, her final words quivering as a lump lodged in her throat and tears welled up in her eyes

"Oh, my God, remember? What a fiasco! I felt so bad for you and Frank. Wasn't that just like Vicky though, to go and do something stupid like that?"

"Yes, unfortunately it was," Allison said blinking back the tears and feeling the bitter irony of that incident with Vicky at her wedding. A cynical chuckle escaped her lips as she thought of what a fittingly bad omen it turned out to be. "She really showed her true colors that day. I never wanted to have anything to do with her after that."

"Well, I figured it was a long shot but if anyone knew you would."

"So what are you going to do about the chest?"

"I don't know. I guess just leave it for now. If I decide to break the lock I'll let you know."

"That's not necessary."

"No, I want you to be there if I ever open it. I don't know why exactly, it just seems like somebody from the old days ought to be there. You never know, there might be something valuable in it."

There wasn't much more to the conversation after that. They exchanged pleasantries about Frank and the kids and Sally's most recent community projects. Allison was anxious to get her off the phone before she broke down and sobbed and completely spilled everything about Frank moving out. She ached to pour out her heart to somebody, but Sally was definitely not the person and now was not the time.

* * * * * * *

The lady at the information desk looked up Vicky's room number for Allison. The lady peered intently at the computer screen over the top of thick framed glasses that were perched on the tip of her nose, her eyes roving quickly back and forth, her hand moving the mouse and clicking until at last she found the information she was seeking. She glanced up at Allison and said something about Vicky having been moved. Allison watched as the lady efficiently but discreetly, with a steady and flowing hand wrote down the name of the patient and the room number on a card.

"She's in the Intensive Care Unit now. That's on the second floor," the lady said handing the card to Allison.

"Intensive Care Unit? What happened?"

The lady behind the desk glanced at her over the top of her thick framed glasses and shrugged. She had the curious smile of someone secretly annoyed; as if she was terribly wearied with questions she couldn't answer, such as the medical status of every patient in the hospital.

"I'm sorry. Could you tell me how to get there again?" Allison inquired, still taking in the shock of the news that Vicky was in ICU. When she spoke with Frank the night before he said she was doing much better, that they were going to keep her a couple more days just for observation and that a social worker was working out all the arrangements to have her moved to a half-way house. What could've gone wrong?

The lady behind the desk gave her directions to the ICU and Allison listened with the heightened alertness of those who must respond to a sudden emergency. She felt a surge of adrenaline, a vigilant sort of feeling. It was the same feeling she had a few years ago when her grandmother was admitted to the hospital right before she died. She didn't know why she would have this feeling for Vicky, someone who only touched upon her life for a very brief period, someone whom she hadn't seen in twenty years, someone with whom she had nothing in common and didn't even like anymore. But all the same, she was strangely grateful for this feeling because it made her visit seem more purposeful somehow, less obligatory. She was able to focus on the present while in this state and that's precisely what she needed to do; for whatever the reason was that brought her there.

The Intensive Care waiting room was an area walled off by glass. Although it had the institutional looking carpet, wallpaper, wall hangings, and upholstered chairs in soothing colored fabric of slate blue with wooden arms and legs, it bore the overall feel of a place more lived in than the rest of the hospital. Chairs were pushed together and in the corner was a loveseat with blankets draped over it. Next to the loveseat was a couch on which lay a tired looking woman of about sixty, her head propped on two pillows with pink bedroom slippers on her feet. The sound of voices in dialogue blared a bit too loudly from a television affixed to the wall. The woman on the couch with the pink slippers stared sleepily and hypnotically at the TV screen, the light from which alternately dimmed and brightened upon her face. A few others sprinkled here and there throughout the room were sitting in chairs, most of them looking as if they'd been there too long, in wrinkled clothes with blankets wrapped around them, either sprawled with heads back and legs stretched out or curled up with shoes off and socked feet. Half drunken coffee cups, water bottles, and pop cans sat on end tables next to a deck of cards, magazines, and newspaper sections. One man was typing on his laptop, his suit coat flung over the back of his chair, his tie loosened to one side, and his dress shoes untied and loosened. Allison felt out of place, like an outsider walking into the middle of a family gathering.

She saw what appeared to be a reception desk in the corner but no one was there. Next to the desk were large heavy double doors that opened automatically at the push of a button. A sign outside the doors read, "Visiting Hours–Every Even Hour–8:00 AM to 8:00 PM–On the hour for 30 minutes. Please sign in before visiting." Allison looked at the foreboding double doors and understood. They were wide enough to get a gurney through. Suffering went on behind those doors, suffering and death and lives hanging in the balance somewhere between.

Allison looked at her watch. It was 12:35 PM. She'd missed the visiting hour. What was she to do? She couldn't get away from work until after 12:00. *What would Vicky do if it was me in there and her out here? She would just march right through those doors, regardless of any signs or rules,* Allison thought. She smiled to herself. Vicky used to call herself a renegade. There were obvious advantages to being a renegade. *What's the worst they could do? Ask me to leave. I could always feign ignorance,* Allison tried to tell herself, one hand holding on to the plant, the other hand reaching out for the door. Certainly distraught loved ones entered the unit without seeing the sign or because there was no one there to stop them and their only instinct was to see that loved one. If it was one of her children in there, nothing would stop her from pulling that door open.

She was just about to open the door when she caught a sudden glimpse of her reflection on the shiny metallic side of the helium balloon. The distortion of the reflection seemed to exaggerate the expression of fear; an expression that no one but the wearer of that expression might read. The reluctance to open that door really didn't have anything to do with breaking the rules. She pulled her hand away from the handle of the right double door; that large steel handle which was only one mere grasp, click and push away from entering the unknown.

Oh, well, she had missed visiting hours. At least she tried. She would come back some other time, but what to do with the plant. Should she leave it on the unattended desk with a note asking that it be delivered to Vicky Dooley. She decided to do just that and was writing Vicky's name on a piece of note paper when she heard a young woman's voice call out to her.

"She'll be back in a minute," the voice said.

Allison turned around and in one of the chairs she saw a young woman in her early twenties curled up in the fetal position, her feet on the seat of the chair, with a blanket draped around. It was indeed a cold day and Allison noticed the temperature in the hospital was a bit chilly, even with her coat on she felt the chill in the hospital. She remembered from her grandmother's illness and death how the hospital invariably seemed cold; particularly for those visitors like the ones she saw here who spent most of their time sitting and waiting, moving about only minimally. The young woman who called out to Allison looked like a caterpillar in its cocoon. She was so tightly wrapped in the blanket that the only visible parts of her were the upper portion of her face (from the tip of her nose to the top of her head) and her feet which were covered by worn, dingy socks.

"Pardon me?" Allison said in response to the girl in the blanket.

"The receptionist. She'll be back in a minute."

"Oh, well, thank you, but I really can't wait," Allison said looking at her watch. "Looks like I just missed the visiting hour and I really have to get back to work. I just wanted to leave this plant for one of the patients."

"She might still let you go back. They're not that strict about the visiting hours."

Allison was about to say something when the heavy double doors opened behind her, startling her. A lady carrying a clipboard came out, immediately spotted Allison and asked if she could help her.

"I told you she'd be back," the young woman wrapped in the blanket cocoon interjected before Allison had a chance to reply. "I was just showing this newcomer the ropes, Gracie. She was looking a little lost," the young woman called out from her blanket cocoon to the lady whom Allison guessed to be the receptionist.

The most prominent thing about the receptionist seemed to be her clipboard, which she held onto like an archangel with a fiery shield, ready at any moment to lift it up in protection of all the sick in her charge. The next thing she noticed was the laminated identification tag which the woman wore clipped onto her collar. Allison did a quick comparison with the picture on the identification tag and the woman's face. The picture looked different than the real face. So often that seemed to be the case, Allison thought. Next to the picture was the woman's name in black bold letters: Grace Courier. Later, all Allison would remember about the ICU receptionist was her name. She would try to recall her face, but no real image would come to mind; just a shadow carrying a clipboard and an identification tag with an indiscernible picture above the one thing that stood out about the woman: her name. How strange, Allison would later think, that most acquaintances faces were remembered but not their names. With Grace it would be just the reverse.

"I was just going to leave this plant for one of the patients, Vicky Dooley," Allison said in response to the receptionist's offer to help. She realized she hadn't signed the small card that was affixed to three purple plastic prongs on the end of a long purple plastic stick which emerged out of the soil of the plant.

"Oh, just a moment, let me sign this card then I'll be on my way." Allison pulled the square shaped envelope off the prongs and pulled the card out which read 'Get Well Soon' in fancy cursive on the top. Allison bent over the receptionist desk, with pen in hand, trying to decide what to write; just a short message to be sure, there wasn't room on the small card for much more than a line or two.

She finally just decided to sign the small card: Sincerely, Allison. It already said 'Get Well Soon' and there was nothing more she had to say to Vicky. Sure it was impersonal and perhaps not truly sincere but social prominence dictated one occasionally stoop to little white lies in order to maintain the image of a gracious lady. And so she signed the card in her perfectly pretty, curly lettered cursive hand. She wrote Vicky's name on the small envelope, enclosed the card, and presented it to Grace Courier.

"Would you see to it she gets it," Allison said, feeling something urging her to leave as fast as she could, something as certain and compelling as the force that had brought her there in the first place. "I'll try to come back later when I have more time."

"You can visit her if you like," Grace Courier said. "She hasn't had any other visitors since she was brought here this morning."

"But I thought visiting hours were over, and besides, I really need to get back to work."

"We do make exceptions, particularly for those that…" Grace hesitated. Allison knew what she was going to say… *for those that have no one.*

"For those patients with very few visitors," Grace finally said looking Allison in the eye as if to make her understand the real meaning behind her words. "Are you a friend?"

"I was. I mean, we used to be friends. We haven't seen each other in over twenty years."

"I think she really could use a visitor if you can spare just a few minutes," Grace Courier persisted, much to Allison's astonishment. Everything seemed topsy-turvy about this visit. When her grandmother was in ICU it was like trying to get past the Gestapo to get in to see her, now here was this woman practically begging her to go in for a visit. "Uh…" was all Allison could say in reply. Not very eloquent for a former Toastmaster and graduate of Dale Carnegie but her wit always seemed to fail her when she was caught off guard like now. She spent the entire morning psyching herself up to see Vicky and now she'd just psyched herself out of it (which hadn't taken nearly so long). She looked at her watch and mumbled something about the time and getting back to work. The thought came to her that perhaps now really would be the best time because it would have to be a short visit in order for her to get back to work on time.

"I can only stay for five minutes."

"That's fine. We encourage short visits up here so the patients don't get too worn out."

"Are you sure it's all right?" Allison asked.

"Listen honey, I have a knack for knowing when a patient needs company more than they need rest. I don't know what that poor gal's situation is but I get the feeling she's got nobody. I just came from back on the unit and they said she was conscious and asking if there'd been anybody by to see her. Last I heard they were still trying to get a hold of her next of kin but they weren't having any luck."

"I don't believe she has any next of kin."

"Hmmm, they said something about a brother out west."

"Brother? No, she's an only child."

"Step brother then, or maybe brother-in-law. I can't remember exactly, but I know there is one male relative."

Allison thought that sounded plausible. Maybe she'd married at some point and did in fact have a brother-in-law.

"Oh, well, you get on back there. Don't worry! They know nobody gets past me without my blessing," Grace Courier said with a wink as she made a playful shooing gesture with her clipboard.

Allison stared at the double doors. Anxiety and apprehension stiffened every muscle in her body. She felt it particularly in her throat; the sensation of a tight hard knot lodged between the pharynx and esophagus. She swallowed hard. She wished she had some water to wash the feeling away. She turned around to ask Grace how to get to Vicky's room. Grace was gone. Who knows where? Perhaps Grace's pager went off and she had to run down the hall to head off the frantic family members of a loved one brought up from the emergency room; those desperate relatives who fretted, cried, or prayed openly while following behind a fast moving gurney wheeled by medical personnel calling out commands to one another in terse, no-nonsense tones, their sights focused on a single goal: to get them safely to ICU where dwelt the one hope of life.

Or maybe it wasn't anything nearly so dramatic that caused Grace's disappearance. Perhaps she just discreetly slipped into the corner of the waiting room where she changed the linen on pillows, propped up cushions on the sofa, or made a fresh pot of coffee. Time moves at two polar opposite speeds around ICU: with the breakneck urgency of those responding to a life or death crisis, or the tiresome standstill of those who can do nothing but wait. Grace had moved on to either one time zone or the other. Allison's eyes scanned the waiting room but she didn't see Grace. Not surprising. It wasn't well lit in the waiting room and Allison's vision had dimmed over the years. With a long quivering sigh, Allison resigned herself to the inevitable. There was only one thing left to do. Go through those double doors and find Vicky.

Vicky's nurse explained that she began to take a turn for the worse the previous night. She said it was one of those things where they could look back and see that it was coming, but at the time, who knew? The nurses had a hard time waking her up yesterday. That was the first clue the nurse told Allison. Hepatic encephalopathy begins to show itself with day/night sleep reversal and decreased responsiveness. Like all things with Vicky, it happened fast. It could have been any number of complications from the liver disease that triggered it, or it could have been hastened by the medication they administered to get her through withdrawal. Had they not caught it and begun treating it when they did, she could have gone into a coma and died.

"Encephalopathy? I don't know much about medical things but I do know that has something to do with brain disease," Allison said as she and Vicky's nurse walked down the long corridor of the unit lined with alcoves, thinly partitioned, where lay the sick and dying, all exposed with sliding glass doors open for easy monitoring and quick access.

"Right," the nurse said in response. They had stopped in between two alcoves and Allison tried her hardest to focus on the nurse's words but she was distracted by the beeping and humming noises from life support machines, the sound of nurses conversing, and worst of all, the cry of a patient moaning in pain.

"I'm sorry, could you repeat that," Allison said, trying to tune out not just the sounds but the disturbing sights and smells as well.

"Her liver can no longer break down toxic substances like ammonia, so what happens is these substances begin to accumulate in the blood and travel directly to the brain and central nervous system. It's a very serious condition." The nurse, who seemed to be of the older more experienced variety of RNs, explained in a clear concise manner.

They were still stopped between two alcoves and during the course of the conversation Allison realized that one of these beds was Vicky's. She glanced at the card with the room number on it–2013. *Of course Vicky would get something with the number 13,* Allison morbidly mused to herself. *Nothing but bad luck.* She looked over her right shoulder and there was room 2013. All Allison could see was a shape that, at passing glance seemed startlingly small, almost as if it was a child. She looked again just long enough for her mind to get a snapshot of the image: a frail form, spidery atrophied legs that stretched out from under a gown and long unkempt hair spread out on the pillow, once a lovely auburn color, now a drab grey, terribly thinned and completely robbed of any former body and luster. The head on the pillow was turned away so the face couldn't be seen from where Allison stood outside the alcove. Judging from what she could see Allison was relieved. She didn't want to see the face. Just the quick snapshot image she'd taken in at a glance was enough of a shock.

"How is she?"

"Better, still disoriented but a bit more alert and responsive; not quite so groggy which is definitely a good sign. She's not out of the woods yet. She's due to have another dose of Neomycin in about an hour," she said looking at her watch. "That's an antibiotic that stops the intestinal bacteria from converting protein into ammonia," the nurse went on to explain. "She's responded pretty well so far so we'll see how she does."

Allison wanted to ask the nurse if she would go in with her, just at first, just until Vicky was aware she was there, but she was shy about asking. It was strange to Allison that she felt this way. She had long since overcome all that awkward shyness and lack of confidence from her fat school girl days. She had learned to be confident, assertive, comfortable with anyone, not afraid to ask for what she needed... until the break up of her marriage. That old awkwardness she hadn't felt since she was a kid strangely crept back into her life. She stuttered and stammered and tripped over her words at times. It made her feel so ashamed, so angry with herself.

The nurse, perhaps sensing Allison's reluctance, stepped into the alcove just ahead of her.

"Vicky, you have a visitor," she said in that higher than usual, sing-song pitch that nurses so frequently acquire when addressing certain patients. It was the same tone that nearly everyone on the nursing home staff used to speak to her grandmother. It seemed to Allison a condescending tone and cadence; one so often taken with the elderly, children, or the simple-minded, none of which Vicky was.

Allison was still so focused on the nurse and her hopes that she wouldn't just leave her there alone, that she really hadn't looked at Vicky yet. She avoided it, but now she knew she had to. Slowly she turned toward the bed.

Chapter 36

Seeing Vicky up close like this triggered a sudden physical weakness in Allison that ran from her thighs up to her chest and back down again. She feared for a moment that her knees would buckle. Usually she wasn't the type to get swoony. In fact she could only recall two other incidents where she was similarly affected.

Once when Alex cracked his head open after jumping from the sofa to the loveseat and crashing into the wall. Allison remained calm at the time as her injured son soaked one dishtowel after another with blood while they waited for the ambulance. It was when she noticed bone sticking out, the sudden shocking glimpse of his skull at the site of the injury, that she reacted so violently. The other time was when she was just a kid and she saw Alfred Hitchcock's classic The Birds on TV. It was the sight of a dead man with two gaping wide hollows where his eyes had been pecked out.

Vicky's eyes were open but they might as well have been lifeless gaping hollows inside the gaunt sagging face. Her color was a pallid grayish-yellow, the color of a four day old bruise beginning to heal. Her body was an odd mix of shrunk and swollen, with emaciated limbs sticking out of a bloated trunk, like toothpicks stuck in a potato. Allison was not at all sure she would've recognized her at this point. Nine and a half months ago on the street there was still something there of Vicky that she recognized, but not now. She tentatively stepped a bit closer to the bed, still afraid to touch her, afraid of getting tangled up in the tubing that seemed so intricately attached to her, tubing that pumped life-giving fluid and oxygen into Vicky's body.

"Hello, Vicky. It's Allison. Remember me?" Allison said, wondering if her voice was too chirpy and sing-song, too loud and condescending.

"Hello," was all Vicky said in a groggy, croaky, weak, and unfamiliar sounding voice.

"I brought you something," Allison said. "It's a plant. I know how you love plants. You always had such a green thumb." Allison put the plant down on a bedside table, and for a brief moment Vicky's eyes tracked the movement of the helium balloon attached to the plant.

The nurse busied herself with changing the IV bag. She made a remark that she would finish up and leave them alone to visit. Allison let her know she didn't have to hurry.

"Remember me from Camelot?" Allison said turning her attention back to Vicky.

"Camelot," Vicky said without expression so that Allison didn't know if it was a question, an affirmation that she remembered, or merely a meaningless poly-parrot repetition of what Allison had just said.

"Yes. Camelot, remember? We lived there a long time ago. We were neighbors. We lived in the same apartment building. You lived downstairs. I lived upstairs." Allison felt more comfortable moving a bit closer to the bed.

"Vicky," the nurse said fixing her attention on the patient. "Can you tell me what day it is?"

"Sunday?" Vicky said in a voice so weak you had to strain to hear her.

Pity began to stir in Allison. Here was someone who once spoke her mind so fearlessly and without hesitation in a voice that could always be heard. Now her listeners were straining to hear her tentative uncertain response.

"What's the date? Do you know what month it is? What year? When is your birthday? What's your social security number?"

Vicky's responses were poor attempts at guessing followed by nervous little chuckles of embarrassment, like what a naughty child might do when caught in a lie. The nurse made brief eye contact with Allison just long enough to give a slight frown and shake her head, a sure signal that this was not good. The nurse made a humorous but somewhat patronizing remark to Vicky about her inability to remember, but then said something about at least she was awake and that was a good sign. The word awake was not the most accurate description of Vicky's state, more like semi-conscious. Her eyelids drooped and seemed about to shut entirely.

"Don't go to sleep on me. We need to give you some more medicine in about ten minutes," the nurse said in that chirpy, sing-song, too loud of a voice that Allison knew Vicky would never put up with if she weren't so sick.

"Not that stuff that makes me crap!" Vicky muttered the words through a thick tongue, yet coherently enough to be understood. It was only there for a moment then it was gone again; but just for that moment, Allison thought she caught a glimpse of the Vicky she once knew in the distorted features.

"No, not this time," the nurse said in regard to Vicky's comment. "We're going to give you another dose of Neomycin. That's the antibiotic, not the laxative."

The nurse turned back to Allison and said in a lower more normal tone of voice, "We had to give her Lactulose, to get some of those toxins out of her intestines."

"Do you need to use the bedside commode?" the nurse asked Vicky.

"No," Vicky moaned, her voice returning to the timid, weak, scratch of a voice.

For the first time since Allison arrived at the hospital her injury from the accident started to hurt. She'd almost forgotten about it.

"Are you all right, hon?" asked the nurse who picked up on Allison's discomfort, despite her attempts at hiding it.

"I've got a cracked rib. The pain kind of comes and goes," Allison said, allowing herself to wince now that the nurse knew.

"So what happened to you?"

"Car accident. I got in a fight with an airbag and the airbag won." It was an over-used and tiresome response to the question, and it wasn't all that funny to begin with, but Allison didn't know what else to say when people inquired about her injury.

"Oh, my! Here sit down," the nurse said pulling out a chair from the corner"

"Seat belts are a great invention, but I'm beginning to think airbags are overkill," Allison said as she sat down slowly and carefully so as not to exacerbate the pain.

"Thank you," Allison said to the nurse; then with a nod of assurance she whispered, "You can go now." Maybe it was the pain that distracted her, but whatever the reason, Allison finally felt brave enough to be alone with Vicky. The nurse departed.

"We're a real pair," Allison said to Vicky as she tried to sit up straight and take a deep breath.

"Cracked rib," Vicky said with a deliberate look, a look meant to communicate something though Allison wasn't sure just what. "Sorry," Vicky said, seeming to use every ounce of energy to get the idea across. Vicky was in there and this seemed to be an intentional apology. She was fighting now, fighting to get back to the conscious world of thought and awareness, like someone trying desperately to stay awake during a boring lecture, or even more urgent, behind the wheel after highway hypnosis sets in.

"Frank told you we were in the accident, didn't he?" Allison said, still uncertain if Vicky even recognized her.

"Yes," Vicky strained to get the words out.

"I think you're trying to tell me you're sorry. Am I right?"

"Yes."

The humane side of Allison was stirred, the part of her that in her youthful naiveté used to pull for the underdog. But pity was not the only emotion tugging at her. The same buried resentment, as rotting and festering as her dead dreams, kept trying to claw its way out of its grave, like some undead ghoul from a B horror movie. She tried to keep it down but it was an unusually strong and vengeful monster.

Sure it was about her personal history with Vicky, but there was also a deep-seated, more justified anger for anyone like Vicky who had allowed their lives to become such a mess without taking any responsibility. These people were the parasites of society and it made her furious that Vicky allowed herself to become such a person. Vicky had probably exhausted the resources of every charitable organization in this city. She knew Vicky just enough to know how this sickness had most likely progressed. She used and abused the system, she lied and she conned everyone who came across her path, with her good intentions and resolve for change weakening with each passing day until only a self-serving instinct for survival remained.

Yet still Vicky suffered. Was it right to kick her while she was down already? The two conflicting emotions wrestled with one another over the excruciatingly slow seconds that followed, while Vicky lay silent and waiting. The internal wrestling match had been going on since that night in the emergency room when Allison first realized it was Vicky in the alcove next to her.

What the hell, Allison reasoned, as her eyes burned and her throat tightened into a hard knot of resolve. Her zombie monster could use a little airing out.

"You always thought you could get off just by saying you were sorry. How dare you, Vicky!" Allison's words erupted through a sudden unrestrained burst of tears. "It's not enough for you to ruin your own life, but you have to go and spread all your hurt and misery to others.

"I suppose I could forgive you for ruining my wedding day, for publicly humiliating me and making me out to be the evil other woman who stole your man when you know damn good and well there was never anything between Frank and me until after you left. I guess I could forgive you for casting a pall over the first weeks, no months of my marriage, so that all I could do was doubt Frank's love for me, forgetting the fact that it was you who left Frank, not Frank who left you. So after you just walk out on him with nothing left behind but a note stuck under his door, without even the guts to explain face to face, who do you think was there to pick up the shattered pieces? Huh Vicky? Who? I was. So he turns to me for comfort and friendship and you take offense to that? He falls in love with me after you drop him like a hot potato and you're so freaking shocked by that? How dare he try to move on with his life and forget about you? It was always about you, wasn't it?" Allison paused a moment, and looking at Vicky she wondered if she was taking any of this in. She wondered if it was wise to continue but felt as if all this venting was like a lid that finally blew off due to the build up of too much pressure. There was no way to put the lid back on.

"Yeah, I guess I forgive you for planting doubts in me, doubts that have lasted our whole marriage, doubts that contributed to the break up of our marriage. Yeah, okay, let's forget about that. But how am I supposed to forgive you for jeopardizing my life and the life of my son, not to mention all those other people? Did you know my fifteen year old son who just got his permit was the one driving? For God's sake, he could have been killed!

"You did it to yourself, Vicky. It's hard to feel sympathy for someone who did this to themselves."

"Sorry," Vicky said, her face dull and expressionless.

Allison's humane side made a brief appearance again and tried to reason this out. Why was she so angry anyway? Why should she take the self-destruction of this poor pitiful person she didn't even know anymore so personally? True, they had been friends once but that was so long ago. Their acquaintance hadn't been a long one really, just a little over a year. What did Vicky have to do with her now? The savage side just wanted to finish her off! Put her out of her misery! It was the same terrible violent instinct to strike back, to punish, to teach a lesson to that she so often got with her kids when they pushed her too far. It was wild and fierce. It was the same instinct that caused people to abuse their children… but of course Allison never acted on it because she was educated, civilized, and self-controlled—not like the Vickys of this world. If she could've screamed she would have. If she could've shaken Vicky out of her lethargy she'd do it. But all she could do was cry.

Glancing at her watch, she saw she didn't have much time before she needed to leave. She couldn't leave yet, not with everything so unsettled like it was. What to do? What to say? How to bring some resolution to this fruitless mission? It was becoming both painful and awkward to look at Vicky's dull face which seemed to communicate nothing.

But then Allison noticed. Vicky was trying to lift her arm, which may as well have had lead weights on it considering the strain and effort invested in this simple act.

Allison said her name and Vicky responded with a guttural noise. Yes, she was definitely trying to tell her something, but what? Vicky turned her head to face the opposite wall, and with one last focused exertion, she lifted her arm again and pointed with a shaking index finger to the wall for just a moment before letting the weak appendage drop with a thud.

"Are you pointing to something?" Allison asked. Vicky muttered something which Allison could only interpret as an affirmative response.

Allison looked at the wall opposite them and her eyes fell on the only possible object that Vicky might be pointing to. It was a crucifix.

Oh, that's right, this is a Catholic hospital, Allison mused. *Catholics are so gory! Just what all the patients and their families want to look at; someone affixed with nails to a wooden cross, bleeding from head to toe, hanging there half naked, just waiting to die.*

"Are you pointing to the cross?" Allison asked Vicky.

"Yes. Pray," Vicky uttered through strained words.

"You want me to pray for you?" Allison asked.

Vicky said nothing. Her gaze was transfixed. Allison didn't know what else to do but sit and stare at the wall too. Maybe in the silence something would come to her to say that might bring about some closure to this botched visit. She looked at the crucifix and thought what a cleaned up depiction of the truth it probably was.

* * * * * * *

Allison had been educated on the gruesome realities of crucifixion. Not that she ever wanted to be. The first time was in college; some professor got on the topic. *What was that class? World History or Civilizations maybe? Or was it an Anthropology class?* They were studying the Roman Empire. Somehow it came up; the cruel and barbaric forms of corporal punishment and execution the Romans employed. She learned that crucifixion was one of the most torturous and prolonged forms of execution. The word excruciating, in fact, comes from crucifixion. She learned that in the class. She also learned that suffocation is what typically killed the condemned. She remembered her professor explaining that the "Y" position into which the arms were stretched expanded the chest and ribcage in such a way that the victim was only able to inhale. In order to exhale the victim had to push up from the feet, bringing the arms into a "T" position. This could go on for days, depending upon the strength of the condemned until finally shock and exhaustion made it too difficult to push up any longer. If the executioners decided to be merciful and speed up the process, they simply broke the condemned's legs so pushing up was no longer an option. Death came quickly at that point.

That was what she learned in college and she hadn't given it much more thought until one night last spring shortly after she and Frank separated. Alex was alone in his room with the TV on. He'd been so quiet for such a long time that Allison thought she better poke her head in the door and check on him, just to see what he was watching. Not that her so-called supervision did any good. The quantity and quality of her children's television viewing had become a battle she just didn't have the energy to fight since the separation. But she had an eerie feeling this particular night that he must be watching something particularly bad for him to be in there for such a long time with the door closed, so quiet and so engrossed.

She knocked gently on the door, stuck her head in, and much to her surprise, there was Alex, absorbed in some program about the crucifixion of Jesus on the history or science channel. Allison noticed there were a lot of Jesus documentaries on this time of year with Passover and Easter rapidly approaching. She didn't think much of it and it certainly never piqued her interest, but never in a million years did she think something of such a religious nature would interest Alex. She wondered for a moment if he was on drugs. Even more astonishing was his response when he finally noticed her there at the door. He didn't snarl at her or make some smart-mouthed sarcastic comment as she fully expected. He said, "Mom, you gotta see this. It's really cool!"

What? Was he actually giving her permission to enter the inner sanctum? Stunned at first, she tentatively entered, stepping over a pile of dirty clothes which she was tempted to say something about but her better judgment told her not to. She cleared some clothes and papers from the end corner of his bed and sat down.

"Are you all right?" Allison asked.

"Yeah, I'm fine," he said quickly turning his attention back to the screen. He didn't seem to be under the influence of anything.

A scientist was pointing to a diagram of the muscular skeletal system and speaking in medical jargon that Allison couldn't quite get her head wrapped around. Then the narrator's voice came on explaining about scourging with an illustration of a man tied to a pole being whipped.

"Eech! I don't like this violent stuff," Allison said.

"No, Mom, you gotta see it," Alex said.

Well, here it was, she thought, an opportunity to make up for all the times she'd been too busy or disinterested to play pitch and catch or a video game or cards with him. He was a teenager now so she didn't think she would ever have that chance again. But here it was! He had placed his dark adolescent self-absorbed cynicism aside for the moment and invited her into this small space where interest, good cheer, and perhaps even a little hope still lived.

"I didn't know you still liked science," Allison said.

"What made you think that?"

"I don't know," Allison said still reeling from the pleasant surprise of it all.

Science was his favorite subject until he lost interest in school completely. When he was little he used to say he wanted to be a doctor. The first present that he ever really wanted for Christmas was a little pretend medical kit. So if this was the one place where they could connect, she would try to make up for all those lost times and sit patiently on the end of his bed and watch this boring documentary.

"What exactly is this program about?"

"How Christ died; like the medical cause of death," Alex said.

Why in the heck does it matter, Allison wanted to say but knew better, not daring to dampen Alex's enthusiasm.

Next they showed an example of a whip the Romans used to scourge their prisoners. It consisted of long strips of leather with metal balls, sharp pieces of bone, and sometimes jagged bits of wood sewn into them. Flogging was often a preliminary to crucifixion. It was designed to lacerate and rip the skin open, usually resulting in ruptured blood vessels and veins which subsequently led to blood loss and dehydration, leaving the victim in a pre-shock state. The maximum was thirty-nine lashes, forty, it being said, was enough to kill a man. Indeed, the scourging in itself did often kill the victim. The narrator said that Jesus felt the pain more acutely than normal because of what he endured the night before.

"What did he endure the night before that made it worse," Allison asked.

"Oh, yeah, you missed it. He sweat blood when he was praying in the garden," Alex explained. "That's actually a medical condition brought about by severe stress. The capillary blood vessels rupture and drops of blood mix with sweat."

"You're kidding?"

"No, seriously! He must've known it was coming and he was totally freaked. Anyway, whatever that condition's called, the sweating blood thing; it makes your skin real sensitive afterwards."

"Wow, that's…"

"Shh, I wanna hear this," Alex said.

The narrator went on to explain about Jesus' second beating, this time from the bare hands of the Roman soldiers who spit on him, mocked him pulled chunks of his beard out, and placed a crown of thorns on his head. Then they struck him on the head with a reed, driving the thorns deeper into his skull. The robe they placed around his shoulders to represent mock kingship, only served to rub against and reopen the scourge wounds on his back, resulting in more pain and more blood loss.

The documentary consisted of comments by medical experts and scientists, interlaced with sweeping panoramic views of current holy sites in Jerusalem, lots of dramatic narrative with plenty of scripture quotes and stirring background music.

They went on about his long and exhausting walk to the execution site carrying the horizontal beam of the crucifix across his shoulders. They told about the nails, seven to nine inches in length and filed to a point which were driven through the median nerve of the wrists, a pain described like that of hitting the funny bone only intensified in magnitude and constant. Then the feet contorted to a 45 degree angle and nailed to the vertical beam, more pain as an artery in the foot is pierced, the spike hitting against the tarsal bones of the feet every time he pushed up to exhale, the scourge wounds reopened and splintered each time his back rubbed against the rough wood of the cross.

"Ooooh!" Allison winced and shivered, trying to regain an objective scientific view of the program, but the part about the nails through the wrist got to her in a way that she could almost feel the pain if she thought about it long enough.

"Harsh dude! You know the band Nine Inch Nails got their name from that?" Alex said.

"How interesting! If I run out of the room suddenly, it's because I have to go throw up."

"Not you, Mom. You got a strong stomach. Remember that time I had to go to the emergency room?"

"Which time was that?"

"When I bashed my head against the wall and cracked my head open."

"I remember."

"I was totally whack from the sight of all that blood but you were, like, so calm. You kept me from passing out."

"I did?"

"Yeah, remember, you kept talking to me, saying 'Stay with me, Al. Stay with me!', slapping my cheeks, and fanning me so I wouldn't go unconscious."

"I guess I am pretty brave when I have to be. It's just that part about the funny bone pain that got to me."

Two medical experts gave their opinions about the actual cause of Christ's death. They agreed that his death after only three to six hours on the cross came more quickly than most who were crucified. All indications would suggest that Jesus, a man in his early thirties who traveled all around the countryside by foot was probably in very good physical condition before his arrest the night before. The fact that he was able to talk right up to the end, seemed to indicate his death was not solely due to asphyxiation. The one doctor said it was a combination of shock, blood loss, dehydration, and exhaustion, resulting in heart failure. The other expert said it was due to a cardiac rupture where a blood clot in the heart bursts, noting that the victims of cardiac rupture cry out in a loud voice, become unconscious then die, exactly what Jesus was said to have done in scripture.

They each argued their case based on the blood and water flow from Jesus' side after the Roman soldier pierced him; the water being a build up of fluid in the lungs and the sac around the heart; the blood from the right ventricle of the heart or leaking of the blood into the pericardial sac if it was a rupture. Although both experts had their opinion, nobody knows for sure which side he was pierced on and which flowed first, the blood or the water. If more of these details were known then the exact cause of death could be determined more readily. They both agreed that the suffering leading up to the final moment must've been quite great to have hastened his death so quickly.

"This guy definitely seems more religious," Allison said of the doctor who argued in favor of the cardiac rupture as cause of death. He said it was the weight of everyone's sins which Christ bore that weakened his heart.

The other doctor had a much more pragmatic view. He said there was no doubt Christ knew his fate was determined, judging from his agony the night before when he sweat blood. This condition weakened him considerably, making him more prone to hypovolemic shock and exhaustion.

"You know these shows are so frustrating," Allison said. "They just give you enough information to make you wonder what really happened then they leave you hanging with nobody really knowing for sure. But I guess that really wasn't the point." The program was over and Alex did an unusual thing. He hit the mute button on the remote.

"Do you think it's really true, mom?" Alex asked.

"Do I think what's true?"

"The part about him being the son of God and taking everybody's sins on himself?"

"I don't know. It seems like kind of a cruel God to ask human sacrifice of his own son. I studied just enough anthropology in college to know that these ancient cultures were obsessed with this whole of idea of sacrifice to appease the gods. They felt like somebody had to pay for evil. Now Jesus may have been a delusional psychotic for all we know, but still there's no doubt that he truly believed he was the one chosen by God to pay for everyone else's crimes.

"I don't know if I ever told you this," Allison continued, "but I went to a Christian youth camp when I was about your age."

"Oh, yeah! Did you like it?"

"No. I was so homesick! I felt like my parents, your mamaw and papaw, just sent me there to get me out of their hair for a week. I thought everybody there were a bunch of self-righteous hypocrites who were trying to brainwash us." Alex looked up from where he sat cross-legged on the bed pulling on a

Odd Numbers

loose thread and gave his mother a chuckle, then with a quick flip of his long bangs he went back to his thread.

"But I do remember one thing this counselor said. He said Jesus had plenty of opportunities to escape or defend himself but he didn't. He walked right into it. I don't know if that's true or not but I remember he tried to prove it from the bible. For some reason I remember that. It's about the only thing I remember from that summer besides being miserable."

"So even if he was a complete psycho, I guess he had guts."

"I guess so. But you know..." Allison stopped herself before she said anymore.

"What?" She saw the last hint of youthful idealism in that inquisitive glance of his. Alex wasn't completely jaded. He still believed in super heroes, and she couldn't squelch that little bit of innocence that she saw glimmering within. She just couldn't infect him with the contagion of her cynicism, not yet anyhow. The world would do it soon enough.

"Oh, nothing," Allison said thinking that there were plenty of psychos out there with guts; terrorists for example, delusional maniacs willing to die for their fanatical beliefs. But Jesus didn't seem to belong in that category. His martyrdom seemed more the tragic death of the hopeless romantic. *Of course, it's what happens to all romantics eventually,* Allison thought. *But why tell Alex?* Why ruin this off guard moment when he dared to let that youthful trusting naiveté leak through?

The TV was still on mute. A thoughtful silent pause followed. The light from the TV flashed varying degrees of brightness throughout the darkened room, but neither one of them was looking at the screen. It was strange, this silence. Silence wasn't tolerated for very long in their house. Noise, no matter how much of an irritant to the nerves, was preferable to the deafening sounds of contempt or distance that invariably shouted their way through the silence.

The reflective moment didn't last long. It became awkward. Normally, she would just get up and make a hasty exit, but instead she decided to take a chance. She thanked Alex for sharing the program with her, reached out and touched his arm. He didn't pull his arm away. His head was still down, still working at that loose thread. She thought she saw the trace of a smile from behind the curtain of those long bangs. He mumbled something in acknowledgement. It wasn't exactly audible but at least it wasn't a surly grunt this time. Allison excused herself and left the room.

* * * * * * *

Allison was still looking at the crucifix on the wall of the ICU room when she realized she was crying. Not just crying, but sobbing and shaking. She put her hand over her mouth to stop any audible cry from escaping. She wasn't sure why she was crying. So many emotions stirring the tears, as if everything ever left unwept for was being brought to the surface. The crucifix on the wall, some sort of cathartic trigger, the source from which all the tears flowed.

A psycho but a brave one. Deluded enough to die like that. A romantic hero to be pitied. A lunatic in love. *No one ever loved me that much. No one ever will.* Bleeding. Suffering. Bearing heavy burdens. *Fool to believe that anyone ever would. No knight in shining armor coming to save me. So why do I want so desperately to believe… in fantasies…in fairy tales?*

Gasping. Dying. Heart literally breaking. *Could I ever love that much? To the point where I'd be willing give up everything?* Rejected. Degraded. Mocked Spat upon. *What would I have to give up? My dreams? My identity? My dignity? Wouldn't that just make me a doormat? Yet why is it I don't see weakness when I look at him? I see strength. I don't see groveling or cringing. I see courage. It's not self-loathing I see. It's self-forgetfulness. Total selflessness. The hero who runs into the burning building to save another. Have I ever come close to loving like that? If only I could forget myself. My pride. My image. My control. Could I ever just relinquish it all and trust that it wouldn't be in vain?*

Betrayed by those he loved. *So what makes me hate Vicky so much? Is it because I fear that Frank loved her more than me and always has? I fear he still loves her. Not Vicky now, of course, but her memory. He's in love with a memory and I can't compete. Why can't I just let it go? Let him be free? Let her be free? I can't love like that because I'm in the way. Father forgive them for they know not what they do.*

"I can't forgive," Allison squeezed the words out softly in a half whisper drenched with tears. "But I want to 'cause I'm so tired of carrying it around. Will you forgive them for me?" She said on her knees at Vicky's bedside, the words spoken to the cross on the wall, the image of a God she wasn't sure if she believed in; her rational side struggling, telling her she's talking to no one but herself. But it didn't feel that way. It felt like someone heard.

The emotions began to subside a little and reasoning returned. Allison reached into her pocket and pulled out a tissue, wiped her face, and looked at her watch.

"Oh, my gosh! My lunch break's over." She started to stand up but her sore ribs made it difficult to move quickly. She had pushed it by trying to jump to her feet and slouching over the bed as she knelt and prayed. A pain in her torso caused her to let out an audible moan and clutch her ribs. Again she was reminded of her injury. She remained on her knees and carefully scooted up toward the head of the bed, closer to Vicky. She was as close to her face as she could get without interfering with tubes and medical equipment.

Vicky continued to stare in a half daze toward the other wall with the crucifix on it.

"We really are a pair, aren't we?" Allison said chuckling back a few remaining tears, her hand supporting her aching side as she tried to kneel up a little straighter. Yes, they were both wounded; a link in their humanity. Something Allison could hold onto.

"Excuse me, Vicky, I have to cough and breathe now, lest my lungs collapse Allison turned her head to force out a painful cough She inhaled and exhaled, slowly and deeply, thinking about what a gift an effortless breath of air is and how much it's taken for granted until something happens, like a broken rib. Her eyes landed again on the crucifix, on the extended ribcage and the wide open arms. He was struggling to breathe right along with her… and Vicky.

"There's just one more thing I've got to do before I leave. Vicky, I don't know if you can hear me or not but I have to tell you something. You remember that hope chest you got from your grandmother? The one you used as a coffee table back at Camelot. I know where it is. Sally has it now. She bought it from an antique dealer. Do you remember Sally?"

It was a moment of surprise for Allison, almost joy when Vicky slowly turned her head and looked at her. It was a look of dawning realization, like someone coming out from under hypnosis or some amnesic state.

"You remember don't you? There's something still in that hope chest, Vicky. I'm sure it's something from your grandmother and we'd open it if we could but we don't have a key. We could break the lock but Sally was told it could damage the chest if we tried. I don't expect you have any idea where the key is so I'm asking your permission to contact Sally and break that lock. Whatever's in there belongs to you. I know your grandmother would want you to have it. My God, you should have something, Vicky, even if you have no where to take it. Let me do something for you. Let me… Oh, geez, I can't stop crying… please let me help." The tears came again.

Vicky stirred a little. She was becoming more alert, more aware of her surroundings. Her eyes were becoming clearer, enough for Allison to begin to recognize the person that she once knew. Vicky reached out and touched Allison's hand, almost as if Vicky was trying to comfort her.

The nurse came in and instantly the feel of the room changed as Allison quickly fumbled to get her psychological armor on and her emotional shield up.

"Excuse me. I was just leaving," Allison said, clearing her throat, blotting, and wiping the last of the tears from her face. "I've overstayed my welcome."

"It's all right," the nurse said in a chirpy voice that sounded so strangely out of place. "I just need to get in there and get her vitals."

"I need to move, don't I?"

"You're fine. I'll go around to the other side." The nurse began walking around to the other side of the bed then suddenly stopped in her tracks. "Well, look at this," she said. "She's awake and responding to our voices. Look at the way she's looking at you. She recognizes you."

"I know. She's really come around just in the past few minutes."

"You feeling better, Vicky? Look at you, you're smiling," the nurse said. "That Neimycyn must be working."

Allison tried to rise to her feet without drawing too much attention to herself.

"You need help getting up, honey?" the nurse said to Allison.

"No, I'm good," Allison said bracing herself on the bed for leverage, but trying not to push down too hard for fear of disrupting Vicky. "I tried to get up too fast earlier. I keep forgetting I got a cracked rib." Allison rose with great effort, having to acquiesce and let the nurse help. Once she was standing, she realized everything from her knees down to the bottom of her feet were asleep. She would have to stand there smiling at the nurse while nonchalantly wiggling her legs and feet until the pins and needles stopped sticking her.

"You know we're still trying to notify her next of kin," the nurse said running a digital thermometer across Vicky's forehead.

"Yes, I heard that."

"So far, no luck. Since you seem to be the closest she has to any family, I was wondering if we could give you her personal belongings for safe-keeping."

"Uh, sure," Allison said as she mentally marveled over the fact that so many things can change in just ten short minutes. This started out a quick obligatory visit, dreaded but nonetheless, something she was bound to do. Now, one quarter of an hour later, she had been named Vicky's next of kin, responsible for the few worldly belongings she owned.

"It's not much of course," the nurse said tightening the blood pressure cuff around Vicky's arm. "Just the clothes on her back when she came, which are in pretty bad shape, and a necklace, well, I guess you'd call it that. It's a chain with a key on it."

"A key?"

"Yeah, a really old looking key."

The nurse stuck the plugs of the stethoscope in her ears and the small metal dial at the end in the crook of Vicky's arm. Vicky flinched ever so slightly and Allison guessed it was because the metal dial was cold. She gave a slight smile to Vicky, and it seemed from her eyes that she tried to smile back. Allison caught herself feeling happy about it all; the fact that Vicky responded to something cold, the fact that she smiled and that life and awareness seemed to be returning to her eyes. And then Vicky did something really peculiar. She nodded her head. The nurse, who was busy monitoring Vicky's blood pressure, didn't see it. The nod was intended for Allison alone. She was trying to communicate with her, to tell her the key on the end of that chain was the one she was looking for and to proceed with her plans to open the hope chest.

"Blood pressure's coming back up," the nurse said.

Chapter 37

As her self-appointed next of kin, Allison took Vicky's personal belongings for safe-keeping and left behind phone numbers so the hospital staff could reach her. Not exactly self-appointed; not sure either just how this lot had fallen to her, but sure of one thing, it was something she had to do. A chance at redemption was all she could think as she left the hospital that afternoon and walked to the parking lot on unsteady legs like a newborn colt.

The phone call came early the next morning. Vicky had rallied, the encephalopathy astonishingly reversing itself as quickly as it had come on. They called it amazing and said if she continued to show signs of stabilization, she would be moved out of ICU that day. That wasn't all the news. They had finally reached Vicky's only known next of kin, a cousin by the name of Robert Miner. He had lived in Oklahoma, but just as recently as the past month had moved back to Kentucky where he was originally from.

Robert Miner. Robert Miner. The name's so familiar. Allison turned the name over and over in her head all morning while getting ready for work. Finally it came to her while she was brushing her teeth... *Chief Bobby. Of course! It's gotta be Chief Bobby! But Vicky thought he was dead. Although she mentioned he had talked about moving to Oklahoma. Nobody but Vicky ever really believed he was dead.* Allison recalled a conversation she had with Tim and Sally about Bobby's sudden disappearance. Tim and Sally speculated that he must've gotten in some trouble with the law while down in Florida. Tim figured he was probably running drugs, got busted, and wanting to shield Vicky from any sort of tangle with the law, he never contacted her. But then there was something about a dream. Allison tried to remember. What was it?

Bobby had appeared to her in a dream, but Vicky convinced herself it wasn't a dream but rather his ghost. Allison remembered while styling her hair, the sound of the hair dryer serving as a sort of white noise to carry her memory back. *He warned her. That was it! What did he warn her about? Gosh, Vicky was so superstitious. He told her to change her ways. And then he said goodbye to her. But they were so close. Surely he wouldn't have just left town and moved to Oklahoma without telling her.* That was Vicky's reasoning for why he couldn't possibly be alive. *But then if he was protecting her he wouldn't tell her he was leaving for good.*

How strange! Chief Bobby still alive! Vicky has one family member left. This is good news. I think it is. I hope it is. Anyway, Vicky will be so happy to see him. I wonder if she knows he's still alive. Surely he's at least tried to contact her over all these years."

With a flip of her head and a flick of the wrist that held the hair dryer, Allison's thoughts turned to her children–to Kristen first who was downstairs eating breakfast and would soon be trudging back upstairs with all of her sound and fury and little girl drama. She would be needing help with her hair and Allison had made the mistake of promising to French braid it last night. Last year at this time she was so clingy and Allison would have given anything for a little space. Since then Kristie had backed off, and her insecurity was no longer expressed in that sweet vulnerable fashion but rather in the lamenting complaints of the budding 'tween drama queen. How quickly they grow up and go from one stage to the next. Allison had a brief moment of angst where she longed for that affectionate little girl to come to her, throw her arms around her waist and hang on for dear life. She hadn't seen her in months.

Her thoughts turned to Alex who was still asleep. Allison puzzled over the fact that he could manage to continue sleeping through his radio alarm which blasted the sound of some wretched alternative grunge rock noise. She would have to try to get him up for school and that was always an ugly battle she dreaded fighting. He seemed even more tired and grouchy since the accident; though strangely enough there had also been little rays of light since then. She had been honest with him about Vicky, though she withheld the facts about Vicky's relationship with his father, she did tell him that she was an old friend of her parents, and he had been intrigued with this poor demented woman responsible for his car accident ever since. Of course Frank had been angry that she told him. She figured Frank just didn't want their son to know that they ever knew or associated with anyone like Vicky.

Alex had asked about Vicky since then and even expressed an interest in going to visit her at the hospital. Of course she had been too sick. He seemed curiously engaged when Allison recounted the details of her visit and Vicky's health the night before.

Finally Allison thought about Matthew as she sprayed her hair into place and fumbled for her mascara brush in the vanity drawer. She wondered how her firstborn was fairing at college. He was still sleeping of course since his first class wasn't until ten. She hoped he got enough sleep and didn't drink last night. Was he eating right? He would be having his finals in a couple weeks. She felt the strain he was under as if she was going through it again herself. She suddenly wanted to text him or e-mail him. She hadn't heard from him in a couple days. She would be glad when he came home for Christmas break. Maybe it wasn't too late to make things up to him. Maybe it wasn't too late to make it up to all the kids.

Her thoughts back to Vicky as she popped open lipstick tube after lipstick tube looking for just the right shade to match her blouse. Of course she called Sally last night about the hope chest and they arranged to get together the following night. It was as soon as Sally could do it. Not soon enough for Allison who had this nagging fear that two days would be too late. Hopefully Vicky would continue to improve or at least stabilize. Allison would have to go see her today after work. So much to do today, she thought making a mental checklist as the inevitable sound of Kristen tromping up the stairs with her request, which was somewhere between a demand and a plea, for Mom to fix her hair.

"Can I help you?" the nurse at the nurses' station asked Allison.

"Yes, I'm here to see Vicky Dooley. She was moved here from ICU earlier today."

"Oh, yes, she's in room 3305."

Allison thanked her and asked to speak with Vicky's nurse. She had a moment of apprehension when the harried looking middle-aged woman who was her nurse approached. The state of Vicky's health it seemed was so precarious and could change so suddenly. The fear came to her off and on again last night that Vicky might die before Allison had a chance to tell her she had forgiven her; or at least was trying to forgive her. Allison was awash with relief when the nurse informed her that Vicky was continuing to improve.

"Thank God," Allison said and realized this wasn't just a phrase she thoughtlessly threw out there as she was so prone to do. It was heartfelt. "I think I just prayed," Allison said. The nurse smiled as if she understood. Medical people must become accustomed, Allison thought, to these spontaneous outbursts of prayer; what with all this life, death, and brushes with the supernatural constantly buzzing around them.

The nurse then went on to tell Allison that if Vicky continued to improve she would probably be discharged in two to three days. Something about this didn't sit well with Allison. Although her recovery seemed nothing short of miraculous it just seemed too soon.

"But she has cirrhosis of the liver," Allison protested. "And it's my understanding she's in the advanced stages."

"Yes, I know," the nurse said sounding a little defeated and frustrated as she bit back the words on her tongue before she had a chance to say them. She didn't need to say anything. Allison understood. This was the way of the world and the way of the health care system. A homeless person with no insurance, no Medicaid, she had already overstayed her welcome. Practically anyone would have by this point. She knew that Mercy Hospital had a poor fund, but how much could possibly be allotted to a hospital stay going into its second week? Then there was the problem of what to do with Vicky after discharge.

"She's homeless for crying out loud. And in poor health. What's to become of her?"

"I wish I could say. Her cousin, Mister…"

"Miner. Robert Miner."

"Yes, that's it. He's going to speak with one of our social workers. In fact, he may have already. He was here earlier and said he'd return later this evening. Interesting character!"

"Yes, I remember him from years ago,". She wondered if Bobby would be a help or hindrance. She almost superstitiously associated him with bad luck for Vicky."

Vicky was not only awake but out of bed and sitting in a chair. Color had returned to her cheeks and her eyes were bright and alert. Her face looked surprisingly radiant as if the grime, filth, and residue of disease had been somehow scrubbed off. Her hair, though much thinner than what Allison remembered, had been washed and neatly combed. There was even a trace of the old auburn detected amidst the drab grey strands. Yes, she was older, yes she was worn and frail; but so much of the old Vicky shone through that there was no way not to recognize her in the immediacy of that moment when Allison stepped into the room.

It was similar to what Allison had experienced at so many high school reunions. The old familiar faces from years past looked the same as they once did. It seemed particularly true of those she had once been close with, as if the bond of friendship created a sort of agelessness in the mind's eye. But she knew this was only an illusion and not reality. And so it was with Vicky. She was the same old girl… until she smiled. Perhaps it was because she was missing a front tooth and so badly in need of dental work, but there was something more, something so fundamentally changed in that smile. It was then the illusion was shattered and Allison brought back to present day reality.

"Well, look at you! If you aren't the comeback kid!" Allison said.

"Hey girl! Forgive me for not standing up but I don't want to show my ass, if you get what I mean. It might make me em-bare-assed!" Together they laughed, spontaneously and joyfully, like they did so many years ago, like no time had passed at all.

"Oh, that reminds me," Allison said, only now remembering the gift bag which hung about her wrist all this time. "I got you a gift."

"What's the occasion? It ain't my birthday and it ain't Christmas yet."

"It's a get well gift."

"But you already got me one. The plant," she said referring to the plant on the bedside table, the helium balloon still floating only a tiny bit deflated.

"But I wanted you to have one where you'd actually be awake and conscious when you received it."

"I get what ya mean. I was pretty ding-dang out of it there for a while. Wasn't I?"

"Yes, you were. Do you remember anything?"

"Just you being there by my bedside. I don't remember nothin' you said but I do remember you seemed kinda upset."

"I swear that plant has grown since yesterday," Allison said changing the subject. Focusing intently on the plant she noticed the stems were in fact drooping less and the leaves seemed to be reaching out more, leaning in the direction of the window and the sunlight. "You been talking to that plant, haven't you?"

"We been conversing all day–better conversationalist than my roommate," Vicky said in a half whisper motioning to the curtain that separated her bed from the one on the back end of the room.

"You still got that green thumb, Vicky. You always had such a way with living things. Here… before I forget," Allison said handing her the gift bag, "your second gift."

Vicky responded with such gleeful surprise, like a kid as she received the bag, opened and read the enclosed card, and pulled out the neatly layered and fluffed tissue paper to retrieve the gift at the bottom of the bag.

"It's beautiful." Tears instantly began pooling in Vicky's eyes as she held up a lavender night gown and matching robe.

"Well, I remembered you liked purple. Figured you might like that more than the standard hospital gown," she said, grateful that Vicky didn't see the gift as a charitable offering as she had feared.

Just then a moaning sound ensued from behind the curtain on the back side of the room. It threw Allison off for a moment until she remembered there was another patient sharing the room with Vicky. The moan was one of pain and it was increasing in volume.

"Can I ring the nurse for you, darlin'?" Vicky said to the unknown person behind the curtain, and Allison marveled at how she could go from heart-wrenchingly pitiful to funny and seemingly so with it in just twenty-four short hours. "Would you grab that nurse call device off my bed for me?" Vicky asked Allison, her old self entirely back again.

"Well, that's nice of you Vicky," Allison said handing her the nurse call.

"No, it ain't," Vicky said in a mischievous little whisper. "I just wanna shut her up. She kept me up half the night." Vicky paged the nurse and with the speaker button pushed down she said, "It ain't for me it's for my roommate. You need to get in here with some Demerol ASAP. And in my opinion she needs a higher dose."

"They're comin' darlin', they're comin'! Just you hang in there," Vicky hollered over to the curtain in a voice which Allison thought a bit too loud. Surprisingly, the moaning lowered somewhat in volume.

"So...," Allison said motioning to the gown in Vicky's lap. "You think it's the right size?" She recalled what a hard time she had deciding on the size. It had to be small enough so that it wouldn't slip off Vicky's emaciated shoulders or hang like a formless drape about her sunken in chest; yet big enough to fit around her distended middle.

"Yeah, I think it'll fit," Vicky said holding the gown up in front of her.

"You sure? Because if it doesn't I can exchange it."

"It's cool. Wish I could try it on now but I'm kinda plugged in if you get what I'm sayin'," she said referring to the IV. "It's enough of an ordeal just to change from one backless nightie to the next. But anyhow, like I was sayin', I really think it's beautiful. I...I," Vicky's words got choked off by a surge of emotions.

"Vicky...please," Allison said feeling a little embarrassed by the unnecessary show of gratitude. "It's not much. I mean, I got a pretty good deal on it," Allison said double checking the gown and robe to make sure she'd cut off the tags marked with the final clearance price. "And besides, I had to..." She stopped herself... *get you something...for Chrissake, Vicky, I had to get you something.*

Allison stopped the words that echoed through her mind from slipping out. Of course, this was her guilt offering. When you don't know what else to do for someone, offer them a gift. And what could she do for Vicky? And why should she? And why on earth did she feel so compelled to anyway? She went over it and over it last night as she tossed and turned in her bed. Unable to sleep, she decided to pray. She dropped to her knees, hurting torso and all, and said the only prayer she knew... the Lord's Prayer. The words "Forgive us our trespasses as we forgive those who trespass against us" stuck in her throat. She had to let Vicky know she had forgiven her, or was at least trying to forgive her, and she had to get the contents of that hope chest to her. She knew she had to do these two things, beyond that, she had no idea.

"Had to what?" Vicky said bringing Allison back to the present.

"I had to get you something." Allison pulled the other chair in the room around so that they could sit face to face; close enough so that their knees were practically touching. She took Vicky's frail hand in hers and said, "Vicky, consider this gift a peace offering. I've been angry with you for a long time; long before the car wreck, ever since my wedding day to be exact. I want you to know I forgive you. For everything. When you wear this gown and robe I want you to remember that you're forgiven."

It was a peculiar moment for it seemed to Allison that with her words and Vicky's tears, God stepped into this sad little institutional room for a moment and offered full and free forgiveness to Vicky for all the thoughtless, irresponsible, hurtful, and deceitful things she'd ever done. Allison couldn't help it. Her eyes welled up with tears too.

"I didn't think you ever could," Vicky said daubing at her damp eyes and cheeks with a tissue. "What I did at your wedding was bad enough. But then I almost kill you… and your son. Hurt so many people and couldn't even kill myself… How's your boy?"

"He's fine. He broke his nose but it's healing. You know how young people are, they bounce right back. He may have a slightly crooked nose before it's all said and done, but I keep trying to convince him that it'll make him look rugged and adventurous, like Clint Eastwood."

"He ain't buyin' it is he?"

"Well, no, he already inherited his father's Roman nose and I really don't think he wants it to stand out anymore than it already does."

"And how about you? How you getting along?"

"Oh, fine. I'm healing. Not as quickly as my son but then that's to be expected."

"You cracked a rib, didn't ya?"

"You do remember some things from yesterday's visit."

"I guess I do. Mostly I remember you kneeling by my bed and crying. I thought you said you forgive me. I wasn't for sure. This morning I thought maybe it was just a dream. But then here you are and you really have forgiven me," Vicky said, breaking into a strange, demented, wounded animal-like cry. Allison didn't know how to take Vicky's emotions which were too raw and real at this moment.

The sound of the moaning from Vicky's roommate began to increase again in intensity and volume, as if this roommate was competing with the sound of Vicky's weeping. The situation struck Allison as absurdly funny and soon she couldn't restrain the laughter that this odd cacophonic dual of agony caused.

Vicky kept trying to reach for something on her bedside table in between the great heaving aftermath of sobs and intermittent laughter that came with her own realization of the absurdity of the situation. She was just weak enough to be unable to stretch that far.

"What is it, Vicky? What do you need?"

"CD player," she stammered in between gasps for air.

Allison tried to reach but realized her cracked rib and sore torso wouldn't let her stretch that far either; not without getting out of her chair, that is.

"We really are a pair aren't we?" Allison said with one gigantic heave-ho push on the arms of her chair in order to catapult herself up. She stepped closer to the table and immediately recognized the small boom box that had once belonged to her oldest son Matthew. The red strip of tape with the name "Matt H." printed upon it was still there on the back. Not sure what to say or do, she looked to Vicky for instructions.

"Just push play," Vicky said wiping her reddened nose. "She likes it…. my roommate. Calms her down."

Allison saw it then, the CD case sitting next to the boom box. She pushed play and lifted the case to see what it was they were about to hear. Pavarotti at the Met. And then on the floor next to the bedside table she saw another gift bag, smaller than the one she had given, a crinkled cellophane wrapper with a bright orange sticker affixed to it overflowed from the top of the bag along side tissue paper. Hers was not the only gift Vicky had received, and of course there was only one possible person she could have received it from. The realization along with the first few strains of Pavarotti singing *Nessun Dorma* caused tears to well up in Allison's eyes. Vicky looked at her as if she knew. Allison quickly grabbed a tissue out of her pocket and began blotting compulsively under her eyes, first under the one eye then under the other, as if to stop the tears and send them back from where they came.

"You know, I never much cared for opera. Except of course for Puccini. I love Puccini," Allison said with a defensive little chuckle. She remembered how Frank had bought her all of Puccini's works, including a recording of Pavarotti singing *Nessun Dorma*. He'd taken her to *La Boheme* and *Madame Butterfly* and she was enthralled for a change; unlike the heavy hard to listen to symphonies that she got dragged to where she spent the evening restlessly shifting around in her seat and struggling to stay wake. Those Puccini operas were different. Beautiful. Beautiful, but oh, so sad. They agreed on that musically; that and the Swing, Big Band era dance music. *Damnit! Those Puccini operas were ours. Bastard!* Allison thought as she blew out hard through her nose into the tissue.

"Allie, don't be miffed at Francis, I mean Frank."

"I'm not miffed."

"Like hell you ain't! Sit down," the old Vicky was back and in charge as usual.

Allison slowly lowered herself into the chair, careful to bend at the knees instead of the waist so she wouldn't put strain on her ribcage. She seemed to feel the effects of the broken rib more when she was in an emotional state.

"Look at me, Al! Look at me! He don't love me no more. You don't got noth... I mean, you don't have anything to be jealous of," she said correcting herself the way she used to.

"I'm afraid he don't love me no more either," Allison said.

"Quit talkin' like a dang hillbilly! You know as well as I do a double negative makes a positive. Now listen that's a lot of horse crap and you know it."

Allison looked at Vicky and with the reemergence of her old self she looked startlingly more like the Vicky she once knew than ever before. Perhaps Frank saw her that way too, like how she saw her old friends at the high school reunions. The illusion of agelessness. Maybe it affected him too, so that he didn't see a haggard, sickly old woman with missing teeth and bad color. Maybe he only saw the memory of that beautiful red head when he looked at her.

"Now listen here, Allison, and listen good. A week ago at this time I had no reason to live. So I'm layin' here in this hospital bed, goin' through withdrawal, half outta my mind, wishin' I was dead. There didn't seem to be no... any reason to keep fighting. Until Francis walked in the room. It shocked me really, the way it made me feel to see him again after all these years. It kinda woke me up; like I was dead but then I came back to life. And I believed, if just for a little bitty second, that there was another reason to live besides drinking. I remembered what it felt like to love somebody. And I wanted to live again."

"I'm not sure I follow you, Vicky."

"Stay with me, Allie," Vicky said as lucid as can be. "So after I see Francis I get this fight back in me, but then yesterday I feel myself slip away again. And I'm fighting it and I'm fighting it and I'm trying with all my might to grab hold of something, some reason to keep breathing in and out. And then you come and see me. And there it was again."

"There what was again?"

"Love. And I thought maybe God hasn't given up on me. Only one thing cures a problem as big as the one I got and that's love. Frank bringing me music; you being here after what I did to you, your forgiveness, the plant, the gown, your offering to help – it's all love and I gotta stay alive long enough to... give it back somehow. Oh God, I hope it's not too late."

Allison looked at that sad sick face that sat before her and saw the tears pooling once again in Vicky's eyes. These tears were different, more subdued, more tired and weighed down, sadder and deeper, all the way down to the core of her being. Layers and layers of regret were buried beneath those tears, and it seemed it would take ages to sift through that salty ocean and finally get to the bottom.

"And then I realized somethin' else," Vicky said collecting her thoughts and pulling her emotions back in with a sigh. "Something about you and Francis. If you two could just wake up again, like how I did, and remember what it was like to love and be loved. I mean really remember. If I could help you remember somehow.

"See, you two were meant for each other all along. Francis wasn't meant for me. I was just lucky enough to get him on loan for a short time. I realized he did love me for a little while, and that was enough."

"So what are you saying, Vicky? That Frank and I should get back together?"

"Hell, I don't know. It just seems like a damn shame… for both of you, as well as your kids."

"I agree with you, it is a damn shame. For all of us. It's not like we wanted it. We tried to make it work. We, well, I actually exhausted all possibilities trying to make it work. I just couldn't do it anymore, couldn't live that way."

"Ain't there any hope of you two reconciling?"

"Not at this point. I don't see how. It's funny, some friends of ours got divorced some time ago then got back together a couple years later. Within three months they were right back where they started and wound up splitting up again. I remember when that happened Frank said the whole thing was like taking a carton of spoiled milk and putting it back in the refrigerator to see if it's better tomorrow. It's gone bad! Just throw it out and move on. Anyway, that was one thing I agreed with him on."

"You still didn't answer my question."

"I didn't. I thought I did."

"Is there hope for you two? Yes or no?"

"I guess there's always hope," Allison said tentatively, weighing the improbability of it all.

"But you don't believe in miracles?"

"Do you?"

"I didn't last week at this time."

The final notes of *Nessun Dorma* swelled to a powerful climax and a pause of silence fell in between tracks. The roommate's moaning had died down to a pitiful whimper. Vicky pointed to the curtain which divided the room.

"See I told you the music helps," she whispered.

"She is better, isn't she? Or at least diverted for a little while. Where is that nurse?"

"You know how it is in hospitals. They wanna see how much you can stand before they give ya any pain meds. It's like a test of endurance.

"It's all right, darlin', the nurse is on her way. We got some more music comin' for ya." The roommate moaned louder in response to Vicky, just in time for the second track to begin playing.

Allison looked at Vicky's face and noted the genuine concern there for her roommate. What an odd combination of good and bad we all are, she thought. *I guess if you divvied it all up, my percentage of bad is no less than Vicky's. Her "bad" is just more interesting than mine.* She believed she had forgiven Vicky, or at least was on the way to it, but could she ever forgive Frank? Could there ever be good feelings between them again. Or at least good memories and some distance from all the bad feelings. Then maybe they could carry on a conversation about their children with all the logistics of where they were supposed to be, and when, and what time they needed to be picked up without it somehow morphing into a brutal battle of fault finding and blame. She would be happy with that. No, she would be thrilled with that.

The nurse finally arrived, bringing relief to Vicky's suffering roommate and assistance to Vicky, helping her get up, move about and change into the new gown and robe that Allison gave her. The nurse suggested Vicky take a walk along the unit floor to get the muscles moving again and regain some strength. Allison said she would be happy to take Vicky for a walk; but first a girl has to get spiffed up before going out and she simply had to get Vicky's face on before she allowed her to step foot outside that room.

Allison brushed Vicky's hair and put a little makeup on her while Pavarotti crooned his tenor heart out in the background. The roommate's medication, soon taking effect, caused the moaning to give way to the sound of deep sleep, steady breathing in and out with a trace of a snore. Allison handed Vicky her compact mirror when the makeover was complete. Her eyes and nose began to redden with the onset of tears.

"Please, don't cry, Vick, you'll smudge your mascara," Allison said immediately pulling a tissue out of the box, blotting Vicky's eyes and holding the tissue to her nose so she could blow just like she did with her children so many times when they were too little and helpless to do it for themselves. Vicky turned her head from her reflection and obediently blew. Then looking back in the small mirror she held in her hand she said, "My God, I look like Dandy Dan."

"Who the hell's Dandy Dan?"

"He's this old transvestite I know from around."

"You're saying I made you look like an old drag queen?"

"Well, hell, I guess I contributed to it as much as you did," Vicky said, and together they laughed just like in the old days.

"You let me be the judge of how you look," Allison said. "Mirrors have been known to lie." She scrutinized Vicky's face from every angle, touching up here, brushing back there. It seemed to her that Vicky had been transformed by the touch of her hand from a drab dull grey to a more colorful creature. The pretty shade of lavender against her skin, along with the little color from the makeup caused hints of the old natural beauty to flicker through. "I think you look terrific! Let's go for a walk."

Allison helped Vicky to her feet and together the two friends walked down the hospital unit hall, Vicky in her long lavender gown, anchored between the IV pole and her old friend's arm made Allison think of a wounded butterfly with a tattered wing.

"Remember when we used to jog together?" Vicky said.

"We went at a little faster pace than this. But you could always out run me with those long legs of yours. Remember how after we jogged you'd always plop down on your couch, or mine, light up a cigarette and pop open a beer."

"Remember that one time, we ran like five miles, came back to your place, ripped open a bag of Oreo cookies and a bottle of scotch? Remember how we was dunkin' the Oreo cookies in our glasses of scotch before we ate 'em. You was…excuse me, you were such a corrupting influence," Vicky said.

"Yeah, right, my one little contribution to your corruption. What did we listen to that day? Remember our pact? Women artists only when the girls of Camelot 3300 got together," Allison said.

"That's right–girl songs only. All I remember about the scotch and Oreo cookies spree is that whatever the music was, we were singing along?"

"Most definitely, at the top of our lungs if I recall correctly. Was it Pat Benatar or Heart?"

"No, that was another time, with Sally I think. The scotch and Oreo cookies time wasn't anything too rockin' if I recall. It was somethin' more mellow and folksie-like. But we was just drunk enough to think we sounded great. Oh, I remember… Joni Mitchell."

"Yes!" Allison blurted out. "Both Sides Now."

"Yeah, that's it. Both Sides Now. I remember. We was… sorry, we were singin' along, takin' ourselves pretty seriously as I recall."

"Yeah, we were quite the divas if I recall," Allison said.

"Must've been a combination of the whiskey and chocolate that did it."

"Do you still remember the words?"

"Hell, yeah!" Vicky bragged.

"No way!"

"It's my short term memory that ain't worth a shit. Don't ask me anything about this past week 'cause it's way sketchy in my head, but the lyrics to a thirty-five year old song by a cool chick artist, now that I remember." Vicky cleared her throat and it sounded to Allison like twenty years of tears, mucous, and bile were caught in her throat and nothing could clear those raw, ragged larynxes and free up her those rough damaged vocal cords.

"*Bows and bows of angel hair...*" Vicky began tentatively but her voice failed her.

"Are you sure it's bows and bows?" Allison chuckled. "I think its rows and rows of angel hair."

"Naw, it's rows and bows,"

"Or is it flows?"

"Hell, we can't even get passed the first line," Vicky said as she clutched her throat.

"Well, let's skip down to the middle," Allison said, slowly leading along the shuffling Vicky. She hoped the reminiscing and silly attempts at singing might distract Vicky from the discomfort she sensed she was feeling.

"Just sing what you remember darlin', I'll jump in when I can," Vicky said.

"*Now it's just another show. You leave 'em laughing when you go. And if you care don't let them know. Don't give yourself away,*" Allison sang barely above the range of a whisper. "Hop in Vicky, but don't hurt yourself," she said gently patting her frail little arm.

"*Now old friends are acting strange. They shake their heads. They say I've changed,*" Vicky spoke the words more than sang them.

"*Well, something's lost but something's gained in living everyday,*" they sang together.

"*I've looked at love from both sides now,*" Allison sang.

"*I've looked at life from both sides now,*" Vicky sang.

"*Its love's/life's illusions I recall. I really don't know love/life at all,*" they sang in unison.

"Kinda maudlin, ain't it," Vicky said and Allison gave her a curious look as if she was trying to process just what was transpiring between them. "Maudlin. M-A-U-D-L-I-N. 'Effusively or tearfully sentimental.' It's a way cool song. I guess it's just not right for now."

"Well, I'll be, Vicky, you still remember your dictionary definitions. Did that come out of the same brain that couldn't remember its own name yesterday.

"Hey, let's sing something more upbeat by Joni. How about Big Yellow Taxi?"

"*Don't it always seem to go that you don't know what you got 'til it's gone. They pave paradise and put up a parking lot.*" The old friends sang together, this time Vicky's voice was a little stronger. An orderly passed by and said, "Don't quit your day job, girls." Together they laughed which set off a coughing fit with Vicky.

"It's okay…." She sputtered out, putting up a defensive hand to block Allison's attempts to help. "I… came pre…I got Klee…" she fumbled in her robe pocket and pulled out some tissues. Allison thought she saw a splatter of red as she coughed into the crumpled up wad."

"Are you all right?" Again Vicky's hand came up to stop any intervention from Allison.

"I'm fine." The words barely came out before Vicky was overcome with another round of coughing so violent it shook her body.

"Let's get you some water. Are you strong enough to get over to that chair and sit for a while?" Allison asked as she approached Vicky, now ignoring her efforts to be left alone. Vicky stopped fighting and willingly gave Allison her arm. Her cough subsided somewhat as Allison steered Vicky's body in the direction of a hallway waiting room area. Allison fished through her blazer pocket until she retrieved enough money to buy a bottle of water at a nearby vending machine. She brought the bottle over to Vicky who poured it into her mouth like a woman dying of thirst. Allison observed the difficulty she had swallowing; the water spilling out from the sides of her mouth, the head tilted back enough to reveal the clumsy obstinate gulping movement of the throat. But she seemed better after getting some water down. She wiped her mouth and chin with the unused corners of the wadded up tissue she held in her fist, then with that old mirthful, mischievous Vicky look, she raised her bottle of water in a toasting gesture toward Allison.

"Thanks for the water, girl! Even though I think you're a dang fool to spend money on bottled water. Some lucky con man's making a fortune outta this," she said eyeing the bottle.

"Somehow I knew you'd disapprove of bottled water. But look at the back of the bottle. It says purified through reverse osmosis. Now as I understand, that process…"

"Reverse osmosis my ass! It's a scam. It's Ohio River tap water with a touch of sodium in it, so folks think, 'wow, I can taste the pure, natural mountain stream minerals'. Not that I'm ungrateful. Thank you for the water," she said taking a smaller sip that seemed to go down somewhat easier. Allison had the strange thought, hope maybe, something like a vision in her mind of the water going all through her, hydrating, cleansing, washing away somehow all of Vicky's past.

Allison sat next to Vicky on the waiting area love seat. "You wanna sit for a while?" She asked.

"Judgin' from your shoes, I think you need to sit worse than me," Vicky said, eyeballing Allison's high heeled pumps.

"Naw, I'm fine. I'm used to walking around in these things."

"You sure, 'cause we can stop and getcha some hospital footies at the nurses station. I'm sure they wouldn't mind."

"I'm good. Let me know when you're ready to start moving again," Allison said, staring into the face of Vicky transformed again from frail, sickly, and aged beyond her years to the old girl she once knew. Maybe it was only Ohio River tap water with a touch of sodium, but the water seemed to help. Little things helped Vicky it seemed; the pretty gown and having a chance to wear it, a simple touch, the little walk just down the hall, conversation, small sips of water, and, yes, though Allison hated to admit it, listening to Pavarotti.

"Okay, I'm ready. Let's walk," Vicky said. Allison helped her to her feet and together they made their way down another unit hall, and though it seemed the one old friend was leaning more on the other, the truth is there was mutual support. Helping Vicky, even just lending her an arm to assist her in walking was helping Allison too.

"I hear they got a hold of Chief Bobby," Allison said only now remembering about him.

"Yeah, I saw him this morning. He was there when they moved me out of the ICU," Vicky said somewhat nonchalantly.

"The last time I remember you mentioning his name you thought he was dead."

"For a long time I believed he was. He let me think that and I ain't sure I've forgiven him for it. On the one hand I understand why he did it. He got himself mixed up in some pretty dirty deals. I guess he figured if I didn't know nothin'… sorry, if I didn't know anything then nobody could hurt me, if you get what I'm sayin'.

"See, he wanted to get his life straightened out. Sorta like me only it didn't take him as many tries to get it right. Well, not exactly, he's had a few backslides, but overall he's managed to get straight. He moved out to Oklahoma so he could get back in touch with his roots—our roots I guess you'd say but he was always more Shawnee than me. Remember I told ya, some of our Shawnee ancestors came back to Kentucky in the 1800's to look for this silver mine."

"I remember."

"Well, so he goes out to Oklahoma and gets himself a college degree and becomes a teacher. He learned a lot from the Shawnee people on the reservations out there and I guess you'd say he kinda became one of them. Then he became one of them…. sorry, one of those re-enactors. He travels around to different festivals and dresses up like an Indian and does this storytelling gig where he educates people about the Native American ways.

"Anyhow, I thought sure he was dead and gone until about, ummm….

fifteen years ago or so. Like early nineties, 'cause I remember I was livin' on Canal Street at the time. That's back when I still had a roof over my head. Anyways, I guess he figured enough time had passed and it'd be safe to come back for a visit. So he tracks me down, shows up at my doorstep and about scares the living shit outta me. I thought sure I was seein' his ghost standin' there. But it was the real Bobby–in the flesh. So he tells me what's goin' on with his life and I didn't know whether to hug him or smack him. So he tries to talk me into goin' back to Oklahoma with him. I just couldn't do it. So anyhow we kept in touch for a few years, but then I guess when I lost my home he never could find me to reach me no more so that was that.

"It's strange, the booze really did a number on my head because there were times I felt so danged mental I couldn't remember if he was still alive or dead. Anyhow, I guess he didn't have much reason to try and come back and find me 'cause I was so mean to him the last time I saw him. He tried to get me to straighten out my life, dragged me around to AA meetings and the like. Anyhow it pissed me off. Pissed me off that he was too danged self-righteous to party with me anymore, and here he waltzes back into my life thinkin' he's got all the answers after he up and abandons me. I thought he was dead and he never contacted me all them years… those years before! So I blamed him for all my troubles 'cause he promised he'd be my protector and look after me from the time we were kids and then he just up and bails on me."

The tears that brimmed in Vicky's eyes dropped down on her cheeks. She and Allison stopped for a little while in the midst of their walk while Vicky collected herself again. "But the truth is I just made myself mad at Bobby so I wouldn't have to be mad at me. It ain't his fault. He was only doing what he thought was right for me. Bobby's just another person I disappointed. I failed him by screwing up my life. He didn't fail me. God, I didn't want to become this person. I don't want to live this way. God, how did I get this way?"

"I ask myself the same question," Allison said.

"Nothin' wrong with you."

"Except for the fact that I have a failed marriage. And failed relationships with my kids. I've got nothing to show for my life. Even the so-called good I've done–community and volunteer work, this board, that board, Junior League… it's really all been for me, my image. It occurred to me while I was looking in the mirror this morning. How much energy I've invested into making the externals look good. It's a good thing I can't see my inner self in a mirror. I'd be horrified. We're really not so different, Vicky. My life just looks neater and tidier on the outside. I'm a socially acceptable screw-up. But my future is as scary and uncertain as yours.

"So where are you going when you finally bust out of this joint? Are you going to live with Bobby?"

"I don't know. Bobby was supposed to talk to a social worker today about that. I don't know if I wanna put that on him. I may have to though. There ain't a shelter or halfway house in this town that I ain't worn my welcome out at. Poor Bobby! He's got him a full life. Why should he be saddled with a chronic drunk in as shitty 'o health as me. And I know I'm sicker than what they wanna tell me. They just gotta pretend like I'm all better so they can get me the hell outta this hospital. This one doctor keeps talkin' like if I stay sober for at least six months they can put me on a waiting list for a new liver. And I know Bobby has to put together this living will for me. I just told him to turn all the dang machines off and let me go.

"Anyhow, I know I really didn't answer your question but the truth is I got no answer. I'm scared, Allie. I don't wanna drink again. I don't wanna die either. I'm afraid I'm in too bad 'o shape for anything else."

"I don't believe that. You're a fighter, Vick We were all wondering if you were going to make it twenty-four hours ago, now look at you. You know the body has an amazing ability to repair itself."

"I don't know. We ain't talkin' about a skinned knee. We're talkin' about a badly damaged liver."

"Even so."

"Now you're talkin' about miracles. Thought you didn't believe in them."

"Just when it comes to myself I don't," Allison said.

"Then maybe we need to believe for each other."

"Sounds like a plan." Allison thought that maybe the best thing she could do for Vicky was to hope.

"Vicky, I almost forgot! I've got your hope chest. Well, actually Sally's got it! Do you remember the conversation I had with you about it yesterday?"

"No! What do you mean Sally's got my hope chest?"

Allison told her the whole story about how Sally had bought it from an antique dealer with contents still in it. She told her all about the lock and how they thought they would have to break it until yesterday when the ICU nurse gave Allison Vicky's belongings, one of those being a key on a chain. Vicky confirmed that it was in fact the key and how she was so drunk and desperate when she hocked the chest she forgot to empty it out or give them the key. She cherished the key and wore it around her neck because it was the only thing she had left of her grandmother.

"Sally's supposed to bring it over tomorrow and open it with me."

"Oh, please," Vicky pleaded. "Bring it here... to the hospital, you and Sally. I just gotta be there when you open it. I never opened it Allison."

"You're kidding me!? You mean you have no idea what's in there?"

Odd Numbers

"Oh, I got an idea. Grandma quilted and sewed a lot. I'm pretty sure it's some stuff she made, but what exactly, I don't know."

"I can't believe this! I just can't believe this! I mean I knew Lamasco was a small town and all, but what are the odds of Sally running across my old hope chest and buying it. I could've kicked myself when I sobered up and realized I'd hocked it. I always hoped I could get it back one day, but I never thought..." Once again, Vicky's words were choked with emotion.

"Vicky, I hate to be the bearer of bad news but I don't know that we can bring the chest in to the hospital. Don't they have rules about that kind of thing?"

"Rules? What d'ya mean?" Vicky asked as if the thought had never occurred to her.

"Well, ya know, it could look suspicious–us haulin' a big ol' chest like that into a public institution like the hospital. They might think we're terrorists or something."

"Yeah, Allie ol' girl, you are one shady lookin' lady; what with that perfectly smooth rich lady blond hair that goes flip on the end and them expensive designer clothes; and them stiletto heels which are just perfect for runnin' and divin' behind buildings and tossin' grenades. Yeah, sure, I'd take ya for a terrorist. Besides, if security stops ya, all ya gotta do is sic Sally on 'em. They'll be beggin' ya to go on your merry way before ya know what hit ya."

"So, Sally and I are just supposed to waltz in here with your chest like it's nothing."

"That's exactly right! If you act like you know what you're doin', ain't nobody gonna stop ya."

"If I recall it's made of cedar. I don't know if Sally and I can carry it all that distance, from the parking lot all the way in here and up to your room."

"I suggest you don't wear your stiletto heels that day. Better yet, getcha some able-bodied men to haul it up here for ya."

"Like who am I gonna ask? Frank!?"

"How about Chief Bobby? I can arrange to have him meet you here. And what about that young-un of yours?"

"Who Alex?"

"He's a teenager, ain't he?"

"Yes, but..."

"So he can help. Besides," Vicky said, her take charge steam suddenly evaporating with the exhalation of a deep sigh. "I would like to apologize to him for causin' the accident and breaking his nose. It's just somethin' I feel I gotta do."

"Well, it's strange you would suggest that because he's asked about you;

you know, how you're doing and that kind of thing. He actually asked if he could come to the hospital and see you."

"Ain't that a coincidence? What did ya tell him?"

"That you were too sick for visitors. At the time you were."

"I'm not now."

"Strange what a difference a day can make. Well, okay then, dear heart, if you're sure about this I'll see what he's doing tomorrow night," Allison said with a smile as they turned around at the end of the hall

"Is there anything I can get you?" Allison asked after they arrived back at Vicky's room and she prepared to make her departure. "Anything you need or want?"

"There's only one thing I want," Vicky said.

"What's that?"

"A drink."

Allison let go a slight chuckle until she saw from the look on Vicky's face that she wasn't kidding. For the first time it struck Allison just how much Vicky was struggling to overcome this addiction.

"The second you leave here today it'll be all I can think about. Somehow it's worse when I'm alone. And at night."

"Oh, God, Vicky, I'm so sorry."

"I ain't tryin' to make you feel bad. I know not you, nor anybody else can sit here with me and hold my hand for the rest of my life, or until it goes away, which ever comes first. I just gotta deal with it."

"What can I do?" Allison asked feeling so completely hopeless.

"You can pray for me."

Chapter 38

Allison, Sally, and Alex rode together in Allison's minivan. The far back seat was pushed down to make room for Vicky's hope chest which took up more space than Allison anticipated. It was larger than what she remembered, which struck her as kind of funny. Most things from the past seemed smaller in reality than what appeared in the memory. Perhaps it was different this time because she had to help lift the big, heavy, and cumbersome thing and maneuver it just so to fit the relatively small space in the back of her vehicle. The moment they closed all the doors of the minivan and departed for the hospital, Allison noticed immediately the scent of Vicky's old apartment.

"My God, it smells like Vicky's place!" Allison said as memories flooded her from every direction. "Suddenly I'm back at Camelot."

"I've gotten used to it I guess," Sally said. "But when I first got it my entire house smelled like Vicky's place; which is weird as all get-out considering she hadn't owned the darn thing in years."

Allison checked her rear view mirror. The middle section of seats was pushed up all the way to allow room for the hope chest. Poor Alex who sat in the passenger side seat barely had room for his long lanky legs. All that Allison could see in the mirror was Alex's face and knees, and the hope chest looming behind him like some strangely auspicious beacon, despite the fact it almost completely obstructed her view out the rear window.

"Okay Al junior," Allison said to Alex. "You've got to check my blind spots for me 'cause that thing is blocking my view.

"You got it, Al senior. I'm the blind spot expert," Alex said kneeling in his seat to look around the hope chest. They hadn't called each other by their nicknames in such a long time, and it felt good to Allison to be doing so again

"Just be careful. You've got your seatbelt off."

"You're clear, Mom," Alex said and Allison flipped her turn signal on to change lanes.

Allison's newfound fear of deploying airbags, combined with this huge thing in the back obstructing her vision, and Sally's incessant chatter made this trip a particularly nerve wracking one. Then she would remember to take a deep breath, and when she did, she breathed in the fragrance of good memories that transported her back to a simpler time before disillusion and dashed dreams. She would smell that scent anew and she had that feeling she hadn't felt in years. Promise. That was it! She smelled the scent of Camelot and Vicky's old apartment and she remembered what it felt like to be young and to have promise. The anxious feeling would cease as she temporarily escaped into the past.

She glanced back in the rear view mirror again. She saw promise there in Alex when she'd catch him in these off guard moments and she wondered if he could still feel promise, or if in those tender years it had been wiped out completely by her and Frank. She had to laugh to herself as she noted the awkward way he was seated with the lack of leg room forcing his knees practically up to his chin. How awkwardly adolescent the whole image was with the knees, the shaggy hair, the head back, the eyes closed, earplugs in place with his ipod drowning out the sound of adult chit chat, his mouth moving silently along to the lyrics, and most funny of all, the white gauze dressing which covered his nose after the surgery where his nose bone was rebroken and set. She felt that familiar pang in this moment when time paused so obviously between childhood and young adulthood.

Allison encouraged Alex to drive that day but he declined. He hadn't driven since the accident. Perhaps this time it was a good thing, Allison thought, because Sally would have made him a nervous wreck.

"It's just like riding a horse," Sally remarked to Alex shortly after they began their trek to the hospital. In her usual uncanny way, she picked up on the one thing he didn't want anyone to know; in this instance, his reluctance to get behind the wheel again. "You gotta get right back on that horse after it bucks you off. It's the only way you'll overcome that fear."

Allison looked in the rear view mirror to see Alex's reaction to Sally's statement. She knew at just what angle to look to catch a glimpse of his eyes behind the ever-present curtain of those long bangs. In between the smug adolescent apathy came another one of those off guard moment when he caught sight of his mother's eyes in the rear view mirror. A spontaneous yet ever so subtle smile of amusement passed over his face in response. She was grateful for this moment of connection, this private joke with her long lost son. After Sally's remark, he turned up the volume on his ipod and closed his eyes again–a signal Sally didn't pick up on. Allison wished for just one moment she could be a rude adolescent and stick a pair of earplugs in her ears.

"I have to say in his defense, Sally, it's only been a week," Allison said turning into the long drive of Mercy Hospital and following the arrow to the Main Entrance sign. "He'll drive again when he's ready. Won't you, Al?"

"Oh, my gosh!" Sally blurted out without responding to Allison's comment. "We're here already. I gotta call Tim and let him know."

"Tim? Are we talking about Tim Schulz?" Allison asked in surprise.

"Yeah, he's meeting us here. Didn't I tell you?"

"No," Allison said feeling resentful that Sally had taken it upon herself to invite Tim without informing her.

"I thought Alex could use some help hauling that thing up to Vicky's room."

"But Chief Bobby's going to meet us here."

"Who?! What?! You mean that crazy cousin of hers! I thought he was dead."

"Apparently not! He's supposed to meet us here at the front entrance and help us unload the chest."

"Well if you can invite someone without telling me then don't get mad at me for doing the same thing," Sally said

"Okay, so Bobby, like it or not, is her family. The only living next-of-kin Vicky has. It's only right he should be here, but why invite Tim Schulz? What was the purpose of that except to stroll down memory lane? Why don't I just call Frank and you can give Barb the intern from down the hall a holler and we can just have a little Camelot reunion?!"

"Great idea! Dr. Barb could be our second medical opinion," said Sally.

"I was being facetious."

"So was I. I don't even know where Barb is anymore. Last I heard it was the Dallas/Ft. Worth area but we stopped exchanging Christmas cards a few years ago so I'm really not for sure."

"You mean *you* actually lost touch with someone?"

"I know, I know. I really should Google her."

"Oh, for crying out loud, Sally! You still haven't answered my question. Why does Tim have to straggle along? This is a very sick woman we're talking about and she doesn't need a room full of rubber-necks standing around gawking while she goes through this chest. You know what an emotional ordeal this is going to be for her."

"Well, you know, you did bring your son. No offense, kiddo," Sally said craning her short neck around to address Alex in the back seat

"That's different! She specifically asked to see Alex. I think she wants to tell him she's sorry... you know about the accident. But Tim? Why in God's name?"

"You're speaking of Tim like he's some stranger I just picked up off the street. He's an old friend. He cares about Vicky."

"Don't take it personally, Ms. Bruckens," Alex piped in, much to Allison's surprise who thought he was still listening to his ipod. She looked in the rear view mirror and saw him with ear plugs off fully engaged in the conversation.

"Please call me Aunt Sally."

"Aunt Sally... don't take it personally. Mom's just embarrassed 'cause Mr. Schultz is handling the divorce."

"That has nothing to do with it!" Allison protested as she slowed down and turned into the U shaped drive under the awning of Mercy Hospital's main entrance.

Tim Schultz and Chief Bobby had already bumped into each other and were standing there waiting together by the automatic doors, conversing like old friends.

"Now that's an unlikely pair of old misfits!" Allison said unable to stifle a laugh. There stood Tim in his suit and tie still looking like the up-to-no-good playboy; still boyishly good-looking in that moment of recognition when he smiled and waved; still very much the same except for the beer gut and receding hairline. It was unmistakably Bobby, his face being much the same as she remembered though his skin was more leathery, and all around each feature were deep etchings where the passage of time had left its mark. His long dark hair still hung past his shoulders but was now sprinkled with a bit more grey. In contrast to Tim's expensive looking wool overcoat and perfectly polished dress shoes, Bobby wore old beat up work boots and what appeared to be a deer skin jacket with fringe hanging down.

"They sure seem engrossed in conversation. What do you suppose those two have to talk about?"

"The old glory days. You know, Tim used to buy cocaine from him back when we lived in Camelot, back when he was public defender and Chief Bobby was one of the biggest drug dealers in town."

"I really didn't want to know that. Please don't tell me these things. Especially not when others can hear," Allison whispered and motioned with her head to the back seat where Alex was sitting.

"He can't hear," Sally whispered back.

Allison looked in the back seat. Alex was listening to his ipod again and seemed oblivious, but Allison wasn't convinced he couldn't hear.

A nurse wheeled a patient out through the automatic door. "Oh, great! Where do I park?" Allison said. "This is where they see discharged patients off and make sure they get safely in their cars. I'm blocking the doggone drive so that I can move a huge piece of furniture into the hospital. Suddenly I've become the kind of person I usually get stuck behind and would like to kill."

"Pull up, pull up!" Sally commanded.

"I'm not going to pull up any further, Sally. I'll block the sidewalk ramp and they won't be able to get wheelchairs to their cars. I'll just stay back here by the curb. They can come to us." Allison tooted the horn to get the attention of the two men. Tim acknowledged with a broad grin and a wave, Bobby with a slight, almost formal nod of the head and an even slighter change in facial expression which conveyed something like a greeting. Allison rolled down the driver's side window as the two approached the car.

"I'll open the back, Mom," Alex said and hopped out of the car before she could even turn around.

"He's a good kid," Sally said.

"Lately he has been. Maybe his hormones are settling down."

"Just say thank you and accept it. You know, we were that age once," Sally said.

"Thanks Sal–for the compliment and the reminder."

Allison greeted Tim with a polite but distant hello. She felt so awkward around him now. She couldn't think of him as an old friend, but rather Frank's lawyer. Since the separation she wasn't sure who her true friends were anymore.

Tim seemed oblivious to Allison's guarded greeting as he reached through the driver's side window and gave her a heartfelt hug. Allison perfunctorily returned it with a few quick rich lady pats to the back. Without a word, Bobby went to the back of the van to help Alex with the chest. Bobby and Alex carried the chest (with Tim following behind) into the main lobby of the hospital where they agreed to meet up with Allison and Sally after they parked the van.

"You know it's too bad Barb isn't here," Sally said as they made their way back to the hospital lobby after parking the car. "That way we could have a doctor, a lawyer and an Indian chief."

"Well, maybe my Alex could stand in as the doctor. He used to want to be one, you know. Maybe he still does. I'm never quite sure what goes on in his mind anymore."

"There they are: doctor, lawyer, Indian chief," said Sally as they spied the strange trio through the glass doors of the hospital's main entrance. The automatic doors opened when Sally and Allison stepped onto the transit. They hurried through to get out of the cold, and brought with them a wintry blast of north wind so strong it blew Bobby's long hair and ruffled Tim's neck tie.

"There they are," said Tim with a smile.

"You ready?" Sally said blowing on her hands and rubbing them together rapidly to warm them.

"I believe so," said Tim. He then turned his attention to his two comrades and addressed them. "Remember gentlemen," was all he said as he shot a knowing glance at Bobby first then Alex. Both of them gave Tim a quick nod in response. The three quickly stationed themselves around the hope chest then solemnly, almost ceremoniously, with as few words as possible; the way men so often do when working toward a common goal, they each grabbed a side of the rectangular shaped chest, lifted it and began moving toward the elevator.

Sally walked ahead of the men with a quick purposeful stride, striking her realtor pose as if she was getting ready to walk them through the Taj Mahal. Allison walked along side Alex who, with furrowed brow, was concentrating very hard on supporting his end of the chest.

"What did Mr. Schultz mean when he said 'remember gentlemen' to you guys?" Allison asked in as quiet of a voice as possible.

"He just told us that if anybody looks at us suspiciously to keep moving and act like we know what we're doing; and if anybody asks us why we're carrying this thing through the hospital we're to let him speak, 'cause you know he's a lawyer and stuff," Alex replied in voice just above a whisper. Allison had to smile to herself the way this whole thing had become an adventure for Alex.

Some people eyed the three males and their cargo curiously while others seemed to mind their own business and walk right by. They made it up to Vicky's floor with no interference other than a few strange looks. But then suddenly, there she was. She emerged from the nurses' station just directly across the hall from Vicky's room. This nurse was not a big woman but you didn't have to look too far beyond her diminutive stature to see the authority she commanded. She was the quintessential larger than life head nurse, the alpha caregiver for the unit, the omnipresent protector of all in her charge.

"Excuse me," the nurse said approaching the band of sojourners. True to Tim's instructions, the three men just kept forging forward. "Excuse me," she tried again. "May I help you?"

"Thanks very much, Ma'am, but I believe we got everything under control," Tim said.

"Excuse me, but where are you going with that," she said persisting, her eye more on chief Bobby than the rest.

"We're taking it to a patient. Excuse me, you'll want to move out of the way Ma'am, this thing is wide and extremely heavy," Tim said as they maneuvered the chest at an angle to get it into Vicky's room. Sally held the door open for them and they walked right through with the nurse following.

"Do you have permission to bring that in here?" The head nurse said as the band of visitors huddled into the room while she successfully blocked the door in a manner that would make Sally envious. All the while Vicky, who was sitting up in a chair, looked on watching the whole scene play out before her, first with a look of shock and confusion on her face then bemusement as it became more clear what was going on.

"We do," Tim answered abruptly and confidently.

"I'd like to know who gave you permission and for what purpose."

"I can't reveal that information to you. To do so would be a breach of doctor/patient confidentiality."

"Are you aware she's sharing a room and there's limited space in here. We can't operate around this big piece of furniture."

"Not to worry. We're simply going to empty the contents and take it back with us when we leave."

"I can't imagine who would give you permission to bring this in here."

"It concerns her Native American heritage Ma'am, a ritual similar to the white man's version of reading the last will and testament." It was Bobby who spoke this time, his manner so calm and serious it would have convinced anybody. "This is her lawyer. He's here to make sure everything's in order."

"That's correct. If you insist we remove this chest you'll be infringing on her religious rights. I suggest you call her primary physician, the chaplain, and her social worker. They'll confirm what we've just told you." Tim spoke with such confidence he almost convinced Allison for a moment.

A brief stand off occurred where the nurse stood with folded arms and attempted to stare down first Tim then Bobby. Finally with a sigh of defeat she bade them to do what they had to do as quickly as possible and get that thing out of there.

"Nurse Ratched lives!" Tim said and everyone let go a laugh of relief.

"Tim Schultz! Well, if you aren't the smooth talking ambulance chaser I remember from years gone by."

"Yes, some things never change," Allison said giving him a skeptical squint as she tried to size him up. At the same time she couldn't help admire him and the way he handled the busy body nurse.

"That was fast thinking Mr. Chief!" Sally said to Bobby.

"It's Bobby," Bobby and everyone else replied in unison.

"Sorry, I just drew a blank," Sally said.

"Yeah, but Mr. Chief? Sounds like one of the hand puppets from Mister Roger's Neighborhood. Or some kid's action figure that might come with a Happy Meal," Allison said, feeling suddenly flippant, like she was back at Camelot exchanging barbs with her old friends.

"Kind of sounds like the name of somebody's pet St. Bernard to me," said Tim.

"I was thinkin' professional wrestler," said Vicky.

"So what brings you here?" Vicky asked Tim. "You're not gonna try and talk me into suing somebody, are ya?"

"Naw! My motives are completely honorable. Chief Bobby and I talked and I want to offer my services–pro bona. I'd like to help you draw up a living will and maybe I can talk to your social worker about finding you some place to stay after you leave here."

Vicky said nothing, only looked down at the floor with a sad far-away expression.

"You'd do that for me? No strings attached," she finally said.

"Not exactly," replied Tim.

"Uh-oh! Here it comes. What do I got to do?"

"Take the first step. Take it for real this time."

"What d'ya mean?"

"Are you ready to admit that you're powerless over alcohol and that your life has become unmanageable?" Tim said bending down and leaning in toward Vicky, who sat like a small frightened child in her chair, with the most solemn expression on her face Allison had ever seen.

"Oh, that step. As in twelve steps," Vicky said.

"You know I'm just like you and Bobby here," Tim said. "I'm a drunk and a druggie. You know, you've seen me at meetings over the years."

"I know. I always tried to avoid you."

"The doctor said if you stay sober for at least six months they'll put you on a waiting list for a liver transplant. But you gotta want it, man," Bobby said.

"A new liver, a new life," Vicky said with an enigmatic smile. She looked far away again, her eyes focused up and out towards the corner of the room, as if she was searching the ceiling panels for the answer. "I do want it and I have taken the first step. It's the second step that gets me into trouble. Is there really a power great enough to save me from myself?"

"You've already taken one step. You just have to take one more step forward and believe," said Bobby.

"A step into the darkness," Vicky said.

Allison listened and it seemed so did Sally and Alex.

"Have you finally hit bottom," Tim said.

"I guess I got a high tolerance for hitting bottom, but I think I finally feel the hard ground under my bruised ass," said Vicky.

"Then you got nothin' to lose," said Bobby.

"You got that right. What haven't I lost? I got no home, no job, no money, no self respect, not even any dang teeth, and only a half a functioning liver. Yeah, I'd say I finally hit bottom. I've lost everything."

"You haven't lost everything Vicky," Allison said. "You've still got friends."

"Yes, wonderful old friends," Vicky said as she looked teary-eyed at Allison. "And I hope a new young friend if he can forgive me," Vicky said looking at Alex.

"You mean me?" Alex said completely caught off guard.

"Yeah, I mean you."

"I forgive you," said Alex shrugging his shoulders nonchalantly as if to shrug off the intensity of the moment and his inability to know how to react to it.

"My God, you look like your daddy!" Vicky said.

"Really? Most people can't figure out who I look like," Alex said with a self-conscious chuckle.

"You even sound like him."

"Thanks… I guess."

"Do you like music and numbers like your daddy too?"

"Well, I like music but I don't have any talent. My little sister got that. My big brother's the math whiz."

"What do you like?"

"Playing video games, listening to my ipod, hanging out with my friends."

"No, I mean in school. What's your favorite subject? And you can't say lunch or recess," Vicky persisted.

"P.E. I like sports."

"Cool! What else?"

"Science… I guess. I'm taking biology this year. Next year chemistry. I like the experiments."

"Oh, a hand's on kinda guy," said Vicky.

"When he was little he used to say he wanted to be a doctor when he grew up," Allison added.

"Is that so? Uh-oh, we better lay off, Allison. His face is turning all red. I think we put him on the spot. I'll take the heat off you kid and put it back on me where it belongs. I got something I just gotta say to you." Vicky held her hand out toward Alex and he grasped it without hesitating.

"Listen, what I did was a real stupid thing. It was a selfish thing. Now that I'm sober and my head's cleared up I can see that. I wish I could talk to every kid and tell' em to stay on the right path but I can't. I'm lucky enough to talk to just one kid though, and I gotta chance to make something right with that so I hope you'll hear me out." Alex nodded and appeared to be listening intently.

"Now, I could give you a big lecture and tell you to just say no to alcohol and drugs, but that don't work and you know it. Sayin' no to something ain't enough. You gotta find something to say yes to. I can't tell you what that is. You gotta figure it out yourself. Promise me you'll find something to say yes to; something decent, honorable, and true; something way bigger than making yourself feel good. Promise me that, 'cause I don't want to see anyone end up like me."

"I promise," Alex said in a surprisingly strong voice.

"You look like your daddy, but you got your mama's heart. I can see that in your eyes," Vicky said before she gave his hand a squeeze and released it."

"I know this comes as a shock to you, but she meant it as a compliment," Allison said to the speechless and self-conscious Alex.

"So what do you say we open this chest and find out what's inside before Nurse Ratchid gets back with the security guards," Sally said.

"I've got your key right here," Allison said grasping the key which now hung around her neck. "I hope you don't mind I wore it today. I was afraid I'd lose it in my purse," she said lifting the silver chain up over her head.

"I don't mind. Thank you for taking care of it," Vicky said as Allison handed her the chain and key. "And thank you Sally for taking care of the chest."

"I was happy to do it," Sally said.

"You do the honors," Tim said as he and Bobby pushed the chest closer to her chair.

Vicky's hand trembled slightly as she put the key into the tarnished lock and turned it. Bobby and Alex helped her lift the heavy lid. Immediately the smell of mothballs, cedar, and a faint trace of cigarettes filled the room.

"Smells like grandma's," Vicky said her eyes filling with tears. She began to sort through the contents: colorful quilts, afghans, a set of needle pointed throw pillows. Each item was held up and displayed as Allison and Sally marveled at the beauty and care of each piece. In the middle, carefully wrapped in old newspaper was a pewter bread tray and water pitcher.

"I knew there was something besides just cloth in there," Tim said with a chuckle as Vicky presented the pewter items.

In the bread tray were recipe cards, bound by an old rubber band that snapped in half the moment Vicky undid the thing.

"Her pumpkin bread recipe," Vicky said wiping her eyes and nose with a tissue.

She came to the last few items–a shawl, a sweater, and some knit scarves.

"Sorry about the smell, y'all. I need to air this stuff out," she said holding a sweater up, folding it, and placing it neatly on the pile in front of her.

"My grandma was way into keeping warm," Vicky said. She hated the cold weather, always said she wanted to move to Florida. Oh, Lord, look at this!" Vicky held up an orange ball of yarn and a pair of knitting needle, still attached to the one was a shapeless swath of tightly knit gold, brown, orange, and maroon yarn. "Grandma was trying to teach me how to knit. I started this when I was about fourteen, and as you can see, I didn't get very far. It was supposed to be a scarf."

"I like the colors," said Allison. "You gonna finish it?"

"I don't know," Vicky said holding up the knitting needle with the swath of autumn colored yarn.

"I believe Grandma Dooley is sending you a message. She's trying to tell you to finish what you started," said Bobby.

"You may be bossing me around now, Bobby, but don't forget I used to outrun and out climb you as a kid."

"Maybe so, but who used to help you down when you got stuck in a tree?"

"Here to talk me down again," Vicky said tenderly looking first at Bobby then everyone in the room. "Maybe God really is giving me a second chance at life."

"Looks like you got a note in there," Alex said pointing to an envelope marked "Vicky Lee". The small square shaped envelope was still astonishingly white, un-yellowed and untouched by nicotine and years of confinement in the cedar chest.

"And something else. Looks like that might be the last item," Sally said looking at the contents in the bottom of the chest. There underneath the envelope lay something wrapped in tissue paper and tied about with a blue bow. Vicky reached in and picked up the envelope.

"From your grandmother?" Allison asked. Vicky nodded her blurred eyes and reddened nose about to erupt again with all those years of locked in emotion.

"Do you want us to leave the room while you read that?" Tim asked.

"Maybe you oughta," Vicky nodded. "Except for Allison," she called out as everyone shuffled toward the door.

"You want me to stay?" Allison asked and Vicky nodded in the affirmative.

"You sure?"

"I'm sure."

"I'll come and get you when she's finished," Allison said to Tim on his way out the door.

"And Tim…" Allison called out to him in the hall. "Thank you!"

Allison closed the door and pulled up a chair near Vicky. Vicky's hands trembled as she worked slowly and deliberately to open the envelope. She opened the folded sheet of paper contained within and smiled through tear drenched eyes.

"It's dated January, 1975. My eighteenth birthday," Vicky said.

M. Grace Bernardin

    She began to read aloud, her eyes moving back and forth on the page, pausing periodically when the emotions got the better of her.

> *Dear Vicky Lee,*
>
> *I know you're a young lady now and it's been some years since you come to believe on the Lord Jesus Christ. I know it's been a hard year what with losing your mama and putting up with your daddy and his troubles. Then to make it all worse you had that terrible accident. I look at your pretty face and every time I see that scar, I think there's a scar inside your heart that no one can see.*
>
> *I know you're angry at the Lord and you blame him for your troubles. I don't know why we have troubles in this life. I don't know why sometimes you pray and it seems like the Lord hears your prayers and everything goes just fine. And other times it seems like he don't hear you at all. I don't know why that is. I only know he's weeping with you and he sees that scar in your heart that no one else sees. I believe if you trust in him it'll turn out fine in the end. Look at his only son. Not even death could keep him down. But you have to trust and you have to come back to the Lord.*
>
> *I know you're angry at your daddy. I'd like to take a strap to him myself but he's a grown man and he's made his own decisions. All the same I'm asking you to pray for him. Don't give up hope. It's never too late.*
>
> *This here was supposed to be your birthday present. But then I got to thinking about it and figured you might think I was nagging you or pushing you if I gave it to you now. I decided to put it in your hope chest because it can be used as a wedding dress. But that ain't why I made it. I made it for your baptism. That's my prayer–that you get baptized and return to the Lord. I will always love you, in this life and the next.*
>
> *God Bless You and Keep You,*
> *Grandma Dooley*

    By the end of the letter, both Allison and Vicky were grabbing for the tissue box, Allison sobbing silently and Vicky wailing out loud in her crazy, demented way.

"I don't know why that letter touched me so. I know it wasn't for me. But still," Allison said. The two women held each other and took turns comforting each other.

"You okay back there?" a voice out of nowhere startled them both, until they realized it was Vicky's roommate calling from behind the curtain that divided their room.

"Yeah, I'm fine, Minnie," Vicky called back.

"She sounds like she's improved," Allison said in a whisper. "I forgot she was back there."

"Yeah, she's having a good day. Ain't ya Minnie?"

"What's that?"

"I said you sound like you're feeling good today. They'll probably spring you outta here before me."

"You don't sound so good. You need to put some of that there opera on to calm your nerves?"

"No, really, Minnie. I'm fine. I'm cryin' tears of joy."

"Is that right? What's the occasion?"

"I'm getting baptized."

"Praise the Lord," Minnie called back from the other side of the room.

"Allison, we gotta get the chaplain in here. His name's Father Mudd. I gotta get baptized."

"Here? Now?" Allison said with surprise.

"Well, I don't know if he'll do it right this second but I gotta talk to him about it anyway."

It wasn't until Father Mudd had been contacted and was on his way, and all the others had been gathered back in the room that they realized Vicky hadn't unwrapped the dress yet. The dress was laid on Vicky's lap and Sally and Allison helped her untie the blue bow which bound the treasure. Vicky removed the tissue paper from the dress, careful not to tear any of it as if it was spun gold. She held up a mid-length ivory lace dress.

"It's beautiful," said Allison.

"Absolutely a work of art," said Sally.

"Grandma's pearl necklace would've looked so beautiful with it, but like a dang fool I went and hocked it. But the good news is…" Vicky said breathing in a deep breath which seemed to bolster some inner spark of optimism. "I never thought I'd ever see any of my grandma's things ever again."

The moment Father Mudd walked through the door Vicky said to him, "we need to talk."

"Is that right?" he replied, giving her a puzzled expression.

"I wanna be baptized," Vicky blurted out.

"She needs it, reverend," the voice of the unseen Minnie piped in from behind the curtain.

Both Tim and Sally gave a sudden start. "Who's that?" asked Sally, more wide-eyed than ever.

"Minnie," both Allison and Father Mudd replied.

"Good evening, Minnie. Sounds like you're feeling better."

"I am, reverend. Thank you kindly. I am, indeed."

"So you think Vicky needs to be baptized, huh?" Father Mudd called back to Minnie.

"As the Lord saith, 'Go therefore and make disciples of all men. Baptize them in the name of the Father, and of the Son, and of the Holy Spirit,'" Minnie replied.

"Amen, Minnie. Amen," Father Mudd said. Then turning his attention to Vicky he said, "You're right. We need to talk."

"Guess that's my signal to shoo everybody outta here," Vicky said.

"Ceptin' me, reverend. I ain't gonna listen to a word. I'll just be over here takin' a little rest. You best be sure to wake me when the baptizing commences."

"All right Minnie. We'll keep our voices down," Father Mudd said.

"Sorry y'all, but I'm gonna have to send you into exile just one more time. Y'all mind waiting in the hall again? Don't let me keep you here if you got things you need to do." Vicky spoke these words though her face betrayed a pleading hope that at least some of the entourage would stay.

"I'm not going anywhere, Vicky," Chief Bobby said.

"What about you, Alex? You got homework or ball practice you gotta get to tonight?" Allison asked her son, giving him an out if he wanted it.

"No, I'm good," Alex said, the usual teenage apathy temporarily trumped by his curiosity as to just how this scene might play out.

"You heard the man," Allison said. "We're good. We'll wait."

"I'm in," Tim said with a shrug.

"Me too. Wish I could say I had some hot date waiting for me but I can't," said Sally. "I guess some things never change."

"Passed up your chance for a hot date with me, Sal," said Tim. "Now I'm a married man."

"Hush, we got a man of the cloth here," said Sally.

Go on. Git!" Vicky said.

"We'll be in the lounge area Fr. Gerry," Tim said giving a handshake to Fr. Mudd.

"How do you two know each other?" Allison asked. She had picked up on the familiar exchange which took place between the two men the moment Fr. Mudd entered the room.

"All these crusty old sober drunks know each other," Vicky said.

Chief Bobby, Tim, Sally, Alex, and Allison shuffled out the door, leaving Vicky and Father Mudd alone to talk.

"Kinda weird to think you were all friends once," Alex said when they got out into the hall. Then more discreetly to his mother he whispered, "Vicky was really friends with you and Dad?"

"Why? Are you shocked?"

"Well, no, it's just... well, yeah, I guess I am kinda."

"A lot has happened to the three of us over the last twenty-five years. The truth is," Allison paused, tentatively placing her hand on Alex's back. He didn't pull away. "It wasn't a long lasting friendship, but while it lasted it was one of the best friendships I ever had." Allison choked with emotion at the resounding truth of those words.

"Drinks on the house," Tim said fishing in his pocket for change as he walked over to the soft drink machine. "Who wants what?"

"I'll take a Diet Coke," Allison said

"Alex?"

"Mountain Dew....please."

"What a weird day," Allison said plopping down on the couch next to Sally. "Ouch," she said clutching her side as pain rippled through her torso.

"You okay?" Sally asked.

"Yeah, fine. I keep forgetting I have a broken rib. I can't plop anymore. I have to sit down gingerly, like how I did when I eight months pregnant."

"What about you, Sal? What'll it be?" Tim, who was still standing at the soft drink machine, asked Sally.

"What I'd like to drink isn't in that machine. All this sobriety talk has made me want to run outta here screaming to the nearest corner bar," Sally said. "But I guess a Diet Coke will have to do for now."

There was some anxiety as the group waited in the lounge without a word from Father Mudd. Tim tried to be good-humored and at ease but every so often he'd fidget and check his watch. Alex dozed off listening to his ipod with his head back on the couch, his mouth open and the faintest trace of a snore exuding from his injured nose. Every so often he would snort himself awake, look around bleary-eyed, touch the gauze on his nose to make sure everything was okay, then nod off again.

Allison and Sally debated back and forth about what they should do. Should they have one of the nurses check to see how much longer? Should they leave? Only Chief Bobby seemed entirely serene as he sat peacefully with his hands resting comfortably on his legs as he periodically assured Allison and Sally that everything was fine and they should just continue to wait.

After about forty-five minutes, Father Mudd appeared in the lounge. They instinctively gathered around him in a huddle, like a team waiting direction from their coach.

"Here's the deal—we're going to baptize Vicky tonight," he said without hesitation. "Which one of you ladies is Allison?" He asked looking back and forth between the two.

"I am," Allison said raising a hand.

"Nice to meet you, Allison, I'm Father Gerry Mudd," he said with a tired but sincere smile as he shook her hand. Brief introductions then took place among Fr. Mudd and the rest. Then turning back to Allison he asked,

"Are you a baptized Christian?"

"Yes, as a kid in the Lutheran church."

"Great! Can you stay?"

"Yes, I think so."

"Terrific! Vicky needs a witness. She asked specifically for you."

"Witness? But I..." Allison began, wanting to explain that it had been years since she stepped foot in a church for something other than a wedding or funeral. Her words faltered and she didn't have a chance before Fr. Mudd quickly moved on to the next order of business.

"Is anyone here Catholic?"

"I am... or was," Sally said with a hint of timidity in her voice.

"Baptized?"

"Yes, as a baby."

"There is a God," Fr. Mudd said looking up at the ceiling like it was a private joke between him and God. "Can you stay tonight?" he asked, turning back to Sally.

"Yes, but I..."

"Good, great! You'll do," Fr. Mudd said cutting her off, almost purposely it seemed because he didn't want anything to change his mind or deter his plan.

"I know you gentlemen here are her spiritual brothers. I'm counting on you to help her out," he said to Chief Bobby and Tim. They assured him of their help and told him they, too, would stay for Vicky's baptism.

"Just curious, Gerry, but what's the rush?" Tim asked the priest trying to keep up with his hurried pace as he led the straggling group down the hallway back to Vicky's room. Allison walked as fast as her injured ribs and strained lungs would allow her, so as to catch up with Tim and Father Mudd. She too wanted to know why he seemed in such a hurry. Did he know something they didn't about Vicky and her condition?

Is she really improved or is death more imminent than what everyone says? Allison thought. She remembered how her grandmother rallied and seemed to be doing so much better right before that sudden turn which led to her demise. *Maybe being in this business he gets a sort of feeling about these things, kind of like a premonition,* the thought occurred to her as she caught up with them just outside Vicky's door.

"It's like this, Tim." Fr. Mudd exhaled the words with a long tires sigh. "She's been waiting for a long time for this; longer than she probably even realizes. I'm not going to make her wait any longer if I can help it. Not this time."

Allison wondered what he meant by 'not this time'.

"Is she in danger of death, Father? Is that why we need to baptize her tonight?" Sally said in a breathless whisper as she caught up with the others just outside of Vicky's door.

"I was wondering the same thing," Allison said, grateful that Sally had the nerve to ask the question.

"No, not imminent death, but I don't need to tell you she's not a well woman. We've got some witnesses here. We've got a community of believers," he said addressing the entourage. "Small community but it's what Vicky needs right now. I don't see any reason to wait. Let's get 'er done."

Together the group entered the room.

"Can we do it, reverend?" Vicky asked, her eyes so full of hopeful anticipation it reminded Allison of a child awaiting the answer from a parent about to bestow a gift.

"Get ready to get dunked, Vicky."

"You mean you got it all taken care of?" Vicky said a reluctant smile just waiting to let loose on her face.

Father Mudd looked at Vicky with reassurance radiating from his eyes. "Sometimes, not very often mind you, but sometimes the Holy Spirit just makes everything too easy. I love it when that happens." Father Mudd smiled at Vicky and she smiled back.

Chapter 39

Father Mudd clasped his hands together to signal the pending start of the ceremony; like church bells calling all who would enter into the presence of God. Suddenly in walked the nurse who had tried to thwart their efforts at bringing the hope chest to Vicky's room.

"Becky, you're just who I'm looking for," Fr. Mudd said to the half harried, half confused looking woman who walked in on this unexpected scene.

"I need a cup, a fairly tall Styrofoam cup like the kind you serve to the patients, filled with plain tap water."

"Do you want ice chips in that?"

"No, no ice, just plain tap water. We don't want to freeze out our poor catechumen here," he said to the puzzled nurse. "Oh, and I also need a clean bedpan," Father Mudd added as she approached the door.

"A bedpan?"

"Yes, make sure it's clean."

The nurse left and Father Mudd stepped over to the curtain which divided the room. Parting the curtain ever so slightly, he said, "Minnie, you want to join us?"

"Lord, yes," came the scratchy old voice. Father Mudd pulled back the curtain to reveal a tiny African American lady who was obviously very old, though just how old it was difficult to tell. Her white hair and dark brown skin, which was still remarkably smooth, made for a startling contrast. Everything about her seemed a contrast of old and young; from her clear, strong, and unstrained eyes which seemed to take in everything as if she'd never needed glasses a day in her life to the contrast of her knotted up arthritic hands, with knuckles so enlarged and fingers so gnarled it was painful to look at. She sat up in a chair, her frail diminutive frame looking as if it might break at the slightest handling; yet her legs which didn't quite reach the floor, swung like a fidgety little school girl. Her whole body swayed slightly back and forth to some unknown rhythm, felt only by her. The padding on the bottom of her socked footies just barely scraping across the floor as she swung her feet, kept time to that internal cue which caused her to sway.

"Yes, Lord! Thank you Lord Jesus," Minnie said over and over again. Minnie's continual stream of prayer along with the swaying conjured up in Allison's mind the sudden image of Jewish men at the Wailing Wall.

The nurse entered the room with the bedpan and Styrofoam cup, complete with plastic lid and straw. Father Mudd took the items from her hands with an amused smile. He graciously thanked her. She said nothing in response, acknowledging him with a quick perfunctory nod of the head, her face stoic and expressionless until she turned to leave the room, at which time she was sure to glare at the others.

"Lovely woman," the priest said. At Father Mudd's direction, Tim and Bobby carefully scooted Vicky, chair and all, out toward the center of the room. As soon as they finished he called out in a voice which so often distinguishes preachers and teachers, "Gather around, everyone. Allison and Sally, you stand on either side of Vicky. Minnie can you see all right?"

"Yes, reverend."

"Very good. All right, Allison and Sally," he said turning his attention to them as soon as everyone had settled in their place. His words were brief but his eyes conveyed the seriousness of the matter.

"I'm going to ask you if you will commit to helping Vicky persevere and grow in her Christian faith. Can you do that?"

"I guess that means I have to start going back to church," Sally said.

"I'll take that as a 'yes'," Father Mudd said then turning his attention to Allison he added; "What about you, Allison? Vicky said you two were very close at one time."

"Yes. She was my best friend," Allison said. "In response to your question," she continued in a whisper as she steered Father Mudd off to the side and away from the others, "I really don't know how to answer. I'm not trying to be evasive or anything but what does that mean really–'to help her grow in her Christian faith?' I mean, I know what it means I guess I just don't know what's expected of me."

"And I can't give you any set checklist of expectations. I only ask for your willingness. If you have that God will show you where to go from there."

"But I'm not very religious," Allison said.

"Me neither," said Sally a little sheepishly at having to make such an admission to a priest.

"God's not looking for the perfectly pious, particularly not for this project; just someone with a little faith," Father Mudd said as he reached into his coat pocket and pulled out a folded piece of cloth which he then proceeded to unfold, revealing it to be a long stole. He kissed it and placed it over his shoulders. "Do you have a little faith?"

"I guess I have a little faith," Allison said.

"Me too," Sally said.

"You know what Jesus said about faith the size of a mustard seed?" Fr. Mudd remarked adjusting the long stole around his shoulders until it was smooth and even.

"No, what did he say?" Sally asked in all earnestness.

"It's all you need to move mountains," Allison replied remembering the scripture quote from Bible Youth Camp years ago.

"So as I understand correctly we're supposed to be Vicky's godparents? Is that right?" Sally asked before Father Mudd had a chance to divert his attention elsewhere.

"Godparents!" Allison exclaimed, startled by the images conjured up and the very different impact that word had on her from the word "witness", which seemed more legal somehow, less spiritual. "Now I really feel unqualified."

"God doesn't call the qualified. He qualifies the called. Okay, God," Father Mudd said changing to a less serious tone as he turned his eyes heavenward, as if he was having an actual conversation with God, "you've got to make good on that. Don't make a liar out of me."

"God doesn't call the qualified. He qualifies the called," Sally repeated Father Mudd's words in a thoughtful, reflective manner; a manner that surprised Allison. "Is that from the bible, Father?"

"No, it's from the Assembly of God church marquis down the street. I love their sayings. I steal them all the time. Use them for my homilies."

Father Mudd turned his attention to the others leaving the two women stunned and somewhat silenced. As he began to explain to the others what they were about to do, Sally turned to Allison and said, "He must be desperate to do this baptism thing."

"A couple of warm bodies with a pulse," Allison whispered back.

Allison looked at Vicky then at the ivory dress her grandmother made her which lay neatly draped over the side of the hope chest. She wished Vicky could have worn it. It wasn't the baptism her grandmother had envisioned for her, but still if she existed somewhere in the outer realms of time she had to be smiling upon this scene. Despite everything, Vicky looked pretty in the purple gown and robe that Allison got her. Her hair was not done and she didn't have a stitch of makeup on, yet an inner radiance lit up her eyes and her skin, making her face glow with a beauty that naturally comes to the truly joyful. In that moment she was beautiful again.

Father Mudd removed the plastic lid and straw from the Styrofoam cup and tossed it into a nearby trashcan. Then with eyes closed and right hand raised, he mouthed what appeared to be a silent prayer of blessing over the cup of water. He opened his eyes and traced the sign of the cross with his right hand over the cup. He then opened a small book that read "Rites of Baptism" on the front and began the ceremony.

"Dear sister," Father Mudd said to Vicky. "You have asked to be baptized because you wish to have eternal life. This is eternal life: to know the one, true

God and Jesus Christ, whom he has sent. This is the faith of Christians. Do you acknowledge this?"

"I do," Vicky replied.

A series of promises soon followed; first from Vicky to live the teachings of Christ and to actively learn more about those teachings upon recovering her strength. Then it came time for the godparents and witnesses to make their promises.

"You have heard Vicky's promise," Father Mudd continued the solemn words of the ritual, now directing his attention to Allison and Sally. "As her godparents do you promise to remind her of it and to help her to learn the teaching of Christ, to take part in the life of our community, and to bear witness as a true Christian?"

"I do," Allison and Sally replied.

"And will the rest of you, who have witnessed this promise, assist her in fulfilling it?" Father Mudd addressed the question to Bobby, Tim, Alex, and Minnie.

The replies came back in various forms of the affirmative; a somewhat frightened but serious "yes" from Alex; a solemn "we will" in perfect unison from Bobby and Tim; and a "uh-hmm, amen, yes Jesus, praise Jesus" from the still swaying Minnie.

"How you feeling, Vicky?" Father Mudd asked softly with deepest concern. "Are you still up for that gospel reading? If you're getting tired we can cut to the chase."

Vicky smiled a slow fragile smile and bade Father Mudd to proceed with the gospel reading. Allison noticed she did look suddenly pale and tired, perhaps from all the visitors and all the emotion of the ceremony.

"Vicky chose this reading herself," Father Mudd continued as he opened an old beat up bible which belonged to Minnie and read the parable of the Prodigal Son.

Prayers continued: Prayers for the godparents; for the family and friends (which Allison realized were those standing around Vicky in that very room); prayers for an increase in faith, prayers for eternal life and salvation, for forgiveness of sin, for Vicky's restoration of health, and for unity of all the baptized. Then Vicky was asked a series of questions regarding rejection of Satan and belief in Jesus Christ. Vicky responded a solemn "I do" to each question. At last it was time.

Vicky scooted to the edge of her chair so she could bend down more easily. Alex assisted Father Mudd by holding the bedpan just under Vicky's chin. Father Mudd then spoke the words of baptism.

"Vicky, I baptize you in the name of the Father," the priest poured some water from the styrofoam cup over Vicky's head as she leaned down over the bedpan. Vicky shuddered a little. It could've been from the coldness of the water or it could've been something emotional, perhaps even supernatural.

"And of the Son," Father Mudd said pouring a little more water over her head. "And of the Holy Spirit," were the concluding words as Father poured the remainder of the water over Vicky's head.

Allison couldn't see Vicky's face because she was leaning forward and her long hair hung down, covering it, but it seemed in that moment that Vicky's body posture had assumed more than just a forward lean to facilitate the pouring of water over her head. It had become a bow of reverence and Allison felt sure that if she could have seen her face at that moment it would have shone.

Alex handed Father Mudd a towel he had draped over his arm and he began to blot Vicky's damp hair with it. She sat up and all could see she was smiling as tears streamed down her face. She took the towel which Father Mudd had placed over her shoulders used it to wipe her damp face. "This is what I call a dish towel crying jag," Vicky said. "Though I've never had one from tears of joy before."

Father Mudd placed his hand on her shoulder and asked, "Are you all right?"

Vicky nodded in response and a chuckle of shared happiness and release rippled through the small band of witnesses as little Minnie continued swaying proclaiming, "Amen. Praise you Lord Jesus. Thank you Jesus."

"God our Father has freed you from your sins, has given you a new birth and made you his daughter in Christ. Soon, God willing, you will receive the fullness of the Holy Spirit through confirmation and will approach the altar of God to share the food of life at the table of his sacrifice. In his spirit of that adoption which you have received today, join us now in praying as our Lord himself taught us." Father Mudd spoke the concluding words of the ceremony then all gathered joined hands and said the Lord's Prayer together.

* * * * * * *

It was one of those warm days that mercifully got inserted somehow at the end of January, reminding all winter sufferers that spring would eventually come. The sunshine was such a relief from the dreary grey days preceding it; days not cold enough for snow, just cold rain and occasional sleet, enough to send a damp chill into one's bones. Allison was more vulnerable to the cold and the grey sunless sky than she used to be; so this sudden burst of warmth and sunshine which allowed her to get out her sunglasses and toss her coat on the passengers seat (without having to put the loathsome thing on) was a delight more welcome than an unexpected check in the mail. And she really didn't care if global warming was the cause of it all. It was good to be alive today and she was thankful; thankful for so many things that were clearer, less obscured on a day like today. Even the irritating and distracting could be seen as gifts; for life viewed in the possibility of their absence seemed colorless and bleak. She thought of her renewed friendship with Vicky, sometimes both irritating and distracting, but mostly a gift that had caused her to toss the downside of it all joyfully aside, like the heavy winter coat on the seat next to her.

"What a gift! What a gift!" She said the words out loud and smiled like a half-crazed lunatic. "Gift! Where's Vicky's gift?" she asked herself, knowing it must be on the seat next to her, buried beneath her winter coat. She threw the coat off the seat onto the floor and there was Vicky's birthday gift wrapped in sapphire blue foil paper with a silver bow bound about it, and Allison had to laugh at her own silly fragile self that had to check everything twice, that had to be in control.

She pulled close to the curb and parked in front of the half-way house where Vicky now lived. It was a dilapidated old frame structure, badly in need of repair and a fresh coat of paint. As she walked toward the house she noticed several layers of shingles missing from the roof, perhaps from some previous storm damage, and she wondered how long it had been that way.

Vicky greeted Allison in the foyer with a hug.

"Happy birthday," Allison said presenting her with the gift.

"I can't believe you remembered the date after all these years," Vicky said, overcome with surprise and joy.

"So I got it right?" asked Allison.

"Right on the dot. You gotta quit this girl. Well, at least you don't get to walk away empty handed today. I finally finished your Christmas present. A month late but you know me. I always was late at everything, including growing up. Thank you," she said with another hug. "I'm gonna wait to open it 'til we get upstairs to my room. That-a-way I can give you your gift too. But first I'm gonna give you the grand tour.

"This is it, Allie. Chrysalis half-way house for women," Vicky said as they walked through the foyer and entered the old living room which now served as a Common Room, and was currently buzzing with life. "We're half-way home, aren't we girls!" Vicky said to some of the women who occupied the room, smoking cigarettes, folding laundry, watching television, working on a jigsaw puzzle. They all responded to Vicky with small gestures of camaraderie which signified a common bond.

Vicky introduced Allison to several of the residents. Everyone she encountered wore layered clothing to stave off the perpetual chill which resulted from poor insulation. It seemed colder in here than outside and

Allison suddenly wished she had her winter coat with her. Vicky continued her tour of the downstairs. The place was kept clean and tidy enough, still everywhere were signs of deterioration. The kitchen walls were stained with what appeared to be water damage. Allison's mind immediately went to work, organizing a board and fund-raisers though she said nothing about this internal scheming to Vicky. She just followed her from room to room… thinking.

"I know it ain't exactly Camelot, or at least Camelot in its hey-day, but it's our castle for now. Right girls!" Vicky said as they passed again through the Common Room.

"Some castle! We need a new flippin' moat!" said one of the residents with a throaty chuckle.

"And I'll bet you're queen of the castle," Allison said to Vicky.

"Naw, I don't want to be queen anymore. Just let me be one of them little pages that gets to carry the king's train and I'll be satisfied. As long as I'm well enough to help out that's all that matters. I tell you, Allison, I'm so grateful for my recovery, my health. I almost feel human again."

"You're amazing Vicky!"

"It ain't just me; we're all amazing. Look how everything was designed to work, the human body and all. I been reading up on medical conditions and stuff, you know 'cause of my liver and all. Did you know the human body has this miraculous ability to heal itself, even from serious illness. Of course a lot of it has to do with your attitude."

"I believe that. Who knows, you might not need that new liver after all. The old one might just be repairing itself."

"I don't know about that. The doctor's warned me not to get too over confident, you know, take it easy. 'Course I was never one for that. I'm trying to learn though."

"I bet some of those doctors are eating their words now. Remember when they discharged you from the hospital, how that doctor and social worker were recommending you get on disability and move in with Bobby."

"Yeah, and they said if I got too sick for Bobby to take care of they'd have to stick me in an institution. That made me wanna get better fast!"

"Look at you! You're proving them all wrong," Allison said remembering how sorrowful she felt upon Vicky's discharge when the social worker proclaimed that under close medical supervision, Chrysalis half-way house would be a way-station only until they could assess where to go from there. "They said this place would be your way-station and indeed it is; your way-station to a new and better life. Not the life of an invalid."

"I believe that with all my heart," Vicky said somewhat reflectively.

"C'mon, let me show you my room," she said with a sudden shift of mood as she motioned toward the stairs.

They made their way up the creaking old staircase which sounded as if it might crumble under their feet. When they reached the top, Allison noticed Vicky was terribly winded. She figured that was to be expected with all the years of smoking and abuse to the body.

Once upstairs Vicky opened the door to a small room; just large enough for the two neatly made twin beds, the small night stand separating them, and the chest of drawers in the corner. "I got a roommate but she's not here right now. She just got a job so we're all real happy for her. She'll be moving on soon."

"And so will you," Allison said.

"Yep, so will I. Have a seat," Vicky said, motioning to the corner of the bed. Allison sat down and Vicky sat down next to her.

"Last time we talked you mentioned you were looking for something part-time so you could start back to school. Is that still the plan?" Allison asked.

"It's still *my* plan," Vicky said.

"You seem unsure," Allison said in response to Vicky's cryptic statement.

"No, not unsure, just...open I guess. In case my Higher Power has something else planned for me."

"Like what?" Allison asked.

"I don't know," was all Vicky said with a nonchalant shrug and a faraway look. There was a moment of silence. Away from the hub-bub of activity on the main floor and all the distractions, Allison could see that Vicky was tired. Perhaps it was just Vicky's way, to hide it from all the others, but here alone in her room with her defenses down, it showed readily.

"You're tired, aren't you?"

"Yeah, just kinda battle weary I guess. Over two months clean and sober and in some ways I never felt better, but in other ways I feel lousy. Don't get me wrong, I'm not complaining. It's like I'm aware of how I feel, both the good and the bad, and I just ain't used to dealing with the bad parts. Does that make any sense?"

"It makes perfect sense."

"Like I still wanna drink. I still got this restless feeling, like I gotta grab hold of something to fix it. Then I realize it's a drink I want and I realize I can't go back there, or should I say I won't go back there, and I just feel sad. Sad and tired. Then I get to thinking about something else maybe, like a man or a big piece of chocolate cake, maybe the whole darn cake, and I think, no, that ain't it either. Then I think what if I just sat here with nothin'; nothin' at all but this empty ache inside my gut that's always been there. And then I realize that's the solution. That's the answer to the problem right there. Because that's where I find him—my Higher Power. That's where God is—at the bottom of that empty ache. And I'm not afraid no more, I mean any more, because I'm not alone. He's walking me through it, just for today. Just for today. Like they say in the program, 'This too shall pass'."

"Wow! No wonder you're so tired. That's a lot to think about."

"Yeah, this new way of living is such a change for me. I guess that's why I'm so tired.

"Let's open our presents," Vicky said with a sudden change of focus. She quickly hopped up from the bed and in one swift movement grabbed a gift bag off the chest of drawers. "You have to open yours first seein' as how it's a Christmas present and should have been delivered to you a month ago."

Out of the bag Allison pulled the knit scarf Vicky had begun so long ago when her grandmother taught her to knit; the very one that sat in the hope chest for so long. It was a bright splash of Vicky's favorite autumn colors; gold and burgundy, orange, and brown. Upon examining it Allison discovered it was completed to perfection. She could scarcely tell where she had left off so many years ago and started up again. The card read "I hope this gift brings you warmth and joy and reminds you of me. I know how you hate the cold."

"It's beautiful, Vicky. And you made it with your own hands. Thank you." Allison said taking a hold of Vicky's hands and squeezing them as a gesture of friendship. They were icy cold.

"Yeah, wouldn't you know it would warm up on the day I give it to you."

"Might be too warm to wear it outside but it's sure not in here," Allison said securing the scarf around her neck.

"Guess you noticed it's a little chilly around this place. I think they used toilet paper for insulation."

"Even you're cold," Allison said, squeezing Vicky's cold hand again. "When that happens, you know it's cold."

"For sure."

"Okay, so now it's your turn," Allison said handing Vicky her gift. "I'll give you a little hint; my gift is also hand made but not by me, which is lucky for you since I have absolutely no artistic ability whatsoever."

"You got my curiosity up," Vicky said shaking the gift as she held it to her ear.

"Careful, don't shake it too hard."

"Must be somethin' fragile."

"Go ahead, open it."

Vicky opened the gift the way she opened all her presents—like a kid on Christmas morning, never carefully undoing the taped corners like how

Allison did, like how most of the refined adults Allison knew did. She ripped away without order or reason in her excited anticipation, until at last she freed the prize from its paper prison. She pulled a colorful stained glass cross from the debris of wrapping paper and held it up to the light with a gasp. "Wow, this is so cool! Where did you get it?"

"Right here in Lamasco– Gott's Stained Glass. One of Lamasco's oldest businesses. You know, you've seen the place I'm sure."

"The one by the river front."

"That's the one."

"It must've cost you a fortune."

"Not too bad. I got connections. Or should I say Sally has connections."

"That Sally!"

"I didn't know if you could hang anything on your walls here, but when you mentioned you had a window in your room I thought 'a-ha'. See, it's got this little suction thingy on the back. You can stick it on your window."

"Cool," Vicky said rising from the bed with just enough strain and effort to make her labored breathing more noticeable.

"Are you okay?" Allison asked.

"Fine," Vicky said dismissively but Allison noticed she was terribly pale. She walked over to the small window that looked out over the dilapidated downtown neighborhood with its run-down, old buildings and signs of deterioration all around. "I just need your keen eye here," Vicky said placing the stain glass cross towards the top center of the window. Allison directed her until it was perfectly centered and even. She helped Vicky affix the plastic suction cup to the glass window. When they were finished they stood back and marveled at this splash of color which so overshadowed the dismal grey landscape of neglect and despair just outside that window.

The two women embraced. But this was not the usual strong bear-hug squeeze that Vicky used to give. It was feeble and strained, and Allison felt as if she was trying to hold onto some cumbersome object that was slipping out of her grasp. Vicky's body felt frail and cold; a coldness that emanated, even through her clothes.

"From now on you have to live somewhere with at least one window, no more cardboard boxes under the bridge or old abandoned warehouses. Promise?" Allison said as she held onto Vicky.

"Don't you worry about me. My next house is going to be a mansion," Vicky said and the embrace concluded with a somewhat cautious squeeze on Allison's part, lest she injure Vicky.

"Sit down, sit down. Take a load off. Can you stay a while?"

"Actually yes, I've got the afternoon off."

"Can I get you some coffee or a Coke?" Allison declined Vicky's offer, thinking even if she was dying for something she wouldn't send Vicky on another trek up and down the stairs again just to fetch a drink. They resumed their seats on the small twin bed facing the wall with the window and the cross.

"Thanks again for the gift, Al. What made you think of it?"

"Well, you know I am your godmother. I'm supposed to help you along in your Christian faith even though I think you're more advanced in that area than I am." Vicky was silent as if she knew this was just a surface answer and there was still more; something Allison didn't even know, at least not consciously. Only in that moment of silence was Allison able to remember. She looked up at the stain glass cross as it caught a stream of sunlight and cast a violet colored spot on the wall.

"I had this weird experience while you were in the ICU. It was the first time I went to see you and I'm sitting there by your bedside not really sure what to do."

"I don't remember."

"I'm glad. I said some pretty hateful things. I was angry because, you know…"

"The accident."

"Yeah, that and just all of our history. So I lost my cool and I really let you have it."

"I don't remember much but I do kinda remember you being mad at me."

"Yeah, well, if anything would've snapped you out of your coma it would've been that. So anyhow, afterward I realized that was a pretty low-down thing to do–to tell off somebody as sick as you were, and I'm thinking, I can't in good conscience just leave like this. I'm thinking of something I can say to smooth it all over and while I'm thinking about it, my eyes land on this crucifix that was hanging on the wall. My eyes are just drawn to it, maybe because there wasn't anything else to look at besides heart monitors, and tubes, and catheter bags. Maybe because it was just too difficult to look at you. But anyway my eyes kind of fixed on this crucifix and it's like I'm in a daze."

"Kinda like when you're tired and you get the stares?"

"Yeah, exactly. So I start remembering how you used to be and how we were such good friends, and then something happened. I found myself looking at this cross; I mean really looking at it, thinking about it…" Allison couldn't find words to go on.

"And then what?" Vicky asked

"I can't say exactly except that something inside of me just melted. Like a dam inside me broke and the next thing I know I'm on my knees praying and crying and wondering if maybe, just maybe it's all really true. I don't know. It started something."

"Go on," Vicky said.

"Something changed...in my mind, in my heart. I'm not sure how to describe it. But I felt hopeful. I guess non-believers would call it wishful thinking."

"Believers call it faith."

"Yes, faith. Weak faith. Faith the size of a mustard seed. I don't know. I still don't have any answers."

"Neither do I."

"Well, I guess we'll just stumble around in the darkness together."

"I can't think of anybody else I'd rather stumble around with," Vicky said and Allison noticed again just how pale Vicky was.

"How's Francis?" Vicky asked.

"Not bad. We've actually been getting along."

"Really?"

"Don't get too excited! I only mean we're behaving civilly toward one another. I think I'm finally letting go, cutting Frank a little slack, just giving him the freedom to be who he is. Even if it means he doesn't behave exactly like how I think he should. Even if it means he falls in love with someone else. I can honestly say I want what's best for him... and the kids."

Allison looked at Vicky. Her eyes were glassy. She touched her hand. It was cold.

"Vicky, are you all right?"

"I'm just real tired. Maybe if I lay down for a second. Would you mind?"

"Not at all. I probably should get going anyway."

"No, please stay. I just need to lie down. I feel a little weak."

"Are you sure you're okay?"

"Oh, yeah! I think I might be catching that virus that's going around."

"Can I get you anything?"

"Just help me scoot up so I can get my head on the pillow," Vicky said, and Allison realized she was too weak to even do that without assistance. Allison pulled the covers back and helped Vicky get into bed.

"Let me get you some water," Allison said noticing her lips were dry.

"Oh, that would be nice. I'm so thirsty."

Allison went downstairs and into the kitchen without feeling at all uncomfortable or intrusive. One of the women followed her and asked if she could help. She got a glass out of one of the cabinets and when Allison told her who it was for, she seemed concerned.

Allison thanked the woman for her help and headed back upstairs with the water.

"You're so sweet to fetch that for me," Vicky said as Allison helped prop her up in bed and handed her the glass of water. "Ain't much of a hostess am I? I should be serving you."

"Shhh, don't trouble yourself. Just rest"

"That water hits the spot," Vicky said with a gasp of relief after two large gulps of water. She leaned back on the pillows and said with a smile, "I feel better already." And indeed, the color was returning to her cheeks.

"Can I get you some more water?"

"No, just sit here with me." Allison sat down on the twin bed. There was near silence for a while with only the dull din of the television downstairs and the sound of a bird chirping just outside her window.

"I love the way the light comes through it," she said, and Allison realized Vicky was looking at the cross which she was just propped up enough to see from her bed. "Thank you." The words came out somewhat muffled as she expelled them in the midst of a deep throaty sounding cough.

"It does sound like you might be catching that virus," Allison said and Vicky coughed again, this time more forcefully.

"Let me get you some more water," Allison said standing up. Vicky didn't respond. She was staring ahead, somewhat blankly, at the stain glass cross that hung from the window.

"I wonder if he coughed," Vicky said.

"Who?" Allison asked a little bewildered.

Vicky coughed again and again, so hard it sounded like it hurt.

"Are you all right?" Allison asked, a cold sense of dread beginning to stir in her.

Again she coughed hard, followed by a gagging noise. She tried to sit up as she vomited into her hands. There was bright red blood on the white pillowcase and more on her hands and face with each painful retching noise.

Allison threw open the bedroom door and yelled downstairs for help. "Oh my God!" She pulled her cell phone out of her pocket and dialed 9-1-1.

* * * * * * *

Allison was dreaming–a dream she'd had so many times before. She discovered a new room inside her house, two new rooms, three new rooms. How wonderful! What a surprise! She would put a long dining room table in the largest room and she would invite everyone she knew for Christmas. Why didn't she know those rooms were there before? Then she heard the sound of hammering. Was there construction going on? She went into the next room to see if she could locate the source of the hammering. Did someone add on these rooms? Was someone building? She saw a ladder outside the window. Was someone working on the roof?

Suddenly, without any realization of how she got there, Allison was outside. Vicky was on the ladder, about half-way up and she appeared to be stuck. People were mulling around on the roof. They must've been working on it but she couldn't see who was hammering. She hollered to Vicky to get off that ladder before she hurt herself. "I can't get down. I'm stuck. I have to go up," she said.

She recognized three people on the roof: Vicky's dad, mom and grandmother. Yes, it was them. Allison recognized them from pictures she had seen. They were trying to help her get up, coaxing her, reaching their hands out toward her. Allison thought how nice it was that Vicky's dad seemed to have changed. He seemed concerned. He was encouraging her, telling her she could do it, just like how a dad should do, just like how her dad did sometimes but never often enough. Her mother was telling her she found the silver mines their family had been searching for and she could show them to her too, all bright and sparkling, if Vicky could just get up to where she was.

The three were talking about how to get Vicky off that ladder and onto the roof. All the while, Allison's just hollering as loud as she can for Vicky to come back down. They all ignored her. Vicky's grandmother commenced to make an announcement, an important proclamation of some kind and everyone had to stand at attention.

"We gotta get the big man to help," she said pointing back over her shoulder with her thumb, as if whoever this big man was he was standing just behind her. Everyone laughed at this remark. It was funny. Of course it was funny–in the strange way things are funny in dreams. The Big Man. It had to be Jesus. Suddenly Allison felt afraid, or was it awe, unworthiness perhaps; some emotion that caused her to shield her face because she knew she just couldn't look at Jesus. She turned away and kept asking if it was safe to look. Asking who? She wasn't sure. But somehow she knew when it was safe to look. The ladder was still there but Vicky was gone. The roof was obstructed from view by fog–no–clouds. Heavenly clouds. Allison knew they were heavenly clouds from the pinkish-violet hue that shone around them. She called for Vicky. She called for her again. And then she was trembling, shaking. No, that wasn't it–she wasn't shaking. It was the ground underneath her. She wondered in her dreamy state if it was an earthquake. No, maybe it was just her shaking, like an uncontrollable seizure. Whatever was causing her to shake, it was annoying and she wished it would stop. She was resisting it with all her might. And all the while the sound of hammering–another annoyance, another variable contributing to her unrest. And then she was aware of someone's voice calling her name. It was a man's voice. A familiar voice. It was Frank and he was shaking her.

"Allison, wake up! You're dreaming. Al, wake up."

Allison opened her eyes. It took her a while to get her bearings. She was laying on a small couch, her legs all cramped up, her back aching, in the waiting room of the Intensive Care Unit. She was back again, and the renovations that had begun at the hospital the last time Vicky was a patient, were still going on. The sound of hammering floated down the hallway from a nearby ward with its unnervingly persistent and rhythmic pound. She wondered how the poor patients in that ward got any rest at all. But then no one really rests in the hospital, she thought.

Frank was leaning over her, sitting on the edge of the couch. "You must've been having one heck of a dream. You were talking in you sleep, you know."

"I was? What did I say?"

"Something about, 'get down from there'. The rest was just incoherent mumbling."

"You seem amused," Allison said in response to the familiar wry smile and slight chuckle in his voice that was so characteristic of Frank.

"I always got a kick out of watching you sleep."

"Oh, yeah, I never knew that. So what's so funny about watching me sleep?"

"I suppose because you're so un-Allison like when you're asleep."

"What's that supposed to mean?"

"Well, let's see: you drool, you snore,"

"I do not."

"You do. You mutter and moan and say odd things. You laugh and cry. Maybe not so much un-Allison as the real Allison. Allison unveiled."

"Allison not in control, you mean. No wonder you think it's so funny."

"I didn't say that."

"No, *I* said that, and it's all right, you don't have to walk on egg shells around me," Allison said finally sitting up. "After all, I did call you and ask you to come. I'm trying to be good."

"Why did you call me?"

"I suppose because there had to be somebody from the old Camelot days here. And I didn't want Sally, you know, she's not the most comforting person in a crisis."

"So you think I'm comforting."

"Not exactly. It's just that your type of hysteria is more familiar to me."

"Gee, thanks."

"Well, you know, it is a very familiar scenario–meeting you in the emergency room because one of the kids is sick or injured."

Odd Numbers

"Usually Alex," they both said in unison and Frank cast his eyes downwards with a sad little chuckle and a bittersweet smile.

"So, it's like Pavlov's dog—mad rush to the emergency room, better call Frank."

"*Exactement.* Pavlov's dog," Allison agreed.

She could see it in his eyes; he wanted her to say it was because she needed him, because she missed him. A part of her did. A part of her just wanted to throw her arms around him and say how ridiculous this whole divorce thing was and couldn't they just find some common ground on which to stand and try again. But it was only because she was feeling tired and vulnerable. *Can't put the spoiled milk back in the refrigerator and expect it to get better,* she remembered Frank's analogy in speaking about the stupidity of divorced couples trying to get back together. But then again, the divorce wasn't final yet. Maybe the milk wasn't spoiled yet and they were throwing something perfectly good away. *Who knows?*

"How long was I asleep?" Allison asked.

"An hour, hour and a half."

"You're kidding! Have you talked to the kids?"

"Just got off the phone with Alex ten minutes ago. They're fine. Don't worry."

"Who said I was worried?"

"You don't have to say it. I can tell by that crease in your brow."

"What did they say?"

"Alex asked about Vicky. And Kristy said to tell you she loves you."

"Thanks for checking on them. How long do you plan on staying?"

"As long as you need me too."

"Thanks," Allison said. She really meant it. She squeezed his hand as the only way she knew to convey her sincerity. Then quickly, as she realized what she was doing, she pulled her hand away.

"By the way, thanks for bringing the change of clothes," Allison said, sticking her hands in the pockets of the sweat suit Frank had brought her.

"Well, I wasn't going to let you sit around in blood stained clothes. I gotta say I was pretty shook up when I saw you. You looked like you'd been shot. It was pretty gruesome."

"I had to help her as best I could."

"I'm glad you were there for her. You always managed to keep your head in emergencies."

"Well, I've certainly had experience with Alex. Where's Chief Bobby?"

"He's back on the unit visiting her. He and the chaplain, Father... what's his name?"

"Mudd. Father Mudd."

"He seems like a good man. He seems to take a real personal interest in Vicky."

"He's the one who baptized her."

"Oh, yeah, Alex told me about that."

"He did?"

"Yeah, I think it must've really had some kind of impact on him."

The conversation was interrupted by the appearance of a doctor entering the waiting room from the big double doors of the unit. Whenever a doctor entered the waiting room, everyone became suddenly alert. Heads bobbed up from deep sleep, eyes looked up from reading material, and turned away from the ever-present flash of the TV screen. People sat up straight as the shadow of either hope or dread spread across faces.

The doctor looked tired and his voice was hoarse and strained with fatigue as he called out: "Vicky Dooley. Family of Vicky Dooley," he said wearily looking around. Allison and Frank rose and quickly made their way over to him.

"Come with me," the doctor said with an expressionless face as he led the way to a small room just off the unit. Father Mudd was waiting in the room for them. It was a simple room consisting of a couch, a couple chairs, an end table upon which sat a box of Kleenex and a bible, a small waste basket, a painting of a soothing springtime landscape scene, and of course, a crucifix. The small room was closed off, no window on the door, very private. In her limited experience with the ICU, Allison had only seen families leave that room crying. The door closed.

"She's gone, isn't she?" Allison began crying.

The doctor nodded and put his hand on Allison's shoulder. "We did all we could to stop the hemorrhaging. She lost too much blood too quickly."

"What caused the hemorrhaging?" Frank asked this medical question of the doctor as he stood stiff and stoic; a pose which he often struck at the initial hearing of something unpleasant.

"A condition called esophageal varices. It's a complication from liver disease. As the blood flow in the liver decreases it begins to build up in the blood vessels of the esophageal wall. Eventually these blood vessels become so dilated that they rupture. It may not have been her first bleeding incident."

"I never heard anything about a previous bleeding incident." Allison said.

"She may have had a mild incident where the bleeding stopped on its own. If it happened when no one else was around she may have decided, for whatever reason, not to tell anyone. The bleeding tends to get worse with each episode if it isn't treated right away."

"I can't believe she wouldn't tell anyone," Allison said.

Odd Numbers

"Well, maybe not," the doctor said. "It could've been her first incident. I'm afraid her health was already compromised by the cirrhosis."

"Thank you Doctor," Frank said shaking his hand.

The doctor said his final farewells and offered to help in whatever way he could before making his weary and slump shouldered exit from the room.

Spontaneous tears streamed down Allison's cheeks. Frank stood, seemingly paralyzed as if he didn't know whether comforting her was the right thing to do. The sad basset hound look returned to his eyes. Father Mudd was at her side in a moment. Allison initiated a hug with the priest which seemed the only natural thing to do. She felt a certain bond with him from the baptism.

"I just don't understand why. They said she was so much better, that her liver was healing itself. She was finally getting her life back on track. Please tell me why, Father. Why did her life have to end so sad?" Father Mudd stood patiently with his arm around Allison, handing her tissues.

"I'm not so sure it ended sad. You know her one wish was to die sober. And that she did."

"I know but I still don't get it. Why? Why did she do this to herself in the first place? And then when she finally gets serious about turning her life around, it's too late. I just don't understand."

"And I don't have any answers," Father Mudd said so humbly and with such compassion that it almost sufficed.

Allison grabbed another tissue, wiped her face, and blew her nose. "Vicky said the same thing to me–I mean about not having an answer to a tough question. How come you people of faith never have any answers for life's tough questions?"

"Maybe that's where the faith part comes in," Father Mudd said. This response seemed to trigger something in Frank, something deep and long lost. He looked up and drew his shoulders back. It was as if he just awakened from a long sleep.

"I'm going to go check on Bobby. He's saying goodbye to Vicky right now. When he's finished you can go back and see her," Father Mudd said opening the door slightly ajar as he stood on the threshold of the small room

"Thanks for everything, Father," Frank said shaking Father Mudd's hand before he made his exit.

"I don't know how to help, Al. Please tell me how to help," Frank said after the door was safely closed.

"You can start by giving me a hug. I could really use one, you know. And I promise I won't bite," Allison said, strangely undone and endeared by his remark. They embraced. It was the first time in such a long time. Allison cried onto his suit jacket as he shushed her and stroked her hair. It was then she remembered the dream. It made her feel better to think of that dream, as if there was comfort in it somehow

"I just gotta tell you about this dream I had when I fell asleep in the waiting room," Allison said, finally ending the embrace.

"I'm sure it doesn't mean a thing, but I don't know, maybe it was a sign or something."

Allison told Frank all the details of the dream and he seemed stunned. "You're kidding me?" he said when she had finished.

"No. Why do you look so taken back? It was just a weird dream"

"Did Vicky ever tell you about the ladder incident?"

"The ladder incident? What are you talking about?"

"She got stuck on a ladder trying to sneak up to my apartment."

"Huh?"

"I don't know, maybe I shouldn't tell you," he said. From the look on his face, it seemed he didn't want to dredge up anything concerning the love affair in Allison's presence.

"No, it's okay, Frank. I don't mind. I promise. I want to know."

"She didn't want to have to sneak past Sally's apartment to come upstairs and see me, you know, because of all the gossip. Remember how Sally used to sleep with her door open?"

"Yeah, I remember."

"So this one night, she decides to swipe a ladder off of some workman's truck and climb up to my apartment." By this time Allison's was laughing and soon the laughter caught on to Frank.

"That is so Vicky," Allison said.

"She about scared the living shit out of me when she stormed through my patio door." They laughed together like they hadn't laughed in years.

"Anyway, the tricky part was when she decided to leave. She insisted on going back down the way she came up. Well, she gets stuck on about the third wrung down."

"What happened?"

"She just got scared all of a sudden. I guess going up was no problem but she had this phobia about going down. She was absolutely paralyzed."

"So what did you do?"

"I talked her down. Literally. Like some guy at the control tower talking to an airplane pilot in peril. She eventually made it down okay. I never will forget that.

Are you sure I never told you that story?"

"I'm positive. I would've remembered that. That is really weird, I mean in light of my dream."

"No kidding! You know I'm skeptical about that kind of thing but maybe it was some kind of message from Vicky," Frank said. "Maybe she's trying to tell you that she's okay–that she's with God. Maybe."

"Yeah, maybe."

A light knock on the door signaled the arrival of Father Mudd and Chief Bobby. They entered and Allison could see from Bobby's reddened nose and eyes that he'd been crying. Her heart went out to him as it might have for her own brother.

"Bobby, I'm so sorry. I know how much you loved her," Allison said placing her hand on his back.

"I just wish I could've done more for her," Bobby said.

"I wish I could've too."

"She loved you, you know," Bobby said. "She told me if anything happened to her, she wanted you to have her things. I don't have any use for any of it. It's strange. It was just the other night she mentioned it. I believe she might've known she was going home to the Great Spirit."

"Thank you, Bobby. There's one item I think should go back to Vicky," Allison said and Bobby smiled as if he understood. "I think she should be buried in her dress; the one her grandmother made her."

"She can go meet Grandma Dooley in it."

"Yes. You know I loved her too," Allison said and Bobby nodded in his quiet way.

Frank shook Bobby's hand and offered his condolences. "I'd like to help with the funeral expenses," Frank said to Bobby, then turning to Allison he said, "That is if you think we should."

"I think we should," Allison agreed.

"You may go back and say goodbye to her if you like," Father Mudd said, addressing Allison and Frank. "I'll be waiting here for you."

Father Mudd stayed behind in the room with Bobby while Allison and Frank made their way to Vicky's room.

All the machines had been turned off, all the tubes removed, leaving behind a stark silence. There lay Vicky with no sign of physical struggle or strain appearing on her face. She looked tranquil and younger. Allison went over to her bedside and squeezed Vicky's lifeless hand and kissed her pale forehead as she wept silently. The coolness of her flesh reminded Allison that she was in fact gone.

"Goodbye Vicky. I'm so glad you came back into my life. I wish we had more time to renew our friendship. It meant so much to me." The tears began to choke off her words. Allison looked up at the crucifix on the wall and said, "God be with you." She gave her one last kiss on her forehead and stepped away.

She could tell by looking at Frank that he was about to cry. Allison squeezed his hand and he smiled at her behind red blurred eyes. She knew at that moment what she had to do.

"I'll be waiting in the room with Bobby and Father Mudd." She turned to walk away. She would give him this moment alone with Vicky. It was the least she could do after all the years she gripped too tightly to him. She would let it go. She wouldn't feel jealous. She would turn, walk away, and leave him with his dignity.

As she walked away she thought she heard him say through his tears, "Goodnight, beautiful Vicky."

Allison stopped in the middle of the hallway and mouthed the words: "Beautiful Vicky."

Afterword

Allow me to pull a Vicky here and give you the Webster's Dictionary definition of the word "miracle": 1) an event or action that apparently contradicts known scientific laws and is hence thought to be due to supernatural causes, esp. an act of God. 2) a remarkable event or thing; marvel.

This book is a miracle. I hope that doesn't sound too presumptuous. I believe most creative acts are a miracle, whereby God, one way or another, breaks through to our world. Let's just say I experienced the miraculous first hand with the writing of this book. Just as surely as the Lord let the lame walk, the blind see, the dumb speak, and the prisoner free, he let me write.

As far back as I can remember I wanted to be a writer. One of my early memories is putting a book together for my mother with scotch tape. It didn't hold together very well. The scotch tape didn't stick and the pages kept falling out. I futilely tried to convey something of my imaginary world on paper, but my poor fine motor skills wouldn't let me form my letters correctly and sent my uncontrollable (yet colorful) illustrations off in wild scribbling directions. Even then I suffered for my art! It was an exercise in frustration yet this crazy dream of writing persisted.

I had a whole cast of characters in my head. There was Sue Norlake, Tom Stuffy, and Linda Puck to name but a few. Don't ask me. I have no idea where the names came from. They each had their own story. Many of them were orphans who lived in our garage and it was my responsibility to help them. They were real to me. They accompanied me during the day and talked to me. And, of course, I talked to them, which I learned early on in school was a social "no-no". I was the weird kid on the playground who talked to people who weren't there. And so I had to stifle my instinct to drift off into this imaginary world and act out these dramas going on in my head. Yet these people who weren't there had stories which burned within me to be told. I was definitely not normal!

And so the social difficulties started early in school and it didn't take long for the academic troubles to follow close behind. I learned to read okay, though I often had no idea what I was reading. I could sound the words out, I knew what the words meant individually, but to see them constructed as a sentence on a page, all comprehension was lost to me. It was somewhere around second grade when Sister Mary Timothy was giving directions for an assignment that I realized I had no idea what she was talking about. I knew the words she was speaking were in my native tongue of English, but somehow they were getting scrambled around in my head and were coming through as Greek, or Swahili perhaps. I was lost from that moment on… lost and scared to death.

I was labeled an underachiever. I just knew I was flawed. I had a giant "F" etched on my forehead for all to see. Then there was the impulsivity. I was too scared to move at school, but at home my actions were as out of control as the jumbled and confused thoughts in my brain. I went through a period where I actually belted myself to my desk chair at home so that I could sit still long enough to finish my homework.

In fifth grade, my mother took me to a progressive pediatrician who labeled my condition Hyperkinetic Syndrome. This was back in the early seventies. Today we know the condition as ADD/ADHD and everyone seems to have it. Never did I imagine that my affliction would someday become fashionable!

I was on Ritalin for three years. Say what you will on the question of medicating children with this disorder, but fact is, it did help. I could concentrate. I could think things through. I didn't interrupt. I waited my turn. And for the first time since I started school, I began to have some self-esteem. The problem was it badly suppressed my appetite and I was losing too much weight. I was taken off the meds sometime in eighth grade. By high school I reverted back to all my old problems.

Years and years of struggles started up again. I won't bore you with all the details, but I will tell you that the only real joy in my life during those tough years was the imaginary characters in my head and their stories. Still this dream of being a writer endured. Yet it seemed so unreal to me. Talk about your pipe dreams! How could I become a writer when I couldn't even put a sentence together?

Somehow I graduated from college. "By the skin of her teeth, the grace of God, and a little pull from me," is how my academic advisor put it. Anyhow, I guess that's how it happened. Determined to do something productive with my life, I decided to pursue a career in the helping profession; a profession which so many of us screw-ups opt for. And I say that with the utmost love and admiration for all the beautiful people in that profession who have helped me over the years. I worked harder than I ever worked before. It took everything I had but I managed to get a Masters degree in Counseling. I landed a job in a mental health clinic and worked there a couple years. A couple years was all I ever managed to work anywhere. I left there as I left so many jobs—feeling despondent, feeling like a failure. It wasn't that I was such a bad counselor, as it was I couldn't stay organized enough to keep up with the paperwork. Here I was almost thirty years old and I still hadn't figured out what I was supposed to do with my life. I only knew I wanted to write, but that was out of the question because how could I?

That summer, unemployed, broke, miserable, confused, and completely lacking in focus, I stayed with my parents at their place in northern Michigan. I wandered around in the woods and by the lake that summer with a bible and a notebook desperately trying to find God, desperately looking for answers. Yes, God literally led me by the restful waters and restored my soul. I read the psalms and wept a lot.

That summer in the woods of northern Michigan I had a very real experience of the living Christ. I was given hope through the words in that bible that, surprisingly, I not only comprehended but seemed to leap off the page at me. Through those words I was washed clean. I experienced healing, hope, and yes, forgiveness for all the sins committed–all the sins that flowed from a wounded self-esteem–all those acts intended to boost myself when all I succeeded in doing was hurting myself and others. That would have been enough, but the Lord is never outdone in graciousness. He whispered that old dream into my heart again. He commanded me to pick up a pen and write, telling me not to be afraid, that it would be okay. He told me that with each word I put on paper, he would rewire my brain.

I sat on this old tree stump in the woods of northern Michigan with that notebook and that bible and I began to write. It was mostly journaling at first, but soon those imaginary characters from inside my head demanded to be set free. And so with one word at a time I began to write.

That was the beginning of my miracle. I realized then that I am a writer. I realized God plants dreams in our hearts at a very early age for a purpose–that we might heal, serve, inspire, refresh, spread the good news and bring others to new life.

That was several years ago and I've had other not so successful attempts at "real" jobs since then, but slowly I am beginning to accept the person that God made me to be; and to recognize that it's all gift. I am nothing special in that regard. That gift is for everyone who wants it. That is my prayer for anyone reading this right now, going through struggles of his or her own. They may be very different struggles from mine, but I'm here to tell you, this is a God of miracles. He longs to call us all forth from our tombs. I know he called me forth from mine and it is a *miracle*. Praised be Jesus Christ.

> *"For I know well the plans I have in mind for you, says the LORD, plans for your welfare, not for woe! Plans to give you a future full of hope. When you call me, when you go to pray to me, I will listen to you. When you look for me, you will find*

me. Yes, when you seek me with all your heart, you will find me with you, says the LORD, and I will change your lot."
- Jeremiah 29: 11-14

M. Grace Bernardin
Pentecost Sunday 2009

Acknowledgements

I believe it only appropriate to begin by thanking my husband, John. Together we've shared this dream of writing, which began the very first night we met. It's so exciting to see the dream finally come to fruition for both of us. A simple internet search for John William McMullen will yield the fruits of his literary efforts. But of all John's achievements, his most challenging to date is getting his fledgling wife through this project. His ever-persistent pushing and prodding (gentle pressure!), undying encouragement, helpful suggestions, endless inspiration and belief in me as I stumbled through this second novel (the first novel was an experiment of sorts and we're all greatly relieved that it will never end up on anyone's bookshelf, although John wants me to scrap it for parts) is one of the greatest graces bestowed on me. Thanks John for everything. I seriously could not have done it without you.

I wish to thank the Writer's Group who endured readings of my earliest drafts; particularly Doug Chambers, who gave me so much confidence in my writing ability and is the spirit of that group.

I have many friends who encouraged and supported me along the way (and you know who you are). I wish to thank two in particular: Susan Milligan for believing in this dream at times when I couldn't. Susan–thank you for the countless times you propped me up and told me I had a gift; especially during those times when I just thought the whole thing was crazy and what the heck was I doing with my life anyway. You are my Barnabas.

Finally I wish to thank my friend Judy Lyden for the ideas, inspiration, and constructive feedback. Thanks Judy for your veritable wellspring of creativity which never fails to get me pumped up. You'll never know how many times you helped get me unstuck. Check out Judy Lyden's brilliant and hilarious book *Pork Chops*.

My love and gratitude to all those who played a part in getting this book to print.